The Diamond Maker

The Diamond Maker

An Extraordinary Love Story

Joseph M. Orlando

 AuthorCentrix

Printed in the United States of America
ISBN 978-1-64133-284-2 (sc)
ISBN 978-1-64133-283-5 (e)

Library of Congress Control Number: 2017963884

Fiction / Romance / Drama
18.03.26

AuthorCentrix
25220 Hancock Ave #300,
Murrieta, CA 92562

www.authorcentrix.com

Dedication

To 'Team Orlando'

The most important decision a man will ever make is
choosing the woman to sail with through life.

There will be squalls and there will be fair seas. It will all be easier to
face every challenge when one's partner is a loyal and loving ally.
I have been so blessed for 42 years. How many
men find their soulmate at 16 years old?

I did! And I thank God every day. I love you, Connie.

To the children who filled our home with laughter, love and sometimes
anguish, Amanda, Lisa, and Joe, I am proud to call you my children.

For Papa's boys, Alex, Sam, Frankie, Owen, J.J., Dylan, Joey
and Rocky. You boys are the best part of 'Team Orlando.'

Acknowledgements

I want to thank Dave Gilliss and Laura O'Shea
for their cooperation in posing for the Book Cover.

Dave Gilliss, is in fact, a golf Professional
and the coach of the Gloucester High School golf team.
His insights and skills were extremely helpful in the writing of this novel.

Laura O'Shea is the banquet manager and all around 'Girl Friday'
who is instrumental in keeping everything in the dining
and grill rooms at the Bass Rocks Golf Club operating smoothly.

As I was writing the character, Angela Curcuru, for this novel,
I visualized a pretty and smiling girl, with long,
curly black hair and warm brown eyes.
One evening while my wife Connie and I dined
with friends at Bass Rocks Golf Club,
Connie smiled and pointed to Laura. "That's your Angela," she said.
And, indeed the smiling Laura did indeed reflect the fictional Angela.

I want to acknowledge Katelyn Burke, Attorney and friend.
Thanks for your insights and suggestions.

Thanks to the people of Gloucester,
that I have had the honor and pleasure to know and represent.

To Toni and Greg White for taking the time
to read and share their thoughts.
Your observations and insights were very helpful.

To Bonnie Waldron who read and offered suggestions on an early draft of
'The Diamond Maker,'
Thank you.

A special thanks to ' Team Orlando,' my children,
Amanda, Lisa and Joe.
You have inspired me to achieve.
You three are my greatest accomplishments.

To my Grandchildren,
Alex, Sam, Frankie, Owen, J.J., Dylan, Joey
and Rocky (That's right all boys).
You all are the best part of my life.

And, above all, thanks to my Connie, wife of 42 years.
The best life partner a man could have.

Author's Foreword

The Diamond Maker is a novel, a work of fiction.

In the novel, names and places which may be familiar to the reader are used for the purposes of realism, to help the reader enjoy the narrative. In no way is the dialogue intended to reflect the thoughts, words or ideas of the individuals portrayed. In all facets, this is a work of fiction.

Bart DeMarco and Angela Curcuru, the main characters of the novel, are wholly fictional, thus any dialogue concerning their actions are, and must be, completely fictional.

'The Diamond Maker' is a novel set in Gloucester Massachusetts, 'America's Oldest Fishing Port.'

The author was born and raised in Gloucester, which sets on Cape Ann, a rocky outcropping of land, rich with granite quarries, handy to George's Bank and other fertile fishing grounds, and blessed with beautiful sandy beaches.

The author is an attorney, specializing in Admiralty law. A 'Proctor in Admiralty' who was born the son and grandson of Commercial Fishermen. As an attorney,

Joe Orlando has represented thousands of individuals who have been the victims of negligence on the seas and land, having been referred to as "Attorney For The Injured' by the New York Times.

Joe Orlando is also the author of 'The Gloucester Trilogy.' That is, 'The Fisherman's Son,' 'The Bastard's Weapon' and 'One Man's Hero.'

The trilogy is also set in Gloucester, in the Italian-American fishing community.

"The Fisherman's Son' was named as required reading at Montclair State University, by Professor Donna Marie Pignone, in her class 'The Many Manifestations of Italian Culture.' To have my novel on the reading list with 'The Odyssey' by Homer and 'Twilight in Italy and other Essays,' by D. H. Lawrence is thrilling and humbling.

Chapter One

Bartolo DeMarco awoke to the sound of wind and rain battering the window of the bedroom he shared with his older brother, Mario. He looked about and saw that Mario's bed was empty. A glance at the alarm clock, and he remembered that Mario, who was nineteen and a recent high school graduate, would have left to meet the captain and crew of the fishing boat on which he had recently secured a site. The howl of the wind, Bart realized, meant that Mario would soon be home, as the small dragger would not be able to fish in such conditions.

As he lay in the warmth of his bed, he thought of the upcoming, opening game of the Gloucester High School football season. He looked at Mario's bed and smiled at the memory of Mario leading the Gloucester High School Fishermen to a state championship. Even now, after three years, Bart felt the surge of pride in his big brother, his protector. Bart adored Mario. Mario's success was his success. Mario's success was a success for 'Team DeMarco.'

At the summer training camp, Bart had impressed the coaches and won the starting Quarterback position over some stiff competition. That competition included a senior, Dave Powers, who had been the Quarterback the previous season.

Bart did not worry about playing the position. He had won the job because he was a bigger, faster, more powerful, runner, and a better, more accurate thrower of the football. He had confidence in his athletic ability, but worried that his nerves would cause his stutter, a lifelong problem, to flare, interfering with calling the plays in the huddle, barking out the adjustments at the line of scrimmage and the snap count.

Bart, age 16, swung his legs around and sat on the edge of his twin bed. He set his feet on the floor. As always, he dreaded the day ahead. School was a challenge. In truth, his whole life has been a challenge. He understood his studies and his teacher's instructions, in fact, Bart was a top student, but worried constantly that he would be called on to respond to a question from his teachers or worse, be asked to address the class.

Bart was afflicted with a speech impediment that caused him to stutter, especially, when he was anxious. Those times were humiliating for him. The ridicule of his peers, the mocking of his classmates and teammates, who called him a variety of disparaging names, was a daily event, and painful to hear. He had been called 'Stutter Boy' by those who mocked him for what seemed his entire life.

So, Bart had long retreated into silence and tried his best to just disappear. The exception for Bart was on the athletic field. He was confident and accomplished on the baseball and football fields. Bart used sports as his avenue to success in an effort to compensate for his handicap, at least that was what his therapist believed. Bart just knew that when he was running or swinging a baseball bat, he was free from self-doubt and able to be himself. He loved to compete and condition his body and mind to be better than his competitors.

Bart had worked with a therapist and a speech specialist for years. As he matured, beyond childhood, his speech, had in fact improved. And, when at ease, his stutter was minimal. Still, when anxious, he struggled mightily. And, that fear always preyed on his mind. 'Would he be able to stay calm and in control?'

His coaches loved his athletic grace, strong throwing arm, foot speed and keen, cool, mind. On these strengths, he had won the starting Quarterback job and was set to start his first game in two days.

Bart was big, already two inches over six feet tall, and a solid 170 pounds. At age 16, he was still growing. He had the rugged good looks of the DeMarco men and, he had their athletic prowess. He also was blessed with the DeMarco work ethic, and their drive to succeed.

Bart's Dad, Franco, had been a Gloucester athletic legend. Tall, broad shouldered, Franco DeMarco had met Rosa Parisi when he was 16 years old, at a victory party. He had been instantly captured by her beauty. Rosa was 14 years old, already voluptuous, in the way some girls who at 14 appear to be so much older. She had the appearance that concerned her Dad, which brought out his protectiveness. Her long wavy auburn hair, framed a beautiful face, soft brown eyes, a full mouth that smiled naturally. Their attraction was mutual and instant, although, she always laughed and professed that Franco fell first.

Franco would smile and agree. "I saw her and I knew!"

Rosa's Dad had vetoed the idea of his daughter dating Franco DeMarco. Rosa was too young, "no dating until Rosa is 16!" He stated emphatically.

And, in truth, he didn't really want his baby girl dating Franco DeMarco. He just didn't trust him. Franco scared Rosa's Dad.

"He's too much for our girl," he insisted. Rosa's mother had argued that Franco was from a good family. Franco was intelligent, a good student, and always respectful.

"Yes," Dominic Parisi agreed. "The DeMarcos were good, hard working and helpful neighbors." He had shrugged, saw the look in Rosa's eyes and just knew that he had to protect his girl from this boy, who had captured his Rosa's heart. 'He'll forget all about her by the time she turns 16,' he thought, hoped.

To Papa Parisi's surprise, Franco waited the 14 months until Rosa turned 16, and called, wished her a Happy Birthday, and asked her on a date. Rosa happily agreed, and, although Rosa's Dad had reservations, they were together from that day forward.

Bart, like his Dad and brother, was a good athlete with excellent hand-eye coordination and a sharp mind, he also loved reading, getting lost in the exploits of great athletes and warriors. Like most young men, he dreamed of performing great deeds and having lovely young women desire him. He enjoyed getting lost in the pages of a novel. In his mind he had no limitations or flaws.

It was a battle on many fronts to win the starting Quarterback position. His coaches, of course, were aware of his pedigree. Mario had been a star and Bart was Franco's son. They also knew of Bart's challenges. But, Head Coach, Bob Nelson, was determined to give him an opportunity, while hedging his bets by working with the young man who had played the position last season.

Bart recognized his opportunity, but was aware that if his speech issues flared, he would be replaced. That reality had him on edge. Head Coach, Bob Nelson, had promoted him to the position, encouraged him and worked with him. And, Bart had won the starting role. Now, he had to prove to himself, to the coaches and team, that he could be the team leader.

In the first game of the season, a home game played on a beautiful early September Friday evening, under the lights at Newall Stadium, before a big crowd of supporters, Bart ran onto the field to lead the 'Fighting Fishermen.'

Bart proudly wore the home jersey of red with the white number 7 emblazoned on front and back. It had been Mario's number, as it had been Franco's. His white football helmet with the Gloucester fisherman symbol in red gracing both sides. A last conference to receive encouragement and final instructions from Coach Nelson, for Gloucester's first possession. Bart was ready to lead.

He felt those butterflies that portend focus and alertness. He felt ready. In the huddle, the players, classmates all, but most who were seniors and juniors, looked to him for the play call. The call was to be a play action pass, where Bart would fake a hand-off, hide the ball then set to throw downfield to a, hopefully, open receiver. His anxiety caused him to stutter in that first opportunity to take command in the huddle. The confused look on faces of the players added to his anxiety. Remembering the instructions of his speech therapist, he took a deep breath then repeated the call. It worked and the huddle broke.

As he stood over center, he saw that the defense was set to blitz, which made the called play less than ideal. But, Bart realized, creating an opportunity to check-off the play and throw a screen pass over the blitzing defensive linemen and linebackers. If executed properly, it could be a big gainer and then would likely have the effect of making the defense more passive. He called out the assigned word for a check-off. Then, began to call the new play. Nerves overtook him and his stutter flared. By the time he controlled his breathing and called the play, the referee blew his whistle and called a penalty on Gloucester for delay of game.

In the stands his mother, Rosa, sensed what was happening. She said a silent prayer, as she clutched her husband's arm. Bart's Dad, Franco, supportively, patted her hand.

The offense went back to the huddle. The coaches on the sidelines yelled instructions, Bart's anxiety level rose as he faced his teammates. Now, he managed to call the screen pass and moved to the line of scrimmage. The center snapped the ball and the defense blitzed. Bart had read the defense perfectly, and threw the screen pass which went for a big gain.

The partisan Gloucester crowd erupted with applause, Bart's family exhaled in relief, the Gloucester bench yelled in approval, but Coach Nelson was concerned. Bart looked over to the bench, saw Coach Nelson speaking to the back-up Quarterback, Dave Powers, who put his helmet on.

The team huddled and Bart was a mess. He desperately tried to call the play in the huddle, stumbling over and unable to communicate the play sequence. A frustrated teammate added pressure by yelling, "Come on Bart, spit it out!"

After a few deep breaths the play was called and the Gloucester offense moved to the line of scrimmage. The Salem High School middle linebacker caught on to Bart's problem and began to yell, "come on stutter boy, speak clearly now." Bart tried to focus on calling the cadence, but heard the Salem player call out; "come on stupid, can't you call the cadence?" He laughed as he jumped about. "Hey stupid, how about I help you," and he began calling out numbers as Bart was trying to do the same.

In the confusion, an offensive lineman jumped and the referee's whistle blew, calling a penalty on Gloucester for illegal procedure.

Coach Nelson called a time out and to Bart's utter shock, he saw Dave Powers trot onto the field and into the huddle. Bart was removed from the game, before the home crowd of six thousand. He had failed! And, this time, before the entire city.

Bart stood on the sidelines, removed his helmet and looked into the stands. He made eye contact with his mother, who read his face. Her face flushed and her eyes filled as she, once again, saw the pain and humiliation on her boys face. Rosa DeMarco held her husband, Franco's arm. Bart saw his Dad whisper to his mother, saw his younger sister, Lucia, set her saddened gaze on him. Bart saw Mario and his girl, Celia, flash smiles of support.

Bart cheered his team on, but felt humiliated before the large Gloucester crowd and utterly useless to his teammates. After the game, he met with the team's coaches and was told that while they were sorry, the team had to come first. Coach Nelson, a tough but kind man, assured him that with his athletic abilities, he could be used elsewhere. Coach Nelson smiled and encouraged Bart to hang in there, that on Monday they would talk. The experienced coach saw the look in Bart's eyes and knew the young man was devastated. Having to remove him from the game, before a crowd of thousands, including his family was hard, but, the Coach felt, necessary. Bart nodded and left Coach Nelson's office, alone, to walk home.

Bart walked along the canal that bordered the stadium, passed the drawbridge and walked onto Stacey Boulevard, where Gloucester Harbor met land and where 'The Man at the Wheel,' the statue which faces the outer harbor and the fishing grounds beyond, was placed in 1923 in honor of all the fishermen who went down to the sea in ships, never to return.

Bart sat alone on a bench, looking at Gloucester Harbor, Ten pound Island which set in the harbor, out to the breakwater. The light at the Breakwater's end, turned throwing a yellow stream of light onto the dark ocean.

Bart felt utterly defeated. He sat quietly, lamenting the torture of being unable to simply speak when needed. He knew his teammates, who had been for the most part supportive and encouraging, were heading to a party to celebrate Gloucester's victory, but his mood did not fit a party atmosphere and he would not dampen everyone's spirits.

"Hi Bart," called out Angela Curcuru, a classmate and neighbor, who Bart had known for a few years. Angela was standing close-by, and was smiling after having attended the game. "Nice win, Huh?" She asked.

Bart sat back and looked her way, "Hi Angela," he managed. "Yes," he nodded, "it was." Angela studied Bart, read the pain reflected in his eyes. "Are you okay?" She inquired. "When you left the game everybody thought you were hurt."

Bart managed a weak smile at the ever kind Angela, who, he suspected, understood why he had been removed from the game. While feeling raw over his failure, he still noted how fresh and cheerful Angela looked, in her red pleated skirt and white wool sweater, which complimented an attractive full figure. Her black hair shone, was long, loose and naturally curly, which she kept back off her pretty face, her smile, which lit her gleaming brown eyes, was radiant.

"I'm fine," he paused. He nodded toward the bench upon which he sat, hopefully, he asked, "can you sit for a bit?"

She flashed a smile, which lit her face and encouraged Bart. "Sure, I can, but if my girlfriends leave, I will need you to walk me home." She shrugged and smiled. "You know my Dad."

Bart grinned, he slowly formed the words as he felt a bit anxious. "PPlease ask them to go ahead without you," he stumbled, hopeful she would stay. "I,I will walk you home."

Angela turned and waved to her friends, "go on to the party, I will stay here with Bart." She turned back to him, offered her warm smile. "I'm all yours now." Bart watched as her friends hesitated, whispered to each other, then climbed into the car and drove off to the party in the Magnolia section of Gloucester.

She saw that he was a bit anxious, saw the pain in his eyes, and took his hand. "Bart, you never need to be nervous with me." She held her smile. "We are friends, grew up in the same neighborhood." She chuckled. "You were my hero who saved me from those bullies who made fun of me, calling me 'Ugly Angela,' remember?" She thought back, smiled. "My family had come to America from Sicily, I was what, fourteen years old, and I felt so alone and scared." She shuddered at the memory. "We had only been in Gloucester for less than two years and my English was shaky for so long."

Angela sighed in memory. "I had no friends, but you were always kind to me, you were there for me."

Bart nodded, relaxed. "You were easy to like." He said clearly. He sat back, felt the soft night air. He smiled, as he watched the gentle breeze blow her pretty hair about.

"After you pounded that Sal Siracusa, and the other two, they never bothered me again." Angela said. "You told him that I was your friend and that if he or his loser friends ever bothered me again, they would answer to you." She giggled. "Then you hit him again in that smug face and he cried that he was sorry and it wouldn't happen again."

She paused, "I think you broke his nose, the blood poured out." She squeezed his hand, smiled warmly. "And, those boys never bothered me again, thanks to you." She paused, smiled. "You saw how upset I was, and, you picked up my dance bag and walked me home." She recalled, but didn't mention, the blood on his hands and clothes.

Bart smiled, "I know the feeling of being seen as different, and being treated like an outsider." He responded, clearly, with no hesitation. "When I saw how afraid you were, I flipped out." He shrugged and smiled, sought her eyes. "Besides, I was trying to impress a pretty girl."

Angela blushed at the compliment, her deep brown eyes flashed and she laughed and squeezed his hand. "I wish I was pretty," she said wistfully. "Sometimes, I see the girls in the pep club, and the cheerleaders, and I wish I looked like them, with their long legs, slim bodies and blond hair." She sighed. "I just have to accept that I'm a short and stocky Italian girl, with my big hips and wild black hair."

Bart flared and rose to her defense, "Don't you believe that!" He stated without hesitation, and looked into her eyes. "I think you are very pretty." He paused, realizing what he had just blurted and flushed crimson. He eyed her, saw her appreciative smile.

"Thanks, Bart." She grinned, her soft brown eyes sparkled. "You don't have to be nervous or embarrassed when you say something so nice." On an impulse, she leaned forward and gently kissed him. "That's for being such a good friend."

Bart's eyes opened wide and a smile bloomed. He paused and studied Angela, seeing something in her smile that he had not seen before. "It's a nice night." Bart said, as he sat back, eyes on Angela, heard the gentle lapping of the sea meeting the shore. Bart realized that her mere presence made him feel better. He took a deep breath to fight off a nervous stutter. Hopeful, he plunged forward. "Wwould you like to go for something to eat?" He paused, studied Angela, noting her smile that lit her eyes and gave him hope. "I was so nervous before the game I ccouldn't eat," he stumbled and flushed. It surprised him just how much he hoped she would agree.

Angela smiled, saw he was anxious. She placed a soft, comforting hand on Bart's cheek. She sought his eyes, ignored the stutter. "How about you walk me home and come in. My Mom made veal cutlets Milanese and a tomato salad for dinner and there's lots left." She grinned and added, "My Mom also made some of her sesame cookies today."

Bart exhaled in relief, grinned and tentatively reached for her hand. He hoped Angela would allow him to hold her hand as they walked. He stood and eyed her nervously. "Mmay I,I hold your hand?" He asked hopefully, his deep brown eyes on her face.

The question caught Angela by surprise. She studied Bart, trying to decipher just what his request meant. Tall and handsome, black wavy hair and piercing brown eyes. She noted the athlete's body, broad shoulders, angling down to a slim waist, powerful thighs and beautiful, clear skin. Above all, he was a kind, compassionate guy. In truth, she had long been interested, but thought that this smart and handsome jock was way out of her league.

"I would love to hold your hand," she responded with a laugh, "but, be careful, I might get the idea you are sweet on me."

Bart blushed, took a breath, "I,I guess I am," he responded clumsily. "I I hhope that's ookay?" He added. He was rewarded with her smile.

Bart and Angela walked slowly, hand in hand, through the granite curbed streets of Gloucester. This old fishing port had long been an area rich with granite quarries. The granite from the quarries of Gloucester and Rockport have been used for over a century in construction across the nation. A gentle, early September breeze blew off the ocean, carrying the clean, clear salt air. Angela's hair blew freely in the breeze and Bart was taken by her aura. Angela was a sweet and open, and to Bart's eyes, beautiful girl. He loved her curves and wondered why women despaired at being blessed with a woman's body.

Together they climbed the twisting and hilly streets of this old New England town. Talking to Angela was comfortable for Bart and for the most part stutter-free. When their bodies bumped together on the narrow sidewalks, he loved her softness and her distinctly feminine aroma. She quietly marveled at the hardness of his muscles. Angela felt safe with Bart and Bart felt calm with Angela.

When they arrived at the Curcuru home it was approaching 10 pm. Angela entered the living room to greet her parents. Bart walked over to

Angela's father, who was relaxing in his recliner, extended his hand in greeting. He shook her Dad's hand, smiled and apologized for arriving at such a late hour.

Angela's Dad, Sal, was familiar with the DeMarco family. He nodded to Bart, then turned to Angela. "You no go to the party?" He asked in his halting English. When fishing, the crew, all Italian immigrants, spoke in their Sicilian dialects. At home he often spoke to his wife, Maria, and his children, in Sicilian, as well. While his English was limited, it was sufficient for his daily needs.

"No Papa," Angela responded. "I met Bart after the game and he was nice enough to walk me home."

Sal looked at Bart with approval. "Grazie," he responded, offered a smile. "It no good for a girl to walk the streets alone at night."

Bart nodded and smiled. "Yes sir, I,I, agree," he stumbled nervously on the words, "and was glad to walk Angela home."

Angela smiled. "Bart didn't have dinner because of the game. I told him he could eat here."

Mr. Curcuru nodded and smiled. "Si, Si, you mangia, enjoy."

Angela's mother rose from her seat, smiled at Bart. "Of course, come, I will make you a plate."

Angela flushed. "Mom, I can take care of it." She looked to Maria. "You can just relax."

Maria studied her daughter, glanced at Bart and smiled. "Angela, you sit with Bart in the kitchen. I will warm the food and then leave you two to talk."

While Maria prepared Bart's food, Angela made up a plate of cookies and placed it on the table, taking a seat next to Bart. When the heaping plate of veal Milanese, tomato salad and fresh baked bread was placed before Bart, he smiled, "Thank you, Mrs. Curcuru, this looks wonderful." He paused. "I'm sorry to be causing you this extra work."

Maria smiled, noted his good looks and polite manner. "It's no trouble, Bart, please enjoy," she responded with a smile.

Bart looked to Angela. "Aren't you going to join me?"

Angela smiled. "I had dinner." She reached over and touched Bart's hand. "You eat, I will keep you company." Angela's mother noted the contact, smiled, but said nothing as she returned to the living room.

Bart dug in. "This is great, Angela. Thank you." As he ate Angela studied Bart. She refilled his water glass and enjoyed watching as Bart relaxed and enjoyed the food and her company.

"Do you want to tell me what happened tonight at the game?" She asked.

His eyes clouded. He looked from the food to Angela. She saw that he was becoming tense. She patted his hand. "Not with me," she said softly. "You never need to be nervous with me."

Bart took a deep, steadying, breath. "I couldn't do it." He managed. "I can play quarterback, I can throw the ball and run, but I can't call the plays, bark out the adjustments at the line and call the cadence." He sighed, closed his eyes. "I gget," he stumbled, "Nervous." He drank his glass of water dry, watched Angela refill it. His eyes misted in frustration. "I,I," he stumbled, "f,failed again, in front of thousands of people." He looked up with eyes wet with tears, born of a soul deep frustration. "I don't know w,what to do."

Angela read the pain of a lifetime of humiliation. She smiled, "for now eat dinner, let's think about this and talk tomorrow." She smiled. "There's an answer Bart, we'll find it together."

Bart took Angela's hands, looked into her eyes and nodded. "Thanks, Angela."

The goodnight kiss was thrilling. Angela settled into bed with thoughts of Bart on her mind. How he had gently cradled her face in his big hands and brought his lips to hers. He had rested his forehead against hers and thanked her for being there for him. At five foot three inches tall, she looked up into his eyes. He was almost a foot taller and so big and strong. And, in his eyes she saw a kind but battered soul.

The idea that he was interested in her was exciting and surprising. That evening, she had approached him as a friend and neighbor as she could see he was hurting. She had not believed that Bart would be taken with her.

Angela saw herself as plain, with her small breasts, wide hips and wild black hair. From the time when she had come to Gloucester from Sicily with her family, so her Papa could fish on a good earning Gloucester fishing dragger, she had heard the 'Ugly Angela' sneers. She hadn't known how to fight back. Her English was halting, at best. So, unable to verbally defend herself, she tried to ignore them. But, those girls, had not let up. It had hurt, and, she came to believe it. So, when Bart DeMarco, who was handsome, athletic and kind had defended her against mean spirited bullies and now showed an interest in her, even calling her pretty, she was enchanted.

She believed he could accomplish anything, if he could overcome the speech issues that killed his confidence. She recalled reading that the great leader and inspirational orator, Winston Churchill, suffered from stuttering, but largely overcame the difficulty.

How could she, a sixteen year old high school sophomore, help Bart deal with and overcome this life obstacle? She pondered the question as she lay in bed, cozy and happy.

She thought about when he stuttered and when he didn't. When he was relaxed, she realized, his stutter was minimal, but when he was anxious or worried, it flared.

Angela thought about Bart's smile. How he had been so careful with his big, hard, but gentle hands on her face, how soft and exciting his kiss had been. She sighed. She knew that she wanted Bart in her life. She also knew that she wanted Bart to be happy, and for Bart to be happy, he would need to find a way to conquer his stuttering. 'I will help him,' she vowed.

She fell asleep smiling.

Bart walked home in something of a daze after kissing Angela. He had long heard the 'Ugly Angela' insults and had simply attributed that behavior to the same mean spirited teens who had relished in embarrassing him.

He thought of Angela, with her long and curly, black hair, dancing eyes, voluptuous body and pretty face, and was excited at the very idea that she would be his girl. He recalled how just hours earlier, he had felt devastated and alone as he walked from the locker room to Stacey Boulevard. Then, Angela had been there with her radiant smile and soft words. He smiled remembering how she had left her girlfriends to console him on what was a humbling experience, then, allowed him to hold her hand, had provided dinner for him and smiled when he held her in his arms and kissed her goodnight.

He felt good, even after his dispiriting performance on the football field. The difference had been Angela. He smiled. Maybe he, with Angela's help, could overcome his stuttering. And, maybe, just maybe, beautiful Angela would be his girl.

Chapter Two

Bart woke at 4am to head down to the docks to hopefully be hired, by the Boss Lumper, for a lumping site on one of the draggers unloading its' catch that day. He wore jeans, work boots and a hooded sweatshirt, against the early morning mist and chill.

When a fishing vessel returned to port, the fish had to be off-loaded. Many times, the crew, after five to nine days at sea, wanted to head home to their family. Thus, they would hire lumpers to unload the catch. When there were multiple boats in port to be unloaded, Bart could often land a job. It was backbreaking work, but for a young, strong athlete, it was no problem. And, it paid well.

Bart stood on the dock, assessing his chances. At this dock, where he expected to find the Boss Lumper, he saw three boats readying for take-out. There were two Western rigged draggers and one Eastern rigged dragger. The biggest of the three was the 'Blue Surf.' Bart knew that the 'Blue Surf' fished for redfish. Across the busy harbor, he saw two other draggers at Aiello's dock readying for takeout. He smiled, his chances to find work looked good.

The boss lumper approached Bart and sent him to unload the Blue Surf, a 100 foot Eastern rigged dragger. "Bart, they will need you in the hold. They have over 300,000 pounds of redfish." He paused. "Think you can handle it?"

Bart grinned, he had worked the docks long enough to know that unloading a big catch of redfish was a task that experienced lumpers would shy away from. "No problem, glad to do it." He eyed Sophie, "thanks for the job, Sir."

The boss lumper was Sophie Frontiero, nicknamed, "Sophie the Bull." The name came from his reputation of hard work and a rather stubborn streak. The Bull was not a big man, but he was tough as nails. He eyed Bart, "get it unloaded in less than three hours and there will be a bonus for you." He saw Bart's smile. "And, maybe, another job on a dragger heading in now."

Bart pulled on oilskins and rubber boots, covered his head with the sweatshirt hood and jumped down into the slaughterhouse of the Blue Surf, with a pitch fork and shovel. All about him were pens filled above eye level with iced redfish, the slang for ocean perch. The fish-hold is a big ice-box. But, it wouldn't be long before Bart would be pouring sweat as he forked and shoveled the fish and ice into baskets to be hoisted up and out of the hold.

Perch are a particularly scaley fish, and when the sharp scales hit your skin, it is painful. It was Bart's good fortune that career lumpers often refused to work the fish-hold when redfish was the catch.

The penboards are six feet long, six inches wide and a solid inch thick. They slide into tracks, on either side of the pen, as the fresh fish and ice are shoveled, by the fishermen, into the pens. One board upon another, and a wall encloses the pen. Depending on the vessels size, there may be as many as twenty-five pens.

Bart used the fork to lift the top penboards out, allowing the iced fish to fall to the deck of the slaughterhouse, where he shoveled the iced fish into a canvas sided barrel with a rope across the top. When the barrel was full, he attached the winch line hook to the rope handle and helped steer the barrel up and out through the hatch.

Then it was penboard after penboard, barrel after barrel, with Bart working tirelessly to empty the hold. Bart took no breaks and worked faster than the hatchman, who guided the barrels through the hatch opening to swing up and across to the dock, could get the empty barrels down to him.

"Let's go!" He called to the hatchman, his eye on that promised bonus.

Bart filled the last barrel and sent it up in less than three hours. Coated with sweat, he smiled, climbed onto the deck and drank down a bottle of water. He stretched his back and viewed the harbor, boats at dock, others cruising through the harbor to berths or out to sea.

He found Sophie the Bull on deck, shaking his head and smiling in approval. "You earned that bonus, Bart." He laughed. "If you want, the St. Theresa just docked and there is a job for you." Sophie shrugged. "A couple of hundred thousand pounds of redfish." He eyed Bart. "Do you want it?"

Bart smiled and nodded, "thank you for the opportunity, the bonus and the extra boat." It didn't occur to him that he hadn't stuttered his words until he had finished. 'Wow,' he thought. 'Maybe I can do it."

"Ok," Sophie responded, smiling at the young athlete. "You earned it."

Bart lumped the two draggers and was home by noon. He smelled like ripe fish, his shoulders, arms and chest were cut and bruised by the sharp scales of the redfish, but his pocket was flush with his days' earnings.

He took a long, hot shower, pulled on jeans and a flannel shirt and sat down to lunch with his family.

His mother, Rosa, offered a cheerful smile. "Did you have a good morning?" She queried, as she watched him closely.

Bart realized his Mom was worried. The previous evening was hard on more than Bart. The DeMarcos supported each other. Rosa DeMarco suffered for Bart. As did his Dad, sister and brother. He smiled, "I did." He met her eyes. "I'm okay, Mom."

Bart cut into his mudiga (breaded) steak, fresh off of the barbeque grill, savored the aroma and taste with an appreciative smile. "I love how you mix the breadcrumbs, Mom." He offered. "So much better than the store bought breadcrumbs."

"Better and cheaper," his Dad, Franco added. "Can you believe what they charge for flavored breadcrumbs?"

Mario laughed. "Dad, you only buy the best cuts of meat, but become annoyed at the cost of the bread crumbs."

Franco acknowledged the seeming inconsistency with a shrug. "Why would I ruin a good steak with second rate oil or breadcrumbs?" He shook his head. He smiled at his wife. "My Rosa flavors the breadcrumbs with Romano cheese, fresh basil, garlic, salt and pepper. She dips the steak in only the best extra-virgin olive oil, and then her magnificent breadcrumbs." He savored a delicious slice. Then swirled his fork in the spaghetti in marinara sauce. "I love my steak with pasta."

Bart's sister Lucia, 14 years old, laughed. "Dad, I can't believe how much you love to eat."

Franco eyed his pretty daughter, her long auburn hair framing a face with sparkling brown eyes, and luminescent skin. "Bambina," he chuckled, "eating is one of life's great pleasures." He winked at his daughter. "A wonderful meal, a good glass of wine and a beautiful wife," he grinned at Rosa. "That is what makes a man happy."

Lucia smiled adoringly at her Dad as her cheeks flushed.

Mario looked at Bart. "Tough game last night, Bart?" He paused, put understanding eyes on Bart. "Sorry, Buddy."

Bart looked to his brother. Mario had been a high school all-conference and all-state, football player. He had led the 'Fighting Fisherman' to a State Championship. He also excelled at baseball. Like Bart and their dad, Mario was over six feet tall and powerfully built. "I,I couldn't," he stumbled. Bart took a deep breath. "Call the plays," he sighed.

Lucia placed her hand on Bart's arm in support. Mario eyed his brother and felt Bart's pain, "maybe you should play a fall sport where your stutter won't be a problem." He offered. He smiled, encouraged. "Bart, you are so gifted."

Bart shrugged, "thanks Mario, I'm just not certain what I am going to do."

Rosa looked on her son with pain showing in her eyes. "Mangia, it will be okay," she assured.

"I heard you lumped two boats this morning," Franco said, moving the subject from last evening's pain to this morning's success. "Sophie told me you moved over three hundred thousand pounds of redfish out of the hold in under three hours."

Bart smiled at his Dad. "Yes, we emptied the hold." He laughed. "The guys on the dock couldn't dump and process the fish fast enough to keep up."

Franco beamed. "The lumpers were impressed." He paused, smiled, "You made me proud." He scanned the table, took in his three children, "you all make me proud."

Lucia smiled at her Dad, then turned her attention back to Bart. "I heard that you walked Angela Curcuru home last night and had a late dinner at her house."

Bart blushed as all eyes turned to him. He nodded, "yes, I did." He studied her, "how did you know that?"

Rosa smiled. "That's good, Bartolo, Angela is a good girl. I like her."

"The Curcuru's are good people." Franco asserted.

"Do you like her?" Lucia asked teasingly, sharp eyes fixed on her brother, and avoiding Bart's question.

Bart smiled at his baby sister. "As a matter of fact, I do."

"Well, are you going to ask her out on a date?" Lucia queried, with a smile.

Bart eyed Lucia, "you think I should?" He paused, uncertain, "so soon?"

Lucia rolled her eyes, looked to her mother, who looked on with a smile, then back to Bart, "yes, I think you should call her and take her out tonight."

Mario grinned. "Well, you have plenty of money after today, Bart, why not?"

Bart sat back, shrugged as he considered Lucia's suggestion, smiled, as he recalled the goodnight kiss and the feel and pleasing aroma of her skin and hair, when he had hugged her, nodded. "I think I will."

Chapter Three

On a warm September evening, dressed in khaki pants and a red polo shirt, Bart, somewhat nervously, knocked on the front door of the Curcuru house.

Angela's mother, Maria, opened the door, smiled up at Bart, and led him into the living room. Bart crossed the room and shook Mr. Curcuru's hand.

Sal Curcuru offered a smile and urged Bart to sit. "So, what to do for tonight?" Mr. Curcuru asked in his heavily accented English. The family, except Angela and her sister, Tina, were in the living room, with Angela's two brothers watching television. Sal looked at the two boys, ages 8 and 6, who immediately turned the TV off. Bart smiled an apology at the boys.

Bart took a deep breath, hoping to tame his racing heart. "I,I thought we would have dinner, then go to a movie." He replied a bit shakily. "M,Maybe, Leonardo's for pizza or Chinese food and then the movie at the S,Strand."

Maria smiled. "That sounds nice," she offered.

The Curcuru house is a modest three bedroom, one bath colonial. The lot is small, just a back deck, a small backyard and a one car driveway. The Curcuru family arrived from Sicily about four years back, with their four children, Angela being the oldest. They found Gloucester to be a comfortable, Italian-American fishing community, which took them in without hesitation.

Sal landed a fishing site and proved to be a skilled fisherman. As hard-working, skilled, fishermen are always in demand, he has twice moved to better sites, on better fishing boats, and the family was beginning to enjoy a few creature comforts. Life in Gloucester and America has been good for the Curcuru family.

Angela came down the stairs wearing a white dress, which skirt fell just above her knees. While modestly cut, it attractively outlined her hourglass shape and the color contrasted nicely with her olive skin and summer tan. She wore strappy sandals, with a heel, which flattered her legs.

Bart, smiled on her appearance as she descended the stairs, rose to greet her. He reached out and took her hands, smiled in appreciation. "You look nice," he offered.

Sal looked at his daughter and smiled broadly. "Bambina, you are beautiful," he stated proudly.

Maria's eyes moved from Angela to Bart. She watched Bart's reaction with interest. She noted Angela's blush as Bart's eyes gleamed in appreciation.

Angela smiled. Unaccustomed to such attention, she certainly enjoyed the compliments. Her eyes never left Bart's as she thanked her Dad for his words.

"We should go," Bart stated, still holding her hands. "The movie starts at eight and we will have dinner first."

"Have fun," Maria urged.

"Angela," Sal added, his eyes on Bart. "You be home by eleven."

Bart met Sal's eyes. "I,I will have her home s,safe, by eleven, Sir." He managed.

As they exited the Curcuru house, Bart took Angela's hand as they walked to Main Street, where both the movie and restaurants were located. They walked a block when Bart stopped, turned to face Angela, "you look beautiful, Angela." He paused. "Thank you for saying yes to our date."

Angela smiled. "I was hoping you would call, Bart." She squeezed his hand. "But, when the morning went by, I thought you wouldn't call."

Bart moved closer. "I worked this morning," he countered softly. He took a deep calming, breath, and, as a bonus, he savored her aroma. Angela smelled of wildflowers and woman. "I wasn't sure that you would agree." He smiled. "I am glad you did."

Angela grinned. "Yes, my Dad told me that you were quite the star this morning."

Bart flushed at the compliment. "Thanks," he responded. "We should go, I'm hungry."

They walked hand-in-hand to China Port restaurant, which was but a block from the theatre. They made small talk and Bart found himself relaxed and comfortable with Angela.

They were seated at a booth. "Does a pu-pu platter and some fried rice sound okay, Angela?" He asked, as they sat.

Angela nodded, smiled into his handsome, expressive face. "That sounds fine, Bart," she responded.

When the flaming platter arrived, it was set between them. The platter was a lazy-susan, with the center flaming and the various egg-rolls, meats and shrimp set around the platter.

Bart smiled as he looked at Angela's face, prettily, illuminated by the glow of the flame. He paused, eyed her. "Angela, you look great." He smiled brightly as she blushed. Bart turned his attention to the food. "Let's eat, I'm hungry."

Angela grinned as Bart dug in. She took one pork strip from the platter and a small portion of rice and placed it on her dish. Bart filled his plate with barbequed pork ribs, chicken wings, fried shrimp, an egg roll and pork strips on which he ladled sweet sauce. He then piled a mound of fried rice on his plate, which he also topped with sweet sauce.

Bart glanced up and smiled as he caught Angela's eye, then surprised, noted her almost empty plate. "Angela, do you not like Chinese food?" He watched her closely. "Should we have gone for pizza?"

"No Bart," she responded, smiling. She reached across the table and patted his hand. "I do like Chinese food." She shrugged, "I'm just not very hungry."

Perplexed, he laughed. "Really? Not hungry?" He paused, shook his head and grinned. "I wonder what that is like."

Angela laughed aloud, provoking a satisfied smile from Bart. "I like your laugh," he said.

On the sound of her laugh, a head turned from another booth. The teenage girl turned in her seat. "Angela, is that you?"

Angela greeted the girl with a bright smile. "Hi Betsy," she responded.

Betsy and her date rose and walked to Bart and Angela's booth. As they approached the booth, Betsy's eyes widened when she saw Bart turn and smile. Betsy was a pert blond, short and slim, but with a bright smile and expressive blue eyes. In looks she was the polar opposite of Angela. But, much like Angela, her ready smile was always welcoming.

"Hi Bart, how are you?" She paused, turned and smiled at the young man with her. "You know Jim Perry, right?" She asked.

Bart rose, smiled and shook Jim's hand. "Of course, since kindergarten." He indicated the booth. "Would you like to join us?"

Jim glanced to Betsy, "shall we?" He laughed. "That platter looks good!"

Betsy looked at the table, then to Jim. "Should we? They already have their food."

"N,no problem," Bart responded. "You'll share our pu-pu platter and rice, then we'll order m,more food." He took a deep breath. "Please sit."

Jim and Betsy slipped into the booth together, Bart moved his plate and sat beside Angela.

The waiter brought two more plates and Jim filled his plate and dug in. Like Angela, Betsy placed very little food on her plate.

Bart looked from Angela to Betsy. "Betsy, please feel free to fill your plate, we'll order more."

Betsy glanced at Angela, then smiled, "I'm fine, just not very hungry."

Jim looked to Bart and grinned, "They're pretty and they don't eat much." He laughed. "Now, that's what I call a date."

They all laughed. Betsy playfully punched Jim's arm. "Cheap date, huh?"

Jim beamed a smile. "Anything you say, Beautiful." He paused, raised his brows. "One can always hope." They all were relaxed and smiling. Jim had a way of lightening what might otherwise be a stressful social situation.

Bart shook his head. "I don't really get this not being hungry thing," he laughed, gently nudged Angela. "Okay, but please feel free."

"Thanks," Betsy responded. Then turned to Angela. "I had no idea that you two were dating. How long has it been?"

Angela smiled, looked to Bart. "I guess this is our first date."

Bart met her smile with a wink, "b,but hopefully not our last." He was rewarded with Angela squeezing his hand and smiling in a way that lit her eyes.

Betsy grinned. "Us too, this is our first date." She glanced at Jim, flashed a smile. "How am I doing?"

Jim winked at Betsy. "So far, you're doing okay." He raised his brows. "You're still on probation, of course, but I'll let you know!"

"Always the clown," Betsy said on a laugh. Angela and Bart laughed with them.

Bart watched the exchange with a grin. Saw the amusement in Betsy's eyes. He looked at Jim. "So Jim, are you playing on the golf team this year?"

"I hope so, tryouts start Monday," he paused, shook his head, "no, actually Tuesday, he shrugged, you know Labor Day is a busy day for the members at Bass Rocks Golf Club." He paused looked to Bart. "I'm practicing and playing at Bass Rocks tomorrow afternoon. Want to join me?"

Bart sat back, eyeing Jim and considering the offer.

"That sounds like fun," Angela offered, before Bart responded. It hit her that golf might be perfect for Bart. 'No need to talk in golf,' she thought.

"I,I haven't played for months." Bart responded, thoughtfully. An idea struck. He glanced at the girls and smiled. "H,H,How about Jim and I, pplay tomorrow, then you both join us for a cold drink."

Betsy looked to Jim, who pleased her by eagerly nodding. "That would be great," he enthused. He smiled at Betsy, "would you like to meet me after golf?"

Betsy smiled. "I'd like that." She responded, as she eyed Jim, with an amused glint in her eye.

Bart turned to Angela and smiled. "Wwould you like to join us?" He asked hopefully.

Angela smiled. "Sounds good, but then you'll need to get me home for Sunday dinner." She flushed with embarrassment. "My Dad is going fishing tomorrow at mid-night and we have to be home for dinner, to sorta say goodbye." She paused, leaned toward Bart, her cheeks coloring. "Would you like to have Sunday dinner with us?"

Bart beamed a smile at her, saw the hope in her eyes, her cheeks reddening and thought how beautiful she looked. At that moment, he so wished he could kiss her. "I'd love to," he responded. He turned back to Jim. "I'll be there."

Bart had chosen a movie he guessed Angela would like. It was billed as a romantic comedy, which Bart thought was more romantic drama than comedy. Still, he was happy to see that Angela was engrossed. Her face was wet with tears which provided a golden opportunity for Bart to put his arm around Angela's shoulders and pull her to him. At a particularly dramatic scene, Bart turned Angela's face and placed a soft kiss on her lips. To his delight, Angela cuddled closer and met his lips eagerly. Their eyes met and Bart saw that his feelings for her may well be shared by Angela. He smiled, kissed her again and said softly; "I,I want you to be m,my girl." He swallowed, nervously. "Angela, wwill you be my girl?"

Angela offered a soft smile. "Don't be nervous with me Bart," she kissed him. "I so want to be your girl."

The movie ended about 10pm. Bart walked Angela home slowly, wanting to spend as much time with her as possible. As they walked he held her hand and used every opportunity to gently tug her closer to his side. Angela smiled and offered no resistance. They were smitten with each other. They each had doubts and insecurities about themselves. Together, they felt differently.

With Bart, Angela felt beautiful, she saw how he looked at her. In his eyes she was not 'Ugly Angela,' she was pretty, desirable and cherished.

Bart felt powerful and confident with Angela. He never feared being embarrassed and ridiculed. Angela always encouraged him in words and deeds, making clear, that with her, he never needed to feel anything but special.

When they arrived at Angela's home, Bart took her into his arms, looked into her eyes and asked; "Is it possible to be in love with a girl this quickly?"

Angela gasped and offered an impish smile. "I hope so, Bart, because I feel the same way."

He kissed her deeply, holding her body to his. "Angela," he whispered.

She kissed him. "I know Bart, I know."

"A cold shower for the kid tonight," he joked.

"Think of me tonight," Angela responded. "Because, I will be thinking of you."

Bart took a deep breath. "How about I pick you up for nine o'clock mass tomorrow?"

Angela laughed, kissed Bart. "Really? Sounds good, about 8:30 in the morning?"

"I'll be here." He promised, exhaled deeply. "Sleep well, beauty."

Angela smiled. "You too."

Chapter Four

Angela believed that Bart attending Sunday mass with her was a statement. In her mind, and her mother's, a man took a woman to mass to quietly proclaim to the community that they were a couple, that his desire for her was spiritual as well as physical.

She dressed carefully in a navy skirt, which fell above the knee and a white sweater, modest enough for church, but which showed her shape. She stood before the mirror, with her mother, and put on gold earrings and necklace. Her hair fell softly to her shoulders.

"You look beautiful, Angela." Maria smiled and squeezed her shoulder.

Looking in the mirror, eyes on her mother, she felt vulnerable. "Mom, I know that I am not beautiful, but," she sighed. "Am I pretty enough?"

Maria knew what Angela was asking. "Angela," Maria spoke softly. "When a man loves you, you will be beautiful in his eyes." She smiled. "And, the rest, do not matter."

Bart just wanted to be with Angela. He found her to be kind, beautiful, and generous of heart. She had been there for him on the most humiliating day of his life. He still shook at the horror of that night. He still heard the mocking of the Salem High School linebacker, and the frustration of his teammates. He very much still felt the humiliation of being taken off of the field before of thousands of Gloucester fans, his neighbors and family.

Bart still saw the pain in his mother's eyes as he removed his helmet and looked to his family. Angela had helped him that evening far more than she could ever know. With Angela by his side, he believed he could do anything. He wanted to be everything to her. He so wanted to make her proud.

Bart, dressed in gray pants, a blue striped shirt and a navy sports jacket, held Angela's hand as they entered St. Ann's Catholic Church. He chose a pew and they took their place. They knelt side by side, Bart's forearm in contact with Angela. When they stood or were seated, he held her hand.

Angela heard the whispers and saw the glances. She held Bart's hand as if he was a life line. Before the eyes of the community, her fears and insecurities rose to the surface. She felt bile rise to her throat. She glanced at Bart's strikingly handsome face. She felt the hardness of his muscular, athletic body, and she doubted whether she was good enough, pretty enough, to be Bart's girl.

Angela tried to reassure herself with the thought that whatever they all thought of her looks, Bart seemed proud to present her as his girl. Her family was relatively new in the community, but well respected. She was known to be bright and happy. To be with Bart DeMarco, who was handsome, athletic and smart, gave her confidence. But, she worried, could it really last? Angela had long been hurt in a very profound way by the 'Ugly Angela' slings. She imagined that many wondered why Bart DeMarco would be with Angela when he could be with other, more attractive girls. Angela harbored the same thoughts and fears.

It has long been said that a man's great weakness is his ego and a woman's, her vanity. A 16 year old girl who feels unattractive, will feel unworthy of being loved.

Bart glanced over at Angela, read her eyes, smiled and leaned in close. "Angela," he whispered, for her ears only, "You look beautiful today."

She turned to him with moist eyes. "Really?" she responded, a single tear escaped and ran down her cheek. Embarrassed, she looked to the altar.

Bart knew where Angela's crippling self-doubt originated, and it outraged him. Still, thinking of Angela's needs, rather than his anger, he managed to flash a bright smile. "Absolutely," he said, without hesitation or stutter. "Angela, please look at me."

They were kneeling as the gifts were brought to the priest by the altar boys. She slowly turned her head and met his eyes. Bart took a deep breath and in a now serious tone, he said, "I am the lucky one." he held her gaze, but spoke with certainty. "I want you to be my girl."

He was rewarded with her smile. She looked to the altar and the priest offering mass. She nodded, "let's pay attention to mass," she urged.

He grinned, resisted the urge to kiss her cheek. "Okay, as long as you walk with me to receive communion with your head held high and a smile on your pretty face."

Angela studied Bart's eyes. She read his sincerity, and nodded. "I will," she paused, took a breath. "You are very special, Bart, please always remember that."

Bart grinned, leaned close, "if I forget, you can remind me."

The line proceeding down the aisle to receive the sacrament moved in single file. Angela walked in front of Bart, a smile fixed on her face. Bart kept his hand on her shoulder, only dropping it when she, then he, stood before Father Capelli, and took the host.

Father Capelli placed the host on Bart's tongue and offered a blessing and a smile.

At the conclusion of mass, the aisle was crowded as the faithful slowly made their way to the exit, before which stood Father Capelli, speaking with parishioners. Bart held Angela's hand as they exchanged pleasantries with friends and friends of their families.

"So, you two are together?" Asked a school acquaintance, Jessica Arnold, surprise in her tone. Jessica, the pretty, blond haired, blue eyed captain of the football cheerleading team, was dressed for church services in a soft cream colored blouse and navy skirt. Angela noted how slim and beautiful Jessica looked, at least four inches taller than she, with her long, sleek, legs. By contrast, Angela felt short and squat, wide of hip and quite unattractive. Exactly, the 'Ugly Angela' that Jessica had labeled her.

Jessica had directed the question to Bart, after giving Angela a long, disdainful look.

Angela was intimidated by Jessica's smile and presence. Angela well remembered how it was Jessica and her clique of friends who first called her 'Ugly Angela' in Junior High school. Those girls saw how deeply the words hurt Angela. In a mean spirited enthusiasm, they used their social prominence and the need of so many pre-teens to be accepted, to spread the insult and make the label stick.

"We are, Jessica," Bart responded proudly to Jessica's smirk, with a smile. He shrugged, "it's new," he paused, flashed a loving smile on Angela. "I just hope Angela doesn't get tired of me."

Angela smiled up at Bart, took his arm, but before she could speak, Jessica turned the subject. "I guess Friday's game was tough for you, Bart?"

Bart held his smile. He took a deep breath as he felt some anxiety. "The important thing is that we won." He eyed her, "everything else will work itself out."

Jessica laughed. "I guess, it was Dave to the rescue," she said, angled her head, offered her pretty smile. "We didn't see you at the victory party," she added. "A bit too painful?" She asked.

Bart nodded, ignored the comment about the party. "Dave did a good job when I came out." He paused, took a breath. "He's a good guy."

Angela heard a meanness to Jessica's words. She eyed Jessica, ready to rise to Bart's defense. But, before she could speak, she felt Bart gently squeeze her arm. Angela looked to Bart and noted that Bart seemed undisturbed, and bit her tongue.

"Well, good luck you two," Jessica said, casually and somewhat dismissively, as she moved up the aisle.

Bart put his arm about Angela's shoulder, and pulled her to him, as he shook his head. 'How sad,' he thought, as he watched Jessica walk away. He looked to Angela. "Are you okay?"

Angela's eyes moved from the departing Jessica to Bart. "She's so pretty." Angela said softly, as she felt envy.

Bart smiled. "Not as pretty as my girl!" He stated. He looked into Angela's eyes. "And, no way is she as nice."

Angela smiled. "You are a good guy, Bart." She said softly. She looked to Jessica, long, lean and beautiful. Angela felt anything but pretty.

When Bart and Angela reached Father Capelli, Angela noted the priest's warm smile. "It's good to see you two together." Father Capelli stated. "Very good indeed!"

"Thank you Father," Bart responded.

Angela smiled warmly, holding Bart's arm. "I enjoyed the mass." Angela offered.

Father Capelli studied Angela, smiled warmly. "Thank you, Angela." He gazed at the young couple. "You two are good people, never let anything or anybody beat you."

Bart laughed. "Don't you worry about that Father, we will be fine." He said smoothly and without a stutter. He turned to Angela and smiled. "Am I right, beauty?"

Angela blushed at Bart's words. Father Capelli laughed aloud. "I always thought you were a smart kid, Bart."

Hand in hand they descended the church's granite steps. Bart turned to Angela and grinned, "Hey, are you up for some breakfast and a little scrutiny, at my house?"

"You want me to come to your house for breakfast? Really?" Angela asked, her surprise showing.

Bart stopped and eyed Angela. Surprised, he took her two hands. "Angela, have I read us wrong?" He paused, felt some anxiety, he took a deep breath. "I,I,I want you t,to be my ggirl." He stuttered out. "I,I thought you wanted that too." Feeling somewhat confused, he searched her eyes.

Angela softly placed her hand to still his lips. Her eyes were warm and kind. "Bart, I'm sorry." She took a deep breath. "There is nothing in this world I want more than to be your girl." She paused. "I thought that maybe you were just being nice." She dropped her eyes. "I thought…," she hesitated, thought of Jessica, as she teared up. "I thought that you would want…"

Bart cut her off. "You, Angela," he said clearly and forcefully. He put his hand on her chin, gently raised her face so he could meet her eyes. "I want you!" Tears escaped to trickle down her cheeks as he kissed her softly. "Angela, I want you, okay?"

Angela's tears ran freely, streaking her face. She managed a smile. "Okay, Bart," she took a deep breath, summoning the courage to hope and to believe. "Okay Bart, I'm yours." She took his hands. Her eyes showed the fear and the doubts she lived with. "But, please, if…" She choked, stopped, and fell into his arms.

He held her tight, stroking his hand over her back tenderly. "My beautiful Angela," he said in a soothing voice. "I love you," he whispered. "I want to be with you, I want you to be my girl." Bart sensed a gentleness, an essential kindness in Angela that was unique in his experience. His heart and his gut told him that Angela was the one.

Bart shook his head, laughed softly. "I don't understand it, I have never felt this way before, but I do love you." They held each other on Pleasant Street, in the very shadow of their church, for a long moment. Then he laughed, kissed her tear stained face. "Now, how about some breakfast?"

Angela insisted on stopping at home before going to Bart's house for breakfast. Bart waited in the living room chatting with Mr. Curcuru, as Angela washed and freshened her face.

Angela re-appeared with a smile for Bart and with her mother at her side. Maria smiled up at Bart, then hugged him. "Thank you, Bart." Maria said, softly.

"Okay," Angela laughed. "I am ready for breakfast."

Bart took Angela's hand, grinned and challenged; "into the lion's den for you, Angela."

Angela laughed. "You can't scare me, DeMarco," she responded light-heartily, "your mother is sweet."

While Angela was a bit uneasy as she entered the DeMarco home, breakfast was wonderfully relaxing. Bart's mother had long liked Angela and her family.

The DeMarco family sat to breakfast together. Angela sat next to Bart, Mario and Lucia across the table. Bart's Dad, Franco, sat at the table's head, to Bart's right and Bart's mother, Rosa, across from Franco.

"These blueberry pancakes are wonderful, Mrs. DeMarco." Angela complimented. She continued to enjoy the pancake, and nibbling on the one strip of bacon she placed on her plate.

"Thank you, Angela," Rosa responded. "I am so glad we could have you for breakfast." She nodded to her husband and son, Mario, "Franco and Mario both head out to sea tonight."

Angela nodded. "Yes, my Dad too."

"The life of a fisherman," Franco offered, looking at Angela. He observed her plate with one pancake and a strip of bacon. "Aren't you hungry, Angela?" Franco queried. "We have plenty," he assured.

Lucia looked to her father. "Dad, Angela may be a little nervous." She offered in a soft tone. "You know, the first time in our home as Bart's girlfriend."

Franco looked from his daughter to his wife. "Why nervous?" He flashed Angela a smile, and Angela saw from whom Bart inherited his dazzling smile. Franco continued, "Angela, I want you to be comfortable in our home." He glanced at Bart, then back to Angela. "We DeMarco's value our friends."

Angela smiled at Franco's words and as Bart squeezed her hand, she found herself relaxing. "Thank you, Mr. DeMarco, I really appreciate that." She found that she liked the sound of Lucia's phrase, 'Bart's girlfriend.'

Lucia looked to Angela. "Did you have a good time last night?"

Angela smiled at Lucia. "Yes, I did." She smiled. "I was pleased, but a little surprised that Bart called, you know, so late in the day." She paused, squeezed Bart's hand. "We had Chinese food with some friends and the movie was very good," Angela added.

Lucia grinned broadly, as did Mario and Franco. Angela noted the grins and questioningly, looked to Bart, as Lucia needled, "so Bart, why did you call Angela so late?"

Bart flushed. "Okay, okay," he looked at Angela and smiled. "I was nervous about asking you out so soon, but my nosy sister told me that it was okay to call." He sat back, held Angela's hand. He looked to Angela. "I'm glad I listened."

"Me too," Angela responded. She smiled a thanks to Lucia. "Lucia, I think we may be good friends."

Lucia returned the smile. "So, you liked the movie?"

Angela nodded. "It was good, kind of a tear jerker," she noted.

Mario smiled across the table at his brother. "Good move Bart, I took Celia there to see the movie on Thursday," he winked. "And, she really enjoyed it."

Lucia rolled her eyes at Mario. "Did you enjoy it Mario?" She asked.

Mario laughed. "Well, I enjoyed that Celia was happy." He responded, with a gleam in his eye.

"Vero, Mario," Rosa offered. "It is good you think of Celia."

Lucia rolled her eyes and laughed. "Yes, Mom, Mario is a saint like that."

Mario laughed aloud. Angela looked to Lucia. "Did I miss something, Lucia?"

Lucia adored her brothers. She laughed and looked to Angela, "I guess you don't have older brothers?" She smiled. "We'll talk later."

Chapter Five

Bart met Jim Perry on the range at the Bass Rocks Golf Club. The Golf Club, while private, allowed the Gloucester High School golf team to use the golf course for practice and matches. As a bonus, Dave Gilliss, one of the Asst. golf professionals at the club was the teams coach. Coach Gilliss was a tall and lanky 22 year old. He had harbored dreams of playing golf professionally, but learned that his skills, while considerable, would never be sufficient to carry him beyond the occasional mini-tour event. At age 20, he went to school to become a PGA Professional. He discovered his real golf talent was as a teacher. And fortunately, he found that he truly enjoyed teaching.

Jim and Bart set up on the practice range. Dave Gilliss, who was on the putting green, adjacent to the range, looked over to see Bart take a smooth swing with his driver and launch the ball down the center of the range, and over 270 yards.

Jim saw it as well. "Nice swing, Bart." He paused. "Don't you bat left-handed in baseball?"

Bart nodded. "I do, Jim." He explained, as Coach Gilliss approached. "I'm a natural rightie, but baseball is a game for left-handed batters and right-handed throwers." He shrugged. "My Dad had me bat left-handed from the beginning."

"Good," Coach Gilliss stated. "Your golf swing won't interfere with your baseball swing." He shrugged. "And the opposite is also true." He nodded. "Your Dad is a smart guy."

Bart laughed. "He'd love to hear that!"

Coach Gilliss smiled. He looked at Bart's golf clubs. "Are you both planning on attending tryouts for the golf team?" He asked.

"I am," Jim responded. "And, I hope that Bart will as well."

The Coach looked to Bart. "I think that you might enjoy the team, Bart." He paused. "I've only seen a few swings, but I see potential." He smiled. "And, we have to do something to upgrade these clubs."

Bart looked at Coach Gilliss. "I don't know, Coach. I am on the football team and the season has started." He paused, reflected, "and Coach Nelson," he paused, looked at Gilliss, "I,I really haven't played much golf."

Gilliss looked at Bart, noted the stutter. "Do you like to play golf, Bart?"

Bart nodded. "I do, bbut," he stumbled.

Coach Dave smiled and broke in. "Look, why don't we play a round together. Let's see, okay guys?"

Bart and Jim nodded.

"I have to check in with Peter in the pro-shop, why don't you keep on getting ready, roll a few putts and we'll take it out on the course." Coach added.

They began on the 1st tee. Jim Perry, at 5' 10' and 150 pounds was not big, but Bart noted that he had a nice tempo to his swing and hit the ball well. Bart followed and rocketed his drive 50 yards past Jim's ball. Coach Dave was impressed at Bart's power, generated from what appeared to be an effortless swing. He watched with interest, bordering on excitement. He saw real potential.

Bart's round was spotty, at best. Big, strong and with excellent hand-eye coordination, Bart's smooth swing produced some big drives, high approach shots, but, plenty of poor shots, as well. Still, the Coach saw enough to realize that with work and coaching, Bart could be a very special golfer. He studied Bart with a teacher's eye. 'I could do a lot with him.' Coach Gilliss thought. He mentally shrugged. 'But, would he be willing to dedicate the time and effort required?' He wondered.

Jim played solid and it appeared obvious that he would be an asset on the team. Coach Gilliss was impressed with Jim, who, did not fall for the trap of trying to out-drive Bart. Jim played his game, kept his head and managed his way around the course. At one point, after making a birdie putt, Jim grinned and said; "golf is not a game of how far, but how many."

That comment produced a laugh from Bart and Coach Gilliss. "That is so true," the Coach offered. "Of course, a long and controlled drive is a great weapon."

"Great work guys," Coach Gilliss commented as they approached the golf shop at the conclusion of the round. "Why don't you have a cold drink, I'll check in to the shop and we will talk on the deck."

It was a warm September day. The guys found Angela and Betsy waiting on the deck, dressed attractively in sun-dresses and sandals, enjoying the beautiful views of Thatcher's Island with its' twin lighthouses, the waves gently lapping the shore. Bart smiled at seeing Angela. 'So pretty,' he thought.

"How did it go?" Angela asked, with a hopeful smile.

Bart met Angela's smile. "Dave did great, he shot an 82," Bart responded. "And, on this course, that's a really good score."

"That's great," Betsy congratulated, flashing Jim a smile.

"And?" Angela asked. Eyeing Bart hopefully.

Bart did fine, for a guy who hasn't played much." Jim offered. "Oh, here's the Coach."

Coach Gilliss joined the two young couples at the table. A waitress took drink orders, "Five Arnold Palmers on me." Coach ordered.

"Arnold Palmers?" Betsy asked.

The Coach laughed. "It is half lemonade and half ice-tea." He explained. "It was the great Arnold Palmer's favorite thirst quencher."

"Should we leave, Coach?" Angela asked, rising. "Do you three need some privacy?"

Coach Gilliss looked to Bart and Jim.

Bart smiled. "I'm good with the girls staying, if Jim is."

Jim nodded, "Okay with me." He looked to the Coach as the cold drinks were served.

Coach Gillis eyed the boys. "Try-outs start Tuesday, but Jim, you are a solid golfer. You belong on the team."

Jim smiled. "Thanks Coach," he responded. He looked to Betsy and beamed. Jim saw Betsy meet his smile.

Coach Gilliss turned to Bart and eyed him thoughtfully. Angela felt herself tense. 'He's been through so much,' she thought. 'Please, give him some good news.'

"Bart," Coach Gilliss began, "I think with hard work and dedication you could be a truly great golfer." He paused. Bart relaxed and Angela beamed a smile. "You naturally generate an unusually fast swing speed. In fact," he offered, "way above what most high school players are capable of generating." He paused. "If you choose to play, I will work with you on harnessing your potential." He eyed Bart. "However, you would need to commit to some hard work."

Bart looked at Angela's beaming smile, then turned to Coach Gilliss. "I need to think about this." He considered, "and I have to speak to Coach Nelson, before, I will make a decision." He eyed Coach Gilliss. "I owe him that." He looked at the Coach, "may I tell you Tuesday?"

Dave Gilliss was impressed at Bart's innate fairness and character. "Of course, speak to Coach Nelson and your family. If you are here Tuesday for try-outs I will know your decision." He rose to leave them, eyed the four young people, flashed a smile at Angela. "You are right, he is pretty special." He looked at Bart. "Let me leave you with one thought, Bart. Golf is a game for life. And for you, it could be the ticket to your future." With that he headed into the pro-shop.

Bart watched him go, then looked at Angela quizzically. He smiled. "So, Angela, what was Coach talking about?"

She flushed with embarrassment, but managed to hold her smile. She looked at Bart, "I will tell you about it on our walk home." She paused, sipped her drink, very aware of Bart's appraising eye. She glanced at the clock. "Maybe, we should head home."

"Of course," Bart rose, shook Jim's hand. "Thanks for inviting me, Jim. I had a good time." He looked at Betsy. "Great seeing you again, Betsy," Bart grinned, "we are having dinner at Angela's house, and, we have a good walk." He flashed a smile. "And, unless I want to eat alone in the basement or outside in her yard, I'll need a shower."

They all laughed as Bart and Angela headed off of the deck, Bart throwing his golf bag on his shoulder as they began a pleasant walk home.

Betsy looked to Jim. "He didn't stutter once."

"No," Jim agreed. "Nor did he stutter on the course." He thought about it. "When he is focused and at ease, it really is a minor issue. It seems that it is when he becomes anxious that he stutters."

"Yes, I think you are right." She reflected. "Remember how bad his speech issues were in elementary school and Junior High school?" She paused and shook her head. "And, how mean the kids were and how often they embarrassed him?"

"I do," Jim nodded. "Both, he and Angela have been treated badly."

Betsy flushed. "Those 'Ugly Angela' taunts were awful." She paused, dropped her eyes. "I'm ashamed that I contributed to her pain."

Bart and Angela walked from Bass Rocks Golf Club to home feeling happy with the day. Bart moderated his stride to accommodate Angela. "This is a good walk," Bart said. "Did you walk here?"

"No," Angela responded. "Betsy's mother drove us." She paused and looked to Bart. "I don't mind walking."

Bart nodded. "I know," he smiled, "but soon I will be able to test for my driver's license. And, then I will escort you in style," he laughed. "If you consider my Dad's Ford as stylish."

That brought a smile to Angela's lips that reached her eyes. "Like a Princess?" she teased.

"Okay Princess Angela," Bart said lightly. "Do you want to tell me what Coach meant when he said that you were right about me?"

Angela placed concerned eyes on Bart. Her cheeks reddened with embarrassment. Bart studied her closely. "Are you okay, Princess?" He asked, hoping to keep it light and easy for her.

Angela spoke slowly, as if she was carefully choosing her words. She took a deep breath, stopped walking and turned to face Bart. "Can we sit?" She asked, motioning to a low stone wall, fronting a gracious colonial style home. Bart nodded and they sat side by side. She took Bart's hands and he felt the tremble in her grasp. He eyed her closely. "You're trembling, Angela," he noted with concern. "Is something wrong?"

Her eyes met his. "I called Coach Gilliss," Angela admitted softly. "See, I thought about what Jim said at dinner." Bart said nothing, but kept his eyes on her face. "And, I thought about Friday night's game." She paused and tears came to her eyes. "I hated seeing you so hurt." Her voice broke and she took a deep breath. Angela took tissues out of her purse, wiped her eyes. "I kept thinking that there had to be some way to solve this problem." Tears ran down her cheeks. Bart used his thumbs to gently wipe away her tears. "Then, I remembered watching you play baseball last spring." She took a deep breath. "You hit a homerun and everybody watching said that you had such a sweet swing."

She took another deep breath. "So, I figured that swinging a golf club can't be that much different from swinging a baseball bat," she eyed Bart as her lips trembled. "So, I called Coach Gilliss and told him that maybe you could be on the golf team." She looked down, away from Bart's gaze, took a deep breath as tears ran down her cheeks. "I told him that you were a special person and a special athlete." She looked at him with her eyes brimming with tears. "I know I should not have done that, but" she paused, wiped at her tears and blew her nose. "Bart, I believe in you, and I wanted to help you." She took a deep breath and kept contrite eyes on Bart. "I'm sorry."

Bart leaned forward and kissed her softly. He flashed a smile. "So, you think I'm special, Princess?"

Angela exhaled in relief that Bart wasn't angry with her, shook her head and laughed. "Maybe, a little," she admitted.

Bart laughed. He kissed her and held her hands. "Angela, thank you for believing in me. This golf thing just might work out." He paused, made eye contact. "But, in the future, talk to me before ever doing anything like that, okay?"

Angela nodded. "Okay, I promise." She hesitated, searched his face. "Are you still coming to dinner?" She asked softly, hopefully.

He looked into Angela's eyes, saw the concern and the uncertainty. He hated what those cruel kids had done to her self-confidence. He shook his head, playfully. "Of course," he laughed. "How could a special guy pass up dining with a Princess?"

Angela laughed and began breathing normally, she wiped her tears and stood. "We should be moving so we can make it in time for dinner." She looked up and into his eyes. "My Mom made a special dinner for tonight."

Bart hoisted his golf bag onto his shoulder, took Angela's hand and began walking. He looked at Angela. "Is it a special occasion?" He thought for a minute. "Should I dress?"

"I'm sure that shorts and a polo shirt will be fine." She paused, thought about her response. "My Mom feels it is a special dinner."

Bart walked a bit, then asked. "So, what's the special occasion?"

Angela looked to Bart, waited, until his eyes met hers, she produced a sheepish smile. "The special occasion is that you are coming to dinner."

He looked into her eyes and studied Angela. "Me! Really? WOW!" He smiled broadly. "That's great."

Showered and dressed in Khakis and a polo shirt, Bart arrived at Angela's house. Mr. Curcuru was relaxing in the living room watching the Red Sox battle in an extra-inning game. Mrs. Curcuru could be heard in the kitchen readying dinner. Bart smiled at the sound of Angela's voice as she conversed with her mother and sister.

Bart shook hands with Angela's Dad and then walked through to the kitchen to see Angela. She was with her sister, Tina, and her Mom, working together, to complete dinner preparations. He wasn't immediately noticed, which gave him the opportunity to watch Angela move about. His smile showed that he liked what he saw. Angela had also changed her outfit. She wore white shorts and a red sleeveless blouse. As she moved to and opened the oven to check on the garlic bread, he cleared his throat to announce himself and caught Angela's eye as she glanced over her shoulder from where she was bent over looking into the oven. Angela blushed at Bart's appreciative smile.

Maria noticed Bart and smiled as she saw Bart take in Angela. To see Bart so captured by Angela made her happy. She knew the tears Angela had shed at the cruel 'Ugly Angela' insults. The nights Angela cried herself to sleep. The worst part was what it did to Angela's confidence. Maria knew that the attention of such a handsome boy would do wonderful things for Angela's self-esteem.

Maria went to greet Bart, throwing her arms around Bart and hugging him. Maria looked into Bart's eyes as she kissed both cheeks, in the traditional Italian greeting. "Thank you for being so good to Angela," Maria whispered. Bart smiled. Maria turned to her daughter, "Angela, aren't you going to greet your boyfriend?"

Angela moved across the kitchen and kissed Bart. With a suggestive flush, she whispered, "Bart, did you enjoy the view of the garlic bread?"

Bart laughed. "Oh, is there garlic bread?" He asked softly, then glanced about, noted Maria was occupied with readying a salad and Tina was setting the table. In a low voice for Angela's ears only, he said "I like garlic bread," he grinned, "and that was the most beautifully presented garlic bread I have ever seen, Princess."

Angela blushed red. Still, she smiled brightly. "Shall we go out onto the deck and have a cold drink?"

They sat on a loveseat with glasses of lemonade. Glancing over his shoulder, Bart could see that Angela's family was not about and he slipped his arm around Angela and pulled her close. "I like holding you." He said softly.

Angela grinned and snuggled closer. "I like you holding me," she responded. She glanced back at the house, "but remember where we are," she cautioned. "I don't think my Dad would like you holding me so close."

Bart nodded. "Point taken," he conceded and loosened his hold a bit. "Did you enjoy today at Bass Rocks?"

"I did," Angela responded with a smile. "It is so pretty there and Betsy and I had a nice chat."

Bart looked closely at Angela. "Do you like Betsy?"

Angela looked into Bart's eyes. She swallowed, "she was one of them," Angela said softly. "We talked about it today."

"Really?" Bart responded. "How did it come up?"

"When Betsy's mother dropped us at Bass Rocks, we were walking to the deck to wait for you guys." Angela looked into the distance. "She complimented me on how nice I looked in my sun-dress, and I just looked at her." She paused. "Betsy began to cry and apologized for being part of that group."

"What did you say?" Bart asked softly as he took her hand and pulled her to him.

"I asked her why she did it." Angela flushed as the painful memories surfaced. "I told her that I needed one girl-friend to stand by me, just one." Angela paused and swallowed. "Bart, I felt so alone." Angela's eyes glistened with the tears of remembered pain.

She sipped her drink to swallow the lump in her throat. "Betsy told me that she was afraid that Jessica and the rest would turn on her." She sighed. "Betsy said that she hated what she did and asked me to forgive her."

"And?" Bart asked with a smile, although he thought he knew.

Angela shrugged. "I hugged her and forgave her." She looked at Bart, who was still smiling. "What are you smiling about?" Angela asked, but found herself smiling as well.

"I'm smiling because I was right." He laughed. "I like being right."

"Really?" She pressed. "And, hot shot, what are you so right about?" Angela asked, amused eyes on Bart.

"That my girl is not only beautiful on the outside, but so good on the inside." He paused, kissed her lightly. "And, that you are mine."

Angela misted with happy tears. "Oh Bart," she said as Angela's mother called the family to dinner.

Chapter Six

Coach Bob Nelson called a practice for the football team at 9am on Labor Day. Bart arrived at 8am and asked to speak with the Coach.

Bart entered Coach Nelson's office to find him seated at his desk and speaking with the team's offensive coach. Coach Nelson, smiled at Bart, "Please sit down, Bart." He concluded his thoughts to Coach Bailey, but asked Bailey to stay for the meeting with Bart.

Nelson turned to face Bart. "I'm glad you asked to meet." He paused, searching for the right words. "I know Friday's game had to be tough for you."

Bart nodded, but said nothing, as it appeared that Coach Nelson had more to say.

"Bart," Coach Nelson began. "I felt that it was best for the team that I take you out and put Dave in." He smiled, "that doesn't mean that you can't contribute to the team in other ways."

"Excuse me, Coach," Bart interjected. "May I speak?"

Coach Nelson sat back, eyes on Bart. He noted that Bart seemed focused and determined. "Of course Bart, speak freely."

"We ran one play when I was at Quarterback," Bart began. "It went for a 58 yard gain." He leaned forward, kept his eyes on the head coach. Bart took a breath and continued. "We were called for a delay of game penalty and a penalty for illegal procedure on our right tackle." Bart sat back, eyes set on Coach Nelson, who nodded in agreement. "Coach, you removed me from the game, but left our right tackle in the game." He paused. "Then Dave came in and threw an interception, in fact two interceptions, and, he fumbled a snap that Salem recovered." Bart paused, Nelson saw fire in his eyes. "But Dave stayed in the game!"

Nelson shifted in his seat as he considered Bart's words, recognizing the point he was making.

Bart kept hard eyes on Coach Nelson. "I was responsible for the delay of game penalty, but not for our tackle jumping off-side." He sat tall in the seat, eyes fixed on Coach Nelson. "I was playing my first game as the starting Quarterback, I recognized that an audible needed to be called and I messed up, no question." He sat forward. "Then, the play I called went for big yards, which seems to have become lost in all this!" He stressed, fixed hard eyes on the Head Coach. "I was pulled off of the field for essentially one mistake." He looked at Coach Bailey, then moved his gaze back to the Head Coach. "Why Coach?"

Nelson looked at Bart. "Bart, I just thought the team was better off with Dave at that point." He paused. "I understand what you are saying, but the team has to come first."

Bart sat back, took a deep breath, shook his head and smiled. "I understand Coach, whatever I think, you have to do what you believe is best for the team." He shrugged. "I guess that means my future with the team is in serious question." He smiled. "Maybe, the team would be better off without me."

"Wait Bart," Coach Nelson interrupted. "I didn't say that."

"I know you didn't say that Coach," He paused, took a deep breath. Bart recognized that he was jelling to a decision, and smiled. "So, Coach, what do you see as my role on the team?"

Coach Nelson studied Bart. "I really don't know Bart. We'll have to figure that out."

Bart sighed, rose from his chair. "I want to thank you Coach Nelson," and turning he added, "and you too, Coach Bailey." He paused, felt a load lift off of his shoulders. "I have wrestled all weekend over what to do, what is best for me and for the team." He shook his head and smiled. "For me, I don't want to be a spare part." Bart extended his hand to Coach Bailey, which the Coach took, shook and held. Bart turned to face Coach Nelson. "And, for the team, I have no role."

Bart sighed. "Coach, you need to focus on your team." He shrugged, "and that will be challenge enough." Bart completed shaking Bailey's hand, flashed a smile, and looked around Coach's office. He faced Coach Nelson. "I'll turn in my uniform and gear and wish my teammates the best of luck. Thank you," Bart offered Coach Nelson his hand.

Nelson shook Bart's hand. He looked into Bart's eyes. "You are a class act, Bart. I'm sorry this didn't work out for you." He stated.

Bart smiled. He thought of Angela and how she had been there for him on that difficult night. How, her kindness led to their date and ultimately to the possibility of playing on the golf team. He recalled Coach Gilliss's words, and the hope those simple and honest statements had instilled in Bart.

Bart looked at Coach Nelson. "Perhaps it did Coach, perhaps it did." He turned to leave, walked to the door. He paused, turned and said, "Coach, good luck with the team and the season." And with that, he headed from the office into the varsity locker room. He spoke to his teammates and paused to speak to Dave Powers. "Good luck, Dave, I wish you the best."

"Thanks Bart," Dave responded, collected his thoughts. "I'm sorry to see you leaving the team."

Bart nodded, "thanks for saying that Dave." He shook Dave's hand, smiled and left.

Bart walked home. He settled his mind on his future course. Once home, Bart called Angela and told her what had transpired.

"Are you okay?" Angela asked. Bart heard the concern in her tone.

"I'm good," he responded.

"Do you want to come over to my house?" She asked. "Talk more about this?"

Bart smiled. "Angela, I always want to be with you." He responded. "But, I think my time will be better spent at Bass Rocks working on my game." He considered possibilities. "I think I will give Coach Gilliss a call and see if I could use the practice facilities."

He relished the thought that she was concerned. "Angela, maybe, we can get together later for dinner." He suggested. "Mario and my Dad are out fishing, I am throwing burgers and dogs on the grill for Lucia, my Mom and me." He laughed. "It won't match the incredible manicotti and brascioli your mother made last night, but, it is Labor Day and a barbeque might be fun."

Angela brightened. "That sounds great," she paused. "Will it be okay with your mother?"

Bart laughed. "Absolutely, for some reason my Mom seems to like you."

Angela laughed. "Surprising huh?"

Now they were laughing together. "I can't figure it out." He relaxed back. "Gee, what does she see in you?" He waited a beat. "She didn't even see that great looking garlic bread."

Angela loved the sound of his laugh. "So, you liked the look of the garlic bread, did you?" She teased.

"Oh yeah," He replied. "I so wanted to get my hands on that garlic bread."

Angela flushed at the image. She loved that Bart was so attracted to her and how he flirted with her. He made her feel desired in a way she had never before experienced. She took a deep breath, closed her eyes and felt wanted and happy. "So what time should I be over for dinner?"

"How about 5pm?" He responded.

"Okay, I'll see you then." She paused. "Good luck at Bass Rocks."

Bart met Coach Gilliss at Bass Rocks. As Labor Day was a busy golf day for the Club members and the golf professionals, Coach Gilliss spent ten minutes with Bart on the putting green working on his stroke and left him to practice. "Remember Bart, in putting you have to be concerned with two things, speed and line. If your line is a bit off, but your speed is good, you will have a tap in." Gilliss eyed Bart, "work on getting the speed right." Bart nodded as Gilliss left to attend to a member's needs.

Bart spent the next hour working on his putting. Totally focused, he did not notice Gilliss watching him. The Coach noted that Bart's stroke was smooth and steady. And, his ability to read the greens and his speed control, was improving as he practiced.

"Very good, Bart." The Coach called. "Now let's move to chipping and pitching." They went to the chipping green and Coach Dave showed Bart how to stand with a slightly open stance, shift his weight forward, about 60% on his front leg and the best way to grip the club. "Pick a landing spot, then just sweep through, and let the ball run to the hole."

Bart worked with various clubs from a 6 iron to a sand wedge. "Each club has a different degree of loft," the Coach explained. "If you need to loft the ball high, maybe over a sand trap or some pond, and so it doesn't roll out as much, you use a lofted club and place the ball forward in your stance. If you have a good deal of green from the ball to the hole, play the ball off of your back foot and use a less lofted club." He showed Bart how to 'pitch and run' the ball. "It takes time and effort to become proficient in this part of the game." Gilliss explained. "But, you will save strokes and win matches."

Bart nodded. "I love practicing, effort will not be a problem." Bart smiled. "You know, Coach, pitching a golf ball is a bit like bunting." He then began working on his chipping and pitching skills. Coach Dave watched for a few minutes and offered, "Bart, I've seen that you are very athletic, with fantastic club-head speed. That is a great weapon, but golf is won from 100 yards in." Bart nodded. "Spend 75% of your practice time on the short game and," he repeated. "You will save strokes and win matches." The Coach then left Bart who worked for the next 90 minutes on this critical aspect of the game.

Coach Dave brought Bart a cold bottle of water, which Bart drank down. "Are you tired Bart?" Coach asked.

Bart finished off the bottle. "No Coach, I'm fine," Bart responded, "what's next?"

"Let's go to the range and hit irons," Coach instructed. They set up on the far end of the range and Bart began to take full swings with his wedges, then his 9 iron and on through to his 5 iron. Coach Gilliss smiled at the smooth, graceful swing, which produced high arcing shots. Bart's swing brought to mind Master's Champion, Fred Couples. "You must know how far you hit the ball with each club when taking a full swing," Coach stated. Bart seemed tireless as he hit 15-20 shots with each club. "We'll work on cut shots, fades, draws and half swings in time," he added with a smile. "There's a lot to learn."

Bart smiled acknowledging the point. "Thanks Coach, I appreciate you working with me." He hit a beautiful 5 iron over 195 yards, with a tight draw. "I want to become good at this game. I want to help the team." Bart added.

"I'm sure you will, Bart." He smiled. "And you're welcome."

After two hours of hitting irons, Bart was instructed to move to his fairway metals and then his driver. Coach Gilliss handed Bart a three club set of metal woods. "Try these Bart," Gilliss laughed. "Club technology has come a long way since the time when your clubs were cast."

Bart nodded, hefted and slowly swung the 5 metal, then the 3 metal. He dropped a ball, set over it and swung the 5 metal and grinned when he saw the result. "Wow!" Bart said with awe in his tone. He looked at Dave Gilliss. "These are great, Coach, "He paused. "How much for these clubs?"

Gilliss smiled. "These are my clubs, Bart." He eyed Bart, "we'll get you properly fit, before you buy a set."

The head professional, Peter Hood, stood watching and smiling as Bart launched drives 275-300 yards, and as important, right down the middle of the fairway.

Peter Hood whispered to Dave Gilliss. "This kid is special." He watched a few more and asked Dave. "Will he work at it?"

Coach Dave nodded. "I think so." He paused, watched a few more drives. "I don't really know him yet, but I sense that he feels he has something to prove." He paused. "He's been practicing for over five hours."

Coach Dave called out. "Okay Bart, I think that's enough for today. I'll see you at tryouts tomorrow at 3pm."

Bart opened another bottle of water, drank it down. "Coach, would it be okay for me to leave my clubs here tonight?"

Gilliss shrugged. "I guess so, but why?"

"If I don't have my clubs, I can run home." Bart explained.

Coach Gilliss laughed. "Okay, Bart, I'll see you tomorrow."

Chapter Seven

Angela and Betsy comprised the gallery following Bart and Jim, who were the designated the number one and two players on the Gloucester High School varsity golf team. Angela, wore a blue pleated skirt which fell above the knee and a light-weight, white wool sweater, which showed her figure off to advantage. As she was walking the course, she wore comfortable walking shoes.

Betsy smiled. "Angela, you look really nice." She laughed. "But, a skirt to watch a golf match?" She asked.

Angela looked at Betsy, who wore jeans and a sweatshirt, with cross-trainer shoes. Angela admired Betsy's petite frame and easy smile. "Bart likes it when I dress this way," she explained.

"He said that?" Betsy asked, surprise in her tone.

Angela smiled. "No," she shrugged. "But, honestly, I wish he would feel comfortable enough to always speak freely." She paused, "maybe in time," she said wistfully. "Still, I've observed that he lights up when I dress more feminine." She smiled. "I like seeing Bart enjoy looking at me." She paused, smiled. "So, if Bart prefers that I wear dresses and skirts, I'm happy to do it."

Betsy studied her. "You've noticed how he looks at you in different clothing?"

Angela flushed. "Betsy," she paused. "Bart's my guy, I want to dress to please him." She eyed Betsy. "Is that wrong?"

They walked along, as Betsy considered Angela's question. She looked at Angela. "Some may think so." She paused. "But, No, Angela, that's really the right way to think." She frowned, considered how she was dressed. She flashed that impish smile. "Maybe, I should be more observant, to dress to please Jim." She paused. "I really like him, Angela."

It was mid-October and the air was still warm, but by late afternoon it could become a bit nippy. Today's match was against a strong Danvers High School squad. Each team played eight golfers in head to head matches. The competition was match-play, with each hole comprising a "match" with the winning player receiving one point. They played nine holes and the points won were cumulative. The team with the most points won in all eight matches were the victors.

To qualify for the State Tournament a team must have a .500 record or better. Gloucester needed to win this match to qualify. The foursome moved to the 5th tee-box. The 5th at Bass Rocks is a long par 4, with the green being the furthest point from the clubhouse. The 6th fairway ran back, opposite and alongside the 5th fairway, separated by a berm that created big problems for a tee shot from either 5 or 6 that hung up on the heavily roughed berm.

Coach Gilliss placed himself, along with the Danvers High School coach at the approach to the 6th green, from where they could monitor all eight matches. Today, Coach Gilliss had placed Bart against Danvers' number one player. It was usually Jim that had that particular challenge, but Coach Gilliss felt that Bart's ability to significantly outdrive almost every high school player, would trouble the very talented and proud Danvers star.

Jim Perry's match stood even at 2 points each and Bart led his match 2 ½ points to 1 ½ points for his opponent. Bart had noticed that the confident and chatty Danvers golfer had become quiet as Bart repeatedly outdrove him. Jim and Bart had no idea what was happening in the six matches being played ahead of them.

As they stood on the fifth tee, Bart felt the breeze off of the ocean blow in his face, took a deep breath and recalled Coach's admonition, "to swing with ease into the breeze." They could see the foursome in front of them heading to the 5th green. Another foursome was waiting to tee-off on the 6th tee, and the foursome that group were waiting on had just hit their shots to the 6th green. Bart studied the players, but was unable to read much.

Having the honor after winning the 4th hole in his match, Bart hit his tee shot and really launched a big drive on this long par 4, flying the berm and watching his drive hit the fairway and run. He accepted the compliments of Jim, Jim's opponent, Tom Kiely, and the girls with thanks and walked over to Angela and Betsy.

Bart had noticed the stony silence from his opponent, he flashed a smile. "You girls look great," he observed. His observation was met with smiles and thanks. He then whispered into Angela's ear, who nodded and walked from the tee to where Coach Gilliss stood. They spoke, and Angela walked back to the 5th tee.

Bart's opponent, Paul Jackson, acknowledged as the Northeast Conference's top golfer, had watched Bart's drive fly to within 100 yards of the fifth green, teed his ball. All on the tee stood quietly as the young

Danvers star waggled his driver over the ball. Then, trying to match or exceed Bart's drive, he began his swing.

In what Coach Gilliss called "testosterone poisoning," he swung harder and faster than his usual smooth takeaway and follow through. It is accepted dogma that a smooth, controlled swing will generate more club-head speed and greater distance and control than a faster, harder, swing which has the player losing balance as his club comes through the ball. Thus, the result was predictable, the drive was pulled left and flew past the white, out of bounds, stakes and into the trees.

The Danvers player raged with frustration. Losing control of his emotions, he threw his club and muttered a curse.

All stood in an uncomfortable silence. Bart quietly picked up the club and handed it back to the Danvers player. In doing so he spoke to the golfer in a voice for his ears only. The Danvers player's face reddened, he glanced at the girls and nodded, then faced Angela and Betsy. He shrugged, "ladies, please accept my apology." He paused. "I am sorry for my childish behavior." The girls nodded their acceptance of his apology and smiled.

Jim's opponent, Tom Kiely, moved to tee his ball as Angela motioned Bart aside. "Coach says that we are in trouble. We are losing the other matches." She paused. "Coach figures that to win, the team will need at least twelve of the eighteen points from these matches." Angela smiled, "sorry Bart," she offered.

Bart grinned into Angela's concern. "Thanks Princess," he responded, "by the way, you look very pretty today." Angela's smile bloomed, as she blushed at the compliment. "I really love it when you come to my matches, thanks for coming," he added. He looked to the tee-box, "now, we know what we need to do."

Betsy eyed Angela. "I guess you do know how to read Bart." She paused, reflected. "Thanks, Angela."

The Danvers player hit a solid drive into the wind, leaving about 170 yards into the green. Bart whispered the news to Jim, who nodded, eyed Bart, and simply said, "Okay, let's do it, Bart." Jim teed his ball, took a nice smooth swing and left himself about 150 yards into the green. Jim and Bart fist bumped. "Let's get them, Bart." Jim urged.

They waited for Bart's opponent, Paul Jackson, to re-tee and hit his shot. Danvers High School's best player, stood behind his ball looking down the fairway. Bart studied his face and saw indecision. He thought of a quote he had recently read from golfing legend, Bobby Jones. Jones had said; "90 percent of the game is 5 inches wide, the length of space between your ears."

Bart realized that Coach Gilliss had seen a potential opportunity when he paired Bart against Danvers best golfer. It was usually Jim Perry who played as Gloucester's number one player, but for today, Coach thought Gloucester's best chance of beating Danvers top player, was to beat him mentally. Bart would outdrive almost any competitor, Gilliss reasoned. A talented player, who had won every match he had played, and who played to a 4 handicap, might be shaken by being outdriven on hole after hole by fifty yards or better.

Bart who played to a 10 handicap, which was rather remarkable for a beginner, but still not in his opponent's league, had to win the mental battle to win the match. Jim, who was an eight handicap, would not likely have the tools to win the mental battle. To this point in the match, it appeared that Coach Gilliss had calculated correctly. Now, it was up to Bart and Jim to raise their game and pile up points for the 'Fighting Fishermen' of Gloucester High School.

Bart's opponent hit a good drive, in fact it landed near Jim's ball. But, he was lying three on the fairway and was fifty yards behind Bart.

Jim's opponent, Tom Kiely, hit his second shot and hit it well, but he pushed it right of the green, near the 6th tee-box. Bart and Jim exchanged a knowing glance. Chipping from above the green was tough. To get it close was unlikely. The chip from the rough would need to be high, land on the fringe and roll slowly down the slope of the green. A yard short and it would stay in the rough, a yard long and it would roll down the steep decline to the other side of the green.

Bart thought of the words of Tiger Woods, who was quoting previous great golfers, like Ben Hogan. That it was the quality of your misses that determined your score. Jim's opponent, had simply missed in the wrong spot.

Bart's opponent then hit his fourth shot. Knowing he had to get it close to have any chance to win or halve the hole. He went pin-hunting, hit a high shot to the back pin position, hoping to have it land close to the pin, spin and stop. From 150 yards out that was a big ask, but Bart respected the effort. The ball landed a few yards past the pin, bounced and indeed did bite. Unfortunately, that bounce landed on the back downslope of the green, which resisted the spin and the ball rolled off the back of the green. Bart saw the frustration build on his opponents face.

Then, Jim hit his shot to the middle of the green. A smart play, by a crafty golfer, who wisely managed his way around the course. That shot, put Jim in the position to putt for birdie, but, almost assured Jim of a par as he was putting uphill. Bart smiled and winked, as he fist bumped with Jim. "Smart play," Bart complimented.

Bart then hit a wedge, landing it on the front of the green. The shot assured that Bart would win the hole and the point. He now led 3 ½ to 1 ½ with four holes to play. As he lifted the ball from the hole, he flashed a grin at Angela, who smiled back. It hit Bart just how calming it was for him when Angela was nearby.

Jim's opponent frowned as he saw the difficulty he faced. Making his decision, he used his most lofted club and took a big swing, hoping to have the clubface pass below the ball in the thick grass, with the highest point on the lofted face making contact with the ball. 'A gutty shot,' Bart thought. And, it almost worked. The ball went high but carried too far and landed by the hole. The downslope caused the ball to roll thirty plus feet down the green and then off the green onto the fringe. He two-putted for a bogey as Jim then two putted for par, winning the point. Jim now led his match 3-2.

The 6th hole at Bass Rocks is the number one stroke hole, or, the most challenging on the course. With the 5th hole that is rated as the 5th stroke hole and the 7th hole as the 3rd, it is Bass Rock's version of Augusta National's, "Amen Corner."

Bart maintained the honor and stood studying his options. He knew that the team needed him to win the next four points. The Tournament hung in the balance. He decided to go for it. Risk/Reward dictated his choices. The scale tipped to taking the risks. He and Jim had to win out for the team to succeed.

The wind was now quartering over his left shoulder. All along the left side was out of bounds for about 200 yards, then the fairway opened up, but ran left to right. Too far right and the next shot would be a blind shot over towering trees. Those trees were about 240 yards from the tee and a tee shot flying into those trees would be in the hazard. It all added up to a very challenging tee shot.

Bart glanced at his opponent who appeared lost. He smiled at Angela and took his driver out of his bag. Jim's brow raised at his club selection. Bart did not need a driver here. He could hit a 5 metal 230-240 yards, landing safely short of the hazard. Bart met his eyes and winked. He then set up at the ball, which was teed higher than usual and further forward. He choked up on the driver grip and took aim along the tree line and swung. His tee shot went high along the tree line, much higher than the trees. It cleared the trees and bounded forward, left of the hazard and up onto the plateau, leaving 80 yards to the center of the green. It was a risky, but brilliant, shot and placed his opponent in a quandary.

Bart had calculated that the Danvers star would likely react to Bart's choice of club by selecting his driver. While, the Danvers star, did not have the fire-power off of the tee that Bart possessed, Bart calculated that he would aim away from the trees on the left and down the center of the fairway.

The combination of the slope of the fairway and the prevailing wind would cause his shot to bounce to the right, and toward the hazard. If thinking clearly, Bart believed that he would have recognized the danger. When his opponent chose the driver, Bart knew that he was not thinking through the likely consequences.

Danvers top player put a good swing on the ball, and hit it well. The wind pushed the ball right. It landed about 190 yards out and the slope of the fairway caused the ball to bounce toward the hazard. Standing with the driver still raised in his follow-through, he watched with a growing concern. His eyes grew large as he watched his very well struck drive, hop into the hazard. As Bobby Jones said, the game is 90% mental. And this fine, but young, player had not thought through his shot.

Jim and his opponent watched and learned. Jim hit his 3 metal down the fairway and watched it settle about 220 yards out. Jim's opponent did the same, with his ball resting about 10 yards to the right of Jim's ball, bringing the trees into play.

Jim's opponent, Tom Kiely, studied the line then lofted his shot above the trees with a hybrid club. It landed just right and short of the elevated green and trundled down into the sand trap. Jim could see the green and flagstick. He also used a hybrid and hit his shot onto the upslope to the green. The ball bounded onto the green and settled about 15 feet from the pin. An excellent shot, which earned another fist bump from Bart and applause, and smiles, from Betsy and Angela.

Bart's opponent took his penalty drop, short of the hazard, and hit an iron high and onto the green. He now lay 3 on the green, approximately 20 feet from the pin. The group then walked up to Bart's ball. Bart felt the wind at his back and hit his sand iron high and onto the green, just short and left of the hole. The ball took the slope and ran down to within 5 feet of the pin. Angela jumped and clapped with excitement. Bart flashed her an appreciative grin, fist bumped with Jim, and walked to the green.

Jim's opponent, Tom Kiely, saw where Jim's ball lay and knew he needed an up and down out of the sand trap. He settled into the trap and hit an explosion shot which flew up, and out of the trap, settling about eight feet from the pin. A very good shot.

Bart's opponent rolled his par putt which missed on the low side. He tapped in for a bogey and walked off of the green. His face told the story. He was lost.

Jim's birdie putt came up just short. He grimaced, tapped in his par putt. Jim's opponent rolled his par put into the center of the hole for a half, leaving their match 3 ½-2 ½ in Jim's favor. Bart then rolled in his birdie putt to shoot to a 4 ½-1 ½ lead.

The 7th hole at Bass Rocks is the courses only par 5. Bart blasted a drive down the middle, it hit above the slope, bounded up onto the flat and ran out to about 300 yards. It was his best drive of the day, which had Angela and Betsy excited and clapping. Jim moved close to Bart and whispered; "chicks dig long hitters." That, brought a laugh from Bart and a questioning look from Angela. Bart's opponent, Paul Jackson, then hit his drive which hit into the bottom of the slope and bounded about half way up.

Jim and his opponent hit good drives which also settled on the slope. As they walked up the fairway, Angela walked beside Bart. She nudged him, smiled brightly and asked; "so what did Jim say that was so funny?"

Bart looked at Angela and grinned. "He said that, 'Chicks dig long hitters.'" Angela grinned and shook her head. "You guys!" She said on a laugh.

Bart paused, studied her and flashed a smile. "Well, is it true? Do Chicks dig long hitters?"

Angela blushed as she laughed. "Well, this Chick, certainly digs this long hitter!"

Bart nudged her, briefly put his arm around her shoulder. "Thanks for coming and walking the course with me." He shook his head and smiled. "This long hitter sure digs you." His words won a radiant smile from Angela.

The battle between Jim and his Danvers High School opponent continued with both hitting good second shots and then third shots that found the difficult sloping green. It would be a putting contest to determine who won this point.

Bart's opponent had an uphill lie on the slope. Bart's ball was about seventy yards ahead, and the Danvers player chose to pull his 3 metal to make up the difference and hit the ball close to the green. Bart looked at Jim and shrugged. He realized that his opponent was taking an unnecessary gamble. Hitting the ball down to 90-100 yards would be the smart play.

Irrespective of Bart's drive, the 7th is not a birdie hole due to the difficult green. Coach Gilliss's constant theme of course management came to mind. Bart was still at least 200 yards out. He knew that his shot would not hold, if he went for the green, so, he planned on laying up to about 60-70 yards, which was a good distance for his 60 degree wedge.

The Danvers player set up to the ball. His left foot was set higher than his right. He aimed down the left side of the slot to hopefully hit it close. He swung hard and caught the ball on the upsweep. It popped up high and went left. He saw immediately that it would not clear the trees on the left side and watched, almost in shock, as it disappeared into the thick foliage. His frustration was palpable and for any golfer, easy to understand. The meaning was clear, Bart would win another hole and extend his lead to 5 ½ -1 ½. Not knowing how his teammates in the six matches ahead were faring, he had no idea if it would be enough.

Bart watched Angela and Betsy holding hands on the side of the green, hoping that Jim would win the point. Bart smiled as he was again struck by how decent and forgiving Angela was as a person. Betsy had been a part of the group, led by Jessica Arnold, who hurt and humiliated Angela, so deeply and for so long. Yet, here she was unified with Betsy in cheering on Jim. Angela, sensing Bart's gaze, turned her eyes to him. She beamed a smile at Bart, which spoke volumes of the character of his girl.

The Danvers golfer easily two putted for a par. Jim set up over his difficult downhill putt. He struck the putt and Bart winced. It seemed on line but Bart feared he had hit it too hard. Bart's concerns played out, as the putt missed the cup and rolled 10 feet past. Now, Jim was faced with a must make, thankfully uphill, ten footer. Jim crouched behind the ball, read the putt and stroked it into the heart of the cup for another halved hole. Jim's match stood at 4 points to 3 in Gloucester's favor.

Bart fist bumped with Jim and nodded, "great putt Jim," Bart observed. Then with a grin added, "I hear Chicks dig gutsy golfers." Jim laughed, looked over at Betsy, flashing a smile at the pretty blond. "I hope you are right, Bart."

The 8th at Bass Rocks is a 150 yard par 3. The pin was forward on the narrow green, bringing the sand trap, just short and left of the green, into play. Bart observed Coach Gilliss standing on the 9th tee-box. He turned his attention back to the challenge ahead. He knew if he hit his tee shot right of the green it would bound down the steep embankment into heavy rough. Left of the green, in addition to the sand trap was also heavy rough. 'Put it on the green, Bart,' he coached himself. He stood behind his ball and felt the wind crossing from left to right. He considered playing the shot left of the green and letting the wind carry it back, but smiled as he re-called the wise words of the great Arnold Palmer. Palmer advised a young golfer that a well struck ball will be little affected by the wind.

Bart knew, if he hit a good shot, the pressure would build on his opponent. A bad shot and he would be opening the door for the strong Danvers player. As Bart had been hitting the ball beautifully today, he chose to go for the flag.

Bart set up over the ball and took a smooth swing, lofting the shot high and hoping to land it softly on the putting surface. Bart finished his swing and stood holding his pose as all focus was on the well struck ball. "Looks good," he heard Jim call out excitedly. 'It's on the flag,' Bart thought. The ball landed about five feet short of the pin, rolled forward and stopped just six inches short of the hole.

Angela could not contain herself and called out, "go in!" as the ball rolled to the hole. Betsy grabbed onto Angela and they held each other as they bounced together excitedly. Bart heard Angela call out. His eyes turned and moved from the girl's reaction, back to the ball until it stopped rolling to kick in distance. Every eye appreciated the sight of the two pretty young girls, bouncing with excitement. Bart's eyes focused on Angela and grinned broadly. 'Wow!!' he thought, 'how lucky am I?'

Bart noted the smile on Coach Gilliss as he saw the ball settle near the hole. Coach fired a thumbs up to Bart, who returned the gesture.

Bart's opponent then hit his shot, which splashed into the sand trap. 'He's given up,' Bart thought. 'Come on, Bart, stay focused, take advantage, finish strong,' he scolded himself.

Bart's eyes settled on Jim, who was playing excellent golf and thus far winning his match. Bart's gut told him that these points on holes 8 and 9 might be decisive. "Come on Jim," Bart called. Jim hit a good shot onto the green, about ten feet above the hole. Jim and Bart fist bumped.

Jim's opponent, Tom, looked from his silent, dejected, teammate to the two balls setting on the green. He took a deep breath then took his swing. He hit a pure shot, hitting it better than expected, flying it to the back of the green. The group walked to the green.

Bart's opponent blasted out of the sand, leaving himself about eight feet for par. He stalked onto the green, studied the positions of his ball and Bart's, scooped his ball up, turned to Bart with a nod, "that's good," he said, striding off of the green. Bart was now up 6 ½-1 ½.

Jim's opponent had a downhill, left to right, putt from more than forty feet. He hit a good putt leaving himself a five foot par putt. Jim then studied and rolled his putt, catching the left edge of the hole, before it fell in for the birdie. That putt gave Jim a 5-3 lead in his match. Jim and Bart exchanged a fist bump, and smiled at their girls, whose support was so appreciated.

The group walked to the 9th tee and final hole of the match. Coach Gilliss approached Bart and Jim and quietly asked how their matches were going. "Great," Jim responded. "I have five points and Bart is killing his guy and has 6 ½ points."

Coach made the calculation in his head. "Okay, that gives us a chance," he responded. "It appears that the team will be down by 8 ½ points after the first six matches." He paused. "By my calculations, if you both win the point on nine, we will win by half a point."

Bart smiled and nodded. "And, we both must win this hole. If either of us halve the hole Danvers will win."

Coach nodded. "You guys are playing great." He looked over to where the Danvers coach was speaking with his team. "Your opponents will know the same. Go get them guys."

The 9th hole is a difficult 345 yard par 4. The tee is set at an angle to the fairway, creating a visually challenging shot. To the left of the fairway, is a pond. Further, it is risky to hit the ball more than 250 yards, as at that point the fairway slopes to the left and into a hazard. As the golfer stands on the tee, the right side of the narrow fairway is a heavily wooded area. So, the golfers faced hazards right and left.

Bart teed his ball. Angela and Betsy had overheard Coach Gilliss and realized that notwithstanding the stellar play of Bart and Jim, it was all coming down to this hole. They both had to win the hole to secure a tournament invite for the team. The confident smiles were gone, and they looked on hopeful, but with concern.

As Bart approached his ball, his opponent, Paul Jackson, called out. "Bart, you've played well," he paused, then smiled. "But this hole is the match." He took a deep breath. "I do not intend to lose."

Bart looked hard at his opponent. "Paul, go for it!" He responded. Bart stepped back from his ball, took a calming breath and then moved back into his set. Bart swung his five metal through the ball, lacing a high arcing shot down the middle of the fairway. It landed and bounded to a stop 100 yards from the green.

"Great shot, Bart" Jim called out. "That is position A." He glared at Paul. "Follow that Paul," Jim challenged.

Bart left the tee box and walked over to Angela and Betsy. "Where are those pretty smiles?" Bart chided. "You know, Jim and I are only playing well to impress our girls." The smiles returned. "That's so much better." Bart stated, then winked, leaned in and whispered. "In fact, if you'd like to jump about again, that would be greatly appreciated," he added with a smile.

The girls blushed through their smiles. "You liked that did you?" Angela asked, meeting Bart's eyes.

"You bet!" He responded, as he looked back at the tee box, where Paul was setting up over his ball.

They quieted as Paul Jackson had his driver, hoping to match Bart's ball. Paul put a nice swing on his ball and hit a wonderful shot, just five yards short of Bart's.

"Nice shot, Paul." Bart complimented. Paul nodded at Bart. "The game is afoot!" Paul responded, quoting Sherlock Holmes. They exchanged smiles and turned to watch Jim.

Jim wasted no time. He set up, squared his shoulders and swung confidently through his ball. He hit a beauty that settled five yards right of Paul's ball.

"That a boy!" Bart called out. Jim tipped his cap to Bart and the girls, stepped aside so his opponent could have the tee.

The Danvers players were aware that merely winning a half point in either match would be enough to lock up a team victory. "Come on Tom," Paul called out. Tom Kiely hit his drive about twenty yards short of Jim's ball.

The four players, two coaches, Angela and Betsy, walked to the balls for their second shot. When they arrived they found a gallery of both teams, twelve golfers, some parents and friends seated by the 9th green, ready to cheer on their teammates. All seemed to know what was riding on the two matches left to be settled.

Tom was away and set to hit first. He was 125 yards away from the center of the green. The fairway ran sharply downhill to where a sand trap and heavy rough guarded the front of the green. The wind was in the golfer's faces. Tom set up and swung his 8 iron. His calculation of the effect of the wind against the downhill lie of the green proved faulty. His ball hit the back of the green and bounded into some high, punishing rough. Tom looked to Paul and shook his head.

Jim hit next and lofted a pitching wedge onto the front of the green, right of the pin. The ball bounced and rolled to within ten feet, just right of the hole. The Gloucester crowd cheered the shot. Bart fist bumped with Jim, who flashed a smile and a wink to Betsy.

Angela nudged Betsy and laughed. "I think, as the guys would say, Jim really digs you."

Betsy smiled, a bit wistfully, at Angela. "I hope so, Angela."

Paul had watched the two shots closely. He chose a pitching wedge and set up, swung and lofted a shot that was left of the pin location, landing in the center of the green and rolled left, away from the pin. He left himself a 25 foot putt.

It was now all up to Bart. Jim's point looked safe. Paul would likely two putt for par, leaving Bart to go pin hunting. He knew the team needed him to birdie the hole, a par for a half would not do. He set up over the ball, glanced up at Coach who gave a confident nod, then focused his eyes on Angela. Angela met his eyes and offered a tentative smile. Her hands were fisted and up near her chin.

Bart backed off the shot. He stood behind his ball, looked at the green, closed his eyes and visualized the shot he wanted to hit. He felt the wind lighten a touch, knew he was no more than 100 yards out, but with the downhill green, he calculated that he needed to hit an 85 yard shot. He had his sand iron in hand, opened his eyes and set up over the ball. He settled into his stance. His eyes went from the ball to the target, then back to the ball. He took his smooth swing and lofted the ball up high, just as he had pictured it. The higher the ball rose, the softer it would land, as golfing legend, Sam Snead observed; "like a butterfly with sore feet."

The ball landed softly and bounced forward no more than five feet, leaving Bart with a ten foot putt. He nodded, happy with the shot. He knew it would have been closer if not for the sudden gust of wind that blew off the ocean, as the ball was at the top of its arc. He grinned, 'that's golf,' he reasoned.

Tom tried to blast out of the heavy rough, but moved the ball just about five feet and left the ball, still in the rough. He tried again, taking a big swing. This time he rocketed the ball out, over the green and into the sand trap which guarded the front of the green. He walked over to Jim, offered his hand, conceding the point. Jim won his match by a 6-3 score.

Paul crouched behind his putt, studying the line. If he made the putt, Danvers was assured of a victory. He moved over the putt and stroked it. It looked promising off the putter head, but went a bit left as it approached the hole, stopping a foot left of the cup. Paul tapped it in for par, then cleared the green to stand with his teammates, now a spectator.

Bart lined up his putt. Betsy moved to Angela and took her hand. "He'll make it," Betsy assured, "believe it!" The Gloucester team, Coaches and supporters, knowing that Bart's putt was their ticket to the Conference Tournament, a tournament that the team had not qualified for in more than a decade, stood together, eyes fixed on Bart.

The Danvers team, already assured of a berth in the Conference Tournament, watched with interest as they were now all aware of the dominating golf Bart had played against their number 1 player. Still, it came down to this putt. And all eyes were fixed on the former Quarterback, who was a newcomer to competitive golf.

Bart read the line, which he saw as just outside right of the hole. But, as always, it would be about speed. If he hit the putt too hard, it would fly through the break. Too soft, and it would be more affected by the break, and might not reach the hole. He needed the perfect read and speed.

The crowd was silent. Bart glanced at the group, his Coach and teammates staring intently. He read the hope on their faces. His gaze sought out Angela. When he made eye contact, he saw her anxiety and flashed a smile.

Bart, then, blocked out everything and focused on the task at hand. Make the putt!

He set up and took three practice strokes as he cleared his thoughts of anything but the line and speed of the putt. He brought his putter back and through the ball. He immediately saw that the ball was on the path he wanted. But, had he read the line correctly?

As the ball rolled, Bart saw that it was indeed sliding left and to the hole. He smiled as he saw that he had judged the speed correctly. When the ball was three feet from the hole, Bart lifted his left hand, holding the putter aloft in the expectation of success. The ball rolled and found the middle of the hole and dropped in for the birdie and the victory, as Bart fist pumped his right hand. The crowd erupted in applause as his teammates stormed the green to congratulate him and celebrate the team victory.

Bart freed himself from his teammates as Paul Jackson, Bart's opponent and Danvers High School star approached. Smiling broadly,

Paul congratulated Bart. "You played great today. I'm looking forward to playing again."

Bart nodded. "Me too Paul, Maybe in the tournament."

Coach Gilliss shook Bart's hand. "Great job, Bart, your game has come a long way in six weeks." He eyed Bart as he formed the words. "Bart, stick with the game, you could be a very special golfer."

"Thanks Coach, it has been fun," Bart responded. "And," he paused. "Thanks for believing in me."

Bart looked over Coach's shoulder and saw Angela standing with Betsy. Angela's face was wet with tears and her smile was radiant. 'Wow!' Bart thought and moved to her. Betsy pushed Angela forward and onto the green. She embraced Bart and hugged him tightly. "I am so proud of you." Angela stated.

Bart held her close, then kissed her. "Thanks, Angela," was all he said.

Chapter Eight

Angela suggested a celebratory dinner at her home for that evening. Bart went home to shower and change, update his family on his and the team's success and tell them he would be dining at Angela's house.

"You really like this girl?" Mario asked, with a smile of approval.

"I do," Bart said easily. "Mario, I like her a lot, she is great." He paused to consider his words. "I feel good when I am with her." He thought a bit more. "When Angela is with me, I feel calm, and, I feel happy." He shrugged. "Does any of that make sense?"

"It does," his mother said. "Bart, I think she is good for you."

"You know," Lucia added. "You barely stutter now." She grinned. "It's amazing."

Bart sat back and smiled. "I hadn't thought about that." He reflected. "It has been so much better." He considered. "Do you think it is because of Angela?"

Bart's father, Franco, looked at his son. "When you were little, the Doctor told us that a big part of your problem was that when you became anxious, you would stutter." He paused. "Then, when you stuttered, you became more anxious." He smiled at Bart. "You were afraid people would laugh at you and that made you anxious." He choked up at the painful memories. He took a deep breath as he searched for the words. "It was like a big, painful circle." He took a breath and smiled. "So, maybe it's Angela, maybe it's the golf, maybe, it's that you are growing out of it." He shrugged. "But, since Angela has been in your life, you seem happier." Franco looked at his wife, fought back the emotion that threatened to overwhelm him. "Bart, I really like Angela, she is good for you."

Bart reached over to touch his father's hand. "Thanks Dad."

"So, big brother," Lucia teased, lightening the mood. "How smart was I getting you to ask Angela out?"

Bart laughed aloud. "Pretty smart, I guess." He looked at his family, smiled broadly. "I'm going now to see my girl." He left and headed over to Angela's house.

Bart entered the Curcuru house to find Angela, Tina and her mother preparing dinner and her two brothers watching television. He walked into the kitchen and was met with smiles.

"Augori, congratulations," Angela's mother called, smiling broadly. Angela and Tina watched with smiles as Maria embraced Bart.

"I hope this isn't an imposition?" Bart asked Maria.

Maria laughed. "No, no, no, it is a pleasure." She gestured to the living room, "my husband is fishing and tonight's dinner is simple." She paused. "Just spaghetti with shrimp sauce and pan fried grey sole."

"That sounds wonderful," Bart responded, as Angela crossed the kitchen to greet Bart.

"I guess I will have to move faster if I want to beat my mother in greeting my boyfriend." Angela said on a laugh. Angela kissed Bart. "Welcome, Champ!" She grinned.

Bart smiled, leaned forward, kissed Angela and asked. "No garlic bread tonight?"

Angela offered a wide smile, while Maria responded with a shrewd eye on Bart. "No, we have fresh Italian bread tonight." Maria continued, while wagging her finger at Bart. "Fresh, like you," she added with a knowing smile.

Bart laughed as Tina looked from Angela to her mother, perplexed at the conversation. She shrugged and smiled up at Bart. "So, I hear you had a great day today?"

Bart nodded. "It was a good day. Our team qualified for the Conference tournament."

"And, Bart was the star!" Angela announced proudly. "He was amazing."

Tina moved to Bart, rose on her toes and kissed Bart's cheek. "Congratulations, I am so happy for you."

"Okay, you two, go relax on the deck." Maria said as she eyed Angela, "Tina and I will finish here. "Angela, don't you want to get your boyfriend a cold drink?"

Angela smiled. "Of course, Mom, I'll take care of it." She turned to Bart. "Why don't you head out to the deck and I'll bring us a pitcher of iced tea."

"Sounds good," Bart responded. His attention was diverted by a flier on the kitchen counter. He picked it up and read about the call for students to participate in the upcoming winter musical production of Grease. Bart held the flier and smiled at Angela. "Are you considering doing this?" He asked.

Angela shrugged and smiled. "Maybe, as part of the crew," she responded.

"The crew?" He asked, skeptically. "Why not play Sandy or Rizzo?" He walked to her and took her hands. "I'd love to see you up on stage." He smiled. "You would be great."

Angela blushed at the compliment. "Those are singing parts," she stated and shrugged.

"Angela," he said as he looked into her eyes. "I heard you sing in Church. You have a good voice." He insisted. "And," he added. "You would be a prettier Sandy than Olivia Newton-John."

Maria beamed at his words. While, she had no idea who Olivia Newton-John was, she saw Bart's eyes and the smile it produced on Angela's face.

Tina watched her sister blush. "He's right, Angela," Tina confirmed. "You do sing beautifully."

"Yes," Maria asserted. "And, all those dance lessons."

Chapter Nine

With Thanksgiving approaching and the school year nearing the three month mark, Gloucester High School Principle, Bruce Collier, called an assembly. Fall sports and activities were concluded or nearing an end, and restlessness among the students was noticeable, he decided that it was time for a talk.

Principle Collier felt that the academic year was arranged poorly. He knew it stemmed from a time when students were needed to harvest spring crops, so there were two to three weeks of "vacation" time in the spring semester, but the fall semester began in late August, before Labor Day, and continued without break until Christmas vacation. Four months without a break placed a strain on students, teachers and staff. His call to alter the school year to create a one week break at the end of October, (The World Series break), and a one week vacation the first week of March, was met with opposition from the Teacher's union. Interestingly, the teachers, almost unanimously, agreed it made sound academic sense and would make their jobs easier. But, their union leaders saw the idea as an opportunity to win other concessions. Concessions the city's budget could not afford, so nothing changed.

Principle Collier stood on the auditorium stage as the students settled into their seats. He called for quiet and began to acknowledge the academic and extra-curricular accomplishments of students, clubs, activities and athletics, both individuals and teams. The stage behind Principle Collier began to fill with students.

The Principle then smiled and announced; "as many of you know I have a special place in my heart for the game of golf." He looked for Coach Gilliss. "This year, for the first time in twelve years our golf team qualified for and won a spot in the Conference Tournament." There was a smattering of applause. For most high school students, golf was a bit exotic.

Principle Collier waved to Coach Gilliss to join him on stage. "Coach Gilliss is a golf professional at Bass Rocks Golf Club. He agreed to coach our team and in his first year as coach led the team to the tournament."

Principle Collier led the tepid applause, stepped back and waved Coach Gilliss to the podium.

Dave Gilliss ascended to the stage and moved to the podium. "It was a very good year for the team," he began. "We had solid senior leadership." He called up the four seniors who were on the team. He shook the hands of each player. He then announced the four juniors who were on the team, who took their place beside the seniors. Coach Gilliss smiled. "We also had two sophomores on the team. These young men, Jim Perry and Bart DeMarco, emerged as true team leaders, played superlative golf and pushed their teammates to improve their physical condition, adding strength, flexibility and stamina."

"Unfortunately, our team was eliminated in the first round of the State tournament." He glanced back at his team, smiled. "But, Bart DeMarco won the individual honor as the tournament's best player, by shooting the lowest score by any player in five years." Angela and Betsy jumped to their feet and led the applause. The team, led by Jim Perry, roared their approval for their teammate.

Bart sought and met Angela's eyes, smiling broadly. Bart approached the podium and microphone. At the back of the auditorium stood football coach, Bob Nelson and Elizabeth Nelson, Bob's wife, and the head guidance counselor at Gloucester High School.

As the applause abated and the students and teachers settled into their seats, a voice called out, "come on stutter boy, give us a speech!" There was a smattering of laughter, and then a stony silence followed in the wake of the comment.

"Oh, my God," Coach Nelson whispered to his wife, who watched the scene closely. Principle Collier began to move to the podium, until Bart shook his head and told him that it was okay. "I'll deal with this."

Angela and Betsy knew immediately that the insulting words came from Jessica Arnold, the laughter from the sheep who supported her mean spirited actions. Angela turned to speak, but it was Betsy who tersely replied, "Jessica, are you ever going to grow up?" Betsy's question was met with applause and whistles.

Angela looked to Bart who raised his hands and asked for silence. When the room quieted, Bart focused his eyes on Angela, who offered a supportive smile. Bart smiled back.

"Thank you," Bart began. "It is true that I have had a stuttering problem for most of my life." He shrugged. "I was mocked and made fun of, and it hurt deeply." He paused, smiled. "But, that is why mean spirited people endeavor to humiliate others. It is about control and inspiring fear."

Bart smiled as he looked at the assembled students and teachers. "But, most of us have some challenge that we have to deal with." He watched heads nod in agreement. "I have had years of speech therapy and psychological counseling. My parents and family have been great and I have slowly improved." He glanced back at Coach Gilliss, then faced the students. "The truth is that 'life is 10% what happens to us and 90% how we react to such events.'"

"One of the most painful events of my life was the night of our football game against Salem High School." He paused. "I was pulled out of the game because it was felt that I could not overcome the challenge my stutter had created." Bart took a deep breath. Coach Nelson listened carefully. His wife Beth squeezed his hand. Bart offered a weak smile. "I was so low. I just wanted to quit." He took a deep breath. "A lifetime of being mocked and dismissed just became too much…" He exhaled.

"But," Bart took a deep breath, smiled and continued, "That night an Angel came into my life." His eyes found Angela. Angela beamed a loving smile. "And, I was steered in a new direction." He glanced back at Principle Collier and Coach Gilliss. "I found golf and maybe with that discovery, I found my future."

He paused, reflected. "I don't necessarily mean that golf will be my future." He took a deep breath as he searched for the words. "I mean, that with what happened that night and the days and weeks that followed, showed me that I had to be open to possibilities that I may never have considered."

"See," Bart continued. "Coach Gilliss worked with me and gave me the sense that he believed in me." He paused. "So often, we all just need someone to really believe in us." Bart smiled, glanced back and thanked Dave Gilliss. He then looked for and found Angela's smiling face. "See, I found two people who believed in me." He laughed. "And, as crazy as it seems, that even helped me in my continuing battle to overcome, or at least, make progress on, my lifelong stuttering problem."

He looked out on the sea of students. "We all can be the person that inspires someone who needs a little help." He smiled. "And, for those empty souls who can only find pleasure in bullying and hurting others, pity them." He raised his hand and pointed at the students, in a powerful voice he continued, "Yes, pity them, but resist them!"

The student body rose to their feet as one and applauded Bart's words.

At the conclusion of the assembly, which included the presentation of academic awards to hard working, high achieving students, Bart approached Mrs. Nelson and asked if he could meet with her.

"Of course, Bart," she checked her calendar. "How about at 2:45pm?"

Bart nodded. "Yes, that will work, I have a last class study block."

"Great, Bart, I will see you then." She paused, looked up into the eyes of the much taller student-athlete, "that was a wonderful speech you gave." She nodded, "truly inspiring."

At 2:45pm, Bart entered the guidance offices and knocked on the office door of Mrs. Nelson. Bart heard her ask him to enter and when he did, was a bit surprised to find Coach Nelson as well as Mrs. Nelson present. They were seated on the couch in the small alcove, which, was away from her desk, and used by Mrs. Nelson to put students at ease when the student was troubled or wrestling with challenges.

"Please sit, Bart." Mrs. Nelson offered, pointing to a chair adjacent to the couch. When Bart sat, he looked at Coach Nelson, a look of concern on his face.

"I hope what I said didn't offend you, Coach." Bart said. "That was not my intention."

Bob Nelson smiled. "I know that Bart," he said. "I just hoped we could talk before you have your guidance conference."

Bart nodded. "Okay Coach," he shrugged. "What can I do for you?"

Coach Nelson leaned forward. "Bart, I want to ask a favor." Bart nodded, but said nothing. Coach continued. "It has been a disappointing football season."

Bart nodded in agreement, watching Coach closely.

"I'm considering retiring from coaching," he started, glanced at his wife and smiled. "I haven't completely decided, but coaching High School football is a big commitment." Bart remained attentive, but silent. "In my fifteen years, we have had some success."

Bart nodded and smiled. "Yes, a state Championship three years ago!"

Coach nodded and met Bart's smile. "That was a great season and a strong team," he paused, eyed Bart. "Your brother, Mario, played a big part in our success."

Bart smiled at the pleasant memory. "Mario is a great athlete and a wonderful brother." Bart stated simply. "He's been a role model for me."

Nelson studied Bart. "I had high hopes for this team, but we haven't realized the success I envisioned." He half expected Bart to interject, and, was impressed at Bart's self-control. "The problem, I believe," Coach continued, "is that our offense is one-dimensional." He sat back. "The defenses stack against the run, challenging us to beat them with the passing game." He paused, considered his words. "We have not been able to mount an effective passing attack."

Bart nodded. "Dave has had a tough year," he responded factually, but uncritically.

"Yes, he has, Bart," Coach sighed. "We are 5 wins against 4 losses, with just the Thanksgiving game left, against a strong Danvers team." He looked to his wife, shrugged and turned to Bart. "Honestly, Bart, I've come to believe that I made a mistake pulling you out of the Salem game."

Bart shrugged. "Nothing to be done about that now," he responded evenly.

Coach Nelson nodded, studied the young athlete. "See Bart, I have coached Gloucester High School to 99 wins in my tenure as Head Coach." He looked closely at Bart. "I'd like to have that 100th win."

Bart sat back, nodding in understanding. "I see," he said.

"You are still on the team's official roster." Coach said. "I did not remove your name." He cleared his throat. "I'd like you to be our quarterback in the Thanksgiving Day game." He paused. "Dave knows that a change is likely after losing our last two games." He eyed Bart. "He doesn't know that I am considering you, but I doubt it would surprise him." He paused. "Will you do it?"

Bart looked at Coach, sat back and considered the request. He knew Coach Gilliss would recommend that he not play. The chance of injury would be too great. He smiled at Angela's likely response. Then considered and realized she would support him, irrespective of her fears, whatever he chose. 'How great is that?' He thought. 'How lucky am I?'

Bart smiled, as he realized that Coach Nelson may have provided him with the leverage he needed to accomplish the goal he had set for the meeting with the Theatre Director, Mrs. Nelson. Bart smiled and looked to Mrs. Nelson. "Maybe," he responded. "But, I'd like a favor as well."

Coach looked puzzled. "What can I do for you, Bart?"

Eyes on Mrs. Nelson, Bart smiled. "Mrs. Nelson, you are the Theatre Director." He stated.

Mrs. Nelson nodded. "Yes, Bart, I am."

Bart continued. "The Theatre group is doing Grease for the winter production."

She smiled, still uncertain, but intrigued. "Yes, that's correct."

"How about we exchange favors?" He offered with a warm smile. "I will help Coach get that 100th win on Thanksgiving, Mrs. Nelson." He leaned forward, determined eyes set. "And, you cast Angela Curcuru as Sandy or Rizzo in the Production."

Mrs. Nelson smiled as it became clear. "Ah, Bart, she's your angel, right?"

Bart nodded.

"Does Angela know of this request?" Beth Nelson asked, intent eyes on Bart.

Bart shook his head. "No, she doesn't, and I'd prefer she never knows." He paused. "Agreed?"

"What if we don't win the game?" Coach Nelson pressed. "What if the girl can't sing?"

Bart looked at Nelson with the fierce look of a Champion. "I will get you that win, Coach! You can count on it." He turned to Mrs. Nelson. "Are we agreed?"

Beth Nelson looked at her husband. "Angela has a lovely voice, I've heard her at Church." She turned and faced Bart with a smile. "Why, Bart?"

Bart sat back, collected his thoughts, wanting to get the words right. "I want Angela to have the opportunity to shine." He paused, looked at Mrs. Nelson with determination. "She is a remarkable girl, and it hasn't been easy for her."

The Guidance Counselor nodded. Thoughtfully, she agreed. "No, it hasn't."

"Those girls!" Bart raged. "They have hurt her deeply." He took a deep breath, this time not to soften his stutter, but to control the rage. "She is the best person I have ever known and she has no self-confidence." He took a breath, then smiled. "I want her to see herself the way I see her." He looked at them. "Do you understand?"

Beth Nelson nodded. "I understand perfectly." She smiled, impressed beyond words with the young man seated before her. "How do you plan to convince her to audition?"

Bart shrugged. "I don't know, I haven't had time to think this through." He grinned. "I guess I'll try to be charming."

Bob Nelson laughed. "So, Bart, do you think that you have enough charm?"

Bart met his laugh with a broad smile. "I don't know Coach, but I've been saving up." He paused, as a thought struck, "maybe, you could help."

Coach Nelson narrowed his gaze. "And, how would we do that?"

"This Sunday at 9 o'clock mass, sit close by." He smiled. "Mrs. Nelson, you could comment on how nice a voice Angela has and…" He shrugged.

Beth Nelson smiled, raised her brows. "And encourage her to attend the auditions beginning the next day?"

Bart laughed, with raised brows he commented. "Wow, Mrs. Nelson, you are pretty devious."

Mrs. Nelson laughed aloud, raising her arm emphatically. "The show must go on!"

Bob Nelson rose. "Bart, practice in 15 minutes. We have a lot to do in one week." He shook his head. "You need to get suited up."

Bart stood, studied the couple, he offered his hand. "Excuse me, but I want to be clear. Do we have an agreement?"

Beth and Bob Nelson exchanged a long look, and nodded. They looked at Bart, Coach Nelson grasped his hand in a firm handshake. "We have a deal."

Bart then extended his hand to Mrs. Nelson, "Yes?"

Beth Nelson shook Bart's hand. "I agree."

Chapter Ten

Dinner at Angela's was becoming a pleasant and regular event. Angela's mother routinely set a place for Bart, and always greeted him with a big smile and a hug. When her husband, Sal, was at sea, she would often ask Bart what he might like for dinner the next evening. Initially, being a guest, Bart hesitated to respond, until Angela nudged and encouraged him. "She really likes you for some reason," Angela teased and smiled. "It's okay, she wants you to be happy."

Bart had smiled into Maria's affection. "I really appreciate this," he responded, flashing Maria a grateful smile.

So, Bart became a regular at the Curcuru table, and a real affection was growing on all sides. Maria, as mother's will, had lived the pain Angela endured dealing with the 'Ugly Angela' insults, the ostracism of Angela by her classmates and peers, the stinging self-doubt Angela suffered. Since arriving in America, Maria had never seen Angela so happy and confident. She attributed that to Bart being in her life.

On returning from school, Angela had happily described for her mother the wonderful reception and honor Bart had received at the assembly. She told her of how Betsy had stood up for Bart, and how the students had cheered him. Angela was bursting with pride.

Tina confirmed Angela's account and acknowledged the pride she felt, for herself, her sister, and her family, that handsome, athletic, Bart DeMarco, was becoming a part of her family. Tina explained, with a broad smile, that she had embraced Bart after the assembly, and told Bart that she was proud of him. Tina beamed a smile as she related that Bart had thanked her, and had referred to her, before her friends, as his little sister.

Bart arrived at the Curcuru house in an upbeat mood. He entered, greeted the family and immediately embraced Angela, laying a passionate kiss on her.

Angela laughed, "Wow," she said, blushing. "You are happy!"

Maria beamed a smile, hugged Bart, "augori, congratulations," she offered. Then, she paused, and scanned Bart's face with concern.

Angela noted her mother's reaction. She moved close, her smile turned to an expression of concern. She studied Bart's face, placed her hand gently on the gash over his right eye. "What happened, Bart?"

Bart laughed. "Oh, that's nothing." He paused and watched Angela closely as he added. "That happened at football practice."

Before Angela could respond, her brothers lit up at the mention of football. "Are you playing football, Bart?" Asked eight year old, Nick. Six year old, Giuseppe, excitedly jumped into Bart's arms, "for Gloucester High?" He asked.

Bart smiled at the boys. Keeping a watchful eye on Angela, he shared their excitement. "You bet," he confirmed as he squeezed and tickled the happy six year old. "I will be the quarterback for Gloucester High School in the Thanksgiving Day game against Danvers High School." The boys jumped about excitedly. "I hope you guys will come and watch me play?" Bart asked.

The boys looked to their mother hopefully. "Can we, pleeease, Ma?"

Maria looked from the boys to Angela, read her daughter's mixture of concern and confusion, smiled at the boys. "Well, I will be preparing Thanksgiving dinner. Maybe, you go with Angela and Tina?"

The boys looked to Angela, who pulled them both in for a hug. "Okay," she said, smiling. "But, you have to stay with me and listen." The boys happily jumped about. "Okay," Angela smiled and kissed her brothers. "Now, go play in your room." The boys headed upstairs to their room. Angela then focused on Bart, who could see the questions in her eyes.

"Come on Tina," Maria called. "Come help me with the dinner." Maria's gaze settled on Bart, who met her eyes and smiled. Maria could not resist and smiled back, then eyed Angela and nodded to the living room. Angela smiled at her mother, turned to Bart. "Why don't I get us some iced tea and we can sit in the living room and talk."

Angela entered the living room, a smile on her face, handed Bart a glass of iced tea. She sat rather stiffly next to him on the couch. "My mother told me to smile, even if I am upset," she explained. "She told me that you had to do what makes you happy and a good girlfriend supports her boyfriend." She placed a hand on his knee. "So, see, I'm smiling."

Bart laughed aloud. "I love your mother." He studied her, "are you upset, Angela?" He put the glass on the coffee table and took her hands, felt them tremble.

Angela took a deep breath. "Why Bart?" She paused. "What happened?" Her eyes bore into him. He saw confusion and uncertainty.

Bart squeezed her hands, kissed her gently. "Let me explain. I thought you might not understand."

The dam broke, her tight grip on her emotions slipped, tears flooded her eyes. "That Coach hurt you!" She raged. "He embarrassed you in front of everybody." Her lip quivered. "I saw how hurt you were standing on the sidelines." Without thinking, lost in her anger, she blurted, "That's why I came looking for you."

Bart brightened, and grinned. "You came looking for me?" He laughed. "Really?"

In the face of Bart's smile and obvious delight, Angela couldn't help but smile. "Yes, okay, I was worried about you," she admitted with a blush. She saw the joy in his eyes. 'Men's egos' she thought, and shook her head.

"I guess Coach did me a favor," He laughed, wiped her cheeks. Kissed her softly. "Okay, today, after the assembly Coach Nelson asked me to do him a favor." He paused. "See, Angela as Head Coach he has won 99 games. And, this Thanksgiving Day game may be his last game as Coach."

Bart was still beaming over the revelation that Angela had actually come looking for him. "Coach feels that Gloucester can't win with Dave Powers at Quarterback." He shrugged. "He asked me to help the team and him, win the game." He paused. "He really wants that 100th win." He squeezed her hands. "So, I agreed to play."

It was difficult to hold onto anger in the face of Bart's smile. Her expression softened, her eyes became tender. She shook her head. "How can you be so forgiving after what he did to you?" She asked, astonished.

Bart smiled. He loved that she was so protective of his feelings. He felt so blessed to have her in his life. "I guess, I learned from the best, most tender, caring and forgiving girl in the world." He kissed her again. "You forgave Betsy after she apologized for all the hurt she caused you." He explained. "Coach Nelson acknowledged that taking me out of the game that night was a mistake." He shrugged. "Not exactly an apology, but as close as he could do." He squeezed her hands. "Angela, I am a Gloucester High School Fighting Fisherman, I felt that it was my duty to help the team." He smiled, looked into her eyes. "It's one game and then I'm through with football," he stated. "I want to play golf and that's what I intend to do."

Angela watched him quietly. She saw through the bravado, read in his eyes that there was more, that he was wrestling with something. She touched his face, softly, she encouraged, "talk to me, Bart."

There was a silence as Bart collected his thoughts. He trusted Angela, so, he took a deep breath, engaged Angela's eyes and admitted the truth. "Angela, I want," he stopped, swallowed. "No, I NEED to prove to myself that I can lead the team." He took a deep breath, "I lost the chance that night when I was pulled off the field." He paused, choked up. "Coach made me look like a failure before the entire city."

Bart sipped his iced tea. He swallowed the tea and the lump in his throat. Bart's eyes blazed into hers. He stated emphatically, "Angela, I'm a DeMarco!" He paused, squeezed her hands. "My father and my brother led the team to big victories." He exhaled, engaged her eyes. "I need to do this for ME." He squeezed her hands. "And, I really need you to support me." He searched her face. "It's important to me that you'll be there to cheer for the team."

Angela fought the emotions that threatened to overwhelm her. She read in his eyes just how important this was to him. "Okay," she responded softly. "I'll be there to cheer for YOU." She paused, exhaled the anger she felt and managed a smile. "Bart, I'll always be there for you." She hugged him to her chest. "I love you, Bart DeMarco." She wiped her eyes, blew her nose. "Look at me, I'm a mess," she stated. "And, I think it is time for dinner." She looked at the clock. "You go ahead, I'll wash my face and meet you at the table."

Bart smiled back. "I love you, Princess." He paused. "And, thank you."

That evening, Bart called Coach Gilliss. He explained to his golf coach that he felt that he wanted to play this one game for Coach Nelson. "I'm a Fighting Fisherman," he explained. "The team needs me." He added. "And the golf season is over, Coach. I hope you can understand? Coach Nelson asked me for this gift. I just didn't want to say no."

"And, what if they ask next year, Bart?" Coach Gilliss pressed.

"I explained that this one game is a gift to Coach Bob." He paused. "Next fall, I play golf, and only golf!" He stated emphatically. "In fact, I'm considering playing spring golf as well." He paused. "I understand that there are amateur events run by the Massachusetts Golf Association." He paused. "If I do enter, will you help me, Coach?"

Coach Gilliss laughed. "Sure I will Bart, but my gut tells me there is much more to this story." He paused, laughed. "Okay, go, win that football game," He sighed. "Then, we go to work!"

"Right, Coach," Bart said. "And, thanks."

Chapter Eleven

Bart arrived at Angela's house, precisely at 8:30 am, to meet Angela and walk with her to Sunday mass. He took her hand as they walked to the Church on a blustery November day.

"It's getting cold." Bart said. "After Thanksgiving, I have an appointment to test for my driver's license." He smiled. "Then I will drive you everywhere."

Angela brushed against him. "That will be nice." She smiled, "but this is nice too."

They entered St. Ann's Church, found a pew about halfway down and settled in. Angela did not notice that Coach and Mrs. Nelson were two pews in front of them.

The service was comforting. Father Capelli spoke to the congregation of life's challenges and how together a community can help each other succeed. Bart held Angela's hand as the organist began to play a favorite hymn; 'On Eagle's Wings.'

Angela sang with the congregation; Bart loved her voice, clear and strong. He smiled as she sang;

"And He will raise you up on eagle's wings,

Bear you on the breath of dawn,

Make you to shine like the sun, and, hold you in the palm of his Hand…"

Bart and Angela received the sacrament and walked back to their pew. At the conclusion of the mass, the aisle swelled with parishioners chatting, while waiting patiently to exit. Bart and Angela stood together, holding hands and smiling. Bart saw football teammate, Dave Powers, with his girlfriend, Jessica Arnold. Bart waved and Dave responded with a wave and a smile. Jessica looked away and said nothing.

"Hi Angela," Beth Nelson called and moved closer to the young couple. "I so enjoyed hearing you sing. You have a lovely voice."

Angela blushed at the compliment. "Thank you, Mrs. Nelson." She paused. "There was a nice selection of hymns today."

"Yes, there were." Beth Nelson agreed. She glanced at Bart. "So Angela, are you and Bart dating?"

Angela smiled, lighting her face. "Yes, we are, Mrs. Nelson."

"You must be very proud of Bart," Mrs. Nelson commented. "His hard work, overcoming disappointment and accomplishing so much." Bart flushed but said nothing. Mrs. Nelson continued. "And that inspiring speech at the assembly." She looked at Bart. "You helped more than a few struggling teens."

"Thanks, Mrs. Nelson, I hope so," Bart responded.

Angela beamed with pride. "I am so proud of him."

Bart saw Coach Nelson move beside his wife. "Hi Coach, how are you, today?"

"I'm fine Bart, yourself?"

"Great, Coach, have you met my girlfriend, Angela Curcuru?"

Coach smiled. "I know Angela," the burly coach said as he shook Angela's hand. "You were in my American History course last year, weren't you?" Coach asked.

Angela smiled. "Yes, I was, Mr. Nelson."

"I remember Angela," He smiled, "I remember Angela as a bright and witty student. A pleasure to have in class." Coach responded.

Angela's face flushed red. "Thank you, Mr. Nelson."

Beth Nelson took Angela's hand. "Angela," she began. "We are starting auditions tomorrow for the winter musical."

Angela nodded. "Yes, I saw the flier. You're doing Grease, aren't you?"

"We are," Mrs. Nelson confirmed. "I hope that you will audition for one of the roles."

"Really?" Angela asked, surprise showing on her face. "I've never performed before."

Beth Nelson took Angela's hands. "I think you would be great. Please consider it." She offered an encouraging smile. "We could certainly use a singer of your skills."

"Thank you, Mrs. Nelson." She paused, looked at Bart, who was smiling at her. She turned to Mrs. Nelson. "I'll think about it, thank you."

The line began to move to the exit. "I'll see you at practice tomorrow, Bart." Coach said. "By the way, you are doing great."

"Thanks Coach, see you tomorrow."

Bart and Angela huddled close against the biting wind blowing off of the ocean. Angela held his arm as they walked, smiled up at Bart and asked. "Okay, Bart, do you want to tell me what you did?"

"What I did?" Bart asked. "What do you mean?"

Angela laughed. "Standing together like that, Coach and Mrs. Nelson, you agreeing to play to help Coach win his 100th game." She huddled closer. "Then, Mrs. Nelson asking me to audition for Grease." Her lips quirked in a smile. "Just a big coincidence, Bart?"

He met her eyes and her smile. "You will be great, Angela. I would love to see you on that stage singing, dancing, and acting."

Angela stopped, gently turned Bart to face her. She looked up at him. "You did all this for me?" She misted. "Why?"

Bart didn't try to deny anything. He pulled her to him, looked into her eyes. "Angela, you're my girl," he said softly, with feeling. "I want you to have the opportunity to shine, like the star that you are." He kissed her. "You need to understand just how special you are." He shook his head and grinned. "And, why do you have to be so smart?"

Angela's eyes brimmed with happy tears. "You really want me to do this, Bart?"

He held her close. "I so want you to be happy, Angela. I think that you would have fun and be great."

She nodded. "Okay Bart, you went to so much trouble." She said softly. "I feel so lucky…" She choked, unable to complete her thought, put her face into Bart's chest.

"No Angela," Bart responded. "I am the lucky one." He kissed her head. "I love you." He squeezed her to him. "Now how about we head home for some breakfast?" He laughed. "I am so hungry and I believe my Mom is making her buttermilk waffles."

Chapter Twelve

There was a good turnout for the first of three days of auditions for the winter musical production of 'Grease.'

Theatre Director, Beth Nelson, separated the students into those auditioning for performing parts and those interested in working on Production.

In the Production area, sets had to be constructed, lighting arranged, costumes designed and sewn, literature printed and so much more. Mrs. Nelson was fortunate to have the talented and very creative Director of Production for the North Shore Music Theatre, Jim Harrison. Jim was available as the Music Theatre closed for the winter after its annual Production of Dickens', "A Christmas Carol."

Jim Harrison was always eager to work with the students and perhaps pluck a talented young man or woman to work on the North Shore Music Theatre's summer Productions.

Mrs. Nelson handed scripts and song lyrics to those seeking to audition for one of the multiple parts that required singing. In the high school production, the singing and dancing roles were far more limited than required for Broadway, or the hugely successful movie, starring John Travolta and Olivia Newton-John.

Still, there were multiple parts for students, both male and female, to demonstrate their talent. The females, seeking a singing role were all given the song, "Hopelessly Devoted to You," sung in the movie by Olivia Newton-John. The males, were given the song, "Greased Lightning," sung in the movie by John Travolta. Mrs. Nelson asked them to rehearse the song at home that evening and be prepared to perform over the next two days.

She sat the group down and told them that after auditions were completed on Wednesday, she wanted them all to relax and have a wonderful Thanksgiving weekend. The roles would be posted on the following Monday, with rehearsals beginning that day.

"I expect perfect attendance as we will have only seven weeks to rehearse and learn our parts." She stated. Mrs. Nelson looked at the group. "I know every boy wants to play 'Danny' and every girl, 'Sandy.' She shrugged.

"But, you all know that only one boy and one girl will win those roles." She smiled, "but I chose this play because there are many singing roles."

A hand went up. Mrs. Nelson acknowledged the question. Kate Jenkins, a senior, asked if seniors and then juniors would be given priority in the selection of the various roles.

"Kate, I'm glad you asked that question." The Director looked over the group. "I will select students for the various roles based on merit." She paused. "And, I will be the person making the decisions." She smiled. "Do your best and work together. Let's put on an outstanding performance."

As the meeting concluded, Angela stood with Betsy. Angela looked around the auditorium and noted. "There are some good singers in this group".

Betsy agreed. "Actually, I would be happy with a speaking role." She laughed. "Not really a great singer."

Angela laughed, was about to respond when Jessica Arnold approached with three of her posse. She looked at Angela, offered a haughty sneer. "Imagine 'Ugly Angela' trying to play Sandy?" She paused, looked about. "What a joke."

Angela, surprised by the nastiness of Jessica's words, felt so much like the scared 12 year old, being insulted and humiliated by the pretty and popular Jessica Arnold. Angela paused, considered retreat, then, she thought of Bart. She saw the love in his eyes, his devastating smile, remembered the taste of his sweet kisses. Handsome, athletic, Bart DeMarco wanted Angela, not Jessica. And, that knowledge empowered her.

Angela smiled at Jessica. "Yes, imagine that, 'Ugly Angela' no longer afraid of your mean-spirited words." She moved closer to Jessica. "You're old news, Jessica, even your friends are embarrassed by you." She flipped her long curly, black hair and smiled, "I have to begin rehearsing, see you all later." She looked at Jessica's posse. "You three could do so much better than being Jessica's sheep." Angela took Betsy's arm. "Ready to go Betsy?"

Betsy's smile was ear to ear. "I am ready, Angela, let's go."

Angela and Betsy left the auditorium and once alone, Betsy hugged Angela. "I am so proud of you, Angela." She laughed. "Where did that come from?"

Angela looked at Betsy and smiled. "I don't know, Betsy, I'm still shaking." But, Angela knew. Bart being in her life was having an effect. The way he looked at her, that look that told her that he valued her, that he so wanted her. It made all the difference.

The girls walked passed the football practice field. They stopped and watched as Bart barked a cadence and the offense ran a pass play, Bart threw a perfect spiral pass forty yards downfield into the waiting hands of his receiver.

"Look at him," Angela said softly, awe in her tone. "Three months ago, he was humiliated in front of the entire city, and there he is battling with the team, getting ready to be the quarterback that leads Gloucester against a really good Danvers team." She smiled. "And, he has no fear."

Betsy looked at Angela. "I read somewhere that courage is not the absence of fear, but the willingness to confront one's fear." She smiled. "Your boyfriend is courageous." She paused as her words settled.

Angela smiled. "Yes, he is, Betsy." She blushed, spoke softly, "he's also hot!"

The girls laughed, locked arms and began to walk home. Angela glanced at Betsy, "and, I've noticed that your Jim is pretty hot, as well."

"Yes, he is," Betsy agreed, smiling broadly. "And, our guys beat a very good Danvers golf team a few weeks ago."

Chapter Thirteen

Thanksgiving dawned bright and cold. The sea scented air was so crisp that it felt about to crack, like a twig underfoot. A stiff breeze blew off of the ocean and you could smell snow in the air. It was a day to curl before a warm fire with a good book. But, Thanksgiving in Gloucester meant football. And today was special, as the local newspaper had reported that Coach Nelson was seeking his 100th win as Head Coach. The story repeated the rumor that it might be the Coach's last game as he was contemplating retirement. The story added, that Coach Nelson was, reportedly, recommending long-time assistant Coach, Nick Bailey, to succeed him.

Of course, Gloucester's traditional rival, the Danvers High School Falcons, would be arriving with the conference leading team, an undefeated record of 9-0 and a few thousand fans to watch their team make athletic history.

The rivalry had seen generations of young men play for athletic glory before thousands of fans, many of whom had watched these tussles for decades. And, many of whom, had taken the field in hopes of victory and a place in the athletic fabric of this community. Bart had spent his week of preparation working with the team's offense, especially the pass receivers, brain-storming with Coach Nelson and offensive Coach Nick Bailey. And, he studied game films of the Danvers High School defense.

Watching the game films, Bart quickly concluded that the Danvers defense was quite formidable. He noted that the team's middle linebacker, Jake Taylor, was especially talented. He had read that the big, quick and smart linebacker was headed to Syracuse University to continue his football career. Bart was impressed. The other player who Bart noticed making one outstanding athletic play after another was cornerback, Derek Chambers.

In the three game films that had been provided to Gloucester, Bart noted that each of Danvers opponents had tried to pass the ball away from the tall, slim and very fast Chambers. It was understandable, Chambers was so gifted that the three teams did not have a receiver who could outrun Chambers or athletically compete with him. After watching the films a number of times, Bart noted that Derek Chambers was gifted, but, may well lack discipline. He used his speed and quickness to compensate for leaving the receiver he was assigned to cover. His most athletic plays were usually seen when he went to support the other cornerback or safety. Those plays had made him a star. Bart thought he might just be able to use the gifted cornerback's tendencies against him.

On Wednesday, Bart met with Coaches Nelson and Bailey to discuss the tactical plan to defeat the talented Falcons. Bart looked at the coaches. "Danvers is very good," he began, "but we can beat them!" He stated. The coaches merely looked at Bart as he spoke. "They expect us to run the ball," Bart said thoughtfully. "We need to strike in our first possession. A play action pass, two receivers to the right." He paused in thought. "My guess is that Chambers will break right when I look right." Bart smiled. "That's his M.O." He sat back. "So, we use his tendencies against him. So, when Chambers moves, we release Dana from the backfield to sprint down the left side." Bart smiled. "He should be wide open."

Coach Bailey nodded. "It makes sense," he looked to Coach Nelson, who was studying Bart closely.

"You want to go after Chambers?" Nelson asked, surprise in his tone. "He's the best defensive back in the conference." Nelson stated.

Bart nodded. "He's a great athlete, but an undisciplined football player." Bart smiled. "I'm guessing we'll burn him for at least two touchdowns."

"Bart, that's not how the league is playing Danvers." Coach Nelson pointed out.

Bart nodded, "and the league is 0-9 against Danvers." He eyed Nelson. "I intend to win."

The bleachers were full, fans stood four deep around the field as the teams took their pre-game warm-ups. Bart looked and saw Angela, her family and his sitting together. He waved and received nervous smiles from Angela and his mother. Angela's brothers waved back excitedly. Mario flashed a big smile and a thumbs-up.

The DeMarco's had invited Angela's family to have their Thanksgiving meal with them, and the families were together in the stands to support Bart and the Fighting Fishermen. Angela was with Tina and Lucia, and was obviously anxious.

Lucia nudged Angela, "he'll be fine. He's an amazing athlete."

Angela nodded, "I just wish he wasn't doing this," Angela said with conviction.

Bart's mother, Rosa, rubbed Angela's shoulder. "I don't want him out there either," she agreed. "But, Bart needs to do this."

Angela nodded, looked at Rosa, concern coloring her expression. "I don't understand men!"

Rosa and Maria exchanged a look and laughed.

Danvers kicked off to Gloucester to start the game. The ball was returned to the Gloucester 25 and the offense huddled. Bart called the play and the offense moved over the ball.

Danvers had reviewed Gloucester's game films and recognized the difficulty the Fishermen had in passing the ball. As Bart had expected, the defense stacked against the run.

The ball was snapped to Bart, who had set up under center, and Bart faked a hand-off to, Dana Hughes, the tailback. They sold it well, and the Danvers defense crashed the line. Gloucester's ends both blocked, spun and released. Bart set in the pocket, the linemen gave him time to throw.

A smile spread across Bart's face. He lofted a pass downfield to his wide receiver who was running and was five yards behind the defender. Bart picked the right cornerback as he had later plans for the left corner, Derek Chambers. The Gloucester end, Jeff Bammarito, ran under the perfectly thrown pass, caught it cleanly and sprinted untouched into the end-zone for a Gloucester touchdown. The crowd erupted and the noise level on the field by the canal was deafening.

The Gloucester offense celebrated as they hustled off of the field and the place kicker, Matt Harden, made the extra-point, giving Gloucester a 7-0 lead with only 45 seconds off the clock.

The Danvers coaches were surprised, but recognized, that this new quarterback was a threat. Good coaches adjust to surprise and adversity, and Danvers was a well-coached team.

Gloucester's defense was fired up and stopped the Danvers offense, after Danvers made two first downs, forcing a punt. Gloucester had the lead and the ball. The huge crowd was fired up and ready for more fireworks. Bart and the offense soon accommodated.

Gloucester started at their 20 yard line. Bart called the play and the offense moved over the ball. Gloucester had two running backs behind Bart. It looked like a set for a running play. Bart took the snap and set up in the pocket. Two ends streaked down the right side of the field. Bart looked right and pumped to throw. Danvers', highly touted cornerback, Derek Chambers, watched Bart's eyes, Chambers saw that the two Gloucester receivers were being single covered by the Danvers right cornerback and safety. He raced across to help.

Bart expected that Chambers would so react. He yelled the signal and the Gloucester back, Dana Hughes, sprinted out of the back-field and streaked down the left side. The offensive line gave Bart the time he needed. Bart threw and hit the wide open tailback, who ran 60 yards after the catch for a touchdown. Bart watched with a smile and it was 14-0 Gloucester.

Before half-time Gloucester scored a third touchdown and kicked a field goal. Danvers scored two touchdowns and at the half the score stood Gloucester 24 Danvers 14.

During the half-time break, Bart watched the defensive players carefully. The big linemen and linebackers were tired. As Gloucester's offense had struck quickly for scores, Gloucester's defense had spent a long time on the field. He calculated that fact might become a problem as the game wore on.

Both teams scored one third quarter touchdown. Bart had once again burned Derek Chambers, who had left his zone undefended. So, with 15 minutes left in the game, the score was Gloucester 31, Danvers 21.

Once again, Gloucester's defense had been on the field for about 2/3rds of the fifteen minutes, of the 3rd quarter. Bart was having a big game, he had thrown for three touchdowns and had run for the fourth, but he sensed momentum swinging in Danvers direction.

Unfortunately, he was right. Danvers had won 9 games for a reason. The Danvers team was talented and well coached. The 4th quarter seemed to belong to the Falcons. Danvers engineered two long and time consuming drives for touchdowns. The well-rested Danvers defense adjusted to Gloucester's up tempo offense and when Danvers scored with 1:45 left on the clock, the score was Danvers 34, Gloucester 31. The only break Gloucester received was a missed extra-point.

With one minute, forty five seconds remaining, the Gloucester offense huddled on the sideline before taking the field. The fans had been shocked into silence.

In that huddle, Bart looked at the Coaches and players. He took charge. "We have two time-outs left." He paused and eyed his team. "Only I call a time out." He looked about, nobody challenged him.

Bart continued. "Receivers, catch the ball and move to the sidelines. Catch the ball, run and get out of bounds." He paused, eyed his receivers and stressed. "We have to stop the clock!"

"They will be playing prevent," Bart continued. "So, short passes will be open." He smiled. "We will take what they give us and win this game." Heads nodded. Bart had earned their trust. "Hands in," he called. "This is for Coach!" He read the determination of his teammates. "On three, let's hear it." He saw their bodies respond. They seemed to grow. "One, Two, Three and 11 players yelled; COACH!!!"

Bart began to march Gloucester down the field. A fifteen yard pass and the receiver moved out of bounds to stop the clock. Then a ten yard pass, a five yard run and Gloucester was at mid-field with 58 seconds on the clock.

Bart saw an opening and ran 20 yards to the 30 yard line before avoiding a tackle and getting out of bounds. The clock stopped with 42 seconds left. You could cut the tension at Newell Stadium with a knife.

"Bart is doing great," Mario commented. He saw the anxiety etched on the faces and in the eyes of his mother and Angela. "Bart will get it done," he assured. 'Come on little brother,' he thought. 'You deserve this.'

Bart saw an opportunity on the next play, when once again, Chambers left his receiver to go play hero. Bart threw a strike to the open receiver, Jeff Bammarito, in the corner of the end-zone. The receiver was wide open and not defended. When he let it go Bart's hands went up, the crowd held its collective breaths, but Jeff dropped the perfectly thrown pass. The collective gasp of ten thousand fans was deflating.

Angela looked stricken. "So close," she said, as she choked up. "So close."

Lucia touched her arm. "You can believe in Bart." She paused, smiled. "He'll find a way."

The young receiver was removed from the field. Bart called him back onto the field and into the huddle. He held the sophomore's helmet, locked eyes with him, "Jeff, shake it off," he demanded. "We are going to score and win this game." He paused. "Got that?"

Jeff nodded. "I don't know how I dropped that pass." He paused. "Sorry guys."

"Forget it!" Bart demanded. "I believe in you, Jeff." He looked at the team. "Let's go."

There were 27 seconds left. Angela's hands were fisted at her mouth. "Dear God," she pleaded, "help him!"

Bart was in control. He called the play and took the snap from the shotgun. The center snapped it low and to Bart's right. The ball squirted past Bart. He kept his cool, picked up the ball and scrambled back to the line of scrimmage before being tackled by Jake Taylor. The clock was ticking and Bart screamed for a time-out. The ball was still on the 30 yard line and only 12 seconds remained. Gloucester's fans were silent. They sensed the game slipping away.

In the huddle, the center seemed in shock. "Jim," Bart screamed. "Are you with me?" Jim Johnson nodded. "Not good enough!" Bart screamed and banged the helmet of the big center, "speak!"

The big senior looked Bart in the eyes. "I'm good."

Bart addressed the team. "No more mistakes, Guys." He made eye contact with all ten. "Okay, maybe, we have time for two plays." He looked at his receivers. "Catch it and get out of bounds, immediately."

Taking no chances Bart took the snap under center, he set, then bolted through a seam for the end zone. He caught the defense all falling back to cover the pass. The crowd were on their feet stomping on the metal bleachers and screaming. Bart angled to the corner, seeking the goal line, counting the seconds in his head. He thought he would make it, but Derek Chambers used that great speed to catch Bart and push him out at the 3 yard line. The clock read 3 seconds. Bart took a breath and used the last time out to meet with the coaches.

Coach Nelson looked at Bart. "Good job, Bart, I think we kick a field goal, and win in overtime."

Coach Bailey remained quiet. Bart was astonished, he looked at the coaches. "No!" He insisted. "We won't win in overtime!" He looked at Coach Nelson. "Our defense is gassed. Nothing left. We have to win now!"

"Bart," Coach Nelson reasoned.

Bart shook his head, silencing Nelson. Even with his helmet on, Angela could see that Bart was arguing something, fiercely. "No, Coach," Bart demanded. "You quit on me once, don't do it again!"

Coach Nelson stood tall. He looked into Bart's eyes and saw a Champion. "Okay, Bart, go for it." He paused. "Who do you want on the field?"

Bart trotted back onto the field. There was surprise that Gloucester was passing up the tie and going for the win. "Gutsy," Mario commented. He smiled. "Nelson believes in Bart."

Rosa DeMarco and Angela exchanged a long look. "It's all on Bart," Angela said. "I feel sick."

Rosa touched her cheek. "Think good thoughts." She urged.

The ball was on the left hash. In the huddle, Bart looked at his teammates. "Let's win this now, guys!" Heads nodded. "Okay, a quarterback keeper, triple option, right." He looked at Jeff. "You set up left, go to the end-zone, cut left, go for the corner. I'm counting on Chambers playing hero and leaving you open, when I go right."

He looked to his halfback. "Dana, you are my pitchman. As I run right I'll be looking for the contain man to come after me. If he does, I'll pitch to you."

Bart looked at his left guard and tackle. "Gary, Phil, I need you to protect my blind side. No one catches me from behind, got it?" The linemen nodded.

Bart paused, looked at his center. "Jim, you have to stop Taylor." They all knew, Jake Taylor could destroy the play.

The big center nodded, eyed Bart. "I'll take care of Taylor."

Bart took a deep breath and looked about the huddle. "This is it guys, for Coach. Let's do it."

The huddle broke, everybody had their jobs and everybody was critical. The big crowd was up and on their feet, hoping to explode, but muted.

Bart took the snap and ran right. The crowd noise was suddenly deafening. Dana went out for the pitch, Bart looked for the contain man to go for him. But, the defender held his position. Bart glanced over his shoulder, looking for Jeff, but Derek Chambers had learned after being burnt thrice by Bart.

Now, Bart was down to one option, he had to run it in. He saw, Syracuse bound, Jake Taylor mirroring him along the line of scrimmage. Bart knew he couldn't run over the 265 pound Taylor. As the thought hit, Bart saw a flash of big Jim Johnson crunching Danvers' great middle linebacker, and now Bart had only to beat the 150 pound cornerback.

Bart turned for the end-zone at the 6 yard line, the Danvers' cornerback was on a collision course with him. Angela watched transfixed and terrified. "Please, please, please," is all she could say. So many thoughts raced through her mind. It appeared impossible. To get so close and fail, just seemed so wrong to Angela. "Go Bart," she yelled. "I believe in you."

Bart powered for the goal-line intending to run over the determined Danvers player, but, then he saw the Danvers player lower his head, preparing to dive for Bart's feet, intending to take the legs out from under the bigger, more powerful Bart. Bart hit the 4 yard line, then the 3, and launched himself for the goal-line as the corner back dove for his feet.

Bart extended his right arm, the ball thrust forward, he was airborne and horizontal, seeking to break the plane of the goal-line.

The photo, by now renowned sports photographer, Bartolo Piscitello, will live forever in Gloucester lore. Bart airborne, right arm extended, the ball breaking the plane of the goal-line. The Danvers' cornerback also airborne, but lower, below Bart's body and in the direct background, the referee with his arms raised signaling a touchdown.

The photo and accompanying story ran on the front page of the Gloucester Times. It also was the sports section cover photo of the Boston Herald and Globe.

Bart landed in the end-zone on his shoulder, then flipped over his back and up onto his feet. His right arm holding the ball aloft. The crowd was delirious, yelling Bart's name. Bart found Jim Johnson and embraced him. "You did it!" Bart screamed. "That block was the play of the year, Jim."

Rosa and Franco, with Mario, Celia and Lucia were hugging and crying with joy and relief. Beth Nelson found Angela holding Tina, and they embraced, all crying happy tears.

The team charged the field, all meeting in the end-zone. Bart led the chant, COACH! COACH! COACH! It was picked up by the big crowd.

Beth Nelson looked on, tears streaming down her cheeks, a brilliant smile affixed, as Bob Nelson had his moment. His team lifted their Coach up on their shoulders and carried him off of the field, to thunderous applause.

Chapter Fourteen

Angela, with Bart's family and the DeMarco entourage, found Bart, as the team headed to the locker-room, and wrapped him in embraces and a cocoon of love.

With Rosa DeMarco looking on happily, Bart held Angela, looked into her eyes, kissed her and proclaimed, "I did it, Angela!" His voice shook with emotion, but his words were clear.

Angela nodded, studied his face, his eyes, and at that moment she knew, how deeply hurt he had been, how desperate he had been to prove himself, to Angela, to everybody, but, above all, to himself. And, he had done it! She saw the triumph in his eyes, on his face, and, Angela understood, really, for the first time, that Bart had needed to play, and he had needed to win!

Angela held his gaze, overcome with relief, happy tears streamed down her cheeks. "Yes, Bart, you showed them all. I am so proud of you." She laughed. "I'm not sure my heart can take the stress."

Bart held Angela, his face grimy, his uniform muddy and his hair sweaty and disheveled. He looked to his and Angela's parents. He locked eyes with his mother. She saw the joy, the triumph in his eyes, on his face. Rosa misted as she smiled. No words were, or needed, to be spoken. Her boy was happy. Rosa was happy.

"Is it okay if Angela waits for me to shower and change and walks home with me?" Bart asked.

"Of course," Rosa DeMarco responded. "We will head home and get everything ready." Rosa smiled at a questioning Maria. The mothers made eye contact and Maria nodded her assent.

Angela's brothers, Nick and Giuseppe, watched their hero with big eyes. Bart saw them and bid them forward. "Did you enjoy the game, guys?" He asked.

"You were awesome!" Nick proclaimed. Giuseppe nodded, smiling from ear to ear.

"Thanks guys," Bart smiled. "And, thanks for coming."

Mario approached with a smiling Celia. He went to Bart and embraced him. "I'm so proud of you, Bart." He brushed a tear from his eye. "If you'd like, Celia and I could wait and drive you home."

Bart smiled. "Thank you, Mario." He paused, saw Mario's eyes charged with emotion. "Thank you for believing in me and encouraging me." He grinned. "But, no, I want to walk home with my girl."

Mario nodded, "Okay, Champ, I'll see you at home."

Celia flashed a teary smile as she embraced Bart. "I'm so happy for you, Bart." She smiled at Angela. "Take care of our hero, Angela." Angela beamed a smile.

Lucia moved into Bart's arms. She laughed. "You may be a hero, big brother, but you're a mess." She held tight. "I'm so happy for you." She said with eyes glistening with pride. Bart held Lucia. "Thanks, Lucia, I love you."

The families left Bart and Angela to head home. Bart held Angela close and looked into her eyes. "Thank you, Angela," he said in an emotion choked voice. He held her close as they walked to the field house, which housed the locker rooms. Once in, and out of the cold, Bart kissed Angela. "I'll take a quick shower and change." He looked at Angela, noted some of the dirt from his uniform had soiled her coat. "Angela, I'm sorry for messing your cloths." He said. "If you want, you can go into the girl's locker room and clean that mud and dirt."

Angela smiled. "No worries, Bart. I'll clean it up." Her eyes danced. "You were wonderful today."

Angela entered the ladies locker room and moved to the restroom. She noted the Cheerleaders were changing and warming after cheering in the cold for hours. As she washed away the dirt from her coat, she was approached by Jessica Arnold. Angela saw her approaching in the mirror and sighed, vowing that she would not let Jessica spoil a special day.

"Angela, may I speak to you?" Jessica asked.

Angela turned to face Jessica and smiled. "Of course, Jessica. Great day, Huh?" she offered, smiling warmly.

Jessica nodded. "Bart was great today." She paused. "You should be proud."

"I am," Angela responded, feeling wary, but her smile held, determined that nothing could dampen her joy on this day.

Jessica lowered her eyes, took a deep breath, and then met Angela's eyes. "Angela, I want to apologize." She paused and choked up. "I have been so mean to you, for so long." She shook her head, and tears pooled in her eyes. "I am truly sorry. I hope you can forgive me." The tears then rolled down her cheeks. "Please Angela, please forgive me."

Angela let out a long breath, eyed Jessica, perplexed at the turnaround. "Of course, Jessica. I forgive you."

Jessica moved to embrace Angela, but Angela held her at arms-length. "Why now, Jessica. Just Monday, you…"

"I know, Angela. I know." She choked. "Why should you believe me?" Jessica conceded. "But Dave…" The tears flowed.

Angela saw what was behind the apology. The same social pressure that compelled so many to torment her, now pushed Jessica into apologizing. Angela felt truly sorry for Jessica. She embraced her. "I forgive you, Jessica." She paused. "Maybe, you should speak to Father Capelli. He might help you sort out your feelings." She stood back. "Have a Happy Thanksgiving, Jessica." With that she left the locker room. She took a seat on the gym bleachers, reflecting on the day and smiling, as she recalled Bart's joy.

It was no more than ten additional minutes until a freshly showered, but still smiling, Bart, found Angela sitting on the bleachers. "Hi, Angela," he called.

Angela flashed a winning smile, rose and came down the bleachers. "Ready to head home, Champ?"

Bart took her hand and gently seated her on a chair. A small group of Cheerleaders and Bart's teammates stopped and stood nearby. Bart reached into his pocket and took out a ring box. He opened it and Angela saw a star sapphire with small diamonds on either side, set into a gold band.

Angela looked at the ring and then at Bart. "It's beautiful Bart," she said softly.

Bart took her left hand, looked into her eyes. "It is you who are beautiful, Angela." He wet his lips, nervously. "Will you accept this ring as proof of my commitment to you?" He gulped. "Angela, I want to pledge myself to you and ask you to pledge to me." Their eyes met. "Will you do that, Angela?"

Happy tears flooded Angela's eyes. "'I've lost my heart to you, Bart." She nodded. "Yes, of course."

Bart slid the ring onto her finger, lifted her into a hug. "I love you, Angela." He held her tight, swung her around in joy.

Angela laughed. "I love you, Bart."

The student group, which included Dave Powers and Jessica Arnold, applauded the happy scene and jubilant couple.

The walk to Bart's house was slow and sweet. Bart held Angela's hand and pulled her close. Car horns beeped, people waved and called out to Bart. Bart smiled and waved.

"I guess my guy is a big hero!" Angela teased. "What can a simple girl do to compete with your fans?" She smiled, felt a thrill, as she looked at her hand and the ring which adorned it.

Bart laughed, looked into Angela's loving face. "You have already done so much for me." He kissed her. "There is so much ahead." He added. "Please ride with me through college and beyond." He sought her eyes. "It may not be easy, but never doubt my love, Angela." He grinned happily. "We are 'Team DeMarco' from today on."

Arriving home, Rosa, Celia and Lucia went immediately to Angela. Bart had told his mother and sister of his plans. When Maria saw the ring and heard Angela's description of Bart's requests, she flooded with emotion, hugged Angela tightly. "I am so happy for you, Bambina." Maria then walked over to Bart, eyes filled with tears of joy. She hugged him. "Thank you for loving my little girl, Bart." She looked at Bart. "Please be good to her." She paused and choked up. "She loves you so much."

Thanksgiving dinner looked outstanding. Angela's mother made lasagna and Bart's mother prepared the traditional turkey dinner.

Franco DeMarco sat at the table's head. He scanned the table, saw his family, The Curcuru family and Mario's girl, Celia. He smiled, stood and raised his wine glass. "Before we offer thanks to God, I would like to say a few words."

"Today, has been an extraordinary day for our family." He smiled, looked at Sal Curcuru and added; "And, I include Angela, her family and Celia when I say our family." He put his hand on Bart's shoulder. "I am so proud of my children. Mario, Bart and Lucia, you are my greatest gifts. I love you."

He looked and smiled at his wife, Rosa. "The most important choice a man will ever make in this life is the woman he chooses to love, marry, raise a family and share his life." Franco misted as he looked at his wife. "I thank God every day for my Rosa." He smiled. "I love you, Rosa." Rosa smiled as her eyes filled. She blew Franco a kiss.

"Today, we all watched our Bart achieve great success for Gloucester, his team and Coach, for our family and for himself."

Bart blushed as all eyes were focused on him. Angela squeezed his hand and smiled.

Franco continued, "Bart, I am so proud, not just because you helped your team win a game, but because of the courage you displayed." He paused, scanned the supportive faces of family and dear friends. "A lesser man would have quit in the face of the abuse you withstood." Franco stood tall. "But, not my Bart," Franco proudly proclaimed. "Bart, went back, faced his demons, and proved, like his brother, that he could lead and he could win!"

Heads nodded and all smiled in support of Franco's words. "You bet, Dad," Mario called out.

Franco then looked at Mario and Lucia. He smiled as he made eye contact. "And, to Mario and Lucia, you have proved what family, real family, means. You stood by and supported Bart through his worse days." Tears filled the eyes of the Patriarch. "I am so proud of you, both." He paused. "Today's victory belongs to you as well as Bart."

Franco smiled, wiped his eyes with his napkin and looked to Angela. "And, I want to thank you Angela." Franco engaged her eyes. "Bart owes his success in large measure to you." He paused. "You were there for Bart at a very low point." Franco added, softly. "You were his angel." Angela smiled up at Franco, wiped her eyes as she recalled Bart's pain that September evening. Angela realized it still hurt to remember the pain in his eyes and seeing him so low. Franco looked at the ring which glistened on Angela's hand. "A Beautiful ring for a beautiful girl." Angela blushed red and Franco smiled. "Congratulations on your commitment to Bart and he to you." Franco smiled at Rosa, then turned to face Angela. "Angela, please understand, DeMarco men do not give their hearts easily or casually."

Angela nodded as her eyes filled. "Thank you," she mouthed softly.

"Please join hands to give God thanks." Franco offered a touching family prayer. He concluded by saying; "thank you God for bringing our families together. Whatever the future holds, our bond is forever strong, Amen."

Bart smiled at his Dad. "Thanks, Dad," he said softly. He turned to his mother, smiled broadly. "Dad, Mom," he said as his voice broke. He swallowed, sipped some water, took a moment and flashed that smile that Rosa and, in truth, Angela could not resist, "thank you for inviting Angela's family to share Thanksgiving with us."

Rosa knew the deeper meaning of what Bart was saying. She had known his pain as a mother knows her children's pain. She knew what Angela meant to her boy. And, she had known that after a mere three months, Bart planned on asking Angela to be his girl with a ring and a commitment. Rosa had helped Bart choose the ring he would offer. She was confident Angela felt the same, so Rosa invited Angela's family to share what she trusted and hoped would be a very happy day. The day proved to be so much more than anyone anticipated.

Bart smiled at his mother. As a boy, when the daily slights, insults and bullying became too much for him to handle, Bart had cried in her arms in frustration and humiliation. Rosa had wiped his tears and told him that they would find a way. Family support, professional help, and Angela's love and compassion proved to be the way.

Bart met Rosa's eyes. No words were necessary. So Bart, smiled and said, "Mom, the turkey looks great, and I see you made my favorite stuffing."

Rosa's eyes filled. "Of course, I did," She choked. "Anything for my boy." She paused. "Bart, I am so happy for you."

"Anything for 'The Prince,'" Lucia teased, provoking smiles and laughter. She shared a smile with Mario. "Right, Mom?"

Rosa laughed. "Oh, you!" She said. "I love all my children." She exchanged a happy smile with Lucia. Both, Mother and daughter knew that Bart held a special place in Rosa's heart. He had been through so much. In truth, Lucia felt the same. She loved both of her brothers, but, Bart's challenges had sewn a bond of love and compassion between them that was special.

Dinner was joyous and as happy as could be. Bart was the toast of the city. More importantly, two families who had faced challenges that had seemed both cruel and insurmountable, knew joy. Bart took Angela's hand, leaned close and whispered, "thank you."

Angela smiled. Misted, "thank you, Bart. I love you."

"Mrs. Curcuru," Bart said, as he finished his second helping. "This lasagna is wonderful."

Maria smiled happily. "Bart, I love that you so enjoy food." She looked at Rosa. "It makes it a pleasure to cook."

Angela watched Bart fill his plate with turkey, his favorite stuffing, a mound of whipped potatoes and cover it all with Rosa's creamy turkey gravy. She laughed. "Really?" She nudged him. "You are going to eat all that?"

Bart leaned over and kissed Angela. "You bet I am." He grinned. "I worked hard today."

With espresso and Maria's tiramisu before them, Bart looked to Lucia. His little sister smiled, "relax Bart, have I ever failed you?"

"What's this?" Franco asked, as he saw Lucia's smile.

All eyes were on Lucia, who rose and surveyed the table, setting her gaze on Angela. "This week, Angela auditioned for a singing role in the Winter Musical." Lucia explained. She looked around, before her eyes settled on Angela. Lucia flashed a smile. "The word at school is that everyone was so impressed by her singing and dancing that she may be in line to win a leading role in Grease."

Everybody applauded as Angela blushed. Lucia continued, "Bart asked me to find the music for the song she sang at her audition." Lucia placed a music player on the table, turned to Angela, whose eyes were big with surprise.

Lucia knew just what to say to overcome Angela's expected objection. "Angela, Bart really wants to hear you sing." She paused and smiled. "Will you sing for him?"

Everybody clapped. Angela looked to Bart, who flashed his winning smile. "I was in practices all week for the game." He said. "I would be so happy if you would sing for me."

Between the applause and Bart's request, Angela could only smile and rise. She looked about, "I have no idea if I will be cast," she offered, then she looked into Bart's eyes and softened. "But, how can I say no to our hero?" She looked at Lucia, narrowed her eyes, "you could have warned me."

Lucia smiled. "No, this is way more fun." She teased with a luminous smile. "And," Lucia continued. "Remember, it was me who pushed Bart to ask you on your first date. You have to forgive me." Lucia laughed, and Angela could only smile.

Angela walked to an open area in the spacious dining room. Bart turned his chair to face her. Lucia pressed play and the music filled the room. Angela closed her eyes, looked down and took a deep breath.

She then looked up and smiled, her heart hearing the music and lyrics. She looked at Bart and sang:

> "Guess mine is not the first heart broken,
> My eyes not the first to cry,
> I'm not the first to know there's
> Just no getting over you

She smiled at Bart, as if there were no others in the room. And, she sang in her clear, sweet voice;

You know I'm just a fool who's willing
To sit around and wait for you,
But baby can't you see, there's nothing else for me to do
I'm hopelessly devoted to you.

She sang the next verse with her head back and arms wide. She then focused her energy on Bart's face. Angela slowly walked to stand before Bart; then she sat on his lap. He put his arms around her waist and listened:

My head is saying, fool forget him,
My heart is saying, don't let go,

Angela put her arms around Bart's neck and sang to him.

Hold on to the end, that's what I intend to do,
I'm hopelessly devoted to you.

She saw only Bart, felt his love and devotion and knew she would love him forever. She sang;

But now there's no way to hide
Since you pushed my love aside
I'm outta my head, hopelessly devoted to you.

She put her hands gently on his face, looked into his eyes and sang with passion;

Hopelessly devoted to you,uuu
Hopelessly devoted to you.

And, before her father, family and all present she kissed her love.

The room exploded in applause. Bart held her and looked into her eyes. "WOW! Angela, I had no idea. You are amazing."

She smiled, "I could not have said it any better than the songwriter, John Farrar." She looked into Bart's eyes. "I am hopelessly devoted to you, Bart. I love you."

Chapter Fifteen

December was a busy month for Bart and Angela. As they were both serious and highly achieving students, both, in fact, recently admitted to the National Honor Society, they worked diligently to prepare for semester exams. Bart was also tasked with delivering an oral presentation to his World History class on the Cuban Missile Crisis. The quality of the content and his presentation would determine his semester grade.

Notwithstanding the progress he had made in his speech, standing before the class and making a presentation still concerned him. Memories of past failures rose in his mind and clawed at his self-confidence. Both Rosa and Angela assured him, that they had faith in him.

"You can do it!" Rosa assured, offering a big smile and confident eyes on Bart.

Angela smiled, "Of course, he can do it." She agreed, placed her gaze on Bart. "And, Bart, I'll be there with you," she promised. Her assurance and support brought comfort and a smile to Bart. And, a sense of relief to Rosa, who smiled her thanks to Angela.

Angela had daily rehearsals for Grease, in which she was playing the coveted role of Sandy. Interestingly, Jessica was playing Rizzo and Betsy had a speaking and chorus role as one of the Pink Ladies.

Bart had taken and passed his driving test and was in possession of a driver's license. While he did not own a car, both the family car and Mario's were usually available, when needed.

Christmas was coming and he needed to buy something special for Angela, it being their first Christmas as a couple. He planned on asking his mother and sister to help him choose Angela's gift. He had his eye on a ruby necklace, but thought it wise to consult the experts on women's jewelry.

Bart was working hard to make and save money. He arose, each morning at 4am, and would hustle to the docks to seek lumping sites. The boss lumper, Sophie the Bull, liked Bart and as Bart was a local hero after the big Thanksgiving game victory, he managed to score on average, three to four lumping sites per week. Sophie appreciated that Bart accepted every job offered, irrespective of the challenges and difficulties.

With Coach Gilliss's instruction, Bart tried to hit golf balls each afternoon after class. Coach Gilliss had set up space in the empty bag room at Bass Rocks Golf Club with a net and a mat. They worked together to refine Bart's swing. Coach Gilliss saw progress and encouraged Bart to try to head south for one of the upcoming school breaks. That drew a laugh from Bart. "Sure Coach, I'll hop on my private jet."

Bart walked with Angela to school on the days he did not secure a lumping job and when not practicing or working, spent time on weekends with her. Dinner at Angela's house was a Friday evening routine, while Sunday dinner was usually at the DeMarco house.

Dave Powers and Bart had become friends, dates were arranged by Bart, Dave and Jim Perry with their girls on Saturday evenings.

The dynamic between Angela and Jessica was fascinating. They rehearsed together daily, and were occasionally on double or triple dates on Saturday nights. Over the weeks, Bart observed a comfort level growing between the three girls. Still, he had a hunch it would take some time.

Jessica seemed sincere in her remorse, she acted appropriately and in a friendly manner to all, but, it was difficult to forget that she had been the driving force in the 'Ugly Angela' insults, and responsible for a good deal of the pain Angela had suffered.

Bart knew well, getting past all that had occurred would always be a challenge. The guys, athlete's all, had much in common. The girls had the play, their guys, and school, but, there were scars. Bart knew that time would be required for healing, but, he was satisfied that all was headed in the proper direction. Angela seemed happy, and that was what he felt was most important.

On the Friday before Christmas, after a wonderful dinner of Maria's spaghetti in a shrimp, marinara sauce, followed by codfish cakes, and, of course, some tasty garlic bread, Bart and Angela sat in the living room of Angela's house. Angela's Dad was at sea, hoping for a big Christmas trip. Tina was helping her mother clean up after the meal and the boys were playing in their room. Angela went into the kitchen to plate some cookies and pour a glass of milk for Bart. When she returned and sat beside Bart, he noted she seemed somewhat tense.

"You okay, Angela?" Bart asked as he sat back, comfortably, and bit into a Christmas cookie, freshly baked by Maria. He sighed, "Wow, your mother is a great baker, this cookie is delicious!" He smiled, "and dinner was so good." He laughed, "I always enjoy the garlic bread." He saw her smile, as he took another cookie, bit into it. "Is this an apple filling?"

Angela smiled and nodded, "yes, that's my Mom's apple, cinnamon cookie." She watched as he made short work of another. She marveled at how much Bart loved to eat, and the quantities of food he ate in a sitting. "I'm glad that you are enjoying that." She smiled. "Tomorrow, my Mom will bake other of her Christmas cookies."

He smiled and pulled her into a kiss. She tasted apples and cinnamon. She smiled and eyed him. "Is that kiss for me or my Mom's cookies?"

Bart laughed. He angled a look at Angela. "Do I have to choose? I really like both."

Angela shook her head and laughed. "The way you eat and not a bit of fat on you." She sighed. "So unfair."

Bart put his arm around Angela, held her to him. "I love your body, Angela. You're perfect." He pulled her close and kissed her.

She thrilled at his words, he spoke with such ease and sincerity. She smiled up at him and shook her head, "I wish," she said as she studied a very contented Bart. She decided that this was a good time to discuss her concerns. Angela snuggled close. "Bart, I was wondering about Christmas."

Bart looked at her, perplexed. "What about Christmas?"

"Well," She hesitated. "Are we just going to be with our families?"

Bart shrugged, bit into another cookie, washed it down with milk. "Sure, why wouldn't we be with our families? Where else would we be?"

Angela studied Bart, who appeared so relaxed and happy. "So, we won't be seeing each other?" Angela queried, with raised brow.

Light dawned. Bart sat up, "of course we'll see each other." He looked at Angela, eyes set on her. "Angela, I plan to be with you on Christmas Eve and Christmas Day."

"Really?" She smiled, relieved. "How do we do that?"

Bart sat back and thought through the question. "We will be with one family on Christmas Eve and the other on Christmas Day, I guess." He paused. "I really hadn't thought about it." He looked at Angela and smiled. "Something tells me that you have thought about this."

She slid close to him, leaned in, snuggled against him. "How About," she kissed him. "We spend Christmas Eve with your family and Christmas Day here with my family?"

Bart held her close, enjoying the feel of her soft body against him, he kissed her, and shrugged, "I suppose," he eyed her. "Why is this so important to you, Angela?"

She smiled up at him, but Bart could read her anxiety. "Bart, there is just the six of us, no extended family." She explained in a soft voice. "If I am not here on Christmas Day, it will be hard on my parents."

He nodded, understanding her position. "Angela, relax," he assured. "We won't disappoint your family." He considered, as he smiled. "You know, maybe there is another way." He kissed her, ran his hands up her arms to her face, then down her back bringing her body flush to his. "You feel so good!"

Her eyes grew large, she glanced about. "Easy Bart, we're in my living room."

He closed his eyes, took a deep breath. "You're killing me, Princess."

Angela laughed. "Sorry," she offered as she kissed him softly, loving that he so wanted her. "How about you think about the plans and we talk tomorrow."

"Okay, but I think I have a lumping site tomorrow. I will call you when I finish."

Angela smiled. "That sounds good."

Bart lumped a dragger and was done by 10am. He hustled home, showered and readied to head to the jewelers with his mother and Lucia. Once there, he pointed out a ruby necklace that he had his eye on. "Ruby is her birth stone," he explained with a smile and a faraway look in his eyes. "She will look beautiful wearing this necklace." He looked at Rosa and Lucia. "What do you think?"

Rosa and Lucia watched him closely as he examined the piece. Lucia smiled, "Mom, I think he's got it bad?"

Rosa nodded. "Yes, I think so," she smiled brightly, "I like Angela." She considered her son, noting how happy he had become since Angela entered his life. "She's good for Bart."

Both his mother and sister liked the necklace. "Pretty expensive," Lucia commented with a teasing grin. "Does this mean my gift is out the window?"

Bart laughed. "Maybe," Bart responded with a smile. "After all you're only my little sister."

Lucia laughed. "I know better, big brother." She stated, with flashing eyes.

Bart bought the necklace and had it gift wrapped. He turned to his mother and Lucia. "How about we stop and I treat you to lunch?"

Over lunch at a favorite Italian deli, Bart asked his mother her thoughts on how he should deal with the issue of Christmas Eve and Christmas Day.

Rosa's head tilted as she studied and smiled at her son. "Do you have an idea, Bart?"

Bart looked at Lucia, shook his head, smiling, "how does she always know?"

"She's Mom," Lucia responded on a laugh.

"Mom," Bart began. "The Curcuru's have no family here." He looked at her. "How about we ask them to have Christmas Eve and Christmas Day with us?"

Rosa smiled on her son, gently touched his hand. "Angela is worried about her family, isn't she?"

Bart nodded. "She is," he paused. "She seemed stressed last night when she mentioned it."

"Angela is a good girl, Bart." Rosa nodded. "Okay, that sounds good, you talk to Angela and I will speak to Maria?"

Bart flashed a big smile. "Thanks Mom."

Later that Saturday, Rosa entered Maria Curcuru's kitchen. She had called to ask if she could meet with Maria. They embraced and the women sat at the kitchen table, a plate of cookies and a pot of coffee between them.

Rosa smiled at Maria. She noted how Angela favored Maria. Maria, like Angela, was attractively full figured, with sensuous curves. Maria's black, curly hair was kept short and framed her oval face. When happy, they smiled freely and warmly. Rosa easily understood why Bart had been so captured by Angela.

"My son loves Angela." She stated as she watched Maria's face brighten. "He is so much like his father," she reminisced. "When Franco was 16 we first met." She smiled. "I was only 14, almost 15 and we were at a party." She sat back. "He spent the entire evening with me, called the next day and asked me on a date." Rosa laughed. "Sound like anyone?"

Maria laughed, her brown eyes danced. "Just like Bart."

Rosa nodded. "I was so excited when Franco called, this handsome boy liked me and wanted to take me on a date." Rosa shook her head. "He didn't even have a driver's license yet, but he was determined."

The women laughed together. "Franco was special," Rosa stated. "But, when I told my parents about our date, my father shook his head and said, NO!" She paused. "He said I was too young and there would be no dating until I was 16." Rosa laughed. "I don't think my Dad approved of

Franco." She added. "My mother told me that my Dad thought Franco was 'too much.'"

"Too much?" Maria asked, perplexed.

"Yes," Rosa laughed. "He was a star athlete, a good student, a hard worker, too much."

Maria shook her head. "But, those are good things." She smiled. "He sounds like Bart."

Rosa smiled, a pleasant memory floating across her mind. "Franco was the first boy who chased me." She eyed Maria. "My father did not trust Franco." She laughed. "He told my mother 'that boy wants just one thing from our daughter.'"

Maria laughed. "Of course, just like every boy." She considered Rosa. "Sometimes, Bart looks at Angela like he wants to eat her whole." She paused and grinned. "It's thrilling for Angela that Bart feels that way, of course." She smiled at Rosa. "I guess it is our job to teach our daughters about men." Maria smiled. "Even the best men are still men."

Rosa laughed. "And, aren't we thankful for that?"

They laughed together. "Yes, we are." Maria agreed.

Maria hesitated, looked at Rosa. "Bart is a good man. He treats Angela so well," she paused, smiled. "Bart calls her Princess." She smiled at the image of Angela's face when Bart looks at her so hungrily, so desirous of holding her, kissing her, and wanting more.

Maria sighed, "I am so grateful." She paused, placed happy eyes on Rosa. "Bart saved Angela." She looked at Rosa. "Bart fought three boys who were threatening Angela, calling her 'Ugly Angela,' pushing her and not letting her pass." She sighed, exhaled, and dabbed at her eyes. "Bart came along and protected Angela." She smiled. "He walked her home." Maria smiled. "They were only 14, but Bart was so kind." She took a deep breath. "I helped Angela clean the blood off of Bart's hands and clothes."

Then, Maria's eyes became cloudy. She looked at Rosa. "Before Bart, Angela had been treated badly." Tears came to Maria's eyes. "They called her 'Ugly Angela.'" She wiped her eyes. "They were so mean to her, those girls, and even some boys, they really hurt her." Maria choked with anguish. "They made her feel ugly." She looked at Rosa. "You know what that means to a girl." The women gripped hands, shared the pain. Maria continued, "Bart," she sighed, and managed a smile. "Bart makes her feel beautiful."

Rosa squeezed Maria's hands in support. She waited for Maria to wipe her eyes and always a good hostess, Maria freshened their cups. Rosa looked at Maria, "Angela is beautiful," Rosa stated. "Her smile has captured Bart's heart." She paused, reflected. "I understand the pain Angela and your family suffered." Rosa trembled. Angela's story hit Rosa hard. 'Why do they have to do that?' She thought. Rosa took a deep breath, looked into Maria's eyes and explained, "Bart wants to have your family with us for Christmas Eve and Christmas Day." She paused. "Bart and Angela talked and he wants Angela to be happy."

"I don't understand." Maria said. "Why would Angela be unhappy?"

"You raised a wonderful daughter." Rosa smiled. "Angela is worried that you and Sal would be upset if she were with us, instead of at home, on Christmas." She grinned. "So, Bart thought that we could all be together."

Maria nodded as the issue became clear. "Ah, I see." Maria shook her head in amusement. "And, you raised a very thoughtful boy, Rosa." She paused, frowned, as she shook her head. "We had Thanksgiving with you. Now Christmas, it doesn't seem right."

"Please Maria," Rosa started. "We are a big family. With my mother, brothers and sister, and Franco's family we will be almost thirty people. Having your family won't be a problem." She hesitated, "And, it would make Bart so happy."

Maria nodded and smiled. "Bart is close to your heart." She offered. "And, I can see where Bart came by his brains," she chided. "Okay, I will talk to Sal."

"That's good," Rosa said with a smile. She took a breath. "There's more Maria." She sipped her coffee as she sought the best way to convey her message.

Rosa placed concerned eyes on Maria. "Franco has a friend, a fish dealer, who has a house in Florida." Again, she sipped her coffee. Maria sensed that she was anxious. "See," Rosa continued. "Bart's golf coach called Franco. He thinks Bart could win a golf scholarship to college. So, Coach Gilliss set up an opportunity for some College golf coaches to watch Bart play."

"In Florida?" Maria asked.

Rosa nodded. "Yes, in Florida." She took a deep breath. "See, the house is on a golf course, a perfect opportunity for Bart." She hesitated. "Franco bought airplane tickets for our family to fly to Florida over February vacation. A good chance to enjoy a vacation and for Bart to audition for the college coaches."

"That's nice," Maria said. She sensed there was more, read Rosa's anxiety, but she waited to be enlightened.

Rosa eyed Maria. "Franco bought seven tickets." She paused, took a breath. "Tickets for our family, Mario's girl, Celia, and for Angela."

Maria sat upright, surprised. "You want Angela to go to Florida with Bart?"

"No Maria," Rosa quickly stated. "We want Angela to come to Florida with our family. She would be in a room with my daughter, Lucia, and with Celia." Rosa looked into Maria's eyes. "I will take care of her like my own daughter." She paused. "You have my word."

Maria thought about the request. She knew Angela would be thrilled. She also knew her husband would be anything but thrilled.

Rosa broke into her thoughts. "Maria, Bart bought a beautiful necklace for Angela. I think he is dedicated to her happiness." She looked at Maria, her eyes implored. "My boy loves Angela."

Maria nodded. "Yes, I think he does." She smiled. "Angela told me how excited he becomes when they are alone together, and even then, he's respectful of her wishes." She paused. "Please don't misunderstand, I believe you." She paused. "But, I don't think Sal will allow Angela to do this trip." She shrugged. "Anyway, it's only a week. And Angela is in the play." She studied Rosa. "And, maybe a week apart might be good for them."

Rosa looked at Maria. "You know Maria, Bart has also had a difficult time." She met her eyes. "As a boy he had a very bad stutter." She paused and relived the pain. "The other kids called him 'stutter boy' and taunted and laughed at him." She choked. "It was awful." She took a deep breath, collected her thoughts. "We sent him to speech doctors and therapists. And, it got a little better. "But," Rosa met Maria's eyes, "Maria, when Bart is with Angela, he is calm and confident, and able to speak clearly." She looked to Maria. "I believe Angela calms Bart in stressful situations." Rosa misted. "Bart may well need Angela there."

Maria nodded, now she understood fully just how Bart was able to empathize with Angela's pain. And, replace it with love. She recalled when Bart defended Angela, and fought the three boys who were tormenting her. 'That was when Angela became devoted to Bart,' she realized.

"This is a big opportunity for Bart." Rosa added. "I really believe Angela being there would help Bart." She looked at Maria. "The trip will not interfere with the play." Rosa explained. "The play runs for three nights, ending on the Saturday before February vacation." She paused, smiled. "Bart would never miss a performance. He encouraged Angela to audition." She let out a pent up breath. "We will fly the next day, on Sunday." She looked to Maria, mother to mother. "Maria, Angela may well make the difference for Bart." She paused, placed hopeful eyes on Maria. "Please, Maria, will you please talk to Sal?"

Maria took Rosa's hands. She nodded, "I think Angela needs Bart and Bart needs Angela." She stated. "They give each other confidence." She smiled. "How wonderful is that?" She offered with a smile. Maria considered Rosa's request. "Does Bart know that you are here?"

Rosa smiled. "He knows that I am asking you about spending Christmas with our family." She smiled and shrugged. "He doesn't know about the trip. Franco wants it to be a surprise."

Maria studied Rosa, nodded. "I will talk to Sal."

"Thank you, Maria." Rosa rose and hugged Maria. "Please be part of our family."

Chapter Sixteen

The 'feast of Seven Fishes' is an Italian tradition. On Christmas Eve, a feast of seafood is prepared, as no meat may be consumed until after mid-night mass and the taking of the sacrament. In Gloucester, America's Oldest Fishing port, the Sicilian population followed the custom with religious fervor.

The Demarco house was replete with platters and casseroles of Italian styled, lobster salad, spaghetti with shrimp sauce, baked, stuffed calamari, fried sole and sweet whiting, baked haddock and, of course, octopus salad. Sal Curcuru supplied fresh fish and his personally, squeezed, aged, and vintage wine. Maria baked her homemade Italian bread and a collection of wonderful desserts.

Maria had confided to Rosa that she had spoken to Sal about the Christmas celebrations. She had also discussed the trip to Florida. Sal assented to Christmas Eve with the DeMarco family, but had insisted on Christmas Day at home with his family.

Of course, the DeMarco's understood. And, it didn't take too much coaxing and sweetness from Angela to convince Bart to share Christmas dinner with her family.

Sal was surprised that Maria was in favor of allowing Angela to travel to Florida with Bart's family. Maria reminded Sal that Bart had befriended and defended Angela when others took pleasure in humiliating her. "Bart has been so good for Angela," she stressed. "Now, when she looks in the mirror she smiles and sees the beauty that Bart cherishes, not 'Ugly Angela.'"

Maria paused, looked to Sal with soft eyes and a bit of pleading in her tone. "Sal, Bart has made our girl happy."

Sal nodded. "Yes," he agreed, recalling how Bart, covered in blood, had walked a scared and distraught, Angela home, after defending and fighting for her. "Bart has been good for Angela." He paused and eyed his wife. "But, you see how he looks at her."

Maria smiled in memory, "just like you looked at me." She hugged Sal. "I believe Rosa when she says that she will protect Angela." She kissed her husband. "And, I trust Angela." She studied Sal with warm eyes. "Please Sal, Bart needs her with him. And, Angela would want to be there for Bart."

Sal sighed, nodded as he embraced his wife. "Okay, Maria, okay, I will trust Angela." He kissed her, nuzzled her neck, spoke softly, "Eight days at sea, I've missed you," he said.

Maria laughed, kissed her husband and smiled. "And, you talk about Bart?"

Christmas Eve in the DeMarco home, found more than thirty family and friends gathered happily together. Tables had been arranged for the adults and for the children. Wine was poured and a feast, that was as much about family love and true friendship as delicious seafood, was enjoyed.

When all were seated and Franco heard the laughter and banter from the adult tables and the giggling and joy from the children, he rose and requested an opportunity to speak. He looked about and smiled.

"This has been a wonderful year for our family. I look about and see all my Compare (dearest friends) here, safe from the perils of the sea." Heads nodded in thanks. "We welcome new friends, Maria and Sal Curcuru and their children to our lives." He smiled. "Sal, we are so happy that you have accepted our friendship." Sal Curcuru smiled back at Franco, and raised his wineglass in thanks.

Franco looked to Mario. "We have Mario's girl, Celia, here with us." Franco pointed at Celia, who rose and with a flourish, made a theatrical curtsy. Franco laughed. "Mario, my son, I think you have your hands full with Celia." That brought laughter from all.

"Of course, my beautiful daughter, Lucia, grows prettier by the day." He grinned. "I'm sure she is the cause of my gray hair." Lucia wagged her finger and beamed a smile at her Dad.

"At least you have hair!" Called out Rosa's brother, Vito, whose bald head glistened in the reflection of the rooms lighting. The group exploded in laughter.

Franco looked at Bart, who sat with Angela, smiling and holding hands. Franco's eyes misted. He smiled at Rosa, then looked at his family and close friends. "You all know that Bart has struggled with speech for almost all his life." He paused. "You have all been so supportive of Bart and our family." He choked-up, sipped his wine, swallowed the lump in his throat and smiled. "My Bart never quit. He never let the mean comments and mocking stop him." Franco cleared his throat. "He won the starting quarterback position at Gloucester High, only to be pulled off of the field, and embarrassed, without really being given a chance."

Franco shook his head, relived that pain, as only a parent can. He firmed his gaze and continued. "Still, Bart pushed on and won the award for best player in the State golf tournament." He grinned at Bart. "Then, you all know what he did in the Thanksgiving football game."

Franco paused, smiled at Bart and Angela, happily smiling together. "Bart, just like my Mario, proved he could lead and he could win." Franco looked to Rosa and theirs eyes flooded with tears. In an emotion choked voice, Franco added, "My boy had to overcome so much. And, he did it! For Gloucester, the School, and his teammates. I am so proud."

The room erupted in applause. All eyes were set on Bart, who flushed at the attention. Angela's face was alight with joy, her eyes sparkled.

Franco looked at Angela. "I haven't mentioned Angela." He smiled. "When Bart was so hurt, Angela was there for him, when he really needed her." Franco's eyes glistened with emotion. "My Bart was smart enough to know a truly beautiful and wonderful girl and to chase her…"

"Ya, until she caught him," Uncle Jimmy called out, as the guests burst out with laughter. Angela blushed, a pretty scarlet, and laughed, but, still played to the room by nodding in agreement.

Franco looked at Bart. "Son, I am so proud of you." He pointed at Angela. "I suggest you hold onto that girl." Bart met his Dad's eyes, as Rosa called out, "I agree!"

Franco held up his hands. "I'd like to finish by letting my family and dear friends know that after we cheer Angela on in her performance as Sandy in the Winter musical, 'Grease,' we will all be heading to Florida." Franco smiled, looked to Bart. "See, Bart's golf coach, Dave Gilliss, has arranged for Bart to play golf for some college golf coaches."

Applause met the announcement. "And," Franco raised his hands, grinned broadly and spoke above the noise, "Celia and Angela will be with us."

Angela beamed, then concerned, looked to her parents. Maria nodded in affirmation. Angela smiled, then hugged Bart. "Thank you, Mr. DeMarco," she called out. Celia looked to Mario, who whispered that he had spoken to her parents and they gave their approval.

"Now, can we eat?" Uncle Vito bellowed.

Chapter Seventeen

The DeMarco family came out in force to join the Curcuru family to support Angela in the Saturday evening and final performance of Grease.

Bart had sat front and center for each performance. He so enjoyed watching Angela sing and dance across the stage. Her confident smile was his reward. Bart witnessed, with delight, how happy she was as she performed.

Each evening Angela sang with joy and emotion. Her eyes were alight with pleasure as she danced and sang with the cast in the group numbers. When the stage lights softened and she was alone on the stage to sing the ballad, 'Hopelessly Devoted to You,' she looked out to the packed house and focused her energy on the face of the young man she loved. The audience could feel her passion as she sang for Bart.

The show was a success. Following the performance, Angela's entourage waited to congratulate their star. Surrounded by so many of Bart's family as well as her own, Angela beamed as she accepted their hugs and compliments. For a young girl who had known so few accolades, it meant so very much to her.

Bart attended the closing night Cast party at the Nelson home. As Theatre Director, Beth Nelson, avoided the dangers of extreme and inappropriate student behavior, by hosting the cast parties herself, with the help of Coach Nelson in chaperoning the students. Bart watched with such joy, as Angela beamed her smile as she modestly deflected praise. Bart was delighted to see Angela shine. And, she had performed wonderfully. He felt enormous pride in and love for Angela.

After the speeches by the Directors and certain of the cast and crew, everyone sipped punch and ate the food prepared by the families of the actors and technical team. With laughter, they re-lived the highs, lows and, of course, the amusing mishaps of the three performances.

Bart stood, with Dave Powers and Jim Perry. He smiled when Jessica rose and offered a toast to the cast and crew. "I so enjoyed this play." She looked about and thanked the cast for offering support and joked with the lighting crew for their restraint in not taking revenge on her, for her pettiness and immature actions over the years.

She then looked to Angela. "I want to especially thank Angela, who was brilliant as Sandy," all clapped in agreement. Their eyes met and Jessica's filled with tears as her voice choked. "Angela, I am so sorry for all my mean spirited insults." She paused, wiped her eyes. "You are the best, kindest, and most beautiful person I know." Tears ran down her cheeks. "I hope to someday earn your friendship." Jessica dropped her head, shame flushed her cheeks. "I was so mean to you and," she looked at Bart, "to Bart." She managed a smile. "But, you found and lifted each other."

Wiping her eyes, she concluded. "You two are the best." Bart smiled and nodded at Jessica. Dave looked at Jessica and flashed a big smile. Angela moved to her and wrapped Jessica in a warm hug. "I'd love to be your friend," Angela said softly.

Bart moved with Dave Powers, Jim Perry and Coach Nelson to Coach's den as the Cast party continued in the living room and kitchen. On the table, before them, was a copy of 'Amateur Sports Monthly' magazine.

The cover photo was the award winning Piscitello photo of Bart, in full flight, right hand and arm extended, the football held in his big hand, crossing the goal line and scoring the winning touchdown. The caption read;

'Superman! Bart, 'Stutter boy', DeMarco, carries Gloucester to victory!'"

Coach Nelson moved the discussion to the Thanksgiving Day game and the magazine piece. The reporter had focused the article on Bart and his two sport success. What was interesting to the writer and editor was that the two sports were played in the same season. Even more compelling, was the story of Bart's battle with stuttering. The writer researched stuttering issues in the young. He quoted extensively from case studies and treatment plans as detailed by YES: The Youth association for Excellence in Speech.

Bart was quoted at length, about the pain and humiliation he felt when mocked by his peers. "They called me 'Stutter Boy,'" Bart explained. "I tried to not speak, to disappear." He said. "It was tough," he acknowledged. "My outlet for free expression was sports."

Coach Nelson held the magazine and looked to Bart. "I want to thank you for the manner in which you handled the questions concerning my game decisions."

Bart shrugged. "Why turn a great day for Gloucester into anything less?" He grinned. "We won as a team."

Coach Nelson studied Bart for a long moment, considered the journey this young man had taken. He frowned as he, again realized, how he, as his coach, had added to Bart's pain. He was in awe that Bart had chosen to rise above the hurt. "You were raised right, Bart." Coach complimented, and was amused that Bart's cheeks flushed at the observation. 'A great kid!' He thought.

In the interview, questions focused on the events in the Salem game that resulted in Coach Nelson's removal of Bart from the game. Bart, then making the golf team and helping the Gloucester high school golf team to qualify for the state tournament. And, his winning the medal for the best individual round in the tournament.

Bart heaped praise, in the article, on Coach Gilliss and his teammates, especially, Jim Perry, for guiding him and for leading the team.

Jim Perry read Bart's quote aloud, and laughed. "You bet your ass, DeMarco! You'd be nothing without me!"

The comment brought laughter, which was heard in the living room, prompting a visit from Beth Nelson and Angela. "What's so funny?" Mrs. Nelson asked.

Coach Nelson grinned up at his smiling wife. "Perry's being a smart-ass is all." He responded.

Beth Nelson scanned the room, then looked at her husband. "Coach, I see that you are not being a very good host." She smiled. "Have you offered these boys some food, a cold drink?"

Bob Nelson shrugged. "We were trying to avoid interfering with the Cast party. That's why we came into my den."

Beth Nelson looked at Angela and offered a pained smile. "You were right, Angela. I guess we have to take care of this."

Angela looked at those gathered. "Shall we make plates of food for you Gentlemen?" She offered, with a smile. Angela caught Bart's eye and brought a broad smile to his face. Looking at Angela, his thoughts went to spending a week in Florida with Angela in the sun and surf. She saw the glint in his eye and blushed.

"A plate sounds great," Coach Nelson replied. "Thank you, ladies." The three young men nodded vigorously at the offer.

Mrs. Nelson and Angela left the den. Once out of the den, Beth Nelson smiled at Angela. "Your young man is amazing," she complimented. "He made everyone look good in the magazine article, deflecting praise from himself and even defending Bob, after Bob pulled Bart out of the Salem game." She paused, waited for Angela to meet her eyes. "Bart must have been devastated."

Angela nodded. "He was." She thought back to that evening, remembered the look of defeat that she saw in his eyes. Angela looked at Mrs. Nelson and managed a weak smile. "But, he just pushed on, tried out for the golf team, ignored those who laughed and mocked him." She continued. "I have never met anybody like him." Then Angela's smile bloomed. "But, Mrs. Nelson, that was the night Bart and I began dating."

Beth Nelson smiled at Angela. "He is a very special, really unique, young man." She considered Angela. "Handsome, intelligent, kind and giving, what a package," she stated, as she shook her head. "And, that smile, WOW!" She exclaimed. "You are a lucky girl, Angela," Beth Nelson added. "And, Angela, Bart adores you."

"Yes, I know," Angela blushed, "I don't really, fully, understand it," she responded. "I mean, I don't look like Jessica or the other cheerleaders." She paused. "I keep thinking that he will want a prettier girl." She sighed. "But, I love him, so much." She looked at Mrs. Nelson, "I auditioned for the play because Bart asked me to try." She dropped her eyes and smiled. "He believes in me."

Beth Nelson studied Angela. "He loves you, Angela." She paused. "Bart sees you as beautiful." She paused. "There will be challenges," she continued. "My husband tells me he will likely win a golf scholarship to college."

Angela smiled. "Hopefully, that would be great."

"Yes, it would." She took Angela's hands, looked into her eyes. "It will probably be a Southern or Western school. He will go away." She paused, watched as her words registered.

Angela nodded, a sadness settling on her face. "Yes, I understand, there will be so many beautiful girls who will want Bart." She shrugged.

Beth Nelson squeezed her hands. "Don't you accept it as inevitable, Angela. You fight for him." She looked into Angela's eyes. "That's what I had to do when Bob went off to play football at Penn State." She nodded. "I was here at Salem becoming a teacher, and I was as afraid as you are, but I did not give up." She smiled, recalling a fond memory. "Bob proposed the day he graduated," she explained, focused her eyes on Angela, took a deep breath. "Angela, think of the lyrics of the song you sang so beautifully tonight." She saw Angela's smile. "So, Angela," Beth Nelson challenged. "Are you hopelessly devoted to Bart?" She paused. "And, will you fight for him?"

Angela smiled into Mrs. Nelson's words. "I am." She paused, set a determined gaze. "You bet, I will."

Mrs. Nelson and Angela found Jessica and Betsy, explained that they should assist in making plates for their boyfriends. "Of course," Betsy responded, rose and moved to the join Angela and Mrs. Nelson. Angela looked to Jessica, who nodded and joined the women in the kitchen.

As they made up the plates with generous portions of food, Jessica looked about at the others, "why are we doing this? Dave could make up his own plate."

Angela continued to make Bart's plate, adding two pieces of fried chicken, which she knew Bart enjoyed. She spoke without looking up, as she ladled a good portion of homemade coleslaw onto his plate. "Because, it makes me happy to do for Bart."

In the den, the guys continued to review the magazine article and reflect on the fall sports season. When the interviewer questioned the choice made by Coach Nelson in pulling Bart from the Salem game, Bart defended the decision. "Of course it hurt," Bart asserted. "But, Dave Powers was a proven quarterback, and the right choice at that time."

"Thanks for that," Dave smiled. "I like that, 'a proven quarterback.'" He quoted with a smile.

In response to the interviewer's questions as to the facts surrounding Bart re-joining the team for the Thanksgiving game, Bart had shrugged. "Dave was banged up and Coach asked me to play." He smiled. "I was glad to help my Coach, Team and School."

The interviewer wrote that Bart had thrown for three touchdowns, ran for two and lead the team to a dramatic come from behind victory. Bart chimed in. "It's important to remember, the win was Coach Nelson's 100th victory."

The reporter had allowed Bart to extol the choices made. But, then he focused his attention to the final play selection. "So, tell us about the last play run, Bart?"

"There were three seconds left in the game, so we had one play." Bart explained. "I called our final time-out and met with Coach Nelson, Coach Bailey and with Dave Powers." He smiled. "We discussed kicking a field goal and taking the game into overtime, or going for the win."

"And how did the conversation go?" The magazine reporter asked, eyes set hard on Bart.

Bart shrugged, "it was pretty intense," he began. "We weighed the factors, the chance of winning now, the chances of winning in overtime and Coach Nelson decided to go for it."

"I heard that you argued passionately that you wanted to go for the win, is that true?"

Bart nodded. "Yes, I believed in our team. I wanted to go for it." Bart sat back. "So, when Coach ordered us to go for it, we called the play and," Bart smiled. "It worked."

"Tell me about the play as it unfolded," the reporter asked. "It was all in front of you, what really happened?"

"Well," Bart began. "We called a quarterback keeper, triple option." Bart smiled as he thought back. "I took the snap from Jim Johnson and rolled right. Dana Hughes was my pitch man, had the Danvers contain man come for me, I would have pitched the ball to Dana," Bart shrugged. "But, the contain man held his position." He paused, the reporter could see in Bart's eyes that Bart was mentally back on the field as he recalled the events.

"My next option was to turn and pass to Jeff Bammarito in the left corner of the end-zone, but Derek Chambers was covering Jeff like a blanket, so I was down to option three," Bart looked at the reporter, "I had to run it in." He paused.

"I saw Danvers line-backer, Jake Taylor, mirroring me." Bart shrugged. "I was in trouble, he is so good," Bart proclaimed. "Then, our center, Jim Johnson, the real hero of this story, flashed by me and absolutely crushed Taylor knocking him out of the play!" Bart smiled. "Jim made a great block. He really saved the day!"

"So, now I had to beat the Danvers cornerback." Bart smiled. "I figured that I would just run over him, but he was smart. He moved to take my legs out from under me." Bart let out a breath. "I saw him lower his head and I guessed he was going to dive low, so I went air-born, above him." Bart smiled. "I had the ball in my right hand, I extended the ball as I dove." He paused. "Nobody touched me, I sailed over him across the goal line."

The reporter was smiling, "Wow!" he said. "I saw the photo."

Bart looked at the reporter, "it was a real team win. Everybody did their jobs." He nodded and added. "Our left guard, Gary Brancaleone, and left tackle, Phil Quince, protected my blind side. It was teamwork!" Bart proclaimed and smiled. "And, Coach Nelson won his 100th game."

The reporter nodded. "So Bart, you are a sophomore, I hear that you are a very good student. What are your plans?"

Bart looked at the reporter. "I hope to win a golf scholarship to college." He shrugged. "Who knows, right?" Bart added with a smile.

"Anything you want to add?" The reporter asked.

Bart looked at him, and with a serious expression, Bart stated, "My parents and siblings helped me so much to overcome my stutter." He took a breath. "It was really bad," he emphasized. "They were always there for me, in good times and really low moments." He smiled. "And, the story will not be complete without my mentioning Angela, my angel." He sat up. "Without Angela, I doubt any of these wonderful things would have happened." He nodded and added. "I could not have succeeded without her." The reporter quoted Bart exactly.

"You did a great job with that reporter," Coach Nelson said with a little smile. "Except, I think you gave too much credit to Perry." That brought laughter from the group and a look of mock indignation from Jim.

The ladies arrived with the food. Dave powers took the plate and cold drink from Jessica with a surprised smile and loving eyes. "Thanks, Jess, I appreciate this." He paused, reflected on her heartfelt apology to the many that she had hurt. He knew that could not have been easy. He had made clear to Jessica that their relationship hinged on Jessica really assessing her actions.

Dave had been livid over her 'stutter boy,' insult at the assembly. "If you want me," he had insisted, "you will be the woman I know you are capable of being." Dave took the plate that Jessica had prepared for him, studied her pretty face and gleaming eyes. "How about having dinner tomorrow with my family?" He asked.

Jessica met his eyes and blushed. "I was glad to do it." She paused, looked at Angela, then looked back and smiled at Dave, "you want me to meet your family?"

Dave nodded. "I do," he smiled. "Will you join us?"

Jessica beamed. "I would love to," she responded.

Beth Nelson watched the exchange with a smile, looked to Angela who nodded and smiled. "Everybody happy?" Mrs. Nelson asked.

"Yes, thanks," Coach responded with a smile. "Go and enjoy your party."

The ladies left the den. Angela looked over her shoulder and smiled as Bart watched her leave.

Chapter Eighteen

The DeMarco family entourage arrived at their Florida destination, in the boating community of Punta Gorda Isles. Entering through the front door, they were looking through a Great-room, containing a spacious living area, a formal dining area and a good-size kitchen, to a wall of triple sliders looking out onto the pool-deck and past the shimmering water, onto the golf course. Rosa smiled at the neatness and cleanliness of the house. The furniture appeared comfortable and in good condition.

On the right of the Great-room was the master bedroom suite and to the left, past the kitchen was the guest wing with three bedrooms and a bath.

"Very nice," Rosa offered, much to the relief of Franco. Franco, Mario and Bart hefted in the suitcases, as Rosa walked through the guest suite sizing up the bedrooms. She considered the layout and told Mario and Bart that they would share the bedroom at the back of the house, overlooking the golf course. From that room there was a large slider opening onto the pool deck. She assigned the middle room to Lucia and the room closest to the kitchen to Celia and Angela.

The men set the suitcases in the assigned rooms and Rosa suggested that everyone get into bathing suits to take a refreshing swim after the long travel day. She found a closet with large beach towels and distributed them to the happy group.

As the excited youths changed into their suits, Rosa knocked on the door of the room shared by her sons. In their suits with the blinds pulled open, Mario and Bart readied to dash through the slider and dive into the pool. Mario opened the door and smiled, "Hi Mom," he noted her look of concern. "Are you okay?"

Rosa sat in a chair and asked her sons to take a seat on the bed. They sat facing the pool deck. "I'm fine, but I wanted to have a talk with you two."

Mario and Bart exchanged a curious glance and then looked to their mother. "Okay Mom, what's up?" Mario asked.

As Rosa was forming the words she wished to speak, she noted her son's attention shift. Their eyes lit and smiles spread across their handsome faces.

She glanced over her shoulder and saw that the girls had come onto the pool deck, wearing bikinis and smiling brightly. Rosa smiled, somewhat begrudgingly, and gave her sons a moment to enjoy the view.

"Mario, Bart, could I please have your attention for a minute?" Rosa asked. She saw Bart wave and noted the girls looking on the scene in the bedroom from their lounges. "I can see this is not going to be easy." She said.

"What's not going to be easy, Mom?" Mario asked.

Rosa rose and pulled the blinds closed, stealing the beautiful view. "Please, give me your attention for a few minutes." She requested.

Bart nodded, glanced at the blinds then looked back at his mother. "Okay, Mom, what's up?"

"I want you two to know," she began, "that neither the Curcuru's nor the Scola's were happy about allowing their daughter to come on this trip." She paused, noted that she had their attention. "I had to promise that I would protect Celia and Angela as if they were my own daughters." She sized up her sons reactions. "That is why I separated your rooms from the girls with Lucia between you."

Mario looked at Bart, Rosa noted their smiles. "Protect them from what?" Mario asked, feigning innocence. The boys observed their mothers stern countenance, eyes set hard on them.

"Bart," Rosa began, "Angela's parents allowed her to come with us because I explained that Coach Gilliss set up this opportunity for you to play for the eyes of golf coaches from at least three colleges. She paused, eyed Bart. "I explained that Angela was important to you, that she was a calming influence." She watched Bart nod. Satisfied, she looked to Mario. "And, I told Celia's parents that we considered her part of our family and wanted her with us."

Mario read his mother's concern. "Relax Mom," he grinned. "Celia will soon be part of the family." He looked at his mother. "I'm twenty now, nearly twenty-one, I have a good site on a good boat." He paused. "Dad and I are discussing buying a fishing dragger so we can work for ourselves." He noted her surprise at that revelation, and continued. "It was the reason that fish dealer loaned Dad this house. He wants to invest with us, so we sell our catch to his company." Mario rose, reached into his bag and pulled out a ring box, opened the box and showed the diamond engagement ring to his Mom and brother. He smiled. "Mom, I love Celia, I plan on proposing to Celia on this trip."

Rosa rose and hugged Mario. "I'm happy for you, Mario. Celia is good for you." Bart shook Mario's hand, smiled, "congratulations, Mario."

"We are still young," Mario conceded, "but, she's the one, Mom." He laughed. "Okay if I go see my girl, now?"

Rosa misted, hugged Mario, "that is good, Mario, that is good."

Mario rose, grinned at Bart. "Our girls look hot in their bikinis, don't they?" He laughed. "I'm out of here, Bart. The lecture is all for you now."

Bart laughed. "Some brother you are, tell Angela that I hope to be out there before dark!"

Rosa watched the exchange with amusement. Mario left the room, as she turned to Bart, smiled, "how do I say this?"

Bart reached out and took her hand. "Mom, are you trying to tell me to be careful?"

Rosa nodded. "I don't want you or Angela to be hurt," she cautioned, concern coloring her expression.

Bart held Rosa's hands, he looked into her eyes. "Mom, do you know what it means for an angel to come into your life?" He paused, smiled. "Angela was there for me when I was at my lowest." He gently squeezed Rosa's hands. "She thinks of me before herself." He shook his head. "I think that's rare. And, I know how truly special she is."

He took a breath, and continued. "Angela loves me Mom. And, I love her." He grew serious. "I know we are only 16, and I know that I will likely be going away for college." He smiled, "and, there will be challenges, but, Mom," he looked into her eyes. "I know I will always love her and want her."

He squeezed his mother's hands, sighed. "Mom, I want her so bad that it hurts." He paused, took a breath. "But, I will always respect her wishes," he stated. "Always!"

Rosa's eyes flooded with tears. "I love you, Bartolo."

"I love you, Mom," Bart responded. He grinned, "so, here's an idea, what do you say we get out there and enjoy that sun?"

Bart pulled the blinds, opened the slider and came onto the deck. He dove into the pool and swam across the length to the far side where the lounges were lined up. He pulled himself from the pool, the water cascading from his tall, lean, muscular form and plopped down beside Angela, who wore a white bikini, which accentuated her hourglass figure, a colorful and attractive straw hat and a questioning expression. Bart read the concern and grinned, "Mom just wanted to give Mario and me a little lecture. You can relax, everything is fine," he assured her. "I'll explain later."

Bart laid back and stretched, he took a long look at Angela, smiled in appreciation, leaned over and whispered, "Princess, you really look great!"

Angela blushed at the compliment, smiled, "thanks," she responded. "Let's go for a swim," she suggested. Angela walked down the pool steps as Bart jumped into the pool, causing a splash which showered her. He laughed at her surprise.

"It is a pool," he commented, grinning broadly. "The idea is to get wet, right?"

Angela smirked. "Everything isn't diving into the end-zone, Bart!" Then, unable to resist the obvious delight gleaming in his eyes, she smiled into his grin.

Mario laughed. "I think you committed a Cardinal sin little brother," Mario shook his head, "you wet her hair." He laughed aloud, looked at Celia who he held as they swam together. "Am I right, honey?"

Celia laughed. "It's rare that you are, Mario," she winked at Angela, "but this time, I think so." She looked at Angela, "little boys!" She sighed, feigning exasperation. "You better get used to it."

"Well, Big brother," Bart grinned. "Angela and I challenge you and Celia to a water battle. You game?"

"Water battle?" Angela queried. "What's that?"

Lucia laughed. "Oh, Angela, You up on Bart's shoulders and Celia on Mario's." She giggled at Angela's expression. "Then you wrestle until one of the teams fall over into the pool."

"You're on!" Mario responded, laughing. "Little brother, you are going down!" Mario flexed his muscles to the amusement of all. In truth, he was as tall as Bart, and as he was older, had more musculature, bigger shoulders, and a broader chest. He was an older, bigger, version of Bart.

"I'm betting on Mario," Franco called out, laughing, thoroughly enjoying his family.

Lucia laughed at her Dad. "Okay, I'm betting on Bart."

A puzzled Angela looked at Bart. "Really?" She questioned.

"Sure, Beautiful," Bart responded, grinning. "It will be fun."

Angela looked to Celia. Seeing Angela's surprise, Celia laughed. "Angela, you're with a DeMarco. Everything is an athletic contest." She sidled over to Angela, spoke for her ears only. "They are studs our guys, and they love to compete." She looked about to guarantee her words were not overheard. "And, they will find a million ways to have their hands on us, that won't upset their mother." She laughed. "It will be fun."

Rosa came onto the deck, greeted the group swimming or lounging about, heard and enjoyed the laughter, looked to Franco and smiled. Franco noted that her smile did not reach her eyes. "We need to pick up some groceries. Would you drive me and give me a hand?"

"Do you want me to come?" Lucia asked.

"No," Rosa smiled at her daughter. "You stay and have fun." She eyed Franco, who felt the chill shooting from her eyes. "I don't know the area. It's better if Dad comes with me."

Franco nodded, glanced at Mario, and rose from his lounge. "I'll get dressed, give me a minute." He walked into the house, followed closely by Rosa.

Mario looked at Bart and shrugged. "I had no idea Dad hadn't discussed buying the boat with Mom." He laughed. "I think he's about to get an earful."

Chapter Nineteen

Coach Dave Gilliss had arranged with Charlie Priester, General Manager and Head Professional, for Bart to have playing privileges at St. Andrews South Golf Club. Bart was up and out on the practice range at 7am. He hit through his bag on the range, noting the difference in ball flight off of the Bermuda grass and the effect of the warm, humid air on the distance he hit each club. He practiced chipping, pitching and putting on the practice putting green. As he had never before played on Bermuda grass, the adjustment was significant.

Bart found the Bermuda greens a bit slower than the Bent-Grass greens to which he was accustomed. He noted, putts did not seem to break as much. When hitting out of the rough, he discovered the Bermuda grass roughs to be stickier than the Bent. He mentally shrugged, 'I can adjust to anything,' he reasoned, and kept practicing.

At 10 am, he came back to the house to find the gang enjoying the pool and the sun bathing. Where February in Gloucester was frigid cold and with a wind off the ocean that seemed to cut through you, the Florida sunshine and warmth were a joy. He walked across the pool deck, smiling broadly, eyes on his bikini clad girlfriend, and kissed Angela. "Hi, I missed you," he said. He turned to the group. "Great morning, isn't it?"

"It is," Angela agreed. "How did your practice go?" She studied him. "You look heated."

Bart laughed. "I'm fine," he looked at the pool. "Although that water looks refreshing." He smiled at Angela. "You look great," he complimented. He looked to Rosa. "Mom," Bart called, "I'm going to shower and grab something to eat, before I go play 18." He left the family on the pool deck.

"He's like a whirlwind," Celia said with a grin.

Rosa rose with a smile. "Three hours practicing and he is heading out to play." She laughed, admiration coloring her tone. "He is dedicated," she said, as she made her way to the kitchen to fix Bart a plate.

Angela followed Rosa in, "I'll help you," she offered with a smile.

Rosa looked at Angela, smiled. "How about I fix Bart some food and you change your clothes and walk with him on the course?" She paused. "You can use the master bath to get ready."

Angela hesitated. "Do you think he'd want me to walk with him?"

Rosa smiled, brought her hand lovingly to Angela's cheek. "Bart told me that he feels better, calmer, when you're with him." She paused. "This is an important week for Bart. In two days he will play for the eyes of college coaches." She sighed. "I want my boy to be happy." Rosa paused, and smiled. "Bart is happy when he is with you. I think he needs you, Angela."

"Really?" She asked, unconvinced. Angela misted as she looked at Rosa, who read some inner turmoil in the sixteen year old girl.

Rosa studied Angela, spoke softly. "Angela, what is it that is bothering you?"

Angela took a deep breath. She looked into Rosa DeMarco's eyes. "Mrs. DeMarco, I want Bart to succeed, I want him to go as far as he is able." She sighed. "I want Bart to be happy with all my heart." She paused. "I love Bart," she stated, her emotion showing in her eyes.

Rosa smiled as she prepared two sandwiches and a fruit bowl for Bart. She looked at Angela. "I know that, Angela."

"See, Mrs. DeMarco," Angela explained. "I know Bart will need to go to a southern school to play golf." She paused, heard the shower finish, and smiled as she thought of Bart toweling dry and dressing. "I think Bart is hoping to be a professional golfer. He will need a great golf school and coach." She paused, fixed determined eyes on Rosa. "I believe he can do it."

"Do you?" Rosa asked, a smile playing at her lips.

Angela looked at Mrs. DeMarco. "I believe Bart is capable of achieving anything he sets his mind to."

Rosa smiled. "Well Angela, I think Bart has his mind set on you."

Angela nodded and choked up. "I know that's how he feels now." She sniffed, fear gnawing at her gut. She looked at Rosa. "Mrs. DeMarco, I know that I am not slim and beautiful like Celia." She paused, swallowed, as her eyes filled. She looked to Bart's mother, "Mrs. DeMarco, am I going to lose Bart when he goes away to college?"

Rosa looked at Angela, read the fear in her eyes, and felt fury at what those nasty kids did to Angela's self-image. Rosa shook her head, "I don't know, Bambina," she said softly. "But, I know my Bart loves you." She paused. "In his eyes, you are the most beautiful girl in the world." Rosa smiled. "He told me how badly he wants you." She raised her brows. "He said he wants you so badly that it hurts."

Angela blushed, but couldn't suppress a smile. "Really?"

Rosa nodded. "He needs you Angela." She swallowed. "I hope he always does." She smiled. "And Angela, I agree with Bart. You are beautiful." She nodded. "Now, go get ready."

Bart came out of the bathroom and into the kitchen to find his mother, a hefty plate of food and a bowl of fruit. He went to the refrigerator and grabbed a bottle of water, drank it down, and grabbed another. He picked up his food and headed onto the pool deck. He looked about, "where's Angela?" He asked.

"I'm here," Angela said with a smile as she came from the kitchen onto the pool deck, dressed in shorts, a sleeveless top and walking shoes.

Bart grinned, but perplexed, asked. "Why did you change? Are you going somewhere?"

Angela met his grin with a smile. "I thought you might like some company as you play."

Bart's face bloomed with a bright smile that had his eyes gleaming. "Really?" He said. "That's great! Thank you."

Rosa exchanged a knowing smile with Celia.

Bart carried his golf bag as they walked from the house, which set on the 10th fairway, to the clubhouse and 1st tee. He looked over at Angela, smiled broadly, "I appreciate you doing this, Angela." He bumped against her playfully. "I know you'd rather be relaxing by the pool."

Angela dropped her eyes. "I'd rather be with you, Bart." She blushed. "I love you."

Bart looked at Angela adoringly. "Thanks, Angela, I love you, too." He laughed. "But, after I play, I'd love to see you in that bikini again."

Angela blushed, her cheeks flushing red. "I think that can be arranged." She glanced at Bart. "We will need to cool down, after all." She laughed. "Maybe another water battle?" She suggested slyly.

Bart laughed. "Yes, that really was fun!" He eyed Angela. "I loved having you up on my shoulders." He thought about holding her legs and catching her as she fell into the pool.

Angela laughed. "Me too," Bart saw her cheeks redden. "Even when we were falling into the water and you almost pulled off my top."

Bart tried to stifle a smile. "I'm sorry about that." He said, attempting to sound sincere. "I was trying to catch you and grabbed your…there, by accident."

Angela studied his expression, remembered Celia's words, saw his smile, and laughed. "I'm not sure I believe you." She glanced about to see if anyone was in listening range. She sought Bart's eyes. "But, I kinda liked it," she responded softly with flushed cheeks.

Playing alone, on a quiet golf course, Bart played all 18 holes in under two hours, even when he dropped a second ball to play a shot differently, which he did often, trying different clubs and attack angles into greens.

Angela watched him with a growing appreciation for his strength and skill. "That's a good shot, Bart," she found herself saying repeatedly. Often, Bart wasn't happy and re-tried the shot over and over, until he felt comfortable. Angela was impressed at how much Bart's game had improved since the high school matches. 'All that practice,' she thought.

Bart played chips from around the greens, even when his shot had landed and settled on the green. "This Bermuda grass is tough," he explained. Angela watched patiently. And, he putted the greens obsessively. "It's all about putting, Angela," he stressed.

As they walked from the 18th green back to the house, Bart smiled and said, "you, know, Angela, this game is amazing." He laughed. "Think about it. I hit a drive 300 yards and its one stroke and a 4 foot putt is also one stroke." He shook his head. "You have to make putts."

It was 1:30pm when Bart and Angela returned to the house. "How did it go?" Mario called out as he lazed in the pool.

"Not bad," Bart responded. "The Bermuda grass is tough, but I'm beginning to get it." He grinned. "I need a swim." He headed into the house to change into his swim suit, but not before he challenged Mario to another water battle. "Angela and I will get you this time." He promised, on a laugh.

Mario grinned. "Not in this lifetime, Bart."

All eyes turned to Angela after he left. She watched him go with a smile affixed to her face. She looked at the family. "He's amazing!" She stated. "He was really good on the high school team," she shook her head, "but now, Wow!" She smiled. "I think that he will be great." She paused, considered. "He's never satisfied," she continued. "He re-played shots over and over, until he was sure he had found the touch." She smiled. "And, he hits the ball so far." She laughed, shook her head. "I'd better go change," she said, as she headed into the house.

Bart and Angela joined Lucia, Mario and Celia in the pool, cooling off, playing around, and laughing happily. They began with a series of water battles. Then, Bart and Mario began a contest, lifting Angela and Celia above their heads and throwing them to see who could throw their girl the highest and farthest. The girls eyed each other and smiled as they happily dove into the pool. Lucia, not to be ignored, was entered into the contest, with the brothers competing to loft and launch her to splash happily into the cool, clear water. Franco, who acted as the judge, and Rosa watched Lucia, her sons and their girls with a feeling of contentment. Seeing one's children laughing and happy is about the greatest joy a parent could imagine.

Rosa suggested a barbecue for dinner. "How about some steak tips and Italian sausage on the grill," she offered.

Heads nodded. "I'll make the salad," Lucia called. Franco suggested that he grill corn on the cob as well.

"An Italian tomato salad, I hope," Bart called out. "You know Sis, with cucumber, red- onion, olive oil and spices."

Lucia smirked at her brother. "Bart, I know how Mom makes the salad."

Bart laughed. "So sorry if I've offended you," he replied, winking at his kid sister.

"What can Angela and I do?" Celia asked.

"Actually, Celia and I won't be here," Mario stated. "Maybe, we'll come later for dessert." He smiled at Rosa, who nodded to her son.

Celia looked to Mario, surprise in her voice, "a barbeque sounds good, what did you have in mind?"

Mario splashed across the pool and laughing, grabbed Celia, held her close, and then lifted her above his head, smiled up at her and flipped her into the water. When she surfaced, he grinned. "Wear a pretty dress, beautiful," he said. "You and I are going out to dinner."

Celia set loving eyes on Mario. She laughed, "Okay, sounds good," she looked about for a hint, but only saw smiles. "How about Mexican?" She suggested.

When Celia saw that Mario was distracted and looking at his mother, she jumped on his shoulders, using her full effort to try to dunk him. Mario laughed, as he let her submerge him, taking her under with him, holding her close.

Angela, recalling Celia's words, and thinking about the water battles, and today's contests, laughed at Mario and Bart's obvious, but nonetheless enjoyable, ploys. Rosa, knowing that young, healthy, adults required some physical release, pretended not to be aware of her boy's intentions.

When they surfaced, Mario held her, looked into her eyes, planting a kiss on her lips. "Whatever you want, my love."

Mario and Celia had gone off happily. Franco and Bart stood at the grill. Rosa had shopped and purchased all the essentials for the dinner.

Lucia looked at her mother as she and Angela cut up tomatoes, cucumber and red onion. Rosa was slicing the Italian bread in thick pieces and filling the bread basket, as she sipped red wine. "Mom, you seem happy tonight?" She nudged Angela. "I guess Mom and Dad made up." She teased.

Rosa smiled at her daughter. "I am happy!" She laughed. "And your father and I are just fine," she insisted. Then, she looked at Angela and Lucia, and shrugged with a smile pulling at her lips. "Remember girls, no matter how long you are with a man, they will always drive you crazy!" Her comment was met with laughter.

They were sitting at the extended dining table on the pool deck, enjoying dinner. "Boy, this is the best tomato salad I've ever had!" Bart proclaimed. He looked at Lucia and smiled, "I'm thinking Angela must have made this salad."

Lucia playfully stuck out her tongue at her brother. Then she wondered aloud why Mario and Celia had gone out for dinner. "It won't be as good as this meal." Lucia stated. Rosa smiled, but said nothing.

A very excited Celia, with a grinning Mario burst onto the deck. All eyes turned as Celia held out her left hand. "We're engaged," she stated, as she joyously danced about.

Rosa jumped up and embraced Celia, with Lucia and Angela right behind.

"Did you call your parents?" Rosa asked, while holding Celia's hand and admiring the beautiful diamond ring. "This is so beautiful," Rosa said, smiling happily. She looked at Mario. "You picked a wonderful girl, Mario." Then she embraced Celia, who was still beaming. Lucia and Angela joined in the merriment as Bart and Franco looked on smiling.

"First thing after I proposed, Celia called her parents." He looked up as if trying to remember. "I think she may have called her mother even before she kissed me." He laughed as Celia grinned and playfully punched his arm. "Anyway, she talked to her mother for twenty minutes." Mario explained, as he laughed. "They're planning an engagement party!" He raised his brows. "We never did eat," he looked around at the platters of steak tips, Italian sausage, salad and corn. "This looks great."

"Sit down, eat Mario, enjoy." Rosa said happily. "And, I have champagne and a cake to celebrate this happy occasion."

Celia looked at Rosa. "Mom, you knew?" She asked, a delighted smile illuminating her face.

Rosa smiled. "Of course, and I am so happy that you will be my daughter-in-law." Rosa replied as she and Celia both filled and spilled happy tears. Angela and Lucia joined in the merriment as they all hugged and admired the engagement ring.

Bart looked on, noted Celia's tears, and smiled. "Hey Mario," he called. "I guess Celia just realized she will have to actually live with you." Mario and Franco laughed.

"I think you're right Little brother," Mario smiled. "It does makes you wonder about her sanity, doesn't it?" Mario responded as he playfully punched Bart's arm.

It was a joyous evening. Dinner was followed with cake and champagne toasts, which all drank, even fourteen year old Lucia. After clean-up, an evening swim was in order. Love was in the air as Mario held Celia close as they swam about and smiled incessantly.

Bart kept his arm around Angela, who whispered to Bart, wistfully, "they look so happy." She looked at Bart and welled with tears.

Bart brushed away her tears. "I know exactly how Mario feels." He kissed her cheek. He nodded to the happy couple, whispered to Angela, "Someday, that will be us."

Angela smiled and said a silent prayer that his words would prove to be prophetic.

Chapter Twenty

The day arrived for Bart to play for the group of college coaches, as arranged by Dave Gilliss. The DeMarco family drove to the Alligator Alley golf course on the University of Southern Florida campus. The course, played from the tips, was a 7300 yard, par 72, professional level challenge.

Bart was surprised to find that he would play with three other high school age players, rather than the college coaches. The U.S.F. golf coach provided the four with caddies, actually, members of the college golf team, to guide the three high school juniors and Bart, who was a year younger and a sophomore, around the challenging lay-out.

The four golfers prepared on the practice range, chipping area and practice putting green before moving to the 1st tee. With the caddies, four college coaches and families of the players, it was a sizable gallery watching the nervous group of aspiring college golfers.

Bart was physically the most impressive of the four. At 6'2" and a leanly, muscular, 175 pounds, he had the look and physical appearance of a younger version of PGA star, Dustin Johnson. And, it did not take long for Bart to impress.

The 1st hole was a 450 yard par four. Bart took his long and smooth swing and rocketed a drive over 300 yards. The coaches exchanged long looks. "This kid is 16?" One asked.

The U.S.F. coach added, "yes, and, he really started playing seriously this past year." He shrugged, "Impressive, but, let's see."

Bart impressed with his talent and his focus. He consulted with his caddy, an amiable Cajun from Louisiana, Jim LeBeau, asking questions that demonstrated sound course management skills and he seemed to shrink the course with his power.

Angela and Bart's family walked the course, anxiously watching Bart. Other than Angela, none had seen Bart play. "He's good!" Mario whispered to his father.

Franco nodded. "Certainly better than these others."

Angela, Celia and Lucia walked together. They noted an attractive, blue eyed, blond, in a short skirt and revealing top, eyeing Bart. "Are you seeing this?" Celia asked, shaking her head. "If she gets any closer, she'll get hit by his club."

Angela watched quietly. Celia noted concern and a hint of fear in her eyes. "Are you okay, Angela?" Celia asked.

Angela looked at Celia, her eyes brimming with tears. "This is how it's going to be, isn't it?" Angela asked softly. "Celia, I think that I'm going to lose him."

Celia looked back at Angela and took her hand. "Bart loves you, Angela." She asserted. "And, the DeMarco's are loyal." She smiled. "There will always be women," Celia stated quietly. "You have to put your faith in Bart." She turned her hand, looked at the ring Bart had given her. "Bart put that ring on your finger, remember that."

By the turn, after the front nine, all four college coaches had spoken to Franco. They gave him their cards and assured Bart's Dad that they would be following Bart's play closely. Franco could read their interest in Bart. One coach even asked if Franco would call before Bart committed to another college. "Please, give me an opportunity to better any offer!" He stated.

The four golfers and their college caddies, chatted amiably throughout the round. Jim LeBeau's joking seemed to help relax Bart. After the 9th hole, refreshments were provided. Bart drank from a bottle of water as he went to see Angela and his family. He moved in and kissed Angela, his joy obvious. "It's going well so far," he stated.

Angela smiled. "Yes, it is, Bart. I'm so happy for you."

Bart studied her. "Are you okay, Angela?"

Angela forced a smile. "Of course, my guy is showing the coaches how special he is." She went into his arms, buried her face in his chest. "I've always known."

Bart looked over Angela's shoulder at Lucia. "What's happening, Lucia?"

Lucia glared at her brother. "It's that girl, Bart." She asserted, almost angrily.

"What girl?" Bart asked. He followed Lucia's eyes to the blond. "Oh, I see." Bart nodded, finally understanding. He lifted Angela's face from his chest and met her eyes. Angela's eyes were wet with tears. Bart shook his head and smiled. "I see only one girl." He kissed her. "There's only you, Princess. You have to believe that."

The golfers were called back to play the back nine. "I have to go," Bart said. "Lucia, Celia, please take care of my girl."

Angela straightened. "Go Bart," She flashed her smile. "Go show them who Bart DeMarco is!" She insisted. She hugged him. "I'll be here for you."

He took her chin, angled her face up to meet his eyes, he smiled. "Do you promise, Beautiful?"

Bart moved to the 10th tee, with the Honor and a bright smile. He ripped a beautiful drive down the center of the fairway. He looked at Angela and offered his dazzling smile, especially for her.

The round ended on a high note for Bart, with a birdie on the par 5, 18th green. He had shot a 68, four under par. The other golfers recorded scores from 74-78. Actually, quite good for 17 year old high school juniors, on a challenging course. But, Bart had outshone them all.

All were treated to a late lunch in the club's grill room. A very happy DeMarco clan took a table for ten, Jim LeBeau, the USF sophomore, who had caddied for Bart and played on the college golf team joined them. He had been directed by his coach to talk up the USF golf team. And, maybe help recruit Bart. As they dined, each coach visited the table to gather information from Bart on his academic standing, other hobbies and other sports played.

Jim LeBeau was free with his thoughts. "Bart," he began in his Cajun accent, "you will be in demand. You are a good student so any of the ACC schools will want you." He grinned, "Bart, you will be able to write your own ticket." He laughed. "Hey, maybe I could caddy for you on the PGA Tour?"

That drew a laugh from Bart. "Jim, from your lips to God's ears."

Jim grew serious, he placed intent eyes on Bart. "Bart, you have it!" He stated forcefully. He paused, noted Angela and Bart's family listening. "These other guys will make decent college golfers, but you," he smiled, "The sky's the limit."

"Thanks, Jim," Bart responded. "You really helped me today." He smiled. "I really appreciate it."

The affable Cajun laughed. "You remember that when you hire a caddy to play on the Tour!" That drew a wide smile from Bart.

Bart was enjoying a grilled rib-eye with sautéed onions, baked potato and a tomato salad, when one of the other golfers approached the table. "Hi Bart, great round today," Charlie Reynolds, from Milwaukee, complimented, as he shook Bart's hand.

Bart smiled. "You too, Charlie, it was a fun round."

Standing with Charlie was his sister. "Bart, I'd like you to meet my twin sister, Janet." Blond, blue eyed, Janet offered her hand and a welcoming smile as Bart rose to greet her.

Bart flashed his smile. "Hi Janet, it's nice to meet you," He began. Bart then turned to the table. "Charlie, Janet, I'd like to introduce my family." He pointed across the table. "This is my Dad and Mom," he pointed to Mario, "my brother Mario and his fiancé, Celia, and my little sister, Lucia." He nodded at Jim LeBeau, "Janet, Jim is a student and golfer here at USF, and was nice enough to help me today." Then he took Angela's hand. He looked into Janet's eyes and smiled. "And this beautiful girl is Angela, my girl," he paused, looked into Angela's eyes, "my love." Angela's cheeks blushed red as she smiled up at Bart.

Bart looked back to Janet and smiled. Janet understood Bart's meaning clearly, glanced at Angela, smiled warmly, "you're a lucky girl, Angela."

Angela rose and stood with Bart. Janet extended her hand, her blue eyes sparkled. 'A true lady,' Jim LeBeau thought. Janet took Angela's hand and patted it, flashing a smile. "Angela, I think you have a good man here, good luck."

Angela smiled in appreciation. "Thank you, Janet." She looked at and took Charlie's hand. "So nice to meet you, Charlie." She complimented. "This was fun today."

"It was," Charlie agreed. Eyes passing from Angela to Janet. Charlie rubbed Janet's shoulder, his smile one of pride. "Shall we get back to the family, Sis?"

Janet nodded and smiled at Bart's family. "Enjoy the rest of your trip," she said as she waved. Charlie and Janet walked away. Bart sat and resumed his meal. Lucia and Celia beamed smiles at Angela, the message clear.

Jim LeBeau grinned at Bart. "I guess you just cleared the field," He laughed. "I think I'll go chat with Janet." He looked at Bart. "I don't think that USF is going to get you, Bart." He grinned. "You are clearly headed for bigger things." He punched Bart's shoulder. "And, I wasn't kidding about being your caddy on tour." He nodded. "You have the tools Bart, good luck and stay in touch." He waved and thanked Bart's family for a pleasant day. Then, Jim glanced at Charlie. "But, Charlie may be a good fit for USF." He walked over to Charlie's table, pulled up a chair next to Janet.

"And Janet may be a good fit for Jim," Mario laughed. "Wouldn't you say, Bart?"

"She is a looker," Bart agreed, smiling. He winked at Angela. "She's no Angela, of course, but then, no girl is."

Angela beamed a smile at Bart. Celia poked Mario playfully. "And, what are you looking at?"

Mario sighed, looked at Celia and planted a kiss. "Oh, just another girl who cannot hold a candle to my fiancé."

Celia grinned. "Good answer, Mario."

"Janet seemed nice," Rosa said, her eyes on Angela.

Angela met her smile. "Yes, she did seem nice." She glanced over to where Janet was engaging Cajun, Jim LeBeau, in conversation, a smile playing on Janet's lips. Angela looked at Bart, who was happily eating and joking with Mario about Jim LeBeau, seemingly oblivious to the drama that had played out. She looked at Rosa, spoke softly. "Have I been silly?"

Rosa leaned close to Angela, took Angela's hand. "You have to choose to believe in your love, Angela." She smiled. "My boy loves you."

It had been an exhausting day for the group. It was a good drive to and back from USF. They had walked the course, Bart, of course, had played. But, it was the stress that wore on the group.

There was also a sense of exhilaration. Bart had wowed the coaches and it looked as if Bart would play golf at a top-rated college. The family lay around the pool-deck after refreshing and rejuvenating swims. As they all had a late and substantial lunch, there was no interest in dinner, but ice cream sounded good. Bart volunteered to drive to Cubby's home-made ice cream and pick up ice cream for the group. Angela took individual orders and Bart and Angela headed out.

Bart had whispered to his mother that they were likely to take awhile, as he wanted to talk to Angela.

Rosa nodded, "she needs you to assure her that your love is real, Bart." She looked at Bart. "Angela doesn't believe that she is good enough, pretty enough to be with you." Rosa kissed her son. "She is good for you, Bart," Rosa paused, focused her eyes on her son. "Now, Angela needs you!"

Bart drove to a secluded spot on Charlotte Harbor. Once they were alone, he parked, lowered the windows to enjoy the feel of the refreshing evening breeze and he pulled Angela close. He took a whiff of her, he loved her aroma, she, smelled of springtime, fresh and all woman. He delighted in the feel of her, savored the taste of her kisses. Bart was infatuated. He was also irritated.

He kissed Angela, she smiled at him. "Bart, I'm so proud of you." She said, elation in her tone. "You are on your way to fulfilling your dreams."

He looked at her. "Maybe, Angela." He paused, relished the feel of her. "What are your dreams, Angela?"

She looked at him. "I don't know how to respond to that," she countered. Her eyes grew large as she watched him closely. Bart waited patiently, saying nothing, but kissing her and holding her. She knew he was waiting for an answer, and would wait. She shook her head. "Okay," she began. "I think that I would like to be an elementary school teacher."

Bart smiled. "Is that your dream, Angela? Really?" He sighed. "Let me help you." He paused, smiled, gently he caressed her arms, down to her hips. Looking into her eyes, he said; "I want to be with you, Angela." He held her, "in time, I want to marry you." He watched as her smile bloomed.

He looked deeply into her eyes. "The truth is, I want to ravish you. I want to enjoy your beautiful body. I love your face, your smile when you see me." He smiled, "I crave you, Angela." He paused, felt frustration. "Do you understand me?"

Angela nodded, but said nothing, loving his words. Still, he read the doubt in her eyes.

He took a deep breath. "Yes, I want to play golf in college and maybe someday on the PGA tour." He kissed her deeply. "That is how I want to support our family. But, none of that will matter if I don't have you, Angela, body, mind and soul."

Happy tears flooded her eyes. She nodded. "Bart, I so want to be your wife. I want to be Mrs. Bart DeMarco more than anything. I really do."

He grew serious. "Angela, it will never work if you live your life doubting me." He shook his head. "Why don't you believe in our love?"

Tears of frustration boiled over, her self-doubt surfaced. In her mind she was still 'Ugly Angela.' In her heart, she knew that Bart no longer needed her. She engaged his eyes and spoke from the heart. "Because, I know that you will want a beautiful wife, and you deserve that." She paused, put her hands on his face. "Bart, you are so beautiful, so special." She spilled tears. "And, I know that I am not special enough." She held him to her. "When I saw Janet following you today, I saw the future."

"What future did you see, Angela?" Bart asked in frustration. "Dammit!" Bart blasted. "I will go away to college, probably a southern or western university." He paused. "If my game grows, maybe I will have a chance to play professionally."

He took a deep breath, and it hit him that Angela just might be saying goodbye. His eyes bore into her, he felt that old panic. "But, I,I,I" he stopped, shocked by the stutter. Her eyes grew large as she saw the pain.

Bart closed his eyes. He spoke slowly. "Angela," he began, and that old fear and anxiety was back. "I,I,I love you, and I,I need you." He paused, fearing his next words as he hadn't in months. His anxiety rose. "I,I,I always will," He stated. He took a deep breath, held her close. "None of this was possible without you."

She read the fear in his eyes, Angela had seen that fear, that frustration, before. It was a stark reminder of how much Bart valued her. She put her lips to his, kissed him deeply, hoping to comfort and chase that fear away. "I'm yours Bart," she promised. "I will wait for you, I will cheer you on, and I will be there for you, always and forever." She swore. "I will never doubt your love again, I promise."

"Angela, please believe me," he said desperately, "I don't want Jessica or Janet or anybody, else." He searched her eyes. "I want you!" He took a deep breath to regulate his breathing and to calm him. "I intend to give you and our babies a good life. I will work hard, do whatever it takes." He gasped. "I,I,I need you to trust our love."

Angela nodded, she felt ashamed at what her self-doubt had wrought and exhilarated that Bart needed and loved her.

"I will Bart, I will." She paused and smiled. Angela stroked his face, kissed him, and held him to her chest. "I'm so sorry I doubted you." She kissed him, looked into his eyes, smiled warmly. "Please love me, Bart, please, love me now."

Bart and Angela arrived back at the house with ice cream orders filled and a feeling of contentment. Angela delivered the ice cream according to each request as Bart went to change into his bathing suit.

"This took some time." Mario stated with a suggestive smile. "Were they still churning the ice cream?"

Angela laughed, even as she blushed. "Bart felt that we needed to talk." She handed Celia her ice cream and asked aloud. "Did I get all the orders right?"

"Yes, Angela, I think you did fine." Rosa responded, watching her closely.

"Great," Angela said to the group. "I'll go and change." She headed into the house.

Rosa and Celia exchanged a long look, with Rosa nodding to Celia, who rose from her lounge and followed Angela into the bedroom that they shared.

Celia knocked on the door, "Angela, may I come in?"

Angela unlocked and opened the door. "Of course, I can change in the bathroom."

Celia took her hands, felt a tremble, and looked into Angela's eyes. "Angela, let's talk." Celia suggested. "You can change in a few minutes."

"Of course," Angela responded, painting a smile on her face. "What about?" She sat beside Celia on the bed, avoided making eye contact.

"Was it your first time?" Celia asked quietly.

Surprised, Angela looked fully at Celia. "How did you know?"

Celia smiled. "It was, wasn't it?"

Angela nodded. She took a deep breath and exhaled. She looked at Celia. "I hurt Bart today." She stated. "It was a big day for him and I let my stupid fears and insecurities take over." She shook her head. "He has been telling me that I was the one, almost since that first night."

"I really think Bart loves you." Celia said. "Why the doubts?" She studied Angela. "Has he given you reason to doubt him?"

Angela shook her head, exasperated. "No!" She let out a breath. She focused her eyes on Celia and explained. "Celia, when I was fourteen years old, I was walking to dance class when three guys stopped me and were mocking me." She paused, dropped her eyes. "They took my dance bag from me, they threw it around, kicking it and were calling me 'Ugly Angela.'" She eyed Celia, "and they wouldn't let me pass, when I tried to get away, they pushed me." She looked at Celia. "I was so scared." She explained softly, the memory painful. Then she smiled. "Bart came along, saw what was happening and went after the guys."

Celia smiled. "That sounds like a DeMarco."

"Bart pounded those guys. He hit one of them and he backed off, another one just ran, then Sal Siracusa fought back and Bart pummeled him. He made Sal apologize to me and told him that if he or his loser friends ever bothered me again they would answer to him."

Angela took a deep breath. "I was shaking." She grimaced. "Celia, it was years of being mocked and being afraid," she paused, shook her head, eyes on Celia. "I didn't know what they were going to do to me." Angela sighed. "They were really cruel."

Celia quietly listened, holding Angela's hands.

"Bart saw the fear in my eyes, on my face. He picked up my dance bag, put his arm around my shoulder, and told me that he would walk me home."

Angela looked at Celia. "I saw that his hands were cut up from hitting those guys, and covered with blood." She exhaled. "Sal's blood, mostly," she explained softly. "So I took a towel from my bag and helped clean him up." Angela smiled. "When he had held me, to calm me, there was blood on my clothes, as well."

Celia watched Angela closely, as Angela spoke. "He walked me home, holding my hand. He told me to call him, if ever anybody bothered me again." She smiled, and looked at Celia. "I wasn't afraid after that." She stated, paused, and smiled. "That was the day I fell in love with Bart DeMarco."

Celia smiled and looked at Angela. "So, what's the problem?" She paused. "Bart was magnificent today, he played wonderfully and handled the situation with that blond perfectly." She laughed. "I don't know many guys who would have handled it better and still deal with all that pressure."

Angela nodded. "Yes, he did." She sighed, "But I let my insecurities overwhelm me." She dropped her eyes. "Bart was really hurt by me doubting him." She took a deep breath. We drove to a secluded spot on the Harbor. "We talked." She shrugged. "I told him that he deserved a prettier girl, that he was special, but that I wasn't special."

"You said what?" Celia asked, with a stunned look. She studied Angela. "Are you nuts?"

Angela shook her head, looked into Celia's eyes. "Celia," she began. "All that 'Ugly Angela' stuff really hurt." She choked. "Until Bart, I believed it." She forced a smile. "But Bart told me from that first day, that I am beautiful. The way he looks at me is thrilling." She offered a radiant smile. "He told me that he craves me so badly that sometimes he can't sleep."

Celia laughed. "I know, it's great isn't it?"

"Celia," Angela explained. "The worst part was that he thought I doubted his love, and that I was leaving him." She eyed Celia. "He panicked," she paused. "He began to stutter." She sighed. "He hadn't stuttered in months and then I caused him so much pain."

Angela shook her head. "On a day that should have been all joy." She squeezed Celia's hands. "His anxiety shot up and he couldn't speak." She shook her head. "I saw the fear in his eyes, just like after the Salem game." She paused, eyed Celia. "That is when I realized how much Bart really needs me." Angela sighed, remained quiet. Then, Bart came to mind and Angela smiled. "We are a team, he said. Bart called us; 'Team DeMarco.'"

Celia frowned. "I had hoped that was all behind him." She paused. "Bart is a very real, a very sensitive man." She sighed. "That 'Stutter Boy' stuff really hurt him."

Angela looked at Celia and nodded. "I know, I hurt Bart today, Celia. I never want to do that again." She thought of Bart's words and felt exhilarated, "Celia, he really needs me." She sounded triumphant.

Celia studied her. Softly, but with a touch of sternness, she said; "he does need you, Angela." Celia focused in. "Bart is a very gifted athlete and a real sweet guy." She paused, engaged Angela's eyes. "He needs you to be there for him. To be his girl, to share everything, good and not so good." She paused, squeezed Angela's hands, bore her glare into Angela's eyes. "Maybe, Angela, you should believe Bart, who loves you, who fought for you, rather than those nasty and cruel girls!" She took a deep breath. "I think Bart deserves that!"

Angela nodded, flushed with shame. "I know that now." She shook her head and sighed. "So, I decided," She paused. "I really wanted to give myself to him. To make certain he knew that he was and will always be, my guy!" She paused and offered a shy smile. "So, I asked him to make love to me."

Celia laughed. "I bet you didn't have to ask twice." She watched Angela blush. "Were you safe?"

Angela nodded as she dropped her eyes. "Yes, we were."

Celia pulled her to her feet. "Go put on your sexiest bikini, I want to see Bart really smile." Then, she laughed. "I guess he already smiled pretty good, right?"

Angela blushed red. "We both did."

Celia laughed aloud as she proclaimed. "I guess he is a DeMarco!" She paused. "Angela, we are very lucky girls."

Chapter Twenty-One

They all returned home to Gloucester with a feeling of certainty and optimism about their collective futures.

Franco planned on buying the fishing dragger he had in mind. Financing needed to be arranged, but the fish dealer whose Florida home they used would help with that. Mario was to be the Mate, and when ready, substitute Captain.

The notion of buying a fishing dragger, borrowing the money to make it possible, pledging their home as collateral, scared Rosa. But, she could not resist the excitement that Franco expressed at being his own boss. He wanted, had long wanted, to be Captain Franco DeMarco. In Gloucester, America's Oldest fishing port, a successful Captain was held in high esteem. He wanted to try, and Rosa knew that he and Mario would work hard to make the boat a success.

On that first day in Florida, when Mario had revealed the plan to buy a fishing boat, Franco and Rosa discussed the investment as they drove to the market. Franco suggested that they complete the shopping and resume the discussion at the house.

When they arrived back at the Florida house, Mario and Bart unloaded the car as Celia, Angela and Lucia filled the cupboards, refrigerator and freezer. Franco and Rosa went to the privacy of the master bedroom to discuss the opportunity and the risks involved.

Rosa read his eyes, heard the hope in his voice, and knew that to hold him back would kill his spirit. She took a deep breath, swallowed her fears, and held her husband close. "I am with you, Franco, all the way." She kissed him. "I love you."

Franco flashed that smile that always reached her heart, "thank you, Rosa," he said with a glance to the closed bedroom door. He laughed. "The kids are putting the groceries away and they are certain you are angry with me for not discussing this with you earlier." He read her look and grinned. "I know that I should have and am sorry for that."

Rosa placed amused eyes on him, flashed a smile. After 22 years of marriage, she knew where this was going. "So," he continued as he began to unfasten her dress, "let's have a discussion about all the merits of our plan." He lifted the dress over her head and off. She smiled as he disrobed her.

Rosa shook her head, put her hands on her hips in a pose that she knew always brought a smile to Franco's face, and feigned anger. "Hey, I learned of this from Mario." She stated. "I am not happy about that."

He smiled, "I was so wrong," he agreed. He looked at his wife, standing gloriously before him. Franco pulled her to him, "beautiful as ever," he said with a delighted grin as he kissed her. "Feel free to scream at me if you like." Rosa laughed. "Oh, I will."

Mario and Celia were discussing wedding plans. Celia wanted to marry the following June, giving their parents fifteen months to plan and arrange the many details of a big Italian wedding. Mario had asked Bart to be his 'Best Man' and as Celia's sister would be her 'Maid of Honor,' she asked Angela and Lucia to be Bridesmaids. It was a happy and memorable trip.

Mario would continue to be a fisherman, a deckhand, on his present boat, until he was to be the mate and substitute Captain of the boat his Dad would buy, and name in honor of his two girls. Franco would Christen and name the fishing vessel, the 'Rosa & Lucia.'

As Mario and Celia desired to buy a home for their family the plan was for Celia to keep her job at the Bank and together create a joint DeMarco home account for the family they planned to start on their wedding night.

Bart and Angela were united in their goals. Bart would work to grow and refine his game. Coach Gilliss stressed that there were tens of thousands of young players who could hit long drives. While Bart had impressed the coaches, and the letters were pouring in from colleges, he cautioned Bart, "You have it, Bart." He paused and repeated, "but, be clear, so do many others. You must outwork them, be more dedicated."

Gilliss eyed him. "You must learn how to win, even when you do not have your best game!" Bart heeded his words, working daily on fitness and improving his swing, under the critical eyes of Coach Dave Gilliss.

For his April birthday, Angela had organized the family to band together and buy Bart a junior membership to the Bass Rocks Golf Club.

At a birthday gathering at the DeMarco house, attended by Coach Gilliss, Dave and Jessica, Jim and Betsy along with all the extended DeMarco clan and, also, Angela's family, Angela handed the envelope to Bart. As he opened the envelope and saw the membership documents he smiled. "Thank you, all. This is too generous."

"Bart," Franco explained. "It was Angela's idea." He smiled. "We helped, but she worked hard to make this happen." He looked at his son. "Bart, make us proud." He exhorted.

Bart looked at Angela. He met her eyes. "I will, Dad, I will," he said, eyes fixed on Angela.

"Happy 17th birthday, Bart," Coach Gilliss began his toast. "You impressed the college coaches and word has spread." He studied Bart closely. "The pressure to succeed, to win, will only grow from here. This summer you will compete in the Massachusetts Amateur Championship." He scanned the room, before returning his eyes to Bart. He smiled, "Bart, it is pressure, great pressure, that turns carbon into diamonds." He nodded, let the words sink in. "I have watched you play golf and football. You thrive on pressure." He paused. "You, my friend, are the 'Diamond Maker.'" He smiled. "You can count on my help year round. Let's do this!" He reached out and embraced Bart.

As always the buffet table was full of homemade Italian delicacies. Maria Curcuru made trays of lasagna and baked fresh Italian bread. Rosa made her thick crust Sicilian pizza and arincini, a special Sicilian treat. There was tiramisu and fresh baked Italian cookies. All had a wonderful time.

Bart cut into the peach and cream cake that Rosa had baked, as it was Bart's favorite. He passed the cake knife to his mother and looked about the room. He felt so fortunate to be surrounded by such wonderful family and friends. He looked at Angela and beamed his smile. She lit up, as if she possessed an internal light, and blushed as if his smile penetrated her soul, baring her deepest, secret desires. Bart loved watching Angela blush. In truth, he just loved watching Angela. He scanned the room and thanked everybody for coming to celebrate with him.

"I came for your mother's arincini!" Uncle Jimmy called out. Appearing perplexed, he asked, "Is it your birthday, Bart?"

Laughter rolled through the room. "And what's all this golf talk?" Uncle Vito added. "Do you play golf, Bart?"

Bart laughed and nodded. "I do play a bit, Uncle Vito." He looked at Uncle Jimmy, "my birthday is only an excuse to have Mom make her arincini," Bart responded. Then Bart shrugged, looked about, eyed his friends, and grinned. "They keep me humble."

After dinner, Bart and Angela relaxed in the living room with Dave and Jessica, Jim and Betsy, Lucia, Angela's sister, Tina, and Coach Gilliss. Dave Powers had been accepted at Georgia Tech University and would attend with an eye on an engineering degree. As GTU was his school of choice, everyone was happy for him. As he acknowledged the congratulations, Angela watched Jessica, who was smiling, but Angela read the doubt in her eyes.

Angela signaled Betsy and as the guys were recounting another tale from the athletic field, they moved with Jessica to a quiet spot across the room. "You okay, Jessica?" Angela asked.

Jessica shrugged. "Dave's going to be in Georgia with all those flirty southern girls and I will still be here in High School." She looked at Dave, then faced the girls. "I'm going to miss him."

"Of course, you will," Betsy agreed. "But, he'll be back."

Jessica looked at Betsy, her crystal blue eyes flooded with tears. "Yes, he'll be back, but will he still want me?"

Of course there was no definitive answer. Angela took her hands, looked into her eyes. "Jessica, I know how you feel." She paused, chose her words. "In Florida, when Bart was playing for the college coaches, this beautiful blond was following him around the course." She smiled. "She was gorgeous, long legs, a tiny skirt and a revealing top." She laughed. "And, she had a lot to reveal."

"You didn't tell me this," Betsy said in a surprised tone. "What happened?"

Angela shrugged. "I came apart. I was certain Bart would want her or another girl like her." She appraised the girls. "You know, there is always another girl to chase our guys." Angela shook her head. "Well, while I was coming apart, Bart was staying focused and playing great golf."

"Really?" Jessica said, a touch of hope in her expression.

"After the round, we were all treated to a late lunch." She laughed. "Bart had this huge rib-eye, with sautéed onions and the works. Everybody was happy for Bart, and Bart was beaming." Angela flushed. "It was a big day for Bart, and I acted like a fool. Celia and Lucia were consoling me when this other golfer came over, with the blond!" She couldn't help but laugh. "The knockout blond was the golfer's twin sister, Janet. And, she was so nice."

"Gorgeous and nice," Betsy said with a smile. "I think I hate her!"

"I know," Angela agreed on a laugh. "So, this other golfer introduces his sister to Bart."

"What did Bart do?" Jessica asked.

Angela grinned, and blushed, in fond memory. "Bart rose," Angela explained. "He took my hand. Introduced his family, then looked at me, smiled and turned to Janet," here Angela closed her eyes and smiled at the pleasant memory. Angela spoke softly, "Bart looked at Janet, smiled and said; 'and this beautiful girl is Angela, my girl, my love.'"

"WOW!" Betsy said. "That's great." She laughed. "I doubt Jim would tear himself away from his steak long enough to say something like that."

Now the girls were laughing together.

Angela took Jessica's hands. "Be the girlfriend Dave will be excited to get home to, make him special." She shrugged. "Then, hope for the best." She paused. "It's all we can do."

Jessica hugged Angela, wiped her tears. "Thank you, Angela."

"And, we'll be here for you, Jessica," Betsy offered with a smile.

Chapter Twenty-Two

That summer, Bart lumped fishing boats in the early morning, practiced and played golf most of the day, and spent evenings with Angela. His focus was on the Massachusetts Amateur Championship. He worked daily with Coach Gilliss on those parts of his game that were most challenging and most critical to success.

Bart's game grew and his handicap plummeted. To enter the Mass. Amateur, a player must have an USGA index of 4.4 or lower. All contestants then competed, at selected courses, in the various regions of Massachusetts. Of the thousands of golfers, the low 144 scores and ties advance to compete in an 18 hole, stroke play event. Of the 144 players, the low 32 scores then advance to compete in a match play tournament.

Bart's index, the method of determining handicaps, plunged to below 1.0. With Coach Gilliss's help, Bart completed the entry form and was assigned to play at the Salem Country Club. Salem's golf course was a 1925 Donald Ross design. Ross is considered one of, if not, the greatest golf course architect of all time. His green designs are considered to be genius in their subtle slopes and surprising difficulty.

Bart had a mountain to climb to even qualify for the field of 144. But, he now had his goal, and he worked at overcoming all obstacles to success.

Angela worked at a day care facility, taking care of the children of working parents. Each evening, Bart and Angela were together. They dined with her family or Bart's, and later, when alone with Bart, she recounted comical and endearing tales of her interactions with the 'Little Ones,' as she liked to call them.

Franco completed the purchase of his fishing boat. In an emotional and exciting ceremony, Father Capelli offered prayers for the safety of the men who would sail on the newly christened, and re-named, 'Rosa & Lucia.'

Captain DeMarco, his mate, Mario, and a crew of four began fishing for ground fish on Georges Bank. Having worked as a deckhand for over twenty years, Franco had closely observed the methods and practices of the Captains he had served under. And, when on watch, in the pilothouse, had studied their fishing charts. He felt ready to take command and from the start, the F/V Rosa & Lucia found a struggling and somewhat shaky, success. He quickly realized that he had much to learn in his new role as Captain, but he was determined to succeed.

Bart's qualifying round for the Mass. Amateur fell on Fiesta Saturday. Bart saw that as a good omen. On that late June day, he drew a tee time of 10:30am. Coach Gilliss was pleased with the late tee time. He hoped to be able to calculate, by chatting with the MGA officials, how the thousands of golfers, who were competing at golf courses across the state were faring in relation to par. Bart was in a foursome, and Coach Dave Gilliss served as his caddie. Salem is a fairly open course with wide fairways. Bart loved the course, as golfer's say; 'it fit his eye.'

The first hole was a 410 yard par 4. Bart stood over his tee ball, took a deep breath as he waggled his driver, exhaled, and launched into his smooth as silk swing. His shot split the fairway and stopped rolling 315 yards from the tee, leaving only 95 yards to the flagstick. He hit a wedge to 10 feet and rolled in the birdie putt.

"Great start, Bart," Dave Gilliss complimented. Bart nodded but said little. He looked into the small gallery of family and friends and locked eyes with Angela. She flashed a happy smile and gave a thumbs up.

Angela walked with Rosa, Lucia and Celia. "Stay close," Rosa urged Angela. "Make sure Bart can see you." Rosa recognized the bond that existed between Bart and Angela. She knew it went beyond love. They were a unique couple, whose passion was beyond the physical. Rosa felt strongly that Bart and Angela needed each other to be at their best. They inspired each other.

After 6 holes Bart was 2 under par. He was launching long straight drives and hitting his irons close to the pins. At the par 5 fifth hole, which at Salem is the number 1 stroke hole (the most difficult), Bart crushed his drive 325 yards, leaving 185 yards to the hole. His second shot found the green, but carried over the green into the rough. He then chipped to 5 feet and made the putt. Bart pumped his fist as the birdie putt fell. He flashed a smile at Angela, who happily, blew Bart a kiss in return.

"Great Bart," Coach Gilliss enthused. "There won't be many birdies on this hole." His gallery applauded and Angela jumped and cheered with excitement.

Celia sidled over to Angela. She spoke into Angela's ear with a light airiness. "I guess, if this continues, someone will need to properly congratulate Bart," Celia laughed as Angela blushed.

Bart stayed focused, worked with Coach Gilliss on managing his round. He attacked the pins when possible, played for the center of the greens otherwise. He played smart and stood on the 18th tee, at 5 under par. The 18th at Salem, is a challenging par 4 of 442 yards. A creek angles across the fairway approximately 125 yards short of the elevated green. Bart, following Gilliss's advice, chose a 3 metal, rather than his driver. Dave Gilliss feared that with Bart's adrenaline pumping, he might launch his drive into the creek.

Bart hit his 3 metal 275 yards, leaving a shot of about 165 to the significantly elevated green. Gilliss stood with Bart. "I'm thinking with the wind, elevation and distance, it will play to 185 yards. Bart nodded, took the club from Coach Gilliss, then, he looked at Angela. He smiled, won a smile back from his obviously anxious girlfriend. He settled behind the ball studying the shot. He then closed his eyes, visualizing the shot he wanted to hit, opened his eyes, smiled at Angela and moved over the ball.

"Middle of the green," Gilliss advised. Bart nodded and swung smoothly. The ball flew straight and true, landing on the front of the green and bounding forward.

Bart's three playing partners were not enjoying success. It appeared none of the three would qualify. Each recognized the stellar round Bart was playing and were cheering for his success.

At the green, Bart found his ball about 20 feet from the hole. He marked his ball and moved aside as his playing partners chipped or pitched into the green from various distances. They each putted out leaving the green to Bart.

Bart surveyed the putt, as did Dave Gilliss, who had huddled with an official of the Massachusetts Golf Association as Bart walked to the 18th green. The MGA official, who was in contact with other officials at other courses, informed Dave that it appeared that the cut line to the top 144 would be about even par. Dave had whispered the information to Angela and Bart's family, who were relieved at the news. He said nothing to Bart, whose focus was on making this putt and finishing strong. Studying the putt, player and coach agreed that it would tend to break right to left, how much it would break would depend on the speed of the putt. Dave cautioned Bart to play smart, at 5 under par he was likely to qualify for the next round, an 18 hole, stroke play tourney of 144 golfers. Bart nodded, but felt he had a good feel for the speed of the greens. He chose his line then stroked the putt. It looked good off of the blade and seemed to seek the hole. The ball dropped in to the cheers of the other golfers and Bart's family who ran to congratulate him. Angela led the way, leaping into his arms and gave Bart the happy news. "You did it Bart, you're in!" She chortled happily.

Bart was in the round of 144. Only 32 would qualify for match play. But the mountain which had seemed insurmountable, now was, at least, in view.

The family gathered at the DeMarco home for dinner and a celebration. Franco and Mario were at sea, but Angela was urged to call Bart's friends to join. Dave Gilliss, as well as, Dave and Jessica and Jim and Betsy came to celebrate with Bart, Angela and the family. Rosa and Maria worked together to prepare the feast on the fly, but were so happy to be working with Angela, Celia, Tina and Lucia that the preparation became a fun event in itself. Homemade pizza and spaghetti with calamari sauce were enjoyed by all. Maria, who had not watched Bart play, had spent the day somewhat nervously, but productively, baking a selection of her Italian cookies. "I knew Bart would win," she proclaimed, with a beaming smile for Bart.

"Bart, your mother is amazing," Betsy offered as she sampled the pizza. "This is absolutely delicious."

Bart laughed. "My Mom is amazing, but Angela's Mom and all the girls worked together." He paused. "We are all so lucky to have our families," and, he added with a smile, "Angela is becoming quite the cook," he complimented. "I especially love her garlic bread," he said with a smile and a wink. Angela's blush told Betsy and Jessica that there was more to that particular comment than immediately met the eye.

Lucia entered the living room and joined the group of Bart's friends with Celia and Tina. Now, 15 years old, Lucia was blossoming into a beauty. At 5 foot 6 inches tall and shapely, she was resembling a young Rosa more every day. Her auburn hair was shoulder length and had a natural wave. Her face was pretty, her soft brown eyes glittered. In short, she was bordering on beautiful. She sat quietly, smiling as the guys teased Bart about how his golf was messing with their Fiesta plans.

Angela caught Lucia's eye, saw concern. "Are you okay, Lucia?" She asked.

Lucia nodded and flashed that DeMarco smile. "Yes, I'm fine." She paused. She eyed Angela, "could you come up to my room for a minute, Angela?"

Once Angela had joined Lucia in her room, Lucia closed the door, sat beside Angela on her bed and looked at Angela. She smiled. "Could you help me choose an outfit for tonight?" Lucia asked.

Angela nodded, "of course, Lucia," then she exhaled, breathing out a sigh of relief. "I thought there was a problem. Do you have a date, Lucia?" She laughed. "You had me a bit worried."

Lucia rose, walked to her dresser. With her back to Angela, she nodded. "I do, Angela."

Angela saw the slump of Lucia's shoulders, saw her eyes mist in the reflection from the mirror atop the dresser. Angela's eyes narrowed. "What is it, Lucia?"

Lucia turned to face Angela. Her eyes filled and her hands shook. "He's coming here in an hour to pick me up."

Angela nodded. "Is there a problem?" She watched Lucia closely. "Does your Dad think that you are too young to date?"

The question stopped Lucia. "Maybe," she reflected. "I hadn't even thought about that problem." She looked at Angela. She took a deep breath. "Angela, I went with some girlfriends to a dance at Bishop Fenwick high school." She paused, used a tissue to wipe her eyes. "I met him there. We had a good time." She sighed. "Angela, we spent the entire time together."

Angela smiled. "That's good Lucia, is he cute?" She watched Lucia nod, but drop her head.

"Angela, I didn't know," she pleaded. Now her eyes flooded and tears ran down her cheeks. She looked up at Angela. "The music was so loud, we really couldn't hear each other."

Angela sat holding Lucia's hands, feeling a chill race down her spine. She said nothing, held her smile and waited. She took a deep breath, as Lucia continued. "When the music stopped, you know, at the end of the dance, when we were alone, he asked me on a date."

Angela nodded.

"He invited me to Fiesta, it turned out he's from Gloucester," Lucia added. "He said he hadn't caught my name beyond Lucia." She paused. "When I told him that my name was Lucia DeMarco, his expression changed."

Angela studied her. "How so, Lucia?"

Lucia spoke hurriedly. "He asked me if I was Bart DeMarco's sister." I smiled and told him that yes, Bart's my brother." Lucia paused. "He frowned, then told me that he had fought with Bart and that Bart had beat him pretty badly, actually broke his nose."

Angela gulped, her eyes grew wide. "What's his name, Lucia?"

Lucia looked at Angela. There was a long pause. "Sal Siracusa," Lucia admitted, in a soft voice. She waited for Angela to speak, but Angela just sat, holding Lucia's hands, so Lucia continued. "He told me what he did to you and how Bart jumped in to protect you."

Angela eyed her. "And, you still want to date him?"

Lucia nodded. "He told me that what happened changed his life."

"Really?" Angela asked in a tone of disbelief.

Lucia nodded. "He told me that when he went home and told his parents what happened, they were furious with him." Lucia paused. "Sal told me that he was bleeding, holding a towel to his face, and instead of taking him to a doctor, Sal's father made Sal explain slowly and in detail how he and two other boys blocked your path and mocked you." Lucia gulped. "His father made him say aloud that he saw that you were afraid and he still continued to mock you." There was a long pause. "His father told him that he was proud of Bart and ashamed of Sal."

Angela's expression became reflective, as she nodded. "Yes," she said thoughtfully. "We never did hear anything from the Siracusa's.

Lucia clutched Angela's hands. "I'm so sorry Angela." She swallowed. "I told him that I loved you like a sister and that I would not date him."

Angela looked confused. "But, you said..."

Lucia nodded. "He called me the next day and again two days later and asked for an opportunity to apologize to you, Bart and our family." Lucia paused, a smile played at her lips. "He said that he would do anything necessary to make amends so he could date me."

Angela saw the joy in her eyes. Angela knew well the feeling of being desired by a man. It is a heady, exhilarating feeling. "So, Lucia, you said yes?"

"I told him that he could come to the house, meet my family, apologize to you, and then I would decide if I would go to Fiesta as his date." Lucia said with a smile. She looked at Angela. "If you or Bart are not satisfied, then I won't go with him." She smiled, squeezed Angela's hand. "I hope you will be satisfied, Angela." She paused, her eyes pleaded. "Think about what he's willing to do just to have a chance to take me out." Her eyes glowed, she smiled plaintively. "I really like him, Angela."

Angela smiled at Lucia. "I understand, Lucia." She shook her head and laughed. "But, Bart may not be so easy to convince."

Lucia flashed a smile. "You can convince Bart." She stated with certainty. "Angela, I've never seen anyone so in love as Bart is with you." She placed pleading eyes on Angela. "Please help me, Angela."

Angela nodded and laughed. "Okay, Lucia, let's pick out an outfit for you to dazzle him." She paused, engaged Lucia's eyes. "Lucia, when Sal arrives, do not say anything. This is between Sal and Bart." She squeezed Lucia's hands. "Do you understand?"

Lucia nodded.

Angela and Lucia re-joined the group in the living room. Lucia was wearing a red mini-dress, gold necklace and earrings, and a bright smile.

"WOW," Celia exclaimed. "Lucia, I think that you will be the prettiest woman at my wedding."

Lucia smiled. "Thanks Celia, but no chance. You will be the most beautiful bride ever!"

Before Bart could question Lucia, the doorbell rang.

"I'll get it," Lucia called. She looked at Angela as she went to the door.

Lucia greeted Sal and walked into the living room holding Sal's hand. Bart immediately rose to his feet, anger flashing in his eyes. Angela placed her hand on Bart's arm. "Easy, Bart, let Lucia explain."

Bart looked at Angela, then Lucia and saw her pleading eyes. "Bart," Lucia said, "you know Sal Siracusa?"

Bart nodded. "Yes, I know Sal." He eyed Sal critically. "Why are you here, Sal?"

Sal looked at Bart, he looked around the room and raised his brow in surprise at the presence of Jessica Arnold. It occurred to Sal that if Angela and Bart could forgive 'the queen of mean,' as she was called by so many, then perhaps he had a chance.

Sal was a well-conditioned six feet tall, broad shouldered young man. He showed no fear, but offered a smile. "Bart, I come in peace." He paused. "Please sit, I would like to apologize to Angela."

Everyone but Sal sat. Bart sat at the edge of the couch, poised to leap to his feet. Lucia chose the seat on the other side of Bart, so he was flanked by Lucia and Angela. Both gently rested their hands on Bart's forearms.

Sal stood before Angela, looked her in the eyes. "Angela," he began, "I want to express my sincere sorrow over my treatment of you." He swallowed. "It was cowardly and mean," He paused, took a deep breath. "I know it was three years ago, but time does not absolve me from my cruel treatment of you." He paused, and looked remorseful. "I hope you will forgive me."

Angela kept her eyes fixed on Sal for a long moment, she glanced at Betsy and Jessica, saw them drop their eyes, thought how strange it was that these people who had been so cruel to both she and Bart are now friends. 'People can change,' she realized. Angela looked at Lucia, saw the hope in her eyes. She turned to Bart, made eye contact, smiled and gently squeezed his arm, then she looked back to Sal. She saw Sal swallow nervously. "Sal," Angela said calmly, "you need to speak to Bart. I take my lead from him." Angela sat back, extending Sal's agony.

Sal nodded, then looked at Bart. "Bart, I am actually thankful that you came along when you did." He paused. "I am also glad that you fought me and," he laughed, "pounded the snot out of me." He offered his hand. "That was the beginning of some real changes for me." He paused, his hand still extended. "I am truly sorry."

Bart stood, looked to Angela, who nodded almost imperceptibly, and saw Lucia's hopeful smile, he took Sal's hand. "Okay Sal, we forgive you." He smiled. "But," he looked at Lucia, "something tells me that you came here for more than to offer an apology."

Sal stood tall and looked at Bart with a determined gaze. "I am hoping that Lucia will allow me to take her to Fiesta."

"Oh, I see," Bart smiled, liking the steel in Sal's eyes. "Sal, that's only partly up to Lucia." He shrugged. "You will have to clear that request with my father." He paused. "Lucia is only 15."

"Oh, okay, Bart, I understand. May I speak to your Dad?" He asked hopefully.

Bart shook his head. "No, sorry, he is out fishing. He'll be home by mid-night."

"It's Fiesta!" Sal said surprised. "All the boats are in for Fiesta."

Bart nodded. "Yes, it is, but he just bought the boat and he is on fish." Bart shrugged. "With my father fishing, you would have to speak to Mario." Bart explained. "He's the oldest son."

Sal smiled and looked about, "Okay, is Mario here?" Angela exchanged a long look and smile with Celia. Lucia sat quietly, but glared at Bart.

Bart shook his head. "Sorry Sal, Mario is out fishing with my father."

Sal now noted the smiles across the room. He looked at Bart, "I guess that's fair to make me squirm," he allowed. "So Bart," he asked patiently, "who do I need to speak to?"

"I guess you have to receive that permission from me." He volunteered. "Of course, that's if Lucia wants to be your date for Fiesta."

A frustrated Lucia, still seated, punched Bart's leg, bringing a smile to Bart and grins from all watching. Bart turned to Lucia. "Lucia" Bart asked formally and with a wide smile, "do you wish to go on a date with Sal?"

Lucia looked up to her big brother, bore hard eyes into his gaze. Still she managed a smile, "yes Bart, I would like that."

Bart turned to Sal, shook his head, "I am sorry Sal, but Lucia is not allowed to date until she is 16 years old." He shrugged and smiled. "But, you may stay here with Lucia and her family for the evening."

Sal looked at Lucia, then Bart and laughed aloud. "Sounds good to me."

Bart looked to Lucia. "Lucia, why don't you make a plate for Sal and introduce him to Mom and the family."

The room burst into laughter as Sal and Lucia walked to the kitchen. "Well done, Bart," Dave Powers called. Jim Perry was almost rolling on the floor with laughter. Celia, trying to keep from smiling, looked at Bart, lost the battle and laughed. "Mario would be proud of you."

Angela, Betsy and Jessica, agreed that Sal deserved what he received, and admired Bart for doing it with a light touch.

"Still," Angela warned Bart with a grin, "you are going to get an earful from Lucia."

Chapter Twenty-Three

At Bart's urging, and with the encouragement of Beth Nelson, Angela auditioned for Summer Theatre, an annual summer musical production of professional quality, annually staged at Gloucester High School.

A professional Director is in charge, and, Beth Nelson worked in the role as Assistant Director. Angela's role in Grease, which had seemed initially intimidating, proved to be fun. Working with the cast and crew, rehearsing her part and working with others to blend their talents to an enjoyable outcome, fit Angela well. So, she decided to audition.

She, Jessica and Betsy all auditioned for parts and, happily, all three won roles as dancers in the Production of 'A Chorus Line,' the Broadway hit that had a good number of singing roles. At auditions, Angela sang two songs for the Director, 'Dance 10, Looks 3' and 'What I did for Love.'

She put her heart into both songs, but was red-faced throughout her performance of 'Dance 10, Looks 3.' The Director chose Jessica to play that role and Angela won the role that would have her singing, 'What I Did for Love.'

Bart had a wonderful time teasing Angela about singing and dancing to 'Dance 10, Looks 3.' "I'd love to see that!" He prodded as he held her. "Would you do it for me?"

Angela's face blushed a deep red as she deftly moved the conversation. "Could you imagine my father's reaction to me doing that song?" She laughed. "I told the Director that it wasn't right for me." She shrugged as she nuzzled closer to Bart. "I think Jessica is more fitted to the part."

Bart laughed as he held and kissed her. "I think I like keeping this beautiful body for myself."

Bart worked daily with Dave Gilliss as the round of 144 was scheduled for the following Saturday. He was on his game and eager to compete with the best amateur golfers in the Commonwealth.

It was a perfect early July day on the venerable course, overlooking the ocean on Cape Cod. Dave Gilliss had secured a local golf professional to caddie for Bart, as neither Dave nor Bart had ever seen the course. Once again, Dave Gilliss had proven to be critical in assisting and guiding Bart.

Thirty-six foursomes were scheduled to tee off, using both the 1ˢᵗ tee and the 10ᵗʰ tee. Dave warned Bart that it was likely to be a very slow round, that he would be waiting on every tee box to hit until the fairways and greens cleared. "This is where focus becomes vital." Gilliss explained. "Bart, if you get caught up complaining about delays or anything other than your next shot, it will hurt you." He paused. "We were lucky to get Mike Brentano to caddie for you. He knows the course and is a very good player." He placed hard eyes on Bart. "Listen to him."

Dave Gilliss, along with Angela, Rosa, Celia and Lucia walked the course following Bart. They could see Bart smiling as his caddie spoke non-stop to him about the course, memories of his rounds on the course and constantly offering encouragement. Mike was filling the gaps with positive conversation, a real plus during a very slow round. Angela stayed close, offering encouragement, smiling supportively and, anxiously, watching the big leader boards that posted the top 32 scores.

As Bart had a later tee time, he had to deal with the greens which have been walked on and marked, sand traps that were not always raked properly and fairways that had numerous unrepaired divots. But, as more than half the players had posted scores by the time Bart had completed the front nine, he had a good idea of what score he needed to post to qualify for match play.

Bart and caddie Mike Brentano stood on the 10ᵗʰ tee waiting to hit, they studied the leader board. It appeared that as the players scores scrolled on the board, the leader had played the course in a score of 4 under par. Of course, there were at least 36 players yet to post, but at the moment the player sitting at the 32rd spot was 5 over par.

Mike looked at Bart. "Okay, you played the front nine in 2 under par." He paused, made sure he had Bart's attention. "I want you to do better." He insisted. "Bart, the goal is 6 under par." Mike took a deep breath. "Make a statement, Bart." He demanded. "If you are the medalist you will play against the number 32 player in the first round." Bart nodded. "Stay focused, remember the finals are July 19ᵗʰ. I want you in that 36 hole, final."

Bart laughed. "July 19ᵗʰ! That's Angela's birthday." He looked over at Angela and his small gallery.

Mike rolled that around, looked over at the group and nodded. "Okay, Bart, let's do this for Angela." He laughed. "That would be a great birthday present."

Bart stroked his drive, into the wind, on the par 5, 10th hole, over 300 yards down the middle of the fairway.

Mike laughed. "Good drive Bart, there won't be any divots there." It was the longest drive of the day on the hole. Bart's three playing partners followed. They hit their drives, considerably shorter than Bart's. Having no chance to reach the green on their second shot, they each hit their second shot to a position short of the hazards and to where they could hit a wedge onto the green.

Bart had 210 yards into the green, which was guarded by water to the right and long, a deep sand trap left, leaving a narrow opening to run his shot up and onto the green. Some would argue that the smart shot would be to lay-up short of the green and all the trouble. Then, hit a wedge close and go for the birdie. Mike could read Bart's body language as Bart stood behind the ball, with a hybrid club in hand. He looked over at Mike. "I'm going for the middle of the green." The words were spoken with such certainty that Mike nodded. "Go for it, nice and smooth."

Bart closed his eyes, mentally picturing the shot. Angela watched him closely, recalling how often she'd seen him do so, breathing easily, before smiling as he set up over the ball. He swung smoothly and lofted the shot high and straight. It landed on the middle of the green and rolled back and took the slope to the right. The ball stopped twelve feet from the cup. Bart fist bumped with Mike. Angela and the family cheered. "Great shot, big brother," Lucia called out.

Angela flashed a thumbs up and gave Bart a big smile. "My guy is something." She proclaimed.

Celia nudged Lucia, as they walked to the green. With a smile, she teased. "I guess you're not still angry at Bart?"

Lucia laughed. "I can never stay angry at Bart." She shrugged. "And, besides, he was right to make Sal squirm after what he did to Angela." She grinned. "I was lucky Bart didn't go after him." She winked at Angela. "He seems a bit protective when it comes to his girl."

Angela smiled. "Yes, he is." She thought back, her eyes a bit dreamy. "He was incredible that day. He took on three guys to protect me." She nudged Lucia, smiled. "And, then, after he chased them away, he was so gentle with me." She looked at Lucia. "So, what did your Dad say about Sal?" Angela asked.

Lucia laughed. "He said that Bart was right, no dating until I am 16 years old." She paused, "but, he said that Sal can come for dinner a few times per week, but no going out."

"And Sal is okay with that?" Celia asked with a grin. "Tough to get close when the family is around."

Lucia smiled. "He is." She blushed. "He said I was worth waiting for."

"I like that," Celia offered with a smile.

Lucia looked closely at Angela. She touched her arm, and waited until Angela met her eyes. "Are you okay with Sal being around?"

Angela nodded. "I am," she took a breath and sighed. "It was a tough time, but in a crazy sort of way, I probably wouldn't be with Bart now if Sal hadn't done what he did." Then Angela laughed. "And, it gives me a reason to maybe extort a favor or two as the years go by."

Lucia laughed. "That seems fair," she added. She looked at Angela. "And thanks, Angela."

They waited for the other players in Bart's foursome to hit their wedge shots onto the green, and then walked up to the green. Each hit the green, but Bart's ball was closest to the pin and he waited for the others to putt. It was to his advantage that two of the players had putts which gave Bart a good read on the break of the green. All three of his playing partners made par. Bart then lined up his eagle putt.

He stood over the putt, confident of the break and rolled his putt into the heart of the cup for an eagle. That brought him to 4 under par and in a tie for the lead. He glanced at the scoreboard and noted that number 32 still was at 5 over par. Things looked good, but Bart wasn't done.

He played the last eight holes in 3 under par, to finish the round at 7 under par, easily the low round of the day. Bart was the medalist and his ticket was punched to the match play tourney of 32 golfers.

When Bart tapped in his par putt on 18, he embraced Mike Brentano and thanked him for all his help. Dave Gilliss and the family who had gathered to congratulate Bart stood back as Mike eyed Bart, "you're a great kid and an exceptional golfer, Bart. Keep at it." He paused. "And, if there is anything I can do to assist you, just call."

Angela raced into Bart's arms, planting a congratulatory kiss on him that brought a huge smile. "I'm so proud of you," she said.

He held her close, smiled and whispered, "Angela, are you proud enough to sing and dance for me that song that makes you blush?"

Angela held tight, her cheeks reddened, but she whispered, "for you, anything."

Chapter Twenty-Four

Bart was in the match play tournament, as the medalist, and was readying for three days of 36 holes (two matches) per day. The 32 golfers would play matches of 18 holes, beginning on the morning of Thursday July 17th. After the first round, the field would be reduced to 16 golfers. And, after the second (afternoon) round, there would be only 8 golfers remaining. Friday, July 18th, there would be 4 morning matches. Thus by the afternoon, only 4 golfers would be vying for the Championship. By days end, the final Championship Match would be set. Saturday, July 19th (Angela's birthday) the two finalists would meet in a 36 hole Championship Match.

On the Monday before the Match Play Tournament, Bart had lumped two boats that morning. That afternoon, he met Jim Perry at Bass Rocks Golf Club to play a round of golf. Bart found Jim to be good company and as he was a solid golfer, always a challenge. That evening Bart and Angela were relaxing together before dinner with Angela's family.

As they sat to dinner, Sal Curcuru looked at Bart and smiled. "Maybe, I come and see you play?" He asked. "My Angela tell me that you are very good."

Bart smiled, glanced at Angela, whose cheeks reddened when their eyes met. He turned back to Mr. Curcuru and nodded. "That would be good, maybe on the first day of the tournament." He paused. "Angela will be performing on the 18th and 19th.

Angela startled. "How is that going to work?" She asked. "My show starts at 7pm."

Bart shrugged. "If I get past the first two rounds on Thursday, I will be playing Friday morning and," he laughed, "hopefully on Friday afternoon." He considered the logistics. "The golf course is about an 80-90 minute drive." He shrugged. "I think you would have to leave after the morning round to get home in time to prepare for the show."

Angela straightened in her seat, surprise registering on her face. "I won't be able to watch you play in the semi-finals?"

Bart shrugged and grimaced. "I don't see how you could and be back on time."

"And, the same for the Championship match on Saturday, I imagine?" She queried, eyes set on Bart.

Bart shrugged. "If I get that far, I guess so." He flashed a smile, "but that's my girl's birthday. I will get back, as quickly as possible, to celebrate with you." He was aware that there was a dinner and trophy presentation after the finals. If he won and attended the dinner, he would miss the play and any after party.

Angela studied Bart closely, but said nothing.

Bart looked at Mr. Curcuru. "If you'd like, I will arrange a ride for you with Angela on that Thursday, Sir."

Later that evening, Bart and Angela took a ride to a quiet, secluded spot overlooking Good Harbor Beach and the open ocean. Thatcher's Island, with its' twin light houses flashing twin beams of light on the rippling water, beckoned. Bart cuddled Angela close, gently turned her face and kissed her. She met his kiss eagerly, but slowly leaned back, watching him closely.

"Please tell me what is going on with the golf tournament." She asked. She smiled and kissed him.

Bart shrugged. "What do you want to know?" He leaned in, kissing her and holding her close.

"Tell me what happens on Saturday, after the finals conclude?" She asked.

Bart laughed. "Then, I shoot home to watch my girl star in her play and celebrate your 17th birthday." He shrugged. "That's, of course, if I am playing on Saturday."

"Bart," she asked in a soft, sweet tone, "is there a dinner, maybe an awards ceremony?" Angela kissed him, watched Bart closely.

He couldn't help but shake his head. He looked at her and saw her studying him. "I've asked this before," he laughed. "Why do you have to be so smart?"

She stayed quiet, but kept her eyes on him.

"Yes," he acknowledged. "If I am playing in the finals on Saturday, there is a trophy presentation and a dinner after the match." He smiled. "They even give us time to shower and change before dinner." He studied her. "But, if I win, I plan to blow all that off and hustle home."

Angela shook her head. "No, Bart," she insisted. "When you win, you will stay, do all the interviews, attend the dinner and receive your trophy." She raised her hand to ward off his objection. "The colleges will be watching," she smiled, kissed him. "This is our future Bart." She paused. "You go out there and win. You go to a great college, become the best player in the country, then," she laughed, "if you want, I will be waiting for you." She kissed him, cuddled close and smiled. "And, if you still want, maybe I'll let you marry me."

Bart laughed. "Oh, Angela, I so want to marry you and raise a family together."

She put her hands on his face, looked into his eyes. "Bart, please understand, I want you to achieve all your dreams. I want you to be happy." She kissed him. "Bart, I'm yours, heart, body and soul, for as long as you want me." She kissed him deeply. She looked into his eyes. "I want you to win this tournament."

He smiled, shook his head in disbelief at how strongly she believed in him. "Okay, I'll go out there and win." He paused. "We'll celebrate your birthday on Sunday."

"It's a deal," she said brightly and with a laugh. "You win and we'll celebrate as if it were your birthday!" Bart beamed that smile that touched Angela's soul.

Chapter Twenty-Five

It was a sunny and hot New England July day, not a cloud in the sky. The golf course was magnificent. Coach Dave Gilliss was caddying. Gilliss had spent the previous day walking the course with Bart.

Bart, the #1 seed was playing the #32 seed, Greg White, from Concord Ma. Greg, a 22 year old college senior at Tufts University, has had a solid college career and is planning on attending law school. The players and their caddies met and shook hands on the 1st tee. Greg had an entourage which included his fiancé, Toni, also a student at Tufts, his parents and his 16 year old sister. His brother, Harry, was his caddie.

With Bart was Angela and her parents, Sal and Maria, as well as Angela's sister, Tina. Bart's parents, Franco and Rosa were there as well as Mario and Celia, and, of course, Bart's sister, Lucia.

As the #1 seed Bart had the honor. The first hole is a 465 yard par 4. Bart teed his ball, stood behind the ball looking down the fairway. He closed his eyes and visualized his shot, moved over the ball and launched a 315 yard drive down the center of the fairway. Greg White looked at his brother and rolled his eyes. "This will be over soon," he laughed, before hitting a good drive of 265 yards.

Toni and Greg's sister walked with Angela, Lucia, Celia and Tina. Toni stood with Angela, and spoke softly, "Greg told me that he drew the #1 seed," she laughed. "Bart DeMarco!" She grinned at the memory. "When he told me, Greg shook his head." Toni smiled. "Angela, your guy is making quite a name for himself."

Angela smiled, "thank you, I'm very proud of him."

Toni nodded, "you should be." She grinned. "I'm proud of Greg as well. He starts law school next September." She looked about, saw that they were out of earshot of Greg's parents and said softly, "he wants to get married after college graduation."

Angela smiled. "Congratulations, Toni, that's great."

Toni laughed, "I'm not sure his parents agree."

Greg was facing a 200 yard shot to a green protected on the right, left and back by deep sand traps. He used his 5 fairway metal and hit the ball flush, landing it on the green, but watching as it ran through the green into the punishing back bunker.

Bart was facing a 150 yard second shot. He hit an 8 iron, high, landed it softly on the green. It rolled out and stopped 10 feet from the hole.

Greg descended into the bunker, which was six feet below the level of the green. He took a big swing and blasted the ball out of the bunker landing it on the green, but past the cup. It rolled out about 30 feet beyond the cup, leaving a difficult putt. Greg made a solid stroke, but missed on the low side. He looked at Bart, smiled, told Bart his putt was good and Bart was 1 up.

Greg's statement proved to be prophetic. By the 9th hole Bart was 3up and then won holes 10 and 11. Greg made a long putt to halve the 12th, but the match ended on the 13th green with Bart rolling in a birdie putt to win the hole and the match, winning 6 and 5. (6 holes ahead with 5 holes to play). Greg White, a solid golfer and a good guy, offered his hand with a grin. "Good luck Bart," he offered. "Go all the way." He laughed. He asked Toni to snap a photo of him and Bart. "Someday, I will brag that I played a match against Bart DeMarco."

Bart shook Greg's hand, smiled. "It was fun, Greg. Good luck."

Angela and Bart's family moved in to congratulate him. "Wow, that was easy," Mario said. Franco embraced Bart, held him and told him how proud he was.

Angela stood back smiling, then came in to embrace Bart. "You did great, Bart, I'm so proud of you." She laughed. "I guess that was an easy round for you." She paused. "Next round at 1pm, right?"

Bart nodded, as his family gathered around. "I will play the winner of the match between the 16th and 17th seeds." He looked about. "We have a few hours to relax and get some lunch. I understand there is a luncheon tent for the players and families." He pointed. "Why don't we go and get out of the sun and relax."

Bart and Dave expected that the afternoon match would prove to be a bit tougher.

Bart's opponent, Mark Fitzgerald, a lobster man from Falmouth, had competed in the Massachusett's Amateur for seven years, but this was the first time he had qualified for Match Play. Fitzgerald was proud to have made the 'Sweet 16' after winning his morning match on the 20th hole. Now, he faced the #1 seed!

Fitzgerald arrived on the tee, eating a sandwich, as he had completed his match only 30 minutes before his 1pm tee time. His gallery consisted of his very pregnant wife, Lindie, a pretty and sweet woman. She embraced Angela, "may I walk with you?" She asked. Bart smiled as he watched the women close ranks to help Lindie walk the course.

Bart found Mark to be a solid golfer and a really nice guy. After six holes the match was all square. Dave Gilliss and Bart had studied Mark's game and realized that he was long off of the tee, not Bart long, but long. His short game was reliable, but Dave thought that Mark's putting was his weak point.

The 7ᵗʰ hole was a long par 5. Mark hit a good drive, not his best, leaving himself 300 hundred yards to the green. Dave noted that Mark was over swinging, trying to keep pace with Bart. The wiry Mark was 5' 10" and a slim 155 pounds. He wouldn't be able to drive a ball the distances that the smooth swinging, 6' 2", 180 pound Bart could.

Bart then launched a big drive of 330 yards, leaving about 220 yards to the green.

As the group walked to Mark's ball, Mark seemed strangely preoccupied. Dave guessed that he was becoming flustered by the difference in tee shots and on this big par 5, the contrast was evident. Mark looked at his shot. Dave thought it was or should be an obvious decision. Hit a safe shot to a comfortable wedge distance. But, Mark kept eyeing Bart's ball which lay 80 yards further down the fairway.

Lindie shook her head. "He has that look," she said. "He's going to try to do too much."

Angela and Celia looked at Lindie, not really understanding her meaning. Lindie watched Mark pull his 3 metal. His caddie said nothing. Mark set up and took a big swing. As he over-swung, he fell off the shot and the ball went way right, landing in some heavy gorse. To make matters worse, he had tree trouble.

Bart exchanged a long look with Dave. Dave tapped his head, Bart nodded as Dave handed Bart an 8 iron, which Bart lofted to about 80 yards short of the pin.

Mark had to chip out of the gorse back onto the fairway. The gorse grabbed his club, slowing his swing. The ball stayed in the gorse. Mark picked up his ball, conceding the hole to Bart. Bart was now 1up.

The 8ᵗʰ hole was a short, 130 yard, par 3. There was water right and a deep bunker left of the green. The front of the green was protected by a heavily roughed mound, which was 8 feet above the level of the green. Simply put, the golfer needed to loft a shot high, to land softly on the green.

Bart hit a 9 iron and he hit it high. All watched as the ball cleared the mound and appeared to land on the green. As the mound blocked the view of the green, it was impossible to know how close it was to the hole.

Mark also chose a 9 iron. He took a big swing and lofted a high shot, frustrated, he called out, "get legs" to the ball, but it landed on the mound and stuck. As the group approached the green, Mark saw that his ball had buried into the mound. Bart's ball was 5 feet to the left of the pin. Moments later, Bart was 2up in the match.

As Bart exited the green he looked to Angela, who flashed an encouraging smile. Bart was feeling it. He went on and won the 9th hole, taking a 3up lead into the back nine.

Mark rallied and halved the 10th and 11th holes. But, Bart was 3up with seven to play. Angela was excited. "He's going to do it!" She exclaimed to Lucia.

"You bet he is," Lucia affirmed. "Bart's the best." Rosa and Maria took charge of walking with Lindie, the two mothers keeping a close eye and making sure she stayed hydrated.

Lucia looked to Angela, who smiled. "You okay, Lucia?" Angela asked.

Lucia nodded. "Sal asked if we could go to see the play tomorrow night." She took a deep breath. "If my Dad says I can go with Sal, will it be okay with you?"

Angela nodded. She took the taller Lucia by the shoulders. "Sal apologized," Angela shook her head. "I want to believe he was sincere." She eyed Lucia, "time will tell on that, but," she smiled, "let's give him every chance to prove himself." She pulled Lucia into a hug. "I hope he has changed Lucia, for your sake, far more than mine."

Bart won the 12th hole, to go 4up. They halved the 13th hole, leaving Bart 4up with 5 to play. Mark's chances were melting away.

The 14th is a medium length par 5. There was water down the left side and heavy rough on the right. Bart only saw the 30 yard wide fairway and blasted an enormous drive that split the fairway. Mark looked at Bart, shook his head and teed his ball. His eyes were drawn left at the large pond. Dave saw it, "that water is in his head, watch what happens," he whispered to Bart.

Mark pulled his drive badly, all quietly watched the ball plunk into the pond. Mark stood on the tee, took a deep breath, he looked at Lindie, she read his disappointment and offered a smile. Mark took another deep breath, squared his shoulders, then flashed Bart a smile as he extended his hand to shake and concede the match.

Bart was in the field of 8. Just 8 golfers left, a win tomorrow morning would leave 4 golfers to play in the semi-finals tomorrow afternoon.

Angela raced to Bart and embraced him. She smiled, "great day, Bart. I'm so proud of you." Bart held Angela close, kissed her. With his arm about Angela they walked to join his family. Mario beamed. "Final eight, Bart. Great going!"

Rosa and Franco beamed smiles. Rosa embraced her boy. "I'm so happy for you, Bart."

Rosa looked to Angela. Her eyes spoke a silent message. Angela's eyes betrayed her dilemma

Chapter Twenty-Six

Of the 32 golfers to make the match play tourney, the eight remaining were all seeded in the top 10. Dave told Bart that it would be a battle from here on. "Focus," he implored Bart. "Tomorrow you play a good golfer," he grinned. "Remember Bart, you are 'The Diamond Maker.' There is no way these guys can beat you, unless you beat yourself."

That evening, Angela had the final rehearsal for the play. Bart escorted her and watched her sing and dance across the stage. He loved watching Angela strut so confidently, a smile on her face.

He drove Angela home and went in for a late snack. Angela, as always, was amazed and amused at how Bart never seemed to get enough food. Angela made him a plate of freshly baked Italian cookies and a large glass of milk and placed it before him on the kitchen table.

"Big day tomorrow," Bart exclaimed. "My girl is singing and dancing on stage." He smiled. "I love watching you move that gorgeous body about." He laughed as Angela blushed. "I hope that I can be back in time to make the play."

Angela smiled at Bart. "It is a big day!" She stressed. "Tomorrow you will play yourself into the finals of the Massachusetts Amateur Championship." She paused. "I won't be there for you." He saw the anguish on her face. "Maybe, I should let my understudy perform for me."

Bart smiled and took her hands. "No, Princess, you made a commitment to perform and people are relying on you." He saw her shake her head and prepare to challenge him. He continued. "I would love to have you with me tomorrow and, if I advance, at the finals on Saturday." He kissed her hands. "But, as hard as it is, you won't always be able to be with me at every match." He shrugged and tapped his chest. "Still, you are always with me here."

"Bart," she squeezed his hand. "I really want to be there for you."

Bart smiled. "You always are, my love." He winked. "And, you will come for the morning round, right?" Angela nodded. Bart laughed. "I'm playing a really good golfer tomorrow. Who knows, we may all be driving home after the morning round."

Angela shook her head. "No way," her eyes bore into his. "You WILL make the finals!" She insisted.

Friday, July 18th was another hot and humid July day. Bart was slotted to tee off against Rob Berry, a tall, leanly, muscular, college Junior at Clemson University. He appeared powerful and the word was that he was a long hitter. The ACC is considered an elite college golf conference. Berry, heading into his junior year, had been asked by his coach to appraise Bart's ability and character. So, while trying to win the match, he was, in reality, also, a part of the recruiting team.

As Bart was the 1ˢᵗ seed, his match went off last. So, the golfers and their caddies stood on the 1ˢᵗ tee for the 9:30am tee time.

Angela was there, with Bart's family. His Dad and Mom, Mario, Celia and Lucia. Angela's Dad was there, as well, and would drive Angela home after the match. The timing was good. The hope was that Bart would win his match by 1:30pm and not begin the semi-final match until about 2:30pm. Angela and her Dad would leave after the morning match as they had to drive through Boston to get home. Early afternoon was the best bet to avoid gridlock traffic.

Rob Berry's girlfriend, Andrea, a pretty redhead with sparkling green eyes, was there with Rob's parents. Andrea, a sophomore at Boston College hailed from Amherst Massachusetts. Berry had qualified for Match Play only once before, but this was the first time he had made it to the 'Elite 8.' Rob's college teammate, Ed Young, was acting as his caddie. A second pair of eyes on Bart.

The MGA official announced Bart, who teed his ball and launched a long and straight drive down the middle of the fairway. He stood aside, handed his driver to Coach Gilliss and stood quietly watching Rob Berry hit a good drive, down the left side of the fairway. It rolled out and hopped into the first cut of rough about 290 yards from the tee. The golfers, caddies and their galleries proceeded down the first fairway.

"Nice drive, Bart," Ed Young commented with a smile. "You outdrove my boy here by 30 yards." He laughed, poked Rob, "and," he added, with a wink. "Bart's ball is in the fairway."

Rob laughed. "Oh, is that a good thing?"

Bart smiled. He felt a bit uneasy in the company of the two college golfers. Their joking relaxed him as they approached Rob's ball. It sat in the rough, but not a bad lie, Bart thought.

"It looks like a flyer lie," Dave Gilliss mentioned to Bart. They all noted the trees that ran down the left side of the fairway, to just short of the green.

Rob set up to draw the ball around a tree about 30 yards ahead. The green was 175 yards away. Berry hit it flush, drawing it around the tree and hooking the ball back to the green. When grass gets between the clubface and the ball it will often affect the contact, causing it to fly further than intended. As a draw always will give greater distance, the ball landed just in front of the green and spun left into a sand trap. The spin and the velocity combined to drive the ball into the sand on the slope of the sand trap away from the green, leaving a buried downhill lie in the sand. Rob shook his head, looked at Ed and commented, "Wow, great start, huh?"

Bart and Dave Gilliss walked to his ball. It was sitting beautifully in the fairway about 135 yards from the pin. Dave handed Bart his 9 iron. Bart stood behind the ball, closed his eyes as he evened out his breathing. With a little smile he set up over the ball, swung smoothly and lofted his ball onto the green to about 10 feet below the cup. He looked at Angela and winked. He fist bumped with Dave.

Angela walked with Lucia, Celia and Rosa. Rosa noted the smiles and winks Bart was flashing at Angela. She smiled. "My boy is so in love with you, Angela."

Angela looked at Rosa, "Mrs. DeMarco, I love Bart with all my heart." She paused. "I hope you know that."

Rosa nodded, looked at Angela with concerned eyes. "I wish you could stay and be with Bart." She smiled wanly. "He really needs you."

Lucia and Celia exchanged a long look. Angela took Rosa's hand. "I wish I could stay." She shook her head. "I told Bart that I would give my part in the play to my under-study, so that I could be with him." She sighed. "Bart wouldn't hear of it. He told me that I had made a commitment to the play and people were counting on me."

Celia rolled her eyes. "That's a DeMarco!" She stated, and laughed. "But, that's one of the reasons I love Mario so very much." She stated. "The DeMarco men are loyal and principled."

Rosa nodded, she squeezed Angela's hands. Angela continued, "In the future, I will check out the dates and conflicts much more carefully." She shook her head. "I want to be here for Bart." She paused. "I hate the idea of leaving."

"Great shot, Bart," Rob Berry called out. He grinned, "I guess, you don't plan to make this easy for me, do you?"

Bart smiled and shrugged, "I hope that I don't make it easy on you."

Rob tried to blast his ball out of the sand. It came out low and skidded across the green and into the rough. He then attempted a wedge from the rough. He managed to leave himself a 15 foot putt for bogey. "Pick it up, Bart," he called with a smile.

Bart was 1up.

The golfers and caddies chatted amiably as they played the front nine. Bart was on his game and was 2up after nine holes.

Rob was having difficulty finding the fairway with his driver, playing shots consistently from the rough, while Bart was hitting fairways and greens in regulation. Bart won the 10th and 11th holes to go 4up. Rob battled back and rolled in a 20 foot birdie putt to win the 12th hole, but Bart responded by winning 13. As they walked to the 14th tee, Ed looked at Bart. "Do you plan to visit Clemson?" He grinned. "Bart, you will love Clemson. South Carolina has a great climate, and the area is beautiful."

Bart smiled. "Maybe, I don't know. I really haven't thought it all out."

Rob Berry joked. "After beating me up in this match, the least you could do is visit Clemson."

Bart shrugged. "The match isn't over."

But it soon was over. Bart rolled in a birdie putt on the 14th hole to close out the match 5 and 4.

The players and caddies shook hands. "Nobody should beat you, Bart," Rob stated with a smile. "You have the magic IT."

"Thanks," Bart replied with a grin. "And, good luck."

Bart was in the semi-finals and Angela and her Dad readied to leave.

Bart walked over to Angela, smiled and embraced her. "Knock them dead tonight, Beautiful," he said. "Oh," he laughed, "I guess the proper expression is; 'Break a leg.'"

Angela looked into Bart's eyes. "Be great, Bart!" Angela urged. "I'll be thinking of you."

Angela and her Dad left the course and drove home in relative silence. Sal looked over and said, "Bambina, Bart will be fine. He is so good."

She looked at her Dad. "Dad, I like that he needs me." She paused, as she misted. "Because, I really need him."

Sal smiled. "Don't be afraid Bambina, Bart loves you."

Angela nodded, but said nothing. Insecurities die hard. The fear that he would discover that he didn't need Angela terrified her.

Bart's family moved out of the sun to the air-conditioned grill room for lunch. "All this walking is doing me good." Rosa said, smiling.

Franco smiled. "You look prettier and younger all the time, my love."

Celia laughed. Lucia grinned and commented, "Dad, please, I'm trying to eat here!" Franco and Rosa exchanged a smile. Lucia's words provoked laughter across the table.

"So, who do you have this afternoon, Bart?" Mario asked.

Bart shook his head. "I don't know."

"Good," Dave Gilliss stated. "Who we play doesn't matter. It only matters how we play."

Chapter Twenty-Seven

The Summer Theatre's production of 'A Chorus Line' saw the curtain rise a bit after 7pm. Jim Perry and Dave Powers saved a seat in the nearly sold out auditorium for Bart. Jim and Dave smiled as they watched their girls dancing on stage. Betsy, much to her surprise, had won a singing role, she sang the song, 'Nothing.'

About 30 minutes into the show, Bart entered the auditorium and made his way to the 7th row aisle seat, as arranged, to join Jim and Dave. While Bart attempted to enter as quietly as possible, the chorus line was all on the stage, and Angela saw him enter and move to his seat. Staying in character, as much as possible, she searched his face. Bart smiled and flashed a thumbs up as he sat. Angela saw the smiles and handshakes from Jim and Dave, and she exhaled in relief. 'He did it,' she thrilled, 'he's in the finals.'

Bart watched the play with eyes riveted on Angela. He smiled as he savored the look of her curves so enjoyably displayed by the leotard she wore. When Jessica moved forward from the line to perform, 'Dance 10, Looks 3,' she exuded confidence. Bart looked on with eyes gleaming as Jessica danced and sang the racy number. His eyes and smile shifted back to Angela, who noted his rapt attention and happily concluded, 'I guess I'll be doing a private show for Bart tonight.'

When Angela moved to center stage to sing 'What I Did for Love,' composed by the great Marvin Hamlisch, their eyes met and spoke of passion. Angela sang for Bart, and Bart had eyes only for Angela. When she finished her song, Bart leaped to his feet, pulling the audience with him. Angela blushed as she bowed her head to the applause.

The three couples celebrated the girl's success with Chinese food. The flaming platters livening an already happy scene. "I'm so glad I made it tonight," Bart said, as he held Angela close. "I doubt I'll make it for tomorrows show." He raised his water glass. "A toast to our girls. Angela, Betsy and Jessica, you were outstanding, you made us proud." The six teens tapped glasses, happiness all around.

Jim Perry looked to Bart. "Tell us what happened?" He punched Bart's shoulder, "My God, you're in the finals of the Mass. Amateur!" He grinned. "My instruction really paid off."

That brought laughter from the group. Jim feigned outrage, "do I need to show you the magazine article?"

Betsy laughed aloud, "absolutely, Honey," she kissed his cheek. "Bart's success, my dancing, it's all about you!"

"Damn Right!" Jim said, laughing through his feigned indignation.

Bart shook his head. "Not tonight, tonight we celebrate our beautiful girls."

Angela cuddled close. "Please tell us, Bart. How did it go?"

Bart looked about, saw all eyes on him. "Okay," he nodded, exhaled, smiled and explained. "It was tough. I was behind most of the match. My opponent could really play." He shrugged. His short game was so precise, it was impressive." He looked at Jim. "This is what Coach Gilliss has been telling us." He shrugged, "so, I was 2 down after 9 holes. Then, we went back and forth. I was still 1 down with 3 to play." He paused. "My opponent," he recalled, "suddenly, seemed to be struggling. On 16 he hit his drive into a creek, giving me the hole."

"So, all square," Jim said.

"Yes," Bart nodded. "The 17th is a long par 3, about 240 yards. I hit a hybrid onto the green and he pulled his tee shot into the bunker left of the green." Bart sat back, pulled Angela close. "He had a tough sand shot, but he made a really good recovery shot to about two feet, which I conceded." Bart shrugged. "He really had a special short game." Bart stated, clearly impressed. "I want to develop that kind of short game."

He tightened his hold on Angela, looked into her eyes and smiled. "I had a 22 foot putt for the birdie and to finally take the lead." He exhaled. "I lined up the putt, closed my eyes to visualize my stroke and the roll of the ball," he smiled. "And, I pictured Angela's face." He grinned into Angela's surprised expression. "And, I ran the putt into the cup." He watched Angela closely. "We halved 18 and I won the match 1up."

"You thought about me?" Angela asked, almost breathless. The surprise and appreciation written in her expression had her body settling into Bart, her eyes gleaming and set on his face.

Bart smiled. "That's what I do Angela. I stand behind my ball, close my eyes and visualize the shot I need to hit." He nudged her. "I relax my breathing and then I picture your smiling face." He grinned. "Looking at you makes me happy and relaxes me." He shrugged. "Then, I hit my shot."

Angela looked at Bart with such love and devotion in her expression, Bart could only smile.

He looked at the group, and stated without embarrassment or hesitation. "See, I need Angela with me," he tapped his head and then his heart, "to succeed." He flashed a smile at Angela, kissed her. "Team DeMarco, right Angela?"

Jessica and Betsy gasped. Angela smiled at Bart. "Yes, Bart," her eyes misted, "Team DeMarco." She hugged him, kept her eyes fixed on Bart's face. "We should go," she said. "You need to sleep. You're playing for the Championship tomorrow."

Bart put money on the table, said goodnight to all, took Angela's hand and together they left the restaurant to head to Bart's car.

"WOW!" Jessica sighed. "He loves her so much." She thought about Angela, her devotion and her kindness. She looked at Dave. "I hope someday, I can earn that kind of love and devotion."

Dave smiled. Jessica put her fingers to his lips. "I know, I have to earn it first, am I right, Dave?"

He looked into her pretty face, her sparkling eyes. "We can all learn from those two." He paused. "We are lucky to have them as friends."

All four heads nodded.

Chapter Twenty-Eight

After the Red Sox, the Massachusetts Amateur Golf Championship was the biggest sports news of the day. Both Boston dailies, as well as the Gloucester Times ran stories with biographies and photographs of Bart and his opponent, Mike Wright, the 24 year old defending champion.

Wright is the great-grandson of Frederick J. Wright, Jr. a five time champion, including four consecutive victories from 1928-1931. The written pieces on the history of the Massachusetts Amateur recalled the glory of Francis Ouimet, a five time tournament Champion and the 1913 U.S. Open champion. Ouimet, an amateur, bested the legendary, Harry Vardon, a former U.S. Open Champion and six time British Open Champion, and Ted Ray, also a British Open Champion, to win the U.S. Open Championship in a play-off. It had all started for Ouimet with his victory in the 1913 Massachusetts Amateur.

The previous evening, the television sports stations covered the Championship featuring the battle between the defending champ, with a long and glorious lineage of achievement, versus "Stutter Boy," Bart DeMarco.

The newspapers also framed the story similarly. The publications and electronic media did run the Piscitello photo of Bart's high school football heroics and his battle with stuttering, quoting extensively from YES, and the article which ran in the 'Amateur Sports Monthly Magazine.' The reporting heavily favored the defending champ, who had handily won his semi-final match 5 and 4.

The DeMarco entourage left Gloucester at 6am. It was already warm and humid. The forecast called for the temperature to rise to 90 degrees, with high humidity, and clear, and sunny skies. This was the heart of summer. Bart rode with Coach Dave Gilliss. Mario drove Celia, his parents and Lucia and was expecting to take Angela, as Angela's Dad was fishing and her mother had no childcare for her young children. Maria told Bart that she would pray for him and make a special Sunday dinner and his favorite dessert to celebrate his victory and Angela's birthday.

To Angela's surprise, Dave Powers pulled up to her home with Jessica, Jim Perry and Betsy. Jessica and Betsy offered smiles. "We're all with you and Bart," Betsy stated. "Dave will drive us to the match and then back for tonight's show."

Jessica embraced Angela, "Thank you for opening my eyes to what is real." She filled with emotion. "Angela, I want you to know, that you can always count on me."

Angela held Jessica, looked at the group. "Thank you Jessica and all of you for doing this." Angela slid into the back seat of Dave's car, where Betsy and Jessica were seated. "I am so nervous." She smiled. "But, I know Bart will so appreciate the support."

"Bart's our teammate," Dave said simply. "We support each other."

Jim nodded in agreement and grinned. "Besides, I need to make sure all my instructions are being followed!" Jim's comment brought smiles, as he intended. "If," Jim added, "Bart follows the Great Perry's instructions, he'll be fine." He winked at Angela.

Betsy nudged Angela and flashed a smile. "Angela, is Bart in a good state of mind for today?" She paused, smiled. "I hope he's relaxed and ready to play his best golf."

Jessica winked at Betsy, flashed Angela a smile, and stated. "Angela knows how to relax Bart, I have faith in Angela."

Angela blushed as she heard the laughter and read the look and grins exchanged between Dave and Jim. She shook her head. "You guys!" she laughed, before stating primly. "I will always be there for Bart. I wished him luck and kissed him goodnight." She looked to Jessica and Betsy, smiled widely and winked. "What can I say, Bart's my guy!"

"Yes, he is." Jessica agreed. She looked to Angela. "And, I would say that he is one very lucky guy!"

Angela looked at Jessica, smiled. "Thanks Jess, that's a nice thing to say."

The golfers who lost their semi-final matches to Bart and Mike Wright, teed off at 9:30 am, with the 36 hole Championship match scheduled to tee off at 10:00 am. As Bart and Mike approached the tee, they moved through a large gallery of fans. Bart exchanged a surprised look with Dave Gilliss. "Why are all these people here?" Bart asked. Gilliss pointed to signs and a banner. The banner was from YES and the signs were supporting Bart.

"It looks like these children and their parents are here to support you, Bart." Dave Gilliss nodded, considered. "Wow! It must be the stories on the news." He said thoughtfully. "You are a role model for them, Bart." He placed his hands on Bart's shoulders, met his eyes. "The support is great, but our focus is on, and only on, the next shot."

Bart nodded. "Got Ya, Coach." He looked over at Angela, his family, and friends and smiled.

Bart and Mike Wright shook hands. "It looks like you brought a gallery, Bart." Mike commented with an approving smile. "Good for you, let's play some golf."

The announcer stood on the tee and proclaimed this the Championship round, between #1 seed, Bart DeMarco and #2 seed and defending Champion, Mike Wright. He turned to Bart, "Mr. DeMarco, you have the tee."

As Bart readied on the tee, a man with a young boy walked over to Franco and Rosa. They all stood quietly as Bart swung and launched his tee ball long and straight. The crowd applauded and Bart tipped his hat and smiled to the crowd. Bart heard the voice of a young boy call out; "GGo BBart!" He looked to the crowd but could not determine who had called out.

Mike Wright was announced. He took his nice smooth swing and struck an impressive drive. The players, caddies and gallery walked down the 1st fairway.

"Mr. DeMarco?" Asked the man who had approached Franco.

Franco nodded, "yes, I am Franco DeMarco."

"Are you Bart's father?" He asked. Franco nodded, while Rosa smiled at the boy. "Hi," Rosa said. "What's your name?"

"I,I, am Hharry," he struggled to respond. Rosa cupped his cheek and thoughts of Bart suffering the same challenges, at the same age, flooded back. She fought back tears.

The man extended his hand. "Mr. DeMarco, my name is Chet Knowlton." He gestured to the boy. "This young man is my son, Harry."

Franco shook Knowlton's hand, smiled at Harry. "It's a pleasure to meet you both." He paused, made eye contact with Rosa. "This is my wife, Rosa," he offered.

"The pleasure is ours, Mr. DeMarco." He paused, cleared his throat. "Your son, Bart, is an inspiration to my son and all these children." He stated. "I am the President of the local YES chapter."

Franco and Rosa made eye contact. "I'm sorry, I don't know what that is." Franco stated.

"YES is the acronym for our organization, 'the Youth association for Excellence in Speech.'" He smiled. "We saw the news reports. They referred to your son as 'Stutter Boy.'" He smiled and eyed both Franco and Rosa. "Was it difficult for Bart?"

Rosa took Chet's hand. She began to cry. "He cried himself to sleep, it was awful what he went through."

Chet nodded. "Mrs. DeMarco, Bart may be a God-send for Harry and all these children." He paused. "After this tournament is over, may I meet with Bart to discuss how he could help us?"

Rosa nodded. "I'll talk to Bart."

Chet offered and Rosa took his card. "Let's cheer Bart on to victory," Chet said. "We can talk later."

They moved up to where Mike Wright's ball lay. Rosa moved next to Angela. "Stay close Angela. Make sure Bart can see you." She paused. "I think he needs to get a good lead while you are here." She looked down, then engaged Angela's eyes. "He wasn't the same yesterday, after you left."

Surprised, Angela looked at Rosa. "But, he won."

Rosa nodded. "Yes, he won, but he struggled."

Mike had hit a good drive, about 30 yards short of Bart's. Mike took a smooth swing with a seven iron and landed the ball on the green, about 30 feet from the hole. There was polite applause.

They all moved up to Bart's ball. Bart stood in the fairway behind his ball, studied the shot, then closed his eyes and exhaled slowly. He opened his eyes, glanced at Angela, smiled and addressed the ball. He lofted a nine iron onto the green and about 10 feet from the cup. The gallery erupted with applause and calls of support. Bart heard any number of stutters.

Mike Wright two putted for a par. Bart lined up his putt, studied the break and the line, closed his eyes to visualize the putt, steadied his breathing, he then rose from his crouch behind the ball, glanced at Angela, smiled and stood over his putt. He rolled the putt into the heart of the cup for a birdie and a 1up lead. The youngsters in the gallery were delighted with their hero. Angela called out encouragement and flashed a smile.

Mike Wright played like a champion, but Bart simply played better. Bart was 2up after nine holes. He picked up one more on the back nine and when they completed the first 18, Bart was leading 3up!

It was time for the Thespians to leave. With a one hour break, the second 18 would not start until 2pm.

Bart went to Angela. "I'm a bit sweaty, so I won't get too close."

Angela shook her head, smiled up at Bart, "no chance," she took Bart in her arms and kissed him. "You are doing great, Bart." The sentiment was echoed by the group with Angela. Bart looked at them, "Dave, Jim, Betsy, Jessica, thank you for coming. It means a lot to me." He paused. "But, you all better get going, traffic can be a bear."

They all looked down, away from Bart's eyes. "Bart," Jim said, "Angela said she isn't coming home with us."

Bart smiled, he kissed her. "I love you, Princess, but no!" He stated firmly. "You can't bail out on the people who are counting on you."

"I want to be with you, Bart." Tears sprang to her eyes. "I want to be here for you."

"You are, my love." He smiled, glanced over to a group of young people lined up to talk to him, collect his autograph. "I have to talk to these kids, then get out of the sun and cool down." He looked at Angela. "And, you have to go wow them on stage." He kissed her, looked to Dave and Jim, "guys, please take my girl back to Gloucester."

Angela looked stricken, but nodded, ran to Bart and kissed him. "Be great, Bart." She urged. "You too, my love," he responded as he moved to speak to the assembled children and their parents.

Bart watched her walk away. He took a deep breath and engaged with the children. Then, he met his family in the grill room for lunch and a cool drink. He sat, looked to Dave Gilliss and Mario. "Not a bad morning."

Gilliss studied Bart. "This morning doesn't matter." He insisted. "One shot at a time."

At 2pm, the golfers and caddies assembled on the 1st tee. Both felt better after lunch and a chance to escape the heat.

Mike Wright approached Bart, smiled and shook his hand. "You played great this morning." He paused. "You have a real future in this game. Stick with it, Bart."

"Thanks, Mike." He smiled.

Bart had the honor and struck a solid drive. The gallery of youngsters afflicted with the challenges that Bart faced and, in truth, would always fight, cheered loudly. Bart looked to his family, who cheered and shouted encouragement.

Celia looked at Rosa and moved close. "Angela wanted to stay." She shrugged. "Bart told her that he wouldn't hear of it. That she owed the cast and crew of the play to be there." She took Rosa's hand. "Angela left here crying."

Rosa grimaced. "Just like my boys." She glanced at Franco. "Just like their Dad." She shook her head. "Stubborn and hard headed they are, just like their Dad!" She repeated with a shake of her head. "Bart needs Angela here!" She stated, her frustration evident.

Celia met her gaze. With a steely determination, she responded. "You and Dad raised good men, men with character." She paused. "You should be proud."

Rosa sighed, embraced Celia. "I am," she smiled. "Of course, I am." She paused, softened. "And, I think both my boys chose wonderful girls."

"Please tell Angela," Celia urged, "she so wants your approval."

Rosa nodded. "I will." She smiled, "I love Angela." She eyed Celia, "and, thank you, Celia."

Mike Wright came to play. He began the second 18 by birdying the 2nd and 5th holes, to slice Bart's lead to 2up. Bart was still playing solidly, Dave Gilliss was in his ear with encouragement and support. The gallery of youthful supporters cheered wildly. A nice surprise, Mike Brentano, the golf professional from Cape Cod appeared in the gallery encouraging Bart. And, as always, his family was there for him. Still, when he looked over, he didn't see Angela.

When they stood on the 9th tee, Bart's lead had shrunk to 1up. Mike had the honor and launched a nice drive which landed on the right side of the fairway. As it was into a breeze, he still had 190 yards into the green.

Bart huddled with Dave Gilliss, "remember Bart," he began. Bart smiled, and continued the thought. "Swing with ease into the breeze." They laughed together. Mike Brentano saw that as a good sign. Bart was loose. He swung smoothly and absolutely crushed his drive. It landed dead center on the fairway and a mere 135 yards away from the pin. The gallery was festive. Bart was in position A and Wright had a challenging second shot.

Mike Wright felt a tinge of panic. He stepped away and took a few deep breaths. When ready, he addressed the ball and swung hard. It was bad right off the face of the club. It flew well right, in the direction of a large pond.

"Oh God!" Mike called out. The ball rocketed to the bank of the pond, where it struck a granite outcropping. The ball bounced high and unbelievably away from the pond and toward the green. The ball hit the green and rolled out toward the hole.

"No," cried Harry Knowlton, as the ball rolled into the cup for the most improbable eagle that either Dave Gilliss or Mike Brentano, golf pros both, had ever seen. The crowd was stunned into silence.

Bart shook his head and smiled. He looked at Dave Gilliss. "I guess they call that 'the rub of the green.'" He looked over to Harry Knowlton and gave the youngster a smile.

With 9 holes to play, what had moments before had appeared certain that Bart would have a 2up lead, the match now stood all square.

Dave Powers picked up Jessica, Betsy and Angela to take them to the school theatre to prepare for their production.

Angela climbed into the back seat with Betsy. She noted that the usual cheer was absent. She looked at Betsy, who looked away. She eyed Jessica closely. "So, Jessica, what are we hearing?"

Jessica glanced back, forced a smile. "They expect a full house tonight."

"Really?" Angela commented, a pit forming in her stomach. "Okay Dave, please tell me."

Dave pulled the car over, turned and faced Angela. "Bart's lead is gone. Something crazy happened on the 9th hole, but the match is all square."

Angela looked stricken. Tears filled her eyes. "This is my fault!" She insisted.

Dave shook his head. "That's crazy talk, Angela." He laughed. "Come on, you know Bart, he likes to win in dramatic fashion." He smiled. "Bart would tell you to do your job, sing great." He paused. "Bart will be fine."

The almost magical break of luck on the 9th hole lit a fire under Mike Wright. He birdied three of the next five holes, while Bart, playing consistently, made par on all five holes. With 4 holes to play, Wright was leading Bart 3up. Bart's family continued to offer encouraging smiles and comments. The rest of the gallery was silent, but still determined to hang in with their hero. The engraver readied his tools to, once again, inscribe Michael Wrights name on the trophy.

On the 15th tee, Dave Gilliss pulled Bart aside. Dave watched Wright, noted his relaxed demeanor, his joking with his caddie. He was acting differently than Gilliss had seen him over the first 32 holes.

Wrights caddie made certain that his player understood. "Win one hole and you are the Champ." He grinned. "Hell, Mike, if you halve two holes, you win." He studied Wright. "DeMarco has to fire at pins, he has to gamble, so you need to play smart, play safe." He glanced over at Bart. "The kid is really talented, but he's only 17, let him dissolve under the pressure."

Dave Gilliss was again Bart's coach. "Bart, you are better than this guy." He fixed Bart with determined eyes. "I know that you have had some bad breaks, but these kids need you to show them what you are made of."

Bart looked at the youngsters, he noted that Harry Knowlton was near tears. He flashed a smile and a nod. "Bart, you are 'the Diamond Maker,'" Gilliss insisted. "It is pressure like this that makes you better, stronger." He poked his shoulder and reached for his ace. "You don't want to let Angela down!" Dave looked into Bart's eyes. "Do It, Bart!"

The cast was readying to take their places, so the crew could set their lights and all the props could be positioned, when Dave Powers and Jim Perry entered the theatre. Jessica ran to Dave, hugged him. He looked over at Angela, and spoke softly to Jessica, "Bart's in trouble. He's 3 down with 4 to play."

Angela saw the expression on Dave's face, read his body language, and walked over with Betsy. She looked into Dave's eyes. "Is it bad?"

Dave forced a smile and shrugged. "Angela, I'm sorry, but Bart's 3 down with 4 to play."

Angela's eyes filled and she ran backstage, followed by Betsy and Jessica. "I should have stayed with him!" The tears flowed. "Bart needed me and I left." She collapsed onto a folding chair.

"No Angela," Jessica retorted, sinking to her knees to be at eye level with Angela. "Bart insisted that you head home and live up to your commitments." She paused. "That's what Bart is doing, and he expects the same from his girl." She looked to Betsy for support. "'Team DeMarco,' remember, Angela."

Betsy jumped in. "That's right, you have to show the same courage that Bart is showing." She took Angela's shoulders. "Do you think Bart is dissolving because he's behind in a match?"

Angela looked at Betsy, "behind? He's 3 down with 4 to play, Betsy. Do you know what that means?"

Betsy laughed. "Angela, do you forget that I am also in love with a crazy golfer?" The girls laughed, even Angela managed a smile as Betsy continued. "After Jim plays, he describes his shots, his putts, everything." She nudged Angela. "He even acts out his swings," Betsy rolled her eyes. "I smile and appear so interested and fascinated by his stories, I even ask questions, so he'll know that I'm paying attention." She paused, grew serious. "I do that because I love him." She stopped and met Angela's eyes. "You taught me how to really love a guy, Angela. Now, you need to believe in Bart, to think good thoughts, and to go on that stage and give a great performance. Do it for Bart, Angela."

Bart dug deep and birdied the 15th, 16th and 17th holes, to square the match. The momentum swinging totally in Bart's direction. The young fans applauded as Bart ran in putts of 8 feet on 15, 25 feet on 16 and a tap in birdie on 17, when Bart's tee shot to the 240 yard par 3 stopped inches from the cup. Harry Knowlton and the other boys and girls looked adoringly on their hero. They now knew in their hearts, that their stuttering, like Bart's, was an obstacle to be overcome, rather than a disability from which they could not recover.

Rosa DeMarco looked at Bart and knew her boy was so special. She walked with Franco, Lucia, Mario and Celia to the 18th tee. She swelled with pride that Bart's siblings were so dedicated to their brother. And, that Bart was interacting and conversing with the children who looked at Bart so adoringly. When siblings support each other, rather than tear at each other, which is all too common in families, it is clear the parents have done something right.

Bart and Mike Wright met on the 18th tee, and like boxers meeting in the center of the ring to begin the final round of a fight, they shook hands. Wright, having experienced so many such battles, smiled at Bart. "Great comeback, Bart."

"Thanks, Mike," Bart responded. "I've learned a lot from this match."

"That's kind of you to say, Bart." He smiled. "Let's finish this and good luck."

Bart nodded, "same to you."

Bart teed his ball on the long par 5. He stood behind his ball, looked down the fairway, picked his target line and closed his eyes to visualize the shot, and to steady his breathing. He smiled, opened his eyes and addressed the ball. He swung smoothly and crushed his best drive of the day, splitting the fairway and opening the door to go for the green with his second shot.

Mike Wright admired Bart's drive. "Great drive, Bart." He said. He then teed his ball and took a controlled swing, hitting his drive onto the fairway, but 50 yards short of Bart's. It would be a three shot hole for Wright and Bart had a decision to make.

As they left the 18th tee, Bart called for his young fans to walk with him down the fairway. The children formed a half circle directly behind and wrapping around Bart in an arc. Their parents fell in behind them, and Chet Knowlton recognizing an opportunity had the 'YES' banner carried behind the group. Photographers snapped photos and TV crews filmed the happy group stride together up the fairway.

The group arrived at Mike Wright's ball. Bart hushed them and made certain they stayed still. Wright hit his second shot safely up the fairway, short of the pond that protected the front of the green. There was also a steep slope after the pond, just short of the green. A ball landing on that slope would roll down into the pond. He smiled at Bart, knowing Bart had the ultimate risk/reward shot upcoming.

Bart had 225 yards to the flagstick, and 210 yards to clear the pond and slope. Bart stood with Dave Gilliss and together they considered Bart's options. Mike Wright stood aside, watching the 17 year old sizing up what would be the toughest golf shot of his young life.

Dave quietly explained that Wright had played the hole strategically. He had hit a drive that required a lay-up second shot. Then, he hit his shot to his best wedge distance. Dave eyed Bart. "He's playing you, Bart. He could not get to the green on his second shot, but wants you to try to hit your second shot 225 yards into the teeth of a two club wind."

Bart nodded. "Yes, I see that." He laughed. "I saw that when he did not put a full swing on his drive." He considered. "But, he may have done me a favor." He eyed Gilliss. "I can get there and be putting for eagle and the win."

Dave Gilliss eyed the confident Bart, looked to Mike Brentano and nodded. "So, Bart, what club do you want to hit?"

Bart put his hand on a hybrid, but nodded to Dave Gilliss's suggestion that he hit a 5 metal instead. Bart pulled the fairway metal and stood behind the ball, eyeing his line and target. Bart closed his eyes and visualized hitting a high fade that would land on the front of the green and roll back to the pin. He saw Angela in his minds-eye smiling. He then moved over the ball. He glanced at his youthful gallery, winked at Harry Knowlton, and readied himself to swing.

The production was playing to a standing room only crowd. The Director had been appraised of Angela's dilemma, and he was proud of how well she had carried on. He had seen Bart arrive the previous evening and watched Angela's eyes light with joy.

As the play proceeded, the Director was approached backstage by Sal Siracusa and engaged in a lengthy discussion. The Director initially shook his head, but Sal persisted. Finally, the Director smiled and nodded. "I'll do what I can." He promised.

Between scenes, Angela tried to discreetly find out what had happened in the match. She worried that Bart had lost and needed her, and she wasn't there to offer comfort. Then, she was back on stage singing and dancing as she and her fellow cast members performed.

It was about 9:30pm when the Director appeared on stage and addressed the audience. "Did you enjoy the show?"

The audience cheered enthusiastically.

He smiled. "As this is the final performance," he began, "Would you like an encore of some of the songs and dances?" The audience applauded heartily and called out various numbers.

Of course, the young men called for Jessica to reprise her song and dance, 'Dance 10, Looks 3.' Jim nudged Dave. "She does look good doing that song." Dave just grunted.

Jessica smiled at Dave and shrugged. The music played and Jessica danced and sang to the delight of the audience. Betsy also had an opportunity to do her song, 'Nothing.' She happily sang and danced, frankly surprised that the audience would want to hear her sing again. The audience called out for Angela's song, 'What I Did for Love,' but each time the Director called on other cast members to sing.

At a bit after 10pm the Director walked to center stage. He looked at the audience. "Did you enjoy the Production?" His question was met with a thunderous ovation. He waited for the audience to settle. "I think we will close the evening with a reprisal of 'What I Did for Love.' He turned to the cast and asked Angela to join him.

With Angela standing beside him, appearing so small next to the tall, robust Director, he smiled, and addressed the audience. "I'll let you in on a little secret. When Angela arrived this evening she was deeply distraught. You see Angela loves a young man, Bart DeMarco, who I am sure you have heard of and read about. He played today in the finals of the Massachusetts Amateur golf tournament." He laughed. "I do not know anything about sports, but I am told that it really is a big deal." He looked at Angela, winked at her and continued. "Angela wasn't sure she could go on and perform tonight, you see Bart was not doing well." The audience groaned.

"In fact," the Director continued. "Bart was just about beaten when she began tonight." He nodded, "Angela am I over-stating?" Sadly, she shook her head.

The Director continued. "It was her friends who convinced her that," he laughed, pointed to Asst. Director Beth Nelson, raised his right arm, dramatically; "the show must go on!" He laughed. "And, didn't Angela perform wonderfully?"

The audience applauded for Angela, who curtsied in response.

"Now, for our little surprise!" He paused for dramatic effect, smiled at Angela, then, he faced the audience. "I have the distinct privilege and honor to present the new Massachusetts Amateur Golf Champion!"

Angela looked up to the Director with a hopeful expression. "Really?" she whispered, almost afraid to voice her hopes.

The Director gave Angela a beaming smile, pointed at the entrance doors and proclaimed, "Gloucester's own, Bart DeMarco!"

In a purely show business display, the theatre doors opened and Bart entered, with his family. He held the trophy, which had the names inscribed of every champion, back to 1895, high above his head. The audience leaped to their feet and applauded as Bart walked down the center aisle, his eyes riveted on Angela, and ascended the stage. Angela had her hands to her face, crying happy tears. Betsy and Jessica came to her and the three friends embraced. When Bart moved across the stage, he handed the heavy trophy to one of the male cast members and embraced Angela. "We did it, Angela." He stated, triumphantly, "We did it!"

The audience and cast applauded wildly. The spotlight was kept on the happy couple, until the Director tapped Bart on the shoulder. "Hey Champ," he began. "Angela has to do her song," he looked to the audience. "Do you think Angela should sing for Bart?"

The audience erupted, proud of their hometown boy and happy for a family so many knew and respected.

Bart smiled and moved aside. He beamed a loving expression at Angela. "I would love that," he stated. "And, today is Angela's 17th birthday." He announced to the audience, which happily applauded Bart's cheerful proclamation.

The cast stood on line, silently, Bart moved to stand on the wing of the stage, giving the stage to Angela. The lighting crew shone a small spotlight on Bart. His eyes were fixed on Angela, who stood center stage. The spotlight on Angela was soft and flattering. Angela turned from facing the audience and directed herself to Bart, smiled and sang to him; 'What I Did for Love.'

"Kiss today goodbye, the sweetness and the sorrow,
Wish me luck, the same to you,
But I can't regret what I did for love,
What I did for love…

She sang for Bart with her heart full of joy. Bart watched Angela with glowing eyes. Rosa, holding the arm of Franco, stood silently watching her son, so accomplished and so in love. And, now, a hero and a role model to a large group of children struggling with speech, just as Bart had. She watched Bart and again wondered how much of the humiliation he endured had help shape the compassionate and mature man he was becoming.

Angela slowly moved to Bart, as she sang, and draped her arms around his neck. She completed the song while looking into his eyes and softly said; "I love you." He held her to him and Angela kissed him with a passion that was all consuming.

Chapter Twenty-Nine

There was much to celebrate and Maria Curcuru prepared an elaborate feast for Angela's birthday and to celebrate Bart's victory.

That Sunday morning, well over 200 newspapers, nationwide, ran the Associate Press photo of Bart, flanked by his gallery of youthful stutterers striding up the 18th fairway. The headlines declared;

"Bart (Stutter Boy) DeMarco, wins the Mass. Amateur."

The article chronicled Bart's battle with stuttering, his efforts to overcome the condition and his championing the drive to help the young overcome the confidence sapping affliction.

In the piece, the writer referenced Coach Gilliss's nickname for Bart, 'The Diamond Maker.' Gilliss was quoted as explaining that Bart never seemed to feel pressure on the golf course. He used Bart's second shot into the 18th green, in the Mass. Amateur, as a classic example of Bart's ability to block out irrelevant fears from his mind.

"It was the biggest shot of his life," Gilliss attested. "But, Bart just lined up the shot, in his usual way, smiled and hit a brilliant shot to within two feet of the hole."

When asked, Bart shrugged. "Playing golf really isn't pressure." He stated. "Standing before a class and trying desperately to pull the words from your mind and speak them, clearly and without stuttering, before a group of peers ready to laugh at you, mock and ridicule you." He eyed the reporter. "That is pressure!" He sighed. "Failing to perform, because you can't speak, when an entire city is watching you fail, again!" He paused. "That is pressure!"

The reporter, moved by Bart's explanation asked, "how did you overcome what I understand, was a serious stuttering condition?"

Bart smiled. "I was lucky, I had the steady support and love of my parents and siblings. I had the help of speech specialists and of therapists, and at a critical moment, when I was emotionally at my lowest, an angel came into my life. She believed in me and offered love and unconditional support."

Maria had urged Angela to invite her friends, Betsy and Jessica, with their boyfriends as Maria had called Rosa to assure that the DeMarco's would celebrate with them. An added bonus was that Angela's father, Sal Curcuru, had returned from fishing to share in the joy.

Maria felt such contentment that Angela now had friends she cherished and who valued her. Maria knew the pain Jessica Arnold had piled unmercifully on Angela for so long. And, in truth, she was still battling with her emotions concerning Jessica. But, for Angela's sake, she was praying for the forgiveness that did not come easily to a mother who had witnessed her child's pain.

They had all been operating under considerable stress over the past weeks. Bart, in particular, had been taxed with the demands of performing for the dozens of colleges that were watching his progress, while competing against experienced and talented players, who were using all their skills and craftiness to defeat him.

Angela, had been wonderful in her performances in 'A Chorus Line.' And, of course, the dramatic conclusion, played out before the community, had been thrilling. And, Bart had never wavered, in his support of Angela and in his commitment to excellence. Bart had directed so much credit to Angela. More, much more, than Angela believed was deserved.

Still, Angela had endured weeks of stress over her feelings that she was letting Bart down, when he most needed her. Angela regretted becoming involved in the Summer Theatre production, which, while fun, had placed her in a quandary. She had seen, and remembered, Rosa's face and her pleas for Angela to stay. Angela felt that Rosa had disapproved of her choices. And, she so wanted Rosa's approval.

While emotionally exhausted, Bart, Angela, Rosa and the DeMarco family had withstood everything thrown at them and battled through to victory.

Maria had spent the previous day making her crepe like, manicotti shells, as well as mixing the special ricotta and egg filling. It was a great deal of work, but she was expending energy to overcome the anxiety that she felt, as she wondered what was happening. Her thoughts were of Bart, and of Angela.

As she cooked, she prayed, asking St. Peter to help Bart. And, she knew Bart loved her manicotti, and her brascioli. So, she prepared the rolled and stuffed steak with care. Maria cherished Bart. To bring a smile to Bart's face and a blush to Angela's, she made garlic bread.

Rosa rose early, strangely energized after the exhausting but exhilarating previous day, to make homemade cannoli and Italian cookies. Lucia worked with her mother, gathering ingredients and assisting in every way possible. As they worked together, Rosa asked Lucia if she needed to discuss any problem or concern. Lucia smiled. 'How does she always know?' She thought. Lucia sighed, looked to her Mom with hopeful eyes. "Mom, could you talk to Dad and see if Sal could join us today?"

"You like this boy?" Rosa asked her daughter, with raised brows.

Lucia nodded. "I do Mom, I really do." She paused. "You know Mom, it was Sal that talked that Director into prolonging the show so Bart could make that entrance."

Rosa laughed, "Bart hated that!"

Lucia nodded, "I know he did, but Bart did it for Angela." She studied her mother. "Bart would walk through fire for Angela."

Rosa nodded, "and Angela would do the same for Bart." She looked at Lucia, "Okay, first, you talk to Bart. If he is okay with this, then I will ask your father." She paused, studied her daughter. "Lucia, is this boy really worth all this?"

Lucia's eyes filled. "I know, Mom, I know. Sal was really mean to Angela." She paused. "I can't justify that, and I'm glad Bart broke his nose." She looked her mother in the eye. "But, I think Sal really regrets all of that. When I called him and asked him to go to the Theatre and somehow give Bart time to surprise Angela, he immediately agreed." She smiled, brightly. "And, he did it for Bart and Angela. He helped give them a special moment they will always cherish." She took a deep breath, her eyes filled, she looked to her mother, "that has to count for something."

The gathering at Angela's was festive and relaxing. The meal was outstanding. Bart smiled, "thank you, Mrs. Curcuru, this meal is delicious." He flashed a smile. "And, this garlic bread is so tasty." He turned to Angela. "Did you make the garlic bread, Angela?"

Angela blushed as she met Bart's eyes. "No, actually, I didn't," she said with a smile. Betsy, leaned close to Angela, "oh, we so have to talk about this." She winked.

Bart made sure that Angela was the center of attention. It was her birthday celebration and he had asked his Dad and brother to refrain from doing more than acknowledging his victory with a toast. "I only won a golf tournament," he stated. "And, I wouldn't have done that without Angela."

Sal Siracusa sat with Lucia. As they dined, Angela made a point of thanking Sal for helping convince the Director to wait and allow Bart to arrive. "Sal," she smiled. "I'll remember last night for the rest of my life."

Sal looked at Angela, he nodded, "thank you for saying that Angela." He met her eyes. "Thank you for everything." He squeezed Lucia's hand.

Bart grinned as he eyed Sal, "I'm not sure I like you holding and squeezing my sister's hand, Sal." Jim Perry and Dave Powers burst out laughing, Betsy and Jessica tried to stifle a smile, as Lucia shot a hot look at Bart.

They sang happy birthday to Angela over a tower of cannoli with a glowing candle atop the sweet treats. Angela beamed as she looked around the room at her family and friends.

"Speech, speech," Dave Powers called out.

Angela nodded and rose. "Thank you, Mom, for making this wonderful meal," She glanced at Bart, flashed a smile. "Of course, all of Bart's favorite dishes." That drew laughter. "I guess you all can see who my Mom's favorite is." She looked at her sister Tina, "it's not you or me, Tina!" She joked.

Tina laughed, "Angela, I just hope I haven't slipped to 5th place." That drew additional laughter.

Angela continued. "Mom, you even made garlic bread," she said, with a sweet smile and raised brows. "How thoughtful."

Maria beamed a bright smile at Angela. "I thought you'd appreciate that."

"Mrs. DeMarco," Angela continued, "The cannoli and cookies are so tasty, and after all that you went through yesterday! Thank you."

Rosa looked at Celia and then Angela. "Angela, you and Celia are like daughters to me." She paused. "Celia calls me Mom," she looked at Maria, "if your mother is agreeable and if you want, I would be honored if you would call me Mom as well."

Maria's eyes flooded with happy tears, she loved Bart and would be thrilled if Bart and Angela someday married. She looked at Angela and nodded her assent. Angela rose and moved to Rosa and embraced her. With joyful tears pooling, she said, "that means so much to me, Mom."

Bart looked on smiling. 'It is a good day,' he thought.

Rosa held Angela close, she spoke softly, "Team DeMarco! Right Angela?" Their eyes met, both were crying. "Thank you for helping my boy, Angela. I love you."

Angela heard those words with sweet relief. Her fears evaporated and she embraced Rosa. "I will always love Bart!" She stated, firmly, but softly. "Thank you, Mom."

Looking about the table, Mario saw that Celia was crying as was Rosa, Maria, Lucia, Tina and Angela's friends. "What are all these tears about?" He asked, nudging Celia. "You'd think the pasta was bad?" Bart, Jim, Dave and the two Dad's joined in the laughter.

Maria looked about, smiled broadly. "You guys are awful," she said amiably. She eyed Bart and smiled. "Did you enjoy the garlic bread, Bart?"

Bart grinned, flashed a glance at Angela, who blushed, "I always do, I love your garlic bread, Mrs. Curcuru."

Maria eyed Bart with an impish smile. "Mrs. Curcuru? Really Bart?" She angled amused eyes at Bart. "Even after Angela tells you that you're my favorite, you call me Mrs. Curcuru?"

Bart smiled at Angela's Mom. "Please forgive me," he started. "I love your garlic bread," He paused, glanced at Angela, winked, returned his gaze to Mrs. Curcuru, "Mom!" Smiles spread across the room.

Sal, Lucia and Tina joined the three couples in Angela's living room. Always, the good hostess, as her mother taught, Angela with Tina's help, brought a pitcher of Arnold Palmers and a large plate of Rosa's Italian cookies. As she looked at the cookies, Angela thrilled at the memory of Rosa whispering, 'Team DeMarco,' to her.

Jim lifted his glass, "to Bart DeMarco, our teammate, our friend, congratulations on the Mass. Amateur, and here's hoping that you are on your way to the PGA tour."

"Here! Here!" the group called out. Angela cuddled close, beaming a smile, kissed Bart's cheek.

Bart flushed, looked at Jim, "thanks Jim, but tomorrow, I hope to lump a couple of fishing boats." He laughed. "That's a long way from the PGA tour." He stated, with a laugh. Bart paused, eyed Jim. "I hear that you made the cut for the club championship at Bass Rocks."

Jim smiled, "I did. In fact, I'm only five strokes off of the lead." He smiled proudly, looked to Betsy, dressed prettily in a flattering sundress, who beamed a sweet smile at Jim.

Bart nodded. "Okay, Jim, next Saturday and Sunday, you play for the Championship." He eyed Jim. "And, I'll be on your bag."

Jim sat back, suddenly, but temporarily, speechless, he swallowed. He looked at Betsy, the petite blond flashed her loving smile at Jim.

"You would caddie for me?" Jim asked, a note of incredulity in his tone.

Bart smiled. "Of course, who knows your game better than me?" He punched Jim's arm. "We're friends, right?"

Jim nodded. "Absolutely, friends forever." It was said with conviction.

"And, we'll be there to cheer you on," Angela stated, as she misted. "Right Betsy?"

Betsy nodded, as her eyes filled. "Of course, Angela," she paused, dabbed at her eyes. "Thank you."

"Jim," Dave added, with a smile. "Jessica and I will be there, too." He looked to Jessica, who nodded in agreement. "Oh God," Dave called out. "Look at them, they're all crying again." Indeed, all five girls were crying happily.

Lucia looked at Bart, took Sal's arm. With tears running down her cheeks, she said, "no matter how mad you make me, Bart." She managed a smile. "You are the best!"

Bart laughed. "Well today is Angela's birthday celebration." He looked into Angela's eyes, melted her heart. "I have a present for you." He paused, raised his hands, "but before we do presents," he turned to face Sal, "Sal, please tell us how you convinced the Director to delay the closing of the play."

"Yes," Jessica nodded. "He's tough, how did you pull that off?" All eyes turned to Sal.

Sal took a deep breath. "Well, Lucia called me. She asked me to speak to the Director, to delay the end of the play, to give Bart and his family time to arrive." Sal grinned. "Lucia instructed me to not let Angela know how Bart had fared." He jokingly saluted Lucia. "Mission accomplished, General!" He teased.

Lucia smirked. "Funny Sal," but her eyes shone and her smirk devolved into a warm smile.

Angela shook her head as she eyed Lucia, who smiled and shrugged in return.

"So," Sal continued. "I went to the Theatre and found the Director and suggested he delay the close of the play so Bart could arrive and surprise Angela." He grinned. "The Director looked at me as if I was crazy." Sal laughed at the memory. In a nearly perfect mimic, Sal quoted the Director, "you want me to compromise our production to announce the winner of a golf tournament?"

Sal shook his head and laughed. "He said 'golf tournament' like it was a dirty, smelly thing."

Everyone laughed. "That sure sounds like our illustrious Director," Jessica sneered. The group was interested. "So, how did you convince him?" Betsy asked.

"I explained that the Mass. Amateur was a big deal." He paused. "I told him that for the first time, a Gloucester guy won the tournament and that the audience for his play were Gloucester people." Sal looked down, seeking to remember the conversation as accurately as possible. He nodded, looked back at the group. "Then, I told him that it would add luster to the play, the newspaper would cover the play in greater detail, because it was the venue for the big announcement."

Sal smiled, nodded. "I added that the media will certainly want to interview you, as the Director, and you will be able to plug your upcoming projects." Sal grinned. "I saw his wheels spinning, then, he said, okay, 'as long as I direct how it plays out.'"

Bart shook his head. "That's amazing, so he directed that entrance?"

Sal nodded. "He sure did, he played it all out for me. And, set up cameras and video to record it all." Sal continued. "So, I waited outside the doors for your arrival," he shrugged, "the rest you know."

Sal paused, looked at the group, and focused his eyes on Angela. "I really wanted to do this for Angela." He met her eyes. "I owed, at least, that, to Angela."

Sal then looked at Bart and laughed. "And, I knew Bart would hate it," he grinned. "But, I was good with that, in light of how Bart made me squirm that Fiesta Saturday evening, when I came to collect Lucia for our date."

Bart laughed and nodded. "I guess that's fair, Sal."

Angela rose and embraced Sal. "Thank you, Sal," she choked out, through her tears.

Sal held Angela. "I'm so sorry, Angela." He spoke softly, "I hope someday you will be able to forgive me."

"Hey, easy there Sal," Bart said with a smile. "Angela's my girl." With that Sal and Angela parted, both choked with emotion.

Bart sat back as Sal re-seated himself by Lucia. "Sal, that was impressive," Bart stated. "Man," Bart continued. "You're a future John Palermo."

Sal nodded. "That would be nice," he said in a still choked voice. He cleared his throat, sipped his Arnold Palmer, looked at Lucia and smiled. "How do you like the idea of me as a lawyer?"

Lucia met his smile. With a casual aloofness, she responded. "You'll have moved on by then. I doubt you'll even remember me."

Sal looked into Lucia's eyes, "I'll be right here, Lucia." He paused. "There'll be college," and he grinned, "maybe law school," he took her hand. "But, I will still want you."

Lucia gulped, patted Sal's arm and smiled, "I hope so," she said softly. She wiped a tear from her eye, looked at Bart, "so, what about Angela's birthday presents?"

Presents!" Betsy exclaimed, as she moved to retrieve and present the gift from Jim and herself.

"Me, first," Lucia called, smiling happily, as she handed a prettily wrapped package to Angela. Angela opened the package to find a framed photograph of Angela perched on Bart's shoulders, her legs wrapped around him as they engaged Mario and Celia in a water battle. Angela was smiling and wet, her eyes shining and her black hair slicked back and glistening.

Angela studied the photo, looked at Lucia, "I didn't know you took photos." She paused, studied the picture, noted Bart's dazzling smile. "That was a great day," she stated. She looked at Lucia, "Thank you, Lucia, this is special."

Bart studied the photo, leaned in and kissed Angela. "I love you in that bikini."

"Stop Bart," Lucia chided. "You're making her blush."

Tina grinned. "Angela, I told you that bikini would be a hit." Tina then handed Angela her gift. Angela opened the wrapped box and held up a sheer, red dress. Tina smiled. "I hear Bart likes to see you in red."

"It's beautiful, Tina." Angela exclaimed. She held it against her, eyed Bart. "Pretty fancy, Tina."

"Something tells me that you will need some big girl clothes." Tina stated, with a laugh. She smiled at Bart. "That guy is going places." She stated. "And, you'll need to be dressed properly."

Angela embraced Tina. "Thanks, Tina," Angela said, as she held her sister. "I love you."

Angela opened the presents from Jim and Betsy and from Dave and Jessica, before Bart handed her a package. He touched her hand and smiled. "I hope you like it."

Angela opened the jewelry box to find a gold and ruby bracelet, which matched the necklace he had given her for Christmas. Angela smiled and kissed Bart. "I love it, Bart," she paused. "And, I love you." She put the bracelet on and showed her girlfriends. "Isn't it beautiful?"

"That will look great with the dress." Tina offered.

"Lumping must be good!" Dave quipped.

Bart smiled, he looked at Angela. "What I do, I do for 'Team DeMarco!'"

Angela loved the sound and the heartfelt meaning behind Bart's statement. She met Bart's eyes and her love for him could not be any clearer.

Jessica looked from Bart to Angela, took Dave's hand and nodded. "It is beautiful, Angela." She smiled. "You are two very lucky people."

Chapter Thirty

Angela arrived home before her 11pm curfew. She moved softly into the bedroom she shared with Tina, so as not to disturb her sister.

"Hi Angela," Tina, now 15 years old, said softly. "Did you have a nice birthday party?"

"Oh, did I wake you?" Angela asked. "Sorry."

Tina lay in her twin bed, wearing a light nightgown, her sheet and blanket were folded back, as the night air was warm and humid. The windows were open, and a cooling sea breeze was detectable. "No, I was awake," she hesitated. "I have been wanting to talk to you."

"Okay," Angela responded, as she changed out of her cloths and into her nightgown. "Give me a few minutes to wash my face and I'll be back."

When she returned, Angela switched on the lamp by her bed and lay back, offering a contented smile. "So, what's up, Tina?" She focused in on Tina's face and even in the shadows cast by the lamp she could see her sister was troubled. Angela sat up, worry surging to her eyes, stiffening her back. "Are you okay, Tina?"

Tina forced a smile, even as tears pooled in her eyes. "I have to tell someone, Angela, I'm so scared."

"Scared!" Angela moved to Tina's bed. "Why scared, Tina? Is somebody bothering you?" She looked closely at Tina. "Do you want me to call Bart?"

Tina shook her head. She managed a weak laugh. "I'm so glad you found Bart." She paused, dabbing at her eyes. "He makes you so happy." Fresh tears flooded her eyes. "But, Bart can't help me with this, Angela."

Angela took her hands. "Talk to me, Tina." She squeezed her hands and felt a tremor of fear. "What is it?"

Tina took a deep breath. "Angela," she began, hesitantly, "I'm gay." The tears flowed. "I don't know what to do." She searched Angela's face, expecting shock or condemnation. She saw neither.

Angela took a deep breath and visibly relaxed. "Oh, is that all." She smiled and pulled Tina into a hug. "Everything is okay, Tina." Angela exhaled letting the fear flow out. "Thank God, Tina. You had me so scared." Angela sat back and smiled as she searched Tina's face. "Tina,"

Angela comforted. "You can only be who you are." She paused. "Is there more?"

"You're not shocked?" Tina asked, surprise in her tone and expression.

Angela smiled. "No, Tina, I'm not shocked or surprised or upset." She paused, held her little sister, "I've suspected for a few years that you were gay." She smiled. "Bart and I discussed it when we were in Florida."

Tina sat up. "You told Bart?" She put her hands to her mouth. "Oh my God!" She exclaimed.

Angela shook her head and smiled. "No, Tina, Bart told me!" She stated. "He's a very sensitive, observant guy." Angela said, as she embraced Tina, soothingly rubbed her back. "Tina, you can trust him. It was Bart that told me that it was important that I accepted you, for who you are." She grinned, eyed Tina, as she sat back. "Bart told me that you can only be who you are." She laughed, leaned forward, in a conspiratorial tone, she added. "Please don't tell Bart that I called him sensitive."

Tina smiled. "No," then thinking of Bart, she laughed, "of course not, we can't have big, tough, Bart DeMarco, the athletic hero, be called sensitive, now, can we?" At that the sisters embraced and laughed together.

Angela grinned, raised her brows. "Tina, you have no idea how stressful it is to constantly need to stroke a guy's ego." She saw that Tina had relaxed.

Tina breathe deeply, let the stress just flow out of her. She felt as if a big weight had been lifted off of her shoulders. Tina was able to breathe freely and to smile. She looked at her sister, raised her brows and grinned. "Angela, I see your eyes when you look at Bart. There is nothing about Bart that you don't just love to stroke!"

"Tina!" Angela exclaimed as she laughed. "I have no idea what you're talking about." The sisters laughed together for a long time.

Finally, Tina looked to Angela. "Will you help me tell Dad and Mom?"

Angela hugged her. "Of course I will. I'm your sister, I will be here for you."

Chapter Thirty-One

Phil Walleston arrived at his office in Manitoba, Canada. He was the President and CEO of Manitoba Oil. His company had recently discovered an enormous oil deposit and working with the Canadian Government was drilling wells and constructing a pipeline. Thousands of jobs had been created and the central Canadian Province was thriving. Of course, there were the environmental terrorists to deal with. Individuals and groups that compared fossil fuels with the Devils work. Of course, these extremist groups, championed by super-rich entertainers and lobbyists, would use their private jets to attend rallies against the production of the very jet fuel that was re-filling their airplanes fuel tanks.

Phil just accepted this hypocrisy as the price of doing business in a developed nation. No, this morning, Phil was distressed to the point of tears over the scene at his breakfast table. Phil's 10 year old son, Justin, had hysterically refused to go to school. Phil and his wife, Heather, while livid, were trying to stay calm and ease Justin's anxiety about going to school. Justin was traumatized and refusing to face the ridicule and humiliation heaped on him by students who mock and bully him over Justin's pronounced stutter.

The previous day, three bigger boys had restrained him and duct taped his mouth. "See, now you won't stutter, stupid!" They taunted. And, sadly, not one student came to his aid. Of course, when a teacher came on the scene, Justin was freed and helped to the nurse's office, but the damage was done.

The three boys were expelled over the protests of their wealthy parents. The Manitoba Academy was always reluctant to lose big donors, but Phil Walleston had threatened, both civil lawsuits and criminal prosecution, if action was not immediately taken. Of course, none of which helped 10 year old Justin. Phil and Heather had finally settled on letting Justin stay home for a few days, meet with his therapist and speech counselor.

Phil sat at his desk when his longtime secretary and friend, Ruth, entered his office to review the day's schedule. Ruth immediately read

Phil's eyes and asked, "Is it Justin?" Phil broke down in re-telling the sad tale. "Ruth, he's terrified!"

Ruth, who loved the Walleston family, felt anger rise to her throat, but knew anger would not help. "One minute," she said and raced back to her desk, returning with the Winnipeg Gazette, and showed Phil the story heading the front page of the sports section of Bart's victory in the Mass. Open. The significant part of the story was the photograph of Bart striding up the 18th fairway, followed by close to 100 youngsters and their families cheering for 'Stutter Boy.'

"Maybe you could show this to Justin," Ruth suggested. "It might give him hope."

Phil wiped his eyes and blew his nose. As he read the story and studied the photo, he began to calculate a way to help Justin, his company and Canada. He looked at Ruth, "thank you, Ruth." He smiled. "Please clear my schedule for the next few days, I won't be in."

Monday, being a busy day on the docks, Bart landed two lumping sites. Then, he went to Bass Rocks to spend the afternoon practicing, with a renewed focus on his short game. Watching certain of his competitors demonstrate superior short games, chipping and putting so effectively, had made an impact. Bart knew he had to improve that critical area of his game, if he wanted to continue to compete at the highest levels. He had won the Mass. Amateur in large part due to his superior ball striking and his length off the tee. He now knew, that to be able to challenge the best players, his wedge game and putting had to improve.

Dave Gilliss was surprised to see Bart. "No need to rest?" He asked the new Massachusetts Amateur champion.

Bart laughed, "I rested yesterday, now it's back to work." He paused, angled a grin at his coach, "the high school golf season is coming, I have a lot of work to do." Bart paused, and grew serious. "Dave, I need to improve my short game." He eyed his coach and grinned. "Okay, I concede that you have mentioned that a few times."

Dave Gilliss smiled. He recognized the heart of a champion and he felt that Bart had the makings of a great golfer.

Bart practiced for two hours, then played a round with a threesome of young players that had been inspired by Bart, and all the publicity that had been generated by his winning the Mass. Amateur. These young athletes spurned football and soccer and sought to play on the Gloucester High School golf team. It seemed that golf was going mainstream.

Coach Dave introduced the young athletes to Bart. The Coach read their surprise, and awe, so, he began by easing the anxiety of the aspiring players.

"Guys, relax," Coach Gilliss encouraged. "When Bart first started, he was all promise and no skill." He grinned at Bart. "Now, he's improving."

Bart laughed. "It's true guys. My game was rough." He paused. "Work hard, listen to Coach and you will be golfers." He smiled. "Just relax, focus and let's have fun."

Bart had a pleasant afternoon. He enjoyed offering tips and encouragement, and noted that the aspiring golfers listened and learned.

As he was a member of Bass Rocks golf club, he left his clubs in bag storage and ran the three miles home. He showered, relaxed a bit as he chatted with his Mom and Lucia. Lucia was insistently pleading with her parents about their 'archaic demand' that she be 16 years old before she was allowed to date. "Mom, that's another seven months!"

Rosa smiled, "you'll have to discuss that with your father," She insisted. Lucia felt that Sal Siracusa had been slowly winning over the DeMarco's, and most importantly, Angela, who Lucia looked upon as a sister.

"Dinner at Angela's tonight?" Rosa asked with a smile.

Bart nodded. "Yes, Angela made a point of asking me to be at her house for dinner tonight." He smiled at his mother. "Mom, since Dad and Mario will be out fishing for about a week, how about we call Celia to join Angela and us for dinner here tomorrow?" He smiled and winked at his Mom, "I guess we could ask Lucia's boyfriend," he looked at Lucia with a look of uncertainty. "Lucia, what's that guy's name?"

Lucia grinned, looked to her Mom with hopeful eyes. Rosa laughed. "Sure, let's invite Celia," she paused. "And, Sal, too."

Lucia jumped up, kissed Bart and her mother and ran to the phone. Bart watched her go, looked at Rosa, "Mom, what do you think of Sal?"

Rosa considered the question. "My children have always shown good judgement." She pursed her lips, "Still, I'm not sure about this one," she shrugged. "But," she paused. "Lucia seems to like him." She sighed. "I guess that we should give him a chance."

Bart casually and happily whistled a tune as he walked to Angela's house for dinner on a beautiful summer evening. He thought of Angela and smiled. When he arrived, he smiled as he knocked at the door and, to his surprise, walked into the eye of a storm as he entered Angela's home.

Angela met him at the door, went into Bart's arms and kissed him. "I'm so glad you're here," she said with a relief that belied the concern he read in her eyes.

"Are you okay?" Bart asked, cautious eyes studying Angela. "What's wrong, Angela?"

Angela nodded. "I'm fine, but Tina just told my parents that she is gay and has a girlfriend." She sighed. "It's not going well."

Bart nodded, "I see," he held Angela's shoulders, looked into her eyes. "Do your parents want me here?" He asked with a sincere concern. "This is family business."

Angela's eyes filled. "Bart, you are family!" She insisted, as she felt a shiver of fear. "I really need you here." She pleaded, as she studied his face.

He smiled, and kissed her. "If my girl needs me, then I am here." He pulled her close, softly and reassuringly, he stroked her back. "God, I love you so much!" He soothed. "Take a deep breath, Princess." He won a smile. "Let's go," he laughed, "into the fire!" Angela took that breath, exhaled and wondered why she had the slightest doubt or concern that Bart would fail her. 'He never has.' She thought, and smiled.

Bart held Angela's hand as he led her into the kitchen. He quickly assessed the room. Mr. Curcuru seemed equal parts enraged and confused. Maria looked stricken, as if she had suffered a loss and was grieving. Tina was crying, feeling helpless. She looked hopefully to Bart, who took a deep breath, flashed her a smile, and walked to greet Angela's Dad and firmly shook his hand.

"Good to see you, Sir," Bart said, offering a smile. He moved around the table and kissed Maria. He winked, "you okay, Mom?" His use of 'Mom' brought a smile and a recognition that Bart was not shocked and appalled. His calm, supportive greeting helped to relax the mother of four. Then, Bart went to Tina, pulled her up and into a hug. He whispered, "Tina, it will be okay. Believe me, it will be okay."

Bart and Angela sat, holding hands. Sal Curcuru sat erect, perched on the end of his seat, hands on the table as he glared at Tina. "You bring shame to our house," Sal stated. He looked to Maria, who began to cry, "Maria," he gestured at Tina. "I don't understand."

Bart reached his hand to still Tina. His eyes instructed her not to respond harshly. Tears flowed down her cheeks, "I'm sorry," she said softly, "I'm so sorry, Papa."

Bart took a deep breath, looked to Angela's Dad and asked, "Sir, may I speak?"

Sal Curcuru nodded. Bart read the pain and the shock in his eyes. He also saw the love for his daughter, that, he was certain, Sal could not, at that moment, verbalize.

Bart looked to Tina. "Tina," he asked softly. "How long did it take you to understand and accept that you are gay?"

Tina eyed Bart, as she wiped her eyes. She sat back, deep in thought, considered the question, looked at Bart. "About two years, I guess."

Bart smiled, reached over and ruffled her hair. That friendly, big brother, gesture brought a smile. "Okay," Bart started. "If it took two years for you to come to understand and accept who you are, isn't it reasonable to give your parents some time to come to terms with this?"

Tina nodded. "I guess so," she agreed. She looked at her Dad.

"Tina," Bart said with a smile, "this is out of left field for your parents." He glanced at Sal and Maria, looked back to Tina. "You have to give them time to process all this." He paused. "They need time to grieve."

"Grieve?" Tina and Angela asked simultaneously, with surprise. Angela squeezed Bart's hand.

"Yes," Bart said, looking at Tina. "They need to grieve the death of their expectations for your life." He saw that Tina was not quite grasping the concept. He took her hands. "Tina, your parents always expected that you would marry, have children." He smiled. "Now, you tell them that you are gay, and everything is different." He glanced at Sal and Maria. "You need to give them time to accept a whole new reality." He watched her closely. "Tina, your Mom and Dad love you," He smiled and patted her hand. "Give them time to grieve and to accept."

Angela looked at Bart with awe. "I hadn't thought about that." She smiled at him. "You're a pretty smart guy for a jock." She teasingly added. All present felt the tension lighten.

Maria studied Bart, even Sal looked at him with a more open expression.

Bart addressed the table. "It will take time to digest all this." He paused. "Maybe, Tina will never have children." He smiled, sat back, glanced at Angela. "I guess, after we marry, Angela, we'll have to quickly give your Mom and Dad grandchildren to love and enjoy."

Angela looked at Bart, surprise, almost shock, registering on her face. Bart had mentioned marriage and children so casually, and with such certainty, as if it were a foregone conclusion. Her surprise quickly bloomed into a dazzling smile.

Angela's joy was contagious. Maria beamed a smile at Angela, loving the sound of Bart's words, and the joy his simple declaration brought to

Angela. Tina saw her Dad and Mom begin to relax and, maybe begin, what would certainly be, a long process of accepting the new reality.

Bart addressed Tina. "Why don't you give your Dad a hug?" Tina tensed, fearing rejection. Bart smiled and nodded. "Tina, your Dad loves you." He nodded. "Go hug your Dad."

Tina rose, uncertainly, she looked to her Dad, who had risen and opened his arms, even as tears flooded his eyes. Tina rushed into Sal's arms. "I love you, Papa," she said as she clung to her Dad. The hug held for a long time as Sal finally managed, "I love you, Bambina."

Angela's eyes were wet, as were Maria's, Tina's and Sal's. Bart looked on smiling. He said nothing as Maria and Angela joined in on the group hug. When they slowly parted, wiping their eyes and faces, Bart shrugged, "wasn't I invited here for dinner?"

Maria nodded as she laughed. "You were!" Then, she raced into Bart's arms. "Thank you, my boy, thank you, so much." She smiled up at Bart. "And, thank you for loving my Angela."

Maria looked to Tina. "Come Tina, help me finish dinner." She walked to her husband, their eyes met, she read his pain, "thank you," she kissed him. "You are a good man." Maria hugged Sal, gently touched his face and wiped the tears from his cheeks. "Please, relax in the living room, I will bring you a glass of wine." Maria looked to Angela, "you make your boyfriend a cold drink and go sit on the deck with him."

Bart and Angela sat together on the loveseat, enjoying the early evening air. "You are amazing," Angela said, with a look of awe.

Bart pulled her into a hug, "even for a jock?" He laughed. He kissed her deeply, passionately.

Chapter Thirty-Two

Dave Powers, excitedly, went off to Georgia Tech to pursue an engineering degree. A new chapter in his life was opening before him, and he thrilled at the challenge. Jessica began her senior year of High School, a bit depressed and uncertain of her future with Dave. She was looking at various fine art colleges, with her target being the exceptional theatre program offered at NYU. Still, she often lamented that if she was accepted into NYU, she and Dave would be on two very different life trajectories.

Angela and Betsy continued to encourage her, reminding Jessica that Dave really cared for her. "Fight for him," Angela urged, remembering Beth Nelson's advice. "There will be challenges," Angela agreed. "But, if you love each other, challenges can be fun rather than defeating."

Bart and Angela continued to maintain their exceptional academic record. They were considered to be the leading candidates to win the Sawyer Medal, the highest and most prestigious academic award given annually at Gloucester High School. As there would be one winner, they often joked about swaying the committee's votes.

"How could I ever expect to beat the wonderful, Bart DeMarco?" Angela would lament, with a grin. "I am just a humble student, hardly a match for the Mass. Amateur Champion."

Bart would laugh and respond; "I know your game, Princess," he would pull her close, to savor the feel of her body against his, "You constantly distract me with your beautiful face and lush body." He'd shake his head and kiss her. "How could I possibly focus on my studies, with such distractions?"

The Golf Team, led by Bart and Bass Rock Golf Club's new club champion, Jim Perry, was providing excitement to the student body of GHS and receiving newspaper coverage usually reserved for the football team. The team was vastly improved under the guidance of Coach Dave Gilliss. Athlete's that might well have played football or soccer were eyeing golf. In many cases, the parents of those student-athletes were delighted that their sons were not exposed to the joint injuries and concussion risks inherent in football and soccer.

Galleries composed of parents, students and teachers were regularly attending matches. Bart, of course, was the draw, hitting his long drives and dominating all opponents. Coach Gilliss hoped that interest would continue to grow in Gloucester. The team glided to the State Tournament, winning more than 90% of their matches. Bart, the designated #1 player, won every match he played. Jim was also dominant as the #2 player, piling up points in every match.

Bart, who was admired by the young and novice golfers, helped Coach Gilliss inspire the younger players, stressing the importance of physical conditioning and mental toughness. For the most part, he left the swing instruction to the Coach. He spent part of every Saturday and/ or Sunday with the children of YES. He loved telling Angela about every breakthrough he witnessed and in which he participated. So many of the children brought back memories of his youth, which Bart believed helped him to relate to their challenges and to help them gain confidence.

Coach Gilliss and Bart looked to the near future. Bart spoke of repeating as Mass. Amateur Champion. Dave Gilliss had bigger things in mind. Gilliss wanted Bart to enter the U.S. Amateur Championship. "Let's go big, Bart," Coach Gilliss urged.

The U.S. Amateur Championship is and long has been, a title cherished and won by some of the greatest golfers ever to play. The Champions include the legendary, Bobby Jones, 'The King,' Arnold Palmer, 'The Golden Bear,' Jack Nicklaus, and, of course, Phil Mickelson and Tiger Woods.

Coach and player discussed the Pacific Amateur Tournament to be held at the Pebble Beach Golf facility. It was a four day tournament to be played at the Spyglass and Pebble Beach golf courses. It was very prestigious and considered a prelude to the United States Amateur Championship.

The tournament, in which Dave Gilliss had registered Bart, as the Massachusetts Amateur Champion, would be played the week following Thanksgiving. Of course, cost would be a factor. Plane tickets, rooms, food and incidentals on the Monterey Peninsula were a challenge, but Bart had worked hard, lumping boats throughout the summer and even when back in school. Dave made it clear that he would be there for Bart. And, Bart, with Dave's constant guidance, worked on his ever improving game.

One evening, after dinner at Angela's, she and Bart sat to watch a movie. Angela cuddled close to Bart on the couch, limited in their ability to do more by the presence of Maria, who was in and out of the kitchen. Angela smiled, kissed Bart, and rose. "I'll make us some popcorn," she said, as she happily went to the kitchen. Bart used her absence to switch to the Golf Channel. The 'Golf Central' announcers were discussing the rumors circulating of a new tournament to be scheduled opposite 'The U.S. Open.'

The U.S. Open has long been recognized by many in the world of golf as the premier tournament in the world. The U.S. Open Championship, a title that eluded the great, Sam Snead, winner of 82 PGA titles, is played in June and is the 2nd major championship played each year. Snead, a remarkable athlete, had won the other three majors, The Masters, The Open Championship (often called the British Open), and the PGA Championship. Snead had seemingly blown golden opportunities to win the coveted Championship, and complete the 'Career Grand Slam.' He once remarked, in somewhat bitterly recalling those tournament losses, that "of all the hazards, fear is the worst."

The shows hostess, a pretty blond, was stating that a meeting, held in Ottawa, Canada, with the Canadian Prime Minister, the PGA Commissioner and a potential Tournament sponsor outlined a plan to hold the tournament in Manitoba in Central Canada. Manitoba Province, is bordered by the Provinces of Ontario to the East, Saskatchewan to the west and the U.S. States of North Dakota and Minnesota to the South. The Tournament, to be called, 'The Manitoba Classic,' would benefit local charities as designated by the sponsor and be given full PGA recognition. The tournament winner would receive a two year PGA exemption, invitations to all the Major championships and all the WGC tournaments.

It would be a life changer for whoever won. With the World's top players competing in the U.S. Open, it was a rare opportunity for a lesser known player to step into the Big Leagues. The PGA insisted that the sponsors provide a full PGA purse, with the winner earning more than $1 million.

The Golf Central analyst, with close ties to the PGA, described the possibility as a "win all around." He looked at the pretty co-host and offered, "Lisa, for the players who did not qualify for the U.S. Open, it is an opportunity to make money and improve their professional status. For the PGA, it is a golden chance to demonstrate that they represent more than the elite players." He nodded, "and for the Prime Minister, it brings another major sporting event to Canada." He laughed. "And, of course, it's great for The Golf Channel, because while the network carries the U.S. Open, we can broadcast the new tournament."

Angela entered with a tray holding a big bowl of popcorn and glasses of ice tea for Bart, Angela and Maria. Bart flipped the channel back to the movie, '12 Angry Men,' which Angela referred to as research for her role in the Theatre's fall production.

Angela noted Bart watching The Golf Channel. "Would you rather watch golf?" She asked. "I can always watch the movie some other time."

Bart laughed. "No, I was just trolling the sport stations." He winked. "I want to watch the movie with you and see how many kisses," he wiggled his brows, "and whatever, I can steal."

Angela grinned and leaned close, she whispered, seductively, "Bart, you don't have to steal what is willingly given."

Bart closed his eyes. "God, give me strength," he said softly, for Angela's ears only. "I think this girl is trying to kill me."

Angela laughed, as she leaned in and kissed him.

Bart lumped as many fishing boats as he could, heading to the docks each morning, Monday- Saturday at 4:30 am. Sophie 'the Bull' made his best efforts to secure lumping jobs for Bart, who continued to average three-four jobs per week. Lumping fishing boats was hard work, but it was lucrative. Bart needed the money to fund the upcoming journey to Pebble Beach. On the days that no lumping jobs were available for him, he would thank Sophie, smile and assure Sophie he would be back tomorrow.

As Bart was something of a local athletic hero, he was treated well, but pushed hard. He would tell Angela how the lumpers would taunt him with calls for 'the Star' to move faster, work harder. 'Come on star, nobody to carry your bag here,' they would snipe.

Bart loved watching Angela's eyes as she would become enraged in his defense. He would smile and hold her. "I love when you fire up to fight for me," he would say. "But, the guys are just treating me like a rookie." He would kiss her. "It's actually a compliment," he'd explain. Angela couldn't really see how being insulted and taunted could be a compliment, but would inevitably laugh as Bart told comical stories of incidents on the docks.

Angela continued in the Theatre group. They were preparing for the fall drama. This year, Mrs. Nelson chose, '12 angry jurors,' an adaptation of the play and movie, '12 Angry Men,' starring Henry Fonda. Angela preferred musicals, but with Bart so busy with school, work, golf, getting ready for the Pebble Beach Tournament, and helping with YES, she was keeping busy and spending as much time with Bart as possible.

Her friendship with Jessica and Betsy continued. Jessica often commented that Dave's calls were becoming less frequent. Angela read fear in her eyes. One day after rehearsal, Jessica looked to Angela and Betsy and said sadly, "I think I'm losing him." The girls did not know what to say, because frankly, it appeared that Jessica's fears may well be grounded in reality.

The next day at dinner, Angela asked Bart if he had heard from Dave lately. Bart hesitated, gave the question some thought. "No, I haven't, but he should be home for Thanksgiving break soon."

Coach Gilliss had been correct, the new head football Coach pushed Bart hard to play quarterback. Bart even had calls and letters from college football coaches. Coach Bailey reminded Bart that if he played football, rather than golf, with his strong academic record and physical talent, he could attend a great University, such as Boston College, which boasted a top 25 national academic standing and an ACC football conference schedule. The added bonus is that he would be close to home.

Bart admitted to himself, that staying close to home had some appeal. However, Bart had committed to golf, as he had promised. And, as expected, the calls and letters from college golf programs poured in daily. Still, interest in Bart, the still blossoming 6'3", 180 pound, fleet footed and strong armed quarterback remained. He was seen as an unusual talent. In discussions with Angela, he toyed with the idea of playing football. "I could be close to my girl," he would say. "If, I play college golf, I almost certainly will head South or West."

One night, after dinner at Angela's house, where this discussion was had, Bart and Angela drove to a secluded spot overlooking Gloucester Harbor. They were alone, away from the world with all the demands and conflicts. At least for the moment, Angela had Bart to herself. She looked at Bart, held his hands and looked into his eyes. "Bart," she began. "I so want you to stay close." She took a deep breath. "I am terrified that you will go away and all those pretty, flirty, college girls will turn your head."

Bart opened his mouth to respond, but Angela put her fingers to his lips and shook her head. Bart understood that Angela wanted to finish her thought. Angela kissed him and continued. "Bart, I want what is best for you," she paused. "And, I think we both know that golf is your future."

She teared up, and was angry with herself for doing so. She took a deep breath and continued. "If you find someone else, it will break my heart, but, I will still want what is best for your future." A tear escaped and trickled down her cheek. "I want that, because I love you."

Angela wiped at the tears, eyed Bart, fire flashing in her eyes. "Just remember, nobody, no matter how pretty, will ever love you like I love you."

Bart smiled, kissed her softly. "Princess, you are my future." He held her close. "We are 'Team DeMarco,' remember?" He kissed her and held her as if he could not get enough of her. "Someday, I am going to make you my wife." He smiled. "I am going to take care of you and our children, I will work hard," he promised. "And, you, are going to be there for our children and," he grinned, "for me."

Chapter Thirty-Three

In, what was becoming a happy tradition, the Curcuru family joined the DeMarco's for Thanksgiving dinner. Celia was also present with her parents, Nina and Joe Scola, and her sister, Jackie. Having the families of his son's girls at his dinner table delighted Franco. There was a wedding to plan and as the Scola's wanted the DeMarco's to be informed and involved, Thanksgiving Day, seemed an opportune time for the families to meet and plan.

In the proud Gloucester tradition, Bart and Angela attended the Thanksgiving Day football game, played this year at Danvers High School. They were a part of a Gloucester contingent of over 3000 fans who braved the crisp, cold day.

"It feels and smells like snow," Bart stated as he held Angela close. Angela, bundled against the cold in a warm coat, pretty scarf and a knitted wool cap and gloves, smiled at Bart, excited at the news that he had been asked to play in a professional golf tournament.

"It's going to happen for you," Angela enthused. "Pebble Beach next week, then next June your first professional tournament." She smiled up at Bart. "I am so proud of you."

Bart gently kissed her lips. He grinned, "Princess, your lips are cold." He snuggled Angela close. "I hope IT," he smiled and searched her eyes, "whatever IT turns out to be, is happening for us, Princess."

Angela nodded and flashed a smile. She so wanted to believe, but insecurities die hard.

Bart and Angela ran into Jim and Betsy at the concession stand as they sipped a steaming cup of hot chocolate. Jessica, the cheerleader captain, was on the sidelines cheering on 'The Fighting Fishermen.' Bart wasn't ready to share the news of the invitation to the Manitoba Classic, just yet. It was all so overwhelming, he wanted to receive the letter and consider the offer, discuss it with Angela, his parents and Coach Gilliss. Bart suggested that the group meet at Bart's house later that day, to have some dessert and catch up.

Over 35 family members and friends crowded the DeMarco home. There was a palpable excitement in the air. The telephone call the previous evening from Phil Walleston, President and C.E.O. of Manitoba Oil Company, was a surprise, maybe, in truth, a shocking development. Manitoba Oil was the title sponsor of the Manitoba Classic. Mr. Walleston had offered Bart a Sponsor's exemption to play in the first Manitoba Classic. He had said a written invitation would soon arrive.

Bart was stunned to realize, that he would play, as an amateur, in a PGA tournament. Mr. Walleston had requested that Bart speak to his son, Justin, and perhaps help the youngster to learn ways to cope with his stutter and the emotional scars he had suffered. Bart stated that he would be happy to try to help Justin Walleston, as he had helped the children of YES. In the conversation with Mr. Walleston, Bart had mentioned his planned trip to Monterey to play in the Pacific Amateur.

Phil Walleston saw an opportunity. He offered to fly Bart and his caddie/coach to California, in his company's private jet, put them up at the Pebble Beach Resort, and attend the tournament, with his family. "It would be an opportunity for Justin to get to know you." The CEO added.

Walleston suggested that after the Pacific Amateur, they all fly to Manitoba, on the way back home from the Pebble Beach Tournament. He offered to have them stay with the Walleston family, study the course and advise him on ways to create a school for young stutterers. "We have to find a way to help these young people," Walleston affirmed. "And, Bart, you are the right guy to help me."

The Manitoba Classic was scheduled for June the 13th through June 16th. The dates were important as Mario, Celia and her parents had set Saturday, June the 15th for their wedding.

It was a splendid Thanksgiving feast. Bart had two servings of Maria's lasagna, and a big plate of turkey, his mother's sausage stuffing, mashed potatoes, all liberally covered with Rosa's creamy turkey gravy. Bart looked across at Mario with a cheeky grin, "so, do you think Celia will be a good cook, Big brother?"

Nina Scola, Celia's mother laughed. "My Celia will be a fine cook," she winked at Mario, "and a good wife."

"Thanks Mom," Celia eyed her soon to be brother-in-law, as Mario laughed. "We'll do just fine," Celia asserted as she kissed Mario and flashed a smile at Bart. Smiles bloomed across the table at Celia's statement.

Eyeing pretty Celia, Uncle Vito chuckled, "I think Mario will be plenty happy with Celia while she learns to cook."

Mario nodded his agreement, pulled Celia close, "remember, little brother," Mario smiled. "Man does not live by bread alone!"

Bart reveled in their happiness. He winked at Celia as he pulled Angela close, "you are so wise, Mario," He grinned. "I'm certain Celia will keep you a happy man!"

"You said it, guys," Uncle Jimmy agreed with a big laugh and a wink. "It is so nice to be young." He sighed. "I remember it well."

Relaxing over espresso and Tiramisu, Mario, Celia and their parents sat in the den discussing the forthcoming wedding.

Celia began, "first thing, Dad, I'm sorry, but we have to push the wedding back one week to June 22nd." She smiled, that smile designed by God, to be used by cherished daughters to melt her Dad's heart. "Bart is playing in a big golf tournament on the weekend of June 15." She sat back and took Mario's hand, and explained. "This is a big opportunity for Bart and he is our Best Man." She shrugged. "And, we really want him at the wedding."

Celia's father studied his daughter. He read her resolve, recognized and appreciated her devotion to Mario's family, nodded and returned her smile. "Celia," he said softly, "that means we will have to cancel and re-book the Church, reception hall, band, photographer, everything" he raised his hands in resignation. "We may lose some of the wedding vendors, Celia." He didn't mention the loss of the deposits that were paid to reserve the date.

Celia smiled at her father, "Dad, we are sorry to cause this problem, but Bart just received this huge opportunity yesterday. And, he really has to play."

Franco patted Joe Scola's knee. "You have a beautiful and remarkable daughter." He smiled at Celia. "I want to help with whatever costs are caused by this change."

Joe Scola glanced at his wife, Nina, and shrugged. "Thank you, Captain," he began. He smiled at Mario and Celia. "Of course, weddings are about family. We will do our best." Celia rose and ran into her Dad's arms. "Thank you, Daddy," she gushed. "Thanks for understanding."

While the wedding discussion was playing out, Bart and Angela were entertaining Jim, Betsy and Jessica in the kitchen. Jessica was in tears as she explained that Dave had ended their relationship the previous evening. "He found somebody else," she cried. "Dave said she was very sweet." Bart and Jim eyed each other, then Bart told Angela they would leave so Angela, Betsy and Jessica could talk. He looked to Jessica, shrugged and offered,

"I'm sorry, Jess." He touched her hand. "I'm really sorry." With that, the two young men rose to leave the ladies.

Bart stopped at the doorway, turned and looked at Jessica. He hesitated before he walked back, knelt before the seated Jessica. He took her hands. "Jess, I'm not too good at this and you know I like Dave." He paused, looked into her eyes. "But, Jess, you deserve a guy who loves you and wants you." He squeezed her hands, glanced at Angela. "If Dave doesn't want you with all his heart, it's better, for you and for Dave that you move on." Feeling parched, he licked his lips. "I know you're hurting, but you have a real goodness in you. The right guy is out there." He insisted. "Give it some time," he urged. "Try to keep smiling and let him find you."

Jessica's eyes flooded with tears. "Bart," she choked. "I really love Dave." She wiped her eyes. "Dave is the reason that you and Angela are now my friends." She sobbed and bowed her head. "He pushed me to do the right thing. To apologize to everyone that I hurt." Tears ran down her cheeks. "Bart, I really want Dave."

Bart smiled. "Give it some time, Jess." He repeated. "Take time to sort out your feelings, don't rush into anything." He rose, flashed a smile at Angela and walked with Jim out of the room.

The three girls watch him and Jim go. Jessica managed a smile, "too much emotion for the guys," she said softly. She looked at Angela, managed a smile, "by any chance does Bart have a brother?" That brought laughter, even Jessica seemed a bit lighter in spirit.

Angela looked at the door. "Yes," she grinned. "He has a brother, and, right now they are planning his and Celia's wedding." She paused, grew serious as she considered Bart's words to Jessica. "He's right, you know," Angela said. She looked to the doorway from which Bart and Jim had left. She looked back at Jessica. "Bart has a knack for really feeling the pain of others." She paused and nodded, flashed a smile. "Pretty amazing for a jock," she commented wryly. The girls all smiled. She grew serious. "It's as if he remembers all the pain and humiliation he suffered," she said softly, almost reverently, "but he is never bitter or angry." She looked at the girls. "He's mature beyond his years, he's amazing!"

Jessica looked at Angela. "So are you, Angela." She took a deep breath. "I was so cruel to you, and you responded with kindness." She shook her head. "Others would be rejoicing in my pain, especially with you having such an incredible guy," she paused, "but not you." She felt tears burn her eyes. "You want to help me." She looked at Betsy. "We are lucky to have you and Bart as our friends."

Betsy nodded in agreement.

Angela wondered at the conversation in the den. She was aware of the conflict, and hoped it could be worked out. She didn't want Bart to be forced to make a choice between family and his future.

Chapter Thirty-Four

The day after Thanksgiving Bart received his official letter of invitation to the Manitoba Classic. He also had a lengthy discussion with Phil Walleston about his son, Justin. The conversation made clear to Bart that Mr. Walleston had conceived the idea of the tournament, then, convinced the Prime Minister of Canada to persuade the Commissioner of the PGA to sanction the Manitoba Classic as a full-fledged event on the PGA Tour schedule.

Mr. Walleston hoped to attract tour caliber players from the PGA and European Tours who had not qualified for the U.S. Open. His goal was to raise millions of dollars to support the education and treatment of young stutterers.

Bart was impressed. Phil Walleston could have focused solely and exclusively on the treatment of his son, but he had a bigger, more noble purpose. Phil Walleston wanted to help children whose families lacked the resources to effectively help the child who stuttered.

Bart vividly recalled the daily humiliation he suffered as a boy. 'Stutter Boy,' that horrible, demeaning insult, that was hurled at him by bullies and the cruel, who always seem to be with us, had hurt deeply. It had made him afraid to speak, his anxiety rising as he was taunted by peers and called on by teachers. But, now, Bart had a different perspective. 'Stutter Boy,' was and would be a badge of honor. He would be a role model for children like Justin Walleston. He would be a shining light, showing them what they could achieve, if they believed in themselves.

Bart saw the hand of God, in the fact that Phil Walleston had come into his life at a critical moment. Just as Angela had sought him out, on that most difficult evening, to raise him from despair and give him hope and the love he needed, to re-direct his life. He also realized that now it was up to him to take these God given gifts and rise to the top, not just for himself, but for all the children, like Justin, whose spirit and hope rode with him.

Bart and Dave Gilliss spent the next days working on his game. On Sunday, they flew from Beverly Airport on a luxurious private jet, owned by Manitoba Oil, to California, to compete against America's best amateurs.

As they boarded the jet, Bart and Dave met Phil Walleston, his wife, Heather, their 17 year old daughter, Rachel, and 10 year old Justin. They would be together for the next two weeks.

When pretty, red haired, green eyed, Rachel saw the tall, athletic and handsome, Bart DeMarco step onto the jet, she knew that she had met the man of her dreams. Bart shook Rachel's hand as he noted how pretty she was, with her peaches and cream complexion, with a splash of freckles across her cheeks and nose. At 5 feet, 5 inches tall, a willowy body, much like her mother, Rachel looked up to the much taller Bart. She was lost in his warm, brown eyes and easy smile.

Bart was quickly corralled by Phil Walleston as he and Dave boarded the jet. They sat at a comfortable conference table with Justin, whose eyes gleamed at meeting his new hero. Bart meshed with Justin comfortably, giving Justin space to express himself. Bart's personal life story and his work with the children of YES had taught him that when given time, many young stutterers would relax and speak more easily. Justin's Mom, Heather, and Rachel sat nearby on a couch listening attentively to Bart joke and laugh with Justin. Heather noted the tears forming in Phil's eyes as he watched Justin connect with Bart in a way he had never before connected with anyone. 'His boy was happy,' Phil thought as he made eye contact with Heather. 'This just might work.'

The flight was very comfortable. Bart and Dave exchanged a meaningful glance and a laugh when Dave whispered, "this beats the crap out of flying commercial." After the first few hours where Bart and Dave had talked with Justin and Phil, Phil excused himself to deal with some work issues.

Heather and Rachel joined Bart, Dave, and Justin in a game of Monopoly. The 10 year old laughed aloud, music to the ears of Phil and Heather, and even jumped up to dance and taunt his playing partners when he took money off of Bart, when Bart landed on Boardwalk, a property Justin owned. "Oh Yeah, Oh Yeah," He sang and danced, "Yyou owe mme $2000 'Sstutter Boy.'" They all laughed when Bart leapt to his feet and lifted Justin off of the floor, flipping him about, as Justin laughed aloud. "Who are you calling 'Stutter Boy?" Bart challenged the happy youngster.

Rachel's attraction to Bart was immediately noticed by Heather. Heather had smiled when Rachel excused herself, and went to the comfortable, and, for a plane, spacious, bathroom, returning with make-up freshly applied and her hair brushed and styled.

Rachel found Bart to be funny and surprisingly intelligent, for a jock. Of course, Rachel did not say that, but she did laugh at his jokes and engaged him in a vigorous discussion about North America's Environmental groups.

Rachel accepted the environmentalist's arguments concerning global warming, while Bart believed and professed that Environmental Groups use junk science to support their conclusions.

"How can you accept their conclusions? Bart asked with a smile. "So often, they are dishonest in their underlying research?" He offered. "And," he continued, "their habit of personally attacking those who challenge their conclusions." He shook his head. "If you dispute their science, they call you a 'climate denier.'" He shrugged. "And worse." He flashed that dazzling smile at Rachel, which had her knees going weak. "They refuse to honestly debate." He winked at Rachel. "That tells me that they are afraid of facts and truth."

Rachel was lost in his words, his eyes and his smile. Heather watched her daughter with an amused grin. Rachel pulled herself together to respond. "You sound like my father!" Her tone was a mixture of surprise and disapproval.

Bart laughed aloud. He looked into Rachel's eyes. "Did it ever occur to you that your father may be right?"

Rachel looked back at Bart with a thoughtful, but perplexed, expression.

The group checked into the Pebble Beach Resort. Bart and Dave shared a room and the Walleston's had a 3 bedroom suite.

As it was clear to Heather that Rachel was attracted to Bart, the mother sat her daughter down and placed a file on the desk before her. "Rachel, as you know, your father is a thorough man. He has invested a great deal of time, money and the Company's prestige into this new golf tournament. He has chosen Bart to be the face of the Manitoba Classic." She studied her daughter. "He didn't do that lightly. He looked into Bart very closely." She smiled. "He liked what he learned."

Rachel smiled. "I really like him, Mom." She stated, and laughed. "Even if he does sound like Dad."

Heather smiled. "I know you do," she sat across from her daughter and smiled. "This is the file the investigators compiled on Bart."

"File?" Rachel flared, as her eyes roved over the folder. "Dad created a file on Bart." She paused. "Mom, that sounds kind of creepy." She crossed her arms across her chest. "I bet Bart wouldn't like that!"

"Relax, Rachel," Heather explained. "This is not CIA stuff, just background material available on line, newspapers, magazines, school records, etc."

"School records? How do you get school records?" She huffed. "Aren't school records private?"

Heather took her daughter's hands. "The school publishes the names and backgrounds of students admitted into the National Honor Society, for example." She explained. She shrugged. "Bart is a very good student, with a high IQ and significant academic accomplishments." She studied her daughter. "Bart DeMarco is no dumb jock." She paused. "Although, he is an outstanding athlete." She laughed. "I guess you could call him a smart jock!"

Heather opened the folder. "Rachel, there is material contained in this file that you should be aware of, if you want to seek a relationship with Bart."

Rachel narrowed her eyes. "Is Dad against me seeing Bart?" She sat back, studied her mother. "Is it because his family are not wealthy?"

Heather shook her head, her anger flared. "Rachel, really, stop the dramatics!" She demanded. "We, your Dad and I, would be thrilled if you married Bart or another man like Bart." She paused. "Bart and his family are good people." She eyed her daughter. "Rachel, you need to understand that, Bart, his family, and his community are also very traditional people." She took a deep breath. "Look at the file, photographs and the investigator's conclusions, and then we'll talk."

Bart felt somewhat lethargic after the long flight and told Dave that he was going out for a run. He ran along the Pacific Ocean, felt the cool sea spray, tasted the salt on his lips and enjoyed the beautiful vistas. He ran hard, burning off the weariness in his muscles. He concluded his run with a long sprint which took him back to the resort. He stood, re-capturing his breath, looking at the ocean and watched the sun set. Bart then returned to his room to shower and dress for dinner.

The group met for dinner at Spanish Bay. They sat by the outdoor fire pit and listened as the music of bagpipes floated in the air. The music getting closer and closer, until the bagpiper stood and played before the guests. Justin sat by Bart, holding his hand and smiling. Phil Walleston watched his son closely, saw the boy's smile, and the relative ease with which he conversed with Bart. When Justin stumbled, Bart assured him that he never need be anxious with him. As Bart gave that assurance, he thought of Angela on the evening she found him on that bench on Stacey Boulevard. The memory brought a smile.

"Are you excited about the tournament, Bart?" Asked Heather Walleston.

"I am, Mrs. Walleston," Bart stated. "Playing at Pebble Beach and Spyglass will be a treat."

"Is it a bit scary?" Rachel asked. She looked at Bart, who looked quite sharp, dressed in navy pants, a cream colored button down shirt and a red sweater. "There will be a lot of pressure, won't there?"

Bart smiled at Rachel. "Playing golf really isn't pressure." He looked at Dave. "I like what Bobby Jones said about the game. He nudged Justin, before looking back at Rachel, who was prettily attired in a sea green dress, which was cut to show her best features. She smiled as she noted the approving glint in his eyes.

"Anyway," Bart continued, "Bobby Jones said; 'Golf is the closest game to life. You get bad breaks from good shots, you get good breaks from bad shots, but you always have to play the ball where it lies.'" He nudged Justin. "See, Buddy, you and I have a bad lie in the rough of life." He shrugged. "But, even though we stutter and sometimes people make fun of us, we have to play the shot as it lies." He hugged Justin roughly, drawing a laugh from him. "And, we can do it, right, Justin?"

Justin nodded, "we can, Bbbart." he stumbled, looked at Bart with big eyes.

Bart took a deep breath. "No worries, Justin, we will beat this and hit a pure shot, right?"

Justin also took a deep breath and managed a smile. "We wwill, Bart."

"That's right, Justin," his Dad said with a smile. "Bart will help us."

Dave scanned the group, settled his eyes on Rachel. "You know, Rachel, pressure is what turns carbon into diamonds." He smiled at her. "That is why I call Bart 'The Diamond Maker.'" He paused. "Bart just doesn't seem to feel pressure on the golf course, big situations that have others crumbling, seem to bring out the best in Bart."

Rachel looked at Bart and smiled. "So, you're not worried about how you will do this week?"

Bart shrugged. "We believe in preparation and conditioning." He looked to Dave. "I have a great Coach, who is an excellent teacher." He paused. "Starting tomorrow, we will study the courses and practice." He smiled. "We are a team, we work together. We'll do fine." Bart stated with certainty.

"The Pacific Amateur is the most important amateur tournament after the U.S. Amateur." Dave Gilliss offered. "It will be a good test for Bart." He paused and eyed Bart. "And, we'll be ready."

Bart sat at dinner flanked by Rachel and Justin. Phil engaged Dave in a conversation on the finer points of Bart's game. Heather was encouraging Justin to eat, finally recognizing that it was time for Justin to go to bed. Heather excused herself, eyed Rachel, she then left with Justin.

Rachel flashed a pretty smile at Bart, and suggested that she and he retire back to the fire pit to relax and talk. Phil Walleston and Dave Gilliss stayed at the table discussing Bart's game and their expected approach to this tournament. For Rachel, it was the perfect opportunity to be alone with Bart.

As they settled by the fire pit, Rachel snuggled close to Bart. "I saw that you played both football and baseball in school, as well as golf," she stated.

Bart studied Rachel. He smiled, "I guess you saw the magazine article or maybe some of the newspaper pieces?"

"I did," Rachel responded. She laughed. "I saw a photo of you wearing what the writer called oilskins. You were unloading a fishing boat."

Bart nodded, studied Rachel. "I guess you also read about my girlfriend."

Rachel smiled, "I did, Angela, is it?" She gently placed her hand on Bart's knee. "I saw a photo where she was singing to you on stage."

"Yes," Bart responded. "That was the day I won the Mass. Amateur. Angela was in the summer Theatre production of 'A Chorus Line.'"

Bart stood. "I need to head to my room and give Angela a call." He paused, looked down to where Rachel was seated. He smiled as he looked into her eyes. "Rachel, I hope that we can be friends." He paused. "Angela is my girl, I would appreciate it if you would respect that."

Rachel smiled up at Bart. "Of course, Bart, of course." She sighed as she watched him walk away.

Chapter Thirty-Five

Bart and Dave spent the next few days practicing and studying the courses they would play. They worked relentlessly on Bart's short game and putting. Bart had never putted on poa annua greens before and found them to be a bit lumpy.

Dave encouraged Bart to block out the negatives. "You will miss some putts because of those poa annua weeds," he laughed. "Just accept it and move on."

By Wednesday evening Bart felt ready. That evening was the annual Pacific Amateur Banquet and Ball. Heather had Bart and Dave fitted for tuxedos, explaining that photos would be used in the marketing for 'The Manitoba Classic.' She laughed, and winked, "there will be no rented, ill-fitted, tuxedos on my watch."

The event was heavily covered by media. Photographs of the Walleston family, one of Canada's leading families, were run throughout the U.S. and Canada. There was much speculation in the media about the tall, handsome young man who escorted Rachel Walleston, an heir to the Manitoba Oil fortune, to the Ball.

Of course, it was quickly discovered that Bart had won the Mass. Amateur and was considered to be a rising star in the world of golf. That Bart and Rachel were an extremely attractive couple was not missed by the gossip columnists. And, the photo of them dancing, Bart smiling for the camera and Rachel's eyes lovingly locked on Bart was run everywhere, even in the Boston papers. The Gloucester Times picked up the story off of the wire services and the photo and story ran on the front page of the Gloucester Times on the first day of the Tournament.

The more time Heather spent with Bart, the more she liked him. "He's a good boy, Phil. You chose well."

Phil laughed. "Don't give me too much credit. When I saw the photo of Bart walking up the 18th fairway with all those young stutterers, I felt he could help Justin." He smiled at Heather, "the rest was dumb luck."

Heather flashed her smile at Phil. "Maybe," she offered. "But, you did do some background on Bart, his family, Gloucester." She paused. "Not, just dumb luck, I'm thinking."

Phil shrugged. "I like what I learned." He acknowledged. "He's already helping Justin."

Heather thought on Rachel. "You know Rachel is crazy about Bart, right?"

Phil laughed. "Now that would be great, but unlikely." He smiled. "Bart has a girl, and he's a loyal young man." He laughed. "He has thanked me at least a dozen times." He considered. "He doesn't completely appreciate that he's doing more for us by helping Justin than could ever be repaid."

Heather nodded in agreement. "Justin is blossoming, thanks to Bart." She shrugged, "Still, Bart's only 17, won't be 18 until April, you never know."

"True," he grinned at his pretty wife. "But, remember, I knew when I first saw you as a high school freshman."

Heather laughed. "Yes, you cradle robber," she went into his arms, "a senior sweeping an innocent freshman girl off of her feet."

The Wallestons walked the course cheering Bart on. Bart made a point of smiling at Justin, a few times taking the opportunity to speak with him and the family. It was a good first round. Bart finished with birdies on 17 and 18 to shoot a 67. At days end Bart shared the lead with three other golfers.

Before dinner Bart called Angela, with the three hour time difference it was after 9pm when Angela received the call. He was in good spirits. "Hi Beautiful, I really miss you," he said happily. "I shot a 67 today."

"Yes," Angela said. "We saw it on the Golf Channel, Congratulations."

"Really? Wow! The Golf Channel, that's something." He fairly gushed. "Can you believe that?" He paused, thought he had heard a catch in Angela's voice. "Are you okay, Princess?"

Angela felt tears burning her eyes. She fought to keep her emotions under control. "I saw that photo of you and Rachel Walleston dancing at the Ball," she said. "She's very pretty." She paused, wiped her eyes. "Is she nice?"

Bart grimaced. He hated that Angela still harbored doubts, but he understood. He laughed. "Yes, she is pretty, but not Angela pretty." He paused, listened carefully. "And," he continued. "Rachel is nice, but no way is she Angela nice!"

Now Angela let the tears flow. "I'm sorry, Bart." She paused, battling to regain control, and lost the battle. "The photo was in all the newspapers." He heard her anguish. "I'm just so scared."

Bart winced, he hadn't realized, that the photo, which he had believed was just one of the many photos taken at the Ball, would be run in newspapers across the country. Nor, had he seen the gossip columns suggesting a relationship between him and Rachel. Of course, all of it, would have tongues wagging. And, that could only upset Angela. He shook his head in frustration. He took a deep breath. He just wanted to play golf, he thought. He wanted to compete against the best and know how he stacked up. Now this? It was infuriating.

Still, he knew, Angela needed and deserved reassurance, rather than anger. In an understanding tone, he said, "Please, don't be afraid, Princess. You are my girl." He paused, considered his words carefully. "You know, Angela, I can't punch this fear away, like with Sal, you have to believe in me and in our love."

Angela took a deep breath, she felt the fear evaporate, at least, she thought, for the moment. She smiled, and realized that Bart had never given her any reason to doubt him. Her tone lightened. "I don't know Bart," she teased, "you might think about re-considering." She wiped her eyes. "Rachel Walleston is very rich. I can't compete with that."

He laughed, relieved that Angela was okay. "That's true," he said, also in a teasing tone. "So," he drew it out. Angela could visualize his smile. "My choice is Rachel's millions or Angela's garlic bread." He paused and laughed. Angela smiled, took a deep breath and laughed with him. His voice was emphatic as he said, "I want the garlic bread, Princess."

She closed her eyes, sighed in relief. She blushed at the image, but reveled in his love. "Sounds good to me." She offered shyly.

Bart laughed aloud. "Thanks for that, Princess." I wish you were here. I miss you so much it hurts." He paused. "And, please remember, there is only one girl for me, Okay Angela?"

"Okay Bart," Angela exhaled her stress. "I love you. Be great tomorrow," she urged. "I will be thinking of you."

"Princess, you'll be in my mind, helping me on every shot." He paused, "Sleep well, my love."

Angela smiled. "I will, Bart. Call me tomorrow?"

"Count on it, Beautiful," he assured.

Chapter Thirty-Six

Bart played Spyglass on Friday, and posted a strong score of 68. Now, halfway through the tournament, Bart, a High School Junior, was tied for the lead with Billy Ray Boyd, a junior at the University of Texas. They had a four stroke lead over their next closest rival.

Billy Ray, a garrulous 22 year old from West Texas, joked that the legendary Monterey winds amounted to little more than a 'mere breeze' in West Texas. He was big and broad through the chest and shoulders, and hit the ball a long way. He also had 'soft hands,' the golf term for the ability to play difficult and delicate shots around the green. The consensus in the golf world was that Billy Ray was a lock to become a star on the PGA Tour.

As the tournament leaders, Bart and Billy Ray would be teeing it up at 2pm on the Pebble Beach course, 5pm on the East Coast. The Golf Channel was carrying the weekend coverage with their crack team of announcers and commentators. The DeMarco's hosted a family gathering to watch Bart play, and Angela invited Jim and Betsy, as well as Jessica.

After the treacherous 8th hole, where the players second shot had to carry the famous chasm, where the sea and waves crashed and swirled before them, Bart and Billy Ray were both three under par, and had stretched their lead to six strokes over three players tied for third place. The color commentator, Sir Nick Faldo, a winner of six Major Championships and numerous tournaments on the PGA and European tours, speculated. "There is still 27 holes to play, Jim," he began. "And, these two are running away from the field."

Angela sat in a tight group and next to Rosa. Franco and Mario were at sea, no doubt thinking about and praying for Bart. Rosa nervously held Angela's hand. Betsy, Jessica, Lucia, Celia and Tina comprised the group of girls staying close and offering support. Tina stood behind Angela with a comforting hand on Angela's shoulder. The tension in the room was thick enough to cut with a knife, but when the camera found Bart, he seemed relaxed and completely in control. Angela smiled when she saw Bart and thought exactly the words Rosa proclaimed; "look how handsome my Bart is." Her comment, coupled with Bart's apparent ease, brought smiles all around.

Bart stood in the 9th fairway. Both Bart and Billy Ray had boomed long drives. Billy Ray had hit first into the green. Bart then stood behind his ball looking down the fairway to the green. The Pacific Ocean crashing waves to his right. The camera angle was a wide shot showing Bart, the so green fairway and in the background the blue/grey ocean crashing into the rocky shore. The camera slowly focused in for a tight shot on Bart.

"So beautiful," Rosa commented, as she teared up. "Imagine my Bart playing golf there and being on television?"

Bart stood still, studying his shot. The announcers commented on his habit of standing behind each shot, focusing on the shot to be made, closing his eyes, then opening his eyes and smiling as he moved over the ball.

The color commentator offered, "I think he's visualizing the shot he plans on hitting, when he stands and closes his eyes," he suggested. "But, what's going through his mind when he opens his eyes and smiles is anyone's guess."

Jessica grinned at Angela, "I know what, or should I say who, he is picturing in his mind."

Angela blushed, her cheeks reddening. Betsy nudged Angela, she whispered for Angela's ears only, "you are one lucky girl, Angela."

Angela smiled and sighed, recalling Bart's words from last evening's conversation. "I am," she said softly. "I am so lucky."

Rosa heard the exchange. She squeezed Angela's hand and smiled.

Both Bart and Billy Ray finished strong, both shooting 65 to remain in a tie atop the leader board and separate themselves from the field.

The Wallestons walked every step with Bart. Justin leaped into his arms after Bart rolled in a difficult birdie putt on 18 to even the match. Bart was interviewed with the Wallestons standing about him. Rachel, stood close to Bart as he was responding to questions, eloquently, and without a stutter.

"That's the girl, Rachel right?" Betsy said with contempt.

Angela smiled, appreciating the support. "Bart said that she is nice," she looked around, found Rosa's eyes. "I'm not worried, Bart loves me."

Rosa smiled. "Yes, he does." She paused, listening to the interview. She teared up. "He's speaking beautifully," Rosa said proudly, as tears of joy ran down her cheeks.

An on course commentator asked Bart if he wanted to make a comment about the round. Bart thanked him, he spoke in glowing terms about Billy

Ray Boyd. "He was such a help to me, today. He's a good guy and," he laughed, "a really good golfer. Tomorrow should be fun."

"You are 17 years old." The commentator, who hailed from Ireland stated. "When I was 17," he stated, smiling broadly, "I was lucky to finish in the top 10 of a junior club event." He shook his head. "You don't seem a bit fazed that you are playing before the eyes of the world."

Bart saw his opportunity. He hoisted Justin into his arms. "When I was 10 years old, like this guy here," he jostled Justin, provoking a laugh from the boy. "My stutter was so pronounced, that I was terrified to even try to speak." He flashed that million dollar smile. "They taunted and embarrassed me, you know how tough kids can be?" He smiled. "They called me 'Stutter Boy.'" He shrugged. "It really hurt." He looked to Phil Walleston. "The PGA Tour does so much good for so many worthy charities." He smiled. "And now, I would like to introduce Phil Walleston, of Manitoba Oil, the title sponsor for the upcoming Manitoba Classic. The Classic will be a brand new tournament on the PGA Tour next summer." He paused, looked to Mr. Walleston. "It will be played June 13th through Sunday June 16th."

Bart smiled. "Mr. Walleston has graciously extended a Sponsors invitation for me to play in the Tournament." He looked into the camera and flashed his smile, "before I turn this over to Mr. Walleston, I want to say a big hello to my family." He paused, smiled. "Mom, Dad, Mario, Celia and Lucia, thank you, I love you." He pulled Dave Gilliss into the shot. "This is my coach, my instructor, and my friend, Dave Gilliss. He has been magnificent in helping me."

Bart took a deep breath and smiled into the camera. "And, to my Princess, I miss you Angela, I love you." His eyes glittered. "Angela, I could not have accomplished any of this without you." He winked. "Team DeMarco!"

Angela gasped as she watched. "I love you, Bart," she mouthed, as her eyes flooded with happy tears.

Bart moved out of the shot and walked to the scorer's tent where he would turn in his scorecard. The camera followed him and focused on the young women who called to him. Bart waved politely and moved into the tent.

Phil Walleston moved forward and gave an extensive interview on the charitable goals behind the Classic. "We will build a school, staffed with the best teachers, as well as speech therapists and psychologists who specialize in dealing with children with stuttering challenges." He began. "We will offer support to YES, and" he looked into the camera. "There will be no charge for any services we provide."

The DeMarco house was alight with pride. Happy tears flowed when Angela and Rosa embraced. "My boy is special!" Rosa proclaimed. She held Angela, looked into her eyes. "Please, take care of my boy, Angela."

Angela smiled. "I will Mom, I promise."

Chapter Thirty-Seven

B art called home before heading to dinner. He also called Angela and had a pleasant, lighthearted conversation. They laughed when Angela told Bart that his Mom had implored Angela to take good care of him.

"That's my Mom, always looking out for her boy." Bart said with a laugh. "Although, it is a good point she makes," He paused. "I mean, Princess, can you cook?" He laughed. "Food is a big issue for me."

Angela could feel and hear how happy and at ease Bart was. She laughed and blushed, felt heat in her cheeks. "Well, I hear that you enjoy my garlic bread."

It was perfect. Bart laughed aloud. "You have no idea how much, Princess." He listened to her laugh. "You doing okay, Angela?"

"I am," she said softly. "Bart, be great tomorrow. I'll be watching and cheering for my guy."

Bart and Dave met the Walleston family for dinner. Bart's Sunday tee time was again 2pm Pacific time, so he could relax that evening. Bart asked Phil Walleston if they could talk. They walked the grounds together and could be seen smiling.

Phil Walleston was exuberant. "You hit a homerun today, Bart." He laughed. "That was a great endorsement of the tournament and the charity. Great job."

Bart smiled. "Thank you, Mr. Walleston. You've been so great." He looked around at the group gathered at the table. "Inviting me to play in the Classic, the private jet, this great resort," he grinned. "WOW, Dave and I are more than a little impressed, right Dave?"

Dave shrugged, attempted an air of nonchalance, "speak for yourself, Bart," he said, tongue in cheek, smiled at the ladies, drew a smile from Rachel, "private jets are a daily experience for me."

Everybody laughed. Heather Walleston pointed a finger at Dave. "I remember my first time on a private jet." She smiled and Bart noted just how pretty she was. He observed that Rachel favored her mother. "Phil had just been hired by an oil company in Texas and we were going to a conference in New York." Heather stated and shook her head. "It blew me away." She laughed. "I actually jumped up and offered to help the stewardess serve drinks."

Phil laughed aloud. "Oh my God, I remember that." He smiled at Heather, who blushed and lowered her eyes as she smiled. "Here I am meeting with a few of the top execs and here comes Heather with a tray of drinks." He actually belly laughed. Rachel and Justin grinned at each other. "So, I rose and introduced Heather as my wife." He shook his head, eyed Heather. "She was so beautiful," he smiled at his wife, "of course, she still is, but, anyway, she served the drinks and left the conference room." Phil and Heather exchanged grins. "So, she left us and the CEO looked at me and said, 'Wow, Phil, impressive. You work fast.'" He laughed. "He actually thought that I just met a pretty stewardess and married her on the spot." He looked at his children, grew reflective, shrugged. "You know, we didn't grow up with luxuries," he grinned at Heather. "We just got lucky."

"Not really," Heather challenged. She addressed her children, "your Dad always worked harder and," she tapped her head, "smarter than everyone else." She smiled at Phil. "He shot right up the ladder to the top."

Justin looked at Bart. "Ddo you think you wwill wwin, tomorrow?" He closed his eyes in frustration.

Bart ruffled his hair, put his hands on Justin's face and met his eyes. "Justin, take a deep breath. Let all that anxiety and fear go, and just speak."

Justin nodded, took and let out a deep breath. He looked up at Bart. "Do you tthink you will wwin, tomorrow?" It was better and Justin could feel it."

Bart grabbed him and gave him a shake, Justin loved the roughhousing. "See, that was so much better." He looked into Justin's eyes. "We will beat this together, Justin." He paused. "As to whether I will win, Justin, I don't know. We'll play tomorrow and see."

"Are you nervous?" Rachel asked.

Bart looked at Dave, then faced Rachel. He shrugged, "its golf, Dave and I will do our best and we'll see."

Sunday in Monterey dawned bright and reasonably warm. Bart went for a morning run, took a long refreshing shower, and had a big meal at 10:30am. By noon, he was at the range loosening up.

Billy Ray and Bart met on the 1st tee a few minutes before 2pm. They shook hands and Billy Ray smiled. "Bart, you are a great talent. Stick with it and I predict great things for you."

"Thanks, Billy Ray," Bart responded. He returned the smile. "I enjoyed our round yesterday." He paused. "Good luck today."

"You know, Bart," Billy Ray drawled. "I really think you'd like playing at Texas. We have a great course, facilities, and a super coach." He grinned. "How about you visit? I will personally show you the sites." He laughed and winked. "They're pretty spectacular."

Bart nodded. "Maybe," he responded. "I will think about it and call you."

"I have an idea," Dave Gilliss interjected, smiling. "How about we defer the recruiting to after the round."

Bart and Billy Ray laughed. "Good idea," the always jovial Billy Ray agreed. "Good luck, Bart."

The DeMarco house was celebratory and packed. Rosa and Maria, with help from their daughters, created a veritable feast. Arincini, pizza, homemade Italian bread, imported, sharp provolone cheese, Sicilian olives and, of course, freshly baked Italian cookies. Word of what Bart was accomplishing out in California had spread throughout Cape Ann.

Father Capelli used his sermon at that morning's mass to laud Bart's hard work and determination to overcome a difficult condition and achieve his dreams. "He is only 17 years old," Father Capelli observed, "he battled an emotionally crippling, stutter, that silenced his voice." He nodded. "But, Bart never quit. And today, he is challenging the most accomplished amateur golfer in America," He smiled. "In an important tournament." Father Capelli took a deep breath, looked at his congregation. His eyes settled on the Palermo family, John and Katie, with their children, Franco, Anna, blond, blue eyed, Kelly and John, Jr. He smiled. "I believe that Bart will need help and guidance." John's eyes engaged the long-time parish priest.

"Bart is blessed with a good family," Father Capelli continued. He smiled at Rosa, who sat with Lucia and Celia. "His parents gave him, Mario and Lucia, an outstanding work ethic." He caught Angela's eye. "And, he is so fortunate to have a young lady of outstanding character and compassion, in his life, who loves him, and," he smiled, "who Bart loves so passionately." Angela beamed a smile.

Father Capelli raised his arms. "I ask you all to be with Bart as he plays today, send your prayers and love his way." He nodded. "Together, we can help our Bart." He paused, eyed his congregation. "I will remind you of the words of Corinthians;

"And, now these three remain: Faith, Hope and Love. But, the Greatest of these is Love."

Across Cape Ann, Gloucester, Rockport, Essex and Manchester by the Sea, TV sets in homes, restaurants and pubs were tuned to the Golf Channel and families who knew little about golf, were cheering for their hometown boy.

At the DeMarco house, at precisely 5pm, all were seated before the television, and listening intently to the words of the golf announcers and commentators, who praised the quality of the competitors. The consensus was that Billy Ray had the advantage of maturity and having played against tougher competition for the last three years. One of the on course commentators cautioned that while it appeared that the older, more experienced Billy Ray had a decided advantage over 17 year old Bart, he had never seen a young man that handled pressure with the aplomb of Bart DeMarco.

Bart and Billy Ray did not disappoint the vast television audience nor the big gallery. After the 6th hole, they were both 3 under par.

"This is amazing," Jim Perry offered. "Bart is playing this guy tough." He laughed. "And, look at him," as the camera settled on Bart standing, chatting with Dave Gilliss, on the famous 7th tee. "He looks as if he is having fun."

"I wish I were," a very nervous Angela said, softly.

The 7th at Pebble Beach is a very short par 3, from an elevated tee to a green surrounded on three sides by the crashing waves of the Pacific Ocean. Standing on the tee box, one is overwhelmed with the beauty on display before his eyes. It is only about 110 yards, downhill, but depending on the winds, which can be fierce or as placid as the name Pacific implies, PGA players have been known to hit from a sand wedge to a 4 iron.

Bart took the club from Dave, teed his ball, about even with the grass, to guarantee a perfect lie. He then stood behind the ball considering the shot. Angela watched as he closed his eyes, then opened them, showed a small smile. In that smile, she felt Bart's love. Bart took his smooth as silk swing and lofted a shot high into the air. It looked good off of the tee.

"It's all over the pin!" Phil Walleston called, excitedly.

The ball descended to the green, landing about ten feet past the pin, took a short hop and rolled out, leaving Bart with a 15 foot putt.

"Excellent," Dave encouraged. He took Bart's sand iron and handed him his putter. Bart and Dave exchanged a smile. The camera scanned the gallery and caught the smiles and excited high fives exchanged by Phil and

Justin, and the broad, encouraging smiles of Heather and Rachel. Betsy noted that Rachel's eyes seemed focused on Bart. She glanced at Angela, who met her eyes. Angela nodded and smiled, choosing to believe in Bart.

Billy Ray had watched Bart's shot closely, nodded his approval to Bart, and teed his ball. He took his swing, which produced a much lower ball flight. Billy Ray's ball also flew directly over the flagstick, landed about 10 feet past, but hopped, bit and spun back to the hole. The gallery watched transfixed as the ball rolled to the cup, kissed the flagstick and dropped to the bottom of the hole for an ace, a hole in one. The roar of the gallery was met with a collective groan from the DeMarco clan.

The camera caught Billy Ray leap and chest bump with his caddie. The camera shot showed Bart smiling and clapping. He shot Billy Ray a thumbs up as he proceeded down the slope to the green, to take, what was now a critical birdie putt.

"This is a big putt," intoned the color commentator. "I'm reminded of the words of the great, Arnold Palmer; 'golf is deceptively simple and endlessly complicated.'" He shook his head. "Now what for young Bart?"

"Yes," the play by play announcer confirmed. "Is this when the tires come off?" He shrugged. "I guess we'll see."

Angela watched Bart stride down the slope to the green. Her fists were nervously balled at her mouth. The DeMarco clan were silent. Angela bowed her head and thought, 'why does he do this?' She looked up and met Rosa's eyes. "Think good thoughts," Rosa encouraged.

Bart crouched behind the ball, considering the putt. Dave stood just behind, studying the slope of the green. They conferred, Dave moved away and Bart took an additional moment to read the green. He closed his eyes, rose, opened his eyes and smiled, moved over the putt. Bart set and stroked his putt.

'Please, please, please,' Angela thought.

Bart hit a good putt, they had read the slope of the green perfectly, but the entire field of golfers had played this green and the poa annua was a bit bumpy from all the feet that had trod over the green. One foot short of the cup, the ball hit an almost imperceptible bump and moved fractionally right. It stopped just on the lip outside the cup. Bart stood, hoping that it would drop. The camera focused on his face, he exhaled, walked to his ball and tapped in his par putt.

"A big swing in favor of Billy Ray!" The announcer emphasized.

"A crazy game," the color commentator intoned. "He hit a perfect putt, just a bad break." He paused. "Remember, there is still eleven holes to play, a lot of golf." He smiled. "You know Jim," he added, addressing the announcer, "this is exactly what tests the metal of a young player." He paused. "We'll see how he responds to adversity."

Rosa fired up. "My Bart has overcome far worse than this!" She proclaimed. "You'll see."

As Bart and Billy Ray moved to the 8th tee, Donna Caponi, an on course commentator, approached Bart. A former LPGA major champion and Golf Hall of Fame member, she grew to adulthood in an Italian-American family, and felt an affinity for this young man from a similar background. She studied Bart's face as she gauged his reaction. Bart smiled, "Billy Ray hit a great shot," he laughed. "He wants me to make a visit to the University of Texas." He winked into the camera. "I told him that he had to show me the mechanics of that shot." He smiled. "Pretty Amazing!"

"What about your putt?" Donna asked.

Bart smiled and shrugged. "That's golf, we have a long way to go."

The announcer grinned. "Anything else?" She asked, a smile playing at her lips.

"Yes," Bart responded, flashing that smile, as he looked into the camera. "Hi Angela, I love you, everything is good, try to calm down my Mom." He moved to the tee box.

"Jim," Donna Caponi opined. "This kid is as solid as a rock. We're in for an exciting finish."

"This could be something," Nick Faldo, the color commentator offered, excitedly. "I think there are some fireworks ahead."

The mood of the DeMarco clan quickly moved from tense to relaxed, smiles replaced frowns.

Rosa laughed, as her eyes filled. "My boy knows his mother," she smiled at Angela, "he's thinking about us." She just shook her head.

Angela was touched by Bart's efforts to re-assure those he loved most. Jessica leaned close to Angela and whispered. "If you get tired of that man, how about you send him my way?"

Angela laughed aloud, met Jess's eyes. "Not much chance of that." They laughed together.

Billy Ray blasted a tee shot down the middle of the fairway. Bart matched it, and a bit more. They walked to their balls. Billy Ray was looking at 200 yards of carry, across the chasm and onto the green. He chose his club and took his swing.

"Oh, he tugged it," the announcer stated. "It settled down in that heavy rough. He'll have a tough shot from there."

Bart stood behind his ball. Dave Gilliss handed him his club. "185 to the middle of the green." He smiled. "The only lay-up is the Pacific Ocean."

Bart laughed aloud. "Okay," he took the club, sized up his shot, closed his eyes, then smiled and stroked a beauty to about ten feet from the flagstick.

"Great shot," declared a very relieved Dave Gilliss. He handed Bart his putter, put the iron back in the bag. "You know what the Old Caddie always says;" Dave stated with a smile, "Happiness is a long walk with your putter." He grinned. "Here we go, Bart."

The players, caddies and gallery followed the path around the chasm. As Bart and Dave passed Billy Ray's ball, they noted the lie.

"Not good," Bart said, softly to Dave.

Dave grinned. "Let's think about your putt."

Bart walked onto the green, placed his marker and flipped his ball to Dave. As Dave wiped the ball, they both watched Billy Ray. The big and sturdy Texan stood studying his shot, he took a few practice swings through the heavy rough to gauge the resistance, then moved over the ball.

"Tough shot," Donna whispered into her microphone.

Nick agreed. "You just don't know how the ball will come out of that rough. There will be a lot of grass between the club-head and ball. It could fly out or the heavy grass could wrap around the shaft and slow the club." He paused. "There could easily be a two shot swing here in favor of young Bart, if the ball doesn't come out as Billy Ray guesses."

"Please!" Angela prayed softly.

Bart and Dave stood off the green watching Billy Ray. Bart was smiling easily.

Billy Ray took a big swing through the heavy rough. The ball came out high, carried onto the green and rolled to the pin.

"Great shot!" Donna called. The surprise evident in her tone. Bart watched with a shake of his head and could only smile as Billy Ray's ball found the bottom of the hole for a birdie. The gallery reacted with a loud cheer.

"Eagle, birdie, on 7 and 8 at Pebble Beach." Jim Nantz announced to the television audience. "WOW! What a shock!"

Billy Ray leaped with joy, fist pumping across the green to retrieve his ball from the cup. He looked at Bart and shrugged. Bart just smiled.

"That was a blow to the gut," called out Sir Nick. "The question now is, how will this young man recover?" He paused. "Was that the knockout punch?"

Bart waited for the gallery to settle. He looked at Justin, who appeared dejected and defeated, Bart flashed a smile.

The emotional roller coaster continued at Casa DeMarco. A groan was followed by silence. Rosa reached for Angela's hand. Tina caressed Angela's shoulders, "it will be okay," Tina assured her sister. "Bart will find a way."

Bart went through his routine. He read the green, closed his eyes, opened them and smiled. He hit a good putt, but missed a bit left.

"Oh, No!" Angela gasped. Bart tapped in for par, but was now three strokes behind with 10 holes to play.

"Donna, what are you seeing?" Jim asked.

"Bart DeMarco just parred 7 and 8 at Pebble Beach and lost three strokes." The LPGA Hall of Famer replied. "That's hard to take, Jim."

Donna approached Billy Ray. "How about this Billy Ray?" She asked.

Billy Ray grinned happily. "I think the Good Lord had to be in my corner on that shot." He shrugged. "But, I'll take it." He walked with Donna to the 9th tee box, looked into the camera. "Don't count Bart out." He smiled. "He's the toughest competitor I've ever seen."

The camera found Bart, Rosa saw the look on his face. She so recalled that look, when he was a boy and all the insults and mocking became too much. Bart was shaken, but he was no longer a scared child. He looked at Justin and flashed a smile.

Dave stayed close, and in his ear. "No problem, Bart, we'll get him on the back nine."

Billy Ray had the honor and hit a good drive.

Bart listened to Dave, took a deep breath and pulled himself together. He launched a big drive that split the fairway. He parred the tough 9th hole. Billy Ray also parred the 9th and recorded a front nine score of 30. Bart was 3 under par, with his 33, but was falling behind.

Billy Ray's words proved to be prophetic. Bart charged through the back nine at historic Pebble Beach Golf Links in 6 under par, to post his best score ever, a 63.

Billy Ray watched Bart with respect and admiration growing with each swing by the 17 year old. The announcers were battling to find enough superlatives to describe Bart's play and his courage. Bart's play pushed Billy Ray, who matched Bart shot for shot. The Big Texan tapped in on 18 to post a career best score of 60 and a three shot victory.

He stood as Bart walked to him with his hand extended. Billy Ray pulled him into a bear hug. "You are going to be great kid. It was an honor."

"Thanks, Billy Ray, and congratulations. You deserved it." Bart responded.

Donna Caponi approached Bart, a sympathetic smile on her face. "May I speak to you, Bart?" She asked, respectfully.

Bart grinned. "Of course," he smiled, but Rosa and Angela saw the look in his eyes. "I wish I could be there for him," Angela said softly.

"Billy Ray played the best golf I've ever seen. He's a deserving Champion." Bart proclaimed. As he spoke, the Wallestons approached. Justin jumped into his arms, tears on the 10 year old's cheeks. Phil shook Bart's hand. "I'm proud of you, Bart." He stated. Rachel stood close between Bart and Dave.

Bart looked into the camera. "I'm okay Angela. I love you all."

Before Donna moved to do an extensive interview with the Champ, Jim, Nick and Donna all heaped praise on Bart. Donna concluded by saying, "Bart DeMarco is a very good golfer, but above all, he is a fine young man." She paused. "His family should be proud."

Rosa's tears flowed. And, Bart had, unknowingly, won a big fan base.

Chapter Thirty-Eight

Later that night, Lucia, Betsy, and Jessica, with bags of night cloths, joined Angela and Tina at the Curcuru house. They were there to support Angela.

They arrived to find a pitcher of Arnold Palmer's and a big plate of cookies. And, surprisingly, a smiling Angela.

"Bart just called," Angela reported, happily. "He's okay, disappointed, but okay." As the girls studied her, she blushed.

Jessica grinned. "Well, well, what did our Bart say that has Angela blushing so?"

Tina poked her big sister. "He only has to look at her, and she blushes." She grinned. "Isn't that right, Angela?"

Angela laughed. "I kinda like him, what can I say?"

That brought laughter from the group. Angela looked to Jessica, considered, "shouldn't you have heard from NYU by now?"

Jessica grinned, her smile lighting that pretty face and sparkling blue eyes. "I heard," she beamed. "I've been accepted into the Theatre program." She stated excitedly.

'That's great, Jess!" Betsy exclaimed. "Someday, we'll see you starring on Broadway or in the Movies."

The girls settled on the living room floor, in their pajamas, chatting and laughing.

"We know Jess's future," Lucia teased. "She's going to be a big star and marry a hot and famous actor."

They all laughed at the image, picturing their favorite actor in the role of Jess's guy.

"How about you girls?" Jessica asked. "How do you see your future?"

Lucia smiled. "I think I'll be going to law school," she stated. "You may have heard that I like to debate, it feels right to get paid for it."

"Didn't I hear that Sal is planning to be a lawyer?" Angela asked, with a grin. "Could that have anything to do with your plans?"

"Maybe," Lucia laughed as her cheeks flushed. "How about you Tina?"

Tina looked at Angela, who nodded her assent. She summoned her courage. "I should tell you," she paused, took a deep breath, "that I am a lesbian." The pronouncement was met with silence. Tina rushed to fill the vacuum. "I think I'd like to go to culinary school, become a chef."

Betsy studied Tina, looked to Angela. "Really, Tina?"

Tina smiled, "being a chef is a good career, don't you think?" She said lightly as she studied the girl's reactions closely. Of course, she knew what Betsy was asking. Betsy's eyes were set on Tina. Angela held her sister's hand. Tina took a deep breath. "It has been so hard, but I feel that I can tell my friends." She smiled. "As Bart said, I can only be who I am."

Lucia eyed Tina. "Tina, I've known you for three years. I thought we were friends." She raised her brows, appeared somewhat crestfallen. "You're a lesbian, and you never told me?"

Angela was about to rise to Tina's defense, when Tina smiled. "Lucia, I wasn't ready to admit to myself that I was gay, let alone tell the world." She smiled. "I hope you understand."

"How did you do it?" Jessica asked. "How did you tell your parents?"

Tina smiled. "It was hard, my mother cried, my Dad was angry and confused." She paused, squeezed Angela's hand. "Angela was with me, but it was Bart who put it all into perspective for our family."

Lucia looked from Tina to Angela. Angela smiled. "Okay," Lucia pressed, a smile pulling at her lips. "What did Bart do?"

"He came over," Tina explained. "Angela called and told him that she needed him."

Betsy laughed, looked to Angela. "Of course," she said appreciatively. "Bart would do anything for Angela."

Angela smiled at the words. She so appreciated that it was true, but still had trouble understanding just why Bart felt that way.

Tina nodded. "Isn't it great?" She paused. "Bart joined the family at the table. It was so tense, and I was so scared." She exhaled, hoping to lessen the tension she was now feeling. Tina looked about, all eyes were fixed on her. "Bart was so calm, he greeted my Dad, Mom and me, then he sat and listened to my Dad tell me that I was bringing shame on the family."

Tina paused, saw that she had the rapt attention of the girls. "Bart let the silence settle, touched my arm and shook his head to stop me from making things worse with an emotional response." She sighed. "I was a mess. Bart saw that and patted my hand." Tina looked at Angela. "I so get why you love him, Angela." Angela smiled. "Then," Tina continued. "Bart asked my Dad if he could speak." Tina smiled. "I think my Dad was happy to give Bart the floor."

"He wouldn't have been able to do that before Angela came into his life." Lucia offered, in a soft voice, recalling how Bart had so struggled with speech, and the pain he endured. She looked to Angela. "He loves you so much."

Angela misted, feeling joyful. She looked to Tina. "Tell them, Tina." She urged her sister.

Tina laughed. "I thought Bart was going to talk to my father, really give him the straight scoop." She laughed, lifted her brows, "no pun intended." Tentative smiles showed on the girl's faces. "Instead, Bart asked me how long it took for me to accept that I was gay." Tina shook her head and smiled in memory. "I told him about two years." She looked at the girls, settled her eyes on Lucia. "It was so hard to accept. I just didn't know what to do." Her eyes filled. "I'm sorry Lucia."

Lucia rose and hugged Tina. "Sorry if I made you feel bad." Lucia said softly. "It must have been so difficult."

"So?" Betsy pressed. "What happened?"

Tina wiped her eyes, took a deep breath, and she managed a smile. "Bart explained that if it took two years for me to accept the fact that I was gay, shouldn't I understand that my parents needed time to come to terms with the new reality?" She looked and smiled at Angela. "He explained that my parents needed time to grieve."

"Grieve?" the girls all asked, surprise registering.

Tina nodded. "Yes, to grieve the loss of the life they expected and wanted for me, Bart explained." She searched their faces as each accepted and nodded their understanding. "He said that I may never have children." She shrugged. "Maybe, maybe not," she paused. "But, Bart got it all out and on the table." She laughed. "Then, he looked at Angela, grinned and said that when they were married, that they would have children quickly, so my parents would have grandchildren to love."

Tina shook her head and laughed, remembering Angela's reaction. "Angela just gawked at him, total surprise," she added. "But, it worked, just as he planned." Tina said with admiration. "My parents smiled. Everything just seemed better, more normal." She looked at the girls. "Then, Bart told me to go hug my Dad." She teared up. "Bart was unbelievable!"

"Grandchildren?" Lucia laughed, picturing Bart as a Dad and discovering that she could. She looked to Angela with a bright smile. "Did you know about this, Angela?"

Angela laughed. "He shocked me, but…"

"You loved it!" Betsy proclaimed with a laugh. Angela's wide smile confirmed Betsy's words.

Tina looked at the girls. She swallowed. "Are we all right?" She asked tentatively. Heads nodded. Then, Lucia rose and again hugged Tina. "I guess we are going to be family, Tina." She grinned. "We DeMarco's take care of our own."

Tina's eyes filled with tears borne of relief. She felt another great weight lift off of her shoulders. "Thank you, Lucia."

Jessica looked to Angela, she smiled. "So, Angela, I guess we know that you want Bart." She eyed Angela. "But, what else do you want for your future?"

She blushed and smiled. Her eyes were dreamy. "I want to be Bart's wife." She said with certainty. "I want to have his children and be there for him," she shrugged. "I wasn't there for him today." She paused. "He needed me and I wasn't there."

"What about a career?" Jessica asked, surprise in her tone.

Angela smiled. "Is there a better or more important career than wife and mother?"

"That's crazy, Angela," Jessica fired up. "You're a member of the National Honor Society!" Jessica stated, surprised at Angela's words. "You may win the Sawyer Medal." She eyed Angela. "You can be anything that you want to be." She paused, perplexed. "You must have some aspirations?"

Angela took Jessica's hands, held them until Jess met her eyes. Angela's calm surprised Jessica. The other girls watched, a mix of confusion and empathy on their faces. "I love Bart DeMarco," she stated. "I have loved him from the day he stood up for me and fought three guys to protect me."

Lucia dropped her eyes, felt shame at Sal's actions.

Angela saw her face, but decided to deal with Lucia later. Now, she wanted to say this out loud, for herself, more than for the girls. "Jessica, you and the others convinced me that I was not pretty enough to win Bart's heart." Angela paused, sighed. "I loved him, was so grateful to him, but knew that I was 'Ugly Angela.' I was convinced that Bart would never want me."

Jessica met Betsy's eyes, neither said a word. The shame showed in their eyes, the flush of their cheeks.

Angela smiled. "That night, after the Salem game, when Bart was so devastated," She looked at Betsy. "We were planning to go to that victory party." She paused, smiled. "Remember Betsy?" Betsy nodded.

"But," Angela explained, "I watched Bart throughout that game, I saw the humiliation he felt." She took a deep breath. "I knew that feeling and seeing him so hurt just killed me." She looked at Jessica, Betsy and Lucia. Tina touched Angela's shoulder in support.

"So," Angela continued. "I went to find Bart." Her eyes filled. "I didn't want him to be alone." She took a deep breath. "I found him, sitting alone on that bench, and I saw the pain in his eyes, on his face." She paused, wiped tears from her eyes. She shrugged. "I didn't know what to say, I must have sounded like an idiot, but he smiled and asked me to sit with him."

She sighed, the memory sweet. "He said that I was pretty." She looked at the girls. "I could see he was sincere. I kissed him."

"You hussy!" Tina said, hoping to lighten the mood. The girls all smiled, their eyes still fixed on Angela.

Angela looked to her sister and laughed. Then, she looked at the girls. "I helped Bart that night." She smiled in memory. "He had a late dinner here. We talked." She took a deep breath. "I knew that Bart needed me. That I could really help him." She closed her eyes and smiled. "I walked Bart to the door. He thanked me, told me that I was special. He put his hands on my face and kissed me goodnight." She sighed. "It was magical!"

"The next day, I hoped he would call," She took a deep breath. "I had about given up hope, but," she smiled at Lucia, "thanks to Lucia he called that afternoon. We went out on our first date that evening." She laughed. "Remember, Betsy?"

Betsy nodded and smiled. "I do, it was my first date with Jim."

"We had Chinese food with Jim and Betsy, then Bart and I went to a movie." Angela laughed. "Bart hated it, but he saw that I was into the love story." Angela smiled. "He put his arm around me, pulled me close." She closed her eyes, smiled sweetly. "He turned my face to his, kissed me, and asked me to be his girl." She paused, smiled brightly, looked at the girls. "Those were the sweetest words ever spoken to me."

"You really love him." Jessica said softly, thoughtfully. "It's not just that he is so handsome and accomplished?"

"Yes, Jess, I do." Angela smiled. "I love Bart with all my heart." She paused, scanned the girls faces. "You're right Jess, I can be anything I want to be." She took Jess's hands, squeezed them. "What I want to be is Bart's wife. I want to have a family with him. I want to help him be everything he can be." She laughed. "I want to be on 'Team DeMarco' with Bart." She sat tall. "That is what I want."

Nobody spoke, each girl was in her thoughts, eyes still on Angela. Finally, Angela said; "I hope that someday you feel for a man what I feel for Bart." She smiled. "Then, you'll know."

Chapter Thirty-Nine

The Walleston family, with Bart and Dave sat at dinner. Justin was still sad that Bart had not won the tournament.

"You okay, Big Guy?" Bart asked. He kept his eyes on Justin. "You know, golfers, even the very best golfers, lose more tournaments than they win."

Justin looked into Bart's face. Bart read his anguish. "He was so lucky!" Justin stated forcefully. "A hole in one, then that chip shot!" Justin seethed. "He was so lucky!"

Bart smiled broadly. He looked at Heather, whose eyes flooded with tears of joy. Phil sat, studying his son, awe on his face.

"He was really lucky, Justin." Phil said. "But, Bart did great. He shot a 63." He looked at Bart. "I'm proud of you, Bart." He looked at Justin, turned thankful eyes to Bart. He choked up and Rachel saw a new side of her Dad. "Thank you, Bart."

Bart smiled at Phil. He knew what it meant for Phil and Heather to hear Justin speak clearly and without fear or hesitation. "There is still a long battle ahead." He warned. He looked to Heather. "It will take time."

"Bart, you have no idea what it means to hear Justin speak so clearly." Heather said, wiping her eyes. "Thank you so much, my boy."

Justin looked from his Dad to his Mother. "Wwhy are you ccrying?" He asked.

Heather went to her son, wrapped Justin in a big hug. "Because, now, I know," she paused, and squeezed her boy. "Justin, it's really possible."

Phil choked back the lump in his throat. He sipped some water, looked from Justin to Bart. Bart met his eyes and smiled. "Thank you, Bart," Phil mouthed. Bart smiled.

Phil addressed the group. "Tomorrow we fly back to Canada." He looked at Dave. "Dave, you will stay with us for a few days to study the course?"

Dave smiled. "Of course, Sir." He glanced at Heather and Rachel.

"Bart, you have to get back to school." Mr. Walleston stated. "But, I hope that you and Dave will come back and stay with us for a few days after Christmas."

Bart smiled and nodded. "That will be fine, Sir."

The Curcuru's were sitting down to dinner. Sal had returned from fishing and had unloaded a good catch that morning. Tina had helped Maria prepare a coming home feast for Sal. Dad and daughter were slowly finding their way together.

As they sat and said their dinner prayer, there was a knock at the front door. "I'll get it," Angela called as she left the table.

"Are we expecting anyone?" Sal asked a smiling Maria. Tina rose to get another place setting.

Maria just smiled and listened. She heard Angela shriek with joy as she jumped into Bart's arms. Angela was spilling happy tears. "Why are you home?" She asked. "I thought you were spending some time in Canada?"

Bart kissed Angela with a pent-up passion. "I've missed you, Princess." He stated, then kissed her again. He grinned. "Why am I here?" He joked. "I'm here for dinner." He laughed, held her with her feet off of the floor, twirling Angela around and holding her close. "And, to see my girl."

He led Angela into the kitchen. She saw Bart's place set. She looked at her mother. "You knew Bart was coming?"

Maria laughed. "Yes, Bart called. I just wasn't sure what time he would arrive."

Sal looked at his wife. "Now, I see, this fancy meal isn't really for me." He tried to feign outrage, but just laughed. He looked at Bart, pulled him into a hug. "We're so proud of you, Son." Sal looked at Tina. "My Tina explained how good you did."

Nick and Giuseppe were bouncing in their seats with excitement. "We saw you on television," Nick blurted. He frowned, "but you lost."

Bart smiled and mussed his hair. "You know, Nick, you can't always win."

"You should try harder," Giuseppe concluded.

Bart nodded and laughed. "Okay, Buddy, I'll try that."

Tina met Angela's smile. The family was coming back together. Bart smiled and winked at Tina. 'There are always challenges,' he thought. 'But love and some kind words go a long way.'

"Sit," Sal called, "mangia, let's eat."

Angela was bubbly with excitement. Her smile just beamed. "So, what happened?" She queried, excitedly. "I'm so glad that you are home, but is everything okay?"

Bart laughed. "Actually, better than okay, Princess." He said, as he sampled Maria's calamari in a rich Marinara sauce. He grinned. "This is delicious." He ate more as Angela waited impatiently for Bart to elaborate. "I've missed your cooking, Mom." He said comfortably. "Those chefs in that fancy hotel should take lessons from you."

Maria smiled. "Thank you, Bart. It's good to cook for you, you just love to eat."

Angela sat, eyed him with a smirk. "Are you trying to frustrate me?" She asked, a glint of amusement in her eyes.

Bart smiled at her. "I've missed that face," he said. "And, especially your sweet words." He teased.

Angela laughed and punched his rock hard arm. She laughed again. "Okay, tell me, Bart, before I hurt my hand."

Bart smiled at her. "You saw the Pacific Amateur Tournament." Angela nodded. "Well, I guess the announcers had some nice things to say about me and my game."

"They sure did!" Angela affirmed with a smile. "My God, that woman announcer, I thought she wanted to adopt you."

Bart laughed. "Donna was great." He paused. "Did you know that she is in the World Golf Hall of Fame?"

Angela shrugged. "They said something about that, but I was focused on this really handsome golfer." Angela paused and grinned. "I think his name was Billy Ray Something."

Bart laughed. Maria noted the love in their eyes. 'He really does look like he'd just wants to ravish her,' she thought, happily.

Bart shook his head. "Let's put your crush on Billy Ray aside for a moment." He flashed a smile that always delighted Angela. Bart continued. "That Sunday night, I started to receive offers of sponsor exemptions into other PGA tournaments, in Arizona, Florida and California." He laughed. "Even a tournament in Hawaii." He shrugged. "I guess they want to give 'Stutter Boy' a chance.

Angela looked pleased. "That's good right?"

Bart laughed. "Yes, it is very good." He paused, became thoughtful. "I also received some offers from companies wanting to sponsor me on tour."

Angela shook her head. "What does that mean?"

"It means," Bart smiled, "that I could give up my amateur status and turn professional." He smiled, drank some water, broke off a hunk of Maria's freshly baked Italian bread, swirled it in the rich Marinara sauce, and popped it into his mouth. He smiled. "It also means that I have to go see John Palermo."

Sal looked at Bart. "Why, Mr. Palermo?"

Bart smiled. "I will need someone I can trust to negotiate for me with these companies." He paused. "My Dad says that Mr. Palermo has taken care of the people in Gloucester for almost twenty years." He paused. "My Dad told me how Mr. Palermo fought for the Scola family to protect their baby." He smiled. "They wanted to arrest Joe Scola, Mr. Palermo protected him, his wife and baby." He looked at Angela. "Joe Scola is Celia's cousin."

Maria nodded. "Vero," she asserted. "It is true, John Palermo is a good man."

Bart looked at Angela. "So, Angela, how would you feel about your boyfriend being a professional golfer?"

Angela smiled, met his eyes. "If it makes you happy, Bart, then, I'm all for it."

The next afternoon, after classes, Bart met with, Guidance Counsellor, Mrs. Nelson. They discussed the best way to handle Bart's absences from school and his need to make up the work, to maintain his high academic standing. Mrs. Nelson suggested that Bart would benefit by having a tutor travel with him. The guidance office could help to schedule exams between tournaments. She smiled. "Bart, it will be challenging." She offered, with a smile. "But, challenging seems to be right up your alley!"

Bart then went with his Dad and brother, Mario, to meet with John Palermo.

John Palermo, now 45 years old, father of four and happily married to Katie, for 11 years, rose to shake Bart's hand. Palermo stood 6'2", looked Bart in the eye. John had black hair, running to gray at the temples. He maintained a youthful appearance by his daily five mile run.

Bart introduced his father, Franco, and brother, Mario. John sat at the head of the conference table, legal pad before him. He smiled. "Good to see you again, Mario." John smiled.

Mario nodded, "I enjoyed working with you, Mr. Palermo. You're a straight shooter."

John smiled a thanks. "Before we begin," John started, as he looked at Bart, "I want to say how much I enjoyed your performance this past weekend." He laughed. "A 63 and you lose by three strokes." He shook his head, looked Bart in the eye. "You handled the disappointment admirably."

"Thank you, sir," Bart responded. He grinned. "Your son, Franco, plays on the High School golf team." Bart stated. "He's a good kid and a pretty good golfer." He hesitated, decided to proceed with his thoughts. "Mr. Palermo, Franco is big and athletic, the football team will want him." He smiled. "If I may, I think with work, he could play college golf, maybe win a scholarship."

John Palermo smiled. "Thanks Bart, I'll keep that in mind." He studied Bart, looked to Franco, "you must be very proud."

Franco smiled. "Mr. Palermo, I'm proud of all my children." He nodded to Mario. "My son, Mario, is the mate on our families fishing dragger and a good man." He grinned. "My daughter, Lucia, is an auburn haired beauty, a good student and a wonderful, respectful girl."

John Palermo heard the pride in Franco's tone. He smiled. "So, what can I do for you, Bart?" The lawyer asked.

Bart looked to his Dad, who nodded. "Mr. Palermo," Bart began, "I have a number of PGA tournaments offering me Sponsor's exemptions. I also have had various companies offering to sponsor me on tour." He paused. "I was hoping that you would represent me in the discussions."

John smiled. "Bart, you do know that I am not an athlete's agent?" He shook his head. "I could line up a reputable agent for you, if you'd like."

Bart looked at John Palermo. "Mr. Palermo, I know that you are a litigation attorney." He smiled. "But, so many people speak so highly of you." He paused, looked into the lawyer's eyes. "I want you to manage my career, my earnings, my investments, everything." He sat back. "I want to play golf, focus on my game and my private life." He looked at John. "I don't want to be meeting with agents, listening to proposals, discussing various investments." He laughed. "I'm 17 years old, but I know enough to focus on my life and my game and let others, who I trust, handle the rest." He paused, eyed the lawyer. "Will you help me, Sir?"

John was incredibly impressed. He smiled, recalling conversations with his partner, Phil Harmon, to whom, he long had acknowledged an inability to refuse to help those in Gloucester who needed him. They were his people.

It had been that desire to help, that brought John into the middle of a battle to save the life of Joe Scola, III. He had helped, Ali and Joe Scola, fight off the power of the U.S. Justice Department, and, of Ali's father, a U.S. Senator, who was determined to kill that young couple's baby in utero.

And, prosecute and imprison the baby's father. Today, that baby is a healthy and robust, six year old, and his father, Joe Scola, Jr. is an up and coming attorney at the law firm of Palermo & Harmon. There were rumors that Joe Scola Jr. was eyeing a run for Congress.

"Okay Bart, tell me what you want to happen." John Palermo asked.

Bart smiled. "Thank you, Sir." He exhaled a deep breath, he hadn't realized he was holding. "I want these companies who want me to wear their logos to pay for our equipment, transportation, lodgings, clothes, and a private tutor." He eyed the lawyer. "I want to graduate high school and figure a way to go to college, if possible."

"Our?" John asked.

Bart nodded. "Yes, my coach, and me. We are a team." He looked at Mr. Palermo. "Sir, also for my family, when I marry."

"Okay, Bart, I get the drift." He considered. "I will want to bring in a sport's agent, who knows the golf world."

"Whatever you think, Sir." Bart responded. "I'm placing my trust in you."

John smiled. "Okay, Bart, give me the contact info on the companies that have offered to sponsor you."

Bart handed over a list to the lawyer. "The top name on the list is, Phillip Walleston, from Manitoba Oil." Bart explained. "Mr. Walleston has been very generous to me." He hesitated. "Please give him every consideration." He then gave the lawyer a second list, of the PGA Tournament Sponsors that have offered exemptions into their tournaments. "I will leave this with you."

John Palermo rose and shook the hands of the DeMarco men. "Bart, you are a very impressive young man." He considered Bart and smiled. "I promise to do my best for you."

"Thank you, Sir," Bart responded with a relieved smile.

That evening John Palermo arrived home to the happy chaos of his family. Katie, John's wife, a willowy blond, with sparkling blue eyes and a ready smile, was at the stove preparing dinner. John went to her, embraced and kissed her.

Katie laughed. "I love it when you come home so happy. A good day?"

John smiled. "Yes, it was." He looked about. "Are the kid's home?"

"Franco should be home soon, he's at basketball practice." She rolled her eyes, "the girls are helping each other decide which make-up products are best for their complexions." Katie shook her head, "first high school dance on Friday." She raised her brow. "I think Kelly has her eyes on a boy, Dad." She smiled. "Good luck."

John laughed. "Okay, I think it's time to send them to a convent!" He shook his head. "Dances, boys, I don't like this!" He looked about, as Katie chuckled. "And, John?"

"He's doing his homework." She laughed. "He's going to try to talk you into letting him stay up to watch the Boston College basketball game." She grinned. "B.C. is playing Duke." She laughed. "He's sure his Eagles will win."

"An easy problem." John stated as he looked up at the heavens. "God help me survive two teenage daughters!"

The Palermo family sat to dinner, they joined hands for a prayer. John happily scanned his family. He looked at Anna, 14 years old, auburn hair, lively brown eyes and the image of her mother, Connie, who they had lost to cancer 13 years before.

John and Connie had a wonderful, happy marriage, two boisterous, beautiful, children, Franco, now 16, and Anna." Seeing Anna grow more every day in her mother's image always hit John. He still loved Connie, always would. He looked to Katie, who read his expression. She smiled, confident in John's love and understanding the pain of loss.

John and Connie had been lifelong friends with Katie and Marc Morrissey. John and Marc, with Peter Novello had found more than their share of youthful mischief. Each was an accomplished athlete, each married fantastic women. Life seemed perfect for the three young couples until the diagnosis of cancer. John and Connie fought and prayed, but the cancer won.

John had been devastated. With the help of Maria and Benny Amico, Connie's parents, and the family that took 10 year old John in as their son, John struggled through, running his law practice and trying to be mother and father to his children.

A year, or so, later, the Fishing Vessel, 'Mio Mondo' sank and took the crew, with the exception of Captain Joseph Amalfi, to a watery grave. Marc Morrissey had been a deckhand. Katie and the two other widows, along with the detestable, Captain Amalfi, had hired John to represent them, in their claim for damages for the wrongful death of the three young men, and, for Amalfi, in the contract action against the insurance company for the loss of his fishing boat.

John had won for the widows and the children, as well as for Captain Amalfi. In the process, John and Katie fell in love. It was difficult for both, they dealt with feelings of guilt and betrayal, families that still mourned the loss of a child, and the challenge of merging three families into a cohesive entity. But, John and Katie loved each other and were determined to make it work.

Katie had the additional challenges of showing Marc's family that they would never lose Kelly, and of winning the heart of the Amico's.

Their efforts were successful, and John Palermo, Jr.'s birth was the glue that bound all into a joyous unit, while never forgetting Connie and Marc.

John looked at his children. "I met a very impressive young man today." He began. "Do you know Bart DeMarco?"

Franco nodded as he chewed and swallowed his mother's delicious fried chicken. "Yes, he's a good guy, a great athlete." Franco stated. "The football team really missed him this season."

Anna and Kelly exchanged a look that Katie did not miss. "Do you girls know Bart?" Katie asked her daughters. The girls giggled. "He's like the cutest boy in the whole school," Kelly stated. "Anna has a big crush on him." Anna blushed, but didn't deny it.

John smiled. "Really Anna?" He shook his head. "Still, you chose a good guy to have feelings for." He winked. "But, I think he has a girlfriend." He suggested.

Kelly nodded. "Yes, Angela Curcuru. She's in the Theatre group." She laughed. "She's crazy about Bart."

"Do you know Angela?" Katie asked.

Kelly nodded. "Yes, she's so nice. She helped me with my lines, she even helps the tech crew." She shrugged. "Everybody likes her."

Franco considered the question. "You know, they always called her 'Ugly Angela.'" He shrugged. "I think she's kind of pretty." He exhaled. "You know, Angela is always smiling." He thought about it, "Angela is really very nice." He paused and shook his head. "They were very mean to her, mostly the girls."

Katie nodded. "Girls can be mean." She studied Anna. "Do you know Angela, Anna?"

Anna laughed. "Yes, I do. I wanted to hate her because of my feelings for Bart." She shrugged. "But, I couldn't, she's too nice."

John looked at his daughters. "You know girls, Franco just said something important."

Anna looked to her Dad quizzically. "Did I miss something?" She grinned. "When does Franco ever say anything important?" She teased.

Franco grinned at Anna. "Oh, every once in a while." He laughed. "Anna, you have to listen carefully." Anna met his smile.

John appreciated that Anna and Kelly loved and looked up to their big brother. "When I arrived home today," he glanced and grinned at Katie, "Mom mentioned that you two are planning on attending the High School dance this Friday."

Kelly nodded and smiled. "Our first High School dance."

"Mom also mentioned," John continued, "that you were helping each other to choose make-up to wear on Friday to the dance."

Anna nodded. "Dad, we want to look our best."

John shook his head. Katie grinned at his unease. "I just want you to know," John quietly offered, "that the best thing that you can possibly put on your face to look pretty, is a smile."

Anna and Kelly flashed their smiles. "Okay, Dad?" Anna offered, to placate her father, much to Katie's amusement.

Katie studied Franco, now 6 feet tall, broad of shoulder, and well-toned from his daily work-outs and the sports he played. Katie grinned. 'He looks like John,' she thought, 'with Connie's coloring.' "You know Franco, you are a very handsome young man."

Franco smiled at Katie, "Mom, take it easy, okay?"

She studied him as she laughed. "Franco, my boy, do you like Angela?" She paused. "I mean for a girlfriend?"

Franco looked at her with a perplexed look. "Mom, Angela is Bart's girl." He stated simply, settling the matter.

Katie sat back, eyed her son, John smiled at her, across the table. "Bart's girl?" Katie repeated.

"Of course, Mom." He reached for another piece of chicken from the platter, served family style. He smiled at Katie, "Mom, this chicken is great."

"Oh," Katie said, with an edge to her tone, looking into John's smile. "What is that, some Italian Guy code?"

John laughed aloud, Katie fixed John with her glare. Franco looked at Katie. "Mom, do you think I would go after another guy's girl?" He shook his head in surprise.

She studied Franco, "Well, my son," she said, the edge in her tone growing sharper. "Isn't Angela free to make her own choices?" She looked at John's bemused expression.

Franco bit into a savory thigh. "This chicken is really delicious, Mom," he repeated. "You're the best!" He reached for and spooned more mashed potatoes into his plate. He smiled at Katie. "Sure," Franco said. "Angela can do what she wants." He shrugged. "I'm talking about what I would or would not do." He looked at Katie. "Mom, do you want me to be the kind of guy that doesn't respect another guy's girl?"

Katie didn't reply. She rolled Franco's question around in her head.

"It really doesn't matter Mom," Kelly interjected, as she looked at Franco. "I think Franco has another girl in mind."

Franco just laughed, as he continued eating.

Katie perked up, "really, Franco?" She looked at her son. "And, who would that be?"

Franco laughed. "Since Kelly, the busybody, knows so much, why doesn't she tell you?"

Kelly laughed and playfully stuck out her tongue at Franco. "I hear that my big brother is sweet on Lucia DeMarco."

Anna nudged Franco and grinned. "That's also, what I hear." She confirmed.

"Isn't Lucia somebody's girl, Franco?" Katie asked with a smile, but, with raised brows and an edge to her tone. "Or, is it open season on Lucia?"

Franco sat back, took a momentary break from a delicious dinner. He smiled at Katie. "Okay, I understand that Lucia isn't allowed to date until she's 16, which won't be until February." He laughed. "While Bart and I were working on my chipping, we talked about this guy, Sal, who has been hanging around." He grinned. "The DeMarco's really don't like him." Franco looked at his Dad, "I plan on calling on Lucia in January," he shrugged. He looked at Katie and smiled. "Mom, she's really pretty." He shrugged. "And, so nice to talk to." He paused. "We'll see." He looked at his mother with an endearing smile, "now, may I finish dinner?"

John smiled at Katie. He looked to Franco. "Franco, while Mom considers your question, and steps off of her 'I am woman' soapbox, could you tell me if Bart is a good student?" John asked.

Franco nodded, "he sure is, I think he's at or near the top of his class." He grinned. "I hear that Angela, his girlfriend, is right there as well."

Katie nodded and considered. "So, Bart is smart, handsome and athletic, sounds like a good package to me." She smiled. John, Jr. just watched the discussion, while Kelly and Anna listened closely.

"I guess that's the kind of guy that Mom likes," John said with a grin. "It is smart jocks that you like, right Mom?" John teased. The comment drew smiles across the table and a smirk from Katie.

Kelly looked at Katie, she paused, spoke softly, surprising Katie. "Mom, was my Dad smart?" She hesitated. "I know he played college basketball." She sighed. Anna took her hand. "Was he?" Kelly repeated.

Caught by surprise, Katie looked at John. He read the look in her eyes.

"Yes, Kelly," John responded. "Marc Morrissey was smart, really athletic, a nice guy and a good friend." He smiled. "Your Dad, Uncle Peter and I were close friends." He laughed. "We had so much fun together." He stated. "Then, we all married these great women." He looked to Katie, read the surprise in her eyes and smiled. "We were really smart guys! Isn't that right Mom?"

Katie smiled, but John saw that her thoughts were of Marc. She eyed Kelly, thoughts of Marc flooded her mind. Marc holding Kelly, Marc smiling and loving her. She felt the pang of loss. She looked at John, saw his encouraging smile, took a breath and rallied. "Smartest thing you ever did, John." She took in her children, eyed John. "And, you married two fantastic women."

John looked at Katie lovingly, and continued. "So true," he agreed. "And, we remained friends as couples." He watched Kelly and Anna closely. "Girls, both your Moms and Aunt Laura loved to take their babies walking, they went shopping, really, they did everything together."

John paused. "I'm so glad you asked that question, Kelly." He smiled. "I want you all to feel free to ask any questions you may have." He studied each child. "Franco, Anna, I so loved your mother. And Kelly, Mom loved your Dad." He smiled. "Now, we love each other." He paused, smiled. "But, we will never forget Marc or Connie. We will love them forever." He saw that the girls seemed content. He looked to Franco. "Franco, you were discussing Bart. Is there more?"

Franco nodded. "He had his issues," Franco informed. "He had a terrible stutter for most of his life." He winced. "They called him 'Stutter Boy,' really gave him a hard time," Franco informed. "He seems to have beat it for the most part." He paused. "I've heard that Angela really helped him." He shrugged. "I don't know how, but that's what I hear."

"You like Bart?" Katie asked her son.

"I do," Franco agreed. "He's a good guy. He's the reason I'm on the golf team." He paused. "Bart is always ready to help any member of the team. He worked with me on my chipping for an hour." He shook his head and smiled. "He really is a good guy."

John laughed. "Your Uncle Peter is not happy about that!"

Franco laughed happily. "Bart made golf cool." He looked at his Dad, smiled. "He's all over the Golf Channel, but he never talks about himself." He shook his head. "When I see Uncle Peter, I will tell him that I may be the 1st or 2nd seed on the golf team next season." He grinned. "That should get him going."

Everybody laughed. They all loved the funny, quirky, and loyal, Uncle Peter. He is the dearest of friends. As John often said. 'Peter Novello is a man you can count on.'

"You can be certain of that." John agreed. "Golf over football, he'll go crazy!" John laughed.

Later that evening, after John and his sons watched the Boston College basketball team play and win an exciting game, and when the children were all settled, John and Katie retired to their bed. When John climbed in, he pulled Katie close. She smiled, "you handled Kelly's question perfectly," she paused, kissed John, "thank you." She cuddled close, her head resting on John's chest. "That caught me by surprise."

"Sure," John grinned. "You were too preoccupied with waging a war for Angela Curcuru, that she has zero interest in fighting."

Katie snuggled close. "I suppose," she said, hiding her smile in John's chest. She looked up at him, with raised brows. "I would appreciate you expounding on the 'I am woman' soapbox?' comment." She paused, kissed him, snuggled close. "Do you care to elaborate on your point, Counselor?"

John held her and laughed. Katie loved the sound of his laugh. "Okay, since we are recounting our stimulating dinner conversation, do you, my dear, want to elaborate on the 'Italian Guy Code' reference?" They laughed together comfortably. He pulled her close, kissed her and grinned. "How about I love you, instead?" They lost themselves in their love.

Chapter Forty

Things were happening quickly. Phil Walleston called Bart to see if he was still planning on visiting after Christmas. Bart assured him that he and Dave planned on the trip.

Bart heard concern in Mr. Walleston's tone. "Is everything okay, Sir?" Bart asked.

"Yes, Bart, everything is fine," Mr. Walleston assured. "It's just that I received a call from an attorney, John Palermo, who wanted to discuss whether Manitoba Oil wished to sponsor you as a professional golfer?" He paused. "Are you planning on turning professional?"

Bart took his time. "I think so, Sir." He paused. "Right now, there are PGA Tournaments that want me to play on Sponsor Exemptions. There are companies that are willing to sponsor me." He considered, and elaborated. "See, Sir, neither Dave nor I have the money to pay for flights, hotels and food and everything else to play in these tournaments." He explained. "And, I have to pay Dave,"

Bart paused, shrugged. "I just don't have the luxury of remaining an amateur and still playing against the best golfers in the world." He considered his next words. "Mr. Walleston, I might not have this opportunity again."

Phil Walleston considered his words, nodded. "Of course, Bart, you're right." He smiled. "You are a smart kid." He took a deep breath. "I hope that I can count on you to play in the Manitoba Classic."

Bart smiled. "Mr. Walleston, even if I am invited to play in the U.S. OPEN, you can rest assured that I will be in Manitoba to play in the Classic." He grew serious. "I will be there for Justin and all the Justin's who need my help."

Walleston was deeply moved. "Thank you, Bart." He cleared his throat. "I'm going to place a call to Mr. Palermo now."

The Golf Channel reported that Bart 'Stutter Boy' DeMarco, has recently given up his amateur status and declared that he was a Professional. The announcer reported that he had been offered, and reportedly, has accepted, the maximum permitted, by PGA rules, of six Sponsor

Exemptions to play in PGA Tournaments beginning with the Hawaiian Open in January.

Bart was interviewed by and appeared on the Golf Channel. Bart explained his reasons for turning Professional.

"You realize," He was asked, that you have six Tournaments to earn enough money to secure a PGA Tour Card?"

"I do," he smiled. "I know that it will be tough," he nodded. "I plan on giving it my best efforts and we'll see what happens."

Bart and his Dad met with John Palermo and the sport's agent, Harry Winston, John had retained to represent Bart.

"Bart," John began. "It looks as if Manitoba Oil wants an exclusive deal with you."

Bart looked from John to Harry. "Okay, is that good?"

Harry leaned forward. "Bart, you must have really impressed this guy, Walleston." He looked at John. "Manitoba Oil is offering to provide everything you need. A private jet, at your disposal, 5 star lodgings. The equipment of your choice, golf clothes, which they will have designed, food, everything, including tutors." He smiled, "in addition they will pay you $1 million per year and your coach and caddie, a guaranteed, $100,000 per year." He paused, studied Bart's reaction. Winston was somewhat surprised that Bart's reaction, was, at that pointed muted.

Harry smiled and continued. "It is traditional for golfers to pay their caddies 10% of their winnings." He shook his head. "Finally, he agreed to pay for the full family health coverage for you and your coach." He smiled. "And, this is huge," he paused. "Walleston, on behalf of Manitoba Oil, has offered a three year commitment." He sat back and smiled at Bart. "Walleston must really have faith in you."

Bart smiled, "Mr. Walleston is a remarkable man." He looked to his Dad, who met Bart's gaze. He addressed Winston. "And, what am I obligated to do?" Bart asked. It sounded too good to be true.

John Palermo laughed, looked at Harry. "I told you he was smart."

Harry laughed. "Mr. Walleston wants you to wear golf clothes and hat with his company's logo in PGA Tour events, and when making television appearances. He wants you to advise him on the development of a school for young stutterers." He paused. "He also would ask, but not require, you to appear in some advertising for his company and for the Tournament his company is sponsoring." He smiled. "He encourages you to play in as many PGA events as you and your advisors believe are appropriate." He shrugged. "And, of course, there are bonuses built in for tournament wins and big bonuses if you should win a major." He laughed. "That's it!"

Bart sat back, looked at John. "Mr. Palermo, what do you think?"

John smiled. "Bart, it's a home run or," he laughed, "a hole in one."

"When does the contract become effective," Franco DeMarco asked.

"Immediately, sir," John responded. "As soon as Bart agrees and signs the contract."

Franco hesitated. "There is something else I should ask," he said.

John smiled. "Please, ask away."

"What does Bart owe you two?" He shrugged, a bit embarrassed.

John Palermo smiled. "You should ask that question, Mr. DeMarco." He looked at Bart. "I plan to bring in specialists to handle your business affairs. Harry will handle your schedule, register you for the tournaments, arrange the transportation, lodgings, everything." He smiled. "For that, he will be paid 5% of your winnings and of future endorsement revenues." He paused, eyed Bart and Franco. "That is fair, Bart." John watched Bart carefully. "And, I will oversee everyone on 'Team DeMarco,' as you requested."

Bart nodded. "I trust you Mr. Palermo." He paused. "But, I also expect to pay you." He stated. "How do I pay you?"

John Palermo studied Bart. He smiled. "How does 5% sound, Bart? I will charge 5% of your future income to oversee 'Team DeMarco.'"

Bart nodded, watched Palermo closely. "Is that fair to you, Sir?" He paused. "You will be the guy in charge, overseeing our team."

John smiled, "I appreciate your concern, but 5% will be fine, Bart." He paused, studied Bart. "Signing this contract will change your life, Bart." The lawyer shrugged. "But, it will be an opportunity that few ever receive."

Bart nodded. "Mr. Palermo, I love to play golf, even more, I love to compete." He smiled. "I have a wonderful family, a girl that I love and who supports me." He scanned the room, eyed the lawyer. "With you, Sir, and Mr. Winston on my team, I'm ready and eager to start this adventure."

John Palermo smiled and nodded. "Bart, I'm proud to be a part of the team."

Franco DeMarco looked at Harry. "Excuse me, please. You didn't say anything about fees on this contract."

John Palermo smiled. "That's because we are not charging a fee on this contract, Sir."

Franco's eye narrowed. "Why not?" He asked.

"In fairness, we really didn't do anything." He smiled. "Mr. Walleston simply laid out extremely generous terms." He looked to Harry. "If Manitoba Oil could be generous, so can your representatives." He eyed Bart. "Are we good?"

Bart smiled. "Yes sir, we're good. And thank you." Bart rose and shook their hands. "I need to call Dave and," he looked at Harry, "we need to plan my travel schedule."

John Palermo smiled. "First, you need to sign the contract with Manitoba Oil and the contract with Harry." He pulled them from the folder. He looked to Franco. "Mr. DeMarco, as Bart is just 17, you will need to sign as well."

Bart and Franco signed where John indicated. Bart looked to Harry, "so, what's the plan, sir?"

Harry laughed. "First, you call me Harry." He poked Bart. "Next, you enjoy your family and work on your game, as best you can in this New England weather, until Christmas." He looked at Bart, "then, you will fly to Manitoba on December 27th, as you promised Mr. Walleston, and stay for a week." He grimaced. "That week would be better used preparing in Florida. Still, he was pretty insistent that you fly to Canada." He sighed. "Then, after Canada, you fly on to Hawaii, for your first PGA Tournament." He smiled. "You will have about a week to acclimate and practice before you start."

Bart watched Harry Winston closely. "You seem concerned, sir." He glanced at John Palermo, then focused on Harry. "Is there something else?"

Harry paused. "Bart, you have been given an amazing opportunity." He paused, eyed Bart. "I have been in contact with the PGA." He studied his newest client. "You do realize that you have these six tournaments to earn the six hundred thousand dollars required to secure a card for the remainder of the season?" He shrugged. "You will be playing against the best players in the world." He paused, eyed Bart. "These guys are killers, Bart."

Bart nodded and smiled. "I guess, we'll see how good I am."

Harry nodded, studied Bart's face, and wondered if the young man would be overwhelmed. 'We'll see,' he thought.

Chapter Forty-One

It was a relatively balmy Saturday, mid-December day. About 35 degrees, with not much wind. Bart thought that while not ideal, his plan would work.

Jim and Betsy drove to Angela's house to collect her. Angela was busy helping her mother and Tina clean the house. A traditional Saturday chore. She wore jeans and a baggy sweat-shirt. Betsy knocked on the door, which was opened by Tina, while Jim waited in the car.

Angela heard conversation in the foyer and was surprised to find Tina conversing with Betsy. "Hi Betsy," Angela smiled. "This is a nice surprise, what's up?"

Betsy looked at Angela, shook her head. "Come on," she urged. "Go and take a shower, fix yourself up, put on some, 'I'm seeing Bart clothes,' and let's go."

Angela looked puzzled. "What's happening, Betsy?"

Betsy stood before Angela, Tina and Maria hovered in the background. Betsy held Angela's shoulders, looked into her eyes. "Angela, I'm asking you to do as I request. It will all be made clear to you very soon, Okay?"

Angela looked from Betsy to the smiling faces of her sister and mother.

"Go, Angela," Betsy urged. "You're keeping Bart waiting."

Angela laughed, nodded and hustled up the stairs to shower and dress. Her mother insisted that she take a warm winter coat, gloves and a hat. "Just in case, Angela," she said.

Jim drove Betsy and Angela around what the locals referred to as the Back Shore, or a more accurate description, Atlantic Road, with its beautiful ocean views. Angela sat comfortably in the back seat of Jim's car, having removed her coat and hat.

"Are we going to see Bart?" Angela asked. She laughed. "Betsy, I don't understand all this."

Betsy looked from Jim back to Angela. Betsy smiled, "be patient Angela, Bart gave us our instructions."

"Ya," Jim complained. "First, I teach him to play golf and now I'm his girl's chauffeur." He glanced back and grinned. "Can you believe this, Angela?"

Angela sensed something important was happening, and was anxious to know, but since Bart had made the arrangements, she sat back, smiling, and enjoyed the company of dear friends and the majestic ocean view. "Hard to believe, Jim," Angela agreed, feigning outrage. "That Bart is out of control!"

"Look at her," Jim said to Betsy, with his easy smile. "Now, she's humoring me."

Finally, and it seemed like forever, Jim drove to Stacey Boulevard and parked. Jim turned around and smiled at Angela. "Why don't you go see who's sitting on that bench?"

Angela looked to the bench, the same bench where Bart was sitting on that long past September, Friday night, after the Salem High School football game. She saw Bart sitting, he looked her way, waved and smiled.

Betsy handed Angela her coat, hat and gloves. "It's cold out there." She smiled. "Good luck, Angela."

Angela exited the car and walked to where Bart was waiting.

"Hi Princess," He called, rose and kissed her. He pointed to the bench. "Can you sit for a bit?" He asked, flashing a big smile.

Angela smiled, remembering that those were the words he had used that evening. Her eyes lit. "Sure I can, but if my girlfriends leave, I will need you to walk me home." She shrugged and smiled. "You know my Dad."

He laughed aloud, took her hands and helped her to the bench. She was glad she wore her coat, it was cold, but Bart's eyes fixed on her in a way that made her feel warm.

"I need to tell you something, Angela." He held onto her hands, looked into her eyes. "You know that I have been invited to play in six PGA Tournaments." He smiled, flashed a smile, excitement dancing in his eyes. "This is my big chance, Angela." He studied her sweet face. "The first Tournament is scheduled for the second week of January in Hawaii." He paused, allowing her to absorb the information. "So, Dave Gilliss and I will be flying to Manitoba on December 27th, staying a week, then on to Hawaii for two weeks."

Angela smiled, but the smile did not reach her eyes. "I guess you will be staying in Manitoba with the Wallestons?" She asked.

Bart nodded. "Yes, Mr. Walleston wants me to see the golf course we will be playing in June and to consult on the school he is opening for children with speech challenges."

Angela swallowed. "Justin will be happy to see you." She said softly. "Will Rachel be there?"

"Oh yeah," he affirmed. "Then, I might be able to get home for a week, but most likely will have to spend the next two to three weeks in Arizona and California." He smiled. "Two great golf courses and Tournaments."

Angela's eyes misted. "So, you'll be gone for six weeks?"

Bart felt bad, he didn't want to upset Angela. "I will," he said. "But, the problem is, I don't want to be away from my girl for six weeks."

Angela took a deep breath. She knew that this was Bart's big opportunity. She vowed that she would not be an obstacle to his success. Even, if it meant losing him. "You must go, Bart." She fought tears. "I will be waiting for you."

He smiled. "Angela, I will go, but I want you with me."

Angela offered a sad smile, gently placed her hand on Bart's cheek. "That's not really possible." She sighed. "I wish, but my Dad…" The tears came.

Bart gently wiped away her tears. He rose, stood before Angela and smiled. He bent to one knee, saw her eyes go wide. He took a ring box from his pocket, flipped it open to reveal a diamond engagement ring. He looked into her eyes. "Princess, I wanted to ask you here, on our bench, with everybody we love present." He grinned as both families and their closest friends moved from cover into view, forming a half-circle around the happy couple.

Angela was overwhelmed. She saw her Mom and Dad, smiling. Bart's parents happily standing with them. Tina beaming a smile. Lucia, Celia and Mario smiling, nodding, and Mario acting as cameraman. Bart gently eased the friendship ring he had given her off of her left ring finger and moved it to her right ring finger. He held her left hand and placed the engagement ring on her ring finger. He looked into her eyes. "Angela," he paused, smiled, "will you marry me?"

Angela looked at the ring, she saw her mother and Rosa crying tears of joy. She looked at Bart, she leaned forward and kissed him as she had that night when they first sat on this bench. "Yes, Bart, oh yes, I will marry you."

They embraced and the sizable group clapped for them. Bart knew that Angela had a million questions. As he held her he whispered. "Angela, my beauty, I have worked everything out." He kissed her. "I will explain everything." He pulled her to her feet, kissed her deeply and passionately. "How did I get so lucky to find you, Princess?"

The group comprised of Angela's and Bart's families, as well as their closest friends gathered at the DeMarco house. Bart sat Angela down in the living room and began the lengthy process of filling in all the blanks and answering all of her questions.

Bart told Angela about the Sponsorship by Manitoba Oil, and all that was involved. He explained that he had met with Mrs. Nelson in the guidance office and that she was arranging with the tutors, who would travel with them, to keep them on track to graduate with their class. He smiled. "I promised your parents, and mine, that we would walk with our class."

He smiled when he described the conversation with her Dad, when Bart asked for Angela's hand.

"You asked my Dad? Really?" Tears flooded her eyes. "What did he say?" She paused. "Was he upset that we're only 17 years old?"

Bart laughed. "You know, I thought that might be a sticking point, but he said his mother was 16 when she married. And they are still married." He pulled Angela into a hug. "He gave me his blessing." Bart paused. "He asked me to please take care of his Bambina." Bart smiled, looked into her eyes. "I told him that I would always cherish you." He winked. "I told him that we would be 'Team DeMarco.'"

Angela beamed, pulled him into a hug. "I love you, Bart."

"So," Bart continued, "our Dads will sign for us, as we're still minors, and Father Capelli will marry us Christmas Eve." He laughed. "By the way, Father wants to see us on Tuesday at 5pm." He grinned. "Then Christmas, and we're off for a six week honeymoon," he laughed, added, "and, of course, a little golf."

Her eyes glinted. "Won't Rachel be disappointed?" She smiled, "when you show up with a wife?"

Bart laughed. "No, I don't think so. I think Dave has his eye on Rachel."

"Really?" Angela replied with a grin. "Bart, you keep disappointing women. There was Janet in Florida and now Rachel." She raised her brows and smiled. "You must be really sweet on me?"

Bart laughed aloud. "I'm glad that you finally figured that out."

Angela went into his arms, feeling safe and cherished. "Sorry for all the trouble," she whispered.

"I'll find a way for you to make it up to me," he said softly.

Angela laughed. "I bet you will!"

"The only thing," Bart explained, "is that we will need to postpone a wedding reception until after Mario and Celia's wedding." He grinned. "I don't want to upstage them or steal their thunder."

Angela nodded. "So, Christmas Eve at St. Ann's Church." She eyed Bart, hopefully. "Will there be bridesmaids and groomsmen?"

"Sure, of course, whatever my girl wants." Bart stated with a smile. "Let's celebrate our engagement and then you can sit down with my mother and yours and plan the wedding."

Angela looked up and saw Celia, Lucia, Betsy, Jessica, and Tina hovering nearby.

"So, should we be thinking of dresses and flowers for the wedding?" Celia asked with a smile.

Angela hugged Celia. "This is all so sudden, and unexpected. I hope this is okay with you."

Celia smiled, "as long as you make me a Bridesmaid, I'll be fine."

Angela held Celia's hand. "Thank you, Celia." She smiled. "I certainly hope my sister-in-law will be a Bridesmaid."

"I'm happy for you, Angela." Celia paused, eyed Angela. "You take good care of Bart."

Angela smiled. "I will, I promise."

Angela walked to Tina, took her hands. "Tina, will you be my Maid of Honor?"

Tina pulled her into a hug. "Of course, I will." Tears flowed. "I'm so happy for you, Angela."

Angela looked to Lucia, Betsy and Jessica, saw their smiles. "I hope you will be my Bridesmaids?"

"I'd be honored," Jessica responded with tears of happiness and a hug for Angela. "And, whom will Bart be pairing me with?" She laughed. "Bart, I hope he's hot."

Before Bart could respond, Betsy wrapped Angela and Jessica in an embrace. Betsy looked at Bart with a queried expression. "Will Jim be a groomsman, Bart?"

Bart shook his head and smiled at the scene. His girl was happy. He silently vowed to keep her happy. As he walked away, he laughed, "I'm pretty sure Angela will have some suggestions for me." He looked at Angela and flashed a smile. "We'll talk later."

Chapter Forty-Two

B art met with Dave at Bass Rocks Golf Club. He smiled at his coach. "Let's sit down, we need to talk."

Dave studied Bart, shrugged, "Okay, let's go to the grill room, there's usually a pot of coffee brewing."

They sat with coffees before them. Bart looked out over the Meadows, holes 15 through 18, which back in 1896 was the entire golf course. He sat back and looked beyond the course, to the breathtaking ocean views to Thatcher's Island and its twin lighthouses. Bart took a deep breath. It hit him just how significantly his life was about to change. He looked over the course, out to the ocean, and sighed. "It's so pretty here."

Dave nodded, studied Bart. "Hey, Bart, are you okay?"

Bart nodded. "I'm okay, just a little uneasy." Dave sat back, sipped his coffee and waited. "Coach," Bart began. "I don't think any of this could have happened for me without your guidance, coaching and encouragement."

The tall, lanky, coach smiled. "I've enjoyed it, Bart." He paused, eyed Bart. "You have a gift, Bart. I've never seen such natural talent." He leaned forward. "Bart, you need to use it, develop it, but understand, it will take a lot of work."

Bart nodded. "Yes, I know." He pursed his lips. "You know that I've been offered Sponsor Exemptions into some PGA tournaments."

Dave nodded. "I know," he smiled. "This could be your big chance, Bart."

Bart eyed Dave, there was hope in his eyes. "I really think that we are a good team." Bart stated. "Together, I think we'll succeed," he paused. "But, without you," he shook his head. "I think that would be tough." He exhaled, nervously, he eyed Dave and asked. "Coach, I'm asking you to be my full-time coach and caddie." He paused. "I want you with me, to help me earn my PGA Tour card."

Dave sat back. "I want to be there for you." He laughed. "What does Angela always say?" He shook his head. "'Team DeMarco!'" He smiled. "You know Bart, Angela is a prize." He considered. "So, you want me to be part of 'Team DeMarco?'" He eyed Bart. "What do you have in mind?"

Bart filled Dave in on the details, the tournaments, John Palermo and Harry Winston, Manitoba Oil's sponsorship. "You could do well Dave, especially if we play well."

Dave Gilliss smiled. He loved that Bart always thought in terms of Team, never Bart DeMarco, but 'Team DeMarco.'"

Dave sat back and considered, nodded. "Okay, Bart, I'm in." He paused. "But, we have to do this right." He looked at Bart, "you do realize," he set a serious gaze on Bart, "that you have six PGA Tournaments to earn a card?" He paused. "If, you haven't done that, the Manitoba Classic will be the end of your PGA season."

Bart nodded and smiled, "I guess we need to win a Tournament, Coach." He paused. "Would that be a solution to our problem?"

Dave laughed. "It sure would." He shook his head. "Let's get to work."

Bart and Dave spent the next days working on Bart's short game. "This is where you will save strokes." He eyed Bart. "This won't be the Mass. Amateur, Bart. You will be battling the best golfers in the world."

Bart smiled. "I'll only be battling the golf course, Coach." He paused, eyed Dave. "I can't control what Bubba, Rory or Phil do. I can only focus on my game."

Dave smiled. "Good, I like the way you think, Bart."

Bart picked up a smiling and exuberant, Angela at about 4:45pm and they happily drove to the Church Rectory to meet with Father Capelli. Angela wore a pretty navy skirt and white blouse outfit, with earrings, the necklace and bracelet that Bart had given as a gifts at Christmas and her birthday, and of course, the rings he had given her. The commitment ring on her right hand and, the engagement ring, shining on her left ring finger.

Bart and Angela were shown into Father's study and took their place, side by side, on the couch. Father Capelli entered and sat across a coffee table in a maroon, leather chair. The priest studied the young couple as they sat, happily, holding hands.

"Thank you for coming in." The priest began. "I thought we would discuss your plans."

Bart nodded. "Of course, Father."

Father Capelli got right to his biggest concern. "Bart, Angela, you are 17 years old." He paused. "What's the rush?"

Bart nodded and smiled. "I know we are young, Father, but I have been presented with an amazing opportunity." Bart filled in Father Capelli on the broad outline. "So, you can see, I will be traveling constantly over the next few years." He looked at Angela, their eyes met and he smiled. "I want Angela with me." He looked at the priest. "In truth, Father, I need her with me." He exhaled. "Angela and I, we are a team."

Angela beamed a smile at Bart. She looked to their priest.

Father Capelli also smiled. "What about school, Bart? Neither of you have graduated High school."

Angela nervously tightened her grip on Bart's hand. Bart smiled at her, "relax, Angela, everything is okay."

"Father," Bart smiled. "My sponsor is paying for tutors to help Angela and I complete our class work, so we can graduate with our class." He leaned forward. "And, we will graduate with our class!" He stated firmly as he eyed the priest. Bart smiled. "We are not your usual couple, Father." Bart acknowledged. "I will be into my career immediately." He smiled, "a bit different from most 17 year olds."

Father Capelli nodded. "You've never been ordinary Bart," he stated.

"After Christmas," Bart continued, "We will be flying to Canada to meet with my Tour Sponsor. He wants to build a school for young stutterers." He smiled, "he asked for my input."

Father Capelli nodded. "I can see that."

"After the New Year," Bart continued. We will fly to Hawaii, so I can play in the Hawaiian Open." He smiled, "it will be my first PGA Tour event." He watched as the priest took in the information. "Then onto Arizona, followed by California." He paused. "Father, I have six tournaments to earn my PGA Tour card." He caressed Angela's hand. "I don't think it's possible without Angela." He sighed. "I need her, Father."

Father Capelli studied Bart and Angela. He sat back. "Angela, what do you have to say?"

Angela smiled. "Father, I love Bart. We are a team, 'Team DeMarco,'" she stated. "Bart's coach, Dave Gilliss is with us, and our families support us." She said. "I need to be with Bart, I want to help him, in any way that I am able." She paused. "You know, Father, it's more than just the golf, it's a whole life." She smiled at Bart. "Bart shouldn't have to do this alone."

Father Capelli nodded.

Bart smiled. "Father, if I may," he sighed and shook his head. "We know people will say that we are too young." He shrugged. "I have found that everybody seems to believe themselves to be an expert on how others should live their lives, while they struggle with their own lives." He flashed a wry smile. "Father, I can't worry about that." He eyed the smiling priest.

"I see couples who wait until they are in their thirties, set in their careers, in theory, mature, and the marriage doesn't work."

Father Capelli nodded. "That's true." He chuckled. "That's so true, Bart."

"The way I see it, Father," Bart added. "When one finds the right person, and the love is there, that is when you marry." He grew serious, thoughtful. "And, it doesn't matter if you are 17 or 70. When it's right, it's right." He paused, looked at Angela and smiled. "Father, I found the love of my life when I was 16." He faced the priest. "When you find your soul mate, you don't worry about the details."

Father Capelli sat back, studied the young couple. He looked at Angela, whose eyes were on Bart. The priest read the love and her belief in his words. He smiled, "Angela?"

Angela smiled. "I love Bart and I want to be his wife." She paused, reached for the words. "I want to help Bart." She looked at Bart, then back to Father Capelli. "Father, Bart and I are a team." She grinned.

"Yes," Father Capelli smiled. "'Team DeMarco!" He stated.

Angela placed serious eyes on the priest. "We will be together and we'll succeed together." She laughed. "Whatever happens, I will be with Bart." She took Bart's arm. "We hope to have a big family, a happy family, just like Bart and I have had." She sighed. "Let them all talk, Father." She paused, a sweet smile emerged. "What matters is our love."

Father Capelli met Angela's eyes. He read the intelligence and her maturity. He felt his confidence and his faith in these two young, but very special, people surge. He rose and embraced Angela, then Bart. "The first time I saw you two together, I thought, there are two wonderful people." He smiled. "If you remember, I urged you to not let anything or anyone beat you." He patted Bart's shoulder. "It appears you haven't." He smiled. "Bart, Angela, go with God. You have my blessing."

Angela beamed and hugged the priest. "Thank you, Father, that's means so much to me."

Father Capelli smiled. "Christmas Eve at 5pm." He smiled. "Angela, I believe you will be a beautiful bride."

Bart and Angela drove back to Angela's house for dinner. Angela was emotionally exhausted. "I was so worried," she told Bart, as he steered through the granite curbed streets.

Bart smiled, pulled to a stop by Angela's house. He looked into her eyes, gently cupped her face. "Princess, we have the blessings of our families. Nothing and nobody will stop me from making you my wife."

She smiled. "I like the sound of that." She proclaimed, with a laugh. "Bart, I am so happy."

He laughed, kissed her. "That's my job, to keep my girl happy." He set his gaze on her smiling face. "I promised your Dad."

Angela cuddled close. "I'll try to make you happy, Bart. I really will."

He grinned. "I know you will, Princess." He paused, grinned. "So, what's for dinner?"

Angela laughed. "I don't know. Actually, Tina is making dinner." She set her gaze on Bart, she blushed, which brought a smile to Bart's face. "But, if you want," she continued, her gleaming eyes set on his. "Your favorite garlic bread is certainly available."

The Curcuru house was buzzing with excitement. Tina had taken command in the kitchen, allowing Maria to spend the day altering her wedding gown to fit Angela. As she worked, Maria thrilled and misted at the thought of Angela wearing her gown. "There is good luck in this gown, Angela." She assured her daughter. "Dad and I have had a wonderful life, I pray this gown will bring the same luck to you."

Angela smiled and hugged Maria. "I know it will, Mom." Angela looked on happily as she explained to her mother the conversation with Father Capelli. Sal was out fishing, scheduled to complete another fishing trip before Christmas.

Bart left them and walked into the kitchen to see Tina and check on dinner.

"Hi Bart," Tina called, with a big smile. "Did everything go well with Father?"

Bart nodded, as he lifted the top off of a pot. "Just fine." He grinned. "What do I smell?"

"That is Veal Saltimbocca," she stated proudly. "That's veal with prosciutto, sage, white wine, extra-virgin olive oil, lots of butter and some lemon juice." She laughed. "I think that you will like it."

"It smells great," he said. He laughed, eyed Tina, "Okay, Tina, I need to know, can Angela cook?"

Tina laughed as she watched Bart poke around. She grew serious, set her eyes on Bart. "Angela adores you, Bart." She paused. "She will learn to cook for you." Tina smiled and misted. "In fact, all the women in this family adore you."

"WOW!" Bart said. "Thanks Tina, that's great, but you know," he said with a grin. "I'm a one-woman man."

Tina laughed. "That's good to know."

They sat to dinner, with joy radiating through all. Bart tasted the veal, and sighed. He smiled, "Tina, this is great," Bart praised. He grinned, "Tina, you just have to teach Angela how to make this."

Angela smiled, feigned aloofness. "A Princess doesn't cook!" She stated haughtily, her eyes gleaming.

All laughed. Maria set amused eyes on her eldest daughter. She wagged her finger. "No Princess's in this family." Maria smiled, the happiness contagious. "Angela, you take care of your husband!" She instructed.

Angela's smile bloomed. She eyed Bart. "Oh, I intend to take good care of my husband."

Angela was ebullient in re-counting their conversation with Father Capelli. She moved into a discussion of the planned wedding, which was only eight days away.

"The girls are all deciding on dresses for the wedding." She stated. "Tina, I love the dress you chose."

Tina laughed. "Thanks, but I'm not sure I chose it," She lifted her brows to her mother and laughed. "Mom does have good taste."

Angela grinned. "It looks great on you."

Bart laughed with the group. He knew that the schedule was tight and that everybody was happily plugging away as the days to the wedding became fewer.

Angela looked to Bart, who was savoring a generous forkful of Tina's Saltimbocca. She watched as he closed his eyes in delight. She smiled. "Have you decided on groomsmen?" Angela asked.

Bart nodded as he swirled pasta on his fork. "All taken care of, Princess."

Angela grinned. "That's great, so who are they?"

Bart sat back and smiled. "Well, Mario, of course, is my best man." He looked to Tina. "I think Tina will look so pretty, nobody will even notice him." He shrugged and laughed. "But, that's his problem."

Tina blushed, "Thanks, Bart." Then, she laughed. "Are you saying that because you like the veal?"

Maria smiled. "My girls will look beautiful." She stated proudly.

Bart eyed Tina with a grin. "The Curcuru girls are beauties." He paused, eyed Angela. "I just hope that the culinary skills are in the DNA!" He laughed.

Angela smiled, leaned over and kissed his cheek. "I guess you'll just have to wait and see." Her eyes twinkled.

Bart met her smile. At that moment, he wasn't thinking of dinner. He shook his head, placed hungry eyes on Angela.

Angela read the look in his eyes and grinned with a feminine satisfaction. "Oh, Bart," she teased. "I believe, you were discussing the Groomsmen."

Bart cleared his throat, lustful eyes on Angela. "Then," Bart continued, "I thought Dave Gilliss would match with Lucia." Angela nodded, still smiling. Bart met her smile and shook his head. He swirled his fork through the spaghetti in the sweet and rich Saltimbocca sauce that coupled so well with the veal. He ate it with such an apparent pleasure, that Tina so appreciated.

He looked to Angela. "I thought Jim and Betsy was a no brainer, of course." He smiled. "For Celia, I asked Justin Walleston. It will be such a confidence builder for a boy who really could use it."

Angela smiled. She knew Bart saw his young scared and uncertain self in Justin. "I like that." She kissed Bart's cheek. "You're really a nice guy, DeMarco."

Bart looked into her eyes and laughed.

Angela shook her head and grinned. "Okay, should I ask for a drum roll?" Bart met her eyes. "And, who did you ask to pair with Jessica?"

Bart cut into the veal, swirled the forkful through the sauce, he smiled, chewed the portion thoughtfully. "I asked the perfect guy," he said with a smile. "I asked Dave Powers." He paused. "He'll be home for the Christmas break and was happy to have been asked."

Maria and Tina exchanged a long look. Angela studied Bart, smiled. "What are you up to?" She asked, suspiciously. "You know Dave dumped Jessica." She paused. "I like Dave," she conceded. "But, he really broke her heart."

Bart shrugged. "Did he dump her?" Bart asked with a grin. "Maybe, just maybe," he smiled, "not everything is quite as it seems."

Angela studied Bart's demeanor. She shook her head, her expression one of frustration. "Do you want to fill me in?" She looked to her mother, shook her head, but managed a smile. "Was Dad this maddening?"

Maria patted Angela's hand, and smiled. "I think with this one, you better get used to it."

Bart watched the exchange and smiled. "Okay, Dave's really crazy about Jessica." He stated. "But, he really hated how cruel she was to so many people." He shrugged. Angela nodded.

"Dave's a good guy," Bart continued. "Dave felt that he needed to know if Jessica's transformation was real." He paused, shrugged. "I mean, how many people really ever change?" He swirled another forkful of spaghetti. Ate it as he thought through his next words. "Dave wanted to see if Jessica really cared for him. And, he wanted to know, really know, if she had changed." He sat back, smiled. "Tina, this is great." He saw Tina's appreciative smile light her face.

Maria nodded, remembering how cruel Jessica had been. "I'm still not sure about that girl, either."

Angela considered his words, her eyes widened. "Jessica hasn't dated anybody since Dave." She laughed. "Half of the senior boys have asked her out."

"And?" Bart prodded.

"She has said no, but always in a kind way," Angela affirmed. She looked at Bart. "And, you, have been talking to Dave, filling him in." She exhaled. "Right?"

"Dave's my friend." Bart shrugged. "He thought if Jessica could get over him quickly, then, they never really had anything." He sat quietly, flashed a smile at Angela. "And, if Jessica proved to be less than honest in her transformation from 'the queen of mean' to a kind person, he wouldn't want to be with her." He shrugged. "Dave felt that he had to know."

Angela's eyes went wide in surprise. "So, he tested her!" Angela stated, with a tone of amazement. She looked at Bart. "And, you knew what he was doing?"

Bart nodded, "I did."

She studied him. "You didn't tell me." He saw hurt in her eyes.

Bart shook his head, reached and took her hand. He smiled. "Angela, please understand," he explained. "Dave asked me to keep his confidence. He needed to talk it out," Bart shrugged. "So, I listened." He exhaled, considered, wanting to get the words right. "Dave wanted to be sure of Jessica, before…" Bart shrugged, he looked Angela in the eye.

With a serious expression, he stated, "Angela, I will always be honest with you about our life." He assured. "But, this was about Dave and Jessica." He smiled. "I know that you understand the difference."

Angela nodded, smiled, "you really are a smart jock, aren't you?"

Bart smiled, gently squeezed her hand. "I was smart enough to cherish my angel, when I found her."

That had all three women misting. Nick and Giuseppe looked on with befuddled expressions.

Dabbing at her eyes, Angela offered a smile. "So what's the plan?" Angela asked. "I'm certain that you have thought this out."

He reached and tenderly cupped her cheek. "Angela, we say nothing. Dave will be at the Wedding rehearsal on the 23th. We provide the opportunity for Dave and Jessica to talk." He smiled. "Then, we sit them together at the rehearsal dinner." Bart shrugged. "That puts the ball in their court." He laughed. "And, we get to watch the show."

"So," Angela concluded, with a smile, "There was no 'sweet girl' that Dave was seeing?"

Bart laughed. "No," he shook his head. "Dave's crazy in love with Jessica." He paused. "That's why he demanded that she apologize to all the people she had hurt over the years." Bart smiled. "Dave had a strong hunch that there was a good person lurking inside Jessica." He shrugged. "In any event, he felt that he had to know, to be certain, if their relationship was going to move forward."

Angela sat back, considered, and nodded. "I see." She eyed Bart, then her eyes lit. "Oh, I do see, tough guy," she laughed as dawn broke. "That's why you came back in when Betsy and I were talking to Jess. You told her that she deserved someone who really wanted her." She laughed, "you crafty guy! You told her that there is a real goodness in her and she shouldn't rush into anything."

Bart smiled as he watched Angela put it all together. "I love it that you are so smart." He stated with a grin. "Anyway, Dave felt that it would take character for Jess to humble herself." Bart explained. "And, he would see if he meant enough to Jessica for her to eat crow, as it were." He nodded. "And, she did it."

Tina looked across at Bart. "You know, it might not work out as Dave hopes. Maybe, Jessica will tell him to take a flying leap."

Bart nodded. "We discussed that very point." He smiled. "But, Dave felt that if she didn't want him, then okay, he would have his answer."

Chapter Forty-Three

B art practiced every day under the eyes of Dave Gilliss. Angela attended, with her mother and Rosa, to the thousand details involved with a wedding.

The rehearsal was scheduled for 4pm on the 23th of December. The plan was to have a small, simple, wedding and then a Christmas Eve Celebration to follow. The traditional 'Feast of the Seven Fishes,' with the addition of the Bridal Party and some very close friends, a celebratory party, rather than a large reception. But, following the rehearsal, Franco DeMarco had arranged a rehearsal party at the newly constructed Beauport hotel, set on Pavilion Beach.

Bart drove to collect Angela to head to Church for the wedding rehearsal. She met him with a big smile and an even bigger kiss. Bart was pleased at how positively bubbly Angela appeared. "Happy, Princess?" He asked.

She threw her arms around him. "I'm so happy!" She affirmed. "Are you happy, Bart?'

He smiled, looked into her eyes. "I'm a day away from marrying my dream girl." He stated. And, he grinned. "I'm so looking forward to our wedding night." He laughed, glanced at her, "should I have held that back?"

Angela smiled brightly, "No, you never need to hold back with me, Bart." She kissed him. "Me too," she whispered.

Bart began to drive to St. Ann's Church. "By the way, we received a wedding gift today, Angela."

"Really?" she asked. "From who?"

"The European Tour," Bart responded with a laugh. "How does March in Bermuda sound?" He asked. He smiled as he saw Angela's look that meant, please explain. "The European Tour has scheduled a Tournament in Bermuda, at Port Royal Golf Club." He explained. "I was invited to play."

"Is that good?" She asked, and grinned. "I mean, Bermuda sounds great, but will it help you get a tour card?"

"Actually, it is great." He explained. "I can only play in six PGA events on Sponsor Exemptions, but this is a European Tour event." he smiled. "It's another opportunity to move closer to earning playing privileges, somewhere." Angela nodded her understanding.

He parked the car in front of the granite church, with its spire spearing into the sky. Bart looked at her. "Do you recall our first time here together?"

Angela smiled. "I do," she looked into his eyes. She bit her lip, recalling her fears and feelings of inadequacy. "Bart, thank you for loving me." She said softly.

He flashed his best, happiest smile. "Princess," he stated. "The pleasure is all mine." He kissed her. "By the way, our girl, Jessica, she still doesn't know about Dave, right?"

Angela laughed. "No," she said a bit nervously. "I hope it works out okay." She eyed Bart. "She asked me again this morning who her partner was?"

Bart laughed. "What did you say?"

"I told her it was Justin Walleston." Angela laughed. "I think she was a bit disappointed. But, she accepted it." She smiled. "Justin will be here tomorrow?" She asked.

"He will," Bart assured with a smile. "He's very excited to be part of the festivities." Bart paused. "The Walleston's fly in tomorrow and will be staying at the Hotel. "They'll be with us for Christmas and we fly together on the 27th."

"So, I will finally meet Rachel?" Angela asked with a happy smile.

"Indeed, you will." He eyed her. "Princess, I think that you will like her." He laughed. "And, I know Gilliss is pumped to see her."

The wedding coordinator for the parish, with the help of Father Capelli, began the process of lining everybody up, in order, to enter to the music that Angela had chosen. The groomsmen, absent Justin, who was Celia's partner, and Jessica's partner, walked down the aisle. Then, the Bridesmaids made their stroll toward the altar.

Bart and Mario stood before the altar, watching the procession. Bart's eyes were fixed on Angela, as she stood in the shadows, at the Church's entrance waiting to slowly, beautifully, walk with her proud father, towards him, and their future.

As the bridesmaids lined up to stand next to Tina, and the groomsmen flanked Bart and Mario, Bart saw Angela's head turn. She quickly embraced a man, it was impossible to see who, in the shadows. She spoke a few words to him, before he scurried down the aisle to join the line of Groomsmen.

Dave's eyes were set on Jessica, who Bart saw was shocked by his presence. She straightened, looked at Dave, then, she looked away.

Angela and her Dad processed down the aisle and before long, they were all headed back, up the aisle, two by two, to the Church's entry room. Dave walked with Jessica, who took his arm, as instructed, but did not meet his eyes.

In a private dining room of the elegant hotel, which looked out to Gloucester Harbor, the granite Breakwater and beyond, the group gathered. The wedding party were placed at reserved tables. A table for six, for the bride and groom, best man and maid of honor and so that Celia could dine with Mario, Celia joined them. Also, and to Tina's surprise, Tina's friend, Katelyn, was seated at the table, next to Tina. At the second table, place cards were set for Jim and Betsy, Dave Gilliss and Lucia, and Dave Powers and Jessica.

Jessica rode from the church to the hotel with Bart and Angela. Jessica was angry, confused, and tearful. "Angela, you know how devastated I've been over Dave dumping me, how could you do this to me?"

Bart pulled the car to a stop. He turned and faced Jess. "Angela knew nothing about me choosing Dave until a few days ago." Bart waited until Jess's eyes met his. "I asked her to say nothing to you, Jess."

"Why Bart?" She asked as tears ran down her cheeks. "I really thought we were friends."

Bart smiled. "We ARE friends, Jess!" He stressed the point as he gently patted her arm. "Angela and I have grown to love you and to believe in you." He sought her eyes. "Would you do me one favor?"

Jessica glared at Bart. She saw his smile, read his sincerity, and took a deep breath. She wiped her eyes. "Okay, Bart, what's the favor?"

"First, give me a smile, please." He grinned. "Jess, you are so pretty when you smile."

Jessica held on to her glare and her anger for only a moment longer. She looked at him and smiled. "Okay, you made me smile. Now, what's the favor?"

"When we go into the hotel, go with Angela, wash your face and pull yourself together." He began. She watched him and nodded. "Then, please have a talk with Dave, before dinner."

Jessica looked at Angela. Angela nodded, "I really think you should, Jess."

Jessica looked from Angela to Bart. She smiled, considered, probed. "What do you know, Bart?"

Angela took her hands. "Give Dave a chance to talk to you, to explain, and think carefully, before making any rash decisions, okay, Jess?" She sighed and smiled. "Think with your heart, Jess." Angela urged.

Angela went to help Jessica, and Bart entered the dining room. Tina was standing with Katelyn and immediately hugged Bart. "Thank you, Bart," Tina beamed. "Thank you for inviting Katelyn."

Bart turned to Katelyn, "it's a pleasure to meet you, Katelyn." Bart smiled. "I'm so glad you could make it to our gathering." He looked to Angela as she arrived. "Katelyn, this is Angela, Tina's sister and," he smiled. "My bride to be," he looked at his watch, "in less than 24 hours."

The slender blond, had a sweet smile. "I appreciate you inviting me." She responded. "Tina has told me so much about you, Bart." She looked at Angela. "Congratulations, Angela, I wish you every happiness."

In a quiet corner of the bar, Jessica moved to seat herself next to Dave on a love seat, before the fireplace. As she approached, Dave drank in her beauty. Her dress showcased her best features. Her blue eyes captured him. Dave rose, reached for Jessica's hand. Jessica hesitated, looked into the eyes of the man she loved, the man who had broken her heart.

Dave smiled, his blue/gray eyes studied her. Jessica saw his broad shoulders, tall athletic body and read a determination in his gaze. 'So handsome,' she thought, as she felt the pang of loss, the ache in her heart.

Jessica wanted him, had humbled herself for him, but, it hadn't been enough. She took a deep breath, vowed to hold onto her dignity. They were a beautiful couple, everybody said so, but even that, hadn't been enough. She sighed. Dave wanted sweet, he had left her for a sweet southern belle. And, it hurt, as she had to admit, sweet she had never been.

Jessica placed her hand in his. They sat, before the fire. "Do you think that your 'sweet girlfriend' would appreciate you holding my hand?" Jess asked, a tad caustically.

Dave smiled. "I'm holding the hand of my 'sweet girlfriend,' Jess." He stated, as he looked into her eyes.

Jess's eyes narrowed. "What are you saying, Dave?"

Dave took Jessica's other hand, caressed them. "I'm saying that there was never another girl." He shrugged, smiled. "Jess, I hope that there never will be another girl."

Her eyes implored. "When you dumped me, I cried myself to sleep every night." She paused, took a deep breath, tears flooded her eyes. "Dave, you broke my heart."

Dave nodded. He searched her eyes. "Jess, you hurt so many people. You were the cause of so many crying themselves to sleep." He paused. "Jess, think of the pain you caused Angela." He took a deep breath. "But, I still believed, or wanted to believe, that you could be good and decent." He watched her, shrugged. "Or, maybe, I just wanted the prettiest girl on my arm?" He paused. "Jess, I had to know."

Jessica nodded and grimaced. She took a deep breath, her mind spinning. "I don't understand, Dave." She studied him. "Why would you break off with me, if…?" She gasped. "You were testing me?"

Dave held her eyes. "Yes, I was." The silence was thunderous. The blood pounding in her ears, she glared at him with a kind of anger, he hoped he would never see in her. "I can see that you are angry, but please let me explain."

She pulled her hands from his. "How dare you?" Her voice rose a few octaves.

"Easy, Jess, please let me explain." He looked into her eyes. She battled to hold onto her anger, but looking into his kind, loving eyes was not conducive to remaining angry."

She knew that she should rise and walk away. She should never speak to him again. But instead, she took a deep breath and remembered what she had promised Bart. "Okay, I promised Bart and Angela that I would listen to you." She fixed him with her pretty blue eyes. "It's their big event, I'm their friend, so I will listen." She paused and challenged. "Make it good, Dave."

Dave smiled. "I'll make it honest, Jess, that's really the best I can do." She nodded. He saw a glimmer in her eye. "Jess, I've cared for you for so long. I watched you hurt so many people, really good people, like Bart and Angela." He paused. "You were mean, Jess, and I never understood it." He sat back and smiled. "Jess, let's be honest." He asked. "The only reason you agreed to date me was because I was a football captain and quarterback." He eyed her, "True?"

Jessica lowered her eyes and nodded.

"One day I decided to stand up and be a man." He stated. "I demanded that you seek the forgiveness of every person you hurt, act like the good person I thought you could choose to be, or I was done with you." He watched her, and he smiled. "And, you did it!"

He shook his head. "I was shocked. But, you humbled yourself and did the right thing. And, as a result, look at the friends we have." He laughed. "Angela, actually, feels close enough to include you in her wedding!" He took and squeezed her hands. "After everything, Angela loves you! How amazing is that?"

Jessica met his eyes, her cheeks flushed. She nodded, "Bart and Angela are remarkable people." She said, softly. "They have been so kind to me." She sighed. "I don't think I deserve their friendship."

Dave met her eyes and smiled. "Maybe not, but we are lucky to have them as friends," he paused. "Actually, they are more than friends."

Dave squeezed Jessica's hands. "I was leaving for Georgia Tech." Dave continued. "I just didn't know. So, I had a long talk with Bart." Dave grinned. "Bart believed in you, he thought you to be sincere." He paused. "But, he urged me to do what was necessary to resolve my doubts." He sighed and shrugged. "So, I decided to dump you, see if you really cared for me." He smiled. "If you would revert to being 'the queen of mean,' or continue being the good person and friend you had become?"

He took her hands, kissed them. "Bart told me that you were asked out by so many guys." He smiled. "And, why not?" He asked. "You are so beautiful." He took a deep breath. "But, you refused every offer," he grinned, looked into her eyes. "You missed me, didn't you?"

Jessica met his eyes and smiled. "Maybe, a little," she conceded. Her smile told Dave the full truth.

"Jess, you are the girl I want, the girl I've always hoped you would be." He smiled, looked into her eyes. "Do you want me, Jess?" He asked. "Because, I so want you."

Jessica looked at him, and recalled Angela's words to think with her heart. She went into his arms. "Yes, Dave, I do want you." She kissed him. "Please, ignore all those 'sweet girls' and be mine." She asked. "I couldn't take it if I lost you again."

Dave and Jessica walked into the dining room, holding hands and giddy with joy. Bart and Angela smiled and slapped a high five, grinning happily as they walked over to Jess and Dave. Angela embraced Jessica as Bart and Dave shook hands.

Bart eyed Jessica. "I have you seated together." Bart stated. He offered a teasing smile. "Would you prefer to be seated separately?"

Jessica kissed Bart's cheek. "Thank you, Bart." She said, with a big smile. "And, no," she looked at Dave. "Nothing will ever separate us again."

Jess embraced Angela. "You're marrying a great guy, Angela." Jess said, grateful eyes on Angela. "Thank you for letting me into your life."

Chapter Forty-Four

Christmas Eve dawned crisp and cold. There was a threat of snow and the hope of a White Christmas had many school children, on Christmas break, happy and smiling. The stores were expecting to do a brisk trade and Main Street shoppers were Christmas cheerful. It was the season for good cheer.

The Curcuru home could only be properly described as being in a state of excited chaos. Angela awoke, early, with a grin. Happiness seemed to radiate off her. Tina smiled at her sister. "Great rehearsal party last night." She paused. "Angela, did you know that Bart invited Katelyn?"

Angela smiled and winked at her sister. "Yes, Bart told me that he intended to invite her." Angela stretched out. "He wants you to be happy, Tina." She lay back, propping her pillows. "He talked to Dad and persuaded him that it would be okay." She grinned. "I just agreed, of course," Angela said with a contented smile. "Will she be attending the wedding?" Angela asked.

Tina looked across the room, surprised at the question. "Is it okay with you, Angela?" She hesitated. "I need you to help me. I don't know how to tell Katelyn that she shouldn't come to the Christmas Eve gathering at the DeMarco house after the ceremony."

Angela stretched and sat up, she studied Tina. "Why would Katelyn not come to the party at Bart's?" Angela smiled. "She's certainly welcome to come."

"Really?" Tina asked. "Would you need to check with Mrs. DeMarco?"

Angela smiled. "Please let Katelyn know that she is welcome." She shook her head, eyes on her sister. "Tina, don't create problems where they don't exist?" She paused. "Everybody will take their lead from you. If you are relaxed and comfortable, they will be as well."

Tina laughed, relieved at Angela's words. She grinned at her sister. "Did Bart tell you that?"

Angela eyed her sister, feigned outrage. "You know Tina, I am perfectly capable of weighing possibilities and arriving at conclusions on my own."

She shrugged, laughed aloud. "And, yes, Bart did mention that." The sisters laughed together.

"I am so happy for you, Angela." She sighed. "You so deserve Bart. I am so happy you found him."

Angela laid back and smiled contently. "Tina, the best part is that, Bart really needs me." She paused, wanted to choose the right words. "It's so much more than the physical," she grinned. "Although, the physical is outstanding!" They laughed together. "Bart has made me so much a part of his success." She paused, grinned, "our success," she corrected. Angela took a deep breath, looked to Tina. "It's like I'm his muse." She looked at Tina. "Does that make sense?"

Tina smiled. "It makes perfect sense. You are a team, what every family should be."

Angela nodded. "'Team DeMarco,' Bart always says." Angela beamed. "And, today I will be Angela DeMarco." She looked at her sister, appraised her. "You know Bart said that you are a very pretty girl." She raised her brows. "He said that you look like me."

Tina laughed. "Did he?" She smiled on her sister. "From Bart, that is high praise." Tina stated as she settled back. "It's still early, but we're both too excited to sleep." She looked at the framed photo, set on Angela's dresser, of Angela atop Bart's shoulders, engaging in a water battle in the pool. Angela was beaming in the way she now regularly smiled, since Bart entered her life. 'What a transformation,' Tina thought. She looked at the wedding dress hanging on the wardrobe. "You look so great in that gown, Angela. You will be a beautiful bride."

Angela sighed. "Bart makes me feel beautiful." She looked at Tina. "He makes me feel desired." She grinned and exulted. "He told me that he intends to ravish me tonight."

Tina laughed. "Good for him!" She looked at Angela. "I'm going to really miss you both." She shrugged. "You will be traveling pretty regularly. We won't be seeing each other very much." She sighed. "Are you even going to live in Gloucester?"

Angela looked at Tina. "We will to start." She explained. "When Bart makes the tour we will most likely live in Florida." She shrugged. "He'll need the good weather." She smiled. "But, Bart said that we will have a home here for the summer months. We both love Gloucester and want to be near our families, when possible." She eyed her sister. "I will still be your big sister, Tina, I promise that I'll be here for you."

Tina sighed. "You won't be sleeping in that bed again, will you?"

Angela smiled. "No, Tina," she closed her eyes, felt contented. "From tonight on, I will be with Bart."

Maria rose early to make sure that the suits that Nick and Giuseppe were to wear were pressed properly. She had been working with Rosa to create an elaborate feast to celebrate 'The Feast of the Seven Fishes,' the traditional Christmas Eve meal and, of course, some extras, in honor of the wedding celebration. There would be champagne and a three tiered wedding cake. She sighed, silently lamenting the lack of an elaborate wedding reception for her daughter.

The DeMarco house, while considerably more spacious than their home, had limits to how many people could attend. She had, begrudgingly, accepted Bart's explanation that he didn't want to upstage Mario and Celia's wedding. And, of course, it was all happening so fast, there really wasn't time to plan a big reception.

Maria smiled, as she recalled just how content was Angela. "Mom," Angela explained. "I want to marry Bart, the rest just doesn't matter." So, Maria pushed on with a smile. If Angela and Bart were happy, then, so be it. Still, she intended to make the event as special as the circumstances allowed.

Bart escaped the craziness of his home early. He went for a run in the crisp cold air. Stopped to have some breakfast at George's coffee shop with Mario, his Dad and Sal Curcuru. They relaxed and drew the breakfast out, having no desire to return home any earlier than necessary. Bart then planned to head to Bass Rocks and put in a few hours of practice, in the converted bag room, with Dave. He planned to then run home about 3pm, shower, dress and head to Church. As he ran, breathing in the clean, cold, salt air, his thoughts were of Angela and the life they would have together. He was happy.

Bart arrived at Church, with Mario at about 4:15pm. He wore his perfectly fitted tuxedo that Heather Walleston had provided for the Pacific Amateur Ball. Mario and the groomsmen wore dark suits with a lapel flower. At about 4:30 pm, the Walleston's arrived. Justin, smiling proudly in his suit, going directly to Bart, who lifted him high above his head. Justin's laughter filled the cavernous church. Rachel stood aside, looking so pretty, in a beautifully tailored dress.

Bart made eye contact with Rachel. "You look very pretty, Rachel." He stated, with a smile.

Rachel grinned, "Thank you, Bart." She paused, looked him over. "Haven't I seen you in that tuxedo before?" She laughed, placed happy eyes on him. "Bart, I wish you all the happiness in this world." She looked about the Church. "Has Dave arrived yet?"

Bart smiled. "No, not yet, but he'll be here soon."

Bart walked to greet Mr. And Mrs. Walleston. "Thank you for coming, Sir," Bart said. "It means a great deal to me."

Phil Walleston smiled, looked to Heather. "Bart, we feel as if you are part of the family." He hesitated, looked into Bart's eyes. "And, I mean more than the Manitoba Oil family, I mean the Walleston family."

Heather moved to him and wrapped Bart in a hug. "It's so good to see you, Bart." She smiled. "I look forward to meeting Angela." She held Bart's hand. "She must be a very special girl to have so won your heart."

Bart smiled. "Angela is very special." He paused, smiled, "Mrs. Walleston, Angela helped me to improve my speech. She's amazing!"

"Bart," Phil Walleston asked. "I hope that Angela will be flying to Manitoba with us on the 27th?"

"Thank you, Sir." Bart nodded, "Angela will be with me." He smiled. "Are the Tournament and School plans going well?"

"I never realized how much preparation is involved in running a PGA Tournament." He commented. "But, we're proceeding nicely." He shrugged, "and, on the school, the architects are designing a campus. There will be classroom buildings, offices, an infirmary with advanced medical facilities, dorms, a cafeteria building." He laughed. "A lot to do."

Dave Gilliss entered the Church, dressed in a new, blue pin-striped, suit. He smiled, eagerly, as he walked to Rachel and embraced her.

Bart looked at Heather, smiled, "did I miss something?"

Phil and Heather laughed aloud. "I think so," Heather said. "Dave's a fine young man." She laughed. "He spent a lot of time with Rachel after the Pacific Amateur."

"Dave is solid, Mrs. Walleston." Bart stated. "You can depend on him."

The rest of the groomsmen arrived and began seating guests. Dave Gilliss took the arms of Heather and Rachel and escorted them to a pew. He also escorted Katie Palermo to her seat. John grinned at Bart and flashed a thumbs-up.

The photographer arrived ahead of the limo that carried Angela and her parents. The cars carrying the Bridesmaids arrived. Each looked beautiful in their gowns. Each gown was different in color and style, but together, they looked elegant and festive.

Curiously, Sal Siracusa and Franco Palermo were in Church, dressed stylishly, in new suits, and with eyes on Lucia.

Katie looked at Sal and Franco, saw them eyeing each other. She smiled, leaned close and whispered to John, "so that's Franco's competition?" She saw Lucia and nodded. "I can see why he's smitten. She's a beauty."

John nodded. "And, if she is anything like her brothers, she's a quality girl." He laughed. "Worth fighting for, I'd say!"

Katie's defenses showed. "Well, she cannot do better than my son!" She stated.

John laughed. "I agree, Mom!" That drew a smile from Katie.

When the guests were seated, the groomsmen moved to the Church's entry. The heavy, exterior, oak doors were closed and the bridal party, with the exception of the groom and his best man, who stood, with Father Capelli, at the altar, readied to travel down the aisle.

The organist played and the tenor sang, Ave Maria, as Maria, escorted by Nick and Giuseppe, proceeded down the aisle to her front row pew. Then, as insisted on by Angela, Rosa, escorted by her husband, Franco, proceeded down the aisle to their front row pew, to the same beautiful hymn. As she walked, Rosa eyed her sons, standing at the altar, and beamed with pride.

The double polished, interior, Maple doors opened. And, at the direction of the photographer, the main, exterior, Church doors were opened to show the lightly falling snow. It made for a special, somewhat unique and seasonal, backdrop, for his photos. From his spot at the altar, Bart saw the snow falling as the groomsmen, to the classic organ music of 'Canon in D,' proceeded in single file down the aisle. Justin Walleston was first, flashing a smile at his family. He approached Bart who took his hand, then pulled the youngster into a hug. The other groomsmen followed and lined up in a straight line next to the best man.

The music changed. Bart, looking tall and strong, stood hoping to get a glimpse of his bride. The Bridesmaids processed down the aisle as the organist played another festive selection of Angela's. First was Celia, followed by Betsy, Lucia and Jessica. Each proceeded slowly and regally down the aisle, smiling brightly, feeling beautiful. Lucia did not miss Sal's presence and was a bit surprised by Franco Palermo, smiling so brightly at her. The Bridesmaids stood in line at the altar. Each flashed smiles at Bart.

Tina stood alone at the head of the aisle, before the now closed doors. Bart smiled at his soon to be sister-in-law. With her bouquet of flowers in hand, she slowly strolled down the aisle. She stood across from Bart. They exchanged a smile.

The organist then played Felix Mendelssohn's, 'Wedding March.' The doors opened and there stood, Sal Curcuru. On his arm was the most beautiful site Bart had ever seen. A vision in white. Angela's smile was all for him. They locked eyes as father and daughter proceeded in the age old ritual, of the proud father, giving his cherished daughter, in marriage, to a worthy suitor.

Each step brought Angela closer to Bart. Bart's face was alight with joy. Angela was radiant.

Sal walked Angela to the altar. Her face covered with a delicate lace veil. Sal lifted the veil over her head and kissed his daughter. In an emotion choked voice, he said; "I love you, Bambina." He turned to Bart, Sal's eyes were full. "Bart, please, take care of my little girl." He asked.

Bart embraced Sal. "I will cherish and take care of her with my life."

Sal sat with Maria and his boys, Maria took Sal's hand. Angela handed her Bouquet to Tina, smiled at Bart and stood beside him facing Father Capelli.

The ceremony was intimate, as there were only 50 guests in the Church. What could have seemed a sad and empty Church, instead felt so very special, so very personal, as each guest was carefully selected and very important to the DeMarco and Curcuru families.

Angela beamed a smile at Father Capelli when he asked the most important question of her life. She looked at Bart, smiled, and said; "I do!"

Bart met and locked eyes with his love. When asked, he happily responded; "I do!"

Father Capelli, then, looked upon the smiling couple standing before him. He raised his arms to the heavens, uttered the age old words which united "this man and this woman, in the sacred bonds of matrimony." Their parish priest smiled. "What God has this day joined together, no man may sever." He placed dancing eyes on them. "Thus, in the eyes of God, you are one!"

And, with those joyous words, Bart and Angela were "man and wife."

Father Capelli spoke softly to the happy couple and asked them to face their friends and families.

Father Capelli placed a hand on Bart's and Angela's shoulder. He smiled and announced. "I now have the distinct pleasure and Honor to be the first, to introduce, Mr. and Mrs. Bartolo DeMarco, may they live in harmony and love."

The family and guests rose and applauded. Bart leaned down and whispered. "Thank you for marrying me, Mrs. DeMarco." He then beamed a smile at his love and brought his lips to hers.

Chapter Forty-Five

The Wedding celebration/Christmas Eve gathering was joyous. The DeMarco house was ablaze with Christmas lights and full to capacity. Franco and Mario had created seating for all the guests. Bart, Angela, the bridal party and their friends were set up in the Living room. Fortunately, the large dining room opened to a spacious Living room through a wide archway.

The Palermo's were seated with the Walleston's, and thoroughly enjoyed each other's company. Heather and Katie bonded, almost instantly, and all were so very impressed by Bart's qualities.

Photographs were taken before the beautifully decorated Christmas tree in the corner of the Living Room. Bart and Angela stood before the tree, smiling happily.

"A beautiful couple," Katie opined. She looked to John. "So young," she said in a hushed voice.

John nodded. "They are young, but, I have never seen so much maturity in a young man, even five or ten years older than Bart." He considered, looked at Phil. "He's known real adversity. He was mocked and humiliated." He paused, thoughtful, "perhaps, adversity either matures or destroys?"

Phil agreed. "That's the reason I want him so badly to help my Justin and the tens of thousands of other children." He sighed. "Bart is a great role model." He smiled at John. "Maybe, I've said too much to Bart's lawyer." He nudged John. "Have I weakened my negotiating position?"

John smiled at Phil and Heather. "You were very good to Bart." He looked over at the young couple, smiling as they posed with the bridal party. "Without your generosity, Bart could not have done this." He paused, a nagging doubt lingering, thoughtfully, John looked at Phil. "Does he have what it takes to win a tour card?"

Phil nodded. He pointed to Bart, smiling happily as he and Angela posed with his parents. "That boy can accomplish anything he sets his mind to." He paused. "And, now that Angela is by his side, I predict great things for them."

Katie pointed out, to the amusement of both women, the mini-drama playing out over Lucia. She noted Franco chatting with Lucia, and Lucia's pretty smile and flashing eyes directed to Franco. Katie smiled as she watched her son's obvious delight at something Lucia said. Heather told Katie about Rachel's disappointment over striking out with Bart. She grinned, nodded to Rachel's flirting with Dave. "They bounce back!" Heather proclaimed.

Katie watched as Sal approached Franco, she saw Franco's eyes, the set of his jaw. "That looks like trouble." She said softly to John. Lucia shook her head and walked away from the confrontation.

John eyed them, rose, and went over to the boys. He spoke quietly, but firmly, and returned to the table.

Katie looked to John, alarm in her tone. "Where are they going?" She watched Sal and Franco leave the house.

"I told them that this was a happy occasion, that if they could not act appropriately to take their issues outside."

Katie's eyes went wide. "Are they going to fight?"

John shrugged. "Maybe, but I doubt it will be much of a fight."

She looked at John. "What is this?" She huffed. "They pound each other like a couple of cavemen and the winner carries off his prize?"

Heather glanced at Phil and smiled. "Katie, I think that's about it." She said casually. She smiled at Phil, laughed, "at least that is how it is in the wilds of Canada."

John took her hand, "stay calm, Mom, your boy will be fine."

"FINE!" She responded. "Are you kidding me? John, you have to stop this!"

John smiled. "No, Katie, I will not." He gently placed his hand on her arm. "They will settle this between themselves." He smiled. "Look at Bart and Angela, Katie." Her eyes went from John to the happy couple, now posing with the DeMarco family. "How do you think Bart won Angela's heart?"

Phil nodded, smiled at Katie's panic. "He's right, Katie. Bart told me how he had to fight three boys who were bullying Angela." Phil grinned. "Bart and Angela were only 14 years old." He paused, shrugged. "And, I believe the ringleader of that group was Sal."

Katie sat back, looked around the table. Amazed at how casually they spoke of such unnecessary violence. "This is barbaric!" She stated.

John smiled. "No, Katie, this is life." He eyed his pretty wife. "Franco is doing what he feels he must do to win Lucia."

Katie's eyes flared. "So, I can expect to see my son, bloodied and bruised, drag Lucia home by her pretty, auburn hair?"

John laughed. "Pretty dramatic, Helen, but as I said, I doubt there will be much of a fight."

"Helen?" Heather asked, perplexed.

John laughed. "Yes, every so often Katie takes out her 'I am woman' soapbox."

"Oh, Helen Reddy!" Heather laughed aloud. She looked to John, "clever, I like that." She saw Katie's scowl. "Sorry, Katie, but John is right."

Katie looked to John. "So, why do you think that they won't actually fight?"

Phil touched John's arm. "If I may, John?" John nodded, sat back and looked to his wife. "Katie, the reason John, and I agree," Phil stated, "and believe there will not be much of a fight, if any, is that Sal is a bully, the kind of boy who would bully a terrified young girl." He smiled. "Bullies are always cowards, they prey on the weak." Phil smiled. "He is unlikely to fight for Lucia." He grinned. "Using a jungle analogy," Phil offered. "He will withdraw from a battle with a challenger, rather than protect his turf."

Katie looked at Phil. "His turf?" She shook her head, but saw Angela smile up at Bart, kiss him with delight. Angela's smile, had Katie recalling when John fought for her and Kelly, risking everything, to protect their future, because he had promised his friend Marc that he would. And, she admitted to herself, that she loved him for that. "Courage,' she thought, 'What women wants a man who would not fight for her?'

Katie looked at John and smiled. She looked over and observed as Lucia smiled and posed for photographs, while she waited anxiously and continued to steal glances at the door. Katie shook her head and laughed. She leaned over and kissed John. "I guess I'll retire that soapbox," she laughed. She lifted her glass of Sal Curcuru's homemade wine. "To Bart and Angela," she smiled. "And, to the law of the jungle."

The group toasted and saw the door open and Franco Palermo return. He was smoothing his hair, brushing off dust and dirt, from his suit coat and adjusting his tie. Katie saw that he had blood seeping from a split lip. Katie looked closer. She saw that the knuckles of both his hands were scraped raw, but her son was smiling as he scoped the room for Lucia. When Franco saw Lucia, and she met his eyes, he beamed a smile at her.

She looked at John. "Is it okay for me to help Franco clean up a bit?" Katie asked. A tear in her eye.

Heather patted her hand, noted Lucia crossing to Franco. "No need, Katie, I think Lucia will take care of that."

Katie watched Lucia approach Franco, take his hand, note the condition of his knuckles and, still holding his hand, lead him to the kitchen. There were tears in Katie's eyes as she watched her son smile at Lucia, and happily walk with her. She looked to John, "our boy is so much like his Dad."

John smiled. "Katie, he's been blessed with two wonderful mothers." He leaned over and kissed her. "I'm so proud of him." Katie nodded agreement and squeezed John's hand.

Phil witnessed the emotional exchange. Looked to John. "So, John, how is the food on Christmas Eve in Gloucester,"

"Pretty spectacular," John promised. "It is called 'the Feast of the Seven Fishes.' And, you will eat the most delicate and delectable seafood that you have ever tasted."

The photo session was complete and everyone sat to dinner. And, the dinner lived up to the hype. Bart was beaming. He held the hand of his bride, who smiled happily. Bart kept leaning over and kissing and nibbling on Angela.

Angela smiled. "You should eat, Bart." She blushed a deep crimson, as she whispered for his ears only. "I want you strong for later."

Bart's eyes glowed at the comment. He looked into her eyes. "I'm ravenous for you, Princess." Her blush deepened, and her smile widened.

"Look, Tina nudged Katelyn, who dressed so prettily for the event. "Bart always makes Angela blush." She sighed. "He makes her happy, Katelyn." She paused, smiled into Katelyn's eyes. "And, he's the reason we can be here together." Tina laughed. "I love my brother-in-law."

Katelyn took her hand under the table. "I agree, he's a great guy. I'm happy for Angela." Tina noticed Franco Palermo sitting with Lucia, he was leaning close, speaking softly, and they were laughing together. She nudged Katelyn. "Now, that looks like a nice change." She laughed, saw Katelyn's blank look. "I'll explain later."

Betsy looked to Jessica and winked, turned and smiled at the Bride. "Hey, Angela" she said across the table, "do you and Bart need a lift to the hotel now?"

Angela grinned, took in the looks exchanged between Dave and Jessica, watched Rachel flirt with Dave Gilliss, felt the love in the room. She smiled, "I think Bart would be okay with that, but maybe we should stay at least until we cut the cake." She looked at Bart, grinned as she nudged closer. "Soon, my love." She teased. "I'm as anxious as you."

Bart laughed. "You're still killing me, Princess, and now you are my wife." They laughed together.

"This is unbelievable," Phil gushed. "What a taste."

"Yes, that's calamari in a rich Marinara sauce." John stated. "Dip the homemade Italian bread in that sauce, it's spectacular." John sampled the calamari. "And, Phil," John added, indicating a large platter placed on the table. "Here we have an Italian lobster salad, baked shrimp, sweet fried whiting, some baked haddock, and more. Eat hardy." John re-filled the wine glasses. "Sal certainly makes a tasty wine."

Katie nudged John. "Franco is sitting with Lucia, eating and laughing. He wasn't invited." She said, a note of alarm in her tone.

Heather looked at Katie. "It appears that he's claiming his turf." She laughed. "I get the feeling the DeMarco family will consider Franco a huge upgrade on Sal."

Katie straightened. "I would hope so!" She insisted, protective of her son.

John laughed, hugged his wife, "how can you not love this girl?" He laughed aloud. "Two minutes ago, she was outraged that her son was fighting for the girl he desires, and now she's ready to fight to defend his right to claim his prize." He kissed Katie as she blushed.

"Of course," Katie stated, a smile on her face. "My boy is a prize."

They all laughed together. The two mothers looked at their children. Justin, glowing as he sat near his hero. Rachel, smiling in the company of Angela and her friends, and, of course, Dave. Katie looked to Franco, split lip, scraped knuckles, and all, and as happy as could be. And, all it took was the smile of pretty, Lucia DeMarco.

"Look at our children," Heather commented. "All because of Bart." Katie nodded, understanding her point clearly.

There were toasts and laughter. Bart rose and delighted his parents by his joy and by speaking so comfortably and so clearly. It was a great night.

By midnight the guests waved goodbye to the happy couple as Bart and Angela drove the few blocks to the hotel. Of course, they would all celebrate Christmas together, but a wedding night is special.

The Honeymoon suite was elegant. Bart and Angela stood at the large French doors which led to their private deck and provided a spectacular view of Gloucester Harbor to Ten Pound Island, the Breakwater and out to the open ocean.

"Beautiful," Angela said, she looked up at Bart, offered a loving smile.

Bart met her smile, he looked into her eyes. He pulled her close, kissed her. His gaze upon her was lustful. "Yes, it's beautiful, but its beauty pales in comparison to my wife."

'My wife,' she thought, and thrilled at the title, met his lips in a kiss as Bart began to slowly undress her. She reveled in Bart's delight as she stood gloriously before him.

He smiled as he took in her beauty. "WOW! How did I get so lucky?" He asked.

Angela beamed a smile, kissed him. "I think you promised to ravish me." She beamed. "Please, Mr. DeMarco, ravish me."

Bart laughed. "Anything for my wife." Bart scooped her up, cradling Angela in his arms, and kissing her, carried her to the bed. He placed her on the bed, smiled. "You are so beautiful."

Exhausted and sated, they laid happily together. Bart on his back and Angela's head cushioned on his chest. His arm tight around her. He kissed her head. "My life is perfect," he said. "I love you, Princess."

She pressed her soft breasts to him, kissed his chest. "I love you Bart." She smiled contently as she dozed. As she was dropping off to sleep, she heard him say, "Thanks for coming to look for me, Princess." They slept, peacefully.

Chapter Forty-Six

Bart and Angela knocked on the door of the Walleston suite. It was mid-afternoon on Christmas Day and though the grinning newlyweds had only a few hours of sleep, they were happily energized.

Heather Walleston opened the door with a smile and an embrace for the DeMarco's. "What a nice surprise." She ushered them into the suite's living room, where they saw a Christmas tree and the remnants of gift giving.

Justin ran to Bart, who hoisted him up. "Here's my best groomsman," Bart said with a grin. Angela looked on with a smile.

"Bbart," Justin enthused. "I,I got ggolf clubs." He beamed a smile at his hero. "Mmaybe, we ccould pplay?"

Bart smiled. "Of course, we'll play, Buddy." He saw Rachel lounging in her bed cloths and laughed. "Rachel, I know you've met my Angela, but I'd love you two to get to know each other." He angled a grin. "From what Dave says," he laughed, "or at least hopes, you and Angela may be spending time together, while Dave and I work."

Rachel smiled at Angela, looked to Bart with raised brows, but an inner delight. "He said that, did he?" She shrugged. "He hasn't said that to me." She met Angela's eyes and smiled. She rose from the couch, embraced Angela, "so nice to meet you Mrs. DeMarco," Rachel said with a smile. She motioned to Bart, "I don't know what spell you cast, but this guy has eyes only for you." She grinned, whispered for Angela's ears only, "I tried, but he only wants you."

Angela smiled at Rachel, "you had me worried, Rachel." The girls laughed together. "But, Dave is a great guy." Angela asserted. "He and Bart are a team, like brothers."

"Can we offer you anything?" Phil asked. "I can call room service."

Bart shook his head. "No, actually, we're here to invite you all for Christmas dinner at Angela's parent's house."

Phil looked to Heather, then, addressed Bart. "I have to tell you that we so enjoyed the wedding ceremony and the Christmas Eve party." He grinned. "And, the food was spectacular."

Heather nodded. "It was all so intimate and special." She laughed, embraced Angela. "We sat with the Palermo's. John and Katie are great." She eyed Angela. "About having Christmas dinner," she cringed. "We'd hate to impose. Everybody must be so tired."

Bart laughed. "You really must come." He eyed Phil, "Mr. Walleston, Angela's parents will be hurt if you refuse."

Phil looked at Heather. "I told you he was smart." He grinned. "Okay," he conceded. "What time should we be there?"

Bart had convinced Maria to keep the Christmas dinner simple. Sal's homemade sweet Italian sausage, his wine and Maria's freshly baked Italian bread and, of course, a tomato salad.

When Bart and Angela arrived at the Curcuru house, they witnessed a scene of happy chaos. Nick and Giuseppe were enjoying their Santa Claus gifts and eager to unwrap the gifts from Bart and Angela, Tina and their parents. The boys eyed the identical large gift wrapped packages from the DeMarco's with excitement.

Maria placed espresso coffee, Christmas cakes and cookies on the coffee table.

Sal surprisingly, embraced Bart. The smaller man held Bart's face in his strong, work callused hands. He looked into Bart's eyes. "Per Favore, (please)" he asked. "You take good care of my Bambina?" Sal's eyes filled. He looked at Angela. "I love my girl."

Bart looked into his eyes. "Papa," he began. "I promise you that I will cherish her, love her, and protect my precious wife, with all my heart and with my life."

The scene had tears flowing from Maria, Angela and Tina. Angela went into his arms. She held tight. "From the beginning you have always been there to protect me." She looked into his eyes. "Bart, I love you, so much."

Tina and Maria embraced Bart. Maria was choked with emotion and speechless. "Mom," Bart said softly. "It's all good. We're happy." He paused. "And, I will work hard to provide for my family." He looked into her tear stained face. "I am happy and proud to count your family as part of my family."

Tina laughed as she hugged Bart. "Papa, Huh?" She whispered. "Are you sure that you aren't a politician rather than a golfer?"

Bart held Tina, looked into her face, spoke softly. "I'm a golfer, but it never hurts to kiss up, a bit, to your wife's family." They laughed together.

"You are smart, Mr. DeMarco." She laughed. "I'll give you that." Bart and Angela sat together on the couch, the same couch he had sat so often with Angela, while stealing hugs and kisses.

"Did you enjoy the wedding and celebration, Tina?" He asked. "Did Katelyn have a good time?" He watched her closely. "Was she comfortable?"

Tina smiled as she sat. "She did, and thank you," she angled a look, a gleam in her eye, and thought she'd stir the pot. "Maybe, not quite as comfortable as Franco Palermo?"

Bart looked at Tina quizzically. "Franco Palermo? Was he at the wedding?"

Tina grinned, leaned forward, spoke softly, "if you weren't so focused on ravishing my sister, you might have noticed that he chased Sal off and spent the party with Lucia."

Bart leaned back, "Tina," he responded, as he put his arm around Angela and pulled her close. Speaking softly, but with a wry grin, he cracked, "ravishing your sister, MY wife, is about all I think about these days." He grinned. "And," he winked at Angela. "I might add, she seems to enjoy it." Bart and Tina watched Angela blush. Bart laughed and squeezed Angela. "Now, back to Lucia. So, Franco spent the party with Lucia?" He looked to Angela. "Princess," Bart asked Angela. "Did you know this?"

Angela grinned. "Yes, I saw, it was quite a show." She paused. "Lucia seemed very happy."

"You didn't say anything?" He asked in surprise. "At the hotel?"

Angela blushed, offered a soft, sweet smile. "At the Hotel, I was preoccupied with other pursuits."

Bart laughed. "Yes, you were." He smiled at Angela, love in his expression, in his eyes. He paused, considered, "Franco?" He thought aloud. Kicked the idea around. "I like Franco, he's a stand-up guy." He considered. "I think he'd be good for Lucia." He looked at Angela. Their eyes met, then he laughed aloud.

"What's funny?" Angela asked.

"Franco is on the High School golf team." He paused, thought. "He gave up football to play golf." Bart laughed. "That devious kid!" He stated, looked at Tina. "Franco told me that I inspired him to play golf." He shook his head, smiled broadly. "He asked me to help him with his chipping." He grinned at Angela. "We worked together for more than an hour, and, all through the lesson we talked about family, his and mine."

Angela laughed, raised her brows. "And, did he ask a lot of questions about Lucia?"

Bart put his face in his hands and laughed. "He played me!" There was admiration in his tone.

Angela and Tina were laughing with him.

"So," Angela summarized, enjoying the moment. "Franco played to and inflated your ego." She glanced at Tina and in a theatrical whisper, commented, "not, hard to do!" She continued. "Then, Franco asked questions about Lucia, without seeming to be focused on her, correct?"

Bart nodded, smiling widely. "That wily guy!" He said.

"And," Angela suggested. "He discovered Sal's interest in Lucia and the fact that the DeMarco family had very mixed feelings about Sal?" She leaned forward, laughed and planted a kiss on his cheek. "About right, dear husband?"

Bart nodded. He couldn't help but be impressed. "I even told him that Lucia was not allowed to date until she is 16 years old."

"And, did you tell him when she would be 16?" Tina asked, a knowing grin on her face.

Bart nodded. "I did! WOW!"

Now Maria was smiling with the group. She poured Bart a double espresso. "Here," she smiled. "This may help."

"I guess," Angela suggested, with a wry grin, "Franco is a pretty smart kid." She flashed her eyes and batted her lashes. "I think he out maneuvered you, Bart." She laughed.

Bart looked at Angela. "I'd say that you are right." He paused, looked at Tina. "That is an impressive young man." He nodded. "Did you say he chased Sal off?"

Tina nodded. "Yes, Franco came to Church," she grinned, "without an invitation." She added. "He watched Lucia very closely." She looked at Angela who was smiling. "I was standing at the head of the aisle, waiting to walk down to the altar," she decided to fan the flames of brotherly protectiveness. "And, I watched him ogle Lucia." She laughed at Bart's reaction.

"Dear Brother-in-Law," She offered, "don't be outraged." She angled an amused look at him. "It was much like the way you have ogled my sister every time you saw her." She laughed. "And, still do, by the way."

Bart laughed. "That's different," he asserted, met Angela's eyes, shrugged and conceded, "Okay, maybe not."

Angela touched his cheek, looked into his eyes. "Don't stop, okay?"

"No worries there, Beauty." He smiled.

"Anyway, Franco, came back to the house," Tina continued, with a shake of her head. "He just strolled in and started chatting up Lucia." She laughed. "We all go to school together." She explained. "So, we all know each other." She shrugged. "Sal saw him with Lucia and got in his face." Tina smiled. "Guys!" She stated, feigning exasperation.

Angela grinned at her sister. Tina winked and continued. "They were about to go at it, when Mr. Palermo told them to take it outside."

"Really?" Bart said. "And, I missed all of this?"

"We were taking photos with the families." Angela grinned. "And, I think your mind was elsewhere." Angela laughed. "You weren't even interested in eating!" She stated, and chuckled. "When does that ever happen?"

Bart nodded and laughed, "I guess that's true," he agreed. He looked at Angela, the desire flaming in his eyes.

Tina saw it and grinned. "Easy, boy," she said, on a laugh. "Anyway, they left and only Franco returned." She smiled. "Franco's lip was split and bleeding, his knuckles were bruised and his clothes were a mess, but he was smiling." She paused and grinned, "and, so was Lucia," She added. "They spent the evening together, chatting and laughing." She flashed a grin, glanced at her watch. "You can ask her about it yourself, your family is coming for dinner."

Christmas presents were exchanged, with Nick and Giuseppe opening brand new sets of golf clubs. The clubs were set in a golf bag, with their names stitched onto the bag. They were delighted, and pressed Bart to teach them. He gave each a hug and promised to teach and play golf with them when the weather warmed.

Bart continued to think through and admire Franco Palermo in his single minded pursuit of Lucia. A good student, a solid athlete, and from a good family. He considered how very much Franco resembled himself in his pursuit of Angela.

Bart angled a look at Angela. "I like Franco, and I like his family." He grinned. "A big improvement over Siracusa, I'd say."

"Of course, we have to see what Lucia thinks," Angela cautioned. "She was pretty interested in Sal."

Bart shook his head. "Sal was the first guy to come knocking." He offered. "That was exciting for a 14 year old." He reasoned. "But, Lucia is a sensible girl."

The Wallestons and DeMarco's arrived almost simultaneously. The two men exchanged a hearty handshake. In truth, Phil Walleston considered

Bart as a surrogate son. Bart's work with Justin had already shown dividends. Phil and Heather admired Bart. His handling of Rachel's advances were dealt with directly, but sensitively. They looked forward to working with him. And, they loved that he was going to be the face of Manitoba Oil, hopefully, on the PGA Tour.

Franco and Rosa embraced Bart and Angela. They saw their gleaming smiles and were happy that Bart was building a life for, and with, his wife and future family. Of course, they were saddened that soon Bart and Angela would be away far more than home, but they were proud of Bart, as a golfer, but even more, as a man.

Angela hugged Lucia. "Did you enjoy the celebration?" Angela asked Lucia. Bart watched Lucia closely as his little sister blushed at the question.

Lucia nodded happily. "You were a beautiful bride, Angela." She looked to Bart.

Bart met her eyes. "So, Franco Palermo, Huh?" He asked with a smile.

Lucia laughed. She looked at Bart with pride. "He fought for me, Bart!" She sighed, smiled. "Something like you and Angela." She paused, spoke softly. "Sal left," she said softly. "He hasn't even called." She looked to Angela. "I thought I meant something to him." Lucia shrugged. "But, I guess not."

"Do you care for Sal?" Angela asked quietly, sympathetic eyes on Lucia.

Lucia met Angela's eyes. "Angela, I stuck up for Sal, when everybody thought I was making a mistake." She exhaled. "I defended him, tried to understand." She paused, had a faraway look in her eyes. "Angela, Franco fought for me. Sal just retreated."

Bart nodded, he hugged his sister, kissed her cheek. "I doubt that my opinion matters," he shrugged. "But, Franco's a good guy." He paused, looked at Lucia. "Be careful, Lucia, but I think that he'll be a man you will be able to count on."

Lucia nodded. She looked to Angela, smiled, Angela could see her excitement. "He really wants to date me." Lucia explained. "He came this morning to talk to my Dad." She smiled. "He left his house on Christmas morning, Angela," Lucia gushed. "His lip is split, his knuckles scraped raw, from punching Sal, but he asked Dad if he could date me."

"And?" Bart asked.

Her smile bloomed. "I think Dad likes him. Anyway, Dad said he could. I'll be 16 in a few weeks." She looked at Bart. He saw that she was nervous. Lucia took a deep breath. "Franco really admires you, Bart." There was a silence, her eyes pleaded. "Franco wants you to be okay with him dating me." Bart realized that Lucia was seeking his approval.

"As I said, Lucia, I like him," Bart confirmed. He looked from Lucia to Angela, who watched attentively. Bart embraced his baby sister, continued, "He's a good guy, from a good family, Lucia." He grew serious. "And, he never bothered my wife."

Chapter Forty-Seven

It was Angela's first flight on a private jet. She looked at Bart, eyes wide, "this is great!" She gushed.

Bart laughed. "For the most part, this is how we will be traveling." He smiled. "But, if we want to travel to quality tournaments, I will have to play well."

Within an hour of take-off, Bart with Dave, Phil and Justin were seated at the conference table discussing the up-coming tournaments, his practice schedule, and trying to fashion a workable calendar to accomplish his purpose. His Sport's Agent, Harry Winston, had informed Bart that to earn a Tour card, he would need to earn $600,000 in the six events. A formidable task. Of course, a win would earn him a Tour card and a two year PGA exemption.

"Wwhat is tthat tthing?" Justin asked. "An exemption?" He managed.

Dave grinned and touched Justin's shoulder. "Justin, an exemption means that Bart will not have to qualify for tournaments. For two years, he can choose to play in any tournament on the schedule."

Angela, Rachel and Heather were on the couches relaxed and engaged in an in depth conversation on any number of topics.

Bart watched Angela laugh and bond with Rachel. He grinned, as he knew that with him practicing and playing every day, Angela would need a girlfriend. He hoped that she might find one in Rachel.

Phil explained that he had secured for Bart and Dave, the use of an indoor football stadium for the week they would be visiting. The facility had a fully equipped gym, a track for running, and a ceiling high enough, he believed, to hit golf balls.

Bart smiled. "Thank you, Sir. I so appreciate your help."

Phil considered Bart. He leaned forward. "I spoke with John Palermo, I explained that we are all in this together." He paused. "Bart, you and Dave are the point men of 'Team DeMarco.'" He sipped a ginger ale, Bart noted with a grin that it was a Canada Dry product. "When you earn your card," the CEO continued, "especially, if you win a Tournament, it will promote

Manitoba Oil and, more importantly, the school for our children." He set his gaze on Bart. "So, if there's anything we can do, just ask."

Bart glanced at Angela, sat back. He looked at Mr. Walleston and smiled. "Sir, is there any chance that your family could come to Hawaii with us?"

Walleston studied Bart, showed surprise. "Why, Bart?"

"Dave and I will be working every day." He explained. "Angela will be at the Tournament, but, she'll be alone." He paused, eager to choose the correct words. "I'd like her to have company." He paused. "Rachel and Mrs. Walleston would be great. They can shop or do spa stuff, or sightsee, while Dave and I practice." He sighed. "Angela won't be alone, and I won't be worrying about her."

Phil Walleston nodded. "I see your point, Bart." He took a deep breath. "What about after Hawaii? We can't go to every Tournament with you."

Bart nodded. "I know that, Sir, but this is my first PGA Tournament." He looked at Mr. Walleston, "I could use the support," he smiled. "And, your family would enjoy a wonderful vacation."

He nodded. "And, you and Angela, Dave and Rachel could enjoy some night life?" He grinned.

Bart smiled. "The truth is that Angela and I are from Gloucester, we're not yet 18, let alone 21." He laughed. "I guess some might say that we aren't very exciting people. Dinner, a movie in the suite, is exciting enough, especially, if we have been going all day."

Walleston nodded. "I'll speak to Heather." He stroked his chin. "The kids are on Winter break. It might work. We'll talk tomorrow."

Bart smiled. "Thank you, Sir."

The Walleston home was palatial by the simple standards of Bart, Angela and Dave Gilliss. Bart and Angela were given a big room with a private bath, a balcony overlooking a pond. And, perhaps most importantly, they were given privacy.

"Relax," Mrs. Walleston advised with a knowing smile. "Dinner will be at 6pm, she looked at her watch, in about two hours." She informed. "Welcome to our home."

Bart and Angela escorted Mrs. Walleston and Rachel to the door. Bart thanked them for their hospitality. He then locked the door, faced Angela and smiled. "How about a shower, Beautiful?" He suggested.

"Should I go first?" Angela asked, innocently. Her smile gave away her expectation.

Bart shook his head. "You know, water supply might be a problem." He grinned as he began to disrobe her. His eyes gleamed as he enjoyed her beauty. "God, I love to look at you," he said excitedly. "We should probably shower together."

She came into his arms. "Whatever you think is best, my Love," Angela said on a laugh.

Central Canada is cold. As they slept, the landscape was freshly covered in a blanket of white from an overnight snowstorm. Bart, programmed to wake by 4am to lump fishing boats, woke and smiled on a sleeping Angela, cuddled up to him, seeking warmth, in the large, comfortable bed. He delighted in her soft, curvy and voluptuous body. He smiled as she pressed against him. He kissed her face and chuckled as she worked her body closer. When her hand began to caress him, he knew she had awoken. She glanced up, planted a kiss on his chin and met his eyes. She smiled that soft, sexy, smile that so thrilled him. "Ravish me, please, my love," she asked. That she still blushed was endearing.

By 7:30am Bart had showered, dressed and stood for a long moment smiling on the resting form of his beautiful wife, burrowing under the covers, her long shining black hair fanned over the white pillow. She opened one eye and smiled. "I'll be here when you get back from practice," she promised. "Bart, you exhaust me," she laughed. "But, please, don't ever stop." They exchanged a lover's smile. "Go, practice," she paused, smiled. "Be great, Bart." He planted a kiss on her sweet lips and left the room.

He smelled bacon frying, and homed in on the kitchen seeking food. He found Julia, the family cook, simmering Canadian bacon, frying potatoes, and readying eggs. He sniffed, "are those biscuits I smell?"

Julia, a mid-fifties, gray haired, pleasantly plump woman, smiled. "Good morning, Sir. Yes, those are butter biscuits baking." She studied Bart. "Did you enjoy dinner last evening?" She asked.

Bart smiled. "It was delicious," he responded. "The glaze on the pork roast was so good." He watched Julia bustle around the kitchen. "May I sit?" He asked.

Julia smiled, "of course, but would you be more comfortable in the dining room?"

Bart smiled. "I usually sit in the kitchen, have coffee, and chat with my mother as she cooks breakfast." He flashed that smile and Julia understood just why the Walleston's were so taken with this big, broad shouldered, strikingly handsome, young man. "So, if you don't object, I'll just sit here and we can talk."

"Absolutely, Sir," Julia laughed, as she poured Bart a cup of coffee, placed the cream and sugar before him, grinned and brought a plate with two of her butter biscuits, hot out of the oven, with a bowl of raspberry jam.

Bart watched her in her work. It helped make him feel at home. "Ma'am," he began, could I ask you to call me Bart?" He shrugged. "Sir, seems just too much."

Julia smiled. "Of course, Bart," she nodded. "As long as you lose the Ma'am and call me Julia."

"Deal!" Bart emphasized with a laugh. He looked about and saw a smiling Mrs. Walleston standing in the doorway.

"You're up early," Mrs. Walleston said as she poured herself a cup of coffee and sat across from Bart. She smiled at Julia, "good morning, Julia." Julia smiled and nodded.

Bart watched the exchange closely. He sipped his coffee, broke open a biscuit, watched the steam escape, and savored the aroma. "Actually, I awoke at about 4am." He said, in a matter of fact tone.

"4am?" both woman repeated in surprise.

Bart nodded, slathered the biscuit with jam and took a healthy bite. He grinned at the cook. "Julia, this is wonderful." He began working on the second biscuit. "Yes, at home, I woke daily at 4am, so I could get to the docks by 4:30am to hopefully lump a fishing boat or two."

Heather nodded, "of course," she said, again impressed by the ease with which Bart accepted hard work as a given. She smiled, "is Angela still sleeping?"

Bart's cheeks flushed, both women noticed, understood and smiled. "Yes, she'll probably sleep for a bit." He offered. "You know, the flight, time difference," he shrugged, smiled, "and everything."

Heather and Julia exchanged a smile. "Of course," Heather agreed. "We'll let her rest."

Dave entered the kitchen, rubbing his hands and grinning. He went and kissed Julia, "how's my favorite cook?"

Julia laughed. "I'm fine, Sir." She responded.

Dave grinned at Heather. "Good morning, Mrs. Walleston."

Heather smiled. "Please sit, it appears we three will be dining here this morning."

Dave looked at Bart. "Ready to go to work?"

Bart smiled. "Yes, I am, Coach."

Julia served Bart and Dave plates heaping with Canadian bacon, fried potatoes and eggs. A basket of biscuits was placed handily on the table. Julia then made a more modest plate for Mrs. Walleston. All began to eat. Bart watched Julia standing by the stove, considered, rose and poured a cup of coffee and pulled out a chair. "Please, Julia, sit and join us." He urged.

Julia froze, looked to Mrs. Walleston, who glanced at Bart, noted that his eyes were on her. Heather smiled graciously, "please Julia, make yourself a plate and join us."

The awkwardness passed relatively quickly as life stories were swapped, laughs were had, and breakfast was enjoyed. Heather and Julia laughed aloud at the stories Bart told of lumping fishing boats in Gloucester.

As Bart and Dave readied to leave for practice, Bart kissed Julia, "thanks for the delicious breakfast, Julia." He then hugged Mrs. Walleston. He smiled. "I hope that I didn't upset you." He stated. "I just wasn't comfortable."

Heather kissed Bart's cheek. "You're a gem, Bart. Have a good day."

Bart began his session with a two mile run. He broke for water, then, he went into the gym to do a series of stretching exercises and weight drills that promoted flexibility and core strength. After about an hour in the gym, under Dave's eye, Bart began to hit golf balls.

Dave had set targets at various distances for Bart to work on his wedge game. "100 yards and in," Dave repeated. "That is how you win." Bart worked on all the facets of his game possible inside the facility. After, three hours of practice, they drove to a driving range with heated tee boxes to take full swings. Dave was pleased with Bart's swing and, as always, loved his work ethic. Bart never seemed to tire. His drive to improve was innate and demanding. After a five hour practice session, topped off with another two mile run, Bart and Dave headed back to the Walleston home.

They entered Casa Walleston to see a suitcase set in the foyer and Angela dissolved in tears. She was in Heather Walleston's arms, the mother of two was offering what comfort was possible. Rachel sat close by, holding Angela's hand, offering whatever support she could.

Bart saw Angela, who dashed into his arms. He held her, looked to Mr. Walleston, "what happened?" Angela's sobbing made it impossible for her to explain. Bart held her close, rubbing a hand over her back. "It's going to be okay, Angela," he soothed. "It's going to be okay."

Phil Walleston sighed and faced Bart. "Angela's Dad was hurt in an accident at sea." He explained. "The Coast Guard air-lifted him to the

Boston General Hospital." He stated with a hint of alarm in his eyes. "They say it's bad," he said softly. "That's really all we know." He paused. "Angela waited to tell you before she left."

Bart took a moment to digest the information. "Okay," he said. "I will take a quick shower and we will fly to Boston." He looked at Dave. "You stay, I'll let you know when I can get back."

Walleston shook his head. "No need, there is a shower on the plane." He looked to Julia. "Did you pack some clothes for Bart?"

Julia nodded. Bart read her distress and nodded his thanks. She hurriedly brought a suitcase to Bart.

Angela looked at Bart, alarm in her eyes. In a voice choked with grief and tears streaming down her cheeks, she protested. "You need to stay, Bart, the Tournament?"

Bart took her face in his hands. He smiled, "Princess, my wife needs me with her." He paused, kissed her. "And, family always comes first."

Walleston looked at Bart, smiled. "I thought you'd say that." He eyed Heather. They exchanged a look of pride. Mr. Walleston turned to Bart. "The pilot is here to drive you to the airport and fly you to Boston." He paused. "He'll stay and wait for you." He smiled. "Now, go!"

Bart considered, looked to Walleston. "Sir, please call John Palermo, tell him that we need him to protect Mr. Curcuru, he will know what to do."

Walleston nodded. "I'll do it immediately.

Bart took Angela and led her to the door. "We'll be praying for you, Angela," Heather Walleston called out.

The flight was interminably long. Bart showered and changed. He assured Angela that all would be well. He read Angela's fears and the panic in her eyes. He held her close.

At Boston's Logan Airport, a limo awaited Bart and Angela, arranged, thoughtfully, by Phil Walleston, to take them to the Hospital. They arrived to find Maria dissolved in Tina's arms, Angela went to hold and comfort her mother. Katelyn was there to support the family. Nick and Giuseppe were with Rosa DeMarco, who organized a prayer session for Sal Curcuru.

John Palermo was in the process of ordering the Insurance Company's investigators out of the Hospital. He shook his head and cursed, "Those vultures!" Who cared not a whit about Sal Curcuru or his family, their only purpose was to find a way to limit or destroy any claim the severely injured fisherman may make.

John Palermo saw Bart and embraced him. "Thank God you're here. Mrs. Curcuru has been distraught, thinking and worrying about Angela." He looked Bart in the eye, with a serious expression, he informed, "It's bad, Bart!" He watched the young man's reaction. "He's heading to surgery." He looked at Bart's face. "All we can do is pray."

"What happened?" Bart asked.

"They were hauling back, the seas were rough, putting extra strain on the gear," John Palermo explained. "Under tension, the tackle bloch snapped, causing the bloch to come crashing to the deck." He paused and his eyes showed alarm. "It hit Sal in the head."

Bart had grown up on fishing boats, he could visualize the terrific force of a thirty pound bloch, under thousands of pounds of pressure, crashing down. "Mr. Palermo?" Was all he said, as he turned and met Angela's gaze. She knew Bart too well, his eyes told the story. Bart went to her, held her tight.

They waited and they prayed. John Palermo never left them. He arranged for food and drink to be provided to the waiting room. Father Capelli arrived and led the group in prayer. It was all they had.

Six hours later the surgeon appeared. Exhausted, he looked at the terrified group. "Who should I speak to?" He asked.

Maria Curcuru looked at the surgeon, her hands trembled and her lips quivered. "You talk to my Son-in-Law," she instructed. John Palermo stood with Bart as the surgeon quietly explained the difficulties and the risks ahead. The desperate group watched Bart shake the surgeon's hand.

Bart and John Palermo walked over to the group. Maria was shaking, her face dissolved. Bart looked at her. "He's going to live." Bart began. Maria fell into Angela's arms, thanking God in her Sicilian dialect. "But," Bart stressed. "He's facing at least three more surgeries and a long period of therapy and recovery."

Bart spoke slowly, sad eyes on Maria, "he has suffered brain damage." Bart explained. "They're still not sure how extensive the damage will be." Angela came into his arms. He kissed her cheek, tasted her tears. "We will just have to wait and see."

Maria looked to the priest and up to heaven. "Grazie, Dio!" She intoned. "Thank you, God, Thank you!" She took a deep breath. "Okay, okay," she repeated, "I will take care of my husband!"

Angela and Tina embraced Maria. They cried together. They cried tears of thanks and of hope.

Maria straightened, looked at her family. "God has smiled on us." She stated. "He gave me back my husband." She took a deep breath, wiped her eyes. "Now, we must move forward." Maria looked to Angela. "You must go back to your life, Angela." She kissed her cheek. "Go help your husband." She managed a smile. "I will help mine!"

Chapter Forty-Eight

Bart and Angela stayed with the family through the next week. Two more surgeries and Sal was able to speak. Hope soared, but he faced another critical surgery. There was damage to his spinal column that, if not repaired, would leave him paralyzed.

Bart had encouraged Dave to go to Hawaii with the Wallestons. He promised that upon the completion of the critical surgery, and when Sal was stable, he would fly to Hawaii.

"You'll be cutting it close, Bart." Dave stated, concern in his tone.

"I know, but Angela needs me." He paused. "Dave, I'll do my best."

The Golf Channel was reporting that due to a family emergency, Bart 'Stutter Boy' DeMarco may well need to withdraw from the Tournament. As the days passed more information became available, Bart had no idea how, but Sal's condition was discussed and Bart's insistence on staying with his young wife was questioned, discussed extensively, and challenged by some.

"He may be throwing away his opportunity to win a Tour Card," a Golf Channel analyst suggested. "I fully understand his desire to support his wife's family, but this is a big risk."

"Bart has said that 'family comes first,'" another analyst, a former PGA champion countered. "I think he's right."

The critical surgery was scheduled for the Monday of the week the Hawaiian Open would be played. Bart was given a late-early draw, where he would tee off late on Thursday and early, on Friday morning. Then, the cuts would be made to the low 70 golfers and ties. On the weekend, the tees times were based on the player's scores, with the leaders going off last.

Bart and the Curcuru family stood vigil on that Monday. Maria was reasonably cheerful and hopeful. She kept repeating, as if it was a mantra she was holding onto; "these Doctors saved his life. He can speak again. I have faith."

Of course, Bart stayed with Angela. As he was something of a golfing celebrity, he visited the children's ward and encouraged the little ones. And, he held onto Angela, helped her to believe.

It was late Monday when the exhausted surgeon approached the family. He met with Bart and they spoke at length. The verdict was wait and see. The surgeon was optimistic, but it would be weeks of recovery, followed by months of physical and occupational therapy to know how much movement Sal would recover.

It was time to fly to Hawaii. On that Tuesday, Bart and Angela saw Sal Curcuru. Angela kissed her Dad and explained that they would be leaving for the Tournament in Hawaii.

Sal looked at Bart, took his hand. "I'm sorry for this," he said.

Bart smiled. "Papa, just get better and stronger." He grasped his hand. "We'll be back as soon as possible."

"No worry about me," Sal insisted. "Go make us proud!" He smiled at Angela. "Bella," he kissed her. "You help your husband."

Angela kissed her Dad, smiled. "I will Papa."

Sal held their hands, looked into their eyes. "I will pray for you."

Bart spoke to Maria before leaving. "Mom," he urged. "You must listen to Mr. Palermo, do as he says." He looked into her eyes. "He will protect Papa and your family." He waited and watched her. "Do you understand?"

Maria, whose emotions had been so battered, who was terrified every minute of the day, managed a smile. "I will do as you say, Bart." She looked into his eyes. "Take care of Angela, please."

Bart held Maria, kissed her cheek. "It will be okay, Mom, you'll see."

Maria held Bart. "God sent you to my Angela and to our family, Bart." She offered a tearful smile. "Now, go and make us all proud!"

They flew all day and into the night, landing in Honolulu after midnight. They arrived at their hotel at 1:30am, exhausted, and collapsed into their bed. Bart awoke at 6am, quietly left the bed and called Dave. "I'm here, I'll go for a run and," he laughed. "Then, maybe you could introduce me to my golf clubs."

Dave laughed. "The Sponsors and the PGA agreed to excuse you from the pro-am today." He paused. "How's Angela's Dad?"

"Not good, Dave," He sighed. "But, he's alive." He thought about Angela. "Are the Walleston's here?"

"Yes," Dave responded. "Why don't you give them a call after your run?"

Bart ran hard and long trying to clear the cobwebs and loosen his muscles. He finished his run at the luxurious hotel and headed to the Walleston suite."

They were delighted to see him and hear that there was some hope for Sal. Bart drank down a water bottle, apologized for his appearance.

He looked to Rachel and Heather. "Do you think that you might spend the day with Angela?" He asked. "She could sure use the support and the company."

"Absolutely," Rachel responded. "I guess you'll be with Dave?" She asked.

Bart nodded. "We'll be practicing," he smiled. Rachel met his smile. "Do I sense something happening here with my Coach?" Bart teased.

Rachel flipped her hair and laughed. "Maybe, just maybe." She looked at Bart. "Go shower and tell Angela we'll be by in 30 minutes to go for breakfast and then to visit the Pearl Harbor Memorial." She pointed her finger at Bart. "And, you, go practice. Dave has been fighting for you all week."

He looked at the family. "Thank you all, so much." He headed to his room.

With Angela pleasantly occupied, Bart and Dave worked on his game.

"Got to knock the rust off." Dave preached. "Two weeks with no golf," he shook his head. "It'll take a miracle."

Bart laughed, "Okay, Coach, one miracle coming up," he promised.

Chapter Forty-Nine

After a long day of practice, Bart and Angela, joined Dave and the Walleston's for dinner. Angela described the awe she felt at the Pearl Harbor Memorial. "I think of all those young men who are still entombed in the hull of the U.S.S. Arizona." She paused. "It was so sad, but at the same time so breathtaking!"

Heather Walleston smiled as she agreed. "It was impressive," she acknowledged. "But, what I thought about was how the Japanese had really knocked the United States to its knees." She looked at Bart. "And, how this country struggled back to its feet, fought and won." Bart met her smile, catching her subtle meaning.

Rachel nodded. "How about that story of how four months after the Pearl Harbor attack, the President ordered, and a brave group of volunteers flew big planes off of an aircraft carrier and bombed Tokyo!" She shook her head. "That was something."

Bart smiled, looked at Justin and ruffled his hair. "What did you think, Big Guy?"

"I,I thought it wwas pretty amazing." He stuttered out. Bart smiled and nodded, encouraging him to continue. 10 year old, Justin studied Bart, spoke what was most on his mind. "Are you going to wwin, Bbart?"

"Well Justin," Bart responded. "I haven't really practiced or played in two weeks." He smiled. "I'm a little rusty."

"A LITTLE?" Dave cracked, with a wide grin. "You're swing is like an old pump handle by the pig trough!"

That brought laughter from all and a belly laugh from Bart. Bart saw Angela's eyes spark, ready to rise to his defense. When she locked eyes with Bart, she softened and grinned. "Well," she said, with a demure smile, "he's not rusty at everything!"

The comment went right over Justin's head, but brought another laugh from the group. It was what they needed after the terrifying and harrowing weeks of worry.

Back in their suite, Bart and Angela lay in bed, holding each other and glowing in the aftermath of passion. She cuddled against him, gently kissing and touching. "I was thinking," she said softly. "With my Dad's injuries, it might be best if we spent more time at home." She kissed his cheek, stroked his leg. "Do you think we could rent an apartment in Gloucester so, when we're home, I could help my mother?"

Bart smiled. He loved Angela's attempts at subtle persuasion. Who wouldn't? "I hate to say anything that might cause you to stop what you are doing," he groaned with pleasure, took a breath. "But, I spoke to Mario. He and Celia are buying a duplex on Church Street." He grinned and kissed her. "They are really nice units, with big rooms, a large yard and more than enough parking." He paused and kissed her. "That feels so great, Princess." He savored her touch. "And, one of the units will be ours."

"Really?" She gushed. "Thank you, so much." She kissed him. "That's right around the corner from my parents," she kissed him excitedly. "Oh, thank you!"

Bart laughed, pulled her close, felt her softness, "two things," he started. "First, when we get home, go with your Mom to furnish our new home." She smiled. "I think it will be good for her to shop with you and help you furnish the house." Angela nodded happily. "And second," he kissed her, "why did you stop what you were doing?"

Angela laughed. "You mean this?" She said coyly. "I was just worried about wearing you out before you play tomorrow," she said on a laugh.

"I'll definitely risk it," he laughed and lifted her on top of him. They kissed and lost themselves in their love.

It was a glorious Hawaiian day as the tournament opened. The Trade winds blew to cool the players, caddies and spectators. The views were spectacular, the sky, bright and clear, white sand beaches, a beautiful blue ocean with waves and surfers painting a captivating postcard. And, being that this was the PGA Tour, the golf was something to see. The big gallery enjoyed the show.

Bart and Dave stood on the 1st tee, wearing identical blue trimmed white golf shirts and hats with the symbol of Manitoba Oil emblazoned prominently. Behind the ropes, Justin and Phil Walleston were dressed the same. Angela wore a cool sun dress and a straw hat. Bart waved to her. She blew Bart a kiss.

"Wow," Rachel said softly to Angela. "That guy loves you so much." She paused. "I hope I have that someday."

Angela laughed, leaned close to Rachel. "Take a look, Rachel. I see a guy, standing with Bart, who can't seem to take his eyes off of you."

Rachel smiled at Dave, and impulsively, blew him a kiss. "He is kind of cute." She said on a laugh.

The morning wave of golfers had completed their rounds and posted their scores. Bart looked at the big scoreboard and was awed by the names. He looked at Dave, "Wow!" he said with a big grin. "Look who I am playing golf with." He laughed. "Bart DeMarco playing with Phil, Bubba and Rory, amazing." He looked about, smiled at Dave, "this certainly beats unloading 300,000 pounds of redfish."

Dave laughed. "They're just golfers Bart, you are as good as any of them." He sized Bart up, liked what he saw. "Let's play some golf."

The miracle didn't happen on this day. Bart shot a 3 over par 75! And, it could well have been worse, but for a chip-in from the rough on the 7th hole and rolling in an improbable 40 foot putt on the 18th.

The DeMarco's joined with the Curcuru family gathered at the Hospital to be with Sal, and cheer Bart on. Franco Palermo was with a smiling Lucia. "It seems the place to be," he whispered to Lucia.

She flashed a grin. "Is that why you are here, because this is the place to be?" She asked with raised brows.

Franco looked into Lucia's eyes. "I think you know why I'm here." He paused, glanced at the television. With a wide grin, he added. "I'm here to watch, my golfing hero, Bart DeMarco, play on the PGA Tour." He shrugged, seemingly perplexed. "What other attraction could possibly get me to drive to Boston to watch golf?"

Lucia laughed, punched his arm, leaned forward and kissed his cheek. "If you think of anything else, just let me know."

A big television was set up in the recreation room, Sal was wheeled in, and as the telecast originated from Hawaii, with the time difference, it was an evening broadcast. It was a quiet and concerned group watching Bart struggle. The announcers repeatedly explained that Bart had not been able to practice, flew in the day before, and was rusty. But, the color commentator, Johnny Miller, opined. "I see the bones of a big time game in him. Don't count this kid out."

As Bart and Dave strode up the 18th fairway, Donna Caponi, the on course announcer, who had been so kind to Bart at the Pacific Amateur, walked with him.

"How are things at home, Bart?" She asked, with a smile.

"Hi Donna," He grinned. "My father-in-law is doing better, he gave us quite a scare, but he's a tough Gloucester fisherman, he'll make it back."

Sal watched from his reclined wheelchair, really a bed, with tears in his eyes. Maria held his hand. Rosa felt such a sense of pride in her son.

"I messed up his chances," Sal said sadly. He looked at Franco and Rosa, "I'm so sorry."

"No," Rosa said, as she squeezed Sal's arm. "There will always be another Tournament, but Bart was right, 'family comes first.'"

"What about your round today," Donna asked Bart. "He smiled easily. "I'm shaking off the rust," he glanced at the scoreboard. "The leaders are at 4 under, I won't be too far behind."

"Well Bart," she asked with a smile. "It's early, but right now the cut looks to be about even par." She hustled to match his stride. "Do you think that you can make the cut?"

Bart flashed his best smile. "I'm playing this Tournament for Sal Curcuru, my father-in-law," he affirmed. The camera flashed to Angela, walking in the gallery with Rachel and Heather Walleston, the caption read, 'Bart DeMarco's wife, Angela.'

The camera flashed back on Bart. "If he can fight his battle, I will make the cut." He looked into the camera. "This is for you, Papa!"

"Quite a statement, Jim Nantz, the fabled golf announcer, commented. "What do you think, Johnny?"

On the 18th green, Bart stood over his putt. Donna spoke quietly, "it's a long, tough, downhill, twisting putt." She sighed. "A two putt would be a victory."

Bart stroked the putt, "looking good," Donna said excitedly. It was three feet from the cup, when Johnny said; "there's your answer, Jim. This kid is for real!"

Bart leaped into the air when the putt fell, pointed at Dave, who had helped him read the putt. In the gallery, Angela and Heather embraced. The big crowd following Bart exploded.

"Don't count out Bart DeMarco!" Donna asserted.

The crowd gathered with Sal at the hospital recreation room erupted in excited applause.

In the post round interview Bart was asked about his choice to remain in Boston rather than prepare for his first PGA Tournament. Bart looked into the camera, smiled, "my wife needed me, and family always comes first," he stated simply.

A golf writer for a prominent golf publication asked if he was offended or troubled by the moniker 'Stutter Boy' which was repeated in television and radio reports and printed in magazines and newspaper articles. In fact the nation's biggest and most prestigious golf magazine had a wonderful photo of Bart on its cover with the caption; 'Will STUTTER BOY succeed on the PGA Tour?'

Bart thanked the writer for the question. He smiled. "When I was a boy and terrified to even try to speak, I hated that I was mocked and called 'Stutter Boy,'" he replied. "Every day was a challenge for me. Every day I was laughed at and bullied." He paused. "The bullying stopped pretty quickly when my older brother, Mario, came upon two older kids pushing me and mocking me." He laughed. "Mario beat them both pretty well and made them apologize."

Bart shrugged, as he continued. "Typical cowards," he looked into the camera. "That is what bullies are, COWARDS," he stressed. "They never bothered me again." He sat back and considered his words. "Now, I see 'Stutter Boy' as a way to help others to succeed." He grinned. "It is a badge of honor, I proudly wear."

A newspaper reporter asked. "My paper has received thousands of calls and correspondence supporting your choice of family over golf." Bart smiled and nodded. "You have a big and growing fan base." The reporter stated. "What's your message to them?"

He pointed at the symbol on his breast. "I play for the hundreds of thousands of children, who like me, suffer the daily challenges and often the humiliation caused by stuttering." He paused. "Manitoba Oil and the Walleston family have pledged to help these children." He smiled, "I play for them!" He paused. "And, of course, for my father-in-law, Sal Curcuru, who's battling back from a devastating injury." He looked into the camera. "I've dedicated this Tournament to Sal Curcuru." He smiled. "Fight on, Papa, I'll do my best for you." He paused. "And, Angela sends her love."

Back at the hotel, Bart felt as if he was ready to compete. At dinner, he told Justin that he needed to hear Justin's voice cheering for him. He poked Justin, eliciting a laugh. "How can I win if I don't hear you cheering?"

Justin smiled. "Okay, ttomorrow, I,I will yyell lloud."

"That's what I want to hear!" Bart proclaimed. He looked around the table. "What a putt on 18, Huh?" He said. Smiles bloomed. Bart raised a finger. "We just talk about my brilliant putt on 18," he said. "Nothing about the other 74 strokes." He laughed aloud. And, he watched everybody relax.

Heather looked at Justin, "okay, Justin, we better get you up to bed. It will be an early and a long day tomorrow." Justin frowned, but rose and ran into Bart's arms. "You'll ddo better ttomorrow, Bart," Justin encouraged.

Bart squeezed him. "Get some rest, tomorrow will be a big day."

Heather with Phil said their goodnights and led Justin to the elevator bank and up to their suite.

Rachel eyed Bart, "you better not let my brother down, Bart." She raised her tiny fist, and with a big, pretty smile, threatened, "or else!"

Bart looked at Rachel, raised his hands in surrender. "Message received." Now, everybody was laughing. Bart shrugged. "Would it be in bad taste to mention all of Dave's mistakes out there on the course?"

Dave laughed. "Always blame the poor caddie."

Angela looked at Bart, with a flirtatious gleam, she asked, "is there anything I can do to help relax you, Bart."

Grins flashed across the table. Bart met Angela's eye. "I'll try to think of something."

Chapter Fifty

B art was off early on Friday, wearing blue with white piping. With the five hour time difference, it was 1pm on the East Coast when Bart hit his first shot at 8am Hawaii Time. Coverage on the Golf Channel would not begin until 3pm, EST, and since he was not one of the leaders, Bart's family was unaware how his round started. But, they were all seated watching as the Golf Channel cued in the Hawaiian Open Golf Tournament.

Coverage began with the camera shot of a smiling Bart striding down the 10th fairway. The announcer's excited report stated that; "on the strength of an eagle and four birdies, Bart DeMarco has shot a front nine score of 30, and is now 3 under par for the Tournament and charging."

A big, boisterous crowd, spiked heavily with the Hawaiian chapter of YES, were leading the cheers. Bart was smiling, as on every hole, every swing, he heard Justin, who was again dressed as Bart and Dave were, and walking with his Dad. Justin was yelling out in support, often stuttering his cheers, but still cheering.

Angela walked with Rachel and Heather. Her smile was as big as Billy Ray's, Texas. Billy Ray had also received a sponsor's exemption into the tournament and was playing in Bart's threesome. Billy Ray was struggling and heading in the wrong direction.

"The pressure of a PGA Tournament is extreme," Johnny Miller, the color commentator stated. "And, the pressure may be getting to Billy Ray," he paused and laughed, "but Bart, looks as if he is playing a Saturday morning round with his buddies."

The on course commentator, Donna Caponi, added to Johnny's statement; "Bart doesn't appear to feel the pressure of the big crowd or really anything that he can't control." She said with a tone of approval. "Jim, Johnny, Bart told me that golf isn't pressure." She paused, collected her thoughts. "Bart explained that pressure is being terrified to speak and facing the mocking and ridicule of your peers, when he stood before them, praying to speak without stuttering." Rosa listened to Donna's comment with tears in her eyes, re-living those terribly painful years, as she watched, with a mother's pride, her son stride confidently up the fairway.

Heather held Angela's hand, she looked at the young bride, "Angela, you are married to a special young man."

Angela nodded. "I am," she smiled, just as the camera cut to her, dressed prettily in a sundress and a colorful and cool straw hat.

Sal and Maria clasped hands as they watched Angela on camera. Rosa smiled at them, "Angela is so important to their success."

Angela, unaware of the camera or the scrutiny, looked at Mrs. Walleston and happily agreed. "Bart is special, but he's not out there alone." She looked at Heather and Rachel. "And, I feel blessed that he loves me," she smiled. "But, Bart's always telling me how important Dave is to the team." She paused, "'Team DeMarco' is more than Bart. Dave's a great coach and a special friend."

Angela smiled, spoke softly, earnestly. "Mrs. Walleston, you and Mr. Walleston have been everything to Bart." She hugged her. "He's so thankful and so am I." Angela nudged Rachel. "Don't blow it with Dave," she advised. "He really likes you." She paused, eyed Rachel, "but, he feels that he has so little to offer to you." She paused, smiled, "but, Rachel," she pushed, "he really has so much." Their eyes met. Angela implored. "Rachel, don't look at his bank account, look at his heart." She paused, studied Rachel, who looked out at Bart and Dave conferring on the next shot. "Think about it Rachel," Angela urged.

The cheers from the Activities room at the Boston General Hospital brought a crowd of mobile patients, Doctors, nurses and staff. Sal was beaming. He looked at Maria, "Bart's going to do it!" He pronounced. "Bart's going to win for me!"

Franco and Mario had gone out fishing. It was painful not to be there, not to know, but radio reports would have to do, they had a business to run.

As Bart neared completion of his second round, he began to feel the wind pick up. "It will be tough on the late starters," Bart suggested.

Dave eyed Bart. "C'mon Bart, stay focused, let's run through the finish line." He urged.

And that's what Bart did. He posted a back nine of 3 under par, to finish with a round of 63, for a total of 9 under par on the day and 6 under par for the Tournament. When Bart left the course, holding Angela's hand, and smiling happily, he was only 1 shot back of the leaders.

The announcers were profuse in their praise. The former great golfer and current color commentator, Johnny Miller, picked Bart to be leading by the end of that round. "He got a gift," Johnny stated. "This wind will kill the afternoon scoring." He paused and reflected. "He deserves a break." Johnny added, "I think golf has a new superstar in the making."

On the course, Donna, the on course reporter agreed. "Johnny," she said, "Bart hits his drives really long and so straight, his short game keeps improving and he has such confidence on the greens." She paused. "I believe Bart DeMarco will be a special golfer." She opined. "I think he's already a very special young man."

Rosa heard those words with a pride that only a parent could comprehend. 'That's my boy!' She thought, as she teared up.

Angela stood with Bart, patient and smiling, as he signed every autograph, and answered every question for his young fans. These youngsters stuttered their thanks and looked on Bart as their hero. Bart gave them a new outlook on their potential and their life.

Bart and Angela with Dave and Rachel and a jubilant Justin, spent the afternoon swimming in the elaborate resort swimming pool. Justin smiled at Bart. "I,I did wwhat you ssaid, Bart." He stuttered out. "I ccheered on every sshot." Bart hoisted Justin, heard the boy's laugh, and jumped into the pool with him. "You did it, Justin," Bart called. "You are my biggest fan!"

Dave joined the fray and the three frolicked, laughed and let off steam. Angela, wearing the bikini that Bart so enjoyed seeing on his girl, watched Bart with Justin and considered Bart as a Dad. She liked her imaging. Bart swam to the pools edge and eyed Angela. "Hey, Beauty," he teased. "You need a date?"

She smiled as he eyed her, then, Angela laughed. She looked at Bart with a grin, and shook her head as she warned him. "Young man, I happen to be a married woman."

"I'd say your husband is one lucky guy!" He responded, offering a wide grin. "If I were he, I'd take you upstairs to your room right now."

"Easy boy," Rachel warned, eyes flashing. "You'll burn yourself out, right Dave?"

Dave, with Justin up on his shoulders, smiled at Rachel, "well, it may be worth the risk." Their eyes met, he summoned the courage to ask. "Rachel, would you like to take a walk?"

Rachel looked at Angela, who nodded and smiled. "Go ahead, Rachel, we'll stay with Justin.

"Okay," Rachel responded to Dave with an inviting smile. She looked at Bart and Angela. "We'll see you at dinner."

Bart looked at Angela as Dave and Rachel walked away holding hands. "Do you think?" He asked, smiling.

Angela shrugged. "I don't know, but look at us," She eyed him and laughed. "'Stutter Boy' and 'Ugly Angela,'" she winked, "you just never know."

Bart ogled Angela in her sleek bikini, smiled. "You are beautiful, Angela." He glanced at Justin swimming with another boy about his age. "How about we dump the kid and take a little nap?" He suggested, smiling.

Angela met his smile, imagined Bart asking the same question in the years ahead. "Sounds good, but why don't we let him swim for a bit, he's having fun."

Bart laughed. "Stymied by a ten year old."

Chapter Fifty-One

The wind, as predicted, had made a difference. Bart was in a three way tie for the tournament lead, with Rory and Phil. They would be the last threesome to go out on moving day. Moving Day, usually the Saturday (or third day) of the four day Tournament, is when golfers, who hoped to win, needed to move up the leaderboard, to put themselves in a position to win on Sunday. Bart arrived at the tee-box early to watch the threesome of Dustin Johnson, Jordan Spieth and Justin Thomas tee off. The 17 year old, was impressed beyond words.

The three Tournament leaders moved to the tee-box as Dustin, Jordan and Justin headed down the 1st fairway. Bart, dressed in a green golf shirt with white piping and a white baseball cap with the logo in green, had run that morning, worked out in the resort's gym and practiced on the range, chipping areas and practice greens for ninety minutes. The leaders were ready to strike their opening drives. On course reporter and commentator, Donna Caponi, was interviewing Phil Mickelson.

"Phil, she asked, with a smile, "what are your thoughts on playing today with a 17 year old?"

The always affable star laughed. "Donna, he introduced himself to me yesterday, by calling me Mr. Mickelson." He laughed. "Mr. Mickelson?"

Donna smiled. "Well, Phil, you are old enough to be his father!" Donna poked the Hall of Fame golfer.

Phil laughed. "That's what Amy told me." He shook his head. "He seems like a nice kid." He paused. "And, Donna, the kid can really play." He smiled, flashed that Mickelson gleam. "But, I have no intention of losing to a 17 year old."

Donna, an unabashed fan of Bart, smiled, "we'll see Phil." Then she moved to do an interview with Rory McIlroy, the world's number 1 ranked golfer.

Bart walked onto the tee-box with Dave, shook the hands of Phil and his legendary caddie, Jim (Bones) MacKay, then Rory and his caddie. Dave watched Bart closely, rolled his eyes and pulled Bart aside. "Hey, Bart, relax," he advised. "They're just a couple of golfers."

Donna moved to Bart. "How are you feeling today, Bart?" She asked.

"Are you kidding," he grinned, "I'm playing a round of golf with Phil and Rory." He shook his head, eyed Donna. "WOW!" He beamed.

She laughed. "Anything to say to the family at home?"

Bart nodded. "Papa, I hope you're watching." He looked into the camera. "I'm going to win this Tournament for you." He smiled. "And, if I can do that, you can get stronger, do your therapy, and walk out of that Hospital!"

The activity room was packed with family and friends. The DeMarco's were there, Lucia with Franco Palermo. Of course, the Curcuru family were all there, and, in a show of support, and at Angela's request, Dave and Jessica and Jim and Betsy were there as well. With all the Hospital staff, the large room was packed. All eyes looked to Sal Curcuru, who upon hearing Bart's words called out. "It's a deal, Bart!"

Donna looked into the camera and smiled. "Bart I've noticed a lot of buttons being worn by adults and children, your fans, have you noticed?"

Bart shook his head, "no," he said. He looked into the gallery surrounding the first tee-box. He smiled at Angela, who stood with the Wallestons. The buttons being worn proudly, read: 'I'm with Stutter Boy.'

He smiled, looked at Donna. "We're going to help these kids." He stated with certainty. His fan base continued to grow.

Bart shot out of the gate on the 1ˢᵗ hole, blasting a drive that split the fairway. His second shot landed safely on the green. He then rolled in a 20 foot putt for a birdie and his first lead of the Tournament. Bart fist pumped in celebration, he saw Angela clapping and jumping joyously. Their eyes met and she blushed. There was a roar from the huge gallery following this threesome. As always, Phil's fans were out in force. It seemed everybody loved Rory's game and character. And, the untested rookie, Bart DeMarco, had a large contingent of youthful fans and their parents cheering his every move.

Phil and Rory parred the 1st and the network's color commentator, Johnny Miller, stated; "Bart has the lead." He laughed. "Why do I feel, Jim," he addressed the play-by-play broadcaster, Jim Nantz, "that we will be saying that phrase regularly in the future?"

"Bart DeMarco is an unusual talent, I agree Johnny." He paused. "We'll see."

Angela and Rachel shrieked their approval for their guys, 'Team DeMarco', "Go Bart," Angela called out as Bart passed by on the walk to the 2ⁿᵈ tee. Bart stopped for a quick kiss, caught by the network cameras.

Donna Caponi, walking with the leaders, laughed. "They're newlyweds, folks," she said in explanation. The crowd in the Activity room applauded when Angela appeared on the screen. Sal and Maria smiled broadly, Rosa beamed.

Franco Palermo leaned closer to Lucia, "your brother is something, Lucia." She smiled at him. "And, his baby sister is beautiful," he added with a smile. Their eyes met and Lucia blushed and smiled, raised her fingers to the remaining blemish on Franco's lip, where Sal had landed, 'a lucky punch,' according to Franco, before Franco pounded him into retreating.

"That's nothing," Franco said. He looked into Lucia's eyes, "the prize was so worth it." Lucia beamed her beautiful smile.

On the par 3 second hole, Rory, up to the challenge, landed his tee shot to within 2 feet. He tapped in the birdie putt to grab a share of the lead. On the long par 4, Fourth hole, Phil, who had been scattering his tee shots, in the words of Johnny Miller, "all over Hawaii," but making miraculous recovery shots, lofted a 64 degree wedge over a pond, to a tucked pin, as only the Great Mickelson could do. He rolled in his putt for birdie and the leaders were, again, even.

Bart walked beside Phil as they moved across to the 5th tee. "That was great, Sir," Bart hesitated, looked at Phil, "do you think that you could teach me that shot?" He asked with a touch of awe in his tone. Phil just smiled, "thanks Bart," he responded.

The battle continued, with each gaining a temporary advantage, but after the 9th hole, they were all 3 under par for the round and 9 under for the Tournament. Dustin and Jordan, also playing well, were now 4 strokes behind.

Bart's youthful gallery was beginning to believe. Their calls of support and applause grew as the match continued. Little voices, racked with stutters, called out. Bart heard the hope in their voices, grew even more determined.

The trio continued to sparkle on the back nine. They seemed to be inspiring and pushing each other. Each played the back nine in 3 under par to shoot a 6 under par score of 66. Bart walked with Phil as often as possible, as Phil explained the science of golf. Bart was impressed. "He really thinks through all of this." Bart said to Dave. "He's amazing!"

Dave nodded. "You can learn a great deal from him." He paused. "But, let's stay in the moment." He eyed Bart. "Only focus on the next shot."

Bart listened to his Coach and rolled a birdie putt in on the 18th hole to end the third round in a tie for the lead with both Rory and Phil. In the process they had opened a five shot lead over the next nearest competitor.

"It looks like a three man battle for the Tournament," Jim Nantz noted. He looked to Johnny Miller. "Johnny, who do you think has the advantage?"

Miller studied the gallery of youngsters who delightedly flocked around Bart as he left the 18th green. "You know Jim, logic says that it should be Rory or Phil, they are both great players, they have both won multiple Major Championships." He paused. "But my gut tells me not to discount this young warrior."

Donna Caponi added, as she stood waiting to conduct interviews with the three leaders, "You know guys, I thought playing with Phil, who Bart idolizes, and Rory, the world's number 1 ranked player, might throw Bart." She shook her head. "He seems unshakable. I'm picking Bart DeMarco to get it done tomorrow." She smiled. "This young man is special!"

Bart's family and friends at the Boston General Hospital let out a cheer on her words. Sal flashed a fist, Bart style. "My boy is going to win!" He stated. "You'll see!"

Bart and Angela, Dave and the Wallestons chose a quiet dinner at the resorts prize winning steak house. As always, Justin took the seat next to Bart. So, Bart sat between Angela and Justin. Angela laughed as Bart ordered a 22 ounce bone-in, rib-eye, with sautéed onions and a baked sweet potato. "You think that you ordered enough food there, Bart?" Angela queried with a grin.

He flashed her a lascivious smile. "I need to build up my strength, I have a lot of work ahead." Angela raised her brows and met his smile. "And, Angela" Bart winked. "Can you believe they don't have garlic bread?" On cue, Angela blushed, causing inquisitive grins from Heather and Rachel.

Justin jumped in, "Bbart nneeds to bbe strong ffor tomorrow." He stuttered.

Bart saw the frustration on the youngster's face, put his hand on Justin's shoulder and looked into his eyes. "Justin, take a deep breath, give me a smile, and just look at me, okay?" Justin nodded, the 10 year old took and released the breath, eyes on Bart. "Now," Bart said with a comforting smile, "take another deep breath and say that again, nice and easy."

Justin exhaled, eyes on Bart, "you need to bbe strong for ttomorrow." He said, looked to his parents and smiled.

"That's great," Bart said. "See, Justin, you can do it!" Bart smiled, put a hand on Justin's shoulders, smiled and met his eyes. "Okay Justin, take a deep breath, let it out slowly and try again," Bart urged with an encouraging smile.

Justin nodded, and met Bart's smile. Bart could see that the boy's anxiety level was much lower. Justin took and released a deep breath, smiled into Bart's encouraging expression and repeated; "Bart, you need to be strong for tomorrow." Justin's eyes lit, he smiled in triumph.

Smiles bloomed across the table, Bart playfully shook Justin's shoulders. "See, you can do it, Justin, you can do it!" Bart repeated.

Heather wrapped her arms around Justin, her tears flowed, as she looked over Justin's shoulder at Bart. "God Bless you, Bart." She said, joyously.

Phil Walleston's eyes filled, he looked at Bart. "Thank you, Son," he managed.

Everyone toasted the proud 10 year old with their water glasses. Justin beamed, looked at Bart. He took and released a breath, "I can do it!" He said triumphantly.

Angela observed the joy of the Walleston's, she took Bart's hand, leaned close and whispered, "Bart, you are something special."

Bart laughed and eyed her. In a soft voice, while the Walleston's were embracing Justin, he winked and responded. "I'd rather you showed me how special you think I am, Mrs. DeMarco." Angela flashed a smile. "Oh, I will."

With everybody back in their seats and as dinner was being served, Bart looked across the table. "I've been meaning to ask, Donna Caponi hinted at it and a PGA official today said to me that they were so glad that they didn't withdraw my invite." He looked at Rachel, and smiled. "And, earlier Rachel, you said something about Dave fighting for me." He paused, eyes on Dave, "who wants to tell me what all that means?"

Dave looked at Mr. Walleston and smiled. "Okay Bart," Dave explained. "When you were back in Boston, with Angela's Dad and all, the PGA began to get edgy about whether you would show." He smiled. "It became clear that they were considering offering your Sponsor's Exemption to a suddenly available PGA Tour player." He shrugged. "So, Mr. Walleston and I decided we needed to act," he angled his head and grinned. "We called John Palermo and between the three of us we decided to put pressure on the Sponsors and the PGA officials by going to the media with Sal's story and how you were supporting your wife and her family."

Phil Walleston jumped in. "Dave was just great," he nodded approvingly at Dave. "Dave," Walleston continued, "cornered media, television and print, and told your story, Bart. All of it, the 'Stutter Boy' angle, the devoted young husband and how you put family before golf, even though you so wanted to play in the Tournament." Walleston sat back and gestured to Dave to carry on.

Dave took Rachel's hand, a bold move before her family, and continued. "I called the Hawaii Chapter of YES." He smiled, "they leaped into action, and began to pressure the Sponsor, whose business is primarily here in Hawaii." He paused and saw that Mrs. Walleston was smiling at him.

"Before the Tournament," Dave explained, "there is not much news, so they ate it up, and made Bart DeMarco, Gandhi like." He smiled at Rachel, turned back to Bart. "Mr. Palermo updated us daily on Mr. Curcuru's condition, so we had fresh news every day."

Bart looked at Angela, and grinned, "I see," he said, "so, Angela, that explains how the Golf Channel knew!" He laughed. He eyed Dave. "Thank you, Dave." He looked at Mr. Walleston. "It seems that I am always thanking you, Sir."

Walleston looked at Bart. "We are all so thankful, Bart." He smiled at his son, who was eating his burger, "for so much." He paused. "Please, everybody, eat, enjoy."

Bart nodded and eyed his beautifully prepared steak, glistening in sautéed onions. He cut a generous slice and savored the taste. "So, good!" Bart exuded.

"Of course," Angela joked, looking at Bart's plate, "Bart eats more at dinner than Gandhi did in a year."

Bart eyed Angela with a grin as everybody laughed. "My mother," Bart responded, "always encouraged me to eat hearty!"

"And, there you have it Ladies and Gentlemen!" Angela proclaimed with a flourish and feigned exasperation. "Italian mothers and their beloved sons. It's always the poor wife who bears the burden."

"Hey, Mother Theresa," Dave laughed, angling a happy glint at Angela. "You're doing okay!" All laughed. Looking at the table of happy diners, no observer would have the slightest clue as to the challenges being faced and battled by this group.

Phil Walleston considered and decided to complete his thought. "Bart, Dave," his eyes scanned the table, taking in everyone. "We are all a team." He smiled at Rachel. "Together, we can do so much." He looked to Heather and met her smile. "Okay, just one last thing." He looked at Dave, noted his caressing of Rachel's hand, recalled the attention Dave had lavished on Rachel when he visited the family in Manitoba, and offered a smile. "Dave, is there something that you should tell me?"

Dave sat tall in his chair, eyed Mr. Walleston. "Yes Sir, there is." He looked at Rachel, who remained silent, but smiled encouragingly. "I'm in love with your daughter."

Angela beamed a smile at Rachel, who, leaned over and kissed Dave.

Phil Walleston looked at the happy couple, flashed a smile at Rachel, who met his eyes and nodded. Then, he looked at Dave. "Good to hear, Son, you have my blessing."

Dave let out a deep breath, smiled from ear to ear, kissed Rachel, and addressed her father. "Thank you, Sir."

Bart shook his head. He smiled at Dave, who beamed with joy. "This is way too much drama for me," he stated with a laugh. "Is it okay if I eat my steak, now?" The question was met with relieved smiles.

"Yes," Angela said, as everyone relaxed. "Bart needs to eat and get back to our room." She eyed Bart, smiled sweetly. "He needs his rest."

"Right!" Dave said, with a laugh. "Rest?" He eyed Angela. "Just take it easy on my boy, Angela." Smiles and laughter rolled across the group. 'Perfect,' Dave thought. 'Let's stay loose.'

Back in their suite, Bart took Angela in his arms, savored her softness and perfumed body. He kissed her sweet lips and smiled. "You know, Angela, I feel so tense about tomorrow and all, I really need something to relieve my stress." With a grin, he began to disrobe his lovely, happy, wife.

When she stood gloriously before him, she wound her hands around his neck, smiled seductively and kissed him. "Please ravish me, my love." Angela offered her best smile. "I'm all yours!"

They cuddled together, happily sated. Angela's head on Bart's chest. Her hand never stopped caressing and pleasing, and she delighted at his response. "I love you, Bart," she cooed. Angela kissed his cheek, met his eyes. "Are you worried about tomorrow?"

Bart kissed her, lifted her easily up on top of him. He loved the feel of her body on his. 'All soft and sweet,' he thought. She smiled, read his eyes. "You're insatiable," she giggled as she wriggled into position and watched his smile bloom.

Later, they laid entwined together, near sleep, when Bart said. "No, Princess, I'm not worried." He shrugged. "It's just golf." He squeezed her. "Whatever happens, I still have you."

They slept peacefully.

Chapter Fifty-Two

Championship Sunday dawned on another beautiful Hawaiian day. The air was warm, the sun was high and bright in a blue sky dotted with puffy white clouds, and there was a cooling breeze. The ocean was alive with surfers, navigating the building waves. In short, it felt like Paradise.

Bart, Phil and Rory, were the final threesome, and moved to the tee for their 2pm (Hawaiian Time, 7pm, EST) Tee time.

YES had come through and brought several thousand children and their parents to cheer for Bart. In truth, they came to cheer for the hope Bart inspired. Many wore 'I'm with Stutter Boy' pins. They came to cheer Bart to victory. Each of the children saw Bart as their personal Champion. And, Bart intended to win for them.

Bart and Dave wore their Sunday apparel. A red, white and blue shirt, with the Manitoba Oil logo on one breast and the American flag on the other. On one sleeve was the Canadian Maple Leaf. Their hats were white, with Red and Blue logos and lettering. Phil and Justin Walleston were dressed identically.

The golfers and caddies exchanged handshakes and pleasantries on the Tee. "Nice crowd," Phil Mickelson mentioned, to Bart. "I respect what you are trying to do for these children."

"Thank you, sir," Bart responded. "I appreciate that."

Rory walked over, smiled. "Let's give them a good show, gentlemen," the popular Irishman urged. They all smiled, shook hands and readied to hit their opening drives. Bart found Angela, standing in a sea of buttoned, 'I'm with Stutter Boy' children, and flashed a smile. He read her anxiety and gave her a wink.

It was 7pm in Boston and the Activity room at the Boston General Hospital was the place to be. Sal was wheeled close to the TV, his family, as well as Bart's family, seated around him. Bart's father, Franco and brother, Mario, were still at sea. Rosa knew how very badly her husband wanted to see this, but, as he said, "we need to make a trip. The boat mortgage and the house mortgage are due." He laughed and shrugged. "The life of a fisherman."

Both, John Palermo and his son, Franco, were there. Franco sat close to Lucia, who simply radiated happiness. John was delighted for his son. The bruises and scrapes were all healed, and he was proud that his son had stood strong and fought for Lucia. John knew and respected the DeMarco family. His gut told John that the pretty, almost 16 year old, Lucia DeMarco, was worth fighting for.

On course reporter, Donna Caponi, was with the three leaders. She stood back and watched carefully. Of course, every golfer has weaknesses. As a Hall of Fame golfer and Major Champion herself, Donna knew what to watch for in each golfer.

Phil had a masterful short game and more creativity on the course than any other three golfers combined. He did, however, have trouble driving the ball in the fairway. Rory was long off of the tee, a great ball striker. If he had a weakness, at times, he struggled on the putting green.

Donna explained the golfer's strengths and weaknesses to the viewers. Then, she came to Bart. "I have not detected any real flaws," she stated. "He's only 17, and the only time he was in a final on a National stage, he shot a 63, but lost to Billy Ray Boyd, at the Pacific Amateur."

"Johnny," she reflected. "If Bart DeMarco has a flaw, it is that he is only 17 years old and not accustomed to the pressure of a Championship Sunday." She smiled into the camera. "I'm a fan," she confessed with a grin. "There are thousands of fans in his gallery." She stated. "Maybe, that helps or hurts Bart?" She paused, thoughtful. "I guess, we'll have to wait and see."

On the 5th hole, Bart rolled in a 15 foot putt to move to 2 under par on the round. Phil and Rory were both 1 under par and playing well.

On the 9th hole Bart's tee shot skipped into a bad lie in the rough. "He missed the fairway there," commented Jim Nantz.

"Nobody, hits them all." Johnny Miller replied softly. "How does his lie look, Donna?" Miller asked.

Donna Caponi studied the lie. She considered his options. "It doesn't look good," she stated. "I'm not sure he will be able to find the green." She opined. "It's a good time to reign in his youthful enthusiasm."

"He needs to play this smart, Donna," Johnny Miller stated. "Get the ball in good position to get up and down from the fairway." He paused. "He has to try and save par."

Bart and Dave studied the lie. Dave noted the clump of grass directly behind the ball. "You won't be able to get any spin from this lie." He exhaled, considered. "I'd suggest that you just try to run it up to the green." Bart nodded in agreement.

Bart settled into his routine, visualized, smiled and addressed the shot. He swung a tad too hard, and pushed his second shot to the right and placed himself in a difficult position. The ball was sitting down in the rough, there was a pond between his ball and the green. To add to the difficulty, the green sloped away from Bart and the pin was tucked close to the pond. He had little green to work with. He faced a very difficult shot.

Donna Caponi studied the shot and commented to Jim Nantz and Johnnie Miller. "This is a tough shot, guys. Phil and Rory are both on the green in two and are likely to, at worse, par the hole. Bart may give back a stroke or more here."

Bart stood studying the shot with Dave beside him. Bart looked over at Phil Mickelson, who smiled at Bart. Bart grinned and reached for his most lofted club, a 60 degree wedge. Bart stood to the side, opened the face of the club and took two practice swings.

Dave moved in quickly, close to Bart, "what are you doing, Bart?" He asked with alarm.

Bart looked at Dave and smiled. "I'm going to hit a Mickelson lob shot, try to get it close."

Dave took a deep breath. "Easy Bart, Phil has worked developing that shot for more than a decade." He paused. You have never tried the shot." He studied Bart. "Why don't you just hit a little pitch shot over the pond onto the green, nice and easy?" He paused. "At worse, you will have a 30 foot par putt, a two putt for a bogey and we're still tied for the lead."

Angela and Rachel watched the intense discussion from a distance. Angela looked at Rachel, "I don't know." She said.

Donna suggested that based on the practice swings, Bart may be thinking of trying a Mickelson lob. "Bart was impressed with Phil's shot yesterday." She added and paused. "I think his caddie and Coach, Dave Gilliss, is trying to talk him out of that idea."

At the Boston General Hospital, there was deep concern. One of the Doctor's watching, Sal's surgeon, and a long-time golfer, shook his head. "Stop him, Dave," he fairly pleaded. "That shot is most likely to end up in the pond."

Rosa heard the Doctor's concern, and studied Bart's face closely. "He's going to try it," she said on a sigh. She looked about, shook her head, concern on her face, "he has the DeMarco hard head."

Bart looked at Dave. "I watched Phil closely, Dave." He grinned. "Come on Dave, it will be fun." The comment was picked up by Donna's microphone.

"I'll say this Jim," Donna laughed. "He's having fun with this, let's see."

Dave looked closely at Bart. "Okay, Bart, go after it hard, a big swing, don't hold back."

Jim Nantz looked to Johnny Miller, "what do you think, Johnny?"

"Jim," Miller started. "This has the potential for disaster written all over it." He sighed. "Not a high percentage shot, for sure." He paused, "but, if he pulls it off?"

Jim Nantz watched closely. "Is this where being 17 and unfamiliar with Championship pressure will rear its ugly head, Johnny?"

"Maybe, Jim," Miller said. "Certainly the safe shot, the smart shot, is to pitch it over the pond, accept the two putt and move on." He paused. "But, this kid has no fear." He watched Bart closely. "He's going for it Jim, get ready!"

Bart settled over the ball. He flashed a smile at Angela. He took a big, Mickelson type, swing under the ball, and shot the ball high. It seemed to climb forever. "There was total silence from the gallery. Angela quietly pleaded, "please, please, please," and closed her eyes.

Donna called, "Guys, it may be good," she took a step closer. "It may be very good," she called excitedly. The ball came down over the pond on the fringe of the green, took a tiny hop onto the green, and gently rolled down the slope and into the hole for a Birdie.

The gallery exploded in a roar not before heard that day. The big crowd at the Boston General Hospital exulted. "He's going to do it!" Sal yelled. "He's going to do it!" The camera found Angela crying happy tears and embracing Rachel.

"That's likely a two shot lead, WOW!" called Jim Nantz. "From disaster to redemption!"

"The kid is special," Johnny Miller stated, excitedly. "I mean, who does that?" He laughed. Bart and Dave embraced.

Phil Mickelson looked at Rory McIlroy, smiled and shook his head. They waited for the crowd to settle, but, both two putted and after 9 holes, Bart had a two shot lead.

"Bart DeMarco," Jim Nantz said, "in his first ever PGA Tournament has a two shot lead on Phil Mickelson and Rory McIlroy, after nine holes on Championship Sunday!" He looked at Johnny Miller. "Will the pressure get to him, Johnny? Will he back up?"

Rosa shook her head. "My boy doesn't back up!" She stated with certainty.

On the 220 yard, par 3, 12th hole, Bart with the honor, struck a beautiful 5 hybrid. It landed on the green, rolled to about 10 feet below the cup. "Great shot, Johnny," Donna called. "He left it below the hole, not a tough putt."

"Not at all," Johnny Miller agreed. "These guys better watch out, young Bart DeMarco may run away from them."

Both Phil and Rory found the green, but were much further away. They both managed two putts for par. Bart crouched behind his putt, Dave stood looking over Bart's shoulder at the putt. They conferred on the line, Dave moved away. Angela's hands were fisted at her mouth. Rachel nudged her. "Relax," she smiled. "There's a great golfer and a great coach sizing up that putt." She winked. "It's going in, Angela."

Bart moved over the putt. He looked up and met Angela's eye. The camera caught the connection.

Rosa smiled. "He's going to make it," she stated. Bart stroked the putt into the center of the hole. He flashed his smile at Angela, who was jumping and clapping. Rachel saw his smile. "You know, Angela, I think that guy likes you." They laughed together. Bart had a three shot lead and his gallery was cheering and screaming his name. Like one of the surfers in the distance, Bart seemed to be riding the wave of support all the way to victory.

Bart was excited, Dave stayed calm and in control. Bart was in the zone, the gallery was frenzied, Bart, simply took the club and Dave's instructions, and swung smoothly.

Phil birdied the 13th hole, to Bart's and Rory's pars, cutting Bart's lead to 2 shots. On 14, Rory hit his second shot to five feet and dropped the putt. Bart's lead was now 2 shots over both Phil and Rory.

"Great Champions don't quit," Miller attested. Bart's gallery quieted, matching the hushed silence at the Boston General Hospital.

They moved to the par 5, 15th hole. A big drive, in the fairway, would allow the golfer to go for the green in two. There was water to the right and a deep punishing sand-trap by the left front corner of the green.

Rory had the honor and hit a good drive, but yanked it a little left, in the fairway, near the left rough. "He may have tree trouble," Donna commented. "If so, it's likely a lay-up for Rory. Phil hit a good drive, about 290 yards, center cut. "Good drive and an excellent lie," Johnny called. "He's about 265 yards away."

Bart eyed Dave, who smiled, "go for it, Bart," he urged, as Dave handed Bart his driver. Bart grinned at his coach, flashed a smile at Angela and teed his ball. He took a deep breath and launched into his smooth as silk swing. "He caught all of that," Donna called. "Absolutely, Jim Nantz agreed. "He hit that about 335 yards, leaving 220 yards to the center of the green, Wow! A great drive."

Bart's gallery of youngsters came alive, calling to him as he strode up the fairway. 'Now!' Dave thought. 'We put it away now!' Of course, he just smiled at Bart as they confidently walked to Phil's ball.

Phil stood behind his shot, discussing options with Jim (Bones) MacKay. Dave watched closely. Phil has the well-earned reputation for being bold. Dave believed that Phil took smart risks. He did not believe going for the green from where Phil's ball lay, was a smart move, especially, considering how truly great Phil was with a wedge in his hands. It seems that Phil and Bones agreed. Phil hit an iron to about 90 yards. 'He'll make magic from that distance,' Dave thought.

Rory grimaced as he finally accepted that he would need to hit a punch shot, under the branches of the over-hanging trees. He hit his shot, which stayed below the branches, but it had a bit too much steam. Unfortunately, it ran into the sand trap, on the front left of the green.

"That'll be a tough up and down," Dave thought, as Bart and Dave, with gallery in tow, marched to his ball.

Dave looked at the trees to see how the wind blew, he smiled and handed Bart his 5 hybrid. "Nice and smooth Bart, aim just left of the flag."

"He could put the Tournament away here." The golfing Doctor suggested. "Go Bart," he called, excitedly.

Sal took Maria's hand. He looked at Rosa. "He's going to do it, Rosa." Rosa smiled. "He's doing it for you, Sal."

Bart nodded, stood behind his shot, glanced over to the ropes, smiled at Angela. He then studied the target line, closed his eyes to visualize the shot, opened his eyes, smiled and stood over his ball. He wasted no time, took a smooth swing and hit an excellent shot, left of the pin, it took the slope of the green and rolled to within eight feet of the cup.

The gallery exploded with a roar that could be heard across the course. "Great shot," called Donna. "He's on fire, Guys," she added. Bart happily jogged over to the gallery and high fived a number of youngsters.

"He sure is," Johnny Miller agreed. "And, you know, Phil and Rory are playing well." He paused. "Bart's just playing incredibly well." He laughed. "Do I have to remind anyone that he is only 17 years old?"

Donna Caponi smiled at Johnny Miller's question. "You know Johnny," Donna stated. "I've talked to Bart, he's not like any 17 year old I've known." She paused. "There's a maturity about him that you just don't see in a teenager." She considered. "He has a real idea of who he is, and what he wants." She stopped to watch Phil set up over his shot.

Phil hit a sand wedge that landed a few yards shorter than intended, it spun back leaving him a 20 foot putt.

"To complete my thought," Donna added. "I've watched him with these young fans, who absolutely adore him." She laughed. "He is playing for them, to help them succeed." She paused. "He loves playing golf, for sure. But, he knows that it's all about more than just him." She shrugged. "He's just not your average teenager at all."

"I agree," Johnny Miller stated. "There is nothing average about Bart DeMarco. Absolutely nothing!"

Rory set up in the deep bunker. "Not a good lie," Donna whispered. "It will be tough." Rory exploded the ball out of the trap, but it had no spin. It ran 25 feet past the hole.

Rory and then Phil two putted for pars. Phil took the ball from the hole, smiled at Bart, who crouched with Dave behind his ball. "Left edge, firm" Dave urged. Bart nodded in agreement.

Bart heard Justin call out. "Go Bart, Go 'Stutter Boy!'"

Bart flashed a smile, stood over his putt and stroked it home for an Eagle. "That, my friends," Johnny Miller called, "gives Bart DeMarco a four shot lead. He's at 17 under par." Bart's gallery was in a frenzy of excitement. The roar was astounding.

"Three holes left!" Stated the excited Doctor, a brilliant neurosurgeon, whose skill had saved Sal's life on that long and terrifying first day. But, at the moment, he was an unabashed Bart DeMarco fan. "4 shots up with three holes to play." He watched the screen, which showed Bart and Dave high-fiving. "Keep him calm, Dave," the Doctor advised. "Just 3 pars and he wins." He smiled. "Absolutely Amazing!"

Rosa took the Doctor's hand, met his eyes. With happy tears in her eyes, she nodded. "My Bart will win!"

The threesome walked to the par 4, 16th hole. Bart hit his drive down the middle of the fairway, leaving 160 yards into the green. His gallery was abuzz. 'Stutter Boy' was going to win. A large banner was unfurled, it had a smiling photo of Bart and emblazoned on the banner it read: Go Bart: YES loves 'Stutter Boy.'

Phil and Rory also found the fairway and all three landed their second shots on the green. Phil nearly holed out, his shot hit the green, bounced up, struck the pin and bounded about 15 feet away. Phil shook his head, looked at Bart and smiled, "the rub of the green, Bart." All three golfers 2 putted for par, and they moved to the par 3, 17th tee-box.

Donna stood by the tee-box as the threesome waited for the green to clear. "DeMarco stands on the 17th tee with a commanding 4 stroke lead." Jim Nantz stated. "What do you see in his swing and game, Johnny?"

"Jim," Johnny Miller began. "DeMarco has a smooth, natural and repeatable swing." He laughed. "We all saw on the 9th hole that he doesn't play scared." He shrugged, "I see a bright future for the young man." Nantz addressed Donna Caponi. "Your thoughts Donna? He asked.

"I am impressed by his game and his character." Donna paused. "Bart's a winner, Guys."

Bart walked over to the ropes, kissed a smiling Angela and ruffled Justin's hair. The YES youngsters, adorned in their 'We're with Stutter Boy' buttons broke into a cheer. One red-headed, freckled faced, boy stammered out; "Ggo Bbart!" Bart smiled and high-fived the smiling boy.

"This young man is as cool a golfer as I've seen." Donna Capone commented. "He's a bit like Arnold Palmer, in that he's able to raise the shade, engage the fans, then, lower the shade, shut everything out and focus completely on his shot."

"And," Johnny Miller added. "Bart has his own version of Arnie's Army." He laughed. "Maybe, we'll call it Bart's Battalion!"

'Bart's Battalion' was itching for an opportunity to explode. With the 17th green clear, Bart lined up his shot. He stood behind the ball, scanned the 235 yards to the green, flashed a smile at Angela, closed his eyes, evened his breathing, then opened his eyes, smiled and stood over the ball. He took his smooth swing and the ball soared to the green. It landed on the front of the green and rolled to the flag.

"He's posing!" Johnny Miller called. "It must be good."

"GO IN" yelled Justin, stutter free.

"Better than good, I'd say," Donna responded. The ball rolled out and stopped within inches of the hole. "WOW!" She exclaimed. "Bart's putting an Exclamation point on this victory."

Rory and Phil were battling for second place. There seemed almost no chance of winning at this point, but they are great players and great competitors. So, they were battling each other. They both hit their tee shots onto the green. Bart walked onto the green, his Battalion cheered as he tapped in his Birdie putt, and smiled and waved to the kids, as he left the green.

Phil struck a good putt that just missed. He tapped in for par, shook his head, and watched as Rory pushed his putt, a bit right of the hole. Rory also tapped in for par and walked to the 18th tee-box.

The entire, massive crowd, was now gathered at the 18th tee, fairway and green. Bart kept an eye on Angela and the Wallestons, concerned for their safety. A security team arrived to escort Angela, Rachel and the Wallestons to the family viewing area beside the 18th green. As they walked a security guard mentioned to Angela that Phil's wife, Amy Mickelson, had directed security to find and guard Angela and her family.

When they arrived, Angela approached the pretty blond, mother of three. "Are you Mrs. Mickelson?" Angela asked.

Amy smiled. "Yes, Angela, I'm Amy, stand with me, I'll show you what to do."

Angela smiled, "Mrs, sorry, Amy, thank you for sending help." She turned to Rachel, "Amy, this is Rachel Walleston." Angela then introduced the Walleston family. Amy took time chatting with Justin.

Amy smiled. "Rachel, are you with Dave?" She asked.

Rachel flushed, looked back toward the tee and smiled. "Yes, I guess, I am."

Amy smiled, "girls, this is my dear friend, Jen Mackay, her husband, Jim, works with Phil." Amy paused, looked at how young Angela was, she smiled. "I want you to know how impressed we are with what you are doing for these children."

Angela smiled. "It's really Bart and Mr. Walleston," she grinned. "But, we're all a part of 'Team DeMarco.'"

Amy touched Angela's shoulder. "Angela, you should see this." They all turned and faced the fairway.

The threesome playing in front of Bart's group was just clearing the green, shaking hands, replacing the flagstick and heading to the scorer's tent.

Phil hit his second shot into the green. Rory followed, but missed the green to the left, his ball settling into some rough. Then Bart went through his pre-shot routine. Angela saw Bart looking toward the green for Angela. Angela waved to Bart, who saw her standing with Mrs. Mickelson, he smiled. Bart hit his second shot onto the green.

"Well Johnny, Bart DeMarco has a 5 shot lead as he strides to the 18th green," Jim Nantz stated, "Did anybody see this coming?"

Johnny Miller laughed. "That's the beauty of this game. You never know where the next Arnold Palmer or Jack Nicklaus is coming from."

The massive crowd erupted into a huge cheering section for Bart. Phil, Rory and their caddies walked close to the rough, to leave the fairway to Bart. Chants of "Bart! Bart! Bart!" rose to an ear splitting level. Bart saw Phil and Rory back off, but when Dave moved away, Bart grabbed the strap on the bag he carried.

Bart looked at Dave and smiled. "We're a team, we walk to victory together!" Bart put his arm on Dave's shoulder. In the cacophony of cheers, Bart seemed to be walking in a joyous tunnel.

"With this victory," Jim Nantz announced. "Bart DeMarco has won a PGA Tour card, a two year exemption on the PGA tour and an Invitation to the Masters in April, The U.S. Open in June, the Open Championship in July and the PGA Championship in August!" A life changing event for the very young DeMarco family."

"No doubt about that, Jim." Johnny Miller added, "Not to mention, all the WGC events and the winner's check of over One million dollars."

Donna Caponi ran to Bart and Dave. Their smiles were ear to ear. "Anything that you want to say, Bart?"

The screen split to show Angela standing with Rachel and Amy Mickelson. Amy was smiling and pointing to the green, explaining in a motherly manner, just how and when Angela was to go onto the green and congratulate Bart, pose for photos, etc. Amy Mickelson laughed. "Angela, when you kiss Bart," she urged, "rattle his teeth!"

Bart smiled and looked into the camera. "Papa," he called. "I won for you!" He paused. "Angela and I will be home soon, and I'm going to be with you when you are ready to walk out of that Hospital." Sal lifted himself on his arms to an upright position, beaming and nodding. "I'll do it, Bart. I'll do it!"

Joyous tears and cheers were the order of the day at the Boston General Hospital. When Angela and Bart appeared on the screen, Rosa hugged Maria fiercely.

"Bart did it!" Maria called happily. "Bart did it!" Rosa held on, crying with relief and happiness. "No, Maria, They did it together." She looked into Maria's eyes. "My Bart needs Angela." She stated.

Maria smiled, nodded. "They need each other, Rosa!" She sighed, contently. "They complete each other."

Celia cheered lustily. She looked to Rosa, "Dad and Mario will be so proud."

Bart walked onto the green, marked his ball and tossed it to Dave. He took a few deep breaths as he stood off the green with Dave as Rory hit a beautiful up and down for par. Bart looked at Dave, and smiled. "Can you believe this?"

Dave smiled. "I knew that you could be a very special golfer the first time I saw you swing a club." He laughed. "So, yes, I absolutely believe it!"

Phil, with Bone's help, read his putt. Lefty stood over the putt and rolled it into the center of the cup to lock up 2nd place in the Tournament. Bart clapped for Lefty, a great Champion, who winked at Bart.

Then Rory and Phil cleared the green for Bart, who stood alone behind his ball, reading his putt. He closed his eyes feeling the rumble of the gallery, drinking in the joyous applause. 'WOW,' he thought. He looked at Angela and smiled.

The cameras caught YES banners all around the grandstands and the ropes. 'Bart's Battalion' was joyously loud. The camera split the picture to show Angela, prettily attired in a form fitting Hawaiian sundress and straw hat. Her smile was radiant and brought such pleasure to her family and friends. "Angela looks great." Celia smiled.

Bart and Dave studied the putt. It was a 15 foot, slightly downhill, putt, with a break from right to left. The DeMarco team agreed on the read. Dave said a final comment and Bart stood over the putt. He looked up and locked eyes and smiles with Angela. Then Bart stroked the put perfectly into the cup for a closing Birdie. The gallery erupted into a loud, sustained cheer.

Bart raised his arms in victory. Dave rushed to embrace Bart. "We did it, Dave!" Bart said. "Thank you for everything."

Angela was joyous. She embraced Rachel, then Heather. She held Justin. "Bart won for you, Justin!" She proclaimed to the happy 10 year old.

Amy Mickelson, who had known 42 such victories, five of those victories being Majors, hugged Angela. "Congratulations to you and Bart, Angela. I hope to see you at Augusta." Amy laughed at Angela's blank look. "Oh, Angela," she laughed. "You'll learn."

Bart shook hands with Rory and Phil, accepted their congratulations and turned to face Donna and her cameraman. At Amy's direction, Angela ran onto the green and into Bart's arms. They held each other with such joy. "You did it, Bart!" Angela cheered, feeling both joy and a profound relief.

Bart held her and kissed her. "We did it, Angela. We did it together." He affirmed as he held her above the green, twirling her about. He met her eyes. "Can you believe this?"

Watching Bart and Angela embrace, kiss and rejoice, had all at Sal's Hospital gathering, beaming with pride and joy. With the victory assured, a victory cake, made by Rosa, was brought out, with homemade Italian cookies, also baked fresh, by Rosa and Celia. Rosa noted, with a smile, how Franco Palermo had used the joy surrounding Bart's win to hold, hug and kiss Lucia repeatedly. He didn't want to let her go. 'Just like my boys,' she thought happily. She flashed a grin at Lucia, and wagged her finger at Franco.

Bart and Angela posed on the green with the beautiful trophy. Bart called Dave and Rachel onto the green to stand with the trophy and pose for pictures. Dave had the flag from the 18th flagstick, which he had removed, according to tradition, firmly in his possession.

The F/V Rosa & Lucia, rolled on ten foot seas as mid-night approached. The Captain and crew worked by the spotty and shadowed light provided by the floodlights affixed to the pilot house, as they hauled back a net, hopefully, full of haddock, cod and flounder.

Captain DeMarco was operating the winch from the pilot house, and overseeing the operation. Mario, as the vessel's mate, was directing the crew in the haulback of the net from the ocean floor. The vessel rolled and pitched as the fishermen battled to keep their balance.

The trawl doors, two large steel, door shaped, devices which used resistance to the water pressure combined with the angle they are pulled through the ocean, to open and spread the mouth of the net, which dragged the ocean floor. The doors, in combination with the floats which lifted the top of the net, and the heavy rubber and steel rollers which kept the nets bottom on the ocean floor and able to bounce over bottom obstructions, effectively allowed the mouth of the net to open wide and high, collect the cod, haddock and sole, (referred by dragger fishermen as ground fish), which is the lifeblood of this historic fishing port. As the net was pulled along the ocean floor, the fish would be pulled down the cone shaped net into the cod end, or point of the cone, where the fish would stay until brought to the surface and onto the deck.

Captain DeMarco watched as the doors broke the surface, one to port and one to starboard. Then, he used the winch to haul the doors to the vessel, where the crew hooked both doors to the gallows frames and freed the wires. Once the doors were hung, Captain DeMarco re-engaged the winch to haul the net to the surface. He watched anxiously as the net broke the surface of the ocean swells, and was pulled alongside the rail. Mario wrapped a strap around the belly of the net and attached the tackle hook, connected to the tackle line, which ran to a bloch (a heavy steel pulley device) high in the mast and from the bloch back down to the winch head.

Mario, then, wrapped the tackle line around the rapidly spinning winch-head and used the hydraulic power of the winch-head to pull the net out of the sea. Once free of the buoyancy of the ocean, the weight of the net required Mario to take another turn on the winch-head. A small smile of satisfaction played on Mario's face as he raised the net to swing above the rail to be positioned over the deck. A crewman, on Mario's signal, then pulled the cod-end strap to open the net and allow the fish to fall onto the deck, to be contained in the checkerboards.

Mario turned to face the pilothouse and flashed a thumbs-up at his Dad, who met Mario's smile as the still flipping sole, cod and haddock overflowed the checkerboards. Mario then directed the crew to tie the cod end tightly and reverse the operation to get the net and doors back into the ocean, so that Captain DeMarco could drag the bottom on the successful course he had just followed. Once the net and doors were properly in the ocean, Franco played out the winch to the desired depth, lock the winch brakes and follow his charts, while Mario directed the crew to rip, gut and store the fresh fish into the fish-hold to be iced for sale.

They fished around the clock, took sleep when possible and battled to fill the fish hold. It is exhausting and hazardous work. For the men who take the risks and brave the sea, it is the life they love. When the sea mixes with your blood, it is an addiction that stays with you for life.

As Franco focused on his fishing line and the crew worked the catch, the radio crackled, "Coast Guard Station Gloucester to the Captain and Mate of the F/V Rosa & Lucia, do you read me, Captain?"

Franco grabbed the hand microphone, "Yes, Coast Guard Station, Gloucester, I read you loud and clear."

"I have a message for you, Captain. It reads; 'Franco, your boy did it!'" He paused. "And, all of Gloucester is proud of its hometown hero!" There was a moment's silence. "Did you receive and understand the message, Captain?"

Franco's eyes flooded with tears of joy. Franco choked out his response. "F/V Rosa & Lucia received the message," He paused, wiped his eyes. "Thank you for transmitting, Coast Guard Station, Gloucester."

Franco took a moment to collect himself. He opened the window overlooking the boats work deck, saw Mario directing the crew. "Mario," he called out. Mario looked up to the pilot house, saw his Dad's eyes and smiled. "He did it, didn't he?" Mario asked.

Franco nodded. "He won, Mario, he won!"

The radio transmission was heard by any number of fishing boats which hailed from Gloucester. Those boats fishing close by blew their horns in celebration. Franco received congratulatory transmissions from numerous captains.

"A victory for Bart, is a victory for Gloucester," called Captain Peter Novello of the F/V Good Fortune. "Congratulations, Franco!"

Bart went to the Media Center with his trophy and took his seat at the podium, facing the large media contingent, next to the PGA official who managed the media event. Angela, Dave and the Wallestons stood at the rear of the large tent.

The PGA official designated who would ask the questions. He called for the first question.

The Writer laughed. "Congratulations, Bart, where do you go from here?"

Bart smiled. "Well, tonight we celebrate, of course, then tomorrow we fly home to see the family."

"How's Angela's Dad doing?" Called out another reporter that Bart could not see due to the lights shining on the podium.

"I understand that he's battling." He shrugged. "I'll know more when I get back to the hotel."

"Bart," called out a reporter, "you had quite a large gallery this weekend, what can you tell us about 'Bart's Battalion?'"

Bart laughed. "Bart's Battalion?" He queried.

"Yes, that's what Johnny Miller was calling that group of button wearing children in your gallery."

Bart smiled. "They are young people with a stuttering problem, who are being helped by an organization called, 'The Youth association for Excellence in Speech.'" Bart paused. "YES, does wonderful work helping young people who stutter to build their self-confidence, so they can fully participate in society." He smiled. "YES runs camps, 'Camp YES,' they provide speech therapy, they have a Confident Voices Program." Bart looked into the cameras, "they do great, important work."

"This means a lot to you, Bart?"

Bart nodded. "It does." His voice softened a bit. "I know what these kids feel." He paused. "They called me 'Stutter Boy' to mock me." He took a deep breath. "It really hurt." He paused, his eyes reflected the remembered pain. "My parents and my siblings were magnificent in supporting me. Still, I was terrified to speak."

Bart smiled. "So, yes indeed, 'YES' and their good work means a great deal to me." He pointed at the logo on his breast pocket. "Manitoba Oil and the Walleston family are committed to extending and helping groups like 'YES' in their work. They are sponsoring a PGA Tournament to raise money for a school where all the essential services will be provided." He smiled. "And, at no cost to the families of these children."

Rosa watched the interview with a mother's pride. When Bart spoke of the pain and humiliation he had suffered, the pain all flooded back. Her eyes filled at the memory and for the man her son had become. Celia took her hand. Rosa squeezed Celia's hand, too choked to speak.

"Are you excited about playing in the Masters?" Called a reporter.

Bart smiled. "Beyond excited." He responded with a laugh. "Augusta National, the Masters, WOW!"

"You played with Phil and Rory this weekend, how was that, Bart?"

Bart laughed. "It was like a dream come true." He said. "They are great guys. They both treated me, an unknown rookie, so well."

"How about the U.S. Open?" Called a voice from the back of the room. "Will you play?"

Bart smiled into the cameras, "I will be playing in the Manitoba Classic that week." He grinned. "Next question please."

"Tell us about your caddie, Bart?"

"Of course," he began. "Dave Gilliss is more than my caddie. He is my golf and swing coach." He laughed. "The only Coach I've had." He shrugged. "He's also my good friend."

"Tell us about the lob shot on the 9th hole, Bart?

Bart laughed. "You saw, I had to get over the pond, the pin was tucked, I thought it was my best option." He laughed again and shrugged. "Well, at least it worked out pretty well." Laughter filled the room.

"Can you tell us about Angela, Bart?"

Bart paused, smiled. "She's my angel, my love, the best thing that has happened to me." He considered his words and shrugged. "I feel better, more at ease, I'm happy when I'm with her." He laughed. "I can't explain it any better than that."

"What's next on your schedule, Bart?"

Bart shook his head. "I don't know. When we get home, Dave and I will meet with our team, and try to set a schedule that makes sense." He smiled and rose. "Thanks everyone." He waved as he left the podium, trophy in hand.

Angela, Dave and Rachel, with the Walleston's were waiting for Bart to head back to the resort hotel. The excitement was palpable. Angela leaped into his arms. "So, you think I'm pretty good, do you?" She smiled and kissed him.

Bart eyed her, feigned nonchalance. "You know how it is, in that situation, you have to be nice." He laughed aloud, releasing the stress, held her close, gently kissed her smiling lips. "Actually, I think you're the best." He smiled, looked at Angela. "How great was that, today?"

Justin was bursting. "You are so ggreat, Bart." He managed, with a look of pride.

"Thanks, Buddy." He put a friendly arm around Justin's shoulder, handed him the trophy, which his Dad helped him to heft. "And, thanks for the cheering." Bart sat back in the limo, closed his eyes. "I'm whipped," he laughed.

"Maybe, you need a nap?" Rachel suggested with a grin. Bart laughed, he winked at Angela. "Now, that's a good idea."

Back in their suite, Bart stood in the shower, his eyes closed, letting the hot water cascade on his neck and shoulders. He smiled when he felt Angela's hands messaging his shoulders.

"Does this help?" She asked, with a brilliant and suggestive smile.

He turned and faced her, took her in his arms. "Oh, you can help me." He assured, flashing a smile and pulling her to him.

It was a jubilant group at dinner. Bart looked across the table. "Dave," he shook his head, with a look of consternation, he said. "What were you thinking about on 9, having me hit that lob shot?"

They all laughed.

Dave shook his head. "Come on Dave, it will be fun?" He mimicked Bart and laughed. "You nearly caused me to have a heart attack."

Phil Walleston was still beaming over Bart's unexpected, but spectacular victory. He looked at Bart, "so, tomorrow, Bart, you and Angela fly to Boston." He looked at Dave and smiled, "what's your plan, Dave?"

Dave smiled at Rachel. "I thought that I would fly to Canada, with the family, for a few days, then on to Gloucester." He looked at Bart. "You'll need a few days with the family and then we will meet Mr. Palermo and Mr. Winston to establish a Tournament schedule." He paused, considered. "We'll need to spend some time in Florida, so we can practice.

Walleston nodded. "You can use my house in Boca, if you'd like." He paused. "I'll contact the pro at my club and make sure everything will be smooth." He laughed. "Of course, who wouldn't want Bart DeMarco practicing at their club?"

Phil Walleston sat back, grew serious and eyed Bart. "There is something we need to discuss." He looked at Heather, who smiled and shrugged. "Bart," Walleston continued. "By winning this tournament, you've qualified to play in the U.S. Open." He eyed Bart. "I don't want to ever hold you back, Son."

Bart nodded as he sampled the Pacific Catfish that was sautéed to perfection. "This catfish is delicious," he commented. He sat back and smiled. "Mr. Walleston, I am playing in the Classic." He nudged Justin, who giggled. "I am playing for Justin and for all the kids who have been there, cheering me on." He paused. "Sir, you've done nothing but help Angela, Dave and me." He jostled Justin, producing laughter from the happy boy. "I will always play for Justin and our kids! Okay?" He grinned at the CEO.

Walleston choked with pride. "Okay, Bart, and thank you."

Bart glanced at Angela, who was smiling. "Mr. Walleston, on the week of June 10th, I will be in Manitoba." He laughed, looked to Heather Walleston. "I hope Angela and I can stay with you. I don't want to miss any of Julia's cooking." And, he cracked. "I don't think Dave would have it any other way." Bart smiled at Rachel, and added. "There seems to be something that draws my Buddy to Manitoba."

Heather laughed, as Rachel blushed. "Of course, the DeMarco's are always welcome and wanted," Heather said with a smile. She met Angela's eyes, who smiled a thank you.

"The following week," Bart continued, "Angela and I will be attending my brother, Mario, and Celia's wedding," he stated. "As I've said, family comes first." He looked at Phil and Heather. "And, I consider the Walleston's as family!" He smiled. "Now, as all of that is settled, may I eat my dinner?"

Phil looked at Heather, and they both smiled. "Thank you, Bart." Heather replied, fighting tears. "That is so good to hear." She paused, dabbed at her eyes, "we feel the same way."

Chapter Fifty-Three

Bart and Angela flew all day on Monday, arriving at Beverly Airport at 2am on Tuesday. Physically and emotionally exhausted, they fell into bed at the DeMarco home at about 3am, and Bart woke at 8am. He left Angela, sleeping peacefully, in Mario's bed and quietly exited the bedroom to head down to breakfast with Rosa and Lucia.

Bart and his mother embraced. Rosa held Bart to her chest as Lucia laughed. "Oh Boy," Lucia commented, laughing, "The Prince is home." Bart went to Lucia and gave his little sister a hug. "You look really happy, Lucia." He grinned. "Could it have something to do with Franco Palermo?"

Lucia beamed a smile. "Actually, big brother, it could." She stated. "He's a really nice guy."

Bart laughed. "And, a smart guy, too." He paused, "Franco was smart enough to see how special my bratty little sister happens to be." Bart laughed when Lucia poked her tongue out at him. He looked at Rosa, "Mom, when will Dad and Mario be home?"

"They'll be home for tomorrow's market." She smiled. "It looks like they had a good trip."

Bart smiled. "That's great, Mom." He paused, studied her. "So, they're doing okay?"

Rosa touched Bart's cheek, as she often did to calm him when, as a boy, he became anxious. "Everything is good, Bart." She grinned. "And, I'm making buttermilk waffles and bacon, just the way you like it." She smiled. "It's so good to have you and Angela back home."

Hearing her name, Angela entered, a bit groggily, into the kitchen. She went to Rosa, hugged her, "Hi, Mom, it's so good to see you." She beamed a smile. "Your boy did okay in Hawaii."

Rosa laughed. "We were all so happy." She eyed Angela, "and, everybody was so impressed at how beautiful you looked."

Angela blushed. "Me?" She showed surprise. "When did anybody see me?" She paused, thought, "Oh, you mean when Bart and I were posing with the trophy?"

"You were shown every day." Lucia said. "Franco kept mentioning how pretty you looked." She smiled. "It looks as if I have two beautiful sisters-in-law."

Bart watched the exchange as he sipped his coffee, a smile affixed to his face. He pulled Angela to him, kissed her, "I keep on telling you how beautiful you are." He laughed. "Nobody ever listens to the husband."

Angela looked into his eyes and smiled. The unspoken message clear as a brisk winter day on Gloucester Harbor. Aware of Rosa and Lucia's presence, and flustered by their smiles, Angela blushed as she looked about. "Is there coffee?" Angela asked. Rosa rose and Angela attempted to stop her, "Mom, I'll get it."

Rosa looked at the young woman who was so important to her son. "No, Angela, for today, you rest." She paused. "We'll have breakfast, then you and Bart go see your mother and take her to the Hospital." She nodded. "Go see your father." Rosa smiled. "He is so eager to see you two."

They sat to a delicious breakfast, with Lucia filling them in on the TV coverage, the daily hospital gatherings, all that had occurred in their absence. Angela peppered her with questions. Rosa and Bart laughed at Angela's surprise that she was seen and discussed.

"Was Mrs. Mickelson as nice as she seemed on television?" Lucia asked.

Angela nodded. "She's great, Bart was beating her husband, and she still made sure we were guarded and safe, and that I knew what to do." She smiled. "A really gracious lady."

"And, so pretty!" Rosa added. "I'd love to meet her someday."

"You will, Mom," Bart stated simply. "When I play in the Masters in April."

The reference to the Masters had little meaning for Rosa. "Tonight," Rosa began, "You all come here for dinner." She smiled, looked to Angela, "Nick and Giuseppe will be here so your mother and Tina can visit your Dad. And, Tina and Katelyn are also welcome." She looked at Bart and smiled. "Would you like me to make fried chicken, with potatoes, biscuits and gravy?"

Bart rose and kissed his mother. "That sounds great." He grinned. "How about your sweet potato pie?" He laughed. "I've missed your cooking, Mom."

Rosa beamed a smile, then she lovingly swatted him. "Okay, sweet potato pie it is."

"Anything for the Prince," Lucia teased. "Right Mom?"

Rosa shook her head, wagged her finger at Lucia. She kissed Bart's cheek. "I missed my boy!" They all laughed together.

Bart drove Angela, Maria and Tina to the Hospital to see Sal. Bart noted that Maria seemed distracted and worried. He looked at Angela, who met his eyes.

"Mom, Papa is doing okay, isn't he?" Bart asked.

Maria smiled. "Better, every day." She looked at Bart. "He wants to make you proud, Bart."

"Mom," Angela asked, concerned eyes set on her mother. "Are you sleeping well?"

"I'm fine," Maria stated and smiled. "Don't you worry about me, it's so good having you home."

When Bart and Angela arrived and entered Sal's room, the patient lit up. He propped himself up to embrace Angela. "I've missed you Bambina." He said.

Angela looked her Dad over, concern coloring her expression. "How are you, Papa?"

He smiled. "I get better and stronger every day." He insisted. He looked at Bart, reached for him. They embraced. "Angela," Sal stated, "Bart and I have a deal. Am I right Bart?"

"Yes sir, you are right." He smiled. "And, I will be here to walk with you out of the Hospital."

They spent a quiet and pleasant day catching up and listening to Angela's descriptions of Hawaii. "The most beautiful place you've ever seen," she insisted.

"So, where will you stay?" Tina asked. "And, how long are you here for?"

Angela looked to Bart. She laughed, "I've been so swept up in all that has been happening, I haven't thought about it." She looked at Bart and smiled. "But, I bet Bart has."

All eyes turned to Bart. "Okay," he laughed. "Tonight, we will stay in my room." He shrugged. "But, tomorrow Mario will be home, so we'll go to the hotel."

"Wait," Tina interjected. "Angela, I know that it's not a 5 star hotel, but why don't you stay in our room." She laughed. "You can push the twin beds together." Bart loved that Angela still blushed. "I'll bunk in with the boys." Tina offered hopefully. She looked at Bart, "I really don't mind." She smiled at Angela. "It will give us a chance to catch up."

Angela smiled at Bart, the smile he knew meant she really wanted his approval. "What do you think, Bart?" He heard hope in her tone.

He smiled, 'saying no to that beautiful, loving, face was not possible,' he thought. "It sounds fine to me." He looked at Angela, "but, it will only be until Monday."

Angela looked at Bart with questioning eyes. "Monday?"

Bart grinned. "We need the week to see family, and to meet with our team. We need to discuss the schedule, what Tournaments I'll play, not play, etc." He laughed, "Of course, we'll stay for Sunday dinner. Then Monday we fly to Florida." He grinned, looked at Sal. "Papa, I have to go to work."

He nodded. "Of course, you do." Sal laughed. "You must work hard to win!"

"While we're traveling, Mario will square away the details on the new house." He smiled. "Angela will fly back between tournaments to furnish it," he smiled at Maria. "Mom, I hope you will help Angela choose furniture and everything we'll need." He looked at Tina, "Hey, Chef," he laughed. "Tina, my dear, will you make sure that Angela has all the pots and equipment to cook wonderful meals." He looked at Angela, smiled. "Princess, I love to eat."

Tina laughed. "Of course, Bart." She smiled at Angela. "I'll help you, Angela." She winked. "Anything for Bart!"

Angela grinned, accepted the challenge. "I'll be a great cook, you'll see!"

Sal watched Bart and Angela with a smile. 'Angela is settled and happy,' he thought. He looked at Tina with concern in his eyes.

"Are you okay, Bambina?" Sal asked Tina. "I worry about you."

Tina smiled and took her Dad's hand. "I'm fine, Papa, really!"

Bart watched the exchange. He understood Sal's concerns. He met Angela's eyes.

Bart patted Tina's shoulder. He looked to Sal and Maria, who sat next to Sal's bed, holding his hand. "The house purchase will take some time," Bart stated, casually, "but when everything is completed, we will have a comfortable place to live, entertain," he looked at Sal and Maria, smiled, "and, to bring your grandchildren home."

Maria beamed, leaped to her feet and embraced Bart. "Just like you said." Her eyes filled, even as she laughed.

Angela watched as Bart thrilled her parents. 'He knows how to make people happy.' She thought. And, she loved him even more, if that was possible.

While they visited, Dr. Howard entered Sal's room. Somewhat tentatively, he looked at Bart. "I heard that you were here, Bart." He smiled.

"You may remember, I was the surgeon you spoke to that first day, Sal was here." He extended his hand. "I'm Rob Howard."

Bart smiled as he rose. "I do remember, Doctor." He nodded. "Thank you." Bart shook his hand. "You are a talented surgeon."

"Thank you," Dr. Howard smiled. "And, you are a great golfer." He paused. "I watched the Tournament here with your family." He looked to Angela, offered a broad smile. "And, this must be Angela?"

Angela smiled. "Yes, Doctor, I'm Angela DeMarco." She rose, offered and shook his hand. "Thank you for saving my father."

"You are welcome, Angela." He stated. He looked at Bart and Dr. Howard flushed. "I may as well just ask," he stated nervously. "Bart, do you think sometime, we could play a round of golf together?" He took a deep breath. "I'm really not terrible, I'm a 14 handicap, but with this job," He shrugged. "I just don't have enough time to play."

The request had Angela, Tina and Maria smiling. 'This great surgeon in awe of Bart,' Angela thought, with shake of the head. She looked to her mother and grinned, 'guys never really grow up,' she thought.

Bart smiled, placed his hand on Dr. Howard's shoulder. "Doc, I'll make a deal with you," he offered. "You help get my father-in-law back up and walking, and I'll play two rounds with you and any two friends you choose." He met Dr. Howard's smile, extended his hand. "Do we have a deal?"

Doc Howard clasped his hand. "Bart, you have a deal!" He stated excitedly. "And, after we play, perhaps you and Angela will have dinner with my wife and me?" He grinned at Angela. "My wife just loved the dresses Angela wore each day of the Tournament."

Bart looked at Angela, who blushed at Doc Howard's compliments. Bart grinned. "Of course, we'd love that."

Doc looked at his watch. "I have to run," he said, still smiling. He looked at Sal, "Mr. Curcuru, I will personally supervise your physical therapy." He winked. "Get ready to work hard."

Sal smiled. "Doctor, I'm a fisherman. All I know is hard work."

Dr. Howard smiled happily, then, he stopped, considered and looked at Bart. His shoulder's sagged, and his eyes were weary. He paused, "Bart, I hate to do this, but I have another request."

Bart saw the change, watched Doc Howard closely. He smiled. "What is it Doc?"

Dr. Howard looked at Bart. He scanned the room, summoned the will to speak, to ask for help. "Bart, there's a young boy." He paused. "He's not doing well."

Bart nodded, watched the doctor's face, read his eyes. "He's a patient of a colleague." Doc Howard continued. He shrugged. "He's a big fan of yours." He cleared his throat. "Bart, he has a bad stutter." Dr. Howard paused, shook his head. "He also has leukemia."

Bart winced and placed concerned eyes on Doc Howard. "How bad is it, Doc?"

Dr. Howard shrugged. "It's bad, Bart. He sure could use a boost." He sighed. "It's been rough."

Bart rose, took Angela's hand. "Would you like me to go see him?"

"Would you?" Dr. Howard asked. "It would mean a lot to him and his parents." He paused. "The boy's name is Peter LoBello."

Angela reached into her bag. "Bart, I have the golf ball that you used to win in Hawaii." She looked to Dr. Howard. "Bart could sign it for him. We'll visit him." She saw the pained look in Bart's eyes, took his hand. Angela realized that this was the difficult challenge of Bart's celebrity. She managed a smile. "I'll be with you, Bart."

Bart took a moment at the door of the Pediatric Oncology unit. He took a deep breath, squeezed Angela's hand, smiled and entered the room. He saw a frail boy, of about nine or ten, laying in the bed. His skin was almost as white as the sheets.

"Hi Peter," Bart said brightly. He saw the boy's eyes widen in recognition. "I heard you cheered for me."

"Sstutter Bboy!" Peter exclaimed, excitedly. "I,I ssaw you wwin!"

Bart smiled at Peter's Mom, moved to the bed, pushed a chair close and sat. "How are you feeling, Buddy?"

Peter's Mom, Gina LoBello, looked at Bart. "Bart DeMarco?" She asked, awe in her tone. "You've come to see Peter?"

Angela smiled. "Of course, when Bart heard that his biggest fan was here, he wanted to say hello."

Peter smiled up at his hero. Angela took Gina's hand. The young mother's hand trembled. Angela met her eyes. "Not long," Gina mouthed, as her eyes misted.

"I'm ggood," Peter managed. And, at that moment, Peter was good and thrilled, and happy. "I,I was sso hhappy when you wwon."

Bart looked into the boys eyes. "Thank you, Peter. I was playing for you." He paused, took a deep breath. "I brought the golf ball I used to make that last putt in Hawaii." He smiled. "Would you like me to sign the ball for you?"

Peter smiled. "I,I ccan kkeep it?" He asked, hopefully.

Bart nodded, smiled. "Of course, Peter. I brought it for you."

Angela handed Bart the golf ball and a sharpie. Bart signed the ball, held it, giving it a few moments to dry, then handed the ball to a smiling Peter.

"Come on guys," Angela urged. "Let's take your photo together."

Gina fluffed up his pillows, helped Peter sit more upright. Bart crouched beside him and put his arm around Peter's shoulders. Peter held the ball, they both smiled as Angela snapped the photo.

"I'll have it printed, Gina." Angela assured. "I'll bring it tomorrow."

Gina looked at Angela. "Please Angela," she took a deep breath, fought back tears. "I'd like Peter to see it, before..." Gina broke and fell into Angela's arms.

Angela held Gina, felt her sobs. "I'm so sorry," she spoke softly.

Bart grinned at Peter. "Girls always cry, Peter." He looked at Angela and Gina. He turned back to Peter. "Did you watch the entire tournament?"

Peter nodded and smiled. "I,I was sso hhappy." He looked up at his Mom. "Ddon't ccry Mmom," he urged.

Gina went to Peter, held her baby to her chest. "I'm okay Peter." She assured, with eyes pooled with tears. "I'm just so happy that Bart DeMarco, our 'Stutter Boy,' came to visit my brave boy."

In Sal's room, Tina looked to her Dad. "Why do you worry, Papa? I'm really okay."

Maria took Tina's hands, looked into her eyes. "Tina, your father worries about you. There will be no man to take care of you."

"Mom," Tina smiled. "I don't need a man. I can take care of myself."

Shaken, having left Peter, Bart and Angela, holding hands, entered Sal's room. They witnessed the exchange, moved in and sat.

"Tina," Maria continued. "Your Papa loves you. He's scared for you." She paused, she nodded to Bart and Angela. "Bart takes care of Angela. Papa's mind is at peace." She sighed. "But you? Who will take care of you?"

Tina looked to Bart and Angela. Smiled at her Dad, addressed her mother. "Mom, Angela takes care of Bart!" She asserted.

Maria nodded and smiled. "Yes, Tina, they take care of each other."

Sal looked at his family. "Tina, when those boys tried to hurt Angela, Bart was there and protected her." He took a breath, choked up. "I'm hurt," tears of frustration filled his eyes. "I can't work!" His eyes met Maria's. "Who's going to take care of my baby girl?"

Tina saw the frustration and read her Dad's fears. She had no answer. She looked to Angela.

Angela studied her Dad, understood her Papa's concerns. She clasped Bart's hand, looked into his eyes, saw him nod and smile. "Papa, we're family, we all will!"

Dinner at the DeMarco house was a treat. As promised, Rosa made Bart's favorite, Southern fried chicken, whipped potatoes, biscuits and gravy. And, of course, two sweet potato pies. Maria and Tina joined Nick and Giuseppe, who had spent the day with Rosa and Lucia. Franco Palermo also joined the gathering.

It was a special evening for Bart and Angela to be with their families. Franco Palermo was excited to be with Bart. He asked question after question. They discussed grips and stance. "You use a baseball grip, a ten finger grip," Franco commented. "Why?"

"It feels more natural to me than the inter-locking grip," Bart explained, with a shrug. "It really doesn't matter what grip you choose, just stay consistent," Bart advised. He rose, "Come on, Franco, I'll grab a club," Bart said. "I'll show you." They went to the living room with one of Bart's old golf clubs. Lucia watched them go with a look of astonishment, feeling a tad ignored by her erstwhile boyfriend. Angela watched Lucia's reaction with amusement, but said nothing.

Bart and Franco were laughing when they returned to the table. All ate heartily, "Mom, this is great," Bart complimented. He grinned. "Do you think that you could teach Angela?" Rosa and Maria smiled at the request. Maria had received similar requests from Bart.

"Of course, Bart." Rosa replied with a smile. It was wonderful having Bart and Angela home.

Angela just smiled and shook her head. "I guess marriage is not all private jets and 5 star resorts," she laughed.

Rosa asked Lucia to go to the kitchen to re-fill the bowl of whipped potatoes and bring in the second sweet potato pie. Angela rose with her, "I'll give you a hand, Lucia," she offered.

Once alone in the kitchen, Angela put her hand on Lucia's arm. Lucia met her eyes, and Angela saw that Lucia was genuinely upset.

Angela smiled, "Lucia," Angela advised softly, "You have to give Franco a break. He is overwhelmed." She rubbed her shoulder. "Franco is sitting at the same table with a guy who will be on the cover of the next Sports Illustrated." She nudged Lucia. "You know guys," she laughed. "That stuff really impresses them." Angela took Lucia's hand. "Don't be upset that Franco looks up to Bart." She paused and met Lucia's eyes. "Franco couldn't have a better role model, as an athlete, a man or a boyfriend."

Lucia considered her words, nodded, and finally laughed. "I guess you're right. Bart is pretty spectacular."

As Lucia's words hung in the air, Bart came into the kitchen, saw them conversing, and flashed his smile. "Hey, ladies, what's with the chit-chat, there are hungry people out there." He caught Angela's eye and winked, and went back into the dining room.

Angela looked at Lucia and shrugged, "Yeah, he's spectacular," she laughed, "but, he's still a guy!" They laughed together. "And, remember what Mom told us in Florida, Guys will always drive us crazy!"

Chapter Fifty-Four

Bart and Dave met with John Palermo and Harry Winston. Dave had spent a few days with Rachel and her family, in Canada, and was flying on an emotional high when he came home to Gloucester.

"Well, Bart, you certainly made my job easier," Harry laughed. "With a two year exemption, we can set a comfortable and workable schedule." He paused. "The officials at the PGA volunteered to waive the 18 year old rule." He grinned. "I didn't have to ask." He sat back. "They love you," he laughed. "Bart, you bring eyes to the screen, grow the galleries."

Bart nodded. He thought of little, Peter LoBello, who had passed away the previous evening. After Bart's visit, Peter's Dad had bought Peter a set of golf clubs, propped them beside his bed. Young Peter had told his parents that 'he was going to get better and play golf, like Bart.'

Gina had told Bart and Angela that Peter had died while clutching the photo of him with Bart. The powerful young star had held and cried with Angela. "What a terrible waste," he said, to a distraught Angela.

"Bart, you made his last days better." Angela had said consolingly, as her eyes filled. "He was a sweet little boy."

John Palermo clasped Bart's hand. "Bart, my Franco told me about that young boy, Peter, I believe?"

Bart nodded, took a deep breath.

John offered a supportive smile "I'm so sorry!" He paused. "If there's anything I can do, please just ask." He paused, read Bart's eyes. "Bart, I'm afraid that this is the most difficult part of fame."

Bart nodded, still a bit shaken, he choked up. Bart gamely swallowed, took a deep breath, and fought the tears that welled. He looked at Harry Winston. "I'll be 18 in April," he said. "Okay, sir, so what do you think?" Bart asked, anxious to move the discussion.

John rose and put his hand on Bart's shoulder. "Bart," he counseled, "don't be afraid to cry. I know how much it hurts."

Bart met John's eyes and nodded. He looked from John Palermo to Harry Winston, "have you determined a preliminary schedule?"

"It's Harry, okay Bart?" He eyed Bart. "I work for you, I am a part of 'Team DeMarco.' He paused, "it would be better if you called me Harry."

Bart looked at John Palermo, then back to Harry Winston. Relieved that the discussion had moved from little Peter, he shrugged and tried to smile, "okay, I'll try."

Harry had been filled in by John. He knew the reality of star athletes. Sometimes, when faced with something as overwhelming as a very sick child, they felt so impotent. Sadly, celebrity didn't come with a magic wand.

"Okay Bart," Harry began. "The PGA requires all members to annually play in a minimum of 15 PGA Tournaments." He shrugged. "That's not a problem, of course." He looked at his list. "You already played in the Hawaiian Open, and, you'll certainly play in all the Majors." He stated.

Bart shook his head, "not the U.S. Open, sir." He paused. "Sorry, I mean Harry. I'll be playing in the Manitoba Classic that week." He paused, felt emotionally exhausted. "I've explained all that in the post-tournament interviews."

Winston was stunned. He looked at Bart, then a watchful, John Palermo. "I don't understand, Bart. Why would you play in a second tier event rather than the U.S. Open?" Harry asked. "If Walleston is the problem, I'm certain I can help him to understand."

Bart smiled. "I gave my word, Harry." He paused. "Also, the Manitoba Classic will benefit children with stuttering issues." He thought of Peter, looked at Harry. "And, the Walleston family has been good to me." He shrugged. "Manitoba Oil is my Sponsor." He shook his head and offered a wan smile. "It's really a no-brainer."

"The USGA Commissioner won't be happy about this." Harry stated.

Bart shrugged. "Come on, it's no big deal, it's the U.S. Open, Sir." He stated, showing irritation. "All the best golfers in the world will be there. They don't need me."

Harry sat back and looked to John Palermo for help. "Sorry, Harry, I'm with Bart." John smiled. "He gave his word."

Harry looked stunned. "You WILL play in the other Majors, won't you?" Harry asked, with an edge.

"Yes, sir, of course I will." He responded, assessed Harry. "I'm not trying to upset you, Sir."

Harry nodded. "So, I have you playing in the three majors, the Manitoba Classic, four WGC events and we should choose six to nine more

Tournaments." He paused. "Have you thought about practice facilities between Tournaments?"

Bart looked to Dave. Dave nodded and addressed the question. "Yes, Harry, Mr. Walleston is making his Florida home and golf club available to us whenever we need it." He paused, smiled. "In fact, we're heading there on Monday." He smiled. "May I suggest that you lay out the schedule you think best, send it to us and we can talk about it?"

Harry Winston laughed. "Okay, you'll have it tomorrow."

Bart looked at John Palermo. "Mr. Palermo, I'd like to have a private word with you if you are free."

Chapter Fifty-Five

B art and Angela moved into Angela and Tina's bedroom in the Curcuru house. Angela and Tina spent time together, Tina filling Angela in on the stresses Sal and Maria were living with. They went shopping and visited their Dad every day. Angela made a point of popping in to see Gina and Little Peter when she visited her Dad.

Angela attended some classes at Gloucester High School, enjoyed seeing the classmates she had performed with and had known since she came to America, at age 12. She, and the tutor, retained by Manitoba Oil, had meetings with Mrs. Nelson about streamlining a curriculum for Bart and for her.

When she walked into the guidance office, she was met with a hearty welcome and a big hug from Beth Nelson. "Angela, Bob and I are so proud of you and Bart," She gushed. "We watched every minute of the Tournament." She smiled. "Bart was wonderful and it was pretty clear that you mean the world to him." She winked. "As he says, you are his angel."

Angela smiled. "Thank you, Mrs. Nelson. It was an amazing week."

"How's your Dad doing, Angela?" Beth Nelson asked. "We heard that he sustained a serious injury."

"He did," Angela confirmed. "We almost lost him, but the surgeon saved his life." She smiled, "but my Dad made a deal with Bart that if Bart won the Tournament, my Dad would walk out of the Hospital."

Beth Nelson smiled. "We heard Bart talking to him and encouraging him during the Tournament." Beth took Angela's hands. "You married a very special guy, Angela." She paused, with a concerned look, she added. "Angela, do your best to help Bart." She paused. "Everybody is going to want a piece of him."

Angela nodded, looked at Beth Nelson. "I will, Mrs. Nelson," she paused. "I will always be there for him." She smiled, considered. "But, you know, I think Bart knows that." She smiled. "Bart may be one of the brightest people I've ever known. He hired John Palermo to oversee and manage his business, so, as Bart said, he can focus on golf," she blushed, "and me."

Beth Nelson smiled. "I like that," she said. "And, listen to Mr. Palermo, he is truly a good man."

Bart greeted the F/V Rosa & Lucia when it docked early the next morning. Franco and Mario were delighted to see Bart standing on the dock with Sophie 'The Bull,' at 4am.

Sophie smiled at Bart. "Your Dad has a fish hold full of quality groundfish, are you looking for a lumping site.

Bart laughed, "I'll pass on that." Bart shook Sophie's hand, looked into his eyes. "Sophie, thank you for all the help. I will never forget you."

Sophie 'the Bull,' just nodded, acknowledging Bart's words. Bart looked up and waved to Mario, who stood on the raised bow readying to toss the bow line to a dock worker. "Hey, Mario," he called and waved.

Mario supervised the docking and securing of the fishing boat to the wharf. Franco spoke to Sophie, "how long until the fish house is ready for us?"

Sophie shrugged. "About 30 minutes," he estimated. "Do you still want lumpers for the men?"

Franco smiled, "Yes, but, Mario and I will be at the scales, making sure the count is right." He looked to Bart embracing Mario. "Sophie, please oversee everything, I want to have breakfast with my boys."

The DeMarco boys walked into the Main Mast, a coffee shop and diner, set across from the docks where fishermen and lumpers met to catch up and sometimes to share gossip and information on available fishing and lumping sites.

The name, 'Main Mast,' was something of an inside joke, and spoke to the owner's outlook on life. Jim Militello, the owner, had been a fisherman. His boat was caught in a storm, the engine seized, and the vessel's main mast snapped falling on his leg and pinning him to the deck. He lay there for two days, delirious with dehydration, until another vessel found him. His leg was too far gone to be saved and was amputated. He adjusted to a prosthetic leg, opened the coffee shop, made the best freshly fried doughnuts in the world, and pushed on with life.

Cheers and jeers greeted the DeMarco's when they entered.

"Fore," someone called. Another fisherman yelled out, "May I play through?"

Bart knew these men, he laughed. "I don't know if you could." He called. That brought a roar of laughter.

They ordered coffee and doughnuts, savored the flavor and enjoyed catching up. "How long are you home for?" Mario asked.

"Until Monday," Bart responded. "I wanted to stay for Sunday Dinner." He laughed, I missed Mom's cooking." He looked at his Dad, "when do you sail?"

"Friday, at midnight, if all the gear work is done." He shrugged, "maybe we'll take another day, what do you say, Mario?"

Mario looked at Bart. He grinned and eyed his Dad. "I say we sail Sunday at midnight." He laughed. "Sunday dinner at home sounds good."

Franco nodded in agreement, considered the successful trip just completed, the hold full of fish. "Yes, Mario," Franco agreed. "It will be good to have the family together."

Franco looked at Bart and took his hand. "We are all so proud of you, Bart." He paused. "I hope we'll see you and Angela."

"You will," he laughed. "We'll have dinner every night at home." He stated. "Mom is making all my favorites."

"Nice!" Mario joked. "How about my favorites?" He smiled, took Bart's hand, held it firmly. He looked Bart in the eye. "You were always a special kid, Bart. You deserve your success." He winked. "Celia and I are so happy for you and Angela."

Bart looked at Mario. "Mario," he said, as he clasped his brother's hand. "No guy ever had a better big brother." He paused. "Thank you."

Franco smiled with pride. He looked at Mario, "we best get back." He smiled at Bart, "I'll see you for dinner?"

"Yes, you will Dad." Bart confirmed, with a smile. "Angela and I will be there."

The Curcuru's were dealing with very hard times. Rosa volunteered to take care of Maria's boys so she could be with Sal. Each evening, they dined with the DeMarco's. Friends brought fish, groceries and baked goods to the Curcuru house. Maria was worried over Sal, as well as their finances. It appeared that while Sal might someday walk again, it was almost certain that he would never be able to go fishing again. 'How would they manage?' She fretted. 'Would they lose their home?'

On Saturday, Bart drove Angela, Maria and Tina to see Sal. It was Sal's off day from therapy. He was on a regimen of three days of intense therapy and one day off. He would be back at it tomorrow, "Sunday be damned!" Sal proclaimed. "I will walk out of this hospital!"

Bart and Angela had stopped and bought Sal's favorite sharp Italian cheeses, Sicilian olives, freshly baked Italian bread and, of course, all his favorite Italian cold-cuts.

"My Dad loves his prosciutto and salami," Tina said happily. Bart even snuck in a bottle of Sal's homemade wine. "We have to keep his spirits up." Bart said with a grin.

At the hospital, the visit was especially happy. Sal was making progress, but the worry lines brought on by the financial stress were no longer. Maria smiled and explained, "Mr. Palermo was here yesterday, he told us that the case is going well." She smiled. "He told us that the Insurance Company had agreed to pay Sal his share of all the fishing trips he has missed since the accident." She paused, thought. "He called it Care or Cure or something?" She laughed.

"Angela, Mr. Palermo brought a check for all the trips your Papa has lost." Maria smiled. "Now, we can pay the mortgage, the oil bill, everything," she told Angela, with a sense of relief. "I didn't know what we were going to do."

Angela smiled, took her mother's hands. "Now, all we think about is getting Papa healthy, right?" She said.

Sal nodded. "That's right, everything will be okay!" He said happily. "I was so worried." He looked to Bart. "You were right to have Mr. Palermo take charge."

"He's a good man, Papa. You can trust him." Bart responded.

That night, after a wonderful dinner of Rosa's roasted lamb, and a relaxing and enjoyable evening, spent with Dave and Jessica and Jim and Betsy listening to music and catching up, Bart and Angela settled down to sleep in her childhood bedroom.

Angela cuddled close, whispered, "we have to be quiet." She pointed to the wall that was common to the boy's bedroom. Bart smiled into her concern, kissed her. As always, he couldn't resist her, not that he tried. Bart kissed her slowly, sweetly, "happy to be home, in your old bed?"

Angela laughed. "I never did the kind of things in this bed that we do now." She whispered. "Although, that first night, when you held me close and kissed me, I sure thought about doing some of the things we now do." She put her face in his chest and laughed. "Although, some of it, I didn't ever imagine doing!"

He laughed, lay on his back as she laid her head on his chest. He kissed her head, luxuriating in her beautiful hair, stroked her back, while she let her hand roam in ways that she knew he so enjoyed. "Thank you, Bart?" She said softly.

He lay quiet, smiled. "No Angela, thank you, and please don't stop."

She grinned, loving his response to her. "I appreciate what you did for my family." She said as she continued to bring pleasure to her love. She looked into his face, smiled. "And, you found a way to protect my Dad's pride." She kissed his cheek. "You are a good man, Bart!"

Bart said nothing, if you don't count the pleasure groans. He shrugged and managed. "It was nothing," he replied. "Angela, that feels so good," he said.

"I guess it was just a big coincidence," she laughed, "that you met with Mr. Palermo on Thursday, and on Friday, he visited my Dad and Mom at the Hospital and informed them of how suddenly reasonable the Insurance Company became?" She smiled and kissed him. "He even brought a rather healthy check."

Bart laughed. "Why do you have to be so smart, my Beauty?" He sighed. "Okay!" he gasped, lifted Angela on top of him. He kissed her deeply and fully as she wriggled into position." She looked into his eyes. "I love you, Bart. Enjoy!"

After their lovemaking, when they laid together happily sated, Bart gently kissed her head. "Are you happy with the Tournament schedule?" He asked.

She cuddled closer. "It doesn't matter, we'll be together." She paused. "My Dad's doing okay, and, thanks to you, my mother isn't scared anymore, and Tina's happy." She sighed, contently. "I can leave comfortably." She sighed, kissed his chest. "Thank you for helping my family," she repeated.

"Our family," Bart responded, his words touching her deeply. He lay quietly for a time, then, he said, "Angela, we have to be careful about how we help." She nodded, listened closely. Bart continued. "Our families always took care of us, Mario was incredible in how he protected me from all the bullies, when I was a boy."

"Like you protected me." She said, softly.

Bart nodded. "I'm so glad that I came along, when I did." He kissed her. "I love you, Princess."

Angela cuddled close. "I love you, Bart."

Bart kissed her. "I don't want us to separate ourselves from our community." He sighed. "I want to keep our friends, I want to stay a part, a real part, of Gloucester." He nuzzled her. "Do you understand, what I'm trying to say?"

Angela smiled into his chest. "I do." She paused. "You want to play golf, because you love to play, and take care of our family." She giggled. "And, ravish me, of course!"

He laughed, "Oh Yeah!"

"But, you want us to be part of Gloucester, try not to stand out, any more than a PGA star would." Angela said, with a shrug. "Is that it?"

He nodded. "It sure is." He grinned. "I am so happy I married such a beautiful and brilliant woman."

Sunday dinner at the DeMarco's home was special, and Rosa felt it deeply. Bart and Angela were traveling so much. Franco and Mario were working long and hard to make a success of their boat. So, for today, with Franco and Mario present, the entire DeMarco and Curcuru family members, except for Angela's Dad, were together.

Franco Palermo, who was becoming a regular at DeMarco family gatherings, was there, seated next to Lucia. Rosa had made her hand rolled, potato gnocchi, one of Bart's favorites, a big Bolognese sauce flavored with sausages, meatballs, pork ribs, garlic stuffed beef, and hard boiled eggs. Big bowls of gnocchi and large platters of the meats were placed on the table family style, and all ate joyously, as good food was meant to be savored and enjoyed.

There was laughter and teasing. Above all, love was on display.

Maria made garlic bread for Bart. She offered the basket to him. "I'll always remember when I learned how much you like garlic bread, Bart." She said with a wink and a smile. Bart nudged Angela, smiled at Maria. "Thanks, Mom, I'll always remember that day."

Angela looked at her mother and blushed. "Thanks, Mom!" She said on a laugh, "I must admit that was quite a day."

Maria looked to Rosa. "Franco, Rosa, I want to thank you for all your help." She smiled. "Rosa, you have been a life-saver for me." She paused, shuddered at the memory of the days and weeks following Sal's injury. "When Sal was so hurt, I didn't know what to do." She sighed, misted. "I had to be with Sal, he needed me," She thought about the fear she had read in Sal's eyes before he regained the ability to speak.

"But," she continued. "I had the boys, and we have no family in America." She met Rosa's eyes. "Rosa, you once asked me to be a part of your family." She scanned the table, looked at Franco DeMarco. "You made my Angela family, and when we needed help, you made us all family."

Maria choked down emotion. "I've heard Bart speak of 'Team DeMarco,'" She now sipped some water, fought for control, as tears flooded her eyes. "I now understand what he means, and who taught him about family and loyalty." She smiled. "Franco, Rosa, thank you."

Franco DeMarco smiled, put his arm around Rosa's shoulders and pulled her close. With his free hand, he took Maria's hand, he looked into her eyes. "You're welcome, Maria," He paused. "We are family, we take care of each other."

Maria smiled a thanks, as she was too choked to speak.

With dinner complete, they decided to sip some espresso and delay dessert for a bit. Nick and Giuseppe went to the basement playroom, where Rosa, who had been helping Maria care for the boys since Sal's injury, had put out many of Mario and Bart's childhood toys.

Bart had his Tournament schedule printed for both families. There would be much traveling and, unfortunately, little time at home. "The nomadic life of a professional golfer," he explained with a shrug. "A lot like being a fisherman." He added, smiling at his Dad and Mario.

Bart looked across the table, looked to his Dad. "Angela and I are hoping that you will all come to the see me play in The Masters, in April, and, then, in June, in Canada, in the Manitoba Classic." He scanned the table. "I've arranged, through my Sponsor, for flights and we rented a big house in Augusta."

Franco listened closely, considered Bart's request. He looked to Mario. While sailing home, after Bart's victory in the Hawaiian Open, Captain and Mate, father and son, had lamented not being there for Bart when he won his first PGA tournament. "It would mean keeping the boat in for a week." Franco observed, as he met Rosa's eyes. Franco saw her smile and knew Rosa wanted to be there for Bart. Never able to refuse her, always reasonable, requests, he winked at his beautiful wife. "We'll see."

Mario nodded, eyed his Dad. "Maybe, we could hire a replacement Captain for one trip?" He grinned. "Dad, it is the Masters!" He smiled, looked at Celia.

Celia picked up Mario's signal, looked to Franco and smiled. "Dad, I'd love to have another family vacation, all together." She laughed. "We had so much fun in Florida."

Smiles bloomed across the table. "It was fun." Bart agreed."

Celia playfully nudged Angela. "Maybe, a few water battles?" She eyed Angela, winked and shook her head. "Those DeMarco boys!" She feigned exasperation. "Always taking advantage of our innocence!"

Angela laughed, glanced at Bart, and recalled the fun they had together in the pool. "Sad to say," Angela agreed, as she shook her head, winked at Rosa. "Your boys can be fresh, Mom!"

Angela looked at Maria, who was smiling and clearly enjoying the conversation. "Mom, I hate to shock you, but, your son-in-law tried to take inappropriate liberties." She smiled, as she shook her head. "He's not the saint that you think he is!"

Bart laughed aloud, looked at his Mom and Maria. "I honestly have no idea of what they speak. Mario and I were always perfect gentlemen!" He protested, with a wide grin. "You saw Mom."

Rosa shook her head and laughed. "Oh, I saw plenty," she eyed Mario and Bart, but could not suppress her smile. Rosa so adored her boys. She wagged her finger at Celia and Angela. "And, I saw you two tempt my boys." Now everybody at the table was laughing. Rosa looked at Lucia, pointed her finger. "And you," she said. "Be careful with that one," pointing to Franco Palermo. "He's too much like your brothers."

"That's right!" Mario slapped the table. He smiled at Franco." Palermo, you better watch your step."

Franco laughed, as Lucia blushed. "I only shake Lucia's hand." He put his hand up. "Scout's honor."

Rosa wagged her finger at Franco. "Oh, Mr. Palermo, I know better!" Franco laughed and shrugged in concession. Lucia blushed as the laughter rolled across the table.

Bart sipped his espresso, feeling so relaxed. He glanced at Angela and nodded. "Time to put operation 'family exodus,' into play." He whispered.

Angela looked to her mother, with a smile. "Mom, it looks as if Dad should be home by April," Angela encouraged. "Bart and I want you all to come to Augusta for Bart's birthday and to watch him play in the Masters." She looked to Bart.

Bart scanned the table, focused on Maria. "Mom, the traveling will be easy, no airport crowds to jostle Papa, he'll sit on a nice, comfortable recliner for the flight."

"A recliner?" Tina queried. "On the airplane?"

Angela nodded. "Tina, it's a private jet, with couches, recliners, a conference table, full bathrooms, even a kitchen, it's amazing." She gushed. She looked at her mother. "It would mean a lot to Bart and to me, if the family was all together." She paused, looked at Rosa, confident of her support. "We'll be in Augusta for Bart's birthday."

Rosa smiled, looked at Franco Palermo. "Franco, your Dad could use someone like Angela to plead a case in court for him!" Rosa looked at Bart, smiled. "You know it's up to your Dad." She looked at her sons. "Give your Dad time to consider this."

Bart nodded, flashed a grin at his Dad. He met his Dad's eyes, saw the pride in his Dad's expression. Then, he turned to Maria. "Okay, Mom? You know, of course, that it would mean so much to Angela and to me, if you all came."

Tina laughed, her eyes sparkled. "Mom, I think Bart has your number." She flashed a smile at Bart and Angela.

Maria smiled at Angela, as she shook her head. "I will talk to your Dad."

Tina laughed. "Angela, Dad can never so no to Mom." She winked at Angela. "I'd say it looks good."

"Not to push our luck," Angela said. "But, the Classic is being played in Canada the week before Celia's wedding." She looked to Celia. "The Wallestons have invited the entire family. They are arranging the flight, everything." She paused, her eyes pleaded to Celia. "I know that might be tough, but you'll be back on the Monday of your wedding week." She smiled. "We all will be back."

Celia frowned. "Angela, I'd love to go, but, that would mean Mario and Dad not fishing for two weeks, then the Honeymoon week." She looked at Mario, glanced at her soon-to-be father-in-law, considered. "I don't know Angela, three weeks?"

Surprisingly, neither Franco nor Mario reacted immediately. Franco always enjoyed allowing his children to think out their ideas, then, state their requests.

Celia sat back and pondered. "Unless," she laughed. "She looked to Mario, smiled. "We had a pre-wedding Honeymoon in Canada," she considered. "We could watch Bart play," she weighed it. "Then, after the wedding, Dad and Mario could squeeze in a fishing trip before Fiesta." She looked at Franco, flashed her pretty smile. "That could work, Dad."

Franco was amused. He nodded, raised his brows, smiled at Celia. "How would your parents feel about, 'a pre-wedding honeymoon,' Celia?"

Celia laughed. "I'll admit, it is a bit unusual," she grinned, eyed Angela. "But, isn't everything a bit unusual with a DeMarco guy?" Laughter broke out across the table at that observation.

Bart jumped in. "I have an idea, that should make your Mom and Dad feel better." He looked about, saw all eyes were on him. "How about if Father Capelli marries you before we head to Canada." He paused, saw

Celia smile. "Then, you and Mario have your honeymoon, stay in one of the beautiful rooms in the Walleston mansion. We'll all be together, I'll play the Tournament, then we all come home, have the wedding ceremony, the reception, everything." He smiled at Celia. "I think my big brother is marrying a very smart lady."

Celia laughed, looked at Mario. "From what I can see, the DeMarco men like their women smart." She observed, mischievous eyes flashing.

Bart looked at Celia, then Angela. "And," he added, "don't forget, sexy as hell!" He looked to his mother and smiled. "Dad taught us that."

Celia and Angela blushed at the compliment. Rosa happily, but playfully, swatted Bart.

Chapter Fifty-Six

It was early afternoon when Bart, Angela and Dave, arrived at Casa Walleston, South. They were surprised to find Heather and Rachel, along with the tutor, at the Boca estate.

Dave lit up when he saw Rachel. "What a wonderful surprise!" Dave exclaimed as he hugged and kissed Rachel.

Heather smiled. "Rachel convinced her Dad that she could study with Angela, while Bart and Dave were busy practicing." She laughed, looked at Dave. "And, I'm here to keep my eye on you!" She stated, with a wink.

"Will Mr. Walleston be joining us?" Bart asked.

Heather shook her head. "No, unfortunately, he has meetings and construction issues to address and deal with." She smiled. "He is hoping to see us in Scottsdale for the Tournament."

Bart looked about the beautiful and spacious house. "Mrs. Walleston, thank you for allowing us the use of your home." He smiled. "It's really wonderful of you and Mr. Walleston."

Heather smiled. "Bart," she looked into his eyes. "Phil and I are so grateful to you." She smiled. "Because of you, the example you set, Justin is a different boy." She paused. "He now believes in his future. So, no thanks are needed." Heather embraced Angela. "Let me show you all to your rooms." She pointed at Dave, feigned a stern look. "You'll be staying on the first floor, the rest of us on the second floor." Rachel rolled her eyes, but, as agreed, said nothing, as that was the deal she and her Dad had reached.

Bart smiled and winked at Dave. "I think I'd like to go for a run and maybe hit the gym." He stretched. "I need to work out the kinks, after the flight." He looked at Heather. "Is there a gym nearby?"

"Yes, Bart," Heather smiled. "The club is about two miles down the road. It has a full gym and is totally at your disposal."

"I could use a workout myself," Dave stated. "I'll join you, Bart."

In their room, Bart changed into workout clothes. He pulled Angela close, "after my workout, I will probably need a massage." He kissed her. "You know to relax my muscles."

She smiled up at him. "I'll see what I can do, Sir."

Bart laughed as he headed out. "I should be about three hours." He winked. "I love you, Princess."

Bart spoke to Dave as they jogged to the club. They agreed that today Bart would do his workout and tomorrow they would hit the range and play, at least, 18." As Bart picked up his pace, he laughed. "We need to work on my lob shot."

Dave and Bart arrived back at the house about 5pm. They headed to their rooms to shower. To his disappointment, there was no sign of Angela. Bart showered, dressed and went in search of the group. He saw Dave, Mrs. Walleston, and the tutor, Linda Cromwell, relaxing in the den, sipping on wine. Linda, a pretty, full figured, forty year old, with brown hair and lively brown eyes, appraised Bart with a teacher's eye. Bart poured himself a large glass of water, and joined them. "Where's Angela and Rachel?" He asked, as he looked about.

Heather laughed, "you look disappointed, Bart," she said. "Oh, I guess, Angela wasn't in your room?"

Bart eyed them, smiled. "Okay, what's up?"

"What's up," Dave responded, with a grin, "is that our girls are in the kitchen cooking dinner."

"Yes," Heather said with a smile. "They sent our cook home for the evening."

Bart laughed. "Really? That's great." He thought about it. "What are they making?"

Heather smiled. "They are attempting, Veal Saltimbocca!" She stated with raised brows. "Angela has been on the phone with Tina, who, I guess is walking them through the steps."

Bart rose, re-filled his glass and smiled. "My girl is cooking!" He said softly, appreciatively.

"How was the run and workout?" Heather asked. "Dave seemed happy."

Bart smiled. "It was great, just what I needed." He took a deep breath. "I so love the weather here." He stood, considered. "I think I'll take a look," he said as he walked to the kitchen. As he approached the kitchen, he heard the sound of Angela singing. She sounded so happy. Bart listened and smiled. Rachel was singing along. They both had their backs to Bart, focused on their tasks. He stood in the doorway, quietly watching Angela.

Rachel stood at the gas range, gently placing the veal into the frying pans. He could see a pasta pot on a burner and watched Angela as she dropped the linguini into the boiling water. Angela, dressed in white shorts and a red sleeveless blouse, opened the oven door and bent over to look in and check on the garlic bread. Bart smiled, almost laughed aloud, but instead, cleared his throat, as he had on that day, which seemed so long ago.

"Really?" Angela said on a laugh. She looked over her shoulder and saw his beaming smile. "It seems we've been here before, Sir," she laughed.

"I loved the view then, and I love it now." He said, as he appreciated that she still blushed. "Although, then, your mother urged you to properly greet your boyfriend, as I recall." He said.

Rachel looked at Bart, saw the gleam in his eye. "Easy there boy," she smiled and wagged her finger. "Between shopping, preparation, and cooking, we've been at this for four hours." She saw the joy on both of their faces, found herself hoping that someday a man would love her so completely. Rachel smiled, but shook her head. "Bart, don't you think, for one minute, that you are taking the chef away from this kitchen!" Rachel warned.

He looked from Rachel back to Angela. "I guess I can wait for that massage," he smiled.

Angela grinned, rolled her neck. "I'm feeling pretty stiff myself." She eyed Bart. "I think that I may need a massage."

Bart laughed, pictured his hands on her body. He looked into her eyes, "I will be glad to provide that service, my Dear."

"Okay, okay," Rachel laughed. "I get that you two are into each other, but right now we're cooking." She glanced at the veal and linguini, nodded. "Bart, would you ask Dave, Linda and my Mom to take their places at the table?"

Dinner was delicious. Bart sliced a generous forkful of veal, ran it through the rich sauce and savored the flavor. "Angela, Rachel, this is great." He reached out and took Angela's hand. "Thank you for doing this."

Dave had his eyes on Rachel. "This is wonderful," he said. "Rachel, I had no idea that you could cook?"

Rachel met his eyes, she saw something that caused her to blush as she smiled. "I can learn," she said. She paused, placed tender eyes on Dave. "I'm glad to learn, Dave."

"I was so happy to see you here when we arrived," Dave said. He angled his head, looked into her eyes. "Rachel, I hope you came, at least in some small part, because you knew I would be here."

She flashed her prettiest smile at him. "Could be," she replied, "Could be."

Heather and Rachel exchanged a smile. Then Heather addressed the group. "You know, Bart, Angela and Dave, my husband and I were discussing just how important you have all become to us."

Angela smiled. "Thank you, we feel the same." She reached for Bart's hand.

"We feel," Heather continued, "that the Mr. and Mrs. Walleston, while polite, does not really express the closeness we feel for you."

Bart smiled. "So, what are your thoughts?"

Heather looked at Bart. "How does PapaWall and MamaWall sound?"

Smiles bloomed around the table. Rachel looked at Dave. "What do you think of that, Dave?"

He met her smile, saw the glow of her eyes. "I like it," he responded. He took a deep breath. "At least for now," he added.

"PapaWall and MamaWall it is," Bart said.

Bart and Dave settled in the den while Heather and the girls cleared the table and loaded the dishwasher. Dave tuned in the Golf Channel and saw the show, 'Golf Central,' re-capping the California Tournaments. One of the golfing analysts was asked by the pretty blond hostess, what he knew of Bart's schedule.

He adjusted his glasses and replied. "Well, Lisa, my understanding from speaking with his team is that he will next play in Arizona and will follow that with the Pebble Beach Pro-Am Tournament." He laughed. "Word is that many of the Amateurs are requesting to play with Bart."

She laughed. "He was rather impressive." She followed up, "is there more information? She smiled. "I'm sure 'Bart's Battalion' would like to plan ahead."

"Actually, nothing firm, but I'm informed that Bart has hopes of playing on the U.S Ryder Cup team." He shook his head. "That may be tough. He would need to make up a lot of points." He shrugged. "Although, he could be a Captain's pick."

Angela, Rachel, Linda, and MamaWall came in and settled quietly. Angela stood behind Bart and placed her hands on Bart's shoulders, gently caressing as she watched the discussion.

"The Golf central analyst continued. "After Pebble Beach, Bart will likely take a week off and then the Florida swing begins." He consulted his notes. "I'm told that he's likely to play the PGA National Tournament, then the World Golf Championship in Mexico."

"How will he prepare for the Masters?" She asked.

"I have to caution that all of this is not cut in stone." The analyst stated. "Bart's team is concerned about burning him out." He paused. "He's only 17. Still, I'm told he wants to play the Arnold Palmer, then the Match Play, if he's qualified." He looked at Lisa. "He's accepted an invitation to play in the new European Tour event in Bermuda." He laughed. "Then on to Augusta," he looked at the camera, "to celebrate his 18th birthday, on April 2nd, by the way, and then the Masters."

"I guess Harry must have filled them in." Bart said. He looked to Dave.

"He did," Dave confirmed. "We want 'Bart's Battalion' in your gallery. It's what makes you unique," he laughed. "Other than that you are one of the few PGA golfers who can't order a drink!"

Angela smiled, she excitedly announced, "We talked the family, even my Dad, into coming to Augusta for Bart's birthday celebration and the Masters." She looked to Heather. "MamaWall, we hope you will all be there for Bart's party."

MamaWall smiled. "I'll talk to PapaWall, but I think we'll be there."

Bart nodded, "that's great," he smiled. "How about we watch a movie?" He pulled Angela onto his lap. She smiled, but slid off to sit beside him. She leaned close, "later," she promised.

"And, we planned for the post dinner entertainment," Rachel said. "We have two choices, both musicals that might appeal to our newlyweds." With a dramatic flair, she pulled two DVD's from her bag. "We have 'Grease,' which, I hear, showed Bart how hopelessly devoted Angela was to him." Bart and Angela laughed. "Or, we have 'A Chorus Line,' where Angela explained just, 'What she did for Love.'"

They all laughed. "Okay," Bart said, "how about we watch one tonight and the other tomorrow?"

"Sounds good," Dave said. "Let's do it!"

Chapter Fifty-Seven

Bart and Dave rose early, met in the kitchen for breakfast, drawn in by the sweet, buttery aroma of freshly baked goods, prepared by the family cook, Rosita. She greeted them with a smile, poured two cups of coffee. "Mrs. Walleston told me that you rise early." She hustled over to the stove, "would bacon, eggs and freshly baked croissants be okay?"

"That sounds great," Dave responded, as he sat at the kitchen table.

Rosita watched as the two smiling young men sat. "Would you be more comfortable in the Dining Room?" She asked.

Bart smiled, "no, if it's okay, I think we'll be happy here." He laughed. "I love the warmth and feel of a kitchen."

Rosita smiled, something Bart could see came easily to her. She placed a basket of croissants on the table, with fresh butter and a tray of jams. "You can start with these." She offered. "Be careful, they're hot."

As they ate, Bart asked if Dave would bring his clubs and golf shoes to the club, as he wanted to jog the two miles.

"Of course," Dave responded, with a smile. "A little jog to loosen up?" He quipped.

"It always helps," Bart responded, laughed. "Especially when I eat like this."

At the club, Dave set up at the end of the practice range. It was a well laid out range with flags placed at distances from 50 yards to 300 yards in progressions of 25 yards. Bart arrived smiling, after his run, and began to do a series of stretches. As it was just 7am, they had the practice range to themselves. He switched out his running shoes for golf shoes and spent the next hour or so, hitting through his bag.

"The swing looks good," Dave said as he watched closely.

They moved to the practice chipping green. First, Dave had Bart work from the two sand traps, then from the rough. "Bermuda grass is sticky," Dave reminded Bart. "Very different from Bent and Poa Annua."

As they worked, club members began to arrive and took an interest in Bart's practice. A small group of eight golfers watched, offering compliments and congratulations on his Hawaiian win. Bart, conscious that these were likely friends of PapaWall, made certain to chat with them and sign autographs, for those who asked.

One man approached Bart, somewhat anxiously. He took a deep breath, then hesitantly asked if Bart would speak to his daughter. He paused, as his eyes sought Bart. "She's eight," he explained with a catch in his voice. "Bart, she has a terrible stutter, I hoped…," he choked, "when I heard…" Tears came to his eyes, he dropped his gaze.

Bart smiled, he saw the pain, thought of his mother and father. "Of course, why don't we meet to have lunch together on Saturday? She'll be out of school, right?"

The man brightened, offered his hand. "Yes, thank you, Bart." He wiped his eyes. "Sorry, I feel like an idiot."

"Please don't," Bart said. "There were plenty of tears shed in my house when I was a boy, fighting the same battle." He smiled. "What's your daughter's name?" Bart asked.

"It's Stacey," remembering that he hadn't properly introduced himself, he continued, "Stacey Nolen, I'm Sean Nolen."

"Great," Bart smiled. "Does Stacey take golf lessons?"

Sean nodded. "Yes, for two years, she loves the game."

Bart thought of Angela and how she had pushed him to golf, partly, because 'you don't have to talk in golf,' she had reasoned. "Good, why don't you bring her clubs, and yours," Bart smiled. "We'll have lunch and maybe play nine."

"Wow," the grateful father said, as he looked up to the taller Bart. "Thank you, I'll do that."

"See you Saturday, at noon?" Bart confirmed as he returned to the pile of golf balls at his feet.

"Yes, noon." Sean gratefully repeated. "And, thank you, Bart."

Dave watched the very grateful Dad walk away. He studied Bart closely. "You really are a good guy, Bart." He paused. "You made that guy's year."

Bart shrugged. He thought of little, Peter LoBello. "Everybody needs help sometimes," he stated softly. "Maybe, I can help that little girl." He smiled. "On Saturday, we'll bring the girls and MamaWall," he laughed. "We'll spend some time with them." He looked at Dave. "Angela is great with kids, and, Rachel knows the problem first hand." Bart lobbed a few shots onto the green, looked at Dave and grinned. "And, we'll get to ogle our girls in their golf skirts."

By 9:30am, Bart and Dave were standing on the 1st tee. Angela and Rachel were sitting with the tutor, Linda Cromwell, who was outlining her plan to keep them current, even ahead, of their classes.

Angela smiled. "Linda, please outline a plan for Bart as well. He won't be as available as Rachel and me, but maybe, you could find a way for him to do the work in the limited time he has available."

Linda smiled, shrugged. "I'll do what I can."

Angela paused. "Linda, Bart's working to support our family. He needs you to find a way for him to learn the information so we can graduate together." She eyed the tutor. "He's very bright and hard working. I don't want to see him disappointed."

Linda nodded. "I understand, I'll find a way, Angela."

Angela smiled. "I'm sorry if I seemed insistent, but between the tour and everyone that is looking to him for help, I have to try to shield him, help him, where I can."

Linda smiled, impressed by this young wife. Her opinion of Angela, who she was just beginning to know, was significantly elevated. She seemed to be everything that Mrs. Walleston had promised.

Standing on the 1st tee, Dave told Bart that he would play two balls, which he marked with the number on the balls. "You play ball #1 as you see fit." He smiled. "You play ball #2 as I instruct." He eyed Bart, "you give me your best effort, and we'll see what works best, Okay?"

Bart smiled. "That lob shot really got to you, didn't it?"

Dave shrugged. "Bart, you are amazingly talented and as smart as any golfer I've ever seen, but you will be competing against the best golfers in the world every week." He set determined eyes on him. "It's my job to advise and try to guide and help you." He paused. "That lob shot was too risky at that point." He smiled, "even, if it was fun!" He emphasized.

Bart nodded, smiled. "Okay, let's do it, Coach."

Bart blasted two excellent tee shots down the 1st fairway. As they walked to the balls, Bart noticed that Dave seemed distracted. "Are you okay, Dave?" he asked.

Dave slowed his pace and looked at Bart. "May I ask you for an opinion?"

"Of course," Bart responded with a smile. "Is this about Rachel?"

Dave, with a look of surprise, studied Bart, "How would you know that?"

He shrugged. "Angela suggested that you seemed somewhat conflicted about Rachel."

Dave exhaled. "Bart, I don't know what to do?" Dave said with a shake of his head.

"Well," Bart asked. "What do you want to do?" He paused. "How do you feel about her?"

Dave looked to Bart. He appeared conflicted. "I really care about her." He responded.

"You care about her?" Bart said, with an incredulous tone. "You mean like you care about your cousins or aunts?" He shook his head. "Dave, you told Mr. Walleston that you were in love with her." He paused, set his gaze on Dave. "Do you love her?"

Dave took a deep breath. "Yes, I do." He paused. "So, what do I do? She's only 17 years old."

Bart just smiled at him. "Too old, Dave, or too young?" He studied his coach and friend, "or are you just afraid?"

Dave considered Bart's words. "I know you and Angela are only 17." He nodded, considered and decided that since they were speaking candidly, they were close enough for him to speak freely. "Okay, Bart, why so young?" He looked at Bart. "Why not wait?"

Bart thought that Dave looked confused. He smiled. "Dave, Angela and me, we are young. And, for most people, I would not advise marrying at 17." He shrugged. "But, with me going away to play around the country, even beyond, I just knew that it was right for us." He exhaled, smiled. "I'm just not going to live my life by other people's rules."

He bore his eyes into Dave. "You know Dave," Bart explained. "That even with all the hate and nasty words," he flared, "all the 'Ugly Angela's' those Bastards threw at her, Angela kept smiling."

Bart took a deep breath. He fixed his eyes on Dave. "When I was at my lowest, when I felt totally defeated, she came looking for me." He eyed Dave, "she was worried about me!" He shook his head and smiled. "What spirit! What a girl!"

Bart took a deep breath. "My beautiful Angela is the strongest and kindest person I've ever known." He smiled. "When I had the chance, I was never going to let her go!"

Dave looked at Bart. He nodded.

"You need to get settled in your head, Dave." Bart said. "You're 23 years old, but it was 17 year old Rachel that made the bold statement by flying from Canada to be here." He studied Dave. "Are you ready, really ready, to do the same?" He paused. "If not, don't play with her emotions." He said softly. "She's a great girl."

They arrived at Bart's ball. "Okay, Dave," Bart smiled. "This is ball #2, what do you want me to do?"

Dave studied the chart. "Okay, 158 to the middle of the green." Dave handed Bart his 8 iron, "middle of the green, Bart." Bart followed instructions and lofted his shot onto the middle of the green, about 20 feet right of the pin.

They walked to ball#1, Bart used the same club, but went pin hunting. He pulled the ball, long and left, over the green, into the heavy rough. He eyed Dave.

"Bart, there's a time to gamble and a time to play smart." Dave affirmed. "Let's go." As they walked, Dave looked at Bart. "What should I do?"

Bart smiled and nudged Dave. "If you love her, make a commitment." He shrugged. "When we started, I knew that Angela was right for me. So, I bought her a commitment ring." He smiled at the memory. "I asked her to commit to me."

"Actually, I'm considering proposing marriage." Dave stated.

Bart looked at Dave. "Have you spoken to her Dad? He asked. "Have you sought his blessing?"

Dave eyed Bart. "Do people really still do that?" Dave asked, perplexed.

Bart smiled. "Respectful people do, Dave." Bart stated.

Dave nodded. "You're right, Mr. Walleston deserves that respect."

Bart eyed Dave and laughed. "You asked, so I'll tell you. When we finish here, let's go to a jeweler and you buy her a commitment ring." He smiled. "Put it on her finger and tell her that you love her and cannot imagine living without her." He paused, smiled. "Tell her that you want to commit to her and you want her to do the same." He grinned. "Then, let slip that you plan on speaking to her Dad in Arizona." He laughed. "She'll understand."

Dave smiled. "Sounds good, Bart." He paused, shook his head. "Thanks," he took a deep breath. "Okay, Bart, let's play some golf."

Bart shot a 68 on Dave's ball and a 70 on his own. As they drove to the business district, Bart acknowledged that 2 shots at the level he was playing was, in fact, 8 shots over a four day tournament. He laughed. "Coach, I guess, I'll have to think about this."

Chapter Fifty-Eight

It was a happy group at Casa Walleston, South. Rachel shared with her mother, Linda and Angela how Dave had taken her for a drive to a secluded spot, in a grove of Christmas Palms, overlooking the sea and asked her to commit to him. "I love you, Rachel," he said. He placed the ring on her finger, kissed her.

"It's beautiful Dave," Rachel had gushed. "I love it." She paused, eyed Dave. "Yes, I will commit my heart to you." She kissed him and held on tight. "Thank you, Dave."

Rachel smiled as she related that Dave had added. "I wish your Dad was here. I need to talk with him." That had Rachel beaming with delight.

Bart and Dave worked diligently on his game. The results were promising. Sal Curcuru, Angela's dad, seemed to be making some progress in Physical Therapy.

Angela and Rachel worked each evening with Rosita on making dinner. Bart heard laughter and singing coming from the kitchen as they created wonderful dinners. MamaWall even helped out, not wanting to miss the fun.

The tutoring was proceeding nicely. Linda was impressed at just how quickly Bart absorbed the material. In the limited time he had to devote to his studies, he was keeping pace with their class, while Angela was racing ahead.

That Saturday, the group all planned lunch at the Golf Club. Bart and Dave had practiced and played that morning and entered the Clubhouse a little after noon, to find the Nolen family sitting with MamaWall, Angela and Rachel.

Bart walked to the table and shook Sean's hand. He crouched, to be at eye level with Stacey. Bart smiled, "and, you must be Stacey," he said as he shook her hand. He held her hand, looked into her eyes, "please don't be afraid to speak," He smiled. "There will be no pressure or impatience here, I promise."

She smiled. "Hhi, Ii'm Sstacey," she managed. He noted that she was still smiling.

"Do you want to play golf, Stacey?" He asked. He glanced at Angela and Rachel, "these pretty ladies will walk with us. It will be fun."

Stacey nodded, enthusiastically. "Yyes," she stuttered. Stacey looked at Bart. He saw that she had a question. He encouraged her with a smile.

"Ddo tthey ccall you sstutter bboy?" She asked.

Bart nodded. "Yes, Stacey, they do." He smiled. "When I was your age, I stuttered just like you." He winked. "Okay, let's have some lunch, and we'll all go play golf." He smiled. "The only thing, Stacey," he whispered, "is that as pretty as you are, I'm already married."

Stacey laughed. "You're tto oold!" she said. Everybody laughed, which had the desired effect of relaxing Stacey.

Bart complimented and encouraged Stacey on her game. "You're doing great," he encouraged. In the circle of family and her new friends all noticed that the 8 year old spoke in a more relaxed manner.

At one point Bart crouched before her and looked into her eyes. "Stacey, I think that you should try taking a deep breath and slowly let it out before speaking." He advised in a soothing tone. "That's what I used to do, and it helps."

She smiled up at Bart. "You ddon't sstutter nnow." She said.

He pointed at Angela. "See that beautiful girl?" Stacey nodded. "She really helped me." He smiled. "But, I still stutter." He smiled. "I will probably always stutter, sometimes." He said. "But, Stacey, I think that if you relax your breathing, it will get better."

As they walked the course, Angela sidled up to Bart, she flashed a smile. "Is this skirt short enough for you?" She asked in a whisper. She shook her head in mock disapproval. "I heard all about your motive for inviting me."

Bart laughed aloud, kissed her cheek and looked into her eyes. "I love you, Mrs. DeMarco."

That evening, for dinner, the girls made a spaghetti with shrimp sauce, the recipe from Angela's Mom. As well as Angela's garlic bread. Rosita helped, but deferred to the girl's growing culinary confidence. As they sat to dinner, everybody was relaxed and happy.

"So, we fly to Scottsdale on Monday," Heather stated.

"Will PapaWall be there?" Bart asked.

Dave looked at Rachel and smiled. "I sure hope so." Rachel's smile was radiant.

Heather looked at Rachel, met her smile, winked, then, she looked to Dave. "So, Dave, you seem anxious to speak to PapaWall."

Dave nodded, smiled, "yes I am."

"Anything that you liked to share?" She asked, with a smile. "I mean, we are all friends here."

Dave laughed, eyed her and said in an aristocratic tone. "Sorry, MamaWall, this is an issue between men!" The laughter bubbled up.

"I see," she said, feigning deep thought. Her eyes went wide in a seeming confusion. "Thankfully, we have men to run everything." She smiled at Angela. "Isn't that right, Angela?"

"Oh, absolutely, MamaWall." Angela agreed as she smiled up at Bart. She batted her eyes. "What would we helpless women do without our men?"

Bart and Dave laughed aloud. "I just don't want to find out what I would do without my girl." Bart stated, and kissed Angela.

After dinner and clean-up, they all watched a romantic comedy with Tom Hanks and Meg Ryan, 'Sleepless in Seattle.'

"This is painful," Bart complained, with a smile. In a stage whisper, he asked, "would anyone want me to tell you how this story ends?" He paused, laughed. "Tom Hanks gets the girl."

Angela playfully punched Bart's arm. "Come on now, we all watched 'The Dirty Dozen' last night, and we all know who won that war!"

"Yes," Bart laughed, "but we didn't know if Telly Savalas survived the raid."

Angela grinned and snuggled closer. "I like this movie." She flashed loving eyes at Bart. "Love stories make me feel romantic."

Bart laughed. He thought how well Angela played him. He had to admit to himself, that it was okay with him. "That's good enough for me." Bart whispered to Angela.

MamaWall watched the exchange with a smile. She hoped the love she saw in Bart and Angela's eyes, would happen for Rachel. Still, that, of course, wasn't a reason to not poke at Dave. "But," MamaWall queried, with raised brows. "What we really don't know if Dave will ever get the girl?" She angled teasing eyes at Dave. "Now do we?"

The laughter rolled through the room.

Dave shook his head, looked to Rachel and smiled. "What girl is that?"

Rachel beamed a smile, kissed Dave. "I think he'll do all right."

"You were great with Little Stacey today," Angela said when they retired to their room.

"Thanks," he responded. "But, at the moment I have other things to consider," as he kissed her and liberated her from her clothing. "Now, Mrs.

DeMarco, doesn't this feel better?" He flashed a happy smile. "It certainly looks great!" He pulled her close.

She smiled up at him, planted a kiss. "I always seem to end up like this."

I think that I owe you a massage," he said, laughed. "And, I always pay my debts." He lifted her, cradled Angela in his arms, kissing her as he carried her to the bed. "I can't get enough of you," Bart whispered. "Thanks for marrying me, Princess."

Sunday morning Bart went out early for a good five mile run. He returned to the house for breakfast and a shower and saw concern on Angela's face. "What happened, Beauty?" He paused. "Is your Dad okay?"

Angela kissed Bart. "Yes, he's fine," She sighed. "But, Tina is really upset."

Bart's radar went up. "Is someone bothering her?" He pressed.

Angela smiled, put her hand on his face. "Relax, Bart, it's not like that." She shrugged. "Tina is really upset with Katelyn."

"Oh," Bart exhaled, in relief. "They had an argument?"

"A bit worse than that." She explained. "Yesterday, Tina and Katelyn walked down to Main Street to do some shopping." Angela sat back, looked at Bart. "I guess that they ran into Katelyn's parents.

Bart watched with a look of concern, but said nothing.

"Katelyn's parents were delighted to see Katelyn with her good friend, Tina." She sighed. "Her parents took them to lunch at the new hotel." She saw Bart's smile at the mention of the hotel, and her face flushed. "Anyway, during lunch, Katelyn's Mom began to ask Katelyn about her boyfriends."

"Boyfriends?" Bart asked. "I don't understand."

"Nor do I," Angela stated. "She asked Katelyn if some boy that Katelyn had professed to be interested in, had called and asked Katelyn out on a date."

"Wow!" Bart said. "Is Tina okay?"

"No," Angela responded. "Katelyn's mother even asked Tina about her dating status."

"What did Tina say?" Bart asked.

"She said that she was in a relationship." Angela shook her head. "Then, Tina said that she had forgotten an appointment and had to go."

"Has Katelyn called to explain?" Bart asked.

"She has, but, she just told Tina that she wasn't ready to come out to her parents." Angela sighed. "Tina took it hard." She paused. "Tina feels betrayed."

Bart frowned. "That's unfortunate." He shrugged. "Maybe, Katelyn needs more time." He looked at Angela, shook his head. "And, after all that Tina went through." He paused. "Tina must feel so alone and betrayed." He considered the situation. "Angela, maybe, you need to fly home, talk to Tina and help her through this." He smiled, "you can go see your Dad," He suggested. "Then, you can meet me in Arizona on Wednesday."

She took his hand, placed loving eyes on him. "Bart, you are such a good guy." She smiled. "Why don't you fly home with me?" She took a deep breath. "I spoke to Gina LoBello, services for Peter will be tomorrow." Angela watched Bart closely. "Bart, I know it's hard, but, it would mean a lot to them, if we were there to offer support." She paused. "You were Peter's hero." She saw the pained look in his eyes. "Bart, this is the hard part, isn't it?"

"There's so little that I can do!" He stated, the frustration obvious in his eyes, on his face.

Angela put her hands on his face. "Bart, you made Peter happy." Tears filled her eyes. "For the LoBello's that was everything." She managed a smile. "Then, after the services, you could fly on to Arizona. I'll meet you on Wednesday."

He pulled her to him, kissed her. "Okay, I'll do it for Peter." He held her close. "I just wish…" He paused, took a deep breath, tears ran down his cheeks.

"I know Bart, I know." Angela held him, and cried with him.

Bart took a deep breath, blew it out. He wiped his eyes and managed a smile for his girl. "When I'm in Arizona, I'll miss you Princess, but I think that your sister needs you."

Chapter Fifty-Nine

Bart and Angela arrived at Holy Name Catholic Church in Providence, Rhode Island, for the services in celebration of Peter LoBello's life. They were met by Peter's parents, Peter Sr. and Gina.

Gina went to Angela and embraced her. "Thank you for coming, we so appreciate all you and Bart have done for our boy." Gina's lips trembled and tears flooded her eyes.

Bart took her in his embrace. "I wish there was something I could have done for Peter."

Peter's Dad, gamely fought to hold back the tears, took Bart's hand. "Bart, you did so much." His eyes glistened. "Those last days were made so much better for Peter. He talked about his friend, Bart DeMarco, 'Stutter Boy,' constantly." Peter broke down. "My boy said that he was going to get better and play golf like Bart." Peter managed a laugh, even as his tears flowed. "He asked me to buy him golf clubs." Then, the young Dad lost all control and Bart took him in his arms.

"I'm so sorry, Peter." Bart offered. The words felt so insignificant on Bart's tongue.

Gina took her husband's hand. "Bart, Peter kept the clubs by his bed." She wiped her eyes. "He would touch the clubs and smile. The photo, of you and Peter, and, the golf ball you signed for him, stayed on his end table." She looked at Peter, moved close to her distraught husband. With tears running down her cheeks, Gina added. "Bart, at the end, he clutched the photo to his chest, gasped for breath, looked at us and, then, he closed his eyes."

Bart's head bowed, as tears flooded his eyes. Angela took him in her arms. The four young adults cried together. Then, Gina straightened, wiped her eyes. "We should go in," Gina said. "Please, Bart, Angela, please sit with us."

"Bart looked at Peter. "That's for family."

Peter grasped Bart by the shoulders. Looked into his eyes. "You will always be family to us." His lips quivered. "You brought sunshine into my boy's life, when he needed it most." He gulped. "Thank you, Bart."

Arm in arm, the two young couples walked down the aisle. The little casket was set on the altar. Leaning against the casket was the set of golf clubs. Golf clubs that Peter would never use. On the casket, carefully placed, was the signed golf ball, encased in a clear plastic box, and the framed 11x14 photograph of Bart and Peter. In the photo, young, frail, Peter, was smiling, joyously."

After the services, Bart and Angela taxied to the airport, had a late lunch and waited for Angela's ride. Bart, who was to join the group flying from Florida, and Angela, waited, for her ride. They were met by Jim Perry and Betsy.

Bart greeted and thanked Jim and Betsy. He held Angela close, kissed her. "I have to scoot, I'll see you Wednesday." He smiled. "Princess, give my love to everybody." He embraced and again thanked Jim and Betsy for taking the long ride from Gloucester to Providence.

Jim looked at Bart, saw that Bart appeared somewhat down. "I was glad to do it, Bart." He paused, smiled. "Have a safe flight."

Angela watched Bart jog to the tarmac to meet the group flying to Arizona. She sighed, then, she embraced Jim and Betsy. "What a nice thing to do. How are you, guys?" Angela asked.

Betsy stood back, took in Angela's Florida tan and quipped. "Well, certainly not as sunny as you, Angela."

Jim watched Angela. "Is everything okay, Angela?" He hesitated. "Is your Dad okay?"

Angela smiled. "Thanks for asking. He's actually doing well." She shrugged. "Bart and I just came from a funeral for a young boy." She forced a smile. "It was tough."

Jim nodded, "that would be tough." He smiled. "Is Bart okay?"

"It was hard on him." Angela took a deep breath. Decided to leave that discussion right there. "Actually, I'm here for Tina." As they drove, Angela explained all that was happening and how upset Tina sounded. "Of course, it will give me the chance to see my Dad and Mom." She added.

"So, you're here because of a lover's spat?" Jim asked, astonished. He grinned at Betsy. "It's a good thing Angela doesn't fly here every time you act unreasonably, Betsy." He laughed. "The poor girl would live in the air."

Betsy eyed Jim. "When I act unreasonably?" She laughed.

Angela was smiling at the exchange.

"Jim," Betsy said, lovingly, "maybe, you should tell Angela about your new friend, Nina?" Betsy raised her brows, looked at Angela. "She's the new co-ed, of loose virtue, who seems to want Jim."

Jim laughed. "Of course she wants me!" He shrugged. "What girl wouldn't? Am I right, Angela?"

"Without question, Jim!" Angela affirmed. She winked at Betsy. "I always imagined you had to give numbers to the girls, like at the deli department at the super-market." She grinned. "How else could you keep all the girls who wanted you in line?"

"Damn right, Angela!" He looked at Betsy. "I always told you that she was smart." Betsy grinned at just how outrageous Jim could be to produce smiles.

Angela was laughing aloud. "Oh, I've missed you guys."

Jim drove the group to the Boston General Hospital, stopped in the car park. "We drove your Mom and Tina earlier," Jim explained, "before heading to Providence."

Angela smiled. "You didn't have to do that, Jim." She felt overwhelmed. "That was so nice."

Jim turned and looked at Angela. "I am told that your Dad does therapy in the morning for three to four hours. He has lunch and sleeps. So the best visiting time is about 4pm to 6pm." He smiled. "I haven't visited your Dad since the weekend of the Hawaiian Open, so, Betsy and I had planned to drive you and your family today and tomorrow after school." He paused. "Wednesday morning there is a car to take you to the airport for your flight to Phoenix." He looked into her surprise and laughed. "It's all arranged Angela, just relax, visit your Mom and Dad, and talk your sister through whatever issues she is dealing with."

"Tomorrow," Betsy added. "Jess, Tina, you and I are going out for Chinese and to catch up." She smiled and shrugged. "And, maybe help Tina." She smiled. "We've missed you, too, Angela."

Angela looked at her friends and smiled. She saw Bart's fingerprints all over the schedule and well-organized support. "Thanks, Guys, I really appreciate all of this."

Betsy took Angela's hands. "We're friends, Angela. Friends help each other."

Bart, and the group, arrived in Arizona on Monday evening. They were met by PapaWall and Justin. PapaWall embraced Heather and Rachel.

Justin ran to Bart, jumped into his arms. Bart, thinking of little Peter, held Justin so tight.

"I,I missed yyou, Bart." Justin said.

"I missed you too, Buddy." Bart said, a catch in his voice.

Dave stood back, smiling, eyes on his would-be father-in-law. Linda, smiled on the scene.

PapaWall held Rachel. "Did you have a good time, Honey?" He asked.

Rachel beamed a smile and showed her Dad the commitment ring that Dave had offered and she had happily accepted. "I had a wonderful time, Daddy."

"She even learned to cook!" MamaWall informed. "She and Angela cooked every night in Florida." She laughed. "While the guys were working, Rachel and Angela attended classes with Linda and did some shopping, bought groceries and cooked dinner." She winked. "They even let the old lady tag along and help out."

PapaWall smiled. "That's great, Rachel, I'm proud of you." He looked at Dave. "It seems that you've been busy, Dave?" He queried.

Dave smiled. "I have, Sir." He stood tall. "I'd very much like to have a talk with you."

"Okay," PapaWall responded, with a smile. "Let's get to the hotel, settle in and we can have a chat." He looked at Bart, noted Angela's absence. "Is everything okay with Angela?"

Bart nodded. "Yes, thankfully, Angela went home to help her sister through a relationship issue." He smiled. "A bit out of my league!" He said. "I'm hoping she'll be here Wednesday."

"I received a call from Harry Winston," PapaWall said. "He's arranged for you to speak to the Phoenix Chapter of YES, on Tuesday evening."

Bart nodded. "Okay, that's sounds fine."

As the group traveled to the hotel, PapaWall also informed Bart that on Wednesday evening he was booked on a talk show that ran nationally on a major network. "They plan on sending the Host, Caleb Lawson, here for the interview." He laughed. "It is Super Bowl Week!"

"Caleb Lawson," Bart repeated. "I've seen his show, he likes to goad and embarrass his guests." Bart said. Bart looked at PapaWall, with raised brows, "all in fun, of course."

"Fun for him," Dave said, considered. "Bart, I don't know about this." He studied Bart. "You know, you don't have to do this, Bart."

Dave and PapaWall watched Bart as he sat back, rolling something around in his mind. "I know Dave, but if Harry set it up, I'd hate to disappoint him." Bart looked at PapaWall, "could you have someone do some digging into Lawson's bio?"

Walleston smiled. "Sure, I can do that." He laughed. "Information to shoot back with, if necessary."

Bart smiled. "Exactly, PapaWall, we always have to be prepared."

When the limo arrived at the resort, Bart suggested that PapaWall and Dave head into the lounge and chat. "I'll take care of the luggage and safely escort the ladies to their rooms."

Bart handled the registration and coordinated the luggage to the proper suites. Rachel and Linda would share a suite, and Bart's suite would be a bit lonely for a few days.

As the group ascended in the elevator, Bart noted Rachel's concern. He winked at her. "I wonder what Dave and PapaWall could be discussing?" He offered.

Rachel looked at Bart and smiled, "I have no idea, of course."

Everybody laughed as the elevator stopped and the doors opened. "Well, Dave is making pretty good money these days," Bart suggested. "Perhaps, PapaWall is trying to float a loan?" As Bart hoped, Rachel laughed and her tension level seemed to drop.

Bart went for a run, while Dave conducted his business with PapaWall. When Bart returned, MamaWall happily informed him that Dave and Rachel had left the resort hotel to take a walk and have a talk.

Bart smiled, "I guess I'll hit the gym," he replied with an amused shake of the head. "I don't think we'll be practicing today."

Before dinner, (Pacific Time), Bart called Angela at her parent's home, where it was approaching 10 pm and as she was readying for bed. "Is Tina doing okay?" He asked.

Angela sat back, enjoying the sound of his voice. "We talked," Angela sighed. "She feels betrayed." Angela explained. "Tina feels that if she could open up to our family, Katelyn should have done the same."

"I can see that." Bart agreed. "But, sometimes people disappoint." He shrugged. "It's all part of relationships." He paused. "So, how's my girl?" He asked.

"Your girl misses her guy." Angela stated, Bart could hear Angela's joy in her words. "By the way, thanks for arranging transportation and everything for my Mom, Tina and me to visit my Dad." She smiled. "You didn't have to do that, but I do appreciate it."

"Angela, I like to help my girl." Bart paused, asked. "How's your Dad doing?"

"I saw Dr. Howard today." She laughed. "He gave me a message for you." She laughed, again. "He said to tell you, The Country Club and the Nicklaus course, at Pinehills golf club."

Bart smiled. "I guess your Dad must be making progress." He laughed. "Doc is planning the two courses we will be playing." He smiled. "Is your Dad in good spirits?"

"He is," she said. "He so enjoyed our visit." Angela laughed. "He really wants to go home."

"Sure he does," Bart stated. "When he's ready."

"How are things going there?" She asked.

Bart laughed. "Well, Dave met with PapaWall today, then he took Rachel for a walk."

"That sounds promising," Angela said happily. "Have you spoken to Dave?"

"No, not yet." Bart responded. "I guess I will hear all about it at dinner." He looked at his watch. "I better go, Princess."

"Will you call me later?" Angela asked.

Bart smiled. "Sure, I will." He paused. "It will be a lonely bed without you, Princess."

She thrilled at his words. Feeling loved is life's greatest joy. "I'll be there Wednesday, my love." Angela assured.

"It may be late, but I'll call you." He repeated, "I'll give you the scoop on Dave and Rachel." He paused. "Give my best to your family."

Dinner was jubilant. Rachel described Dave's proposal and showed her beautiful engagement ring. Dave was all smiles and was now referring to his future in-laws as Mom and Dad. Bart was happy for the joyous couple and for the Walleston family.

"Back to work tomorrow." Dave said to Bart. "Big Tournament starting on Thursday."

Dave and Phil Walleston accompanied Bart to his talk to the Phoenix Chapter of YES. Bart thanked them for all the support, encouraged them to come out to the PGA Tournament being played this week. "It's great for the visibility of YES, brings the issue of young stutterers before the public and, of course, helps me."

Bart recounted his life story and his struggles with stuttering. He looked into the large group of young stutterers. "I am committed to helping all of you to improve your speech." He paused. "With the help of the good people of YES and what Manitoba Oil is doing, all of you can succeed."

His comments were met with enthusiastic applause.

One of the adults in the audience raised her hand. Bart acknowledged the woman, and smiled. "Please, Ma'am, what's your question?"

"My son has a stuttering problem." She began with a nervous catch in her tone. "He looks up to you." She paused. "You are a hero to him."

Bart thought of Peter, nodded and smiled.

"But, it upsets him," she continued," "when they ridicule you by calling you 'Stutter Boy.'"

Bart smiled. "Thank you for the question, ma'am." He responded. "I now use 'Stutter Boy' as a badge of honor." He stated. "When I was younger," he smiled, engaged her eyes. "And, I was referred to as 'Stutter Boy,' it hurt and embarrassed me." He paused. "I have given this a great deal of thought. And, I've decided that I will not allow words, even when they are used with cruelty, to control me."

He saw the young mother nod. "I once let the words, or even my anticipation that I would be ridiculed, cause me great anxiety." He paused and smiled. "That anxiety led to a worsening of my stutter." He explained. "It was an awful, painful, cycle." He smiled. "Please tell your son to smile into those words. Take the power of those words away." He paused, smiled, and gestured to those gathered. "And, I believe, he will have an easier time."

The large audience gave Bart a standing ovation.

Tuesday and Wednesday Bart and Dave worked on Bart's game, studied the course, and prepared for Thursday's 1st round.

Bart was delighted when Angela arrived on Wednesday afternoon. He met her as she came off the jet and embraced her. "I've missed you, Princess." He held her close in the car on the drive to the hotel. "I have to appear for an interview for the Caleb Lawson show at 5pm." He kissed her. "You can watch it at the hotel and then, I'll be back." He smiled. "We should have at least an hour before dinner to get re-acquainted."

"Sounds good," He saw that she was troubled. She eyed Bart. "Really?" She pondered. "Is this a good idea?" She paused. "Lawson's really rough on his guests."

Bart laughed. "Harry thinks so." He paused. "We'll see."

The group all met at PapaWalls suite to watch the Caleb Lawson show. Rachel embraced Angela. "A lot has happened, Angela, in your absence." Rachel said happily as she showed Angela her engagement ring.

"I'm happy for you two," Angela smiled, took her hands. "All the best." Angela laughed. "We'll be together on tour, Rachel. We'll have so much fun."

They tuned in the show. It was being shown in prime time in the east. It was to be a 15 minute interview and Lawson had no intention of sparing Bart.

"So, Bart," Lawson began. "Congratulations on an exciting win in Hawaii." The audience cheered. "That was your first PGA Tournament and you schooled Phil Mickelson and Rory McIlroy!"

Bart shook his head, flashed a smile. "Phil and Rory are great players. Nobody wins every tournament and believe me, nobody, schooled Phil and Rory." He paused. "I just managed to win."

"Bart looks good." MamaWall offered. She noted Angela's anxiety, took her hand. "He'll be okay, Angela," she assured.

Watching at home in Gloucester, John Palermo looked to Katie, "I don't like this," he said quietly. "This may have been a mistake."

Lawson looked at Bart. "I understand that you're married?" He asked.

Bart nodded and smiled. "Yes, Sir, that's correct."

Lawson smiled at the audience. "Bart, you are 17 years old, are you and your wife hillbillies from the Ozarks?" The audience laughed. "Was it a shotgun wedding?" The laughter continued. Angela was stunned. The room was quiet.

"No, Sir, we are from Gloucester, Massachusetts, actually." Bart responded evenly. "And, I chose to propose, because I love her and wanted Angela to be my wife."

Lawson gave a leering look to the camera. "Look what you are missing out on." He spread his arms. "All those women!" The audience laughed with the host.

Rosa DeMarco, watching at home was outraged.

Bart smiled. "I don't feel as if I'm missing out on anything." He looked at the audience. "When you are in love, everything is better."

"What can you know of love?" Lawson smirked. "Bart you're 17 years old." Lawson shot back and laughed, the audience followed with laughter. "You can't even order a drink." He paused. "Although, I think that your parents may be using drugs to have allowed this!" He smirked and drew a response from the audience.

Angela rose from her chair, anger in her eyes. "How dare he?"

Bart sat back and let the laughter roll. "That's funny, Sir," He said comfortably. "I understand, you were 30 year's old when you first married," he paused. "And, with all your maturity, wisdom and experience, the marriage was a total failure." He eyed Lawson and shrugged.

"Then," Bart continued. "You married again at age 37." He smiled. "I was sorry to learn, that marriage also failed!" He let the silence settle.

Bart sat back, smiled at Lawson. "Sir, my parents have been married for almost 25 years, and they are still happily married." He paused. "Sir, so, who do you think is doing drugs?" The audience was silent. Lawson shifted in his seat.

Rosa clapped. "That's my boy!" Angela smiled. "I love that man." Heather took her hand. "He is something."

Lawson squirmed. "Did a little research did you, 'Stutter Boy?'" There was a meanness to his words. It was not lost on the studio audience, which grew very quiet. Lawson's 'Stutter Boy' dig rolled off of Bart's back.

"Yes sir, I did." Bart continued to smile. "I love my wife, and I love my life." He smiled at Lawson. "I consider myself extraordinarily lucky to have found Angela." He smiled into the camera. Angela beamed.

Bart continued. "I'm going to do my best to keep her happy." He smiled easily, as he faced the host. "Sir, why do you think it is, that so many people seem to be so certain about how others should live, while their own lives are in chaos?"

Lawson looked at Bart, forced a smile, he didn't even try to respond. "We have to take a break, thank you Bart for coming on the show." Bart received a respectful ovation as he left the stage.

PapaWall smiled, recalling Bart's request for information on Lawson. 'Smart kid,' he thought. He looked at Heather. "I think we picked a winner!"

John Palermo let out a breath. "Thank God!"

"Who was the genius who arranged that?" Katie Palermo asked.

"It was Harry Winston." He paused. "I better keep a closer eye on things in the future."

Heather embraced Angela. "Wow!" She shook her head. "That was something. Bart did great." She laughed. "Now, you be nice to him, Angela," Heather quietly admonished. Angela laughed and whispered, "I will be so nice to him."

At dinner, Bart made certain all attention stayed on Dave and Rachel. He looked at Dave. "My dear friend," he smiled. "So, you're going to marry this beautiful girl." Bart shook his head, a look of consternation coloring his face, he turned his gaze to PapaWall. "It pains me to say this Sir, about my dear friend and coach," he shrugged. "But, there is no way that he is good enough for Rachel!"

PapaWall heartily agreed, as he flashed a happy smile, "but, Bart, she really seems to like him!" He shrugged. "What's a guy to do?"

Dave and Rachel beamed smiles. Bart continued. "So, Dave," he grinned. "The day you actually marry Rachel, you need to understand, that you are merely excess baggage." Laughter rolled across the table. "I mean," Bart continued. "They could put a cardboard cut-out of you next to the altar and nobody would even notice or care."

Bart paused. He looked at Angela, met her smile. "The day we married, all you heard was how beautiful Angela looked." He grinned. "And, she really did." Now, he feigned outrage. "Nobody, even noticed that I was there!" He laughed. "Okay, maybe my mother." At that, all were laughing.

"So," Bart rolled on. "You will marry this beautiful girl." Rachel smiled and accepted the compliment with a nod. "I'm thinking that we should just make it a practice day." He smiled. "Of course, we'll be there for the dinner."

Rachel wagged her finger. "No way, Bart." She laughed. "You will both have to be there." She looked to Angela, smiled. "Angela, your husband is a bad influence, I'm sensing."

Angela shook her head, pointed her finger at Bart. "I'll do my best to keep him in line, Rachel." She laughed. "But, no promises."

Justin watched all the laughter with a smile. "Dave, am I,I going to be in your wedding too?"

Dave smiled. "You bet you are."

Chapter Sixty

The weather was warm and dry, ideal Arizona weather. Of course, Bart having lived his life in America's oldest fishing port, preferred living close to the ocean, savoring the clean, crisp, salt air. He enjoyed the beauty of the how the rocky outcroppings of Cape Ann met the sea, and, of course, the wonderful sandy beaches.

Still, he would admit, that he enjoyed the humidity free warmth of the desert, especially as February in Gloucester was windy, snowy and bone-chillingly cold.

Bart had a late-early draw and was in a threesome with Dustin Johnson and Bubba Watson. Dustin and Bubba, both, Major Champions, are incredibly gifted players and two of the longest hitters on tour.

Dave was concerned that Bart would watch these long hitters take their big powerful swings and be pulled into a long drive contest. He pulled Bart aside, after the players and caddies greeted each other and shook hands. "Bart, don't get caught-up in trying to outdrive these guys." He paused, made sure he had Bart's attention. "Remember, Bart, Golf is not about how far, it's about how many."

It was as if Dave had not spoken, Bart was pulled into an effort to out-drive Bubba and Dustin. In the process, Bart did not find one fairway on the front nine. He was over-swinging and losing the ball both right and left. The vastly more experienced Bubba and Dustin reigned in their competitiveness and played golf. After nine holes, both Bubba at -2 and Dustin at -1 were playing their powerful, but controlled game. Bart, suffering from what Dave called 'testosterone poisoning,' stood on the 10th tee at +4. He had shot a 40!

"This is not a good pairing for Bart." Johnny Miller stated. He laughed. "The kid is great, but, he has not been able to control his emotions on the front nine." He looked to Jim Nantz, and smiled. "Someone might get the idea that Bart DeMarco is only 17 years old."

The on course commentator, Donna Caponi, approached Bart on the 10th tee. "Hi Bart," She smiled. "Why are you swinging so hard?"

Bart paused, shook his head, and smiled at Donna, and into the camera. He looked at Dave, before responding. "Maybe, because, I'm an idiot, Donna." he said on a laugh. He took a deep breath, shook his head, he flashed a smile at Angela, noted the worried look in her eyes. "Okay, Dave, how about we play my game on the back nine?"

Dave smiled. "Sounds like a plan, Bart."

Bart listened to his caddie and coach and played the back nine in a controlled, -3, shooting a 33, for a +1 score of 73 for the round. Bubba shot a -1 on the back nine for a -3 score of 69 and Dustin, hitting on all cylinders shot a back nine -4 for a -5 round of 67 and the Tournament lead after the first round.

At dinner that evening, the conversation danced around the Tournament and Bart's play. Heather, Rachel and Angela discussed wedding dates, dresses, flowers, music for the reception. Everything, except the elephant in the room.

Bart smiled. "Okay, do I really have to be the one to state the obvious?" All eyes were on him. "Come on Rachel, you saw it." He paused. "Dave really messed up out there today."

Smiles bloomed at the table. "Absolutely, Bart, you are so right," Rachel agreed. "Dave should have warned you about getting pulled into a driving contest with those two guys." She smiled at Dave. "Oh, that's right, you did warn him." She pursed her lips. "Sorry Bart." She broke into a smile.

Angela jumped in. "I have to defend my husband here." She offered Bart a sweet smile. "It only took him nine holes to figure out how stupidly he was playing."

PapaWall and Dave laughed aloud, as, except for Justin, they all relaxed and smiled.

Heather joined in. "Wait just one minute. Bart gets to play with Dustin and Bubba again tomorrow." She smiled at Bart. "Before, Bart misses the cut."

Bart looked at Dave and the good friends burst out laughing. "What was that game we played in Florida, Dave?" He grinned. "You know, the day you bought Rachel that commitment ring." Dave smiled at Rachel.

"Yes," Dave responded, with a grin. "The one where we showed how listening to your coach will lower your score? Do you mean that game, Bart?"

"That's the one." Bart agreed, smiling. He pointed his finger at Dave, grinned. "Don't mess up again, Dave."

Smiles and laughter returned to the table. Justin finally spoke up. "Bbart," he said. "Yyou rreally played llousy today!" He paused, took a deep breath, looked into Bart's eyes. "Do better tomorrow."

Bart grinned. "Okay, Justin, but only as long as I hear you cheering for me."

Bart, Dustin, and Bubba had an early tee time. The children of YES were out in force, in part, fearing that Bart would miss the cut and this would be their last opportunity to watch their hero play. They cheered for Bart on every swing.

Fortunately, Bart found his natural silky smooth swing. He played the front in 32 shots, or -4. That brought his total to a -3 for the tournament. A 33 on the back nine and Bart had shot a 65 for the second round and was at -6 for the Tournament. He still trailed Dustin Johnson, who was at -9 and Bubba at -7. Phil Mickelson and Jordan Spieth were also a shot ahead of Bart at -7. Bart was tied with a rejuvenated Tiger Woods, who was also at -6.

Bart was in a tie for 5th place with his score of -6. He had easily made the cut. And, on moving day, he would be paired with Tiger Woods.

Jim Nantz looked to Johnny Miller. "What do you think Johnny?"

Miller looked at Nantz, "you know Jim, Bart is so young. He made a mistake yesterday that I'll wager he won't make again." He laughed. "But, Donna," he added. "They'll be plenty of other mistakes."

"I think so," Donna Caponi agreed. "This is a tough game. He, like all golfers, will have to navigate many pit-falls." She laughed. "But, he is so gifted. It will be fun watching."

Bart spent time with his young fans, signing autographs, posing for photos and most importantly, talking with the youngsters. He, patiently listened to their stories, worries and concerns. His encouragement brought smiles to the children, and hope for their parents.

Bart, Angela, Dave and Rachel, along with Justin, spent the afternoon, by the massive resort swimming pool, relaxing and enjoying the spectacular weather.

Bart looked at Angela, "you spoke to Tina, today?" Angela nodded. "First, how's your Dad doing?"

Angela smiled. "Dr. Howard said that he was ready to go home and do his therapy at a clinic near home." She paused, eyed Bart with an appreciative gleam. "But, my Dad said that he would wait for you to return home, so that you can walk with him out of the Hospital."

"That's great," Bart exulted. "That is so great," he laughed and put his hand on Angela's leg. He smiled. "Monday or Tuesday, we take your Dad home." He paused. "And, Tina?" He eyed Angela, "how is she doing?"

Angela shrugged, an unhappy expression clouding her face. "She's really upset." She paused. "She's so disappointed." Angela sighed. "She really cared for Katelyn."

Bart eyed Angela. "Tina's only 15," he paused. "Okay, almost 16, but there will be others." He smiled. "Tina deserves someone who will love her, and need her, the way she will love and need that person." He winked. "You know, Angela, the way, I love and really need you."

Angela laughed. "Aren't you tired from just playing and walking 18 holes of golf?" She shook her head. "I'm exhausted from the stress of watching you."

Bart smiled. Angela saw the happy glint in his eye. "Maybe, you need a massage?" He offered.

Angela shook her head, but smiled. She turned to Rachel, grinned. "We're going to head in for a rest, see you at dinner?"

Rachel laughed. "Bart, have a nice rest."

The happy couple lay together, relaxed and thoroughly sated, gently touching and kissing. Angela grinned into his chest. "Here's a question," she asked. "How can a guy be mature enough, smart enough, to outwit Caleb Lawson and at the same time be so dumb as to let Bubba and Dustin get into your head?"

Bart smiled as he stroked her beautiful, long, thick and curly black hair. "You are so gorgeous, I could touch you forever," he said softly.

Angela smiled. "Well?" she pushed.

Bart laughed, languidly, "Dave called it 'Testosterone poisoning.' Probably a good description."

"Excessive male ego!" She laughed. "Bart, it will be the death of you."

He laughed with her.

Chapter Sixty-One

The cuts having been made, the field for Saturday's, Moving Day, round was reduced to 72 golfers, playing in pairs. Bart was paired with Tiger Woods, who was recovering from two surgeries, but had played well in the first two rounds.

Tiger Woods is unquestionably the greatest golfer of his generation. And, in many minds, along with Bobby Jones and Jack Nicklaus, one of the three all-time greats. In an eleven year span Tiger won 14 Majors, and over 70 PGA Championships. He had accomplished multiple career grand-slams and at one point had held all four major trophies, (The Tiger Slam).

Of course, Bart was awed. In the gallery, PapaWall, dressed as Bart, Dave and Justin were, in a maroon golf shirt with gold and white trim, looked at Angela. "Is he okay?" He paused. "Playing with Tiger can be overwhelming."

Angela watched as Bart shook hands with Tiger. "I think so," she replied softly.

As always, Tiger was gracious with young players. "So," Tiger smiled, as he shook Bart's hand. "Bart, I hear that you are the new me!"

Bart and Dave laughed aloud. "Well, sir," Bart responded. "I've played in one PGA Tournament. We should, maybe, wait a few weeks before we decide that."

Tiger placed amused eyes on Bart. "Sir?" He laughed. "So, you think I'm a relic, do you?" He playfully punched Bart's arm. "I'll show you, young man." Bart met Tiger's smile. "Just play your game, Bart." Tiger encouraged. "It's you against the course, forget all about me, okay?"

Bart smiled. "I will try, Sir, I mean, Tiger."

"So," Jim Nantz asked. "It's Bart playing with Tiger. What do you think, Johnny?"

"It's hard to know, Jim." He paused. "He handled playing with Phil and Rory without any real problem."

Donna Caponi was on the 1ˢᵗ tee, waiting to walk with the leaders. She watched the exchange with a smile. "I think that he'll be okay, guys." She offered. "He appears pretty relaxed." She paused. "And, he is comfortable playing before a large and enthusiastic gallery."

No golfer attracted galleries the size of Tiger's galleries. The fans loved Phil, but Tiger set the standard, and golf fans idolized him, or, even if they disliked him, had enormous respect for his game. And, every golf fan sought to watch him.

Still, Bart's Battalion was out in force. He had a large gallery of fans, many sporting the 'I'm with Stutter Boy' buttons. Others waving signs proclaiming themselves a part of 'Bart's Battalion.' YES had delivered and it was noticed by Tiger.

Knowing that he would be playing with Tiger, Bart had asked for security to walk with Angela and the Wallestons.

It was clear, early, that Tiger was feeling pain. He was suffering back spasms, continually bending and stretching. It affected his game, but, he kept up and enjoyed watching Bart play. After the 9th hole, Bart was -4 and -10 for the Tournament. Tiger, who simply could not turn without pain, was at +2 for the nine holes. On the 10th tee, Tiger walked to Bart and extended his hand. "Sorry, Bart, but I have to withdraw." He smiled. "Go get them, Tiger." He joked.

Bart clasped his hand, looked into Tiger's eyes. "It was an honor, Tiger. I hope you feel better."

"It appears that Tiger will be withdrawing." Jim Nantz stated. "Johnny, do you think playing alone for the remainder of the round will have an effect on Bart?"

Johnny Miller shook his head. "Playing with Tiger for the first time can be overwhelming for a 30 year old, Jim, let alone a 17 year old." Miller said. "The galleries are huge and noisy." He laughed. "But, except for Thursday, when Bart forget he was playing a golf tournament rather than a long-drive contest, he has been rock solid." He paused. "My guess is that he'll be fine."

The back nine was up and down for Bart. He had two birdies, but, two bogies, as well. So, as Bart and Dave walked through the tunnel under the viewing stands from the 15th green, onto the famous par 3, 16th tee, he was losing ground to the leaders, his name sliding down the leader board.

"It's not an easy game." Jim Nantz stated to Johnny Miller. "Bart's not used to going backwards. Do you think that he can recover?"

"His confidence is high, coming off of a win in Hawaii." Miller stated. "Something tells me that Bart DeMarco will be in the mix on Championship Sunday."

"You bet he will!" Rosa stated, with a mother's confidence, to the family and friends gathered in the DeMarco living room.

"We'll see," Nantz stated. "Now, he's at 16," he laughed. "And, it's crazy there."

Bart and Dave stood on the tee, of 'The Coliseum.' The entire hole from tee to green was wrapped with covered bleachers, where over 20,000 well lubricated fans cheer or jeer the player, depending on the quality of his shot into the green. 'The Greatest Show on Grass' draws more fans than any golf tournament in the world, with over 600,000 fans for the four day tournament.

Angela and Rachel locked arms as they looked about. They had heard the cheers and the booing cascading down on the golfers after they struck their shot. "Wow," Rachel said in awe. "Every day there's more people."

Angela watched as Bart stood on the tee box, calmly conversing with Dave. They were waiting as Matt Kuchar and Rory putted out on the green. Matt was applauded for making his birdie putt, while Rory was lustily booed, for lipping out his putt. Angela saw that Bart was smiling. He turned to face her, made eye contact, and beamed a smile. "Look at him," Angela said to Rachel and MamaWall, with a smile. "He's loving this."

Heather laughed. "If 25,000 fans might boo me, I think that I would run for cover." She looked at Angela. "Why is he so relaxed?"

Angela smiled at MamaWall. "The night before the final round of the Hawaiian Open, we were in bed, holding each other." She paused. "I was scared for him." She related. "Now, remember, he still had to earn his card." She smiled and waved to Bart. "I asked him if he was worried about the final round." She smiled as she recalled his words. "He said, 'no, Princess, it's just golf. Whatever happens, I still have you.'"

Rachel gasped. "He loves you so much, Angela."

Angela looked at Rachel and Heather. Her eyes misted and she smiled. "And, he needs me as much as I need him." She wiped away a tear, still smiling. "How great is that?"

Bart stood with Dave, conferring on club selection, gauging the wind. The fans began chanting; "Where's Tiger? Where's Tiger?"

The announcer called out; "Now on the tee, the winner of the Hawaiian Open, Bart DeMarco."

The bleacher crowd abandoned their Tiger chant and began chanting; "Stutter Boy! Stutter Boy!" The children of YES happily joined the chant, waving their signs and boldly proclaiming their support for 'Stutter Boy.'

Dave handed Bart his club and backed away. Bart teed his ball, smiled at Angela, as he stood behind the ball. He looked down the fairway at the green. He closed his eyes, visualized the shot. He evened his breathing, opened his eyes, smiled, set up over the ball and launched into his smooth swing.

When a golfer hits a shot pure, he tends to hold his finish, eyes on the flight of the ball. When he begins to look up at the ball, then at the flag, up at the ball, and then at the flag, it is the clearest indication that he believes the ball is right on the flag.

"It's all over the flag!" Dave called, excitedly. The crowd liked what they saw and began to roar. The ball landed just short of the hole, took a small hop and tracked the hole.

"Go in!" Justin screamed. "Go in!" And into the hole it went, gently kissing the flagstick as it fell to the bottom of the cup. The crowd exploded with a roar not heard that day. On their feet the crowd chanted; "Bart, Bart, Bart, Bart!"

Bart raised his arms aloft, then removed his hat, waved it about, and made an exaggerated bow to the crowd, in every direction, causing a further roar.

"How about that?" Jim Nantz called out. "After playing the back nine in even par, Bart DeMarco posts an Eagle, Ace, to go to -12 for the Tournament!"

"This kid is a thrill a minute." Johnny Miller called excitedly.

Danna Caponi, walking with the leaders, three holes behind Bart asked, "What happened, Guys, we heard the roar back on the 12th fairway." She paused. "Was it Bart?"

"It sure was, Donna," Johnny replied in an excited tone. "He aced 16!"

The DeMarco living room was joyous. Franco Palermo, always ready, embraced and kissed Lucia. Rosa watched the kiss, while smiling, wagged her finger at Franco.

Angela and Rachel embraced, laughing aloud. In their excitement they jumped about, clapping and hugging Justin, Mama and PapaWall. Angela looked over and saw Bart smiling at her. She blushed, looked at Rachel, "he loves when I get excited and jump about." Angela waved to Bart, smiled and blew him a kiss. It was all caught live on camera and Rosa, as well as Sal and Maria laughed delightedly. Is there anything better than watching your children loving life?

Bart, with Dave by his side, walked from the tee to the green in a tunnel of cheers and chants. Bart waved his hat the entire way. He walked onto the green and plucked the ball from the cup. He looked over and saw a group of the children of YES, (Bart's battalion) smiling and clapping. He tossed the ball into the group, waved and walked off to the 17th tee.

He then parred 17 and 18, posting a score of 66. And, at the end of the day, he had lost ground to the leaders.

At dinner, Dave was smiling, "I pulled the right club on 16," he stated, grinned at Bart. "Bart only had to swing." Laughter permeated the table and even nearby tables. So many present thrilled to be dining in proximity to this rising star.

"So true. Honey," Rachel smiled, kissing Dave. "What would Bart do without you?"

Bart shook his head and laughed. He looked about the table, jostled Justin, who adored Bart's attention. "I don't know what I'd do without this team!"

PapaWall stood, lifted his water glass. Everyone at his table followed, and slowly, every diner in the room, stood, hoisting a glass. "To 'Team DeMarco;'" PapaWall toasted.

Bart was at -12, but trailed seven golfers. Bubba and Dustin lead the Tournament at -17, Phil and Jordan Spieth stood at -15, Justin Thomas and Australian, Adam Scott, at -14. At -13 was a compelling story, Kevin Hall, playing on a Sponsor's exemption, was in his early 30's and deaf since the age of 2. Hall, the very pleasant, Ohio State graduate, was a past winner of the Big Ten Championship. A big hitter, he would be paired with Bart on Sunday.

The conversation, steered by Rachel, moved to the possible dates for Dave and Rachel's wedding. Rachel wanted a summer wedding, at home, and smiled at her Dad. "How about on Monday, June 17th?"

"This coming June?" Heather asked, surprised.

Rachel nodded, looked to Angela for support, who smiled. "Mom, Angela and I were discussing the date. It would be the day after the Classic." She smiled. "Bart and Angela's families will all be at our house." She smiled at Bart. "Dave's family could come to the Tournament, and stay for the wedding." Her eyes danced with excitement. "Dave's sister will, hopefully, be a Bridesmaid."

"Have you even discussed this with Dave?" Heather asked, on a laugh.

"Of course, I have, Mom." She took Dave's hand. "Dave thinks it will be fine."

"Would that cause a problem or concern for Celia?" MamaWall asked. "She's getting married that Saturday in Gloucester."

"Actually," Angela said, "I spoke to Celia, and she is fine with the plan."

"The only thing," Rachel added, looking hopefully at her Dad. "I told Celia that you would be happy to fly everybody home on the company jet that Tuesday morning."

PapaWall looked into his daughter's eyes, smiled and nodded his head. "Sure baby, of course." He rose, walked to Rachel and embraced her. Father and daughter clung to each other. There was a tear in his eye when he addressed his wife. "Heather, I'll be busy with the Tournament."

Rachel jumped in. "Mom and I will do everything, Daddy." She flashed him a loving smile, and he melted.

"Okay, Baby," he looked to Heather, a question in his eye.

Heather smiled. "Don't worry, we'll take care of everything, Dad." She beamed a smile on the happy group. "Phil," she winked. "You, Dave and Bart take care of the Tournament and the children we want to help, we'll plan the wedding." She met his eyes. "You just think about walking your daughter down the aisle."

Bart smiled and caught Dave's eye. "See, Dave, I told you." He laughed. "They don't need us." That brought laughter from all.

"One thing, Rachel," Heather suggested. "You do realize that your wedding will be on a Monday?"

Heather laughed. "Angela and I discussed that." She looked at her mother. "Mom, the Classic will be a huge event in Manitoba. The wedding guests will welcome a day off."

As they excitedly discussed wedding plans, a young boy, hesitantly, approached the table. Mmr. DdeMmarco," he stuttered. "Mmay, I,I have y,your ssig,sig,nnature?" He held out an autograph book and a pen.

Bart took the book and pen, smiled at him. "What's your name?" He asked.

"Jjimmy," he responded, nervously. Justin slid over on his chair, "Jimmy," he said, "pplease sit down, I,I'm Justin." Jimmy looked at Bart, who smiled and nodded. "Please, Jimmy, sit down."

At that point, Jimmy's parents approached the table. Jimmy's Dad, offered his hand. "Bart, I'm Carlo Venuti," he stated. He spoke well, but with a heavy Italian accent. "This is my wife, Cara," he added. "Of course," he smiled, "you've met our Jimmy." He shrugged. "I'm sorry if Jimmy disturbed your dinner."

Bart signed his book. He turned to Angela and smiled. "Please take our photo?" He asked. Angela smiled as she rose, posed Jimmy and Justin with Bart. "Smile you handsome guys," she encouraged, as she snapped the photo. She looked to Cara Venuti and smiled. She offered her hand. "Hello, Mrs. Venuti, I'm Angela DeMarco. If you give me your address I'll send you the photo for Jimmy."

"Thank you, Angela." She paused. "Please call me Cara."

Bart shook Carlo's hand, smiled at Jimmy. "Jimmy did not disturb us." He smiled. "Please, Mr. Venuti, won't you join us for dinner?"

Jimmy's eyes lit. Carlo hesitated. His wife squeezed his hand and Carlo smiled. He addressed Bart. "If it isn't too much trouble, I know it would be a thrill for Jimmy."

Bart signaled to their waiter, "please, Sir," he called. "Could we arrange to have the Venuti's join us?" As the wait staff extended the table, added and positioned the chairs, Bart introduced the Walleston's, and, Dave and Linda, who was dining with the family.

Heather took Cara's hand. "It's so nice to meet you, Cara, please call me Heather." The mothers, who each dealt with the challenges of a son who struggled with speech, bonded immediately.

Phil shook Carlo's hand. "So glad that you can join us." He paused. "Are you here for the Tournament?"

Carlo smiled. "Yes, we live in Tucson, but when Jimmy heard that Bart DeMarco, 'Stutter Boy,' was playing in Arizona, he just had to see his hero."

Jimmy was indeed excited about sitting and dining with his hero. Excitedly, he asked Bart questions, stumbling badly with his stutter. It was Justin that touched Jimmy's arm. "Jjimmy," Justin began. He took a deep breath and exhaled. "Pplease, relax," Justin smiled. "Bart, sshowed me to breath and try to relax before sspeaking." He smiled. "It hhelps."

Bart looked and caught PapaWall's eye. The silent message was clear, 'this is what we're playing for!'

"It sure was a big night," Bart said to Angela as they entered their suite. He smiled, pulled her close. "When did you speak to Celia?"

Angela laughed as they kissed. "I called her yesterday." Angela shrugged. "We had a long talk. I worried that Celia would feel that we were minimizing her big day."

Bart kissed her neck. "And?"

Angela laughed. "She was amazing." She grinned as Bart picked her up, cradling her in his arms. Angela wrapped her arms around his neck, kissed him. "Okay, Celia was fine with it all." Angela giggled as he dropped her on the bed.

"You just relax," he smiled as he slowly disrobed her. "You are so beautiful," he said. "I could look at you all day."

Angela smiled, raised her brows, "look at me, you said?" She teased.

Bart laughed as he disrobed. "I need to be relaxed for tomorrow, Angela." He kissed her. "You do want to help me, right?"

She laughed. "Are you trying to take advantage of me, Mr. DeMarco?"

He savored her body, smiled. "Absolutely," he stated.

"Good," she laughed. "Never stop, my love." She kissed him. "I want you so relaxed."

Wonderfully relaxed, they laid together, in their favorite position, Bart lying on his back and Angela resting her head on Bart's chest, gently touching. "We fly home tomorrow," Bart stated with a smile. "And, right to the hospital to bring your Dad home."

"That will be wonderful, Bart," she paused, caressed him lovingly. "Thank you for helping my Dad and my family."

Bart kissed her head. "Oh, that feels so good," he said softly. "Our family, Angela, okay?"

"Okay," she said softly. "It's just so kind." She paused, smiled. "How do I re-pay you?"

He met her smile, lifted Angela to lay on him, enjoying her soft body settling on him. "Two things, Angela." He said. "Never tell them about the money."

She looked into his eyes, nodded, and smiled as she wriggled into position, "and, two?"

He closed his eyes and groaned with pleasure. "Just, always love me."

Chapter Sixty-Two

It was Super Bowl Sunday and the final round of the Phoenix Open. The crowd topped 200,000 on a beautifully bright and sunny day.

Bart and Kevin Hall stood on the 1st tee. Bart approached Kevin and offered his hand. Bart saw that Kevin and his caddie spoke in sign language. The golfers and caddies exchanged pleasantries when Donna Caponi approached.

"Bart," she began, "you are 5 strokes behind the leaders. Do you think that you can catch them?"

Bart smiled. "Donna, I don't think it's the 5 strokes that is the problem." He shrugged. "I have seven great golfers that I need to jump over." He paused. "I'm just going to try to post a low score and see what happens."

Donna smiled. "Good luck today," she offered, and moved off of the tee box.

Bart's Battalion was on hand to cheer him to victory. Bart saw the mass of his kids, sporting their buttons and waving their signs. Bart calculated that there were a few thousand children and parents standing on the first tee and down the fairway. Smiling, he waded into them, high fiving and greeting and thanking them all. "After the round, I'll wait and sign autographs and take photos with all of you," he promised.

Dave and Bart, as well as PapaWall and Justin, wore their Sunday colors, of red, white and blue, with the U.S. flag and the Manitoba Oil logo on his chest and Canada's Maple leaf on the sleeve.

Bart was eager to give chase. Dave and he had agreed to take reasonable risks to set up birdie opportunities. And, thus far, it was working.

"After the 5th hole, Bart DeMarco is -3 and charging." Jim Nantz stated. "Johnny, do you think Bart can catch them?"

"I think Bart can and will post a low score, but," he hesitated. "There are quality golfers ahead of him, Jim. I think winning will be tough."

Bart just kept on posting birdies and after the 9th hole he was -5 for the day, -17 for the tournament. Of course, certain of the leaders were also playing well. Bart was three shots back, and had overtaken half of the players ahead of him. But, Dustin Johnson, Jordan Spieth and Adam Scott were also playing well.

Playing the home nine, Bart kept on rolling, and was -8 when he and Dave passed through the tunnel and onto the 16th tee.

When Bart came into view, the crowd, who had been enjoying the sun washed bleachers and the adult beverages, for over 6 hours, began to cheer; "Ace, Ace, Ace," Bart waved to the crowd, smiled at Kevin Hall, who was playing well at -3 for the round.

As a non-exempt player, Hall was striving for a top 10 finish to assure him a spot in the next PGA Tournament. He presently stood in a 7th place tie on the scoreboard. With a top 10 payday, if he again played well the following week, he would climb the world rankings, making it far easier to qualify for PGA and European Tour events. Bart was quietly cheering for Kevin. He felt that Kevin was a kindred spirit.

"If Bart birdies two of the last three holes," Johnny Miller explained, "he will have shot a ten under par score of 62, a personal best in his brief career, and will likely be the clubhouse leader with a -22 score."

"But," Jim Nantz questioned, "will that be enough, Johnny?"

In the DeMarco living room, Franco and Mario, were present after having had another successful fishing voyage. The family and friends gathered, listened carefully and anxiously.

When the green cleared, Bart, with the honor, teed his ball and went through his pre-shot routine. He smiled and moved over the ball.

"I'd love to know what he's thinking that brings on that smile." Rachel whispered to Angela. "I just don't think we have that whole story."

Angela glanced at Rachel and smiled. "No?" Angela queried, with raised brows. She laughed. "Some things are best kept in confidence."

Bart took his smooth and sweet swing. "Pretty swing," Johnny Miller said, quietly. "Never change that swing," he counseled. The ball soared high and landed and rolled out 10 feet past the pin. Loud cheers greeted the effort.

Kevin Hall hit a beautiful shot that landed inside of Bart's ball, and on the same line. The crowd rose and roared its approval. Bart tapped Kevin's shoulder and pointed to the crowd. Kevin's eyes lit, he smiled and waved to the gallery.

On the green Bart, with Dave's assistance, lined up the putt. Kevin Hall watched closely as Bart's putt would teach him the line.

Bart stroked his birdie putt dead center of the hole. The crowd roared and Bart smiled and tipped his cap. Kevin followed Bart into the hole with his birdie. Things were looking up for Hall.

Bart birdied the 18th hole to post a score of 62 and, at the moment, a tournament leading score of -22.

Bart's battalion exploded in jubilation. "Well Johnny," Jim Nantz stated for the vast television audience. "Bart DeMarco is in the clubhouse, with the lead."

Mario wrapped his arm around Celia. He beamed a smile, kissed Celia, "he's doing great."

Celia looked into Mario's eyes. "Just like his big brother!"

Franco took Rosa's hand, looked at Mario with Celia, and Lucia, happily sitting next to Franco Palermo. He smiled as he looked into her eyes. "Rosa, you did great!" He said softly.

Rosa smiled, "we did it together, Franco. You are a good father." She squeezed his hand, 'Team DeMarco,' she said quietly and kissed her husband. She, then, looked at those gathered. Excitedly, she asked, "Is Bart going to win?"

Franco Palermo smiled. "I certainly hope so, Mrs. DeMarco," he paused, looked at Lucia, and shrugged. "But, there are three golfers within 1 stroke, and they have 4 holes to play."

Rosa smiled at Franco. "Thank you, Franco, we'll pray for Bart and then, if he wins," she raised her brows, "you can celebrate." Franco laughed and Lucia blushed.

Bart left the 18th green and embraced Angela. Donna Caponi was conducting the interviews and approached Bart, who smiled and held Angela close.

"Hi Bart," Donna began. She smiled at Angela, looked back to Bart. "A 62, a great round. Do you think it will be enough?"

Bart smiled. "Donna, I'd like you to meet, my wife, Angela," he turned, holding Angela about her waist, "Angela, this is Donna Caponi, a great LPGA Champion." They smiled at each other.

Bart turned to Donna and shrugged. "I hope it will be enough, but, there are some great golfers still out there." He laughed. "You know Donna, I've often heard that you cannot win a tournament on Thursday, but you sure can lose one." He shrugged. "That front nine on Thursday may have cost me."

Donna smiled and nodded. She knew, and appreciated, that Bart brought the subject up to spare her needing to appear negative in the interview. Another example of his innate kindness, she thought. "So, Bart, what happened on Thursday?"

Bart flashed a smile that showed just how young he really was. "Well, my coach, Dave Gilliss, described it as 'testosterone poisoning.'" He laughed. "My beautiful wife, here, thought it a case of excessive male ego!"

Donna, surprised by the comment, laughed. Still laughing, she looked to Angela.

Angela's cheeks blushed red. She looked at Donna, hoping to defend Bart. "You know Donna," she said. "Bart's still young!"

Donna still smiling, looked at Angela with amusement in her eyes. "Angela," she responded. "That excessive male ego thing, doesn't really go away as men age."

Angela, caught by surprise by Donna's words, laughed aloud. Donna could not help but laugh with the young bride.

Bart, still holding Angela, looked on smiling. Seeing Angela laughing and at ease was a wonderful sight.

"Johnny," Jim Nantz chuckled. "I think we need to re-direct this conversation.

Johnny Miller laughed aloud. "I think my wife might just agree with Donna."

As expected, Dustin Johnson and Jordan Spieth both came in at -23, to edge Bart. The Champion to be determined in a play-off.

"Hard heads," Rosa said, as she eyed her husband and son. "The DeMarco men have hard heads." She smiled at Celia. "You know, Celia, Mario is just like his father and brother."

"And, proud of it!" Mario asserted with a laugh and kissed Celia, who laughed with him.

As promised Bart met with the children and parents of YES and for 90 minutes, signed autographs, posed for photos, and started a new tradition by taking a group photo of Bart's Battalion. All the children, many wearing their 'I'm with Stutter Boy' buttons, holding up YES signs, beamed as Bart put them front and center. Justin stood with Bart as Mama and Papa Wall looked on with a deep satisfaction.

"You guessed right with Bart," Heather said.

Phil smiled, held his wife. "I sure did!"

Chapter Sixty-Three

Angela and Bart walked into Sal's room at the Boston General Hospital's physical therapy unit. They found and embraced Sal and Maria, Tina was at home with the boys, and preparing for their return. Also present was Dr. Howard, who smiled brightly.

Bart smiled at the Doctor. "Shall we see my father-in-law walk?" Bart challenged with a smile.

Sal reached out for Bart, who clutched his hand. Sal pulled on Bart's arm and slowly lifted himself to his feet. He released Bart's hand and walked gingerly and carefully across the room to Maria. They stood embracing each other, tears of joy rolling down their cheeks. Sal put his arm about Maria's shoulders. "Bart," he raised his chin proudly. "I am ready to walk out of this hospital with you."

Angela overcome with emotion embraced Dr. Howard. "Thank you, so much, Doctor." She wiped her eyes. "I will always be thankful to you."

Doc Howard released Angela. "You are very welcome, Angela." He smiled. "I think that Bart and I have dates to discuss."

Bart laughed. "You bet we do, Doc!" He paused, embraced the Doctor. "I will send you my schedule and when I'll be home." He smiled. "I look forward to hitting the links with you." Bart took Doc Howard's hand. "Thank you for everything."

The limo, Bart had arranged, was waiting to receive the happy family. Bart and Sal walked through the grand doors of the Hospital, Sal holding Bart's strong arm, smiling as he felt the, bracing and invigorating, February chill.

"This feels good," he said. A few sportswriters and photographers were present to record the moment that Bart had challenged Sal, so publicly, to accomplish. Sal was delighted and smiled for the cameras.

"Anything to say, Bart?" Asked a Boston sportswriter, a smile on his face. Everybody enjoys a happy ending.

Bart, with Angela's help, settled Sal comfortably in the limo. He turned and smiled. "This is a great day for our family." Bart began. "My father-in-law has a long and painful road ahead, but we will all be there for him." He waved, thanked the reporters for sharing a happy event with his family, and ducked into the limo. He faced the driver. "Please, Sir, take this fisherman home to Gloucester,"

Tina, Nick and Giuseppe greeted their Dad at home. Sal, already feeling weary, held Bart's arm, as he ascended the few steps to the front door. Bart walked him to his comfortable recliner, where Sal settled with a smile. Sal opened his arms to Tina and the boys, who happily embraced their Dad.

Angela hugged Maria, who shed tears of thanks that Sal was home. "I only dreamed and prayed that this day would come," Maria whispered to Angela.

Then, smiling happily, Maria looked to Angela. "Angela, you get your father some wine and Bart a cold drink." She faced Tina, "come on, we need to get dinner started." Bart smiled in happy recognition that order had returned to the Curcuru home.

Maria and Tina hustled to the kitchen, where Maria discovered that Tina had been busy preparing some of her father's favorite dishes. Angela entered the kitchen to the aroma of a simmering shrimp sauce to be served over spaghetti. On a tray was a platter of her Dad's favorite cheeses, Sicilian olives, prosciutto, salami and fresh Italian bread. Angela added a glass of wine for her Dad and a tall Arnold Palmer for Bart. Smiling, she hefted the tray and went into the living room.

"Papa, look what Tina did for your homecoming." Angela said proudly, kissed her Dad and smiled. "She, also, cooked a wonderful meal for you."

Sal smiled. Recognizing that Angela was supporting her sister, he was proud of his family.

Dinner was joyous. Sal had more of an appetite than one would expect. He sipped his wine and smiled from the head of the table. "It is good to be home," he expressed. He smiled at Tina. "Thank you, Bambina. Dinner was wonderful!"

Tina smiled at her Dad. "I'm so glad you are home, Papa. I love you."

Sal's eyes filled with pride. "I love you, Bambina." He looked about, thinking how in a challenging time, his family had pulled together. "Thank you all, I am so proud of my family."

Sal looked to Bart, "you and Angela will be staying here?"

Tina jumped in. She looked to Bart and Angela. "I made up our room for you two, just like before." She smiled, raised her brows hopefully.

Angela smiled at Bart, who laughed, knowing that Angela was seeking his ascent.

"Yes," Bart said, with a smile for Angela. "Of course, we'll stay." He looked to Sal. "After dinner, Angela and I will go see my family." He paused, looked to Maria, "will you be okay settling Papa in for the night?"

"Of course," Maria stated. "Tina and I will be fine."

Tina smiled at her Dad. "I'm here for you, Papa," she said with feeling. The look exchanged between father and daughter spoke volumes of family pride.

Bart and Angela entered the DeMarco house to discover that his Dad and Mom, Mario and Celia, Franco Palermo and Lucia, were there to greet them. It was a warm reunion. Of course, Rosa embraced her son and daughter-in-law. She smiled at Angela, "so, you think my boy has a big ego, I see?"

Angela laughed, "Oh, absolutely, the biggest," she stated.

"I don't know," Celia said with a laugh. "It would be tough to have a bigger ego than Mario," she joked. "They're two of a kind."

"Hard heads," Rosa stated on a laugh. "The DeMarco men have hard heads." She paused, and smiled at her husband. "But, they have good hearts." She pointed her finger at Angela and Celia. "You two, make sure that you take good care of my boys!"

Angela and Celia accepted the good natured scolding with a smile. "Yes, Mom, of course," they said in unison and laughed aloud.

"I'm so glad you are here," Franco Palermo interjected. "Now, at least, Mrs. DeMarco is wagging her finger at you two." He laughed, took Lucia's hand. "I have been her target for weeks now."

Lucia nudged him and flashed her smile. "You seem to be doing okay," she said.

Rosa shook her head and wagged her finger at Franco. "You, Mr. Palermo, I'm keeping my eye on you." That brought laughter as Lucia squeezed Franco's hand.

Mario announced that he and Celia had closed on their new home. "Your apartment is ready to be inspected, Sir," Mario joked, as he handed Bart the keys to the apartment at 11 Church Street. "We aren't sailing until tomorrow night, but, I have to do a few things in the morning. So, how about you and Angela check out the house tomorrow morning?"

Bart smiled at Angela. "Sounds good," he responded.

"That was fun!" Bart said as he lay back in bed, with his arm around Angela, whose head rested on his chest.

Angela grinned. "Exactly what part was the most fun for you?" She asked, unable to contain her laugh. "My Mom directing me to serve you or your mother scolding Celia and me?"

Bart laughed as he gently stroked her back. Well," he began. "Seeing your Dad walk so proudly out of the Hospital was great." He stated. "Watching the connection between your Dad and Tina was special." He continued as he kissed her head. "Of course, there was the great sense of relief on your Mom's face as she, so happily," he stressed on a laugh, "took care of your Dad."

Bart pulled Angela to him, enjoying the warmth and softness of her body. "Then, you counseling Tina on dealing with her broken heart." He kissed her. "You did great, by the way."

"Thanks," Angela said, snuggling closer.

He laughed. "Then, there's the guilty pleasure of enjoying my wife in her childhood bed." He added.

Angela laughed with him. "You like that, do you?"

"Oh yes, Princess, I do." He kissed her. "We egotistical guys just love having beautiful and loving wives."

"And," Bart added with a laugh. "It was great when my Mom scolded you to take better care of your dear husband."

Angela playfully poked him in the ribs. "Italian mothers and their sons!" She let out an exaggerated sigh. "What's a girl to do?"

"That wasn't very loving," he joked. "I might just have to tell my Mom."

Angela laughed as she climbed on top of Bart. "Oh, please Sir, don't," she pleaded with a grin, as she wriggled into position. "What can I do to make up for my transgression, Sir?"

He kissed her. "I'll think of something," he promised with a happy smile. He kissed her again. "Angela, I love you so much," he affirmed, to her delight.

At bit before 9am, Bart unlocked the front door of their new Church Street home. He threw the door open, then scooped Angela up into his arms and carried her across the threshold, closing and locking the door.

Angela wrapped her arms around his neck as he walked in to the entrance hall, then through the empty rooms. "You can put me down now," she exclaimed, on a laugh. "Hey, why do you look so disappointed?" She looked about, "this is a great apartment."

Bart kissed her, "I was hoping to put you down on a nice soft surface and have my way with you."

Angela laughed. "Oh, I see, that's why you locked the door?" She kissed him. "Soon enough, I promise." Bart set her down and in her carefully deliberate way, Angela walked from room to room, jotting down a list of necessary purchases. She had Bart measuring to determine the length of couch, loveseat, and chair for the living room. She measured and calculated the size of the dining set that the kitchen would comfortably hold.

She walked from the kitchen to the spacious dining room. "This is a good sized dining room." She smiled. "We will have wonderful dinner parties."

She tapped the pencil against her chin, thoughtfully, as she strolled happily to the living room. "Would you prefer wood or glass tables for the living room?" She asked. Angela stopped and smiled, as she looked at the fireplace and hearth. She rose on her toes to kiss Bart. "It will be cozy to cuddle together before a glowing fire."

Bart smiled, "it will." He took Angela in his arms, kissed her sweetly. "Princess, you furnish our home as you see fit." He paused. "Except, I will choose my recliner for the living room and we'll choose our mattress together."

Angela held him close. "Sounds good to me, my love."

He smiled. "I will spend the day with your Dad, while you take your Mom and Tina to furnish and outfit our home." He laughed. "Ask Tina to shop in the kitchen store and help you select all the pots, pans and gadgets you will need to create fabulous meals, like you did in Florida."

Angela smiled at Bart, overwhelmed by his kindness. "Really? You'll take care of my Dad and my brothers?"

Bart smiled, pulled her to him and kissed her deeply. "Of course, I want you to have a great day with your mother and Tina." He paused. "I think your Mom needs a break." He stated.

Angela smiled up at Bart. "Do you think that your Mom would be interested in joining us?"

Bart smiled, picked up Angela, kissed her and twirled her about. "I think that she would love that." He kissed her. "Especially, that you thought of her." He held her close. "You are so great, Princess!"

Angela laughed, she kissed Bart. "As you always say, Bart, our family, not mine or yours."

Bart nodded. "I love it that you are so smart." He smiled, "and, so kind." He pulled her close, kissed her. "And, of course, so sexy!"

Bart arranged an early morning meeting with John Palermo and Harry Winston to tweak his schedule and do some planning. Dave, who was in Manitoba, was present by telephone. Bart wanted to be home to settle his household and give Angela some time to help her mother care for and pamper her Dad.

"A win and a 3rd place finish!" Harry congratulated Bart. "Very good, indeed." He grinned. "You are really climbing in the World Rankings.

Bart shrugged. "I should have won Phoenix," he stated with a touch of anger. "I lost my head."

"Bart, give yourself a break." John Palermo advised. "It's a learning process, you were carried away, but, you dealt with it all so well." He laughed. "And, you really handled Caleb Lawson." He shook his head. "That mean spirited hypocrite was really put in his place."

"Where did you get the background on Lawson?" Harry asked.

Bart shrugged. "I asked Mr. Walleston to look into his background. I figured that he would come after me on my age." He smiled. "It wasn't that difficult. He walked right into it."

"He sure did," Harry responded with a laugh. "Still, it was a mistake on my part to agree to have you appear." He shrugged. "I'm sorry about that, Bart."

Bart shrugged. "We all make mistakes, no worries, Harry."

John Palermo looked on quietly. Once again impressed at the inherent goodness of Bart, but even more-so at his maturity and intelligence. John recognized that Bart wanted no conflicts or ill-feelings within 'Team DeMarco.'

Harry nodded and smiled. "So, Bart, what do you think about the upcoming schedule?"

"Well, Mr., sorry, I mean, Harry," he laughed. "I thought I'd play the Pebble Beach Pro-Am next week." He shrugged. "Since, I'm not ranked high enough to play in the match play tournament, I will play in Bermuda." He sat back. "It should be a good tune-up for the Masters." He smiled. "And, maybe, I can recruit a few European Players to play in the Classic." He paused. "Then, down to Augusta to prepare for the Masters."

"Sounds good," Harry agreed.

"So Bart, I'll see you at Pebble Beach on Monday?" Dave Gilliss asked.

"Yes, Dave, we'll see you at the hotel." Bart responded. "Will Rachel be there?"

"No, Bart, not this trip." He said, some regret in his tone. "But, the family will be at Augusta for the Masters."

Bart quickly considered his options. He didn't want Angela to be alone in Monterey, while Bart and Dave practiced. Then, have to walk the course alone. He smiled. "Okay, Dave, see you in California." He laughed. "This time we win!"

"Sounds good," Dave responded. "See you Monday." He hung up.

"What will it take for me to qualify for the Ryder Cup team this fall?" Bart asked. "I'd love to be on that team."

Harry shrugged, he sat back and eyed Bart. "Win the Masters, Bart. I think that should do it."

Bart nodded and smiled. "I'll see what I can do." He rose. "Thanks for meeting so early. I have to get home to take Angela's Dad to physical therapy, then relax for the day with him and the boys."

John smiled. "Where's Angela and her mother?" He paused. "Why not hire a home health care aid?"

Bart shook his head. "It may come to that, but right now my father-in-law needs his family." He paused. "He's been through so much." Then, Bart laughed, "as for Angela, Tina, and her mother, and mine, for that matter, they are going shopping to furnish our new home."

John Palermo nodded, eyes on Bart. He felt a new layer of respect and admiration for this young man.

"Good move, Bart." Harry said with a smile. "That kind of shopping is brutal."

"My thoughts exactly," Bart agreed. "But, Angela is excited," he shrugged. "So, everyone will be happy." He headed out, John watched him leave with a smile.

Bart arrived at the Curcuru home by 8:30am. He found the women assembled, ready and excited for their shopping day. He glanced at his watch. "Wow! You are all ready to go?"

Maria grinned. "Papa and the boys have had breakfast," she handed Bart a sheet of paper with instructions. He looked at it and smiled. "I made lunch and dinner and left them marked in the refrigerator." She continued as she eyed Bart. "There's enough food for all four of you." She pointed her finger. "Preheat the oven to 350 degrees and warm the food for 30 minutes." She paused, eyed Bart. "30 minutes, Bart, okay?"

Bart nodded. He looked at Angela and smiled. Angela did her best to stifle a laugh.

"Papa's therapy appointment is at 10:30am." She studied Bart. "Make sure you leave early, it takes Papa a long time to get in and out of the car." She hesitated, fretted. "Maybe, I should stay home?"

Sal laughed. "Go Maria, help your daughter." He paused and smiled. "Bart, the boys and I will be fine."

It was clear that Maria was unconvinced. She looked to Angela, who grinned and took her mother's hand. "They'll be fine, Mom, come on, let's go." She paused. "I have to furnish six rooms and two baths." She eyed Maria, spoke softly. "Mom, I need your help."

Angela's plea was the tipping point. "Okay, okay, we go."

Bart took the boys and Sal to Physical Therapy. The session was, a tiring and physically challenging, 90 minutes long, with the Therapist pushing Sal hard. By the time that the group arrived home, Sal was exhausted and the boys were hungry.

Bart settled Sal in his recliner. Satisfied that he was comfortable, he looked at the boys. "How does pizza sound?"

Nick and Giuseppe smiled and nodded in approval. "Okay, how about I order a cheese pizza for you guys," he looked at Sal, who was reclined and dozing, decided to not wake him. He also ordered a large sausage, pepper and onion.

When the pizzas arrived, Sal awoke to a living room picnic. Bart had spread a blanket on the floor, where the boys sat with their pizza and lemonade.

"Bart, Maria cooked food," Sal said as he looked at the boys, happy and smiling as they watched 'Jurassic Park' while seated on the blanket.

Nick smiled up. "Papa, Bart ordered pizza and said we could have a picnic."

Sal laughed. "Too much trouble to warm the food?"

Bart laughed. "We used to do this on Friday evenings when we were kids." He shrugged. "I thought the boys would enjoy it." He grinned. "Besides, it seemed to be a bit too much trouble, pre-heating the oven, setting the timer." He shrugged and smiled. "Pizza is easy and fun."

Sal nodded. He smiled at Bart. "I bet the girls are having fun." Sal suggested, as he accepted a plate with two slices of pizza from Bart and a glass of wine. "Maria loves to shop, especially with her daughters." He laughed. "And, they will go out for lunch." He paused, looked at Bart. "Maria deserves the break."

"She does," Bart smiled. "I hope sausage, pepper and onion is okay?"

Sal nodded, "Oh, the pizza is fine, Bart." He looked at his son-in-law and smiled. "Thanks for doing this. Maria really needed a day to relax and enjoy."

Bart smiled. "My Dad always said, 'family takes care of family.'" He winked. "And, I'll bet they are having a great time."

The shopping went into the evening, with the ladies also enjoying a dinner out. Bart ordered Chinese food for dinner and repeated the picnic, as they watched 'Superman.' It was a happy pair of boys that washed, brushed their teeth and settled into bed.

At 9pm Bart helped Sal up the stairs and to bed. It took a bit of time, but Bart managed to settle Sal comfortably and return to the living room, where he put on the Golf Channel. He relaxed from what had been a strenuous day. He chuckled as he thought that he was more exhausted by taking care of Sal and the boys than he was after playing a round of golf, on the tour.

It was after 10pm when Angela, Tina and Maria arrived home, alight with a buoyancy that Bart hadn't seen in his mother-in-law in months. Maria hugged Bart and thanked him. She looked about the room. "What happened here?" She asked. Then, she laughed. "Oh, I don't care, did everything go well?" Not waiting for a response, she started up to the bedrooms to check on Sal and the boys.

"Everything went fine." Bart laughed, as he called out to Maria as she hustled to the stairway. Looking to Angela and Tina, he added, "we had a picnic, the boys loved it, your Dad just stayed in his chair," he explained. "It went okay." He smiled, at the positively bubbly, Angela. "So, how did it go for you?"

Angela went into his arms. "It went great, we furnished the house." She twirled. "I bought a king sized bed for us." She looked at her sister. "I bought everything for the living room." She eyed him. "The salesman showed me a recliner that I just knew you would love, big, and with soft leather." She waited for his objection, but he said nothing. Angela noted however, with concern, the set of his jaw. "I told the salesman that if you didn't like it that they would have to take it back." She explained. "He asked if the recliner was for Bart DeMarco." She shook her head. "Bart, he recognized me, can you believe that?"

Bart said nothing, merely eyed her.

"The salesman was great," she turned to Tina. "Wasn't he, Tina?"

Tina forced a smile. "Bart, you have all the best kitchen equipment, Angela will be able to cook anything." She laughed. "I even picked up some cookbooks." She smiled at Angela. "The salesman was nice." She looked at Bart, saw the set of his jaw. Sensing the imminent need for a marital discussion, Tina looked from Angela to Bart. "Should I go?" Tina asked.

"When he discovered the furniture was for Bart DeMarco," Angela continued, in a rush, "he showed us the best stuff in the store." She paused, winced. "He showed me a mattress and box-spring that felt just like the one you liked so much at MamaWall's house."

"So, you bought a recliner and a mattress?" He looked at her with a surprised expression. "As I recall, Angela, it wasn't the mattress that I enjoyed at the Wallestons." He set hard eyes on her. "It was the girl."

She looked at him. "He promised delivery on Friday." She hurriedly added. "I just thought that we could have the house set up before we fly to California." She cringed, sought his eyes. "Are you angry?"

"So," he said, with a quiet intensity, "I specifically asked you not to buy my recliner and our mattress, and you simply ignored me." He paused, eyed Angela. "He must have been some salesman."

Bart turned his back on Angela and looked at Tina. "How about this Tina, my wife has a great day shopping with her sister, her mother and mine. I stay here take care of her Dad, and she completely ignored my wishes." He paused, his voice rose a few octaves. "She disrespected her husband, because the salesman was a nice guy!"

Tina's eyes went wide, as Bart winked at her and flashed a smile. He turned back to face Angela with anger flashing.

Angela looked stricken. "I didn't intend to disrespect you, Bart. I'm so sorry."

"Tina," Bart continued. "You're her sister, what do you think that I should do?"

"Bart, I honestly think that Angela is sincere in her sorrow." She paused, tapped her chin. "Still, you cannot just let this pass."

"No?" Bart asked. "What do you feel is fair?"

"You know Bart, both my Mom and I told her that she should not buy what you specifically asked her not to buy." She paused. "We told her that to buy those items in defiance of her husband's requests was simply wrong." She thought for a long moment, smiled. "You know, Bart, in the gay community, Angela would, at the very least, get a paddling." She nodded. "I think that you should take her to your room and paddle her bottom. Make it smoky red."

Shocked at the suggestion, Angela blurted, "Tina! Are you crazy?"

"No, Angela, I think that's fair." Tina eyed her sister. "You did totally disrespect your husband." She paused. "And, Bart has always been there for you." She nodded. "Really, for all of us."

Angela paused and absorbed Tina's words. She nodded, looked at Bart. "You have been there for all of us, Bart, I love you so," she flushed, "please don't do this." She pleaded.

Tina looked at Bart. "I suggest you take her to your room, I'll bring you a paddle."

Maria returned to the living room, walked through to the kitchen and returned, smiling. "Pizza and Chinese?" She asked.

Bart smiled. "Cooking seemed to be too much trouble, so we had picnics, watched movies. Everybody had fun."

Maria looked around at the mess, "yes, I can see that." But, she smiled at Bart. "Thank you for today."

Bart smiled. "Did you have a good day, Mom?"

"I did," she exulted. "And, your Mother did too. It was wonderful shopping all together." She nodded. "And, Angela bought beautiful things for your home." She grinned. "And, we went out for lunch and dinner, too!" She laughed, delightedly, did a little twirl, "thank you for today."

Bart hugged Maria. "I'm glad you had a good day, Mom." He turned to Tina and smiled. "Tina, thanks for helping, today." He looked at Angela. "How about we head upstairs, I'm tired."

Angela exchanged a look with her mother and Tina. She took a deep breath. "Okay, good night, Mom, Tina, we'll see you for breakfast."

Tina smiled at Bart, trying to help. "Bart, how about I make eggs Benedict for breakfast tomorrow?" She smiled. "I make a great Hollandaise sauce." She paused, eyed Bart. "I'll stop by your room directly."

Bart smiled. "That sounds great, Tina, Thanks."

When they entered the bedroom, Angela faced Bart. "Bart," she began. "I'm sorry, I just got caught up in the shopping and the salesman knew all about you." She pleaded. "He's a big fan." Her eyes misted. "How about I call tomorrow and cancel the recliner and mattress?" She watched him closely. Her eyes filled. "You wouldn't really...would you?"

He heard panic in her voice, knew the joke had gone far enough.

Bart walked to her. "Please stand still," he instructed. With a serious expression, he began to disrobe her. Her cheeks reddened in nervous anticipation. He looked into her eyes, planted a kiss on her sweet lips. He put his hands on her face. "Princess, as long as I breathe, nobody will ever hurt you." He smiled. "You are my love. And, I will give my life to protect you," he smiled. "And, our children."

Angela caught his eye, she began to smile. She stood gloriously before him, as he savored her body. "You look great," he said as he scooped her into his arms, carried her to the bed and gently set her down. "Tina was just joking, Princess."

Angela studied Bart's eyes. "But, you are angry with me?" She asked, her eyes pleaded. "Bart, I would never disrespect you. I hope you know that." She paused. "I just got caught up in the excitement. I'm really sorry!"

"I don't know," he grinned, drawing a smile from his love. "Why don't I give you the chance to apologize, properly?" He shrugged, as he undressed. "In the way that you think is right. It only seems fair."

Angela breathe out a sigh of relief, "I'm going to kill Tina." She said. She smiled at Bart. "For you, my love, I'll do my best." She smiled, raised her arms. "Please come to me," she asked. "Let me earn your forgiveness." As he took her in his arms, Angela kissed him. "I'm sorry, Bart. I was wrong."

Bart laughed. "Enough said." He paused. "I was surprised," he admitted and shrugged. "But, we all stumble."

Angela looked into his eyes. "If I stumble, again, I hope to always land in your arms."

They lay in the aftermath of passion. Bart held her, as she lay her head on his chest. He whispered, "I would never hurt you, Princess." He laughed, kissed her head. "Although, Princess, the image of your smoky red bottom has some allure." He laughed. Angela blushed. "Anyway," Bart continued, "we fly to California on Monday. Dave will meet us there."

"Will the Wallestons be there?" She asked, hopeful.

"No," he stroked her back. "But, I thought I would ask Lucia or Celia, or both, to join us." He smiled as she caressed him. "How does that sound?"

"That sounds great," she paused, realized that Bart was concerned that she would be alone. "But, Bart," she offered, hoping to re-assure him. "If they can't come, I'll be okay by myself."

"I would ask Tina," he laughed, "your sweet sister," he teased, "But, right now your Mom can really use her help." He groaned. "That feels good, Princess." He exhaled. "You're making it tough to converse."

She looked up at him, with a grin, she innocently asked, "should I stop?"

"NO!" he said.

She laughed and snuggled closer. "Whatever you say."

When they lay sated, he smiled. "Oh, where was I?" He kissed her. "Right, I thought we'd ask Tina to come with us on the Bermuda trip." He paused. "Maybe," he joked, "she could bring her paddle." He laughed and Angela laughed with him.

"I swear I'm going to kill her." Angela laughed. "She really had me going." She looked up at Bart, grinned. "And, you went right along with her." Angela's eyes gleamed. She kissed Bart and smiled. "But, maybe, I deserve a few swats, if you like." She laughed, placed a grateful gaze on Bart. "Thank you for today." She smiled. "My mother really needed a day like today." She shook her head. "But, you knew that, didn't you?"

"I'm glad it went well." He responded, kissed her head. "Did my Mom enjoy herself?"

Angela smiled into his eyes. "She did, she thanked me for including her."

Bart looked at Angela, he smiled. "It was kind of you to think of her." He paused. "Princess, she was there for me when I was a boy." He sighed. "Sometimes, it all became too much. When it did, she cried with me and soothed me." He looked into Angela's eyes. "Then, you came along, Princess!" He smiled. "How did I get so lucky?" He asked with a big grin.

Angela smiled into his chest. "I asked myself that question every day." She sighed. "I guess, we should just enjoy our good fortune in finding each other."

He pulled her tight to him. Angela gently stroked him, producing a corresponding groan of pleasure. "The Bermuda Tournament is a few weeks away and your Dad should be doing better." Bart offered as they lay quietly holding and caressing each other. "Maybe, getting away would be good for Tina. I hear Bermuda in March is beautiful."

Angela smiled. "Then, we all go to Augusta to celebrate your birthday and," she laughed. "I think that they have a golf tournament in early April." Angela kissed him. "I think I heard something about that!"

Bart laughed. "That should be a great trip. The family will be there and the Wallestons."

Angela ran her hand over Bart's chest. "I was thinking that we might invite Mr. Palermo and Franco?" She paused. "The Walleston's have an extra room for them and Lucia would be so happy."

"I'll have to clear that with my Dad before we say anything to Lucia or Franco." Bart said. He laughed. "Unless, of course, you already discussed it with Lucia?"

Angela grinned into his chest. "We might have discussed it, a little."

"I'll talk to my Dad." He paused, kissed her. "I'd suggest you tell Lucia to stay quiet until I have a chance to work it out." He smiled. "My Dad will want all the details." He chuckled. "He doesn't trust Franco."

"Really?" Angela was surprised. "I thought your parents liked Franco."

"Oh, they do." Bart stated. "But, my Dad doesn't like the way he looks at Lucia." He shook his head, grinning.

She laughed. "I remember hearing the same thing about you."

Bart smiled and nodded. "And, your father was right to not trust me." He laughed and squeezed her. "My motives were very self-serving when it came to you, Princess."

She smiled at Bart. "You were there for me, Bart, you were my hero." She paused. "You protected me, you make me feel safe." She paused, kissed him. "Bart, you make me feel beautiful and desired." She smiled and kissed him. "I will always love you and cherish you."

He lifted her to lay on his body. He wrapped his arms around her. "And, you saved me, Princess, you gave me the confidence to speak, to live."

Chapter Sixty-Four

Bart's Dad and brother, Mario, were at sea, so Celia, Lucia and in a nice surprise, Bart's mother, Rosa, joined Bart and Angela and boarded the private jet at Beverly Airport for the flight to Monterrey, California. They all sat on comfortable couches facing each other. As the jet flew across the country, Celia happily investigated. "There's a kitchen here, and a bathroom with a shower." She laughed. "This is great." She looked at Bart. "Is it okay if I make a pot of coffee?"

Bart nodded. "Sure, Celia. I think there are muffins, croissants and bagels, as well." He grinned. "I'm sure hungry," he said. "In the refrigerator there should be butter, jams and all that stuff."

Rosa rose, smiled at her son. "Celia, I'll help you make some breakfast." Rosa poked around and discovered bacon and eggs in the refrigerator. "Bart," she called. "How about I make us bacon and eggs to go with the pastry?"

Angela rose, "I'll help," soon Bart heard laughter from the kitchen. It brought a smile.

The aroma was wonderful. They all sat at the conference table for breakfast. "This is great," Bart smiled and kissed Angela.

"Hey," Celia called with a grin. "Don't you be giving Angela all the credit, here," she protested. That brought laughter from all.

"So, Bart," Rosa asked, as she sipped her coffee. "How do you like the furniture for your house?" Rosa smiled. "Angela bought some beautiful things."

Bart smiled as he tucked into his eggs. "Yes, she did." He paused. "I especially like the recliner, and that wonderfully soft and comfortable mattress." He glanced at Angela, who blushed.

Rosa saw the exchange and smiled. Seeing Bart so happy made her heart sing. "I think you found a good girl, Bart." Rosa said, with a grin. "You be good to her," she instructed.

Bart laughed. "Of course, but Mom, this whole weekend in our new apartment and Angela didn't cook even one meal." He shook his head, but couldn't stifle a smile. "I'm worried."

Rosa smiled, eyed Angela. "Are you taking care of my son, Angela?" She winked. "You know he loves to eat."

Angela smiled at Rosa. "I'll always take care of your boy, Mom, I promise." She sighed. "But, it's not easy. For instance, this jet usually comes with an attendant to do the cooking and clean-up." She smiled. "Bart turned down the help." She smiled at Bart. "It seems Bart doesn't really like having strangers around, he prefers his wife to do the work."

Angela was surprised when Rosa nodded. "Vero," she said. "My Bart is right." She wagged her finger at Angela. "We take care of each other in our family."

Celia laughed. "You walked right into that one, Angela." She shook her head and tsked at Angela. "The DeMarco's are self-sufficient," she smiled at Rosa. "Right, Mom?"

"We take care of each other and we do our jobs!" Rosa stated, proudly.

Angela looked from Celia to Rosa. She noted Bart's big smile. "Liked that did you?" She asked Bart, trying, but failing to stifle her smile.

"We're DeMarco's, my love." Bart responded with the smile that Angela cherished, even when she was the butt of the joke.

Angela just smiled, looked to Rosa. "You are right, Mom." She glanced at Bart. "I'll try to do better."

Everybody thoroughly enjoyed breakfast. Once completed, they sat sipping coffee, enjoying the smooth flight.

Rosa looked at Lucia. "Lucia, you clean-up and do the dishes. I want that kitchen sparkling when we land in California."

Lucia rose, smiled. "Of course, Mom." She gathered the plates and platters and moved to the galley. Angela rose to help, eyed Lucia and smiled. Once in the kitchen galley, Lucia looked at Angela. "My Mom made it clear that I'm expected to help Mrs. Palermo when we eat there." She shook her head and laughed. "I'm not to embarrass the family. 'Only bring honor to the DeMarco name,' Mom insisted."

Angela laughed. "The DeMarco's are hard workers and good people." she shrugged. "I hate to admit it, but I think Mom's right." She shrugged. "Look how hard Dad and Mario work to make their boat a success." She paused. "And, Bart, he never stops trying to improve." She glanced at Lucia and grinned. "In everything!"

Lucia laughed. "Angela!" She said, feigning astonishment. "I don't know what you mean."

"I hope not," Angela laughed." She eyed her sister-in-law. "Lucia, Franco also comes from a good, hard working family." She paused. "It's pretty clear that he's headed to Law School and a career with his Dad." She debated with herself, but decided to speak. "Franco is infatuated with you."

Lucia sighed and smiled. "I hope so, Angela."

Angela stopped in her task, looked at Lucia. "Make sure his future isn't derailed." She paused. "You know, that's up to you."

Lucia nodded. "I know."

They arrived by limo at the Spanish Bay Resort at Pebble Beach. They found Dave, and Linda, their tutor, waiting for them. Rosa, with Lucia, Celia and Linda shared a two bedroom suite. Bart and Angela had a separate suite and Dave a suite of his own.

Everybody settled in and Bart went for a run, to work out the kinks after the cross-country flight. The plan called for some relaxing time by the pool, dinner and then a good night's rest. Bart and Dave would begin work in the morning.

On that Tuesday morning, Bart left Angela sleeping as he went for a run, followed by a workout. He returned to the suite at 8am and found Angela just awakening.

"Did you already run?" She asked, noting his sweaty clothes.

Bart smiled at his sleepy-eyed Princess. "You look so beautiful, all mussed and sleepy," he said. He nodded, "just finished my workout." He smiled at her, "rest Angela," he encouraged as he jumped into the shower. He changed into golf clothes, kissed Angela and headed out. "Have a good day, Princess. Dave and I will be practicing and playing all day." He gave her another kiss. "See you later."

On a beautiful and sunny California day, Angela was lounging by the pool with Rosa, Lucia and Celia, when Bart and Dave returned. She noted Bart's troubled expression. "Are you okay, Honey?" She asked.

Bart shook his head. "I need a shower, I'll be back and will tell you all about it." He promised, as he headed into the resort. He loped off, leaving Dave smiling and four confused women in his wake.

"What happened?" Angela asked Dave, who was still smiling as he watched Bart head into the hotel.

"Okay," Dave began. "This tournament is a Pro-Am, meaning each golfer is paired with a celebrity, an actor, singer or athlete or maybe a CEO."

Angela nodded. "Is there a problem, Dave?"

"Yes," Dave responded, shaking his head. "They paired Bart with Amy Winthrop." He shrugged. "Bart's not happy to be spending three rounds of golf with her all over him."

"The movie star?" Lucia blurted. "Wow!" She smiled. "Will we get the chance to meet her?"

Angela smiled at Lucia, nodded. "I see," she said. Angela looked to the rest. "Amy Winthrop has the reputation for using men to get publicity."

"So," Celia nodded. "I've read that she's a slut, right?" She thought. "Does she even play golf?"

"She does," Dave nodded. "She was there today." He laughed. "You should have seen her golf outfit," he shook his head. "Not much to it, and she kept asking Bart for help." He laughed, mimicked Amy. "Bart, am I holding the club right?" He looked at the women. "So, Bart would come over and help her and the photographers were everywhere." He shook his head. "Angela, there will be photos of Bart with his arms circling Amy, instructing her."

"Why doesn't he say no?" Rosa asked, with annoyance in her tone.

"He really can't," Dave explained. "Bart asked if he could be paired with an athlete, but they said it just wasn't possible to change now." He shook his head. "It's pretty clear that the Tournament officials want the photos of the beautiful couple. The magazines will run the photos suggesting a relationship." He shrugged. "The publicity will sell tickets and bring eyes to the broadcast." He shook his head. "Bart's in a no win situation. Either, Angela and his family is upset or he looks like a bad guy."

Angela sighed, smiled and rose. "I'm going to go talk to Bart." She shook her head. She looked at Rosa, "Mom, this is no big deal. We just can't over-react." She laughed. "Poor Bart, I'll go and try to make him feel better. We'll see you all at dinner."

Rosa smiled as she watched Angela walk into the hotel. She looked at Celia, "Angela's a good girl."

Celia smiled and nodded in agreement. "She's the perfect girl for Bart."

As Angela walked to the suite, she considered how troubled Bart had looked. She knew his concern was for her. Remembering her panic over Janet in Florida and over the photo of Bart dancing with Rachel at the Ball, she realized that she had to put his mind at ease, if he were to be able to focus and play well. She grimaced, as she accepted that his anguish had little to do with Amy Winthrop, and everything to do with his concern for Angela's insecurities. She considered, and then she smiled.

Bart was still showering when Angela entered the suite. She smiled and waited. Bart left the bathroom and walked into the bedroom as he toweled himself dry. He was surprised when he saw Angela waiting and smiling at him. She had disrobed. He scanned her lovely body, smiling broadly. Her curly black hair cascaded over her soft, creamy shoulders. Her beautiful, voluptuous body called to him. Her eyes sparkled. He smiled. "Princess, you are so beautiful."

She noted the look in his eyes, the smile on his face, as he admired her. As she hoped, he was no longer worried about Amy Winthrop and totally focused on her. She saw the lust in his eyes as he scanned her body.

"Amy Winthrop, Huh?" She asked with a grin.

Bart's eyes were on Angela. He didn't even notice the paddle she held in her hand. Bart just shrugged at the question. "I don't know what to do, Angela."

She smiled. "You know, I spoke to Tina. She told me that I really deserved and needed a paddling." She flashed her eyes at Bart. "Would you like me bent over the bed or across your lap?" She extended her hand and the paddle to Bart.

Bart grinned as he took the paddle. Angela bent over the bed, looked over her shoulder. She met his eyes and smiled. "I'm ready, Sir."

Bart took in his beautiful wife. He shook his head, tossed the paddle aside. "Princess, the last thing I want to do is bruise your luscious skin." He touched her. "I'd much rather caress your bottom."

They fell into bed together, laughing, holding, touching and thoroughly enjoying each other. Bart lost himself in the joy of loving his wife. He felt his troubles melt away. He held her close, stroking her back.

"You don't want to paddle my bottom until its smoky red?" She teased with a smile. Angela looked into his eyes, touched his face. "I'm yours Bart, I love you and I trust you." She paused. "All the doubts and all the fear that you would want another girl are gone." She kissed him. "You asked me to trust our love." She nodded. "That's what I am doing."

"There will be photos and stories suggesting all kinds of things." He paused, sighed. "You know how the media works. It will be worse than the newspaper photo with Rachel."

Angela nodded. "Bart, there's a price to be paid for everything." She smiled. "I happen to love and be married to a handsome, charismatic, athlete." She shrugged and grinned as Bart flushed at her words. "I plan on being so friendly and sweet to Amy Winthrop." She winked. "The worse thing I could do is appear troubled or jealous."

He lifted her to lay on his chest. He reveled in her softness, her willing smile. "Thank you, Princess."

She looked into his eyes as she wriggled into position, watched his smile bloom. "You just be so nice to her, and I'll be waving to you from behind the ropes." He gasped, closed his eyes in delight, "we'll just make the best out of this." She kissed him and flashed her saucy smile. "Now, my husband, please love me."

When they lay happily sated, Angela with her head cradled on his chest. She spoke softly. "One more thing," she added. "Focus on your game and win this Tournament, okay?"

Bart laughed. "I'll do my best, Princess."

As Bart and Angela walked to meet the family for dinner, Angela nudged Bart. "You might want to tease Lucia about the guy who was hovering around our lounge chairs and flirting with her."

Bart laughed. "Really? How did she handle it?"

Angela grinned. "She was so flustered. At first, she tried to ignore him." Angela laughed. "When he persisted, she told him that she had a boyfriend." Angela looked at Bart and grinned. "So, this good looking guy, he smiled at Lucia, looked around, 'I don't see any boyfriend, Beautiful,' he responded." Angela shook her head and laughed. "Lucia didn't know what to say or do. So, she looked for help."

"What happened?" Bart asked, amused, thinking about his usually feisty and confident sister.

"Finally, your mother chased him away." Angela explained.

They entered the steak house Bart so enjoyed. The family were all present, as was Dave and Linda. Dave caught Angela's eye. "Everything okay, Angela?"

She smiled and nodded. "Everything is just fine." She eyed Dave. "I'll deal with Amy," she laughed. "And, you help Bart win the Tournament, okay?"

"Sounds good to me." He looked at Bart. "I told you that Angela was way too smart to panic about some trollop."

"You did," Bart agreed as he smiled at Angela. He looked at the group. "Did everybody have a good day today?"

Celia smiled. "I sure did, what a fabulous resort. Thanks for including me."

"No thanks needed, Celia." He smiled. "Having you here makes us all happy." He smiled as he addressed Lucia, who met his eyes. "Lucia, I hear that Franco has some competition?"

Lucia shook her head. "No way, Bart." She flashed a smile. "Just like my big brothers, I know when I have found a good thing." She sat up. "And, Franco's my guy."

Bart grinned at Lucia. "I'm glad to hear it."

Rosa eyed Lucia, "you be careful with that one," she directed. Rosa smiled. "I like Franco," she said, "but, he's like your brothers," She pointed to her head. "Too many ideas."

Bart feigned surprise, "Mom, I have to defend Mario and myself here." He stated. "We never harbored an impure thought concerning our girls."

Angela and Celia laughed. Rosa paused, pointed her finger at Lucia, "and, your father doesn't like the way he looks at you."

Lucia looked at Angela and Celia for help, but found only amusement. "Sorry, Lucia," Celia said with a grin. "If Franco is like your brothers," she wagged her finger in imitation of Rosa, "you better be careful."

All at the table laughed aloud. "Yes, Lucia," Dave added. "Tomorrow, I'll have to be diligent to protect Amy Winthrop's virtue with Bart around." He shook his head. "The hard work of a Coach!" He offered with an air of despair.

Angela laughed. "That's right Dave," she agreed. "After all, Amy is as pure as the driven snow." She saw Bart laughing and relaxed, and exchanged a smile with Dave.

Chapter Sixty-Five

B art had an early tee time. A scantily clad, Amy Winthrop, met him on the first tee with a smile and a kiss on the cheek. Angela noted that the descriptions of Amy as a 'blond bombshell' were no exaggerations. She was both slender and well endowed. Her blue eyes sparkled from a beautiful face, her skin flawless. The Paparazzi were flashing away as Bart smiled at Amy, "I'd like to introduce you to someone." Bart said. They walked the few feet to where Angela stood with the family. Angela was attractively dressed in a fitted sundress and a wide brimmed straw hat. She flashed a big smile and kissed Bart. The Golf Channel cameras were focused on the meeting, as Donna Caponi stood by to do an interview of Bart and the movie star. In the background and along the first fairway were 'Bart's Battalion,' the children of YES. They waved banners proclaiming themselves to be 'Bart's Battalion,' and wore their 'I'm with Stutter Boy,' buttons.

"Amy," Bart began, "I'd like to introduce my wife, Angela." Angela smiled broadly and extended her hand in a warm shake.

"So nice to meet you, Amy," Angela offered. "I loved your last movie."

Amy looked at Bart, glanced at Donna Caponi, realized, with chagrin, that Angela was standing with Bart in the camera shot. She shook Angela's hand and smiled. "So nice to meet you, Angela."

Donna looked into the camera. "I'm standing with Amy Winthrop and Bart DeMarco, as well as Bart's lovely wife, Angela." She faced Amy, "so, you get to play with the hottest name on the PGA Tour, Amy, any thoughts?"

Amy flashed her million dollar smile. "I'm excited to play with the boy wonder," she complimented. "You know, his Coach, Dave Gilliss, calls Bart, 'the Diamond Maker,' because, he deals with pressure so well." All around the Paparazzi flashed photos of the gathering.

Donna turned to Bart. "So you're back at Pebble Beach, Bart, any thoughts?"

Bart smiled, pulled Angela close. "I had a great match on these courses with Billy Ray Boyd." He grinned. "Unfortunately, I finished second, but I love the courses, and this time my Angela is with me." He paused. "And, with Amy with us, Dave and I are surrounded with spectacular beauty, Angela and Amy."

"BOOM!" Rachel Walleston laughed from her living room, where she watched with her parents and Justin. "I think Bart and Angela handled that slut perfectly." She looked at her parents, "Dave told me last night that Bart was really flustered by that floozy." She smiled. "I guess she was all over Bart yesterday, it really threw him off."

"So, what happened?" PapaWall asked.

"I called Angela last night after I spoke to Dave." She smiled. "I guess Angela managed to relax Bart," she grinned. "And, then they formed a plan to deal with her." She shrugged. "Angela didn't want Amy throwing Bart off his game." She paused, shook her head. "Look how she is dressed." She looked at her mother. "How can she possibly play golf in that outfit?"

"I guess it's all for the cameras," PapaWall suggested. "Hey, look, isn't that Rosa, Celia and Lucia there with Angela?"

"Yes," Rachel responded. "Angela told me that Bart worries about her being alone, when he's practicing and during the Tournaments." She sighed. "I wish I could be there for her."

"For her?" Heather laughed. "Maybe, there's someone else you'd like to see?"

Heather engaged her Mom's eyes. "Mom, I miss Dave."

"What Rachel said is true," PapaWall nodded. "Bart asked me to bring the family to Hawaii so Angela wouldn't be alone." He smiled. "Rachel, you know I can't be at every Tournament. I have a business to run. But, we'll all be at the Masters for Bart's birthday and for the Tournament."

"Dad," Rachel asked. "How would you feel about Mom, Justin and me going to Bermuda and then flying on to Augusta?"

Justin excitedly leaped off of the couch. "Ccan wwee, Ddad?" He pleaded.

Phil looked at Heather. "What do you think?" He paused. "It would mean more time out of school for Rachel and Justin."

Heather considered the question. "If we brought a tutor for Justin and his speech therapist, it would be okay." She paused. "Rachel and Angela could work with Linda." She winked at Rachel. "And, maybe we'll see Dave," she laughed. Heather watched the screen, saw Bart and Dave conferring. "That is a smart team." She looked at Rachel, "Who's that good looking guy working with Bart?"

Rachel laughed. "Dave and Bart are a great team." She paused. "I so appreciate that Bart is always acknowledging Dave's role in their success." She smiled. "And, it is their success, not just Bart's."

"Absolutely," PapaWall agreed. "They are a great team!" He grinned, and eyed Rachel. "Dave is a very sharp young man. His early coaching of Bart was critical to their success." He nodded. "Add Angela and you, Rachel, along with Manitoba Oil, YES, and all the children, I'd say 'Team DeMarco' has a great future." He paused, smiled. "And, Bart and Dave are going to shoot a few commercial spots for Manitoba Oil and the Classic."

"Really?" Heather asked. "How did that happen?"

"It's a funny story," PapaWall began. "I called Bart's agent, Harry Winston, to request that Bart shoot a spot." He laughed. "Harry demanded a big fee to use Bart." He shrugged. "I agreed, and we set a date to shoot after The Masters." PapaWall shook his head and smiled. "But, Bart declined, he insisted on setting his own conditions."

Heather looked quizzically at Phil. "What did Bart demand?"

Phil laughed. "He said that we, the Walleston's, had been good to him and his family. He refused to accept payment, which drove Harry Winston crazy, and he suggested we do two spots." He looked at Rachel, and smiled. "Bart insisted that Dave be used with him in the spots, since they're a team. And, that Dave be paid for the spots."

Rachel smiled, her features softened. "He did?" She misted. "He's such a good guy."

"He is that," PapaWall agreed. "With Bart, when he speaks of 'Team DeMarco,' he and Angela, and Dave and our family being a team, he really means it." He shook his head. "Bart's the rarest of people. He's genuine."

Amy Winthrop accepted that using Bart wasn't going to work as her publicists had hoped. Angela showed no jealousy or concern, she even invited Amy to dine with them that evening.

Bart was paired with PGA star, Rickie Fowler. Fowler's Amateur partner was Mike Dench, CEO of a major international energy company. Dench approached Bart with hand extended. "I see you are with Phil Walleston, Bart." He grinned. "Phil's doing a great job with Manitoba Oil."

Bart nodded as he shook Dench's hand. "It's nice to meet you Mr. Dench." He grinned. "Mr. Walleston is a great guy."

Rickie Fowler walked onto the tee and shook Dave's, then Bart's hand. "Great to meet you, Bart." He smiled. "You are making quite a name for yourself." Rickie Fowler, one of 'The Golf Boys,' an impromptu singing group, comprised of Rickie, Ben Crane, Bubba Watson and Hunter

Mahan, that has recorded off-beat songs that have been a boon to various charities.

Rickie is and has been an accomplished golfer since his amateur days. He was the #1 ranked amateur golfer in the world for 39 weeks. He was a PGA rookie of the Year, he has won multiple PGA Tour titles and European Tour Championships, and in one season finished in the top 5 in all four majors. He also attends weekly Bible Studies when on tour. He's a well-liked and highly respected golfer and young man.

"Thanks, Rickie," Bart laughed. "I played in Arizona with Bubba, one of the 'Golf Boys,' he's a good guy." He paused. "I love the way he plays."

Rickie grinned. "I heard that he got a bit into your head."

Bart laughed. "Yes, he and Dustin both." He shrugged, "lesson learned."

Rickie smiled. "We all learn a lot of lessons on the tour." He nodded. "Let's go out there and have some fun."

The professionals hit from the tips, or the longest tees, the male amateur will play from the men's tees and Amy Winthrop will play from the ladies tees.

Bart was announced, teed his ball and rocketed a drive over the trees on the corner of Spyglass's 1st hole landing it on the downslope of the fairway and it ran out to over 350 yards from the tee.

Rickie was announced and also hit an impressive drive. Rickie is not a big man, but he is long off of the tee. He's not Bart long, but he's long.

As the group walked from the Professional's tees to the men's tee from which Mike Dench would hit, Dench fell in beside Bart and Dave. The three chatted away about the energy industry, which conversation Bart enjoyed. Amy Winthrop, having given up on Bart, sidled up to Rickie, flashed her smile, hung on to his arm, and sweet talked the young PGA star.

Bart and Rickie enjoyed playing together. Rickie handled Amy's advances casually and politely, as he made a point of waving to his attractive girlfriend.

On a warm and sunny Monterrey day, the two young men pushed each other to play superior golf. Dave kept Bart focused on the next shot, only. Bart, with Dave's guidance played smart golf. When Rickie tapped in for par on the 18th hole, they each had posted rounds of -8, for a 64. At the end of the day, they would be tied for the lead in the Tournament.

In the post round interview, Mike Dench smiled at on course announcer, David Feherty, a former PGA and European Golf Professional, now turned announcer and widely believed to be the most entertaining of the television golf announcers. A famous television comic, after playing a round of golf with Feherty, described him as; "a comic with a golf swing." Mike Dench smiled at David. "I so enjoyed playing with Rickie and Bart." He shook his head. "We all knew how great Rickie has been, but, Bart, WOW!" He laughed. "Bart is a great golfer and a really good kid." He paused. "I think we will see great things from him."

As they would be playing together the next day at Pebble Beach, they all shook hands warmly, with Amy planting kisses on all three men. She smiled at Bart, "is that invitation for dinner still good?"

Bart nodded. "It is for you Amy, but don't bring the Paparazzi, okay?"

Amy nodded. "You have my word, no cameras, just a chance to get to know you, Angela, and your family."

"Okay," Bart said. "We'll meet you at the fire pits at Spanish Bay at 7:30."

Bart walked over to meet with his young fans. He signed programs, signs, golf balls, you name it. And, he posed for photos, with 'Bart's Battalion.' The numbers seemed to grow with every tournament, and the smiles on the faces of the children and their parents, showed hope for the future. Bart took time to speak with every child who longed to address him. His patience seemed endless. Bart just never forgot, and he's determined to help these young Stutterers. The group photo, a developing tradition, excited his young supporters.

By the time Bart concluded his interviews and time with the children and families of 'Bart's Battalion,' Bart and Angela had to hustle to get back to the resort, shower and dress for dinner. Bart teased Angela as she spent extra time applying make-up. "You don't need that stuff, Princess, you are naturally beautiful."

Angela laughed. "Are you kidding? I can't believe she's really coming to dinner." She sat looking into the make-up mirror, frowned, grabbing another product and applying it to her eyes, she added. "A movie star we have to compete with." She lamented. "Why did I think inviting her to dinner was a good idea?"

Bart laughed, moved behind Angela and planted kisses on her neck and shoulders. "You are so gorgeous," he said.

Angela laughed. "And, Bart, if you mess up my make-up, you are so dead!" She looked at him and smiled. "After dinner, whatever you want, but not now!"

He laughed. "Second place to a movie star. What's a guy to do?"

Angela rose, smiled at Bart. "You can take your wife to dinner."

The family gathered at the fire pit, seated on soft, comfortable couches. In the distance, the sound of bagpipe music played, gradually growing louder and more compelling as the bagpiper walked closer to the assembled group. It was a soft night. And, Celia, Lucia, Linda, even Rosa, took extra care to look their best.

Amy Winthrop was escorted to the group by the dining host. Bart and Dave rose to greet her. She was dressed attractively, but conservatively. Bart smiled, "Amy, I'm glad you could make it to dinner." He looked about, introduced his mother, Celia and Lucia, as well as Linda, who were all very impressed to be dining with a movie star. "You look very nice, tonight." He nodded to Dave. "I'm sure you remember my coach, Dave Gilliss."

"Thanks Bart." She smiled. "It's nice to meet you all." She said. Amy sat and addressed the group. "I know that you'll find this hard to believe, but I really don't like to dress so provocatively." She shrugged. "But, in Hollywood, I am always competing for the next part in the next big movie." She paused. "So, my agent, my manager and my publicist, insist that I play the harlot, so the paparazzi follow me and I'm all over the magazines and television shows." She shrugged. "They say it keeps me current with my fans and the movie executives." She sighed, frowned. "Although, my Dad isn't very happy about it."

"Are you looking for a new movie role now?" Celia asked, hoping to lift Amy's spirits.

"Yes, I certainly am." She said excitedly, as she sat up, sipped on her soda water and grapefruit juice. "Me, and it seems, every young actress, are testing for the lead, female role, in the movie adaptation of that novel, 'The Fisherman's Son.'" She sighed. "We all want to play Connie!"

"I read that novel," Celia said. "It was great." Angela and Lucia agreed with Celia's comment. "I really enjoyed it," Angela said. "I like the way that author writes." She paused, looked to Lucia. "What was the author's name?"

"Joe Orlando," Lucia responded. "It's a great novel." She looked at Amy. "I hope you get the part."

Amy looked at Angela. "I'm sorry if I made it seem that I was trying to steal your husband, Angela." She laughed, eyed Bart. "Although, I could be convinced."

Angela laughed, pointed her finger at Amy and winked. "You stay away from my husband."

They all laughed. "I didn't know that I was so popular." Bart said with a grin.

"You really played wonderfully today," Amy said. "I understand that you and Rickie are tied for the lead."

"That's right," Dave responded. He grinned. "And, Amy, if there's anything you can do to distract Rickie tomorrow, I'll be good with that." Everybody laughed and began to relax.

"Amy," Bart asked. "Is it okay if I take your photo with the girls?" He smiled, winked at Lucia. "I believe that is a photo they will cherish."

"Of course, I will be happy to pose with these ladies." Amy smiled. "But, only on one condition. You and Dave have to be in the photo and send me a copy for my Dad." She flashed her smile. "He's a big 'Team DeMarco' fan."

Bart laughed. "No problem." Bart posed the group, asked a waiter to snap the photo, as he moved and stood between Angela and Amy. "Dave," Bart observed, with a grin, "what beautiful women we are dining with."

Dinner was relaxing and amusing. Amy told tales of hijinks and mishaps on the sets of her movies. She made herself the butt of most of the jokes and all enjoyed her stories. She seemed to be a warm and friendly young lady.

"I have to ask," Lucia offered. "How can you play golf in those outfits?" She laughed. "I thought, at times, you were going to give everything away."

Amy shrugged. "You know Lucia, I'm actually a decent golfer," she stated. "I was captain of my high school golf team." She shook her head. "But, I can't play my game in those clothes. My agent and manager insist that I dress that way and provoke racy photos." She sighed. "So, I do."

"It just goes to show," Bart said to Angela as he happily undressed her, planting kisses on her shoulders and neck. "Things aren't always as they appear."

Angela laughed. "Well, this seems pretty clear," she said, as she stood gloriously before Bart.

He eyed her with a lascivious smile. "'After dinner, anything you want.' I believe those were your words." He grinned. "And, Princess, I want you."

Angela feigned exasperation. "I guess I must," she responded with a laugh. "But, you have to play tomorrow." She grinned. "Maybe, it would be better if you rested."

Bart laughed. "Not possible, Princess." He stated, as he eyed her lovely, voluptuous body. "Besides, I don't tee off until 2pm tomorrow." He kissed her. "We have all the time in the world, to love each other, then rest, then love each other." He pulled her close. "Over and over again." He added. He pulled her into a deep and passionate kiss. "I love you, Princess."

She held Bart to her tightly. "Never stop, Bart," she paused. "Please, always love me."

Chapter Sixty-Six

I n the words of the 'Golden Bear,' Jack Nicklaus, "if I had only one more round to play, I would choose to play it at Pebble Beach. I've loved this course from the first time I saw it. It's possibly the best in the world."

Bart was awed by the beauty. The Pacific Ocean crashing the shore at the feet of the golfers and spectators, the magnificent homes set about the course, and the course itself. He loved playing on this historic and legendary course, where all the greats, from Bobby Jones to Tiger Woods had walked these fairways. And, now, he had the thrill of playing this breathtakingly beautiful course, while competing against the world's best golfers. Bart felt honored, and blessed.

The wind was up, with gusts to 35 mph, and scores were high. The morning wave had played and Bart and Rickie still stood atop the leader board.

Dave stood on the 1st tee deep in thought. He turned to Bart. "I think we let Rickie take the risks today." He smiled. "Bart, we play smart, take our opportunities when presented, but in these winds, we play for pars."

Bart nodded. He smiled at Dave. "You're the coach, let's do it."

Rickie, Mike Dench and Amy Winthrop, dressed even more sexily than yesterday, met on the 1st tee box to shake hands. Amy kissed the three men and whispered her thanks to Bart for the pleasant dinner.

Dave's call proved absolutely correct. The winds and especially the gusts, which seemed to blow just as the player swung, was killing scoring. Almost, everybody seemed to be backing up, except Bart. Bart's driver rarely left his bag. Dave knew that Bart's length, with all his clubs, would play positively to their game. When playing into the wind, Dave had Bart using irons off the tee to keep his shots below the wind. When the wind was at his back, Bart used high flying hybrids to ride the wind. At day's end, Bart had mixed three birdies with fifteen pars to move his tournament leading score to -11. Rickie, a bold player, in the mold of Arnold Palmer and Phil Mickelson, bogeyed three holes, had a double bogey, when a crossing gust of wind caught his ball and hooked it into the great Pacific, and recorded five birdies, to shoot an even par round and remain at -8 for the tournament. Still, Bart and Rickie remained at the top of the leader board and would be last out on Saturday, Moving Day, at Pebble Beach.

Walking off the 18th green, Donna Caponi, asked Bart, how he managed to post one of the few sub-par rounds recorded that day. Bart smiled into the camera. "The credit goes to my coach, Dave Gilliss. He formulated the strategy, pulled the clubs, directed my swing, and I swung." He laughed. "It takes a team, Donna," he paused. "And, I am so lucky to have a great team."

Rachel beamed as she watched with her parents and Justin. "My Dave is the best!" She proclaimed.

"He is," PapaWall agreed. "But, Rachel, please remember, Bart, Dave, you, Angela, all of us are part of a team." He paused. "We all win together, but if we become individuals, we will all lose."

Rachel nodded. "I understand, Dad, 'Team DeMarco,' right?"

"Absolutely," Heather agreed. She looked at Justin. "What do you think, Big Guy?"

He looked at his mother, there was passion in his voice when he spoke, "Mom, I love, Bart!" He stated clearly.

Heather embraced her boy, as all laughed. "Yes," Heather agreed as tears of joy filled her eyes. "We all love Bart."

That evening, the group sat out by the fire pits, enjoying the opportunity to relax and sip a cold drink, as they prepared for dinner. Rosa enjoyed a nice California red blend. She looked at Bart. "This wine is wonderful, Bart." She said. "This has been a wonderful trip." She sat back, thinking of her husband, Franco, and how his boat should be in for Monday's market. She so wished he could be here with her.

The group was approached by a tall, silver haired, smiling man, he appeared to be about 50 years old. "Excuse me," he began. Bart smiled from his seat. Being interrupted by golf fans was becoming routine, and he always responded in a welcoming way. 'The King,' Arnold Palmer, always admonished golfers to remember that the good life they were able to live was because of golf fans. Arnold Palmer treated fans as if they were royalty. He expected the same from young players. Bart took his words to heart.

"Hi," Bart said, with a welcoming smile, as he rose to greet the man, with hand outstretched. "What can I do for you, Sir?"

The gentleman smiled at Bart politely, took and shook his hand, but he showed no signs that he recognized Bart. He looked to Rosa. "Excuse me," he said, with a little bow. "May I buy you a drink?"

Rosa put her hand to her chest. "Me?" She asked with surprise. "Are you speaking to me?"

Celia and Angela smiled, Lucia and Bart narrowed their gaze. All looked to Rosa.

"Yes," he smiled. "I hoped that I could buy you a drink, perhaps dinner?"

Rosa beamed a smile. "That's so nice, Sir." She paused. "I'm Rosa DeMarco," she offered her hand.

The silver haired gentleman took her hand, bowed and kissed it. "I'm Aldo Cello," he smiled. "I have a vineyard in Napa and am here for a conference." He scanned the group. "I noticed you last evening, and as I am here alone," he forced a smile. "My wife passed away last year." He cleared his throat. "I vowed that if I saw you again, I would approach you." He smiled. "I hope that I'm not being too forward, but I see you here with your children, and sometimes it's nice to be with friends from our generation."

Rosa felt so complimented. She smiled up at him. "Aldo, I so appreciate your kind offer. But, I'm a married woman. My husband is Captain and owner of a successful fishing vessel." She saw his disappointment. "I'm here to watch my son, Bart, play in the Pebble Beach golf tournament."

Aldo bowed to the group. "I'm so sorry to have interrupted." He smiled, and turned to leave."

Bart rose. "Mr. Cello," he called. Aldo turned to face him. "Please, join us for dinner." He smiled. "I appreciate your good taste. My mother is a beautiful woman."

Aldo smiled. "You are not offended?"

Bart looked at his family, gathered and comfortably relaxing at the fire pit. The fire cast his mother in an attractive glow. "Not at all. I believe my father would be proud." He smiled. "Please, don't eat alone, join us."

He smiled at Bart. "Thank you," he studied Bart. "I think your father would be very proud of you, son." He paused. "I would love to join you, as a friend," he stressed. "I look forward to someday meeting the lucky man that married this beautiful woman."

Celia, Angela, Linda and Lucia smiled as they watched Rosa flush and glow at the compliment from this attractive man.

Bart signaled to a waiter. "We are ready for dinner, if our table is ready." He said with a smile.

The waiter smiled. "Your table is ready, Mr. DeMarco."

Bart nodded and smiled. "And, please, would you add a place for our friend, Mr. Cello?"

"Of course," he said. "I'll take care of it, Sir." The waiter placed a seat for Aldo Cello between Rosa and Linda. Bart watched as the three chatted amiably throughout dinner.

Back in their suite, Bart looked at Angela and smiled. "How about that?" Bart asked with a laugh. "My mother getting hit on, WOW!"

Angela laughed as she readied for bed. "Your mother is a beautiful woman." She smiled, "could you help me with this zipper, please?"

He grinned. "What am I thinking?" He approached Angela, took her in his arms. He smiled as he kissed her. "It seems that I am just surrounded by beautiful women."

Angela laughed. "You handled that situation so well, Bart." She shook her head, kissed him. "I didn't know what you were going to do." She smiled. "Your mother was so complimented. It's nice for a woman to know that she is still attractive to men."

Bart laughed. "Easy there, Princess, you're speaking of my mother." He lowered the zipper on her dress, smiled and freed her from her clothes. He held her hands and stood at arms-length admiring her. "You are so beautiful."

Angela blushed. "Thank you, Bart." She smiled. "I never tire of you saying that." She paused, moved close, rose on her toes and kissed him. Her eyes gleamed. "Please love me."

Bart's eyes lit, his smile bloomed. "Nothing would give me greater pleasure, Princess."

Chapter Sixty-Seven

Saturday's round would be the last for Mike Dench and Amy Winthrop. Neither Bart's nor Rickie's team would qualify for the Sunday Pro-Am finals.

Amy's manager and publicist recognized that fact and as the Saturday viewing audience would be large, she was attired in her most revealing outfit.

"Poor Amy," Lucia said, softly. "She's a huge star and it's as if she's trapped by the image they are creating for her."

Angela looked at Lucia. "Maybe, she needs someone, like Bart, to help her see that she is beautiful, without appearing cheap." She smiled. "Bart completely changed the way I see myself."

Lucia smiled. "Angela, you did the same for Bart."

They all met on the 1st tee. Mike Dench shook Bart's hand and commented that he'd like to meet Phil Walleston. Bart shrugged. "I'm sure he'd take your call, Sir."

Amy kissed Dave, Rickie, Mike and Bart. "Play great today, Bart," she whispered.

YES had brought out 'Bart's Battalion' in huge numbers. The eager children looked at their hero with confidence. Bart walked over to the crowd gathered around the 1st tee and thanked them for coming.

"Wwin, Bbart," a youngster called out. Bart smiled and winked.

It was another windy day on the Monterrey peninsula. Bart had completely bought into Dave's sound advice. 'Team DeMarco' was clicking, and Bart was comfortable with his coach, Dave Gilliss, at the helm.

Bart was -1 for the day when he stood on the 7th tee. Rickie was at +1, giving Bart a five shot lead. Again, the windy conditions were causing players, playing boldly, in hopes to catch the leaders, to lose strokes and fall further behind.

Bart smiled as he re-called the day Billy Ray aced this hole to take the lead in the Pacific Amateur. A lead Billy Ray grew and never gave up. Bart took the club Dave offered.

"Hit a knock-down, Bart, right over the flag and suck it back," Dave advised. He eyed Bart. "The wind is at you, and the green is receptive, just do as we practiced."

Bart nodded, lined up behind the ball and analyzed the shot. He closed his eyes and visualized the shot, opened his eyes, looked at Angela and smiled. He addressed the ball. He launched into his smooth as silk swing.

"It looks good, Johnny," Jim Nantz called. "It's right on the stick," Donna affirmed. The ball flew over the flag-stick, hit, bounced and then spun back to the hole. The crowd roared.

"GGo In!" screamed a young fan. Angela watched wide eyed, with her fists bunched nervously, at her mouth.

Bart held his pose, watching the shot. He smiled as it began to spin back to the cup, stopping one foot to the right of the hole. He fired his fist pump and smiled. The gallery erupted.

"It's a kick in Birdie, Johnny," Jim Nantz stated. "Remind you of anything?" He laughed.

"He's running away from the field," Johnny Miller stated.

Angela bounced with delight. She turned from watching the shot to see Bart's eyes caressing her, his smile beaming. The fact that she blushed, Bart found endearing.

"I think my big brother digs you, Angela." Lucia laughed.

Amy smiled at Angela and walked to Bart. She placed a chaste kiss on Bart's cheek. "That's from Angela," she said with a smile.

Rosa beamed. "That's my Bart." She scanned the sea of young boys and girls, with their parents, clapping, cheering and calling out to Bart. 'And, he's helping these children,' she thought, feeling a surge of pride.

The round ended with Bart leading Rickie Fowler by eight shots. Rickie lead the next closest competitor by four more. It looked to be shaping up as a route for Bart.

Donna Caponi approached Bart as he exited the 18th green. "A score of 66 playing in this wind, Bart, a great round." Donna stated. "What's your secret?"

"Thanks Donna," he grinned, He eyed the LPGA legend, "I have a great team." He paused, smiled. "Dave has been right on, I'm very lucky," he looked at Angela and smiled. "But, the tournament's not over."

Mike Dench approached Bart, shook his hand and patted his shoulder. "Bart, Rickie," he called. "Can we get a photo of the four of us?" He grinned. "What a coup, two great golfers, a beautiful movie star and little ol me!"

The foursome posed for the photo and it seemed hundreds more. Bart was relaxed and happy, because he knew Angela was sure of him.

Amy asked if she could take a photo with Bart and Angela. "My Dad is a big fan, Bart. It would mean a lot to him." Rosa smiled and gave Amy a sweater to cover her overly revealing outfit. "I think your Dad would like the photo better if you were a bit more covered."

Amy nodded, smiled and wore the sweater. After the photo was taken, Rosa took her hands, looked into her eyes. "I think it's time for you to take charge of your life, Amy." Rosa smiled. "Make your Dad proud." Amy began to remove Rosa's sweater to return it. Rosa shook her head. "No, Amy, you keep it, wear it home, think about what I said."

Bart was truly happy when he waded into Bart's Battalion to sign autographs, talk to his kids and pose for photos.

Back at the hotel, Bart and Angela enjoyed sharing a shower. "Do you think that there's a water shortage here, Bart?" Angela asked, smiling innocently.

Bart laughed. "Actually, I think so," he laughed. "But, I just want to be close to my girl." They laughed and held each other.

Amy surprised the group by appearing by the fire-pit to have dinner with the family.

"You look lovely, Amy." Rosa smiled, as she complimented Amy on her properly modest and attractive dress.

"Thank you, Mrs. DeMarco." She smiled. "I thought about your advice. From now on, I will dress and act to make my Dad proud." She smiled and misted up. "I spoke to my Dad. I told him that I was so sorry for embarrassing him." She engaged Rosa's eyes. "My Dad started crying, he told me that he was always proud to be my father, but that he was so happy that I finally realized that I didn't need to lower myself to please others."

Rosa took her hands. "Good for you, Amy, I'm proud of you."

Amy smiled a thanks. She looked to Angela, "do you think that I could come to Gloucester for a visit." She flushed. "I've heard so many great things, and I have enjoyed the time with your family."

Angela smiled. "Of course, Amy, we would love to have you." Angela met her eyes. "You could be our first houseguest, it will be fun."

Amy looked at the welcoming, smiling faces of 'Team DeMarco,' and felt that she belonged. "I'll call you, Angela."

Back in their rooms and settled for the night, Angela lay on Bart's chest. She snuggled close, happily sated. "That was great, Bart. I love you so much."

Bart grinned as he kissed her head. "I love you, Princess."

Angela casually stroked Bart's chest. "Bart, your mother asked if we could fly home tomorrow night after the final round of the tournament." She hurried to add. "She knows that you have to stay for the interviews, the trophy presentation and, of course, spend time with the kids."

Bart laughed. "My Mom sounds confident." He tipped her chin up to see her eyes. "She wants to fly all night?"

Angela smiled. "She wants to be home when your Dad pulls into port." She kissed Bart. "She wants to greet him." Angela smiled and batted her eyes, suggestively. "She really misses your Dad."

Bart smiled. "Of course," he did a quick mental calculation. "We should be able to take-off by 10pm." He kissed her and groaned as she caressed him. "Will you let everybody know to be packed and ready?"

"Yes Sir, I will." She grinned up at him. "Is there anything else I can do for you?"

He closed his eyes and emitted a groan of pleasure. "As always, you're doing fine."

Chapter Sixty-Eight

Bart's Battalion came out in huge numbers. In an interview, the California director of YES explained; "that 'Stutter Boy,' Bart DeMarco, was a living, breathing symbol of hope for these children and their families. He inspires confidence and we want to support him." He paused. "Bart is giving voice to his God given gifts and the hope of so many young people."

Amy surprised Bart's family by attending the final round of the Pebble Beach Tournament. She walked with Angela, Lucia, Celia and Rosa, cheering for Bart. She wore a pretty sundress, much like the dresses worn by the DeMarco girls. Rosa smiled and winked at Amy. Linda had chosen to relax and not attend the final round. She had been working Angela and Bart hard on their studies. Impressed by their intelligence and dedication, she was aiming for them to graduate with their class in May.

Bart and Dave, wearing their Sunday, Red, White and Blue, golf shirts and hats, teamed to play the course with an eye of being intelligently aggressive. For the challenging Sunday pins, the smart play was to shoot for the middle of the greens. "Let the chasers take the risks," Dave wisely counseled.

After nine holes Bart's lead had grown to ten shots.

"What a performance by Bart DeMarco," Jim Nantz proclaimed. "Johnny, does this make Bart the favorite for Augusta?"

Miller considered the question. "One might think so, Jim, but Bart has never before played in a major, has never seen the rolling hills and lightning greens of Augusta National." He paused, laughed. "But, he keeps on surprising and impressing me. So, I'll say, he's one of my favorites."

"Bart seems unfazed by pressure, guys," Donna contributed. "He has a great team." She paused. "His caddie and coach, Dave Gilliss, is superlative. I think that Bart really is the guy to beat."

Rachel, watching in Manitoba, beamed at Donna's statement. Heather saw her smile and was delighted.

Bart stood on the 18th green with a twelve shot lead. It was a rout for the ages. Still Bart and Dave studied the putt. "Run through the finish line," was Dave's mantra, and that is what Bart did, finishing strong and winning.

Angela ran onto the green and into Bart's arms. She planted a kiss to 'rattle his teeth,' as Amy Mickelson had jokingly advised. Bart, once again, was a winner.

"Bart has played three PGA Tournaments and has won two." Jim Nantz stated. "And, he had a third place finish in the other." He paused. "He's hot, I wonder if there will be anyone to stop him, Johnny."

"Players sometimes get on streaks," Johnny Miller responded. "Seldom, with the exception of Tiger Woods or Byron Nelson, does that streak continue beyond three or four weeks." He laughed. "I like his swing and his approach, Jim, but we'll have to wait and see."

Bart brought Angela and Dave in for the trophy ceremony. He thanked the Tournament sponsors, the PGA, the volunteers and the fans. Then, he addressed Jim Nantz, "Mr. Nantz, none of this would be possible without my team." He paused. "I have a great coach, and wonderful sponsor, the most supportive family and, of course," he smiled at Angela, "the greatest wife a man could have." He kissed Angela.

Following the trophy presentation and media interviews, he spent two hours with Bart's Battalion, the children of YES. He seemed to never tire of meeting with the children, answering their questions and listening to their stories. He would pose for photos, with the children, their families, and YES officials. The group photograph, showed a growing contingent of fans. 'Bart's Battalion' was thriving!

Bart and Angela barely had time for a shower and change of clothes before racing to the jet. When they boarded, the family were all seated and waiting, except Linda. Bart told the pilot to ready for takeoff.

"We can't leave without Linda," Angela said, concerned. "Bart, Linda's not here."

Bart smiled. "Linda is taking a week off," He smiled, "and possibly longer."

Angela studied Bart, caught his eye, saw his smile. "Okay, what's up?"

Dave smiled at Bart. "Do you want to tell them or should I?" Bart nodded, giving Dave the floor.

"She's spending some time in Napa with Aldo Cello." Dave laughed. "I guess, after Mrs. DeMarco broke his heart, he managed to rebound."

Rosa smiled, her cheeks flushed, but she remained silent.

"Good for her," Celia said. "He seemed like a nice guy." She noted Rosa's reaction and flashed a smile to Angela.

Bart grinned. "How about some dinner. I am hungry."

Rosa rose and went into the kitchen. "Well, it looks as if someone ordered pizza and garlic knots for everybody," she said. "Let's eat while the pizza is still hot."

As they dined, Dave added, with a smile. "And, there's more good news. Rachel, MamaWall, and Justin are joining us in Bermuda."

"That's great, Dave," Angela smiled, reading Dave's excitement. She looked at Bart. "What about Tina?"

Bart grinned. "Angela, Tina is coming to Bermuda with us. Nothing changes, except there will be more fun people to enjoy Bermuda." He grinned at Dave. "And, Tina can room with Rachel."

Dave nodded and sighed. "How long until June?" He asked, bringing smiles to all.

"Funny," Celia added, with an appreciative grin. "Mario keeps asking the same question."

They landed at 7am EST. And were home by 8am. Maria Curcuru had stocked Rosa's kitchen with food so that the cupboard was not bare. And, all could gather for dinner that evening. Bart and Angela kissed Lucia and Rosa, dropped Celia, then Dave at home, and headed to their new home.

Exhausted, Bart and Angela slept for a few hours then headed over to see Sal and Maria. Sal lit up when he saw Angela, wrapped her in a hug. "I missed you, Bambina." He kissed her. He grasped Bart's hand, smiled. "You will stay for lunch?

Of course, we will." Bart responded, as he moved to and embraced Maria. He laughed. "Did you make something good, Mom?"

Maria laughed. "Of course, my boy," she responded. She smiled up at Bart. "Cooking for you is always a pleasure." He noted a look of concern in her eyes.

Bart flashed his smile at Maria, put his arm around her shoulder and walked with her to the kitchen. "Is everything good here?" He paused, eyed Maria. "Mom, you look worried."

Maria nodded. "We get along, but Papa is getting restless, sitting home, not working." She shrugged. "A man needs work," She shrugged. "Papa needs work, a reason to get up each day."

Bart nodded, grew thoughtful. "Mom, I'll think about that."

Tina came into the kitchen, smiled at Bart. "Congratulations Bart, nice win," she winked. "Did you like being so close to Amy Winthrop?"

Bart and Tina exchanged a grin. "I saw the photos in the magazines, and I saw her kiss you." She raised her brows, teasingly. "Did Amy inspire you?" Maria looked on, worry playing in her eyes.

Bart grinned at Tina. "Angela told me that you are a troublemaker." He put his arm around Tina, glanced at Maria. "Tina, I told you that I am a one-woman man." He kissed Tina's cheek. "Angela is my girl," he stated, simply.

"The truth is," Bart continued, "that Amy, shook me up, more than inspired me." He laughed. "But, Angela helped me handle the situation." He winked at Maria. "And, it turns out, that Amy's actually a very nice girl." He paused, eyed Tina. "You'll like her."

Tina scoffed. "When will I ever meet her?" Tina asked, surprised. Maria looked on smiling.

Bart laughed. "When she visits Gloucester." He winked at Tina. "She and Angela have become quite friendly." Maria softly exhaled in relief. Bart noticed and flashed a smile, meant to reassure his mother-in-law.

"Really?" Tina showed surprise. "Amy Winthrop is coming to Gloucester?"

"I think so," Bart responded, as Angela walked into the kitchen. "Talk to Angela."

Tina watched Bart closely, shifted her glance to Angela, who grinned at her sister. "I will." She shook her head. "So, when do we leave for Bermuda?" Tina asked, excitement lighting her face.

"We'll collect you at about 7:30am tomorrow." Bart stated. "We should be in Bermuda by 9am." Bart loved that Tina was excited.

Tina leaned close to Angela. "Should I bring my paddle?" She whispered.

Angela laughed. "No need," she responded, quietly. "I bought one of my own." She winked and laughed. "And, it certainly served its purpose."

The DeMarcos gathered for dinner that evening. Bart's Dad and brother were present with hugs for all and congratulations for Bart.

"I'm proud of you, son." Franco said as he pulled Bart into a hug. He looked at Mario. "And, Mario, I am so proud of how quickly you are learning." He grinned and addressed the family. "Mario will be able to Captain the boat by this time next year." Franco laughed. "I'll be able to take some time off." He smiled at Rosa. "Maybe, take a trip with my Rosa."

Celia beamed a smile and embraced Mario. She held him close and asked, "Mario, will I have to call you Captain?" She teased, proudly.

Mario held her tight. He kissed her, smiled. "Of course," he grinned, "actually, Captain, Sir," he added, with a grin. He looked into her eyes. "I just want to call you my wife." He pulled her close.

Bart stood and raised a glass, set proud eyes on Mario. "To Mario, my big brother, the soon-to-be, Captain DeMarco!" All cheered and toasted.

A smiling Franco Palermo was there as well. Franco Palermo looked as if he had really missed Lucia, like a man in the desert misses a cold, refreshing, drink of water.

As they sat to dinner, Bart's Mom and Dad seemed happy. There was something different about this reunion. As a fisherman, they were accustomed to being apart for 7-10 days, when he was at sea. Yet, Rosa seemed to have an eagerness to see her husband that he really appreciated. As they settled around the table and offered a prayer, Bart felt a connection with everyone present. For this special dinner, Rosa made her stuffed pork chops, a favorite of Franco's. Franco smiled at his wife, leaned over and kissed her, bringing smiles across the table.

"Oh," Franco said with a grin. "I have something for you, Rosa." He jumped up and left to return with a bag, containing two bottles of wine.

Rosa smiled, appeared confused. "Thank you, Franco. You never bought me wine before."

Franco grinned. "This is a special wine, my love." He paused. "I heard it was your favorite."

Rosa picked up a bottle, studied the label and blushed. She smiled at Franco, looked at those at the table. "From the vineyards of Aldo Cello," she read aloud, and she winked at Franco. "Thank you, Franco." She smiled. "It brings good memories."

Bart, Angela, Lucia and Celia all laughed.

"You almost lost her, Dad," Bart stated. "He really liked Mom."

Franco met Rosa's eyes. "Never as much as I love your mother," He stated. Rosa beamed a smile at Franco. That look between husband and wife, had Angela, Celia and Lucia, happily misting up.

"Did I miss something?" Mario asked.

"You did, Big Brother," Bart offered with a smile. "When we were having dinner at the hotel, one, Mr. Aldo Cello came to the table to ask if he could buy Mom drinks and dinner."

Mario laughed. "Really?" He angled a devilish grin at his Mom. "So, what did Mom say?" He winked at his mother. "Was Mom gone long?"

Rosa swatted Mario. "I told him that I am a married woman, that my husband was a successful fishing captain." She smiled at Franco. "He knew I had no interest!"

Bart beamed. "Who could blame any guy for wanting to be with a beautiful woman like Mom?" He grinned, took Angela's hand. "But, DeMarco's are loyal, right Mom?"

Rosa smiled, exchanged a loving gaze with Franco. "That's right, Bart. Any woman should be proud to be with a DeMarco man."

"Hey," Lucia piped up. "What about a guy with a DeMarco girl?" She smiled at Franco Palermo.

That brought laughter. Bart smiled, he looked at Franco Palermo. "Did Lucia tell you about the guy hitting on her by the pool?"

Franco looked at Lucia and smiled. "I'm surprised it was only one guy. My Lucia is beautiful."

Lucia beamed, she took young Franco's hand, looked into his eyes. "Franco, you have nothing to worry about." She stated. "DeMarco's are loyal."

He gently, lovingly, squeezed Lucia's hand. "I'm glad to hear that, beauty." He grinned, "Palermo's are also loyal."

Chapter Sixty-Nine

B ermuda was beautiful. Tina stood on the balcony of the suite she shared with Rachel and was awed by the brilliant colors of the ocean. "Look Angela," she said, "the blues blend with the green ocean in an amazing turquoise color that I've never seen before." She smiled. "Thanks for bringing me with you."

Angela grinned. "I'm happy to spend time with my sister, especially with all you are doing for Mom and Dad." She shrugged, looked at Rachel. "Tina is really carrying the load, helping my Mom, while dealing with a bruised heart." She sighed. "I should be doing more."

Rachel moved from the railing to the glass patio table. She poured out glasses of lemonade for the girls, as each sat on the comfortable padded chairs. "I'm sorry Tina." She shrugged. "Angela told me what happened." She offered a sympathetic smile. "I guess it's not just guys who break your heart."

Tina offered a smile. "Thanks, Rachel," she shrugged, her eyes filled. "It really hurts." She sipped some lemonade, swallowed the lump in her throat, as she looked at the view through tear clouded eyes.

Rachel sighed, "I know, Tina. But, you deserve someone who will love you, completely." She sat, feeling Tina's pain. "The right person is out there, Tina." She smiled. "When you find her, you'll know it was worth the pain, the wait."

Tina wiped her eyes, managed a smile. "You sound like Bart and Angela. Thanks."

Rachel eyed Angela. "Angela, don't beat yourself up. You're helping your husband to succeed for your family, and for all those kids, like Justin, who he gives hope to." She paused. "You know, Dave tells me how much Bart depends on you." She smiled. "You're his rock." She looked at Angela, narrowed her gaze in thought. "Even strong guys need someone to lean on."

Angela looked at Rachel and smiled. "I know, Rachel, I love that he needs me." She paused. "But, in truth, it was Bart who saved me," She stated. "Until Bart came along, I believed that I was 'Ugly Angela.'" She sighed, sat back and smiled sweetly, as she recalled what now, is a joyous memory. "Bart looked at me like no one ever had." Her eyes went soft and dreamy. "Bart made me feel beautiful and desired." She paused, her eyes lit at the thought. "Bart wanted the world to know that I was his girl." She shook her head and smiled. "Do you know how amazing that was for me?"

Tina nodded. "Bart brought real joy to Angela." She grinned. "I love what he did for her." Tina laughed. "Angela has this photo on her dresser. She is sitting up on Bart's shoulders in a pool. Celia is on Mario's shoulders, and they are wrestling." Tina looked at Angela and smiled, then, turned to Rachel. "Angela looks so happy, she's absolutely beaming." Tina sighed. "Everybody should have that."

Rachel smiled, shook her head. "You are so pretty, Angela. You are always smiling and happy." She laughed. "I tried to steal Bart from you. Boy, did I strike out!" She grinned. "Bart has eyes only for you, Angela."

Angela met her smile. "Rachel, when I saw that photo of Bart dancing with you at the Ball, I was sure that I had lost him." She shook her head, a smile spread across her face. "But, Bart told me that he wanted me." She grew thoughtful. "You have no idea how that meant everything to me."

Rachel smiled. "I think that I do." She said softly. "I pleaded with my parents to go to Florida to be with all of you. I was so afraid that Dave would forget me." She looked at the girls. "Bart and Dave always have hundreds of pretty girls following them on the course." She shook her head and laughed. "Bart is so focused on his next shot and on the kids he wants to help, he pays the girls no real attention."

Tina laughed. "Rachel, I'm sure he notices the pretty girls." She shook her head and smiled. "He is a guy!"

Angela laughed. "He certainly is!" She sat back, a contented smile played at her face and eyes. "It took me forever, to really believe that Bart loved me." She grinned. "So, if he looks," she shrugged, "I know that's all he's doing. I know that he'll always come back to me."

Rachel nodded. "Yes, Bart will always want you, Angela. But, I was terrified that Dave would notice those girls, and forget about me." She frowned. "I mean, I'm not exactly the kind of girl Dave is accustomed to."

Angela smiled. "Rachel, you can be whatever you choose to be."

Rachel nodded in agreement. "That's true." She paused, considered Angela's words. "So, I made a deal with my Dad, for Mom and me to fly to Florida." She smiled. "Thanks to Bart, it worked." She looked at Angela and laughed. "And, it didn't hurt that we started to learn to cook." She laughed. "Gloucester guys seem to cherish girls with traditional values."

"Yes," Angela added. "Thanks to Tina's help, we began to learn to cook."

Tina smiled, "I don't think Dave will break your heart, Rachel. He's crazy about you." She looked at Angela. "I think Dave's a lot like Bart, hardworking, loyal, and dedicated to each other, golf, and the women they love."

Rachel sat back, looked at the magnificent view. "My Dad thinks Dave has learned a lot from Bart." Rachel stated. She paused, considered her words. "I agree with my Dad. Dave is focused on me now, in a way that he wasn't before he and Bart had that talk in Florida." She smiled, wistfully. "You know, when your family is as rich as mine, it tends to create issues and distractions. You wonder if the guy wants you for you or the money." She shrugged. "Your perspective gets twisted and blurry." Rachel sat back, her face brightened. "But, Dave told me that while he really likes my parents, he will be supporting his wife and family, not my father."

"Angela smiled. "What did PapaWall say about that?"

Rachel laughed. "He loved it. He told me that was exactly what he told my Mom when he proposed." She smiled as she recalled the conversation. "My Dad told me that a man must take responsibility for the protection and support of his family. He's delighted that Dave agrees."

"He sounds like Bart," Angela said. She looked at Rachel, grinned. "Rachel, I think we did okay."

Rachel took a deep breath as she nodded. "We did." She eyed Angela, nervously. "Angela," there's something that I need to ask you," she exhaled, her nerves showing. "Will you be my Matron of Honor?"

Angela jumped to her feet and embraced Rachel. "I so hoped that you would ask." She squeezed Rachel. "I would love to." She paused. "You know that Dave asked Bart to be his best man?"

Rachel nodded. "I did, but I was worried that you would not feel close enough to accept."

Angela embraced Rachel and laughed. "Are you kidding, we're family Rachel." She smiled. "Bart and Dave are like brothers." She paused, eyed Rachel. "Let's make sure that you and I never mess that up."

Rachel nodded and smiled at Angela's words, exhaled the tension she had harbored. "Come on girls, the guys will be practicing for hours yet, let's go sit by the pool. My Mom took Justin to see the Crystal Caves. So, we can just enjoy the beautiful Bermuda sun."

"Okay," Angela agreed. "I'll go change and meet you there."

As they sat by the pool, stretched out on padded lounges, Tina told Rachel the story of her suggesting that Bart paddle Angela's bottom for disrespecting him. Tina laughed. "I told him to make her bottom, smoky red."

Rachel looked at Angela and laughed. "Were you really afraid, Angela?"

Angela eyed Tina, scowled. "I should really paddle your bottom, Tina."

Tina laughed. "Promises, promises," she looked at Rachel. "Yes, Angela was shocked and afraid." She grinned. "It was all a joke, of course," she looked at Angela, considered. "You surprised me, Angela. How could you ever think Bart would hurt you?" She paused. "He would die for you."

Angela nodded. "You're right, of course, but I was feeling pretty guilty about having ignored his very reasonable requests, especially, after he stayed and took care of Dad, and our brothers, while we had a good time shopping and going to dinner." She shrugged. "I guess that I thought I deserved a paddling." She remembered back, smiled. "Instead, Bart made me feel protected and loved." She paused. "I'm not sure that I deserve him."

"You deserve him, Angela." Tina stated. "You deserve all the happiness in this world." She paused. "You are a great person and a special sister."

Rachel grinned. "Wow!" She looked at Angela who had misted up at Tina's words. "Now, that's a compliment!" She smiled. "It makes me wish that I had a sister."

Angela wiped her eyes, beamed a smile at Tina. She then looked at Rachel. "If you want, you do." She smiled. "You, Tina and I can be sisters from different mothers."

Rachel smiled. "Thanks, girls, I like that!"

Chapter Seventy

Port Royal Golf Course, (The Home of the 'PGA Grand Slam of Golf'), is a challenging golf course with slopes and elevated tees and greens, that Dave thought might well be a good preparation for Augusta National. On both courses, one seldom had a flat lie. The ball was often above or below your feet. The ball would invariably set on the so green fairways, in an uphill or downhill lie. It was a good challenge.

As Bart stood on the first tee, he thought of the words of Mark Twain; "You can go to heaven if you want, I'd rather stay in Bermuda."

Bart was in a great mood. He enjoyed the course, which as they say, 'fit his eye.' For three days Dave and he had practiced. He was thrilled to have secured commitments from a group of European Tour players to compete in the Manitoba Classic. Bart had passed on the information to PapaWall through Dave.

Bart was happy to see that Angela and Tina were spending time together. Angela happily related the tales of the adventures of Angela, Tina and Rachel, (The Fabulous Trio). They shopped, explored the beaches and coves, and went deep into the Crystal Caves. Their dinners included amusing stories of the day's adventures. Angela laughed aloud, which was sweet music to Bart's ears.

Bart loved watching and listening to the very happy and animated Angela. After dinner Bart loved his Princess, with the French doors thrown open to their private balcony. They felt the cooling breezes and enjoyed the spectacular views.

"I love Bermuda!" Angela stated with an air of contentment as Bart held and loved her. She smiled into his gaze, "let's come back every year."

In the first and second rounds Bart would be playing with Italian golfer, Francesco Molinari, and legendary Spanish golfer, Miguel Angel Jimenez. Both were talented and emotional players. As they shook hands in greeting, the garrulous Spaniard congratulated Bart on his recent wins. "Tonight we have some wine." He said. "I bring a beautiful wine from Spain." He winked at Molinari, "so much better than Italian wines!"

Molinari laughed. "Bart, my friend," he said in his heavily accented Italian version of English, "be careful of that one."

Bart laughed. "Mr. Jimenez, I'm only 17 years old."

Miguel Angel laughed. "You Americans!" He said disdainfully. "In Spain, even our babies drink wine!"

On the 1st tee, a downhill, dogleg right, 438 yard, par 4, Bart hit an easy hybrid off the tee to the flat at the bottom of the fairway. He left himself a second shot of 130 yards to a green protected with a pond, short and left and sand traps right and long. He then hit a high 9 iron onto the green and rolled in his birdie putt. Jimenez and Molinari parred the hole. Bart laughed when Miguel Angel bowed and doffed his cap to Bart, flipping his ponytail about.

Bart was surprised to find his gallery heavily sprinkled with YES youngsters. Bart's three-some had, by far, the largest gallery. It seemed every golf fan on the island wanted to see 'Stutter Boy,' play. He played well and was -4 after the 15th hole. The golfers walked onto the 16th tee. A 235 yard par 3. The tee box was set on a small peninsula jutting out high over the ocean, the waves crashing below. The green was also a peninsula and in between, it was all Atlantic Ocean. The prevailing wind was from the water, blowing left to right. It is a pretty, but somewhat intimidating, challenge.

As Bart had the honor, he stood with Dave judging the wind to determine the club to be used. "It's blowing pretty steady Bart," Dave stated. "I think we go with a high hybrid, played just left of the green and let the wind carry it over the center of the green."

Bart nodded, took the club and set into his routine. He glanced up to see Angela, Rachel and Tina watching from an elevated perch. Angela wore a form fitting sun-dress and a colorful, straw hat. He flashed a smile, set over the ball and hit the ball, just as he had visualized the shot. He hit it high, just left of the green, flirting with the ocean, the wind pushed it right and the ball landed on the green and rolled to the pin. It stopped five feet short of the cup. The crowd erupted in applause.

Not willing to trust the wind, neither, Jimenez nor Molinari hit the green, both were caught in the heavy, gnarly, rough, right of the green.

Bart watched as his competitors took bogey, before Dave and he lined up his putt. Bart rolled it home for a birdie. Bart birdied the relatively short par 5, 17th hole to move to -6. A par on the 18th had him posting a score of 65. A score that would lead the tournament after Day 1.

Bart followed the round with a photo and autograph session with 'Bart's Battalion,' Bermuda. The group photo had the glorious background of the Turquoise Atlantic. He then went for a two mile run and a work-out session in the resort's gym. He hustled back to the hotel to shower and dress for dinner. He stood under the shower letting the warm water soothe his muscles.

He smiled when he felt Angela's hands working his shoulder muscles. "How does that feel?" She asked, smiled at his pleasured response. "Is there anything else that should be messaged?" She asked on a laugh.

He turned and took her in his arms, kissed her. "How much time do we have before dinner?" He asked, as he kissed her neck.

Angela laughed. "About an hour, I guess," she responded. "Will that be long enough, Sir?"

"We'll make it work." He said, smiling. "By the way, you looked hot in that outfit today."

The group met for dinner in the resort's dining room. The view out to the ocean was spectacular.

"We play late tomorrow," Dave said. "Tee time at 1:44pm."

Bart nodded. "About 11:30 on the range, Dave?"

"Sounds about right." Dave laughed. "What a group today, Bart." He shook his head. "That Miguel Angel Jimenez is a character." Dave said. "Did you see the way Molinari was looking at him?"

Bart nodded. "Yes, Miguel waving that big cigar and offering me red wine from Spain." He laughed. "He was fun."

A waiter came to the table and whispered to Bart, who nodded and rose. He looked at the group. "Just some business that I have to take care of," he explained, kissed Angela. "I'll be right back." About fifteen minutes later Bart returned to the table and dinner. It was a pleasant meal and conversation.

As everyone concluded dinner, Bart pulled Dave aside. They spoke for a few minutes and Dave nodded, embraced Bart and they returned to the table.

Bart smiled. "Okay, I'm sure you are all wondering what's going on?" He stated. He looked at Angela and Tina. "Your Dad took a fall today." He saw the distress in their eyes. "Your Mom couldn't lift him, so she called an ambulance. He's at the hospital." He paused.

"I should have been there!" Tina stated, as tears filled her eyes.

Bart put his hand on her shoulder. "Let's not panic, we aren't sure what's going on." He looked at Heather. "MamaWall," he explained, "Tina, Angela and I will be heading home. They're readying the plane now." He smiled. "Dave will withdraw me from the Tournament and you all should just enjoy the weekend. Hopefully, we'll see you all Monday in Augusta. I'll call you."

Heather embraced Angela and Tina. "Please, if there's anything we can do, just call."

Bart saw that Justin looked a bit scared. He picked up the 11 year old, and tossed him about until Justin was laughing. He lowered Justin, put him on his feet. "Don't you worry, Justin, everything will be fine. I'll see you in Georgia."

Angela and Tina hustled to their suites to pack their bags. Bart arranged a car to the airport. He looked at Dave, shrugged. "My girl needs me, Buddy."

Dave nodded. "Of course," he paused, smiled. "Bart, what do you say that we win the Masters?"

"Sounds like a plan." Bart stated. "We'll see you in Augusta." He grinned. "Hey, MamaWall, you keep an eye on Dave." He angled a smile at Dave. "I don't think he can be trusted around Rachel, now that he has time on his hands."

Heather managed a smile. "I'll watch him closely." She pulled Bart into a hug. "Please call us."

Heather watched him walk to the lobby, on their way to the airport. 'How much does one young man have to deal with?' She thought.

They flew home and were at the Curcuru house by 9pm. They entered the house and, fortunately, discovered, to their relief, that Sal was bruised but had not suffered a fracture. He was sitting in his recliner, surprised when Tina, Angela and Bart entered.

"Why are you here?" Sal asked. "I was going to watch you play on television tomorrow."

Bart smiled. "Hey, you look good." He paused. "We received a call and your girls wanted to see you and make certain everything was okay."

"Who called you?" Sal asked with an edge to his tone.

"I did," Maria explained. "I thought you were hurt, so I called Bart."

Sal shook his head, anger flared. "Why didn't you tell me this?"

Maria took Sal's hand. "Sal, you are the head of this family. But, when you are hurt or not able to make decisions, I count on Bart." She paused, stroked Sal's arm. She began to cry. "When you were so hurt and we thought..." She wiped her eyes. "It was Bart who sent Mr. Palermo to take charge. And, look how good he's doing?"

Sal nodded, looked at Bart. "I'm sorry Bart, I keep interfering with your work."

Bart laughed. "No problem, Papa, my agent dealt with the tournament officials, they understood and even refused our offer to return the appearance fee." He shrugged. "All I had to do is commit to playing next year." He glanced at Angela and smiled. "Something Angela would like me to do." He grinned. "Right, Princess?"

Angela smiled. "I'm glad that you are okay, Papa."

Sal nodded. He looked from Angela to Bart. "Are we still going to Augusta?"

Bart grinned. "We sure are, I think we should leave Saturday, so Dave and I can begin practice early." He put his hand on Sal's shoulder. "It will all be fine, Papa." He paused, smiled. "Family always comes first."

Sal smiled. "Thank you, Bart."

"One thing though," Bart said. "Tomorrow for dinner I expect a great meal, right Mom?"

Maria laughed, embraced Bart and whispered, "thank you, Bart."

Chapter Seventy-One

Bart spoke to PapaWall and they agreed to meet in Augusta on Saturday. PapaWall had rented two houses. Each house had six bedrooms and were adjoining in a shared development with a swimming pool, tennis court and a state of the art barbeque facility.

All twelve bedrooms were occupied, Rosa coordinated the room assignments, assigning the men to PapaWall's house and the women at Bart's house. The married couples, of course, had their rooms, with Dave Gilliss and Mario envying Bart.

Bart had invited Dave Powers to come from Georgia Tech for the Masters. Jessica was also invited, as were Jim Perry and Betsy. John Palermo, with a great deal of nudging from his son, Franco, had agreed to spend the week in Augusta and enjoy the Tournament. Franco Palermo was delighted to spend a week with Lucia. Of course, it would be under Rosa's watchful eye.

With twenty-five people to feed, Rosa, Maria and Heather, joined by Lucia and Tina bought out the supermarket. As Monday, April 2nd, was Bart's 18th birthday, a big barbecue and birthday celebration, was planned. The Masters would be played from Thursday April 5th to Sunday, April 8th.

The weather was beautiful, so Franco and Mario, with help from the guys, set up two dining tables on the pool deck between the houses. Justin, Nick and Giuseppe enjoyed the pool, while all spent Sunday relaxing. Except, Bart and Dave, of course, who were practicing and studying the Augusta National golf course, the brilliant creation of Bobby Jones and famed golf course architect, Alister MacKenzie.

Augusta National is a shrine to golf. Bart was surprised by the slopes of the rolling fairways. He laughed when his first putt rolled out 15 feet past the cup. "It's going to be fun," Bart laughed.

"That's why we practice, Bart, that's why we practice." Dave responded.

Bart played all 18 holes, smiled at the names given to each hole. Some were named for flowering bushes, others for trees. In all, the beauty took one's breath away. He started on 'Tea Olive," and finished on 'Holly." He played Amen corner, with a touch of reverence. Rae's Creek runs through

'Amen Corner,' and many a golfer's heart has been broken on that stretch which includes the 11th hole, 'White Dogwood,' then the 12th, 'Golden Bell,' with pretty Rae's Creek that continues through the 13th hole, 'Azalea.' Bart loved the course.

"WOW!" Bart said. "This is unbelievable, Dave."

Dave laughed. "Let's be amazed and excited today. Starting tomorrow, this is just another golf course." He eye Bart. "Okay, Bart?"

"Sounds good, Coach." Bart responded with a grin. "But, I don't think this will ever be; 'just another golf course.'"

Sunday dinner was an Italian feast. Rosa and Maria, who had given the cooks assigned to the houses the week off, with pay, at PapaWall's insistence, combined to prepare so many favorites. Bart found homemade potato gnocchi, Franco DeMarco loved Rosa's brascioli, Sal was delighted with the calamari in Maria's flavorful marinara sauce, and, of course, Mario smiled when he saw Rosa's Veal Milanese. There was something for everybody, and all enjoyed the balmy air, wonderful food and happy company.

Mario looked at Bart. "Did I hear that you have a practice round scheduled with Tiger Woods tomorrow?"

Bart smiled and nodded. "We are going off at 6am." He looked at Dave. "He likes to play early."

"I'd love to see that," John Palermo said, with a smile. "Any chance I could watch?"

"Me too?" Franco Palermo asked. He met his Dad's smile. Lucia noted the father-son connection, smiled and took his hand. "Have fun," she whispered.

Bart shrugged. "I think that could be arranged." he looked about. "Anybody else interested?"

"Yes, I am, Mario called out."

"We're in," Jim said. Referring to Dave Powers and himself.

PapaWall raised his hand, "I think Justin and I would enjoy that."

"It looks like most of the guys," Angela said with a laugh. "I think that I'll lay by the pool."

Bart laughed. "I remember when you just loved walking the course with me."

Angela smiled, met Bart's gaze, but said nothing. Betsy saw the look and smiled, 'that smoldering exchange could light a fire,' she thought. She grinned at Bart. "True," Betsy said on a laugh. "But, Bart, she's got you now."

Bart smiled at Angela, watched her blush. "She sure does."

Maria saw the joy in Angela's eyes, looked at Rosa. They exchanged a smile.

"I'll hang here and drink wine with Sal," Franco DeMarco called. "Four days of golf is plenty for me."

"Okay," Rosa called out. "Mario, remember, you have to help your father on the grill for dinner tomorrow." She smiled. "It's Bart's birthday."

"Oh, Mario, don't you forget Mom's Prince!" Lucia teased with a smile. "Now, don't you be late."

"Oh you!" Rosa said with a smile.

Mario laughed. "No problem, Mom, I'll be here."

"We'll all help," Dave Powers called. "I'm great on the grill." He pulled Jessica close. "I am so glad you came, Beauty," he said softly to Jess. "I've missed you."

Jess smiled into his grin. "I wouldn't miss a chance to spend the week with Angela and Betsy!" She laughed, as he eyed her with a knowing grin.

"Angela and Betsy, huh?" He held her close, smiled and kissed her. "Why am I so crazy about you, Jess?"

Jessica smiled and with raised brows, responded. "Maybe, it's because I'm so sweet?" She laughed. She leaned in close. "I kinda like you too, Dave." She said softly.

Bart looked at Dave Gilliss. "We should be there by 5am, at the latest, right, Coach?"

Dave nodded. "I'd say even earlier, but it's difficult to practice in the dark." He laughed. "So, we leave here at 4:45am."

Bart and Angela turned in early, after all, Bart needed to rise at 4am.

"This is great, Princess," He smiled as he held her tight. "Everybody together."

Angela's head lay on Bart's chest. "It really is great, Bart." She smiled. "I feel so blessed."

"We are blessed, Princess." Bart affirmed. He kissed her. "I'll dress quietly tomorrow, Princess, not to wake you."

Angela cuddled closer. "I laid out your clothes for tomorrow," she said. "Take the sweater, it may be chilly at 4am."

Bart smiled. "I will, my love."

Bart rose, without the need for an alarm clock. 'Still a lumper,' he thought as he quietly moved to the bathroom. He re-entered the bedroom and looked on Angela as she slept. Her long, curly, black hair fanned out on her white pillow. The smile on her face, that made Bart think that she was enjoying a pleasant dream. He felt so happy in that moment, smiled, took the sweater that Angela had laid out and headed downstairs to meet Dave by the car. The rest of the guys would arrive at 6am.

The practice round with Tiger was challenging and relaxing. Tiger proposed side bets throughout the round that helped both stay focused. Being fierce competitors, Tiger and Bart battled as if it was Sunday at the Masters. Of course, it soon would be. "So, I hear today is your 18th birthday, Bart?" Tiger grinned.

Bart smiled. "Yes Sir, that's right."

Tiger laughed and winked. "I have wedges older than you."

Bart grinned. "I hope you brought them with you, Sir. I think that you will need all the help you can get!"

Tiger bellowed out a deep laugh. "So you brought your gallery, I see?" Tiger shook his head, as he scanned the group. "Even for a practice round, Bart?" He stuck in the needle, for which he is legendary on tour. "I guess I'll just have to school you, youngster, before your family."

Bart laughed. "We'll see, old fellow!" He met Tiger's eyes. "Before you become exhausted and drop off to sleep, I'd like to introduce my family to you."

Tiger, ever the class act, graciously, met and shook hands with all there. Bart's family was awed. "Tiger Woods!" Jim Perry said to the group with a look of astonishment. "I shook hands with Tiger Woods!"

Mario jabbed Jim. "Bart's going to kick his ass." He laughed, as in truth, Mario was as impressed by the 14 time major champion as any there.

Dave worked to keep Bart focused. "This isn't just a fun exercise Bart. We have a major to win!"

Bart smiled. "I've got it, Coach." He eyed Dave. "But, it is awesome!" Dave smiled and nodded.

Bart stayed focused, even as Tiger teased and thrilled. At the same time, Tiger demonstrated his generosity by helping Bart read the greens. In the words of Augusta National's long time caddy master, Freddie Bennett; "you don't read Augusta's greens, you remember them."

Tiger, a four time Master's Champion, told Bart where the traditional pin placements were for all four days. Dave scribbled the info into his course book. They practiced putts to each area. "And, remember," Tiger repeated. "When in doubt, the putt will break to Rae's creek." At the rounds end, by 9am, Bart had shot a 68 and taken some money from the great Tiger Woods."

Bart's group shook hands with Tiger. Mario smiled as he eyed Tiger. "Tiger, thanks for helping my brother."

Tiger smiled. "Your brother is a very special player." He paused, eyed Mario. "Mario, that's what we do here. We help each other in practice," he laughed. "Then, we try to crush our opponents in the tournament." He glanced at Bart who was chatting with the guys. "Bart will do fine."

The group headed back to the houses to relax and rest. They called out Birthday greetings to Bart as they left. Dave and Bart hit the range, chipping areas and practice greens. Dave had Bart concentrating on practicing from the sand traps.

"It is so easy for a chip to get away from you on these slick and very sloped greens," Dave repeated. "Everybody talks about putting these greens," Dave intoned. "But, chipping, to the right spot, to give yourself a good putt is critical."

They worked for three hours, when Dave said, "Okay, that's enough for today. Let's go celebrate your birthday with the family." He laughed, eyed Bart. "I hear they bought some good looking rib-eyes for the grill."

Bart grinned. "How about you take the car, I'll get in a light workout and jog back."

Bart had a cold drink with Tiger and greeted and shook hands with a host of previous Master's Champions. Fred Couples greeted him, as did Phil Mickelson."

Mickelson approached with a big grin and his hand extended. "Watch out guys, this young Buck is a killer." He winked at Bart as they shook hands. "So, Bart, are you planning on stealing any more of my game?"

"Just the part where I can win three Green Jackets, Sir." Bart responded with a smile.

"Hey, Bart," Fuzzy Zoeller called out, with a laugh. "Do you plan to give these guys a chance?"

Bart grinned. "I hope not!" He responded. He thought how much this felt like being at the Main Mast with the lumpers and fishermen. He shook his head, 'guys are guys,' he thought, 'whether eating fried doughnuts on the Gloucester waterfront or much fancier fare at the clubhouse of the famous, Augusta National Golf Club.'

It wasn't until 4pm that Bart arrived home, sweaty from his workout and run in the humid Georgia air. He greeted Angela, who was relaxing by the pool, with a kiss. "I know that I am a bit sweaty from my run," he apologized. "I'll catch a quick shower and put on my suit for a swim."

Angela beamed a smile, while Rosa hugged Bart. "Happy Birthday, my boy." She paused, flashed a huge smile. "Have you had a good day?"

Bart nodded. "Yes, I have," he looked around. He eyed Maria, who was beaming a smile and whose eyes were brimming with tears. He checked to see that Sal was okay, then he looked at Angela. "What's up, Princess?" He smiled. "Do you have something special for my birthday?"

Angela glowed with joy. "I do, Bart. Let's take a little walk, okay?"

Bart took her hand as they walked to the circle before the two houses. "Hey, Princess, do you remember the first time I held your hand?"

Angela smiled in memory. "I do," she nodded. "I remember being surprised that handsome, Bart DeMarco, would want to hold my hand."

He looked into her eyes. "Princess, I never want to let you go."

Angela misted. "Bart, I have something to tell you." The family all watched from their spots on the pool deck. They were not able to hear the conversation, but could see body language.

Bart took both her hands. "Is everything okay, Princess?" He asked, concern showing in his eyes.

'Bart, I've been feeling a bit queasy, you know an upset stomach, no appetite, nausea, for the last few weeks or so."

Bart's eyes grew intense. "Are you okay? Maybe, we should go see a doctor?" He paused, feeling a sense of panic. Losing Angela flashed through his mind. He took a deep breath, trying to remain calm. He thought, "I met a doctor today at Augusta National, "I,I,I could call him." He stuttered.

Angela read the panic, heard the stutter, looked into his eyes and smiled. She put her hands on Bart's face, gently kissed him. "Don't worry. I went to a doctor today, with your Mom and mine." Her eyes filled with joyous tears. "Bart, we're going to have a baby!"

Bart exhaled. His immediate reaction was relief. Then, her words hit him, he laughed aloud, wrapped his arms around her and lifted Angela off the ground. Twirling her in a happy circle, then, cradling her in his arms. "A baby!" he repeated, excitedly. "We're having a baby?"

"Yes," she laughed, kissed him. "We're having a baby."

The group watched the celebration with laughter, tears, smiles, and joy. Bart held Angela, grinning madly, lovingly, cradling Angela in his arms, as he soon would his baby. He saw the happiness on the faces of his family, and carried Angela back to the group, before setting her down. He looked to Rosa, in an emotion choked voice, he said, "Mom, we're going to have a baby!"

Rosa spilled tears of joy. All that he had suffered as a boy flooded back. Now, he was happy and, she believed, due to Angela, coming into his life, free of the stutter that destroyed his confidence and his joy. Rosa embraced them both. "I know Bart, I'm so happy for you." She looked at Angela, kissed her cheek. "Thank you, Angela."

Maria joined the happy group. The Nonnas-to-be, spoke joyously about helping Bart and Angela with the baby. Bart smiled at the happiness the baby was already bringing to their family.

Bart's Dad and brother embraced him. "Congratulations, Son," Franco said in an emotion choked cheer. "This is a nice birthday present."

Mario and Celia embraced Bart and Angela. "So, happy for you two," Celia cried. Mario held his brother. "I'm so proud of you, Bart."

"How about we fire up the grill, Dave Gilliss offered, as he held Rachel, kissed her and enjoyed her smile. "We have a lot to celebrate."

Jessica and Betsy embraced Angela. Jessica smiled. "I'm so happy for you, Angela." She paused. "You are a remarkable woman, you deserve all the happiness this world offers. I'm so proud to count you as a friend." She looked to Dave Powers and flashed a smile.

Betsy took Angela's hand. "I want you to tell me all about how Bart reacted." She smiled. "He seemed to have gone from worried to totally happy in the blink of an eye."

Rachel and MamaWall joined the girls. "Tomorrow," Rachel said, "when, Dave and Bart go off to practice, we need to sit and talk. I want to hear all about it." She grinned. "You know, I'm getting married in a few months." She raised her brows at her mother. "Who knows?"

Heather grinned. "You take it easy there, Rachel." But, she laughed, realizing that a baby would be wonderful. She whispered in Rachel's ear. "Please, for your father's sake, get married first, okay?"

Rachel embraced MamaWall. "Okay, Mom," she laughed. "But I think Dave has other ideas."

"They always do!" MamaWall laughed. "June will be here soon." She paused. "Your Dad deserves to be considered."

It was a joyous party. Bart held Angela all evening. He smiled at her, "we're having a baby." His delight was obvious. Angela's smile was fixed. It seemed her dreams were becoming a reality.

Franco, Mario, Dave Gilliss and John Palermo manned the grill. Pasta dishes whipped up by Rosa, Maria and Tina filled the table.

All ate hearty and the conversation was lively. The young couples, Mario and Celia, Dave and Rachel, Jim and Betsy, Dave and Jessica, even

Franco and Lucia felt the pull that joy and love brings. Franco and Rosa, as well as Sal and Maria smiled throughout the evening. "Grandparents," Maria said. "It's just like Bart said," she looked at Sal. "Bart and Angela are going to give us a baby to love."

Rosa laughed. "I am so happy that they found each other." She looked at Bart, smiling, talking freely and laughing with his friends, his arm around Angela. "My boy is happy."

The cake was brought out and Bart rose to give a speech. "This is a happy day," he said, as he kissed Angela. "My wife tells me that we are looking at a Thanksgiving baby." He laughed, again, kissed Angela. "Who could be more thankful?" He paused. He looked at his Dad and Mom. "So, we can expect little Franco or Rosa to be born this year." He looked at their parents. "Do you remember our first Thanksgiving together?" All four grandparents-to-be nodded and smiled.

Angela smiled up at Bart. The Sicilian tradition of naming the first boy after the paternal grandfather and the first girl after the paternal grandmother, with the next being named for the mother's parents, had long been observed in the Sicilian-American community of Gloucester. Bart and Angela were raised with and cherished their traditional values.

Bart lifted his tall glass filled with an Arnold Palmer. "Today, is my 18th birthday," he looked at all present. "Angela and I are with our family and dear friends in Augusta Georgia." He smiled at a happy Angela. "Thank you all for coming." He paused. "Dave and I are playing in the Masters starting in a few days. WOW!" He took a deep breath. "But, today, I received the best birthday gift of my life." He laughed, kissed Angela. "Thank you, Princess!"

"I think that you had something to do with it," Dave Gilliss called out. "I see you smiling all the time." Everybody laughed.

Angela laughed aloud. "Oh, he sure did!" She called out, as she caught Tina's eye and the sisters exchanged a smile.

"Yes," Bart agreed, "who wouldn't smile to have such a sweet and beautiful, wife?" He grinned. "But, Angela will be doing most of the work." He smiled. "My role was totally a pleasure."

Angela flashed a grin at Bart. "I enjoyed it, too!" She kissed Bart. "Happy Birthday, Honey."

Bart and Angela settled into bed. He pulled her to him, looked into her eyes. "Is it okay?" He asked and grinned. "It is my birthday."

Angela laughed, "It's so okay," she assured him. "Bart, please feel free to love me." She stroked his leg. "Please love me." She asked with a smile.

Bart laughed, kissed her lips. "Whatever makes my girl happy," he responded.

Later, as they lay together. Bart stroked Angela's back, with a light touch. "We're going to be parents." He said, a touch of amazement in his tone. He kissed her. "I think that you will be a great Mom."

Angela stroked him. "I'm so happy, Bart. Thank you for loving me."

He laughed, as he groaned with pleasure from her touch. "Thank you, Princess, for coming to find me." He said. "I have been happy since that night."

Chapter Seventy-Two

The week was spent practicing, learning the course, doing a score of interviews and mentally preparing for his first Major Championship. Bart laughed when he learned that he would be playing with Bubba Watson and Dustin Johnson on Thursday and Friday.

At a media interview, Bart was asked about the pairings. "You are with Dustin and Bubba, Bart. Do you think that you can avoid another debacle like in Phoenix?"

Bart laughed. "I'm pretty sure my coach, Dave Gilliss, will kill me if I even consider getting pulled into another long drive contest." He paused, grinning. "But, playing with Bubba and Dustin will be great fun."

"Bart," a reporter called out, "you are one of the favorites to win the green jacket. What are your thoughts?"

Bart shrugged. "None of that matters. This is a great golf course that we all will be challenging." He shrugged. "I hope that I play well."

"You just celebrated your 18th birthday, Bart. The youngest winner of this Tournament, ever, was Tiger Woods at age 21. Do you think you can do it?"

Bart laughed, "Tiger was the youngest, the best, had the most wins, all those majors, WOW!" He shrugged. "Tiger Woods has had quite a career." He smiled. "We'll just have to see what happens."

"Bart," a reporter called out, "you just withdrew from the Bermuda Classic. You're representatives said that you withdrew for personal reasons, family issues, we were told. Can you tell us what happened?"

"Fortunately, not much. But we were concerned about my father-in-law." He smiled. "But, he's slowly improving, so everything seems fine."

"Bart, you have an early tee time tomorrow, do you feel that is good or bad?" A television reporter queried.

Bart smiled. "I'm good with it. I will get ready then head to the 1st tee to watch golf's legends hit the ceremonial first shots." He grinned. "I'm excited about that. Where else but Augusta National?" He asked. "I am so happy to be here."

At the conclusion of the interview Bart left the media center and saw Donna Caponi. "Hi Donna," Bart called with a smile. "How are you?"

Donna eyed Bart. "I'm good Bart," she studied him. "You look really happy."

"I am," his smile beamed. "The Masters starts tomorrow, and," he laughed. "I have an invitation." He looked around. "I keep expecting security to show up and ask me to leave." He met her smile. "I'm playing with Tiger, Phil, Dustin, Bubba, Wow!" He shook his head. "Last year, it seems, I was playing in high school."

She pursed her lips, studied him. "I'm beginning to know you, Bart. I don't think that smile is because of any golf tournament." She smiled. "Am I right?"

Bart laughed. "Okay, Donna, I'm bursting." He moved closer, spoke excitedly, but softly. "We found out Monday that Angela is expecting!"

Donna embraced Bart. "Congratulations, Bart. You two will make wonderful parents."

"I hope so, Donna." He smiled. "It's a little scary for me."

Donna shook her head. "I've seen you and Angela with the YES kids." She smiled. "You two are naturals."

"Thanks, Donna," he kissed her cheek, gave her a hug. "We are so happy."

"And, your entire family are here with you." She laughed. "A screenwriter couldn't write a script this corny."

Bart smiled. "I guess not."

"You know what this means, Bart?" Donna asked, with a big smile. "You have to win to make the movie perfect!"

Bart smiled. "I'll do my best, Donna." He waved and walked to meet Dave on the practice greens.

Dinner was festive. Rosa and Maria had no kitchen duties as Tina, with the help of Angela and Rachel volunteered to make Veal Saltimbocca for the group. Heather, Lucia and Celia were in and out of the kitchen, setting the tables for 25 hungry people, while Betsy and Jessica were doing sous chef duty, cleaning and tidying behind the 'chefs.'

Bart stood outside the kitchen, smiling, as Angela and Jessica led the girls in 'songs for the galley slaves.' The racy lyrics, created spontaneously, by the young, musically creative minds, and sung to the music of 'Let's Hang on to what we've got,' caused laughter to emanate from the kitchen. The joy and laughter was sweet music to Bart's ears and he was alight with happiness. It all seemed so perfect.

In one of her trips out of the kitchen with plates and silverware, Heather saw Bart hovering. Heather smiled. "You okay, Bart?" She asked.

Bart nodded, concern coloring his features. "I am, but I worry that Angela may be doing too much." He eyed MamaWall, "shouldn't she be resting?"

Heather patted Bart's shoulder. "I'll keep my eye on her, go relax with the guys." She smiled, touched his cheek. "I hear that you and Dave have a big day tomorrow."

Bart smiled. "We do," he paused, looked at Heather, who read his anxiety. "Please make sure that Angela doesn't overdo, okay?"

"I will, I promise," she assured. "Now, please go and try to relax."

"This is great, Tina," Bart said with a smile. He sliced into his veal, savored the flavor. "So good," he added.

Sal smiled at his younger daughter. "Beautiful, Bambina!" He complimented, raising his wine glass in salute. Tina beamed. Maria misted as she saw the connection between father and daughter growing stronger.

The platters of veal and bowls of pasta emptied as all enjoyed the wonderful dinner. Seeing the empty platters, Angela and Betsy rose to head to the kitchen and refill the platters for the hungry group.

Bart put his hand on Angela's arm, to keep her in her seat. He smiled into her questioning gaze. "Please sit and rest, I'll help Betsy."

Rosa, Maria and Heather smiled, as Lucia and Jessica rose to help Betsy. "It's okay Angela," Jessica smiled. "You relax, we'll help Betsy refill the platters."

Angela smiled at Bart. "Bart, I'm fine, really."

Bart looked into her eyes. "Angela, please, make me happy and try to rest a bit, okay?"

The mothers of multiple children were amused by Bart's concern. Each remembered when they were expecting a second, third or even, a fourth child, and caring for crying children, preparing meals, shopping, carrying groceries and taking care of the house. Still, they appreciated that Bart cared.

In the kitchen, as Betsy and Jessica filled the platters with veal and Lucia refilled the pasta bowl, Jessica looked about. "Wow," she said, "Bart has it bad." She looked at Betsy. "He has no idea," she smiled, "but, it's awesome just how much he loves Angela."

Lucia smiled. "Bart is the best." She paused. "He protects the people that he loves." She explained as she looked at the girls. "Look how dedicated he is to those children of YES?"

Betsy smiled. "Angela is so lucky to have Bart." She paused. "He adores her."

Lucia nodded, "Angela deserves his love. She's a great girl." Lucia, became reflective, she looked at the girls. "Bart became different, more confident, when he started dating Angela." She sighed. "Angela really helped Bart." She paused. "I hope to someday mean as much to Franco."

After clean-up, taken care of by Celia, Jessica, Betsy, Tina and Lucia, while Angela sat on a love seat with Bart and a grinning Rachel sat with Dave, the discussion turned to the Tournament. Angela whispered to Bart that she was feeling fine and would prefer to help the girls.

"You did a lot today," Bart responded. "You helped Tina cook a great meal, served us all." He searched her eyes. "You're carrying our baby, you need to stay strong." Angela just smiled and nodded.

Heather and Tina took the young boys to bed by 8pm. They would all be walking the hilly, heavily sloped course in the morning and they needed their rest. Each of the boys hugged Bart.

Bart looked at Justin, "I hope I hear you cheering on every shot tomorrow." He smiled. "And, since you're older than Nick and Giuseppe, you teach them how to cheer, okay?"

Justin nodded, he placed concerned eyes on Bart. "Ddo ggood tomorrow."

Bart smiled. "I'll do my best, Justin." He squeezed the anxious 11 year old. "You get some sleep, I need you strong." The boys were taken off to bed.

"So, Bart," Mario asked. "What do you think?"

"Let me," Dave Gilliss responded, as he looked at the group. "Bart is a better player than any of them." He shrugged. "He just has to play his game, stay focused," he smiled at Bart. "And, we have to play smart."

Bart grinned at Dave, dramatically pointed his finger. "And, Dave, don't you try to push me into trying to outdrive Dustin and Bubba!" Rachel and Angela laughed aloud. PapaWall and John Palermo smiled and were satisfied that Bart was loose.

Dave laughed. "I'll never make that mistake again, Bart." He paused. "And, how about we stay away from 'fun shots,' and focus on smart shots?"

Bart laughed as he hugged Angela to him. "Okay, if we must."

Angela nudged him, "why don't we go and get some rest." She smiled. "You have an early day tomorrow."

Bart nodded, looked at Dave. "6:30 tomorrow morning?"

"Sounds right, Bart, see you in the morning," Dave said. He watched them rise and begin to leave the pool deck, he glanced at Rachel and whispered. "I can't wait until I am as eager to go to bed as Bart and Angela".

Rachel leaned close, put her hand on Dave's leg. "I feel the same way," she whispered with a seductive smile. "But, June's almost here."

He shook his head and smiled. "You are killing me, Rachel." Prompting a laugh from his pretty fiance'.

Bart and Angela said their good nights. Angela kissing her Dad and Mom, as well as Bart's. "See you all in the morning."

"Now, you get some rest, Bart," Jim Perry called out, with a grin. "And, leave that girl alone!" He called.

Angela wagged her finger at Jim. "No way, Jim," she smiled. "I need to be certain Bart is sooo relaxed!"

All laughed as Jim hoped. As a golfer, he knew that being confident and relaxed paid dividends. "Bart," Jim shook his head, disapprovingly, "haven't you done enough damage there?"

Bart smiled, "I'll consider that Jim," he shook his head, "but, I don't know, she's so pretty." He laughed.

Bart and Angela settled into bed and embraced, kissing each other with passion. Once they were sated, she laid her head on Bart's chest. With a laugh, she said; "You know Bart, I'm pregnant, not disabled." She paused. "Someday, we'll have two, three or even four children and I'll be pregnant." She grinned at him. "I'll still have to take care of them all."

Bart lay there enjoying Angela's gentle caresses. "If our baby is a girl, I hope she looks just like you, Princess." Bart said.

Angela realized that Bart was facing his greatest professional challenge and he just wasn't in the frame of mind for a heavy discussion. Her mother had watched Bart's gaze, how he hovered and kept concerned eyes on Angela. Maria told her that, "Bart was just being Bart." She had explained. "He worries about you. Give him time, Angela, he'll figure it out." Angela knew that she was right. In any event, his concern was endearing.

Angela kissed his cheek. "I want all our children to look like the DeMarco's," she replied. "Your family is beautiful."

Bart kissed her, looked into her eyes. "Princess, you are the most beautiful girl in the world." He said with conviction. "I love your face, I love your body, I love the way you look, most of all, I love who you are."

She smiled as she continued to pleasure him. He lifted her to lay atop him, loving the softness of her body, her eager response. She kissed him and wriggled into position. "Please love me, again," she cooed.

Chapter Seventy-Three

Bart was smiling when he shook Dustin Johnson's and Bubba Watson's hands as they met on the 1st tee. The weather was warm, with only a slight breeze. For Friday and Saturday, cooler temperatures and significant wind was in the forecast. Dave hoped to take advantage of the favorable conditions today and survive the following two days.

"So, Bart, whose fault was it? Bubba asked. "Was it me or Dustin?"

Bart grinned. "Fault? Bubba?" He laughed. "I don't know what you are talking about, but," his smile widened. "I guess it was your fault." The three men and their caddies laughed.

Dustin picked up the theme. "All the media guys say that we caused you to lose the Phoenix Open." Dustin shook his head and smiled. "Hearing that has made me so depressed."

Bart laughed. "I could tell that you were depressed when you hoisted that trophy." He looked at Bubba. "Bubba, didn't your heart go out to poor Dustin?"

"Hey," Bubba urged, "how about we have a long drive contest?" He grinned. "Dustin, I don't think that we'd have a chance against such a big, strong and young stud like Bart." He grinned. "But, I'm willing to give it a try."

Bart laughed. "I think that you two are trying to take advantage of my youth and inexperience." He shook his head. "That's not nice!"

Donna Caponi stood by the 1st tee. "Bart seems loose," she said to play-by-play announcer, Jim Nantz and color commentator, Nick Faldo, 'Sir Nick,' knighted by the Queen of Great Britain, to honor a golfer, a six time Major Champion, who had brought honor and glory to her kingdom.

Bart is a cool customer," Faldo stated, "DeMarco is one of my favorites to slip on the green jacket on Sunday." Said the man who had twice won the Masters.

"Bold prediction, Nick," Jim Nantz offered. "Does he know the course well enough?"

"Well guys," Donna interjected. "He played with Tiger on Monday, Phil and Rory on Tuesday and he played nine holes with the great Jack

Nicklaus on Wednesday." She laughed. "Bart and his coach, Dave Gilliss, asked a million questions." She paused. "Then, after the matches, they went and practiced and applied what they learned."

"That's the way to do it." Faldo laughed. "Pick the brain of 6 time, Masters Champion, Jack Nicklaus, 4 time winner, Tiger Woods, and 3 time Champion, Phil Mickelson. That's smart."

The 1st tee announcer introduced two time Master's Champion, Bubba Watson, who, always popular, waved to the gallery and struck his drive on the 455 yard, par 4, called 'Tea Olive.'

Next it was U.S. Open champion, Dustin Johnson, who rocked his drive over 300 yards down the fairway.

Then Bart took the tee box, to the happy roar of his gallery. He smiled and waved to the children of 'Bart's Battalion,' grinned at Angela and his family, teed his ball, then went through his routine, visualized the shot, smiled and launched a drive that split the fairway, 335 yards down the center. He was 20-30 yards longer than Bubba and Dustin. As they left the tee box, Bart smiled at Dave, "nice and smooth," he repeated, Dave's mantra. Dave smiled and winked.

"This is a tough opening hole. Par is a good score," Dave stated. "Middle of the green, Bart." He urged.

Bart two putted the 1st for par. Dave nodded, "Good work."

Angela was walking with Rachel, Celia, Rosa and Lucia. Maria and Tina were helping Sal try to walk at least the first nine of the heavily sloped course. Bart had spoken to Rosa, "please Mom, make sure Angela's okay," he had asked, concern on his face.

Rosa had placed her hand on Bart's face, to reassure him, as she had when he was a boy. "We'll take care of Angela, Bart. You must go and do your job."

Bart smiled and as always trusted the woman who had been a constant in his life. Rosa had cheered him and shared his pain, even crying with him when the daily humiliation became too much to bear.

Dave cut Bart loose on the 2nd hole, a 575 yard, par 5, 'Pink Dogwood.' "We can birdie this one," Dave explained. "A nice drive is what we need."

Bart delivered another perfect, center cut drive, leaving 240 yards to the center of the green. Bart was in a zone, oblivious to his playing partners, focused on Dave's instructions and the shot at hand. He lofted a high, cut, with his 5 fairway metal. It was beautifully struck and landed softly on the green. Dave smiled. Bart would be putting for eagle.

"This looks promising," PapaWall said softly to John Palermo.

"Is he a good putter?" John asked.

"He is," Franco Palermo stated. He shrugged, "but Dad, these greens are slick."

Bart and Dave studied the putt. Dave consulted his course book, covered with notations from Tiger, Phil, and Jack Nicklaus. He looked at Bart. "It will be quick, one ball left, is my read." Bart stood behind the putt, looked up and smiled at Angela. She met his eye and smiled.

"Eagle putt," Jim Nantz called. "What do you see, Nick?"

"It's a bit downhill, and slick." He paused. "It's all about speed, Jim." Faldo added. "If he's too aggressive, he could easily run it 10 feet by the cup."

Bart stood over the putt and started it to the hole. "Speed looks good," Faldo called, paused, "real good!" as the ball fell into the cup for an Eagle. The crowd roared. Somehow, YES had secured hundreds of admission tickets. Bart's Battalion was in good voice. Angela leaped for joy, Franco DeMarco beamed and embraced Rosa. Mario and Franco Palermo high fived.

Bart was -3 after his birdie on the par 5, 570 yard 8th hole, 'Yellow Jasmine.' And, his name was atop the big leader boards. Rosa looked at her son's name on the leaderboard, smiled at Franco, "our boy!" is all she managed to say as she choked up. Bart had the honor on the 9th hole, 'Carolina Cherry,' a 460 yard par 4, with a false front on the green. A good drive and Bart and Dave hoped to be able to hit a high shot into the green, just beyond the pin, with little spin. If his shot landed on the front of the green, or, had a hard spin, the ball would come back off the front of the green and roll as much as 50 yards back onto the fairway.

A 310 yard drive, left Bart with a 150 yard second shot to the center of the green. Dave studied the wind, tossed grass into the air, closely considered the breeze through the trees. He nodded and handed Bart his 8 iron. "Middle of the green, Bart, with a little spin."

Bart nodded, went through his routine. The pin was set just above the false front. Dave was gambling that if Bart could hit past the pin and suck it back, he might just be looking at another birdie. Bart hit a beauty. It flew over the pin, hit, hopped and then bit. The backspin drew the ball back to the cup.

"Oh God," Jim Perry said aloud, "stop, please," he pleaded. Dave watched with concern. Too much spin and it would catch the false front and be pulled off of the green. But, Dave considered a long downhill putt even riskier. Bart's ball spun back, slowed and stopped about one foot right of the hole. The gallery cheered, John Palermo smiled. "He's amazing!"

PapaWall nodded and smiled. "John, the only person who doesn't know how great Bart really is," he laughed, "is Bart." He looked at John. "Dave is equally gifted." He smiled. "And, I'm not saying that because he will soon be my son-in-law." He paused as they readied to move to the back nine. "Dave weighs everything. He wants to take advantage of today's great weather. The forecast for tomorrow and Saturday is for cooler air and wind gusts up to 35 mph." He looked at John. "They are a great team." He paused. "And, my Rachel is a lucky girl."

Bart stood on the 10th tee at -4, after a great front nine. Dave thought about the upcoming, brutally difficult, 'Amen Corner,' holes 11, 12 and 13, where many a golfer's dream has died.

Bart lipped out his birdie putt on the 10th hole, then faced the 11th, 'White Dogwood,' what Master's Champion, Ben Crenshaw, calls the most difficult hole on the course. Bart made a 10 foot par putt and was happy to walk to the par 3, 12th, 'Golden Bell,' still leading at -4.

'Golden Bell' is a difficult, short par 3. The distance ranges from 145-155 yards, but the elevated green is guarded by Rae's Creek. A ball hit short, into the shaved slope will almost always trundle down into Rae's Creek. The notable exception was the 1992 Masters, when eventual champion Fred Couples hit short into the slope and the ball, somehow, stayed on the slope. Freddie, made his up and down for par, and went on, happily, to slip on the fabled green jacket.

Between Rae's Creek and the green is a good sized sand trap, which if hit, will save the ball from Rae's Creek, but leave a tough sand shot. One of the big challenges is that the green is so shallow. A ball hit long will likely find trouble, the same is true, left and right. Some refer to 'Golden Bell' as 'the best par three, pound for pound, in the world.'

On a day with little breeze, 'Golden Bell,' is a reasonable challenge. Bart looked down at the green from where he stood on the tee, smiled at how truly beautiful was the picture before him, took his pitching wedge from Dave, smiled and winked at Angela. He lofted his shot high and right at the flag, in the sage words of Sam Snead, 'it landed like a butterfly with sore feet,' no more than five feet from the cup, bit and stopped. The gallery erupted. Justin shouted encouragement with only a minor stutter. Bart smiled. Moments later, Bart ran in his birdie putt to move to -5.

Bart then birdied the two par 5's, #13, 'Azalea,' and #15, 'Firethorn.' He completed his round with a birdie at #18, to shoot what would be the day's best round of 64. Bart's -8, would find him three shots better than the trio of Rory McElroy, Jordan Spieth, and Dustin Johnson at 67 or -5.

Bart had finished before the afternoon wave went out. "A great start for the young man!" Nick Faldo stated. "We'll see how it holds up," he laughed. "But, Jim," Sir Nick offered. "Bart has shown the ability to go low and run away from the pack."

As he walked off the 18ᵗʰ green, Bart embraced Angela, his mother and the family. Donna Caponi waited to interview Bart. "Why don't you all head home," he suggested. "I'll do the press and spend time with the kids.

Donna approached. "Great round, Bart," she stated with a smile. "You lead the Masters at the moment. Are you excited?"

Bart laughed. "Certainly better than Phoenix!" He stated, emphatically. Donna laughed, as Angela walked over and moved close to Bart. Bart put his arm around Angela's waist. His eyes met Angela's, "are you okay?" He asked. Angela smiled and nodded. Bart looked to and smiled at Donna. "It's so early, Donna, really nothing to get excited about." He shrugged, looked about. "This place is great. I feel so lucky to be here."

Bart and Angela walked over to his young fans. He spent time with each child, signing autographs, posing for photos, and listening to the children who needed to tell Bart their story and share their pain. He encouraged each child to believe things can get better. "Don't let them get to you," he encouraged. "Words, even cruel words, can't hurt you if you don't let them."

Angela, Dave and Rachel stayed with Bart for the two hours he spent answering reporter's questions and talking to 'Bart's Battalion.' They then entered the dining room to have a relaxing lunch.

"Isn't this place beautiful?" Rachel asked. She looked at Dave and Bart. "You know, if you guys win, we can come back every year!"

Bart laughed aloud, still laughing, he glanced at Dave. "Okay, Dave, now we have a reason to win!"

Dave laughed with Bart. It was as if built up pressure was released. Dave took Rachel's hand. "That's perfect sweetheart. I needed that!"

Rachel grinned and kissed him. "Glad I could help."

Angela laughed, leaned over and kissed Bart. "You guys did great, today."

Bart studied Angela. "This is a very hilly course, Angela. Are you okay?"

Angela read the concern in his eyes. "I'm fine, Bart." She smiled. "I love that you're concerned, but the Doctor said the exercise is good for me and the baby."

"Hey Bart," Rachel poked with a grin. "Maybe, you should just let Angela sleep peacefully tonight." She winked. "You know, no strenuous activity."

Bart laughed aloud. "Rachel, you heard the girl, the doctor thinks that exercise is good for her." He winked at Angela. "I know it's good for me!"

Angela laughed, took Bart's hand. "Bart, don't you listen to Rachel," Angela winked at Rachel. "I think that she's jealous."

"I know I am!" Dave said. "Very jealous!"

The good friends, now relaxed, all laughed together, Rachel leaned close to Dave, smiled, "soon, my love, soon."

Chapter Seventy-Four

The weather forecast was accurate. The family awoke to a cool and breezy day. Bart, Dustin and Bubba, were scheduled to tee off at 1:52pm.

The Golf Channel's 'Live from the Master's' show posted the leaderboard, with Bart leading, at -8. Rory McElroy, Dustin Johnson and Jordan Spieth were tied at -5, Phil Mickelson and Sergio Garcia were at -4 and Justin Rose was at -3. The announcers and commentators all mentioned that the group chasing Bart were all Major Champions and this Masters is Bart's very first Major. The consensus was that Bart had a mountain to climb to the coveted green jacket.

Hearing the commentary, the family grew quiet. Jim Perry, however, laughed. "These guys don't realize that I taught Bart how to golf and how to win!" He smiled at Betsy. "Am I right, beautiful?"

"Absolutely," Betsy declared, smiling broadly. "Bart would be nothing without you, Jim."

Smiles blossomed across the room. Bart shook his head. "And, Dave and I intend to win even with that handicap!"

"Boom!" Dave Powers exclaimed. All were smiling at the exchange, worry and concern replaced by good cheer.

Jim feigned shock. "It's like a knife in my heart!" Jim lamented. "Betsy, you see how soon they forget!" He paused. "Where's that magazine?" Bart was laughing aloud.

Angela looked on happily. "So sad, Jim," she said as she feigned outrage. "After all you did for Bart." She shook her head. "I'm so disappointed that my guy has forgotten your enormous contribution to 'Team DeMarco.'"

Jim smiled at Angela. "As you are in a delicate condition, and being the big man that I am, I will forgive Bart." He paused, smiled. "On the condition that he mentions my name during the presentation of the Green Jacket!"

"That's all?" Bart asked, grinning. "Jim, you are too good to me."

"So true," Jim said. "So, true!"

Tina looked on with a smile. "Okay, gang, breakfast is served."

Rosa, Maria and Tina, prepared a wonderful breakfast of buttermilk waffles, bacon, eggs and hash browns. As it was a bit chilly, the group, with the exception of Dave Gilliss, who continued to study the TV coverage, gathered in the dining room and kitchen, before retreating to the Living room for a second cup of coffee and to watch coverage of the Tournament.

Dave sat quietly, with his course charts, watching the breaks of putts at the days pin locations, trying to determine the effect the wind was having on shots into the greens. He dined alone before the TV, with Rachel and Angela bringing breakfast, juice and coffee.

Bart looked on smiling. He felt blessed to be working with such a team.

Bart and Dave arrived at Augusta National at noon. The morning wave had passed through and Bart at -8, was still atop the leaderboard. The wind and chill made scoring difficult, and very few sub-par rounds were posted.

Dave advised Bart that they would play as they had at Pebble Beach. "Fairways and greens, Bart." Dave preached. We'll keep the ball below the wind and ride the breeze when possible.

Bart nodded. He remembered well, how effective Dave's strategy had been and was comfortable giving him control. He was swinging well, playing stingers that flew low and ran down the fairways.

Jim Nantz commented that Bart was shunning the driver and using irons and hybrids with good results.

"He may be young," Nick Faldo offered. "But, he plays smart." He paused. "It's clear with the swirling winds that nobody is going low today, so Bart is playing for par and taking whatever opportunities that may be presented. It's a smart move."

"Guys," Donna interjected. "Bart is allowing his coach, Dave Gilliss to direct his game." She laughed. "They are truly a team."

Bart played the first nine holes in -1, and approached 'Amen Corner' cautiously.

Sal Curcuru was exhausted from walking the first nine holes on Thursday. With the cold and wind, he and Maria decided to stay in the house and watch on television. Angela and the group were on hand, dressed warmly and cheering Bart on.

Bart parred both 10 and 11. He came to 12, the par 3, 'Golden Bell,' and was again impressed by the colors and slopes. Dave had trouble reading the swirling wind. His gut told him that the wind would likely hurt. He handed Bart his 9 iron and suggested that he aim at the left side of the front sand trap. "Let it go, Bart," he instructed.

Bart lofted his ball high, the wind caught it and knocked it down into the sand trap. "Wow!" Bart said. "Thank God that I didn't hit the wedge." He grinned at Dave. "That's why we work so hard on sand saves."

Bart blasted out of the sand, his ball landed on the green and spun. When it came to rest, it lay 15 feet from the cup. Bart missed the putt and tapped in for bogey. He was back to even par for the day.

Angela winced when the par putt lipped out. Still, she found a smile as Bart passed on the way to the par 5, 13th tee. He grinned, took a moment and kissed her. Angela blushed as she smiled. "Keep smiling, beautiful," Bart said. "Things are fine."

As both Bubba and Dustin had parred 12, Bart would hit third off the tee. He noted the wind seemed to be at his back. After Bubba and Dustin hit, Dave handed Bart his driver. "Let's make Eagle here." Dave said with a smile.

Bart launched a mammoth drive, the wind carrying it out past 350 yards. He would have only 160 yards into the green, a golden opportunity. With the wind at his back, Bart hit a 9 iron, lofting it high and watching it land within five feet of the pin. The ball rolled out past the flag, leaving Bart a 4 foot putt for Eagle, which he drained!

Finally, Bart's Battalion had reason to roar. He was -2 on the day and -10 for the tournament. He now had a 5 shot lead.

"He could do this," Nick Faldo stated. "Nothing seems to faze him."

Donna Caponi chimed in, "Bart is 'the Diamond Maker," she stated.

"Donna," Jim Nantz asked. "Could you explain the nickname 'the Diamond Maker,' to the patrons watching at home?

"Certainly, Jim," she responded. "Bart's coach, Dave Gilliss, says that it is the enormous pressure of the earth that turns carbon into Diamonds." She laughed. "And, as Bart thrives under pressure, he's the guy who makes Diamonds."

"Well," Jim Nantz agreed. "He doesn't seem to get rattled easily."

The wind picked up. Bart battled through the last five holes in even par and completed an exhausting day at -10, and firmly in the lead.

At days end, it was Bart at -10, and five players, all Major Champions at -5. "Tomorrow promises to be interesting," Jim Nantz speculated. "Could Bart DeMarco, at age 18, be the youngest Masters Champion in history?"

"36 holes left to play," Faldo warned. "It's a long way to that Green Jacket."

Ignoring the chill, Franco, with the assistance of John Palermo and his son, as well as Mario and Dave Powers, manned the grill to barbeque Sal's homemade Italian sausage, corn on the cob, and roasted bread. Rosa and Lucia made a tomato salad. Maria, with Tina's help, was busy making a spaghetti carbonara.

A frustrated Angela was told to relax. Betsy and Jessica were charged with keeping her company. Angela looked at her mother and Rosa, "this is silly. I feel fine!" She pressed, "I can help."

Rosa and Maria exchanged a knowing smile. "Bart is worried about you doing too much." Maria said, with a smile. "You walked the course in the wind." She shrugged. "Why don't we humor him?"

"Yes," Rosa added. "And, right now he has all the pressure of this Tournament." She smiled. "We should be understanding."

Angela smiled. "I guess that I should be flattered, but, I'm used to helping."

Rosa laughed. "Of course, you're right. One day, you'll be pregnant and caring for children and running the house." She paused. "You'll look back on today with a smile." She shrugged. "Just try to enjoy it." She paused, sighed, took Angela's hands as she engaged her eyes. "Angela, please help Bart," she urged, a mother's concern showing. "This is all so big, I think he needs our help."

Angela nodded. "He acts as if he is unaffected by all the fuss," she shook her head. "But, how could he be?" She paused. "The golf is the smallest part, but all the kids counting on him. He feels that. He doesn't want to let them down."

Rosa welled up. She squeezed Angela's hands. "My Bart loves you so much, I am so happy that he found you."

Maria put her hand on Rosa's shoulder. "They are good for each other, Rosa."

Dinner was delicious and most importantly, relaxing. Jim Perry was at his outrageous best. The group was convulsed with laughter, with Bart and Betsy being the butt of his good natured jabs. Both relished the humor and were fine with Jim's frantic and sometimes crazy, observations on relationships, sports and life.

The group laughed openly. "Betsy, how do you deal with him?" Celia asked, as she wiped laugh tears from her cheeks. "He's crazy!"

Further provoking his hilarity, Betsy sighed. "I have no real choice. There are thousands of women who want Jim." She smiled sweetly. "Isn't that right, Honey?"

"Absolutely," Jim responded. "It's only my self-restraint that holds back Jessica and Celia." He grinned. "Look at me, what girl wouldn't want this?" He grinned at Rachel. "Am I right, Rachel?"

Laughing, Rachel nodded. "Jim, I was hoping Dave wouldn't find out my secret longing for you."

Dave held Rachel and laughed. He pointed a finger at Jim. "Perry, you keep away from my girl."

The young couples laughed and relaxed. Exactly, what Bart and Dave needed, to face the challenges of the weekend battles to come. The Masters is not for the faint of heart. The pressure has broken many a golfer.

Bart and Angela sat together enjoying the comfort of family and friends. Bart held Angela close, laughing, asking if she was tired from the stress of the day.

"I'm fine, Bart." She smiled. She winked at him. "I can't wait to settle in for the night." She moved closer, whispered for his ears. "I'll show you how much energy I still have." With that she won a smile from Bart, as she hoped.

As Bart was leading the Masters, he and Sergio Garcia would be the last pairing out at 2pm. He was looking forward to playing with the flamboyant Spaniard.

Masters Saturday dawned even cooler and with a bigger breeze. The forecast called for the wind to continue to freshen as the day wore on, promising the leaders a difficult challenge.

Bart and Dave sat watching TV coverage of the Tournament. Once again scoring was challenging. Not one golfer was playing better than at par, and many were rapidly going backwards. It was moving day, but most of the competitors seemed to be moving in the wrong direction.

Dave was furiously making notes on the breaks of the greens and the effect wind was having on shots hit into greens. He noted that chips were being affected, and putts were being blown off line. He quietly ruminated on a strategy.

It was decided that Sal and Maria would stay at home and watch coverage of the tournament. Sal embraced Bart. "Tomorrow, I will be there to help cheer you to victory, Bart," he promised.

Sergio greeted Bart warmly. "It will be tough today," the major champion and likely future Hall of Fame golfer stated. He looked at Bart. "Keep your head, Bart. Weird things can happen in the wind."

Major Champions are always a threat. The last four groups out were battling the conditions and seeking par. To get off the incredibly challenging course with a par 72 or better, would see a golfer pass many competitors.

Bart recognized that as a European Tour star, Sergio Garcia knew how to play and adjust to big weather shifts, which was commonplace on the ancient links courses of Scotland, England and Ireland. After the first nine holes, Sergio was even par and Bart was +1.

"You're doing fine," Dave counseled. "They are chasing us, let them make the mistakes."

The leader board at the 10th tee, had Bart at -9, with Sergio and Spieth at -6, the rest packed closely behind. Bart's large gallery was itching for a reason to cheer, but as Bart battled par, he was in survival mode. Angela and Rachel walked together. Rachel assuring Angela that they were on Dave's schedule. "We're leading Angela, let them come after us!"

Having parred holes 10 and 11, Sergio and Bart stood on the 12th tee, 'Golden Bell'.

Sergio had the honor and selected a club. Dave saw it was his pitching wedge. The winds were swirling and in Dave's mind hurting rather than helping the golfer. He looked at Bart. "I don't think that will be enough club."

Bart stood back, watching closely. Sergio has the well-earned reputation of being a great ball striker. Tee to green, he is considered to be one of the best. Sergio struck the ball on the screws and they all watched the wind knock it down. It hit above the front sand trap and ran down into the bunker. Bart smiled at Dave and accepted his club.

Bart struck the 9 iron beautifully, the ball rose and tracked the pin. His gallery began to stir.

"It's on the pin!" Donna Caponi called. Bart held his pose as he watched the shot descend. He looked up at the ball, then at the pin. A smile creased his face.

"It looks good!" Faldo called excitedly.

'Birdie coming,' Dave thought with a grin as the ball descended to the green. It struck the narrow green inches before the hole, a roar began from 'Bart's Battalion.' The ball bounced up and struck the anchored bottom of the pin squarely and solidly.

"Ggo in!" yelled Justin. But, instead of dropping into the cup, or settling close by, the ball ricocheted back, high into the air. It landed on the front fringe of the green, bounced down onto the slope and spun back into Rae's Creek.

There was a stunned silence on the tee. Angela's hands went to her mouth, in shock. The camera caught Bart shaking his head.

"What an awful break," Nick Faldo called. "It should have been an ace or at worse a birdie." He paused. "Now, Bart's looking at a 5 or 6."

"Golf is anything but fair," Jim Nantz stated. The camera found a shocked Angela. "It looks like DeMarco's lead will be gone, Nick." He paused. "Will this cause the 18 year old to unravel?"

The question angered Sal, who watched at the house with Maria. "Bart's tougher than that!" He yelled and pointed at the set.

Bart looked at Dave and shrugged. They began walking down to the drop area.

"Walk slowly," Dave advised. "Deep breaths, Bart." He put his hand on Bart's shoulder. "Just a bad break. We'll be okay."

Bart looked at Dave and smiled. "Rub of the green, Dave." He eyed his coach. "I'm not going to let a bad break beat us." Bart took his drop and looked at a difficult 50 yard shot. He lofted his 60 degree wedge and watched the ball land on the green about 15 feet behind the pin.

Sergio settled into the front bunker and struck a solid sand wedge to 5 feet. Sergio marked his ball and moved aside. Bart and Dave lined up his putt. Bart crouched behind the ball, closed his eyes, stood, smiled at Angela, and set up over his putt. He struck a good putt, perhaps with just a touch too much speed. The ball hit the lip too hard, and spun out, stopping 5 feet from the cup. Bart's ball lay just longer away from the cup than Sergio's.

"He hasn't lost his turn." Sir Nick Faldo stated. "Words no golfer ever wants to hear."

"Is he rattled, Donna?" Jim Nantz asked Donna Caponi.

Donna nodded. "I think he is a bit rattled, guys." She shook her head. "What an awful break." She paused. "His Coach, Dave Gilliss is talking to him, slowing him down."

Bart took a deep breath as Dave closed in to settle Bart. "Easy Bart, let's look at this." Dave urged. Player and coach read the putt. "It will break to Rae's Creek," Dave reminded Bart. "My read is just outside right." Bart studied the putt, nodded his head in agreement, then he closed his eyes to visualize the putt breaking just slightly left and into the cup. He smiled at Angela, set up over the putt and stroked it just outside right. He struck the putt well, but, it didn't break, and stopped and settled one inch from the cup. The gallery gasped. Bart took a deep breath and tapped in for a triple bogey 6. His lead was gone.

Sergio rolled his putt into the heart of the cup for par. They were now tied on top of the leader board at -6.

"It can be a cruel game!" Nick Faldo stated. "How's he doing Donna?"

Donna chuckled. "Guys, it appears he's more upset that he hit his putt too hard than what happened with his tee shot." She walked over to Bart. "Tough break, Bart," she said. "What now?"

Bart grinned. He caught Angela's eye and winked. "Donna, bad breaks are part of the game." He shrugged. "Now, we move forward."

Angela looked at Rachel, she managed a smile. "Look at him, I'm dying and he's smiling."

Rachel kept her eyes on Dave, who signaled that Bart was okay. She took Angela's hand. "He'll be fine. Maybe tomorrow he'll catch a good break." She laughed. "Dave always says, that it is the golfer who keeps his head that usually wins."

As the groups ahead of the DeMarco, Garcia match played on, they heard groans and gasps from the crowd. "Look at that," Justin Rose said to his caddie. As the leaderboard reflected the new reality.

"It's a new game!" Rose's caddie stated. "Come on, Justin, let's go get him."

The wind continued to swirl and gust. Bart and Sergio dug in and played the round out in even par. As they exited the 18th green, the leaderboard showed that Masters Sunday would be exciting. Bart and Sergio stood atop the board at -6, then came McElroy, Spieth, and Mickelson, (chasing his 4th Green Jacket), at -5, and Dustin Johnson and Justin Rose at -4.

Bart sat for all the interviews. He refused to give in to negativity. "Just a bad break," he repeated. "That's golf, we'll be ready tomorrow." After the interviews, he met with 'Bart's Battalion,' the children of YES. He saw their long faces and he smiled. "I hope you will be here tomorrow." He encouraged. "I need your support to win." He looked at a child of about seven years old, he saw her lip was quivering. He took her hand, met her eyes. "What's your name?"

"I,I'm Bbeth," she stuttered and began to cry. "I,I wwanted you tto wwin!" She pleaded.

He lifted her chin, looked into her eyes. "Cheer for me tomorrow, Beth. I'll win for you!" He won a big smile from brown eyed Beth and grateful thanks from Beth's parents. He looked at the group, "who thinks 'Stutter Boy' can win the Masters?" He asked. Smiles emerged and cheers erupted from the gathered group, which counted in the hundreds. He posed for photos, talked to the children. Then, they took the group photo.

Bart clutched Angela's hand as they left the course to head home. He was facing Championship Sunday at the Masters. And, 'Team DeMarco' had no margin for error!

Arriving at the house with Angela, Dave and Rachel, Bart walked into a somber gathering. He noted that Justin, Nick and Giuseppe were off playing. He smiled, "What's this?" He looked about. "Dad, PapaWall, Papa, have you all lost faith in me?" Smiles began to emerge. He looked at Dave, "hey Coach, did I misread the leaderboard or am I still leading this Tournament?"

Dave smiled. "No, Bart, you read it correctly." He affirmed.

He looked to Rosa, smiled. "Mom, do DeMarco's let a bad break beat them?"

Rosa beamed. "No!" She laughed. "DeMarco's are too hard headed to quit!"

"That's right," he said as he kissed Rosa. "Okay, now here's an important question," he looked to Maria, "Mom, what's for dinner?"

"See that," Jim Perry stated. "Bart always asks the right question." He smiled, looked about. "I taught Bart that."

Everybody's mood was lightened. Bart looked to Maria, "well, Mom?"

Maria laughed. "I made spaghetti with calamari sauce, spettini, and," she grinned, "Garlic bread, for my favorite son-in-law!"

Bart's eyes, along with numerous others turned to see Angela blushing. Angela looked into Bart's eyes. She saw that he was shaken.

Angela turned to Maria. "Thanks Mom," Angela said, with flushed cheeks and a forced smile.

Bart moved and kissed Maria. "Mom, I love garlic bread!"

"I'm going to catch a shower," Bart said. "Dinner in about 45 minutes?" Seeing Maria's nod, Bart took the stairs two at a time.

Rosa watched him go. She knew her boy, looked at Franco. "Tough day," she said quietly.

Dave Gilliss watched Bart leave. He shook his head and eyed Angela. He glanced at the stairway. "They all think he's going to fold." He looked about. "Time for 'Team DeMarco' to rally!" He stated.

Rachel moved close and put her arm around Dave's waist. "He just needs time," she smiled. "Some dinner and maybe a few laughs." She looked up to Dave. "We can give him that." She looked into Dave's eyes and read his emotional exhaustion, she also saw panic. She rose on her toes and kissed him. "I love you," she said softly. Dave held Rachel tightly to him. "Hold me," he said softly.

Maria had read Bart, heard Rosa. She looked at Angela, "maybe your husband needs your help?" She asked with raised brows. There were laughs and grins across the room.

"Yes," MamaWall agreed, as she flashed a smile. Seeking to raise everyone's spirits, she added. "Angela, why don't you go and, ahem," she raised her brows and winked, provocatively, "help your husband!" Now, everybody was grinning.

Angela smiled at her mother, her cheeks flushed. "I'll go and try to raise his spirits." She rose from her chair to leave. She met Dave Gilliss's's eyes. Solid Dave, who was never shaken, looked a bit rattled. "He'll be okay, Dave." Angela stated.

"His spirits?" she said, "right?" Jim Perry laughed. "Angela, you are going to raise his" he leered, "his spirits, you say?"

Angela blushed crimson, but flashed a winning smile, shook her head and hustled up the stairs.

Entering their room, Angela found Bart in the shower. His hands flat against the wall, the spray cascading on his head, she heard him sobbing, felt a stab to her heart. She paused, quickly and quietly removed her clothes and entered the shower. "I'm here, Bart." She said, softly, putting her hands on his shoulders.

Bart turned and embraced Angela. "I'm letting them down, Angela. You saw Little Beth," he shook his head, she felt his chest heave. "I just can't let the kids down." He choked. "They deal with enough."

She held him tight. "You won't Bart. Tomorrow will be better," she assured. She put her lips to his. "Kiss me Bart, please love me."

A much calmer and relaxed Bart re-joined the group. He entered the dining room, smiling and holding Angela's hand. "Something smells good!" He called. "I'm hungry."

Rosa and Maria looked from Bart to Angela, who smiled and nodded.

"Come on, my husband's hungry. Let's eat." Angela called, with a smile. It was a far more upbeat group that shared a dinner, before 'Team DeMarco' faced its greatest challenge to date.

Chapter Seventy-Five

M asters Sunday dawned bright, sunny and with a forecast of warmth and light winds. Once again, as the leaders, Sergio and Bart were last off at 2pm.

The leaderboard was packed with Major Champions. Bart stood on the 1st tee with Dave, Sergio and Sergio's caddie. The leaders were approached by on course commentator, Donna Caponi.

"Bart had a truly bad break yesterday, Nick," Jim Nantz stated. "In the process, he brought a pack of great players onto his heels."

"He did," Nick Faldo agreed. "I'm still shaking my head over what happened at the 12th, Jim." He paused. "Bart could well have a three or four shot lead, instead of being tied at the top of the leaderboard."

"Hi Sergio," Donna greeted the flamboyant Spaniard. "How do you see today taking shape?"

Sergio grinned. "It's hard to say, Donna." He paused. "In truth, we should all be chasing Bart." He laughed. "But, you know what they say; 'every shot makes somebody happy.'" He looked across the tee box to Bart, who was conferring with his coach. "That bad break on the 12th yesterday, made a bunch of golfers happy." He eyed Donna. "But, don't count that kid out." He nodded. "I see a toughness there."

Donna moved to Bart. "Hi Bart," Donna smiled. "You ready for a big day?"

Bart flashed his smile. "We're ready." He looked into the crowd of patrons gathered at the tee. He waved to little Beth and her parents. "Donna, I'm playing for that little girl and all those kids." 'Bart's Battalion' was out in force. They looked at Bart with a hope that spoke to their dreams. If 'Stutter Boy' could succeed, so could they.

"Any thoughts about what happened on the 12th green?" She asked.

Bart shrugged. "Sometimes good shots produced unlucky results." He grinned. "That's behind us. Now, we go forward." He eyed Donna and the millions of viewers. "Donna, we have to play the ball as it lies." He shrugged. "Sometimes," he looked at the children, carrying signs and proudly wearing their buttons, "life knocks you down. I need to show these children how to recover and rise to their feet."

"Wow!" Sir Nick commented. "He's quite the young man!"

The golfers went out in pairs. About forty minutes before the leaders, Patrick Reed and Justin Thomas, both at -3, teed off for their final round. Then, Dustin Johnson at -4 and Adam Scott at -3 began their quest to win the green jacket.

Next out, two groups before Bart and Sergio was Phil Mickelson and Justin Rose at -4. The pairing just before the leaders were Rory McElroy, seeking the completion of his career grand slam, and Jordan Spieth at -5.

It was a glorious day for golf on America's greatest shrine to the game. The players, the gallery, the volunteers, that do so much to make the Masters so grand, could all feel the aura of Bobby Jones, the legendary golfer, who conceived this great course from a fruit tree farm. It was his vision that made Augusta National and the Masters so special.

Great players will take advantage of favorable conditions, and that is exactly what the eight who played before the leaders set out to do.

Bart and Sergio played the front nine in a -2, to stand at -8 as they approached the 10th tee. It was not close to good enough. As they studied the leaderboard, they saw that four players had surged past them.

As is so often stated. "The Masters begins on the final nine on Sunday." Bart and Sergio intended to prove that statement to be true.

Bart stood on the 10th tee, 'Camellia,' a long par 4. The green set about 100 yards below the level of the tee. He smiled as he admired the pinks, purples and fuchsias of the azaleas and the white dogwoods that were everywhere to be seen on this beautiful golf course.

Angela saw the smile, she looked to Rachel and the group. "He's settling," she said softly. "He's slowing his breathing, readying to go after this course."

Sergio bogeyed the 10th, as Bart parred the challenging par 4.

At 'White Dogwood,' the 11th hole, which many believe to be the most difficult hole on the course, Bart saved par with a wonderful up and down. Unfortunately, Sergio began 'Amen Corner' with another bogey. He was sliding backwards as the golfers ahead were going low. Bart was still at -2 on the round and -8 on the tournament, but he also, was losing ground to the field as he stepped on the 12th tee, 'Golden Bell.'

'Bart's Battalion' felt some anxiety as Bart stood on the 12th tee box studying his shot. 'Golden Bell' was the site of yesterday's disaster. It is also thought to be one of the best par 3's in golf. Only 155 yards, today, with a shallow green.

Dave stood before Bart, locked eyes. "Now, Bart!" He insisted. "You are 'the Diamond Maker,' we go after this pin."

Bart smiled. "Whatever you say, Coach."

"What's he thinking, Nick?" Jim Nantz asked. "Is it really possible to clear your head of what happened here yesterday?"

"I think so," Sir Nick responded. "Golf requires mental toughness for one to succeed." He paused. "Bart hit a brilliant shot yesterday." He considered. "You can see his coach, Dave Gilliss, talking to him. What are you hearing, Donna?" Nick asked.

"He's going after the pin, Guys." Donna stated. "He's fearless."

Angela was knotted up. She clutched Rosa's hand as wife and mother agonized together. "Think good thoughts," Rosa counselled, but Angela heard a pleading tone to her voice.

Bart had the honor and stood behind his ball. He looked into his gallery, which was silent and smiled at little Beth. He then closed his eyes, visualized the shot, glanced at Angela and flashed a smile as he addressed the ball. He took his smooth swing and the ball flew high and on line. "It looks on line," Donna called. The ball landed just onto the green and rolled out to the pin, "Ggo in," Justin called. The ball rolled toward the cup, but it stopped just one foot short.

'Bart's Battalion,' exploded. Finally, they had something to cheer. "Yes," yelled Sal, he clutched Franco DeMarco's shoulder. "Our boy's going to do it!"

"A brilliant shot!" Nick Faldo called. "It's amazing that Bart was able to block out yesterday's disaster and go after the pin again."

"It's a kick-in birdie," Jim Nantz stated. "He'll be at -9, Nick, still two strokes behind the leaders." He paused. "It may not be enough. But, it's a bit of solace after yesterday's bad luck."

"Yes," Jim," Nick Faldo responded. "But, remember, Bart has two par 5's ahead." He laughed. "I think we are in for an exciting finish."

As Bart and Sergio who had managed a par walked to the 13th tee, the leaderboard showed Phil and Rory at -11, Spieth and Scott at -10 and Dustin Johnson, Justin Rose and Bart, at -9.

"Birdie hole," Dave stated. The 13th, 'Azalea,' is a par 5, but is gettable as the pros say. Phil and Rory had both birdied 13 as had Dustin Johnson. "We need a good drive."

Bart delivered a booming drive, center cut, putting him in position to go for the green in two.

"He's feeling it!" Faldo stated. "He hits his drives so long."

"And, so straight." Donna Caponi added. "There's a bounce to his step," Donna called.

The camera found 'Team DeMarco,' following Bart, grouped together in a protective circle around Sal, who was being helped by Franco DeMarco and Mario, and, of course, with Angela, who had the mothers, Maria, Rosa and Heather walking with her.

Rachel, Betsy and Jessica were teasing Angela. "Should we carry her?" Betsy asked. "You know like Cleopatra in one of those cushioned litters?"

"Better be careful," Jessica added, laughing. "If Bart looks over and Angela looks tired, we'll all be in trouble."

Angela laughed. "I'm fine, ladies, really!"

"We know that," Tina replied with a grin. "But, our boy Bart, needs to be assured." The women all laughed.

"He doesn't have a clue!" Heather laughed. "But, how sweet is it that in the middle of all this," she waved at the huge crowd, the TV cameras, thousands of volunteers, "Bart's worried about his wife?"

Rosa smiled. "My Bart's a good man!"

Maria took Rosa's hand. "Bart is the best!" Maria stated. "He takes care of Angela." She paused, forever grateful. "He always did."

Angela laughed. "I guess that I better be good to Bart or I'll have both mothers after me."

"I think that you're doing all right," Jim Perry said on a laugh. "I've never seen a guy so happy."

Bart and Dave stood at his ball. He was only 180 yards out, after Bart's 330 yard drive. Still, as Rae's Creek rings the front of the green, care had to be taken. Bart lofted a 7 iron high, it landed soft and rolled out to 20 feet.

"An eagle opportunity here." Nick Faldo called. "But, this is a slick, tough green," he cautioned. "Bart better be careful."

Bart and Dave studied the putt closely, conferred and then Bart stroked a solid putt, which just missed left. He tapped in for birdie and moved to -10. As 'Bart's Battalion' cheered, ahead on the par 5, 15th green, Johnson and Scott were rolling in birdie putts. And, Bart was still 2 behind Phil and Rory.

Bart parred the long par 4, 14th hole, 'Chinese Fir.' Sergio, the defending Champion, posted another bogey and was essentially out of contention. They walked to the 15th hole, 'Firethorn.'

'Firethorn' is the last par 5 on the course. Bart and Dave stood on the tee waiting for Rory and Spieth to clear the fairway and considered their options.

"Bart needs to make something happen here, Jim." Faldo stated. "He's running out of holes."

Jim Perry looked at Franco Palermo. Speaking softly, "Bart's gotta go for it!" He paused. "These guys aren't going to let him in."

Franco agreed. "He needs an Eagle here." He paused. "I don't think a birdie will be enough."

Lucia, walking with Franco, looked on with big eyes. "Franco, is Bart going to lose?"

Franco smiled, leaned over and kissed her worried lips. "I have faith in Bart, you just watch, beautiful, Bart will find a way."

Bart launched a big drive on 15. He was again in position to go for a par 5 green in two shots. Bart and Dave walked down the fairway. Bart looked over at Angela with questioning eyes. Angela smiled and waved, "I'm good," she called out. She smiled. "You be great, Bart!"

He smiled and waved, returned his focus to the next shot.

"Good job," Rachel said with a grin. "Keep Bart relaxed and focused."

Bart had 200 yards to the pin. As it was downhill it would play to 185 yards. Dave noted the flag on the 15th green was standing straight out to the right and a bit at them. The wind had freshened and was quartering against them from the left. 'The green runs right to left," Dave reminded Bart.

A large pond wraps around the front, left side and behind the green. The pin was left of center. A big sand trap was right of the green.

"The wind is hurting." Dave stated. "I think it will play to about 210 yards." He paused, thought aloud. "You can bail out in the bunker right of the green and get up and down for birdie."

Bart looked over at the YES children in his gallery. He looked at Dave. "We need an Eagle here!" He stated with conviction. "We're running out of golf course." He paused. "We have to go for it, Dave." He looked at the green. "I'll cut a hybrid, try to ride the wind to the flag."

Dave looked at Bart, then the trees to gauge the wind. "It's a delicate shot, with the wind, that pond, fronting the green, could catch a high cut." He paused, considered the options, nodded. "Bart, I agree, go for it!"

Bart nodded and smiled. "I promised Little Beth, I have to go for it."

Bart stood behind his ball, studied the shot, closed his eyes and visualized the high cut he planned on hitting. He opened his eyes, smiled at Angela and settled over the ball.

"He really needs a bit of luck here," Faldo stated. He laughed. "Thus far, the only luck he's had is bad luck."

Donna interjected. "I'm not sure Bart would agree, Nick."

Bart launched into his smooth swing. "That looks good," Donna stated. "It's right on line."

Dave saw it instantly, Bart had pured the shot. "Get down!" Dave yelled. "Come on wind!" He pleaded. "Knock it down."

"It looks like he pured it, guys." Donna said. "This may fly the green."

Bart held his pose. But, he had hit it pure and he saw that while it was heading at the flag, it would hit the green, past the flag, and bounce over. His eyes locked on the shot as it flew at the pin, Bart grimaced, as the ball flew past the pin and then, seemingly disappeared.

There was silence. All eyes sought answers. "Where's the ball?"

"I think it hit the flag," Donna called out, excitedly. "Oh my God, what a break!"

The ball was wrapped by the flag, losing all momentum. There was absolute silence as the flag finally relaxed and the ball fell to the green, it bounced one tiny hop, took the right to left break and fell into the cup.

"It went in!" Jim Nantz called. "A double Eagle, 2! Move aside, Gene Sarazen, you have company!" He proclaimed. [1]

It took a moment to register, but when the ball disappeared into the hole, the crowd erupted in a roar not heard since Tiger's heyday. Bart and Dave high-fived, laughing joyfully. 'Bart's Battalion' screamed their joy. Little Beth jumped into her Daddy's arms. "Bart's ggoing to wwin, ffor mme!" She cried happily.

"The Golf God's taketh," Nick Faldo stated, on a laugh. "And, sometimes the Golf God's giveth! WOW!"

Team DeMarco was stunned silent, then suddenly delirious with happiness. There were screams of ecstasy and there were tears of joy. Angela jumped for joy and held Rachel, they happily jumped together. When the two young beauties looked at Bart and Dave, they saw appreciative smiles.

---

[1]   Gene Sarazen had hit 'the shot heard round the world,' a double eagle on the 15th in the 1935 Masters. The shot tied Sarazen with the tournament leader, Craig Wood, and Sarazen would win the playoff. In honor of Gene Sarazen's historic shot and win, and his placing the Masters on the sporting map, the Sarazen-bridge was built over the pond and dedicated in 1955.

Rachel beamed a smile at Dave, waved and glanced at Angela. "Shouldn't they be thinking about golf, rather than ogling us?" Rachel asked as she laughed, hugged Angela, and resumed their celebration.

"Let's hope they never stop ogling us." Angela replied.

Franco Palermo embraced Lucia and kissed her passionately, "I told you Bart would find a way!" He looked up to see a smiling Rosa wagging her finger at him. He laughed aloud and again kissed Lucia.

Up ahead, Adam Scott stood on the 18th green, reading his birdie putt, leading the tournament at -12. The roar was heard clearly, Scott's gut told him it was a Bart roar. He rose from his crouch, stood and looked to the leader board, expecting that Bart had eagled the 15th and was now at -12.

The names and scores shuffled on the leaderboard, until DeMarco's score changed from: -10 to -13, placing him on top of the leader board. The gallery at 18 began to clap, stomp the bleachers and cheer. Adam Scott walked over to his caddie, Steve Williams. "He just double Eagled 15," Williams explained. "He pulled a Sarazan!" The legendary caddie put his hand on Adam Scott's shoulder. "Take a minute, calm down and let's make this putt."

Adam Scott did exactly that, posting a final score of -13 to take the clubhouse lead. Dustin Johnson had finished at -12.

It wasn't over, Phil was at -11 as was Rory with two holes to play. But, for the first time since Saturday on the 12th green, Bart was alone on top of the leaderboard. And, he had three holes to play.

Phil and Justin Rose each birdied one hole coming in to finish at -12. The tournament was now between former Master's Champion, Australian, Adam Scott, and 18 year old Bart DeMarco.

Bart and a smiling Sergio walked to the 16th tee, 'Redbud,' is a 170 yard par 3, 'Redbud' is a heavily guarded green with various plateaus. Both Bart and Sergio made par and they moved to the tee box on the17th hole, 'Nandina.'

Sergio approached Bart and Dave. "Bart, take a few deep breaths, focus," urged the reigning Masters champion. "You still need a birdie to win."

'Nandina' is a par 4, 440 yard hole, famous for the Eisenhower tree. While the tree no longer stands, it was long a thorn in President Dwight Eisenhower's side. The green, designed by Perry Maxwell, is a particular challenge. Bart hit his second shot to inside ten feet. He had a birdie putt to take the lead.

Bart and Dave read the putt. 'Team Demarco,' collectively held their breath. His gallery readied to explode.

"He's going to do it!" Lucia said with conviction.

"Left edge, Bart," Dave read.

Bart crouched behind the putt, blocked everything out. He stood, glanced and smiled at Angela. He set over the putt, evened his breathing. The gallery was silent. He struck the putt. It was on the line he and Dave had read.

Bart liked it, but, it moved left, caught the edge of the hole and lipped out, much to the agony of 'Team DeMarco.' Disappointed, Bart tapped in for par, and moved to the famous 18th hole.

"So close," Angela whispered, "so close."

'Holly' has been the site of many an exciting Masters finish. This day might well top them all. The anxiety level for 'Team DeMarco' was off the charts. "Bart's Battalion' believed and cheered lustily.

'Holly' is a long, significantly uphill, par 4. A big drive is needed and a second shot onto the proper tier of the green. Then, Bart would need to make his birdie putt.

Bart blasted a beautiful drive. All Masters Patrons were now either ensconced in the bleachers at 18, or on the hills surrounding the 18th green.

"There must be 30,000-40,000 thousand people crowding the green." Faldo stated. "Can Bart do it?"

"And, maybe a few hundred million watching around the world." Jim Nantz added.

"Don't bet against him!" Donna Caponi stated. "This kid is magic!"

Bart and Dave conferred on the fairway shot. He had 175 yards into the sloping, elevated, green. "It's uphill Bart," Dave stated. "It will play like 190 yards." He handed Bart the club, smiled and encouraged, "Relax, Diamond Maker, you were born for this." He smiled. "Just put a smooth swing on it."

Bart set up behind his second shot. He studied the fairway and green ahead, closed his eyes to visualize the shot's trajectory, opened his eyes, smiled at Angela and addressed the ball. Angela squeezed Rachel's hands, "please!" She implored.

Bart put a smooth swing and hit a high cut shot. The ball found the green, leaving him a 15 foot putt for birdie and to win the Masters.

There were shouts of encouragement as Bart and Dave walked up to the green. Sergio ascended the green and finished out a disappointing round.

After he dropped his putt, he looked at Bart and flashed a thumbs-up. "You can do it!" Sergio called, and he then left the green to 'Team DeMarco.'

Bart and Dave stood studying the putt. "This looks like Mickelson's putt from '04," Dave said. "I'm reading one ball outside right."

As Bart and Dave continued to study the putt, from every angle, walking the circle around the ball and the hole, looking for the break, Justin called to 'Team DeMarco,' "let's help Bart." He called "Let's all hold hands." Heather choked up as she noted that Justin's words were stutter free.

'Team DeMarco' linked hands, it was immediately picked up by 'Bart's Battalion,' who joined hands. Then, the gallery rose, took the hand of the person on either side, family, friend or stranger.

Rosa stood with Franco, looking on as Bart and Dave studied the putt from every angle. "Our boy," she said softly, with pride, as tears of happiness flooded her eyes. Franco leaned close and kissed her. Mario and Celia, with Lucia and Franco Palermo moved close. They would see this as a family.

"Jim, there must be 20,000 people holding hands," Nick Faldo stated. They are ringing the green. The camera panned the gallery, memorializing the amazing site.

"They are all standing and holding hands." Jim Nantz stated. "It is something to see."

"They are sending their joint strength to Bart." Donna Caponi stated. "This is amazing!" She smiled. "They are a solid wall of support for Bart."

The camera focused on Angela, who stood among 'Team DeMarco,' with her left hand on her belly and pointing her right arm and hand at Bart. On the green Bart stood and looked at the gallery. His solid wall of support. His eyes then found Angela. His smile met hers.

"I don't understand, Donna." Nick Faldo stated. "Angela DeMarco is not holding hands with anyone." He paused. "What do you think the meaning is?"

"Guys," Donna explained. "On Monday, Bart's birthday, Angela learned that she is expecting a baby." She smiled. "She is linking the baby, through her, to Bart."

"What are we in a novel?" Jim Nantz laughed. "Or, is this a movie script?" He paused, silenced, considered, then, he spoke reverently. "No, it's the Masters, where magic happens."

"That's so true," Nick Faldo said quietly, "just look at all those children that Bart is helping to speak, to believe in their future?" He paused. "Now, they are helping him."

The gallery stood silently, holding hands. Angela joined their baby to Bart. Bart closed the shade, focused on the challenge, and again conferred with Dave. "One ball right, coach?"

"That's what I read." Dave stated. "Nice and smooth."

Bart stood over the putt, set his feet, closed his eyes and evened his breathing. There was no sound from the gallery. The silence was astounding, birds could be heard chirping. Bart opened his eyes, smiled, then he stroked the putt.

"It looks good!" Jim Nantz stated, excitedly. When it was three feet from the hole, Bart saw that Dave's read was perfect, as the ball took the break. He raised his putter to the sky. At one foot away, it was dead center and it fell into the cup as the crowd roared, a roar to equal any ever heard at Augusta National. Bart leaped for joy. Angela spilled happy tears as she embraced all who had meant so much to them.

"Bart DeMarco is a Masters legend!" Proclaimed long time play by play announcer, Jim Nantz. "His name will live forever in Masters Lore."

Dave sprinted to Bart, and Coach and player embraced. "You are special!" Dave proclaimed.

Bart held Dave, looked into his eyes. "None of this was possible without you, Coach." He choked up, "Thank you."

Angela came running onto the green and into Bart's arms. "You did it, Bart, you did it!"

Bart held Angela, her feet swinging above the green. "No, Princess, we did it!"

Dave signaled Rachel to join them and the two young couples embraced, in a group clinch. "Thank you all," Bart said. "Thank you!"

Chapter Seventy-Six

The traditional Green Jacket presentation ceremony was held in Butler Cabin. Jim Nantz acted as the Master of Ceremony and the Chairman of Augusta National Golf Club, Billy Payne, was the host.

Bart sat with defending Champion, Sergio Garcia, to his left and the low Amateur to his right. He politely listened to Mr. Nantz recount some of the ups and downs of the grueling and exhausting four days. The Chairman offered congratulations to both Bart and the Amateur Champion. He then presented the medal to the Amateur Champion, a young man, who was four years older than Bart.

Chairman Payne then smiled and asked Bart to stand, to have Sergio help him into the Green Jacket that signified golfing excellence, and marked him forever, as a Masters Champion.

The Ceremony moved to the 18th green, where the Green Jacket presentation was repeated. A delighted, 'Team DeMarco' were all front and center to watch Bart, who had overcome so much, in his young life, be declared the Masters Champion. Bart had asked that Little Beth and her parents be present for the ceremony. Standing behind those seated was Bart's Battalion, proudly wearing their buttons and grinning from ear to ear. Bart locked eyes with Rosa and mouthed a thank you. Rosa did not need an explanation from her boy.

Angela beamed as Sergio helped the taller Bart into his jacket. Bart locked eyes and smiles with Angela. He loved her smile, the gleam of her eyes and her total devotion. It so well matched his feelings.

Bart stood before the bank of microphones. "What a day, what a great tournament." He paused looked at the sea of Green Jackets worn by the members of Augusta National Golf Club.

"Thank you for inviting me to play on your magnificent course, in your great Tournament." He paused. "I will always try to make the committee and members of this special golf club proud." He smiled, looked at the Chairman of Augusta National. "Sir, is there any chance that I could have the flag from the 15th green?"

The request was met with laughter. The affable Chairman moved to the microphones. "Actually Bart, the plan is to have that flag framed and hung in a special case in our Hall of Fame museum." He paused. "We will have a plaque below explaining your incredible shot." He smiled. "Maybe a video, as well."

Bart nodded and smiled. Exhaustion sweeping over him. "Sounds good, Sir."

Bart sat for the media interview in his Green Jacket. He saw Angela, and all of 'Team DeMarco' at the rear of the large room.

The Masters director of media relations sat with him, controlling the interview process.

"What will you have served at the Champions dinner next year?" A reporter called out.

Bart laughed. As the Masters Champion, tradition dictated that he set the menu for the annual pre-tournament 'Dinner of Champions.' "Well, I'm from Gloucester and, of course, I'm Italian, so I guess it will be an Italian seafood feast."

"Congratulations on the baby, Bart." A golf magazine writer called. "Have you and Angela chosen names?"

Bart nodded and smiled. "Yes, we have," he responded. "Following our tradition, it will be Franco, after my dad, if it's a boy and Rosa, for a girl. Rosa is my Mom's name."

"That was quite an image, Bart, all the thousands of Patrons holding hands in support of you. What were your thoughts when you saw that?"

Bart smiled and shook his head. "I was really surprised. I'm told that the idea came from 11 year old, Justin Walleston, my dear friend." He grinned at Justin standing with the group. Bart shook his head. "I didn't expect anything like that, I was surprised, but, it was great."

"What about Angela, Bart?"

Bart beamed a smile. "This past Monday was my birthday." He sought Angela's eyes. "When Dave and I returned from practicing and trying to learn the course, Angela told me that she had seen the doctor, with my Mom and her Mom, and we were having a baby." He took a deep breath. "It was the best birthday present imaginable."

"Tell us about the putt on 18, Bart?"

Bart grinned. "It was basically Phil Mickelson's putt from '04, to win the Masters." He paused. "My great Coach, Dave Gilliss, had studied the putt, gave me the read and I knocked it home."

"How does the Green Jacket feel?"

Bart laughed. "Green is now my color!"

"Bart, you are the only player who could win the Grand Slam. Will you play in the U.S. Open?"

Bart smiled. "No sir," he stated. "I will be playing that week in the Manitoba Classic."

"Would your sponsor release you to play in the U.S. Open?" A TV commentator asked. "Bart, no golfer has won the Grand Slam (winning all 4 Majors in a calendar year) since Bobby Jones in 1930." He paused. "Many think that you could do it."

Bart sat back. "That is kind of you to say, Sir." He paused, smiled. "But, I do not need to be released. I am free to do as I wish." He paused, looked at the hundreds of reporters, from every medium, present.

Bart grew serious. "I will play in the Manitoba Classic. I will be playing for my kids." He grinned. "I guess they call it Bart's Battalion." His expression was intent. "I am dedicated to helping Manitoba Oil, a great company, run by an inspirational man, Phil Walleston, to raise the many millions of dollars needed to open and run a school for young stutterers." He paused. "On this, there is no room for discussion. I WILL play in the Classic."

Heather took Phil's hand and smiled. PapaWall misted as he looked into her eyes. "He's a great young man." He turned to Angela. "Take good care of that very special Champion."

Angela smiled. "I will PapaWall." She looked to Heather, laughed. "I kinda like him."

PapaWall smiled at Dave, "I hope you know, Dave, just how important you are to this team?" He eyed his soon to be son-in-law, "Bart doesn't win without you."

Dave took Rachel's hand. "I do know, Dad." He paused. "I will take care of my girl and of Bart."

A reporter called out. "Bart, tell us about your shot into the 15th green?"

Bart laughed. "That was something." He stated and winked. "I played the shot to hit the flag so that I could get a double eagle, just like Gene Sarazen." He grinned. "I bet you didn't realize just how precise my game is?"

The room erupted in laughter. When it settled, Bart continued. "I was just lucky." He shrugged. "But, you know what the great Bobby Jones said. He paused and smiled into the cameras. Bobby Jones said:

"Golf is the closest game to life.
You get bad breaks from good shots;
You get good breaks from bad shots;
But you always have to play the ball where it lies."

Bart smiled. "We sure saw all of that, didn't we?" Heads nodded.

"There is one more thing that I would like to say." He paused and smiled. "I play to help the millions of children, who like me, suffer from speech issues." He took a deep breath. YES, a great organization, has a confident voices program. Please help YES help these wonderful, bright children. Thank you." He rose. "Now, I want to go celebrate with my Angela and our families."

Bart found Angela and 'Team DeMarco' waiting for him. He looked into Angela's eyes and wrapped her in a hug. Exhausted from the stress and emotion they clung to each other. "We did it, Princess!" He said softly. "We did it!" He held her for a long moment, then Bart looked at her, saw that she was crying. "Are you okay?"

Angela nodded, as she smiled through her tears. "I'm so okay, Bart. I'm so proud of you."

He looked at his mother and the family and friends surrounding the jubilant couple. "Let's go home," he said. He smiled at his mother and mother-in-law, "I'm really hungry!" He paused, laughed. "Why don't you all head home, we have to see the kids."

Bart, Angela, Dave and Rachel went to see 'Bart's Battalion.' The children and their parents were bursting with joy. It was a hugfest. Bart spoke to every child, signed every program and smiled for every photo. The group photo was, and always would be, special.

The next days were a whirlwind of interviews and television appearances. Bart, always wearing his 'Green Jacket,' and sometimes with Angela, appeared on the nationally broadcast morning shows from New York. Bart opened the Stock Exchange, and he even threw out the ceremonial first pitch before a game at Yankee Stadium. It was something they would always remember.

The young couple was excited, but exhausted. Rising early, to appear on the many morning shows, then moving to daytime shows and even appearing on the late night shows, had Bart worried for Angela.

On their last day in New York, Bart insisted that they rest, have a late breakfast at the hotel, before he did an extensive interview on the Golf

Channel. Angela breakfasted with Bart, rested, and after Bart left for the interview, headed onto 5ᵗʰ Avenue to do some shopping. Angela loved to shop.

Bart appreciated the depth of knowledge the Golf Channel analysts brought to their coverage of golf. The interview was given to Rich Lerner, a noted golf historian. Bart agreed to the interview, but explained that Angela was back at the hotel resting. "It's just me guys," he joked. "My girl needs to rest."

The Golf Channel interview was conducted in New York, rather than at the Golf Channel's Orlando studio, as Bart and Angela were looking forward to heading home the next day.

Angela thoroughly enjoyed her shopping. She bought presents for her family and Bart's. She wanted all the family and friends, who shared that remarkable week in Augusta, Georgia, to always remember this very special time in their lives.

After shopping, Angela returned to their suite, elevated her legs, sipped a cold glass of water, spiked with orange juice, and settled comfortably to watch the Golf Channel interview of Bart.

The interview began with Lerner, somewhat dramatically, setting the stage for the viewers. He then ran the clip of Bart's winning putt, and the proclamation by Jim Nantz that; 'Bart DeMarco is a Masters legend.' Bart enjoyed the video, the roar of the crowd, and, of course, Jim Nantz's call, which will be forever remembered.

Bart sat back as Rich Lerner asked his thoughts on Nantz's pronouncement.

"That was very nice of Mr. Nantz to say." He paused. "But, in truth, I do not consider myself to be a legend." He took a deep breath. "See, Mr. Lerner, I didn't win the Masters, 'Team DeMarco' won the Masters."

The Golf Channel host, eyed Bart, nodded and smiled. "We've heard you frequently reference 'Team DeMarco.' Please, if you would, explain to us, just what is 'Team DeMarco?'" He asked.

Bart smiled. "Team DeMarco includes my Coach, Dave Gilliss, The Walleston family, who have been so generous and so supportive, our families, Angela's and mine." He grinned. "Our dear and supportive friends and, Dave's fiancé, Rachel and, of course, my Angela." He flashed a smile. "Mr. Lerner, none of this success was possible without my Angela."

Angela watched happily. Eyes set on Bart.

"Bart, you seem extremely dedicated to helping children suffering from the effects of stuttering. You are even passing up the U.S. Open to pursue that goal, would you tell us your story? And, how you acquired the 'Stutter Boy' nickname?"

Bart smiled and nodded. "When I was a boy, I had a terrible stutter. It was painful to speak." He took a deep breath. "Even as a boy, I could see people losing patience with me as I stuttered out my words and my thoughts." He paused. "Every day, other children would mock me." He paused, thought back. "Older boys bullied me and embarrassed me." He sat back, lost in the painful memories. "School was so awful. I didn't want to speak." He paused, looked at Lerner. "I was afraid to speak, because I knew that I would be mocked and ridiculed." He paused, swallowed.

"I would come home upset, day after day. Some days, I would see my mother and break down." He paused, sighed. "I felt broken and worthless."

Rich Lerner nodded, but said nothing. Angela was hearing this entire story for the first time, as she watched the TV in their elegant suite. She felt bereft for Bart. Tears flooded her eyes.

Bart smiled. "My baby sister, Lucia, would see me crying and she would climb onto my lap, hug me and cry with me." He took a moment. "My big brother, Mario, fought for me. Bart smiled. "Mario challenged all the bullies to try and protect me." He took a deep breath. "Nobody, ever, had better siblings than me, nobody!" He stressed.

Lerner smiled. "You don't stutter now. Do you have the problem beat?"

Bart smiled. "I wish." He shrugged. "But, no, Mr. Lerner." He paused, collected his thoughts. "I'm afraid that I will always stutter. See,' he explained. "I weigh my words. I stay away from words that I have trouble with." He sighed. "It's exhausting." He shrugged. "And, it's every day."

Rosa watched the interview at home with Lucia. Tears ran down her cheeks as she re-lived those painful days. She hugged Lucia. "I am so proud of you, Bambina."

Lucia cried with her mother. "Bart is the best!" She stated. "He's doing this to help all those kids. I'm proud to be his sister."

"My mother would encourage me," Bart continued. "'Your special, Bart,' she always said. She always encouraged me, 'believe in yourself,' she preached."

"My Dad, was and is a commercial fisherman, a very strong man, in all the best ways." He smiled. "Now, he is an excellent and respected fishing Captain." He looked into the camera. "My parents are not wealthy, but still, they sent me to speech therapists and psychologists." He smiled. "They did everything that they could do." He paused. "I was lucky to have the support of a loving family."

He sipped some water. Lerner sat back, loathe to break Bart's recitation of his life story.

"It slowly got better," He smiled. "Sometimes, it wasn't really bad." He paused. "I grew big and strong. The bullies left me alone, but the snickering and cruel names didn't really stop."

Bart sat back, reflected on those years. "I was a good athlete, I excelled at baseball and football, my confidence grew, but it was always there. My fear never really left." He sighed. "'Stutter Boy' always lurked when I was anxious." Angela watched in silence.

"As a sophomore at Gloucester High School, I won the starting Quarterback position." He frowned. "It was a great moment for me." He paused, Rich Lerner could see that he was lost in the memory. "Our first game was at home against Salem High School." He sighed. "There were thousands of people at the game on a beautiful Friday evening. I played one play, which went for a big gain." He paused, took a deep breath. "I was anxious and my stutter flared, so, after one play, I was pulled off of the field." He looked at Rich Lerner. "I was humiliated before the entire city." He forced a smile. "And, I had to stand on the sideline for the rest of the game."

Angela recalled the evening vividly. The look of humiliation on Bart's face. The pain in his eyes. She remembered that she sat in the bleachers with her gaze on Bart, and how, as she sat in the big crowd, she thought back to the day Bart had saved her from those three bullies and their 'Ugly Angela' taunts. And, she recalled making the fateful decision to go and find Bart, to try and raise his spirits, to assure that he would not be alone.

Bart continued recounting the events of that evening. "Mr. Lerner, after the game, I walked to our Boulevard, it's where the Fisherman's Statue is set, where the ocean meets the shore. A beautiful place." He paused. "I sat alone, on a bench, facing the outer harbor, ten pound island, the breakwater, to the open ocean."

"It sounds pretty," Lerner offered, with a smile.

Bart smiled. "It is, Gloucester is absolutely beautiful." He paused, and continued. "I was so low, I was so emotionally exhausted. I wanted to give up."

Angela cried as she heard and watched Bart re-live those painful memories. She knew he was doing this to help his kids, 'Bart's Battalion.' Yet, she knew that it still hurt. "He's so brave," she muttered. Angela felt a wonderful sense of pride in being Bart DeMarco's wife.

Bart smiled. "Then, Mr. Lerner, at that precise moment, God sent me an Angel."

"Angela?" Asked Lerner, with a smile.

Bart beamed his smile. "My Angela, my beautiful Angela, came into my life. And, she lifted me." He paused. "That night my life changed," he smiled. "My Angela made the difference for me." He laughed and addressed the Golf Channel host. "We walked to her house," he smiled in memory. "And, she let me hold her hand." He laughed. "I think she liked me, in any event, she gave me dinner, and a shoulder to cry on." He paused. "I felt relaxed with Angela, at peace."

"You know, Mr. Lerner," Bart continued. "Angela encouraged me to play golf. She inspired me to hope, to believe." He looked at Rich Lerner. "It turned out that in trying golf, I found my coach, Dave Gilliss." He smiled. "From that first day, Coach Gilliss told me that with hard work and dedication, I had the potential to be a very good golfer."

"I'd have to say, your coach was right," Rich Lerner stated with a smile.

Bart smiled. "I'm sure Dave will love to hear that!" He laughed. "I owe so much of my success to Dave's instruction and patience." He paused. "He's an important part of the team."

Bart took a deep breath. "You know, Mr. Lerner, Angela always encouraged me, she always repeated, 'be great, Bart.'" He paused. "Angela helped me to believe." Bart exhaled and smiled. "Mr. Lerner, whatever I am, whatever I have or will accomplish, I owe to Angela and to our team."

Rich Lerner smiled. "So Bart, what's next?" He asked.

Bart laughed. "The last few days have been so great, but so crazy." He said. "Angela is exhausted. So, for tonight, we'll have a nice dinner, get a good night's sleep and fly home tomorrow." He smiled. "We both need to get home to Gloucester."

"For me, I'll spend the rest of the week in Gloucester enjoying some great food, seeing my friends and family and letting Angela rest." He thought of the baby and he smiled. "Then, on Monday, I will fly to Canada to shoot a few commercials for Manitoba Oil and for the Manitoba Classic."

"By the way, Bart," Rich Lerner smiled. "Congratulations on the baby."

"Thanks, Mr. Lerner," Bart responded with a smile.

"That was some scene around the 18th green, all those Patrons holding hands in unity with you."

Bart smiled. "It was amazing!" He paused. "You know, that it was the idea of young Justin Walleston?"

"So, Bart, what does the future Tournament schedule look like?" Rich Lerner asked.

Bart sat back. "Dave and I will be meeting with our representatives, Mr. Palermo and Mr. Winston, to set a schedule." He laughed. "There's certainly a lot of exciting events in front of us."

He grinned. "But, Angela and I will head back to good old, Gloucester High School." He smiled. "While we have been traveling, we have had a wonderful tutor, who has been working with the guidance office at our High School." He paused. "We need to take all the tests, and hopefully pass those tests, to graduate with our class."

"When will that be?" Rich Lerner asked.

"In May," Bart responded.

Rich Lerner's eyes popped. "What about the Players Championship?" He considered. "Is there a conflict?"

Bart shrugged, "I'm afraid so." He eyed Rich Lerner. "I doubt that I will be able to play, Sir." He smiled. "Angela and I promised our parents that we would graduate and walk with our class." He paused. "So, that's our immediate goal."

Rich Lerner sat back, studied Bart. "Will you play in the Ryder Cup?" Lerner asked.

Bart beamed. "I would love to be on America's team!"

Chapter Seventy-Seven

It was the first week of May and the Academic Awards Committee met to discuss the upcoming Commencement.

The first agenda item was to choose the Commencement Speaker. Quickly, two camps emerged on the subject. One group supported the idea of Gloucester's Mayor giving the Commencement Address. The second, led by American History teacher and Athletic Director, Bob Nelson, urged the Committee to ask Bart DeMarco to give the Address.

"Bart DeMarco, revived the golf program at this school." Bob Nelson stated. "He is an excellent student, a world class athlete, and a lifelong resident of Gloucester." He paused, eyed his wife, Beth. "And, as to character, there are none better."

"Bart was embarrassed, by me, before the entire city." Nelson acknowledged. "And, I was so wrong." He sighed. "That young man was devastated, but when I asked him to come back and help the team, he responded in the most positive way possible." He looked about the table. "Further, he is in demand. Colleges are calling to ask him to be their Commencement Speaker and too many High Schools to name." He shook his head. "Those schools all recognize that Bart is a New England success story. And, they want him." He looked at Principle, Bruce Collier. "Bruce, this should be a no-brainer." Nelson smiled. "Bart's a Gloucester boy, and a great credit to our school."

"We will always have a Mayor," Nelson continued. "And, I realize it has been our tradition to have the Mayor give the Commencement Address, but, how often will Gloucester High School be able to boast of having the reigning Masters Champion as a member of the graduating class?"

Collier laughed. "I think this will be a first, a member of the graduating class being the chosen Speaker." He sat back. "And, it will be 'Stutter Boy' who overcame incredible challenges to stand before this community and deliver this address. I love it." He looked at Bob Nelson. Will you make the motion to authorize me to extend the invitation to Bart?"

The nine person committee voted unanimously to invite Bart to be the Commencement Speaker. Principle Collier smiled. "I will officially extend the invitation to Bart DeMarco."

"Maybe," Beth Nelson suggested, "you should do it in person?"

Principle Collier nodded. "Good idea."

The second issue, before the Committee, was to whom to award the prestigious Sawyer Medal. The Sawyer Medal is the single most important award presented by the Gloucester Schools. It was given to the student who achieved academically, in extra-curricular activities, and brought honor to Gloucester's schools in the community. It was often, but not always, awarded to the student whose grades placed the student, 1st in the class.

On merit, it appeared, that a good case could be made for Angela DeMarco to win the Award. She had completed the examinations with grades that placed her at the head of her class. Her thesis paper written on great American Heroes, was superlative. Still, some on the Committee argued that she had not attended class for the bulk of two academic years.

Mary Quinn, Science Department head, objected. "Angela is a bright, wonderful girl, but while she was jetting around the world, other students were in school, participating in activities and bringing credit to the school and community.

Beth Nelson challenged that perspective. "Angela was enrolled and a member of this class." She began. "Like others, over the years, her life required her to be away, but she and her tutor were in constant contact with my office. She sat for every test required by the Commonwealth and this High School, and had the highest scores, by far." She paused, sat back. "For her first two years, when she was here, she participated in numerous activities, including Theatre, Debate, DECA, and numerous clubs." Mrs. Nelson smiled. "Angela starred in the Musical, Grease, playing Sandy, and was not only excellent in her performance, but helpful to every member of the cast and crew." She paused. "Angela is liked by everybody. She deserves this award."

She looked about the room and continued. "Every member of this committee that has taught Angela or even just knows her, would acknowledge that she has been a credit to her family, to her school, to Gloucester and an inspiration to Bart DeMarco."

"Beth," Jim Harrison, a soft spoken committee member interjected. "I agree with you, Angela is a wonderful girl, but, she's pregnant. She's 17 years old and pregnant." He paused. "Haven't we had enough issues in this

City with teenage pregnancy?" He shrugged. "Do we really want to put that issue on center stage, again?"

A number of heads nodded, in agreement with Jim Harrison's concerns.

Jenn Sabella, mother of four and owner and operator of a fashionable women's boutique, looked to Principle Collier. "Bruce, I'm sorry, but I agree with Jim." She paused. "Angela is a great girl, but really, after the stories and even a movie about teen pregnancy in Gloucester, I think this would be a mistake."

Beth Nelson smiled. She genuinely liked Jim Harrison, a CPA, and lifelong contributor to the Community. "Jim, Angela is a married woman." She paused, wanting to choose her words carefully. "Married women have children, the fact that she is a teenager is really irrelevant."

"Beth, I'm not sure it is irrelevant," Luke Noble, a financial advisor and a supporter and close ally of Gloucester's Mayor. "We will be telling the Mayor that he will not be giving the Commencement Address." He smiled. "Do you really want to tell him the Sawyer Medal will be presented to a pregnant teen?"

Committee members, all recalling the negative publicity the city and Gloucester High School received over the made for TV movie; 'the pregnancy pact,' shifted in their seats. Beth Nelson read their eyes and knew that this was an uncomfortable issue. She met Bob's eyes and saw his determination.

"Excuse me," Bob Nelson leaned forward. "Is anyone here really arguing that this young girl, a girl of superior character, who has brought nothing but credit to herself, her family and this school, is ineligible to win this award because she and her husband are expecting a baby?" He paused. "Are you nuts?"

"No, Bob," Luke responded. "I don't think that we're nuts to guard the city's reputation."

"What about her long absences from school?" Asked another committee member, Mary Keane, head of the Mathematics department. "Why not award our most prestigious award to a student who has been here for all four years?"

Principle, Bruce Collier, sat back, eyed the table. "Do you all remember Ahmed Muhammed?" Heads nodded. Principle Collier smiled. "Ahmed was a great kid, he came to us as part of the refugee program, after his family escaped religious persecution in Syria." He eyed the committee, "they didn't like Arabs who were Christians." He paused, looked at Mary. "Ahmed was a brilliant scholar, and a math whiz."

Mary Keane smiled, knowing where Principle Collier was heading.

"Mary," Bruce Collier asked. "How long was Ahmed with us, before he won a full scholarship to M.I.T?"

Mary Keane smiled. "Less than two academic years," she raised her hands in a mock surrender. "And, yes, Bruce, before you ask. I recommended Ahmed for the Sawyer Medal."

"But, did he win the Medal?" Asked, Kieran Kelly, Chair of the Social Studies Department. He paused. "He didn't win, because of his short time in our school system."

"Angela has been with us since she came to America, when she was 12 years old." Beth Nelson retorted. "It really is a different situation."

Principle Collier scanned the table. "It appears that Angela has earned this distinction." He looked at Jim Harrison. "Jim, this is not 'the pregnancy pact.'" He smiled. "We all have family, ancestors, who married young. I just cannot see that Angela's marital status and pregnancy should cut against her." He paused. "So, I will ask two questions. First, is Angela DeMarco ranked highest in her class?"

The Asst. Principle, Karen Cifuentes, a non-voting committee member, nodded. "She is first in her class." She grinned, "Second in the class is Bart DeMarco." All smiled.

"The second question is; has Angela DeMarco ever brought any disgrace on herself, her family or this school?" He smiled. "Mary, I'll let you answer this question."

Mary Keane smiled, looked at Beth Nelson. "No, Bruce, Angela is a credit to this community."

Bruce Collier smiled. "So, I guess Bart will have to accept being the second smartest DeMarco in their household." He grinned, attempting to lighten the mood.

"They're great kids," Collier continued. "They are a true credit to this High School. He sat back and smiled. "Okay, I put this committee together for a reason." He scanned the table, and shrugged. "But, I see that there are legitimate concerns." He sighed. "Let's put it to a vote."

"I would like to make a motion that we award the Sawyer Medal to Bart DeMarco." Luke Noble stated. "He's a top student, he is also, the Master's Champion." Luke smiled. Bart has put Gloucester on the map," he paused. "In a positive way!" He smiled, as heads nodded. "Bruce, you can present the award after his Address."

"Wait," Beth Nelson pleaded. "This award should go to Angela." She scanned the table. "I guarantee you, Bart would agree." She looked about. "I move that the Sawyer Medal be awarded to Angela DeMarco."

Beth looked plaintively to Bob. She scanned the table looking for support. "Please, before we vote, I want to add, that Bart is a remarkable young man." She exhaled. "He overcame abuse and humiliation to climb to the top." She paused. "There is no question that Bart is worthy of this award. But," She looked to the three women seated at the table, "Bart would tell you, as he has stated, that he, Bart DeMarco, did not win the Masters. 'Team DeMarco' won the Masters."

Beth Nelson paused, she spoke with passion. "And, Angela was the heart and soul of 'Team DeMarco.'" She looked at those assembled and smiled. "In the words of philosopher and physician, Albert Schweitzer:

> "In everyone's life, at some time, our inner fire goes out.
> It is then burst into flame by an encounter with another human being.
> We should all be thankful for those people who rekindle the inner spirit."

> "Bart told us at the Thanksgiving assembly that Angela was his angel. That it was Angela that saved him from despair."

Bob Nelson looked about the table. "My actions in that football game devastated Bart." He eyed Beth. "I was only thinking about Bob Nelson." He continued. "But, Angela, saw Bart's pain. She went to him and gave him hope and direction."

Bob looked into the eyes of all assembled. "Acts of selfless service, should be recognized, applauded and awarded." He smiled. "I love Bart DeMarco, and I know he would urge everyone seated here to recognize his angel." He took a deep breath. "In Bart's place, I ask you to vote the Sawyer Medal to Angela."

Bruce Collier smiled. "Are there other nominations?" He waited, looked about.

"Okay, hearing none, I guess we'll vote."

Beth Nelson looked at her husband and smiled a thank you. Eyeing the committee, she realized that her plea, Bob's words, would not likely carry the day, but, she was proud that the Nelsons had banded together and tried.

Chapter Seventy-Eight

Commencement Day at Gloucester High School fell on the Sunday of the Players Championship. Many Golf Channel hosts and Commentators took issue with Bart for skipping what many consider to be the Tournament with the best field of players, of the golf year.

"Many students do not walk with their class." Stated the always well-coiffed, Golf Channel Analyst and former PGA player. He shook his head. "Skipping the Players Championship to walk in a graduation procession is not acceptable."

"Acceptable to who?" Replied another commentator, and former European Golf Tour star, in his New Zealand accent. "Bart DeMarco is a young man who promised his parents that he would finish High school." He shrugged. "He is giving his family a gift." He smiled. "Bart lives up to his word, to his family and to the children battling with speech issues. I think that's a good thing."

"So, he skips the Players Championship and will not play in the U.S. Open," well-coiffed retorted, with a tone of exasperation. "Doesn't Bart owe the PGA tour and golf fans anything?"

"The other golfers all speak well of him," interjected the hostess. "It seems that he's living his life and trying to help a lot of kids." She smiled. "I think that Bart DeMarco is a wonderful example of the spirit of charity at the heart of the PGA Tour." She laughed. "In any event, it appears that he will do what he believes is right, whatever others say."

Bart and Angela went to his parent's home to have breakfast on the Sunday morning of Commencement. They carried their caps and gowns so they could pose for photographs with the family.

When they sat down for breakfast, Angela grinned at Franco and Rosa. "Mom, Dad," she smiled. "Bart has something to tell you."

"Are you having twins?" Franco queried with a smile.

Lucia grinned, eyed Angela. "Now, that would be great!"

Angela laughed. "Not that I know of," she responded, her eyes gleaming.

Bart smiled at Rosa. "Mom, Dad," he set his eyes on Rosa. "Principle Collier asked me to give the Commencement Address."

Rosa's eyes met Franco's, as the meaning of Bart's words hit. She looked to Bart, as she began to cry. "Do you mean that you will be the Graduation Speaker, Bart?"

Bart embraced his Mom, the woman who had been his rock in those difficult years. "Yes, Mom, they want 'Stutter Boy' to be the Commencement speaker."

Rosa's tears of joy flooded her eyes and rolled down her cheeks. She held onto Bart in a fierce hug. The usually eloquent mother and wife was too choked to speak. Franco, Lucia and Angela looked on with big smiles.

Lucia laughed, as she teased. "Angela, I feel sorry for you. The Prince is the Graduation Speaker," she shook her head. "I don't think Mom will ever believe that any mere woman will deserve her Prince."

Angela laughed. Her eyes met Rosa's. Rosa released Bart and moved to Angela.

Rosa wiped her eyes and hugged Angela. "Lucia is right," she leaned back, held Angela's shoulders and looked into Angela's smiling eyes. "No mere woman would ever be good enough for my Bart." She cleared her throat. "But, Angela you are no mere woman." Rosa smiled. "Bart always called you his Princess," she pulled Angela into a hug. "I think that's exactly what you are, Our Princess." She held Angela, "thank you, Angela."

Commencement Day at Gloucester High School was bright and sunny. The football bleachers were full to capacity with the family and friends of the graduates. Bart and Angela's families sat together and beamed smiles.

"My girl graduates from High School." Sal said in an emotion choked voice. "I'm so proud." He held Maria, tears of joy and of pride flowing.

The graduates marched into the Stadium and onto the field in their caps and gowns. The boys wore red caps and gowns, the girls wore white. As they processed, in alphabetical order, Angela walked directly in front of Bart. She had insisted that her diploma read, Angela Curcuru DeMarco. "I am a DeMarco," she told the registrar, "I want my diploma to so state."

The large contingent of DeMarco's and Curcuru's applauded joyously when they spotted 6' 3" tall Bart, with his hand resting gently on the shoulder of a beaming Angela, as the graduate candidates walked to their seats.

Bart had agreed to speak, but insisted that Principle Collier allow him to march in with his class, walk and sit with Angela, and when it was time for him to ascend the stage to give his Commencement Address, the Principle would signal him. Bruce Collier was delighted to comply.

When the graduates were seated, the teachers and dignitaries proceeded to take their place on the raised stage. One seat was left vacant, directly next to the Mayor, so that Bart could sit after he spoke.

Principle Bruce Collier opened the proceedings with the playing of our National Anthem, which was followed by the prayer offered by Father Capelli of St. Ann's Catholic Church. Father Capelli looked on the graduates with pride. So many, from his congregation.

"I am so very happy to offer this prayer for this class." He stated. "I see so many who will follow the great Gloucester tradition of sons following their fathers to sea." He scanned the rows of smiling graduates. "I will pray for your safety every day."

Following the prayer, Principle Collier spoke to the class and all those in attendance. He concluded his remarks, smiled and stated; "this year our invited speaker is a member of the graduating class."

"Our Commencement speaker has distinguished himself and brought honor to our fair fishing port." He paused, stood tall. "I take great honor in introducing a young man of great accomplishment, a young man of great character and, as we say, a Gloucesterman. Please, greet our Commencement speaker, Bart DeMarco."

Those seated on the packed bleachers and the students seated on the field rose to give Bart a standing ovation. Rosa and Franco DeMarco rose, and applauded, as tears ran down their cheeks. Mario, Celia, Lucia and Franco Palermo, cheered lustily, so proud of their brother, who had overcome so much in his young life.

Bart stood at the podium as the cheering continued. Behind the graduate candidates, a group of children rose and spread a banner, which read:

'YES' loves 'Stutter Boy' Bart DeMarco!

The unfurling of the banner prolonged and intensified the applause. Bart looked out into the seated candidates and locked eyes with Angela, who was applauding enthusiastically. He looked into the bleachers and smiled at his family. He saw that Dave Powers was back from Georgia Tech and Jessica from NYU, they were seated with his family group. As he saw his mother, he thought back to that football game against Salem High School, played on that very field, on that difficult Friday evening. Bart saw joy replacing the pain in his mother's eyes. He smiled, as he recalled that was the night, Angela came into his life.

He raised his hands to request the crowd settle. As they sat, he looked at the children of 'YES.' "I love you guys, thank you for the banner." He paused. "We are in this fight together." He raised his arm, thrust his big fist forward, "and together we will win!"

A new round of applause greeted his opening remarks and applause peppered his address.

Rosa held onto Franco, tears streaming down her cheeks. In a voice choked with pride, Rosa said, "Look how beautifully my Bart is speaking!"

Bart began his Address to his classmates, with the words of Aristotle:

> "Excellence is an art won by training and habituation.
> We do not act rightly because we have virtue or excellence,
> But we rather have those because we have acted rightly.
> We are what we repeatedly do.
> Excellence, then, is not an act, but a habit."

Bart looked on his classmates. "We all have the ability to be excellent." He smiled. "We, just need to make acting virtuously a habit."

He concluded by looking at Principle Collier, the teachers and staff, seated on stage. His gaze caught the Nelsons sitting together and holding hands. He smiled and mouthed a thank you.

"As I conclude my remarks, I would like to acknowledge the inspired leadership of our Principle, Bruce Collier." He smiled. "Mr. Collier always worked to make GHS a positive place to learn. He supported hard work and accomplishment and urged every student to give their best efforts." He turned and pointed to Principle Collier. "Thank you, Sir, for this honor," he smiled. "Now, I think it is time to award the diplomas that my dear friends have earned."

Principle Collier moved to the podium, he embraced Bart and shook his hand. As Bruce Collier waited at the podium for the applause to settle, he looked out on what he would always believe was a very special class. Bart quietly moved to his seat, next to Gloucester's Mayor, who embraced him.

"You have made us proud," Gloucester's Mayor stated. "You bring honor to our city."

Bart smiled. "Thank you, Mr. Mayor." He moved to the Nelsons. Bart kissed Beth Nelson and embraced Coach Nelson.

Principle Collier smiled at Bart. He faced the students and said; "Before I present diplomas to the graduates, I would like to award the Sawyer Medal. As many of you know, the Sawyer Medal is the most important award given each academic year." He paused. "It is presented to the student who excels academically, in extra-curricular activities, and who brings honor to himself, his school and his community, in a way that distinguishes himself above his peers and exceeds expectations." He smiled, looked back at Bart, turned to face the graduates.

"Bart," he smiled, "would you please join me at the podium." When they stood together, Principle Collier continued. "This year's winner of the Sawyer Medal is a student who has achieved in the highest levels academically. This student also participated in extra-curricular activities and was considered exceptional in so many areas.

He paused, smiled at Bart. "The winner of the Sawyer Medal was caused to miss significant class time and do the required work with the aid of a tutor." He paused. "That class work was performed completely and on time. And further," Collier smiled. "The student returned to take all the tests required and scored at the highest levels seen in decades."

Angela smiled up at Bart, "Bart's going to win," she happily stated to those seated about her.

The large group of Bart and Angela's family and friends stood and focused on the stage.

"The winner of the Sawyer Medal is an outstanding student and has met every criteria required. The winner of the Sawyer Medal is," he paused for dramatic effect, smiled at Bart, then, turned back to all assembled, "Angela DeMarco!"

Angela's hands went to her face in surprise, Bart laughed in delight. Sal and Maria embraced, Tina cried the happiest of tears. The students and guests applauded.

"Please come forward Angela, and receive your Medal from our Commencement Speaker."

Principle Collier handed the Medal and citation to Bart, for the presentation.

Angela ascended the stage and went into Bart's arms. "I'm so proud of you," he said happily.

As Bart and Angela embraced, Principle Collier spoke. "I want to congratulate Angela," he began. He smiled, suppressed a laugh. "Bart, as a man, I regret to say," he shrugged. "Angela finished number 1 in the class, and you finished at number 2." He sadly, shook his head, as laughter rolled across those gathered. "How will you ever live that down?"

Bart laughed aloud, took the medal, unfurled the ribbon in the red and white colors of Gloucester High School, and necklaced the medal on Angela. Then, he kissed Angela. "My angel," he said, softly.

Bart adjusted the microphone down to her height. "Speak to the class," he encouraged.

Angela looked out at her classmates and all those assembled. "I want to thank Principle Collier and all those on the committee who have bestowed this honor on me," she smiled, placed her hand on the medal. "This is a wonderful surprise," she looked at Bart and grinned. "Bart, you will always be number 1 with me!"

Bart beamed his smile. Applause spread throughout those assembled.

Angela continued. "Bart and I, our families," she placed her hand lovingly on her belly, "and our baby, are all part of 'Team DeMarco.' And, I accept this wonderful medal and honor on behalf of 'Team DeMarco.'"

Angela paused, looked into the bleachers and smiled. "Mom and Dad," she looked up at Sal and Maria, who wept happily, "you did great, I'm proud to be your daughter!" She waved, kissed Bart and together, Bart and Angela walked back to their seats, to be with the graduating class, and to process up and receive their diplomas.

Bruce Collier watched Bart and Angela walk back to sit with their classmates. He addressed those assembled. "We can all learn a great deal from this young and accomplished couple." He stated. "When life gives you lemons, you can still make lemonade," he paused, "or, you can make greatness."

"Life was not always kind to Bart and Angela, but they never quit, they never stopped fighting to excel. They kept smiling." He grinned. "And, they always recognized that success has many contributors."

"So," Principle Collier, urged. "Let us give a cheer for 'Team DeMarco!'"

A roaring applause followed. Bart held Angela close and smiled. "Thank you, Princess."

The graduation party was a private matter for the families and friends of Bart and Angela. A number of sports reporters and film crews sought entry, but were told by John Palermo, that this was a special family day. And, that Bart would agree to interviews later in the week.

Still, wearing their robes, with the Sawyer Medal around her neck, hundreds of photos were taken with family, friends and every possible combination.

Rosa laughed and pointed to Franco Palermo, "I guess we should have Franco in some photos."

Franco held Lucia, flashed a beaming smile at Rosa. "You may as well, Mrs. DeMarco," he smiled at Lucia, "because, I plan on being with Lucia for a very long time!"

Lucia offered a bright smile, as Mario shook his head and laughed. "That sounds like trouble to me!"

The buffet table was resplendent with wonderful Italian treats. Homemade Sicilian style pizza, Maria's lasagna, Rosa's arincini, and so much more. Tina, contributed a tasty chicken in a lemon caper sauce. All ate happily and heartily.

Relaxing in the living room, following dinner, the TV was set to the final round of The Players Championship. Angela entered carrying a double espresso for Bart, and saw him, chatting with the guys, watching the action. The leaderboard was flashed on the screen. Bart smiled as he saw so many familiar names.

"If Bart were there," Mario stated, "he would be leading and winning this Tournament!"

Bart smiled. "Thanks Mario, but you just never know."

Angela watched the exchange, studied Bart's face. "Are you sorry that you missed this?" She asked nodding to the TV.

Bart laughed. "Sure, I'd like to be playing, but," he stood, took the cup from Angela, placed it on the coffee table and pulled Angela close, "today, I had a once in a lifetime event with my beautiful wife." He kissed her, nodded to the dining room, where their parents sat, laughing and joyful. "Family always comes first." He grinned. "The Players Championship is played every year."

Chapter Seventy-Nine

B art's magical year continued. The Manitoba Classic was a huge success. The Golf Channel carried the four day Tournament and still ran its 'Live from the U.S. Open' show. Bart had attracted a good contingent of European and Asian players to play with and against many PGA professionals, who had not qualified for the U.S. Open.

Mario and Celia enjoyed their 'pre-wedding honeymoon' at the Walleston estate. They had been married by Father Capelli before heading to Canada. And, they enjoyed a beautiful and private suite. Of course, while PapaWall handled all the details of running a PGA Tournament, and Bart and Dave practiced for the Thursday start, the newlyweds spent a relaxing week together with Angela, Rachel, Dave's sister, Margaret, Lucia and the families. Their official ceremony and reception would be the next Saturday in Gloucester.

On Sunday, with the entire DeMarco, Curcuru, and Gilliss families in Bart's gallery, along with Dave and Jessica and Jim and Betsy, Bart won the inaugural Manitoba Classic by five shots. The Canadian crowds were large, YES was present in big numbers to support 'Stutter Boy,' and the Tournament created to help the very children YES served.

Bart was the sentimental favorite and enjoyed watching the Tournament sponsor, Manitoba Oil, represented by its CEO and President, Phil Walleston, bask in his success and most importantly, the success of the new school for young stutterers.

It was a special moment when CEO, Phil Walleston, presented the beautiful trophy to the Champion, Bart DeMarco. Angela, Dave and Rachel stood with Bart to accept the award. The photo of PapaWall presenting the trophy to the smiling foursome, will always be proudly displayed at the Headquarters of Manitoba Oil and hung above the fireplace at the Walleston home.

Then, it was Rachel's day. Heather and Rachel, as promised, had taken care of everything. The Church shone, decked out with flowers and with candles glowing. The light wafted through the stain glass windows, throwing a special aura on the participants.

While the DeMarco's and Curcuru's along with friends stayed at the Walleston estate, the Gilliss family were accommodated at a nearby luxury hotel. Heather, adhering to her traditional beliefs, wanted to be sure that Dave didn't see Rachel, in her wedding gown, until she walked down the aisle on the arm of her Dad.

Leaving nothing to chance, Heather arranged for Dave to have a nice room, but the Honeymoon suite, was left vacant, and prepared for Dave and Rachel for that very special night.

That morning, Bart left a happy Angela at the Walleston's home. "I think that I'll dress at Dave's hotel." He said. "You can help Rachel get ready."

"Are you planning to make Dave even more nervous than he already is?" Angela asked on a laugh, as she checked to assure all that Bart needed was packed in his bag.

"Of course not," he grinned. "I'll just give him some sage best man advice."

Angela held and kissed Bart. "I'll see you in Church, Champ," She replied.

The groom, Dave Gilliss, and his best man, Bart DeMarco, dressed in the tuxedos Heather had them fitted for at the Pacific Amateur. Bart came into Dave's room to support his dear friend and coach.

"Don't worry Dave," he teased with a smile. "Nobody will even know we're there." He laughed. "We could wear bathing suits and all you'll hear is how beautiful Rachel looks!" He laughed. "And, no doubt, she will look beautiful." He moved to Dave, embraced his dear friend. "I am so happy for you, Dave."

Dave embraced Bart, then, gripped his hand firmly. "It has been a great year, Bart. All our success and meeting Rachel." He paused. "Thanks for helping me get my head on straight in Florida." He exhaled. "Had you not opened my eyes, I might have lost a fabulous girl."

Bart grinned. "Dave, you deserve a girl as special as Rachel." He paused. "You are a solid, loyal and talented guy." He laughed, eyed Dave. "And, I'll deny it if you ever quote me."

Dave laughed. "You're secret is safe with me." He embraced Bart. "Team DeMarco, Bart." He paused. "It has been an honor."

Dave and Rachel's wedding was elegant and joyful. Bart stood with Dave as Best Man and Angela with Rachel, as Matron of Honor. As the couple exchanged their vows, Bart caught Angela's eye. A bond was being forged between the couples that Bart believed would be strong enough to weather any storm.

Bart made the traditional 'Best Man's' speech. He spoke of his friendship and devotion to Dave and to the Walleston family. He smiled and mentioned Justin's contributions to 'Team DeMarco.' "These are truly special people." He stated. "Angela and I are blessed to have them in our lives."

Dave rose, kissed Rachel. He laughed. "Mom, Dad, can you believe this, I'm married!" His mother blew him a kiss, as laughter swept the ballroom.

Dave looked at Rachel. "Mrs. Gilliss, my sweet Rachel, I promise to do everything in my power to keep you as happy as you are today." He paused. "I love you, Rachel." Rachel teared up, but smiled happily.

"There is something I feel I must say." He looked at Bart, who sat with Angela. "Bart, you are the reason for all this!"

Dave continued. "Bart, you always speak of 'Team DeMarco,' and how you could never have achieved all that you have achieved, without me, without Angela, without PapaWall." He smiled. "And, all of that is true!"

He paused, grew serious. "But, Bart, it is you!" He took a deep breath. "Angela helped you, maybe, even saved you." He smiled at Angela. "But, it was you who made her life happy!"

"PapaWall helped you, and you helped Justin to gain confidence and dignity." He smiled. "And, together 'Team DeMarco' will help so many kids."

"Bart, it was that photo of you at the Mass. Amateur, surrounded by all those YES children that sent a charge into PapaWall and brought the Wallestons in."

He pointed his finger. "You, Bart, are the engine!" He smiled. "You are the planet we all revolve around."

Dave smiled. "Bart, you made me a rich man." He paused. "Thank you." He met Bart's eyes. "You, Bart, tied helping the children of YES with big oil!" He laughed. "Now, the hypocritical protesters are afraid to protest Manitoba Oil." He shook his head. "They would be hurting kids!"

He looked at his father-in-law. "Bart, you may not know this, but you have elevated the value of Manitoba Oil." He shrugged. "Sorry, Dad, but Bart should ask for more money!"

PapaWall laughed and called out. "Already done!" PapaWall grinned. "Bart has very good representation." Laughter swept through the ball room.

Dave moved and embraced Bart. "Thank you, Bart." He paused. "I am honored to be a member of 'Team DeMarco.'"

The next day, a private jet carried the large group back to Massachusetts. Dave and Rachel would continue their honeymoon with a week in Gloucester at the Beauport Hotel, attend Mario and Celia's wedding and reception, before flying to Tuscany for another week. Then, off to London, to meet Bart and Angela, where after enjoying London, they would head to Scotland for Bart to play in the Scottish Open, as preparation for the Open Championship, being played at Carnoustie, Scotland.

The week following the Tournament and wedding in Manitoba was Celia's week. Bart was to be Mario's Best Man, as Angela, finding her gown a bit snug at her thickening middle, and needing adjustment, would be one of Celia's Bridesmaids.

It was a joyous wedding. At the reception Bart rose to deliver the Best Man's Toast. He smiled at the happy couple. "Holding a champagne glass, Bart began by saying, "I am so happy to be here toasting my Big Brother, Mario, and his beautiful bride, Celia."

He paused. "Celia came into our family four years ago," he grinned. "They were high school sweethearts and Celia won our hearts almost instantly." He looked at Mario. "Brother, I was amazed, I always thought Celia was way to pretty to be with a guy as average looking as you." The room rolled with laughter. Mario, laughed, kissed Celia, and nodded in agreement.

Bart met Mario's eyes. "But, Mario, you were always smart, you saw Beauty and goodness, and you held on." He looked at his sister-in-law, "Celia, please take care of my big brother." He paused, choked-up and misted. "Mario always took care of me."

There was applause. Bart waited, then addressed Mario. "Mario, no one ever had a better, more supportive and stronger, big brother than you." He stopped, choked, took Angela's hand. "I know a lot of people think that I am some important guy, a golfer that you see on television. But," Bart continued. "Let me tell you about important."

Bart looked at the guests in the beautiful ballroom. "Important is a man who would walk his scared little brother to school to deal with bullies who enjoyed tormenting 'Stutter Boy.'" He cleared his throat. "Important is standing tall and always making Lucia and me know that he was there for us." Bart paused, looked at Mario and Celia and smiled.

He set his gaze on his parents. "Mom and Dad, you always worried about me and my problems." He paused and swallowed. "It was Mario who was the rock, the man we could all depend on." He smiled. "The amazing thing, is that Mario never resented me, was always there for me, was always in my and Lucia's corner." He smiled. "Mario even recruited a group of his friends, guys like Vince Grillo, to keep an eye out for me." He looked at Vince. "Thanks Vince."

Bart raised his glass to the happy couple. "Please raise your glasses to my beautiful sister, Celia, and my hero, my big brother, Mario." Tears ran down Bart's cheeks. "You two deserve all the joy this life can give. I love you." Bart looked at Angela who rose to embrace him. His toast was met with emotion and applause.

Chapter Eighty

It was a cold November morning, Thanksgiving Day, when Bart awoke, at 4am, holding Angela close to him. He smiled as he felt the bulge of her pregnancy, their baby, as she cuddled. 'Still a lumper,' Bart thought with a contented smile as his early morning internal clock readied him for another day.

"You awake, Bart?" Angela asked softly. She nestled close, seeking warmth and comfort.

Bart kissed her head, gently stroked her belly. "Yes, Princess, I'm awake." He smiled. "Happy Thanksgiving!" He stretched and sighed happily. "Are you okay?" He asked casually.

Angela smiled. Bart asked that question of her every day as she approached her time. "How about you take your wife to the hospital." She smiled. "I think it's time."

Bart bolted up. Looked at Angela. She saw the panic in his eyes. She kissed him. "Don't worry, Bart, this is all natural." Her efforts to soothe him, also helped to remind her of all the advice from her mother and Bart's, the teaching of the birthing instructor.

He kissed her, took a deep calming breath, and smiled. "I'll try to remember that." He kissed her again. "My beautiful Angela. Let's go and have our baby."

The Addison Gilbert Hospital was quiet as Bart helped Angela into the maternity receiving room, where an orderly and obstetrical nurse took charge. The nurse, Karen Doyle, who had known Bart since birth, and was a lifelong friend of Rosa's, took and squeezed his hand. "Go relax in the waiting room, Bart, call your parents and Angela's." She smiled. "I will take good care of Angela," she winked, "and your baby." She wheeled Angela off and Bart began to make his calls.

It wasn't long before the waiting room was full to bursting with family and dear friends. Mario and Celia, herself pregnant, were the first there. Mario wrapped Bart in a big hug. "I can't think of a better way to spend Thanksgiving!" Mario chortled. "I'm going to be a Godfather!"

Bart hugged Celia. He studied her. "You okay, Celia?" He asked.

Celia laughed. "Always worried about everybody," she said, as she kissed his cheek. "I am so good and so happy."

The DeMarco's and Curcuru's arrived with joy lighting their faces. Angela's mom and sister headed into Angela's room, where she was being prepped to birth their baby. Rosa embraced Bart. "I always told you that it would all be good."

Bart misted, hugged his Mom. "You did." he agreed. "Thank you for always being there for me."

Rosa's eyes filled. She hugged Bart. "I'm your mother, Bart." No further explanation was needed.

Dave and Rachel arrived with a large tote of coffee, with all the fixings, and trays of pastry and doughnuts, which were placed on the table. Dave hugged Bart, looked into his eyes. "What a year, Bart." He smiled. "Thanks."

Bart pulled Rachel into an embrace. "Are you doing okay?" He asked with a grin. "It seems this baby thing is contagious." That caused a laugh to spread through the room.

"I'm doing fine, Bart." Rachel grinned. "How's our girl doing?"

Bart smiled. "They're getting her ready." He looked at Rosa. "Mom," Bart said happily, and with a sense of relief. "Mrs. Doyle is taking care of Angela." Anxiously, he looked to the door of the waiting room. "In a few minutes, she should be out to give us an update."

Rachel read Bart's concern. She smiled and embraced the worried father-to-be, almost giddy with joy, she gently encouraged. "Try to relax, Bart. Angela will be fine." She looked up into his eyes. "I called my parents, they will be here today with Justin." She paused. "My Dad told me to tell you that he has arranged for everybody to have Thanksgiving dinner together tonight, at the Beauport hotel."

Rachel laughed. "My Dad said to tell you that Thanksgiving is an American holiday." She paused, smiled. "But, if the baby is born today, the Wallestons will adopt the tradition." She grinned. "Thanksgiving will be the baby's day." She looked at Dave, placed her hand on her mildly rounded belly. "As a Gilliss, I have already adopted the holiday!"

Nurse, Karen Doyle came into the waiting room, saw the gathering crowd, which now included Franco Palermo, who had been called by Lucia, as well as Jim and Betsy and Dave and Jessica. She moved to Rosa and embraced her. "Congratulations Nonna," she said, with a smile. "Angela is doing fine, and asking for you, Celia and Lucia."

She looked at Bart. "You are free to come, if you like, but Angela seems to think that you'd rather hang here with the family." Nurse Doyle laughed. "She's worried about you, Bart." She shook her head, put loving hands on his cheeks. "You found a gem!"

The nurse looked at Rosa, pulled her aside. "I asked Angela if she wanted me to call Bart in." The long time obstetrical nurse smiled. "Angela looked me in the eye, just as a contraction hit, she breathed through it, holding her mother's hand. When it passed, she smiled. 'It's hard for Bart to see me in pain,' she said. He's really very sensitive like that.'"

Karen Doyle laughed. "Tina teased her about the fact that she was in labor, and she was worried about Bart."

"Angela looked at us, she rose to Bart's defense. 'Bart would fight an army of men to protect me,' she said. 'I don't need him to prove he loves me.' Angela stated. 'I know he loves me!'"

Nurse Doyle sighed. "Angela then added, 'I love Bart, and if I can spare him from all this, then I will.' She was definite and very loving. I think Bart found a real gem."

"With that," Karen Doyle laughed. "Angela looked at all of us in the room. 'But, please don't tell Bart that I called him sensitive.'" The nurse smiled and shook her head. Angela took my hand. 'Let's spare him all of this,' she said. 'But, please call him in to see his baby being born.'"

Rosa laughed. "Angela's a good girl. I'm so happy Bart found her."

Rosa, Celia and Lucia followed Nurse Doyle to Angela's room. Time passed agonizingly slowly for Bart. He paced, looked at the wall clock, and paced some more.

Moments later, Lucia came back to the waiting room, she look around. "Rachel, Angela is asking for you." Rachel smiled, rose and followed Lucia. Lucia met Bart's eyes, stopped and kissed his cheek. "I'll keep you informed," she assured her big brother.

Family members continued to arrive as word spread. Bart found himself pacing the hall outside the crowded waiting room. Dave Gilliss, Jim Perry, Dave Powers and Franco Palermo, stood with him, talking golf, Gloucester High School football, it was, after all, Thanksgiving, and anything to divert his concerns from what Angela was experiencing.

Sal Curcuru came into the hall and walked to Bart, enveloped him in a hug. He then put his hands on Bart's face. "Thank you, my boy." He said. "For everything!"

Bart was delighted that Katie and John Palermo arrived to share in the joy. Katie brought hot, homemade rolls, with butter, jams and jellies.

"Nothing like fresh, homemade bread to settle your stomach," she grinned. She watched her son, conversing and laughing with Bart and the guys, and smiled that her boy was involved with such a good family.

With so many of the women in with Angela, John left the waiting room, to call Bart and the guys to return. "I think that you're blocking traffic," he smiled. They all re-assembled and sat together in a section of the waiting room and began reviewing the golf season.

John Palermo seeking to divert Bart's thoughts from worrying about Angela, smiled at Bart. "Was it fun battling Sergio on Sunday of the Ryder Cup?" John asked, hoping to distract the obviously worried young father-to-be.

Bart smiled. He had been selected, by Captain, Jack Nicklaus, for the U.S. Ryder Cup team, in the bi-annual match against Team Europe. The match had been played in Paris. Angela and Rachel had loved the shopping, the restaurants, the Louvre, the sights. So, while Bart and Dave, and all the other U.S. team members worked, the wives of the players, caddies and captains had a wonderful time.

As Bart had hoped, Angela and Rachel had become very close. It was wonderful for them to have someone to pass time with, while Bart and Dave practiced. That, they would have babies within months of each other, along with Celia, was an added bonus.

Bart's golf season had been a 'smashing success' in the words of David Feherty. After winning the Masters, Bart won the season's 4th Major, The PGA Championship. He had also won the Manitoba Classic and three other PGA Tournaments.

Bart had been happy to see that Phil Mickelson had won the U.S. Open, to complete his career Grand Slam.

Bart had a top 10 finish in the Open Championship played at the Carnoustie golf club in Scotland. He also advanced through the FedEx Cup events and won the Tour Championship at East Lake Golf Club, the home course of Bobby Jones, to win the FedEx Cup.

The FedEx Cup, something of a World Series for golfers, awards the winner a $10 million bonus. With that and his six tournament wins, as well as his 12 top ten finishes, Bart and Dave earned over $20 million. Adding the bonuses earned from his sponsor, Manitoba Oil, for Tournaments won, including two Majors, they collected an additional $12 million.

Bart never discussed money. He rarely thought about it, as he had the trusted attorney, John Palermo, managing and overseeing his career. He loved to play golf, compete against the best players in the world and enjoy his family and friends. He appreciated the financial security, but just wanted a normal life, where his career was playing golf.

John Palermo sat back casually, and directed Bart's thoughts to his first Ryder Cup team. The Ryder Cup teams from the U.S. and Europe are composed of 12 players each. On the first two days of the tournament there are two sessions. One session will be a four ball competition where four, two man teams compete, in head to head matches. Each man plays his ball, and the lowest score recorded on each hole, counts as the team score. Bart was assigned, by Captain Jack Nicklaus, to play with Jordan Spieth, another young gun, who like Bart, was seldom rattled and possessed a strong game.

The second session is an alternate shot match format, where one player hits the tee shot and his teammate hits the second shot and they alternate shots until they hole the ball. Alternate shot is a challenging format. In both formats, four teams compete while four players on each team do not play or sit out. On the third day, all 12 players play head to head, in a match play format. Bart drew Sergio Garcia for his match.

Bart and Jordan Spieth were the only U.S. players to play all five sessions. And, they played winning golf.

"They are the hot hands," was Captain Nicklaus's explanation to the team and the media. Jordan had won the Open Championship for his third Major Championship and finished second in the FedEx Cup race. After the first two days, the teams stood even, with eight points each. As the U.S. team had won the previous Ryder Cup, they would retain the Cup with 14 points. The Europeans had to have a minimum of 14 ½ points to win the Cup.

In the Sunday head to head matches, Bart and Sergio were placed in the anchor positions, playing last. If it came down to the final match, Captain Nicklaus wanted Bart, the world's hottest player, to carry the fate of the U.S. team.

Angela, into her 8th month of her pregnancy, walked the course with Rachel. Keeping a watchful eye on the young mother-to-be, were Amy Mickelson and Jen MacKay.

"Why does it always have to be Bart in the pressure situations?" Angela asked Rachel, with a sense of exasperation. Amy Mickelson looked on and smiled.

"Because, as Dave always says, Bart is 'the Diamond Maker.' Rachel laughed. "Get used to it, Angela. It will be Bart and Dave fighting these battles for a long time."

Amy Mickelson smiled. "Girls, ask yourself, would Bart and Dave want it to be different?"

Angela shrugged. "Most of the time, it really doesn't seem to bother him." She laughed. "But, it's tough on me."

"I totally understand," Amy Mickelson agreed with a laugh. "Believe me, I totally understand."

As it turned out, the 11 matches preceding the Bart-Sergio match had Team Europe winning 6 of the 11 points. To win the Cup for Europe, Sergio needed to merely halve the match with Bart. For the U.S. team to win, Bart had to win the head to head contest against the renowned Match Play Warrior.

John Palermo sat back and smiled. He saw that Bart was mentally back in Paris, at the Ryder Cup event, rather than worrying about Angela as she prepared to birth their first child.

Katie Palermo moved closer to the group, to be able to listen to the discussion. She recognized that John was distracting Bart from worrying over something that was now out of his control. Being married to John Palermo, she knew how stressful these situations were to someone with control issues. She brought rolls and baked goods with fresh coffee to the guys helping John to keep Bart relaxed and distracted.

As they walked in the gallery, Angela sighed. "It's up to our guys, again." Angela said to Rachel, with frustration oozing from every pore.

Rachel laughed. "They've played great, Angela." She nudged her. "You need to relax." Then, Rachel smiled and whispered. "Angela, I think that I'm pregnant."

Angela's eyes flew open and she embraced Rachel, all thoughts of the golf match gone. "That is so great, Rachel. Our babies will grow up together."

Amy Mickelson and Jen MacKay looked on smiling. "See, you do know what's important!" Amy said on a laugh.

"Sergio is an amazing golfer." Bart explained. "In Match play, he's so tough." Bart nodded, recalling his thoughts. "We were just starting the back nine when we learned how pivotal our match had become," Bart said, with a shake of the head and a glance and smile at Dave Gilliss. "We were all square, and suddenly our relaxed, laid back, round, was critical."

"It went back and forth," Bart continued. "And, after the 16th, we were still All Square." Bart laughed, "I had to win, if we halved the match, it meant a European Team victory."

"As we stood on the 17th tee, here comes Jack Nicklaus." Bart grinned. "An 18 time Major Champion, the greatest golfer of all time, and here he comes!"

The group was laughing. Bart continued, showing a wide grin. "It was like the Principal at school coming after you." He raised his brows. "You know, it can't be good!"

"So, what did he say?" Jim Perry asked.

"I half expected a reassuring pep talk," Bart said, with a smile. "Instead, he moved real close, looked me in the eye and growled, 'Bart, what the hell are you doing? You're better than this guy, finish him off, now!'"

Dave Gilliss was laughing aloud. "That's exactly how he said it." He couldn't control his laughter. "Bart looked like a middle schooler, scared to death!"

"So, Bart, what did you say?" Dave Powers asked, grinning.

Bart shrugged, "what could I say?" He laughed. "I said, yes sir!"

"And, you finished him off, by winning 17 and 18!" John Palermo stated. "I guess, it's a good thing to have 'The Golden Bear,' put you in your place!"

The guys all laughed. Katie Palermo smiled at John.

Lucia came running into the waiting room. "Bart, come now, it's time!"

Bart hesitated, looked at Lucia, she saw the worry in his eyes. "Is Angela okay?"

Lucia smiled. "She's fine," Lucia paused and eyed her big brother, she knew the whole birthing thing scared him. She took his hand, looked into his eyes, spoke softly. "Angela needs you!" The magic words.

Bart jumped to his feet, "Let's go."

Lucia and Bart entered the delivery room. The birthing bed was surrounded by family and friends who were as close as family. Angela's mother was holding her hand and encouraging her with soft words. Tina stood opposite, gently encouraging Angela, and stroking her arm. Maria moved aside for Bart, who took Angela's hand, studied her closely. "Are you okay, Princess?"

Angela was breathing heavily, panting between pushing. She saw his face and smiled. "I'm good, Bart." She paused. "Our baby is coming."

"Okay, Angela," Dr. Stelluto urged. "One more big push and your baby will be here."

Angela pushed, squeezing Bart's hand. Tina gently stroked her head. Bart met his mother's eyes. Rosa knew Bart was afraid. Seeing Angela in pain, a pain he could do nothing about, upset him. She winked and Bart saw her encouraging smile. Angela gasped and laid back, and instantly smiled, as the baby came into Doc Stelluto's capable and experienced hands.

"It's a girl," Doc Stelluto exclaimed, with joy. "A beautiful girl." Bart and Angela smiled joyously.

"Our baby," Angela said softly. "I guess you have a new girl, Bart?" She laughed.

His baby girl, Rosa DeMarco, was born in a circle of love. Bart was awed when Nurse, Karen Doyle, beaming a smile, placed the baby in his arms. He looked down at his little girl, bent and kissed her softly, looked into his baby's sweet face. "Rosa," he said to his beautiful baby girl. "I will love you forever!"

Angela smiled at Bart. "She looks like you, Bart."

Bart smiled, looked at Angela, then back at his baby. "Maybe, she'll get lucky and outgrow that handicap."

Smiles bloomed throughout the room. Bart looked at a beaming Angela, leaned in and gently, kissed her. "Are you okay, Princess?"

Angela flashed a smile at Bart and took his hand. "I have never been better or happier." She paused, misted. "Thank you, Bart. You've made my dreams come true."

Bart held his baby girl, looked into her sweet face and kissed her cheek, then he kissed Angela. He flashed that devastating smile. "It's only just beginning, Princess!"

CPSIA information can be obtained
at www.ICGtesting.com
Printed in the USA
BVHW03*0742190618
518908BV00008B/1/P